FLORENCE MACARTHY: AN IRISH TALE (1818)

Forthcoming Titles

Ann Gomersall, *The Citizen*
edited by Jennifer Chenkin

Frances Brooke, *The History of Lady Julia Mandeville*
edited by Enit K. Steiner

Eliza Haywood, *The Rash Resolve and Life's Progress*
edited by Carol Stewart

Sydney Owenson,
Florence Macarthy: An Irish Tale (1818)

EDITED BY

Jenny McAuley

Routledge
Taylor & Francis Group

LONDON AND NEW YORK

First published 2012 by Pickering & Chatto (Publishers) Limited

Published 2016 by Routledge
2 Park Square, Milton Park, Abingdon, Oxfordshire OX14 4RN
711 Third Avenue, New York, NY 10017, USA

First issued in paperback 2016

Routledge is an imprint of the Taylor & Francis Group, an informa business

BRITISH LIBRARY CATALOGUING IN PUBLICATION DATA

Morgan, Lady (Sydney), 1783–1859.
Florence Macarthy : an Irish tale. – (Chawton House library series. Women's
novels) 1. Ireland – Politics and government – 1800–1837 – Fiction. 2. Ireland
– Social conditions – 19th century – Fiction.
I. Title II. Series III. McAuley, Jenny.
823.7-dc23

ISBN 13: 978-1-138-23541-0 (pbk)
ISBN 13: 978-1-8489-3168-8 (hbk)

Typeset by Pickering & Chatto (Publishers) Limited

CONTENTS

INTRODUCTION

I.

In William Trevor's 2002 novel *The Story of Lucy Gault*, the heroine – who has been brought up alone, in a decaying Ascendancy mansion in Co. Cork – reports on her explorations of the household library, in a letter to her sweetheart: 'I have found another book, Lucy wrote. "Florence Macarthy" by Lady Morgan. I didn't think it would be good. But it is far better than I could have guessed.'[1] *Florence Macarthy* is discussed no further in Trevor's fiction – so the reader never finds out how far the appeal to Lucy Gault of Lady Morgan's 'Irish Tale' of shifting national identities has to do with her own confused experience of growing up in the care of Irish servants, following her Anglo-Irish parents' abandonment of the estate shortly before the establishment of Home Rule in 1922. Moreover, and as a young woman reader in the Irish Free State during the late 1930s, Lucy also encounters *Florence Macarthy* at a period of still-incomplete establishment of a new national identity – just as Sydney Owenson, Lady Morgan, had evoked in her novel the troubled condition during the two decades following the absorption of Ireland into the United Kingdom following the passage of the 1800 Act of Union. At the same time – and although the grounds of the fictional Lucy's initial prejudice against *Florence Macarthy* are not made clear – her change of mind parallels the experiences with it of the novel's first critics, and those, possibly, of many of its subsequent readers. The critic who reviewed *Florence Macarthy* for the *Edinburgh Review* described having initially found its 'reflections' on political and other topics to be 'more numerous than valuable', only to have proceeded with the reading of what turned out to be an intelligent, romantic comedy, as well as an Irish patriot polemic, 'more from a feeling of pleasure than a sense of duty'.[2]

The expectations, and the opinions, with which *Florence Macarthy: An Irish Tale* was met on its publication by Henry Colburn in November 1818, are vividly dramatized in another, and more contemporary, work of fiction. This text was an anonymously-authored novel, *Varieties in Woman*, which appeared during November 1819,[3] almost exactly one year after the publication of *Florence Mac-*

arthy. An apparently liberal-spirited work, *Varieties in Woman* features a scene set in a provincial English circulating library, where the principal characters overhear a conversation concerning Owenson's works between the library's proprietor, and two of its young women customers. Having informed one of these customers that the copy of Walter Scott's *Tales of My Landlord* that she has requested is unavailable, the librarian offers 'Lady Morgan's "Florence Macarthy"' as an alternative, 'if you have not read it'.[4] The customer, named only as '1st Lady', is emphatic in her denial: 'Oh, no! we have no intention of reading it: it is all about *Ireland*, and *pedantry*. I never read any thing of her's, since I found a Latin quotation in one of her works, – it is so dreadfully affected'.[5] Her disinclination to read *Florence Macarthy* increases when she learns that among the 'first literary people of the place' who have been 'enraptured' with it is 'Miss B.', a local, published novelist. This individual's satirical bent and radical political views have already incurred the disapproval of the '1st Lady', who dismisses Miss B.'s admiration for Owenson as 'just what I expected', going on to opine: '*All* authors are Democratic and Jacobinical; there ought really to be a law to put them down'.[6] She decides to try *Florence Macarthy* after all, though, on learning that 'Miss B's' verdict was prompted by her finding that the novel had 'the same splendid imagery, the same glowing enthusiasm, the same touch that gives a life and a breathing to every syllable, – which is conspicuous in all Lady Morgan's writings'.[7]

This passage encapsulates many of the aspects of the public reputation Sydney Owenson had acquired by the time of the first publication of *Florence Macarthy*, in a career as a novelist which had begun fifteen years previously, with her writing of *St Clair, or, The Heiress of Desmond* (1803) when she was aged about twenty-five, and working as a governess in Tipperary.[8] The instant popularity of *Florence Macarthy* is indicated in the fictional librarian's consideration of the likely possibility that the customer may already have read it – the demand for the novel having been such that it had gone into a fourth edition by mid-January 1819;[9] while the reviewer of Thomas Dibdin's 1819 stage adaptation had considered it unnecessary to summarize the plot, as the novel was 'in the libraries of most, and the memories of all'.[10] The fictional library customer has also already observed two of the major hallmarks of Owenson's writing: its preoccupation with Irish nationhood, and the conspicuous display in it of literary and antiquarian allusion, drawing upon a wide (and multilingual) frame of reference. Through the opinions of this character and 'Miss B.', meanwhile, the author of *Varieties in Woman* shows his or her awareness of the sharp division of critical opinion on Owenson, between those who admired the lyricism and 'enthusiasm' (whether sentimental, erotic, or political) of her descriptive writing in particular, and those who condemned both her 'pedantic' displays of classical and antiquarian learning, and what they perceived to be her subversive political views.

With her sixth novel, *O'Donnel: A National Tale* (1814), the first she published under her married name of Lady Morgan, Owenson had initiated a progression away from the conventional, sentimental plots, and romanticized view of Irish history, that had characterized her earlier fictions. She stated in the preface to *O'Donnel* her view that 'literary fiction' had always, in its 'most genuine form', served as a 'mirror' to reflect the manners and morals of the time in which it was produced; and announced her decision to '[venture] on that style of novel, which simply bears upon the "flat realities of life".[11] With this project undertaken, in *Florence Macarthy* Owenson achieved a still more sophisticated fusion of historical and antiquarian erudition, political comment and densely-layered literary allusion, with all the heady emotion, and picturesque 'local colour', that had characterized the courtship narratives of the earlier works she published under her maiden name, most notably *The Wild Irish Girl: A National Tale* (1806), *Woman, or Ida of Athens* (1809) and *The Missionary: An Indian Tale* (1811). Whilst testifying to the increased experience and assurance in non-fictional and political writing that Owenson had developed in *Patriotic Sketches of Ireland* (1807) and *France* (1817), *Florence Macarthy* also displays a new confidence of artistry, in its intricate plotting, and the often broad comedy and linguistic flair, of its authoritative third-person narrative voice. It thus marks an important stage in Owenson's progression toward the formal and stylistic virtuosity achieved in *The O'Briens and the O'Flahertys* (1827), her final 'national tale'.

While she had long presented herself as an Irish patriot, Owenson's politics had become the more prominent in public attention following the banning of *France* (1817), her account of French society since the defeat of Napoleon, in France itself, largely on account of its sympathy with the French Revolution and Napoleon. Foremost among critics taking, and influencing, the 'anti-jacobin' view of Owenson was the Irish-born critic and Tory MP John Wilson Croker. Beginning with his review of Owenson's novel *Woman, or Ida of Athens* in 1809, in which he questioned her literacy and accused her of libertinism and atheism,[12] Croker's scurrilous and patronizing reviews of, or mentioning, Owenson's work in the *Quarterly Review* which he had founded proved as compelling a provocation to Owenson, in her composition of *Florence Macarthy*, as did the condition of Ireland under its post-Union, Westminster-based Parliament. However, and as modern critics from Thomas Flanagan onward have noted,[13] rather than being jacobinical, *Florence Macarthy* is fully informed by the liberal Whig principles with which Owenson had grown up in the 1780s and 1790s, and which had been most notably instanced in the campaigns of figures such as Henry Grattan for the increased legislative independence of the Irish parliament, and the improved liberties of all Irish citizens (including the majority Roman Catholic population). With its concluding union between members of the old Gaelic Irish (and Catholic) aristocracy, and the Norman, or Anglo-Irish, Protestant

Ascendancy, *Florence Macarthy* is 'radical' only in its insistence that with or without a Union with Britain, Ireland should be privileged with its own governing elite, rather than having this absorbed within that of England; and that Ireland should produce its own, resident leaders for the improvement of the education and prosperity of the rest of its population. Most especially as expressed in *Florence Macarthy*, this view of Owenson's contrasted with the promotion, in Maria Edgeworth's Irish novels, of the idea that the Irish people should be guided through education, and the incentive of improved material conditions, to acceptance of the solely British-governed Union.[14]

Owenson meanwhile balanced the historical objectivity of *Florence Macarthy* with an elaborate system of more personal, both coded and more overt, references to her memories of her father, the Irish actor Robert Owenson, who had died in 1812, as well as to her feud with Croker. While all of Owenson's novels would feature authorial self-portraits in their spirited, accomplished heroines, its inclusion of a professional, novel-writing heroine at the centre of its action makes *Florence Macarthy* the most frankly autobiographical of all Owenson's fictions – and thus perhaps the most important of them to the understanding of her life and work within the broader context of women's authorship in Regency-era Britain. As she had already begun to do in *O'Donnel*, in *Florence Macarthy* Owenson also drew heavily upon her personal experiences as the long-term houseguest, from 1810, of the lavishly hospitable, and socially elitist, James Hamilton, ninth earl of Abercorn, and his wife Anne, of Barons Court, Co. Tyrone, and Bentley Priory, Stanmore. Through these patrons, Owenson had been able to associate with figures from the centre of English and Irish government, and the leaders of the Regency-era *ton*, or fashionable society, experiencing also all the high ceremonial and rigid protocols of that world. The couple had also encouraged Owenson's marriage, early in 1812, to the English physician and philosophical author Charles Morgan, who had also been resident in the household as Lord Abercorn's medical attendant.

II.

While she entered upon it with ambivalent feelings, Owenson's marriage does seem to have provided her with a more secure social standing, the value of which to her career she would appear to have recognized.[15] In both *France*, to which he supplied four appendices on French law, finance, medicine and political opinion, and in *Florence Macarthy*, in which he provided the preface advertising its patriotic motivations, Charles Morgan appears as having been cast by his wife in the role of guarantor of her respectability both socially, as a married woman, and on the professional level, as an intellectual colleague worthy of his collaboration. As 'Lady Morgan', Owenson seems to have been enabled to exercise to a fuller extent than previously, the matured satirical talents which she had, of course, been developing quite independently of either the Abercorns or Charles Morgan, throughout the early 1800s. Not least among the benefits of freedom from the Abercorns' hospitality were the new opportunities, which Owenson seized in *O'Donnel*, and continued to exploit in both *Florence Macarthy*, and *The O'Briens and the O'Flahertys*, of confronting the habitués of the viceregal circles at Westminster and Dublin Castle with their extravagance, vanity, corruption and apparently willed ignorance of the conditions endured by the poorest of the Irish people.

Just how conscious Owenson was of the worst tendencies of her patrons' friends is made clear in her letter of 18 January 1810 to her friend and mentor, and fellow Irish novelist, Alicia LeFanu. Writing after participating in a series of glittering Christmas festivities at the London suburb of Stanmore, she remarks:

> I hear of nothing but politics, and the manner in which things are considered, give me a most thorough contempt for the '*rulers of the earth*;' I am certain that the country, its welfare or prosperity, never, for a moment, make a part in their speculation; it is all *a little miserable system of self-interests*, paltry distinctions, of private pique, and personal ambition. I sometimes with difficulty keep in my indignation.[16]

In the same letter – and with her own, often impoverished, upbringing by a professional actor apparently in mind – she also declares, regarding an invitation from the Abercorns to stay for the 'private theatricals', that she would rather 'fly to the end of the world from a species of amusement to me, of all others, the most faded and egotistical'.[17] Having previously presented a sentimentalized, picturesque view of Irish nationhood in *St Clair* and *The Wild Irish Girl*, in the novel she published after moving in with the Abercorns later in 1810, *The Missionary* (1811), Owenson encoded more specific concerns about British rule in Ireland in a lushly sentimental, orientalist romance based in Portugese-ruled Goa – though this work also functioned as a broader critique of imperialist rule and religious intolerance, seen as not confined either to Britain or Portugal. In her 'national tales' *O'Donnel*, and *The O'Briens and the O'Flahertys*, as well as *Florence Macarthy*, however, Owenson spared neither the theatricals, nor any other fad or foible, of the social circle that had surrounded the couple she described, again in 1810, as '*keepers*' who possibly wanted only 'to exhibit her [as the 'Wild Irish Girl'] for her intelligence or ferocity, like the learned pig at Exeter Change, or the beautiful hyena at the Tower, which never was tamed'.[18] Moreover, by 1817, when Owenson began *Florence Macarthy*, conditions in Ireland were such as to enable her easily to overcome her 'difficulty' in restraining her indignation at those in power there, and in England. As Claire Connolly has also recently commented, in 1818 *Florence Macarthy* '[addressed] its own moment', through frequent references to specific, repressive legislations such as the Peace Preservation, and Insurrection Acts of 1814; to the extent of corruption within the viceregal establishment, and to such crises of the 1810s as the famine of 1816, and the typhus epidemic which developed in 1817, spreading to all parts of Ireland by 1819.[19]

III.

While critics as recent as James Newcomer, in 1990, have complained about the apparently confused structuring of *Florence Macarthy*, its unrealistic contrivances and the slowness with which certain major plot strands, such as the hero's purpose for being in Ireland, are revealed,[20] Terry Eagleton has been among those who have noted the appropriateness of its diffuse narrative, which draws upon many generic styles, and linguistic and social registers, for conveying the state of a country whose own identity was still in flux.[21] The first of the novel's four volumes presents evocative descriptions of Dublin city, and peasant life in rural Cork, in the years following the Act of Union, which both indulge and critique the aestheticizing and picturesque views of Ireland that had become prevalent in published travellers' accounts since the late eighteenth century.[22] Volume I begins with the arrival in Dublin, by sea, and 'early in the nineteenth century,'[23] of Owenson's Anglo-Irish hero, General Walter de Montenay Fitzwalter. He is there with the purpose of recovering his usurped estates and aristocratic title, following a period of service as a guerrilla leader in one of the Spanish American independence movements, at their height between 1808 and 1819. He is accompanied by the foppish, philosophizing Adelm Fitzadelm, whom he has befriended without realizing that he is the son of Lord Dunore, the deceased uncle who had deprived him of his inheritance. Both men are travelling incognito, their personal missions being secretive; and their appearance in the identities of 'the Commodore' (Fitzwalter), and 'De Vere' (Fitzadelm) is only the first instance in a long series of disguises and assumed characters to figure in the novel.

Throughout her first and second volumes, Owenson's narrative seems to establish Fitzadelm at the romantic centre of the plot, his presence in Ireland being due to his interest in discovering the identity of a mysterious woman who has been writing to him. At the same time, Owenson generates further mystery around the relationship between Fitzwalter and the eccentric, Gaelic-speaking hedge-schoolmaster and local antiquary Terence Oge O'Leary, whom he has apparently known in his childhood. In the second volume of the novel, Owenson also continues Fitzwalter's journey of discovery through the varied social scenes of the country he has not seen since his boyhood, with the introduction of the *parvenu* Crawley family, ultra-Protestant Unionists whose members include Conway Townsend Crawley, a grasping lawyer with literary aspirations, and his land-agent father Darby, source of much of the novel's comedy with his vulgar tastes and malapropisms. The second volume is dominated, however, by the arrival in Ireland of the excitable, sensation-hungry Lady Dunore herself, to assist in canvassing for Fitzadelm in a forthcoming local election – accompanied by a retinue of London and Dublin 'fashionables' looking forward to an autumn of private theatricals.

It is only in the third volume that readers are introduced to Florence Macarthy, Lady Clancare, imagined by Owenson as being the partly-Spanish descendant of the historical Florence Macarthy More, one of the Irish Catholic earls who fled Ireland in the 1580s, following the failure of their rebellion against Elizabeth I. Having been necessitated to work for her living by the decayed state of her family's fortunes, the vivacious Lady Clancare has achieved celebrity as an author of novels of Irish life, and been adopted as a protégée of Lady Dunore, to the resentment of young Crawley. She has also gradually begun recovering her family's lost lands through the courts, and relieving the poverty of the tenants on them. The novel's fourth, and final, volume charts Lady Dunore's preparations for a performance of *As You Like It*, alongside the development of Fitzwalter's attraction to Lady Clancare. As the narrative also reveals, however, Fitzwalter feels himself to be still bound in honour to complete a previously interrupted marriage-ceremony he had entered upon in Spain, with the daughter of another Irish freedom-fighter, killed in South America, whom he had promised to protect without having seen her face before – or during – the wedding.

In a series of intimate encounters with Lady Clancare, Fitzwalter learns of her impassioned patriotism, her ambivalence about making a living from writing about her country's distresses, and the challenges she has faced as a woman writer trying to correct the faults of the Ascendancy class that has momentarily made her its pet. He also discovers that she is in fact the daughter of his dead friend, and in love with him; and that she has been pursuing him back to, and through, Ireland, in the guises of characters including 'Mrs McGillicuddy', a grotesque old woman encountered by Fitzwalter and Fitzadelm on their travels in Volume I, and Fitzadelm's mystery correspondent. These disguises have had the additional purpose of humiliating Fitzadelm, in revenge for his earlier abandonment of Lady Clancare's cousin (also named Florence Macarthy), whom he had courted whilst touring Portugal. The novel's closing chapters see the exposure –through the efforts of Fitzadelm, O'Leary and a network of sympathetic peasants – of the elder Fitzadelm's, and the Crawleys', plots against Fitzwalter. It concludes with the completion of the wedding between Fitzwalter and Lady Clancare, which enables the establishment of jointly Gaelic and Norman Irish proprietorship of the Dunore estates, and the local implementation of non-absentee government by Irish-born, aristocratic leaders.

IV.

The progression of the narrative of *Florence Macarthy* is interspersed with 'set piece' incidents and dialogues which, rather in the manner of the conversations in Thomas Love Peacock's directly contemporary *Nightmare Abbey* (1818), although far more naturalistically, provide dramatic commentary on literary, cultural and political issues. Such episodes includethe dispute between Fitzwalter and Fitzadelm, in Volume I, concerning Edmund Spenser's colonialist representation of Ireland in both *The Faerie Queene* and *A View of the Present State of Ireland*; the trial of some suspected rebels at Dunore Castle in Volume III, where the Crawleys fabricate a charge based on documents relating to a sixteenth-century rebellion; and Lady Clancare's account of her life to Fitzwalter in Volume IV. Numerous other debates also arise between Lady Dunore's houseguests concerning contemporary and recent authors, and various popular-cultural fads. Recurrent topics include such current affairs as the Spanish American independence movement – some expressions of which, as in Venezuela under Francisco de Miranda, mirrored aspects of eighteenth-century Irish patriot politics, with an elite 'creole' class claiming freedom of trade and legislation from its 'mother country', while championing 'natives'' rights to enfranchisement.[24] A less prominent, but also recurrent, motif in the guests' repartees is supplied by the court of imperial China, the high ceremonial and rigorous protocols of which had been widely reported on in the British press following William Pitt Amherst's embassy there in 1816–17, apparently inspiring Lord Frederick Eversham's running joke comparing China's elaborate court rituals, and network of officious mandarins, with the intricate hierarchies and pompous officials of the British viceregal administration in Ireland. It is also through these conversations that the novel's particular, literary and autobiographical subtexts emerge, with references taking in such antecedent fictional and dramatic works as Hannah Cowley's 1781 comedy *The Belle's Stratagem* (the plot of which is also concerned with female courtship, through disguise, of a man who has returned from residence abroad), and the notorious critique of Owenson's *France* in the April 1817 number of the *Quarterly Review*. Sections from this article – including the epithets 'audacious worm' and 'mad woman'[25] – are quoted verbatim by Conway Crawley, as Owenson's obvious caricature of Croker, in a tirade against her self-portrait, Lady Clancare.

Within her conversational set pieces, and throughout the rest of her narrative, Owenson meanwhile adds further layers of allusion and intertextuality, through dialogues and authorial annotations dense with quotations from, and paraphrases of, a range of historical and antiquarian accounts of Ireland. These include both the highly conjectural studies of antiquaries such as Charles Vallancey, who had claimed an originally Phoenician (North African), and subsequently Spanish-derived, racial origin for the Irish (and which are always associated with the obsessional antiquary O'Leary); and more recent, documentary accounts of Ireland, such as Arthur Young's *Tour in Ireland* (1780), and Charles Smith's *Ancient and Present State of the County and City of Cork* (1774), citations of which texts typically appear both within the body of Owenson's narrative, and in her extensive notes. Also cited are histories and biographies concerning other countries, and a plethora of both canonical, and more marginal, or ephemeral, literary texts, ranging from the works of Shakespeare, Spenser and Milton, to Irish popular songs. These literary and antiquarian references collectively function as a critique upon previous textual representations of Ireland by successive waves of colonists and commentators. In their dominance within the text – as interpolations in the narrative, or in characters' dialogues, and in Owenson's apparatus of footnotes and endnotes – the citations, quotations and allusions also serve to emphasize the extent to which Ireland had, by the early nineteenth century, come to be itself constructed from, and in, texts, many of which contradicted each other.

The plot motif of Ascendancy private theatricals – which Owenson had already deployed in *O'Donnel* (1814), and which she would resume again in *The O'Briens and the O'Flahertys* (1827) – offers an especially fertile pretext for sustaining the novel's continuous accumulation of dramatic quotations and allusions. Through their references to works of Shakespeare, Milton and other dramatists, the houseguests' subconscious intimations of the troubled political state of Ireland emerge – the hollowness and artifice of their play-acting having already been exposed through Fitzwalter's exploration of the derelict private theatre of his own Ascendancy forbears, in Volume I. With such a consideration in mind, the apparent refusal of the especially stagestruck Lord Rosbrin to speak in any other words but (usually) Shakespeare's seems like an attempt to seek refuge in English literary language, as well as in a succession of pretended characters, from the anxious realities of life in Ireland beyond Dunore Castle – which, as the play rehearsals proceed, are to include a typhus epidemic, in addition to the ongoing food shortages and agrarian unrest. In almost all cases, and as Susan B. Egenolf has noted with reference to *The O'Briens and the O'Flahertys*,[26] Owenson's dramatic allusions may also be read as glosses upon her novels' plots or politics – a most notable instance in *Florence Macarthy* being the choice of Shakespeare's *As You Like It*, with its themes of usurpation, and female disguise, as the play to be performed in Lady Dunore's private theatre. Other quotations and citations relate to Robert Owenson's contribution to Irish culture, as an actor, singer and committed Irish Patriot theatre manager in England and Ireland between the 1770s and 1790s. Including several references to stage roles which he performed, such as Macheath in John Gay's *Beggar's Opera*; and Leander, hero of Isaac Bickerstaffe's popular comic opera *The Padlock*, these allusions assert a hereditary claim, on Owenson's part, to a role in British, as well as Irish, cultural history, while also paying tribute to her father's own contribution, through the transmission of dramatic texts, to Ireland's cultural life.

Further literary citations, parallels and intertexts highlight the extent to which Owenson regarded not only Ireland, but also women in her society, as having been constructed (and possibly distorted) by texts – which idea is most spectacularly instanced in the voluminous lists of the pious tracts, and manuals for the cultivation of ladylike accomplishments, that are observed by Fitzwalter in the boudoir of Conway Crawley's prim and narrow-minded aunt. Lady Clancare herself is constructed, as a character, from elements of previous Owenson heroines clearly intended to be recognizable by readers – the 'wild Irish' aristocrat Glorvina, the Greek patriot Ida, the governess-turned-duchessLolotte O'Halloran in *O'Donnel.* Combining with these antecedents is Owenson's own 'construction' of herself, in her preface to *France,* as having been a 'young and unprotected' woman writer, 'struggling in a path of no ordinary industry and effort, for purposes sanctified by the most sacred feelings of nature', at the time of Croker's savagely personal critique of *Woman.*[27] As Ina Ferris has shown, in the most important feminist discussion of *Florence Macarthy* to date, the characterization of Lady Clancare as a woman who serves the cause of patriotism through her creativity, and who refuses to be identified with any single, feminine role (she sits spinning literal yarn, as she tells Fitzwalter about her literary career), also represents a further stage in Owenson's ongoing, critical engagement with Germaine de Staël's influential conception of such a character in *Corinne; ou L'Italie* (1807).[28] Owenson's sense of the continuous nature of the textual construction of women, as of Ireland, is most clearly highlighted in the novel's conclusion, where the newly married Marchioness of Dunore (still also Lady Clancare in her own right) announces her intention to 'take the liberty of *putting myself in my own book,* and ... record the events of this last month of my life under the title of – *Florence Macarthy'.*[29] Lady Clancare's plan to title her book after both herself and her rebellious Gaelic ancestor makes clear Owenson's view, expressed in the novel as a whole, that women, and the Irish more generally, should be creating and controlling their own textual representations – even if these must be partly constructed out of the fragments of others' attempts. Just as she engaged with the authors who had produced Protestant-biased accounts of Gaelic or Catholic Ireland, so in *Florence Macarthy* Owenson also incorporated into her narrative the most inflammatory phrases of the *Quarterly Review's* responses to *Woman* and to *France,* appropriating them as part of the professional identity she was creating for herself from her experiences, at the same time as throwing them back at Croker.[30]

V.

No retaliatory review of *Florence Macarthy* appeared in the *Quarterly*; though the author of its review article on Henry Bradshaw Fearon's *Sketches of America* (1818) referred to it as 'that last sooterkin of dullness and immorality, *Florence Macarthy*', and accused Fearon of 'grossly [libelling]' the female readers of England, in having claimed that they shared the enthusiasm for Owenson's fiction that he had discovered among American women.[31] 'If this woman ['Lady Morgan'] has any readers', the reviewer continued, 'they are not among the *ladies* of England'.[32] They were, however, among both the women and men readers, including Lafayette and Benjamin Constant, with whom Owenson socialized and corresponded during 1818 and 1819 on her travels researching her next assignment for Colburn, a non-fictional account of Italy – having completed *Florence Macarthy* only as she passed through London and Paris, in the late summer of 1818.[33] The gossip of the London salons in particular provided her with plentiful material for the social satire of Volumes III and IV, mainly revolving around new fads such as the kaleidoscope, and exhibitions of human curiosities – 'original matter' being still needed to 'fill out' Volume III as late as August 1818, as Owenson confessed during that month in a letter to her sister.[34]

French and German translations of *Florence Macarthy* appeared in 1819, and in 1823 Dibdin's stage adaptation was succeeded by another version by Michael Bryant.[35] Owenson would also live to see the reissuing of *Florence Macarthy*, in a single-volume form, in Henry Colburn's 'Standard Novels' series in 1839. She had also, by this time, lived to see not only the passage of the Catholic Emancipation Act (in 1829), but also the rise of the radical Catholic lawyer Daniel O'Connell's movement towards mass democracy in Ireland – her Whiggish distaste for which was among reasons for her permanent move to London in 1837.[36] Although the 'Standard Novels' edition diluted the original, political character of *Florence Macarthy* by omitting Charles Morgan's preface (which was, after emancipation, also partly obsolete), and by including illustrations suggestive of a more picturesque, romantic quality to the portrayal of Ireland than its text conveyed, it clearly testified to Colburn's sense of the novel's undiminished potential as an engaging, entertaining fiction.

There is a certain aptness in the recurrence of citations of *Florence Macarthy* in the fictions of the anonymous author of *Varieties of Woman* in the nineteenth century, and of William Trevor in the twenty-first, given that Owenson's novel is itself also so rich in literary allusions and intertexts. Like the mention of *Florence Macarthy* by Owenson's anonymous, novelist contemporary in 1819, and possibly like Trevor's allusion to it, too, these references serve above all to locate the novel within its British, and more specifically Irish, contexts, as well as within the history and tradition of the novel form itself in both Ireland and England. In this work, as in all her mature 'Irish' fictions from 1814, Owenson used quoted and fragmented texts, and multiple languages and registers, and drew upon discourses ranging from antiquarianism to picturesque aesthetics, to achieve exuberant, innovative and learnedly witty fictional forms that entitle her to a place alongside Jonathan Swift and James Joyce in particular, as a contributor to a specifically Irish art of the novel.

Notes

1. W. Trevor, *The Story of Lucy Gault* (2002; London: Penguin, 2010), p. 126.
2. Review of *Florence Macarthy* in *Edinburgh Magazine*, 82 (1818), pp. 551–6, on p. 551.
3. *Varieties in Woman* was advertised as due to be published on 10 November 1819 in the *Morning Post*, Thursday 21 October 1819, p. 2.
4. Anon., *Varieties in Woman. A Novel*, 3 vols (London: Baldwin, Cradock and Joy, 1819), vol. 2, p. 132.
5. Ibid.
6. *Varieties in Woman*, vol. 2, p. 136.
7. Ibid., p. 137.
8. For the purposes of this discussion, I accept the dating of Owenson's birth, about which she was extremely reticent, to *c.* 1778 or 1779, the reports of her death in 1859 having stated her to be then aged about eighty. Her parents were the Irish actor and theatre manager Robert Owenson (1744–1812), and his English wife Jane Hill (d. 1789), from a Shrewsbury merchant family, in whose Protestant faith their children were brought up. Their only other surviving child was Owenson's sister Olivia. Owenson is generally accepted to have been born in Dublin, and was certainly brought up in Ireland, following her father on his tours of the provinces, as well as residing in Dublin (*ODNB*).
9. An advertisement for the fourth edition as 'just published' appeared in the *Morning Post*, 16 January 1819, p. 2.
10. Review of the performance of Thomas Dibdin, *Florence Macarthy, or, A Tour in Hibernia*, on 31 May 1819, at the Royal Circus and Surrey Theatre, London, *European Magazine*, 75 (June 1819), p. 544.
11. S. Owenson, Lady Morgan, 'Preface', dated 1 March 1814, in *O'Donnel: A National Tale* (London: Henry Colburn, 1814), pp. vii–xii, on p. vii, p. ix.
12. The reviewer referred to *Woman*, about the romantic adventures of a young, Greek heroine, as 'licentious and irreverent in the highest degree', and recommended its author acquire a spelling-book; see review of S. Owenson, *Woman; or, Ida of Athens* (1809), *Quarterly Review*, 1 (1809), pp. 43–5, on p. 45.
13. See T. Flanagan, *The Irish Novelists 1800–1850* (New York: Columbia University Press, 1959), pp. 138–46; and T. Dunne, 'Fiction as "the Best History of Nations": Lady Morgan's Irish Novels', in T. Dunne (ed.), *The Writer as Witness: Literature as Historical Evidence* (Cork: Cork University Press, 1987), pp. 133–59.
14. For fuller discussion of how *Florence Macarthy* challenges Edgeworth's exclusionary model of Protestant Ascendancy rule in Ireland, see T. Tracy, 'Transcending Ascendancy: *Florence Macarthy*, Irishness and Womanhood in Nineteenth-Century British Writing* (Farnham: Ashgate, 2009), pp. 51–63.
15. For the fullest account of Charles Morgan's courtship of Sydney Owenson, and Abercorn's arranging for him to be knighted so that Owenson could be compensated for her

loss of independence in marriage by an elevation in social status, see W. Hepworth Dixon (ed.), *Lady Morgan's Memoirs: Autobiography, Diaries and Correspondence*, 2nd edn, 2 vols (London: W. & H. Allan & Co., 1863), vol. 1, pp. 526–7.

16. Sydney Owenson to Alicia Lefanu, 18 January 1810, in H. Dixon (ed.), *Lady Morgan's Memoirs*, vol. 1, p. 403.

17. Ibid.

18. Sydney Owenson to William Cavendish, Marquess of Hartington (1810), in H. Dixon (ed.), *Lady Morgan's Memoirs*, vol. 1, p. 422. Owenson continued to draw an analogy between herself as literary celebrity, and any other animal or 'human curiosity' exhibited for public entertainment, with several references to contemporary freaks and prodigies in the narrative of *Florence Macarthy*.

19. See C. Connolly, *A Cultural History of the Irish Novel, 1790–1829* (Cambridge: Cambridge University Press, 2012), p. 75. For an excellent overview of social and political conditions in Ireland during the 1810s, see S. J. Connolly, 'Union Government, 1812–13', in F. X. Martin et al. (eds) *A New History of Ireland*, 10 vols (Oxford: Clarendon Press, 1989), vol. 5, pp. 48–73; on the structure and culture of the Dublin viceregal establishment, see R. F. Foster, *Modern Ireland 1600–1972* (1988; London: Penguin, 1989), pp. 226–40.

20. See J. Newcomer, *Lady Morgan the Novelist* (Lewisburg, PA: Bucknell University Press, 1990), pp. 55–6.

21. See T. Eagleton, *Heathcliff and the Great Hunger: Studies in Irish Culture* (London: Verso, 1995), p. 182.

22. These passages, in which Fitzadelm's detached, aestheticizing perspective upon urban and rural poverty in Ireland is set against Fitzwalter's more realistic view, have been the focus of most of the recent critical attention to the novel; see especially K. Trumpener, *Bardic Nationalism: The Romantic Novel and the British Empire* (Princeton, NJ: Princeton University Press, 1997), pp. 56, 143–6; J. A. Stevens, 'Views of Georgian Dublin: Perspectives of the City', in G. O'Brien and F. O'Kane (eds), *Georgian Dublin* (Dublin: Four Courts Press, 2008), pp. 156–64; F. L. Price, *Revolutions in Taste, 1773–1818: Women Writers and the Aesthetics of Romanticism* (Farnham: Ashgate, 2009), pp. 162–4 and Connolly, *A Cultural History of the Irish Novel*, pp. 38–41.

23. *Florence Macarthy*, p. 5.

24. On the background to the Spanish American independence movements in the period, and their significance to English and Irish Whig culture, see R. C. Heinowitz, *Spanish America and British Romanticism, 1777–1826: Rewriting Conquest* (Edinburgh: Edinburgh University Press, 2010).

25. Review of Sydney Owenson, Lady Morgan, *France* (1817), *Quarterly Review*, 17 (1817), pp. 260–86, on p. 284.

26. See S. B. Egenolf, *The Art of Political Fiction in Hamilton, Edgeworth, and Owenson* (Farnham: Ashgate, 2009), pp. 177–9.

27. Sydney Owenson, Lady Morgan, 'Preface', in *France*, 2 vols, 2nd edn (London: Henry Colborn, 1817), vol. 1, p. viii.

28. See I. Ferris, *he Romantic National Tale and the Question of Ireland* (Cambridge: Cambridge University Press, 2002), pp. 76–8. Not only the character of Lady Clancare, but also other aspects of *Florence Macarthy* clearly mirror *Corinne*, including the characterization of Fitzwalter, who resembles Stael's 'lord Nelvil' not only as a solitary, melancholic traveller who assists in others' causes while still mourning the loss of his father, but also

in his association with a more irresponsible, hedonistic aristocratic type (with Fitzadelm resembling Stael's comted'Erfeuil in this respect).

29. *Florence Macarthy*, p. 364.
30. For further discussion of Owenson's directness in confronting her detractors in print, throughout her career, and her absorption of critics' attacks into her other writings, see J. E. Belanger, *Critical Receptions: Sydney Owenson, Lady Morgan* (Bethseda, MD: Academic Press, 2007), pp. 2–5; 12–13.
31. Review of H. B. Fearon, *Sketches of America. A Narrative of a Journey of Five Thousand Miles Through the Eastern and Western States of America* (1818), *Quarterly Review*, 21 (1819), pp. 124–67, on p. 143. In the period, 'sooterkin' was used in the senses of a mythical, rat-like afterbirth supposedly produced by Dutch women; and ofan imperfect literary composition (*OED*).
32. Ibid., on p. 144.
33. See journals and correspondence to 1818 and 1819 reproduced throughout Sydney Owenson, Lady Morgan, *Passages from My Autobiography* (London: Bentley, 1859).
34. Owenson, *Passages from My Autobiography*, p. 46.
35. See M. Bryant, *Florence Macarthy; or, Life in Ireland: A Grand Melodramatic Romance in Three Acts* (London: G. Heaton, 1823).
36. For discussion of Owenson's 'distress' over O'Connell's mass politics, see Dunne, 'Fiction as "the Best History of Nations"', in Dunne (ed.), p. 154.

SELECT BIBLIOGRAPHY

Anon., Notice of *Varieties in Woman. A Novel, Morning Post*, Thursday 21 October 1819.

Anon., Review of *Florence Macarthy, Edinburgh Magazine*, 82 (1818), pp. 551–6.

Anon., Review of performance of T. Dibdin, after S. Owenson, *Florence Macarthy, or, A Tour in Hibernia, European Magazine*, 75 (June 1819), p. 544.

Anon., *Varieties in Woman*, 3 vols (London: Baldwin, Cradock and Joy, 1819), vol. 2.

Belanger, J. E., *Critical Receptions: Sydney Owenson, Lady Morgan* (Bethseda, MD: Academic Press, 2007).

Bryant, M., after S. Owenson, *Florence Macarthy; or, Life in Ireland: A Grand Melodramatic Romance in Three Acts* (London: G. Heaton, 1823).

Connolly, C., *A Cultural History of the Irish Novel, 1790–1829* (Cambridge: Cambridge University Press, 2012).

Connolly, S. J., 'Union Government, 1812–13', in F. X. Martin, et al. (eds.), *A New History of Ireland*, 10 vols (Oxford: Clarendon Press, 1989), vol. 5, pp. 48–73.

Croker, J. W. (attrib.), Review of S. Owenson, *Woman; or Ida of Athens, Quarterly Review* 1 (1809), pp. 43–5.

—, (attrib.), Review of S. Owenson, Lady Morgan, *France, Quarterly Review*, 17 (1817), pp. 260–86.

—, (attrib.), Review of H. B. Fearon, *Sketches of America, Quarterly Review*, 21 (1819), pp. 124–67.

Dunne, T., 'Fiction as "the best history of Nations": Lady Morgan's Irish Novels', in T. Dunne (ed.), *The Writer as Witness: Literature as Historical Evidence* (Cork: Cork University Press, 1987).

Eagleton, T., *Heathcliff and the Great Hunger: Studies in Irish Culture* (London: Verso, 1995).

Egenolf, S. B., *The Art of Political Fiction in Hamilton, Edgeworth, and Owenson* (Farnham: Ashgate, 2009).

Ferris, I., *The Romantic National Tale and the Question of Ireland* (Cambridge: Cambridge University Press, 2002).

Flanagan, T., *The Irish Novelists 1800–1850* (New York: Columbia University Press, 1959).

Foster, R. F., *Modern Ireland, 1600–1972* (1988; London: Penguin, 1989).

Heinowitz, R. C., *Spanish America and British Romanticism, 1777–1826: Rewriting Conquest* (Edinburgh: Edinburgh University Press, 2010).

Hepworth Dixon, W. (ed.), *Lady Morgan's Memoirs: Autobiography, Diaries and Correspondence*, 2nd edn, 2 vols (London: W. H. Allan & Co., 1863).

Newcomer, J., *Lady Morgan the Novelist* (Lewisburg, PA: Bucknell University Press, 1990).

Owenson, S., *Florence Macarthy: An Irish Tale* (London: H. Colburn, 1839).

—, *France*, 2nd edn, 2 vols (London: H. Colburn, 1817).

—, *O'Donnel: A National Tale*, 4 vols (London: H. Colburn, 1814), vol.1.

—, *Passages From My Autobiography* (London: Bentley, 1859).

—, *Patriotic Sketches of Ireland, Written in Connaught*, 2 vols (London: R. Phillips, 1807).

—, *St Clair; or, The Heiress of Desmond* (London: E. Harding, 1803).

—, *The Missionary: An Indian Tale*, 3 vols (London: J. J. Stockdale, 1811).

—, *The O'Briens and the O'Flahertys; A National Tale*, 4 vols (London: H. Colburn, 1827).

—, *The Wild Irish Girl: A National Tale*, 3 vols (London: R. Phillips, 1807).

—, *Woman: or, Ida of Athens*, 4 vols (London: Longman, 1809).

Price, F. L., *Revolutions in Taste, 1773–1818: Women Writers and the Aesthetics of Romanticism* (Farnham: Ashgate, 2009).

Tracy, T., *Transcending Ascendancy: Florence Macarthy, Irishness and Womanhood in Nineteenth-Century British Writing* (Farnham: Ashgate, 2009).

Trevor, W., *The Story of Lucy Gault* (2002; London: Penguin, 2010).

Trumpener, K., *Bardic Nationalism: The Romantic Novel and the British Empire* (Princeton, NJ: Princeton University Press, 1997).

Stevens, J. A., 'Views of Georgian Dublin: Perspectives of the City', in G. O'Brien and F. O'Kane (eds), *Georgian Dublin* (Dublin: Four Courts Press, 2008), pp. 155–64.

FLORENCE MACARTHY:

An Irish Tale.

BY

LADY MORGAN,

AUTHOR OF 'FRANCE,' 'O'DONNEL,' &C.

Know thus far forth:
By accident most strange, bountiful fortune,
Now, my dear lady, hath mine enemies
Brought to this shore: and by my prescience,
I find my zenith doth depend upon
A most auspicious star, whose influence,
If now I court not but omit, my fortunes
Will ever after droop. SHAKESPEARE.[1]

Les femmes ne sent pas trop d'humeur à pardonner de certaines injures, et
quand elles se promettent le plaisir de la vengeance elles n'y vont pas de *main-
morte.*
DE GRAMMONT.[2]

IN FOUR VOLUMES.

VOL. I.

LONDON:

PRINTED FOR HENRY COLBURN,
PUBLIC LIBRARY, CONDUIT STREET, HANOVER SQUARE.
1818. /
B. CLARKE. Printer, Well Street, London. /

ADVERTISEMENT.[a]

THE Irish have been accused of making an ostentatious display of their injuries, and of clanking their chains to excite compassion. But, however humiliating it may be deemed to reiterate complaint where there is no commiseration, and to urge claims where there is no redress, the alternative is less intolerable than that silent acquiescence, which malice or self-interest is but too ready to construe into tacit approbation.

The appeal to public opinion belongs to the age in which we live; and it is the certainty of its ultimate success, not the abject hopelessness of its repetition, which has excited this affectation of disgust. The *ratio ultima regum*[3] is too expensive an instrument to be often wielded by the citizen; nor / is it very likely that the detractors of the Irish nation would be more satisfied with an overt act of resistance, than they are with the tameness of annual petitions.

But be that as it may, the '*national tale*', with which the reader is here presented, is no pathetic appeal to public compassion. It is, indeed, impossible to speak of Ireland, still less to take it as the scene of a narrative, without frequent allusion to its starving, squalid, and diseased population. The people form too prominent an object in the landscape to be wholly passed over by the most indifferent observer. But it is chiefly from among the master cast[4] that the author of Florence Macarthy has drawn her characters and her incidents; and it is in the reaction of the execrable system of '*divide and govern*', in the demoralization and insecurity which that system inflicts upon the agents, no less than on the victims / of oppression, that she has found materials for another Irish story.

For the fidelity of her delineations, whoever has resided in Ireland will readily vouch; and if the features are sometimes deeply tragical, and sometimes broadly ludicrous, the fault lies in the originals, and not with their illustrator.

The manners she has described, and the society she has represented, belong to a peculiar epoch; they arose under a particular political combination, and they will cease with its dissolution. But wherever a possibility exists for bringing that combination again into action, the tale will have an interest: and as ridicule will reach those who are impregnable to reason, this picture of the aristocracy of the bureau may not be without a contingent utility to other countries, beside that for whose service it was more expressly undertaken.

In the composition of the series of tales, of which FLORENCE MACARTHY / forms a part, the author has hitherto endeavoured to sketch the brilliant aspect of a people struggling with adversity, and by the delineation of national virtues, to excite sympathy, and awaken justice. In the portraiture of a party, a cast, a faction, the colouring must necessarily vary. The opposition between the natural characteristics of the Irish temperament, and those peculiarities, which a false policy, operating for six hundred years, has impressed upon a portion of the population, must not be confounded with contradiction in statement, or versatility in opinion: nor the Crawley family be taken as derogating from the Glorvinas, O'Donnels, and Mac Rorys, of former compositions.[5]

T. C. M.[6]
La Grange:
Département de Seine et Marne,
September, 1818.[7] /

CHAPTER I.

Whom when I asked, from what place he came,
And how he hight himself, he did y-cleep
The Shepherd of the Ocean, by name,
And said he came far from the main sea deep.
Collin Clout's come home again. – SPENCER.[8]

EARLY in the nineteenth century, in an autumnal month, a corvette, a light built Spanish vessel, passed the Bar of Dublin, and, with all her canvass crowded, rode gallantly into the bay, after having weathered, for a period of five days, one of those tremendous gales, which occasionally agitate the Irish seas. A southern port of Ireland had been her original destination. Stress of weather had driven her up the Channel;[9] and the injury she had received in / her unequal contest with the elements rendered it necessary that she should undergo repair, before she proceeded on her coasting voyage. On her stern she bore the name of '*Il Librador;*'*[10] and, though now unarmed, and the property of a private individual, she had evidently been a sloop of war in some foreign service.

The dawn was breaking in tints of gold and hues of crimson, as the corvette cut her way through the brightning waves; and the happiest aspect of the Irish coast presented itself to the view of two persons, who stood in silence at the helm; – who had stood there since the first pale flush of light had thrown its silvery line along the eastern horizon.

The elder of the two was the master of the vessel. He was still in the very prime of life and flower of manhood; / and as each lovely feature of the Irish shore gradually developed itself, and arose bright and fresh from the mists of the morning upon his eager gaze, he presented, in his own person, an image, that denoted the intention of the creator, when he made man supreme above all, to reign over his fair creation.

He stood erect, his arms so folded as to give to his square chest and shoulders a peculiar muscularity and breadth of outline. His fine bust, indicating extraordinary strength, would have been almost disproportioned to his stature, which rose not much above the middle height, but that the loftiness of his air, and the

---

*   The Liberator.

freedom of his carriage, conferred an artificial elevation on his figure, and corrected what might be deemed imperfect in his actual structure. His large eyes were rather deep set than protuberant; and their glances, rather side-long than direct, flashed from beneath his dark impending brows, like / the vivid lightnings which fringe the massive vapours of a tropical atmosphere. His mouth had a physiognomy of its own: it was what *the eye is* to other faces: and the workings of the nether lip, in moments of emotion, indicated the influence of vehement passions, habitually combatted, though rarely subdued. The expression of his countenance was more intellectual than gracious, and calculated to strike, rather than to please. But his rare and singular smile (a smile so bland, it might well have become even a woman's lip) wholly changed its character; and the full displayed teeth, of splendid whiteness, produced perhaps even too strong a contrast with a complexion, which southern suns, and climes of scorching ardor, had bronzed into a dark, deep, but transparent olive. No tint, no hue warmed or varied this gloomy paleness, save when the tide of passion, rushing impetuously from the heart, coloured / for a moment, with a burning crimson, the livid cheek, and then, as promptly ebbing back to its source, left all cold, pale, and dark as before.

From his accent or manner it would have been difficult to assign him to any particular country. He seemed rather to belong to the world; – one of those creatures formed out of the common mould, whom nature and circumstances combine and fit for deeds of general import and universal interest. Neither could the term *gentility* be appropriately applied to an appearance which had a character beyond it. He might have been above or below heraldic notices and genealogical distinctions, but he was evidently independent of them. His mate, an old but hale man, with whom he conversed in Spanish (but who had English enough to work the ship, and sufficient knowledge of the Irish seas to steer it with skill), respectfully addressed him by the title of / 'the Commodore;' and the crew (a few English sailors, to whom he seemed, even by name, a stranger) adopted the same appellation. But he issued his clear prompt orders with the air and decision of one to whom higher titles of command were familiar. He was a good sailor, fearless in danger, calm and self-possessed in difficulty; and, to the only passenger who accompanied him, (one courteously and accidentally admitted on board his ship), he spoke of himself as a man fond of the sea from boyhood, making voyages of pleasure when he could, and now uniting an old habit of recreation with the urgency of pressing business. He was on his way from a West India island, on a secret mission, of importance to himself; but he neither mentioned his own name, nor inquired that of the young passenger he had taken up out of a wherry in Plymouth Sound,[11] the port whence he had last sailed, and where the stranger had / vainly sought a passage to Ireland, now granted him by the commander of *Il Librador*.

The appearance of this person, who had voluntarily announced himself by the name of De Vere, was less equivocal, and though infinitely interesting, was perhaps less striking than that of the Commodore. It was also of a more definite stamp and character; more assignable to a class, a cast, a country. Though there was little of conventional mannerism about him, though his elegant and thorough bred air was wholly unmarked by the overcharged fashioning of any country, yet, to those acquainted with the first class of British distinction, he was easily cognizable in accent, dress, air, and physiognomy, as an Englishman of rank and fashion, the *homme comme il faut*[12] of the highest circles.

There was, however, in the countenance and modes of this distinguished young stranger something more than / the mere characteristics of country and rank: – a sort of fantastic pensiveness, a real or affected abstraction, a something imaginative and ideal, in his manière d'être,[13] that indicated great eccentricity, if not eminent peculiarity of mind. He seemed a compound of fancy and fashion; a medium between the consciousness of rank, and the assumption and possession of genius, which placed him out of the common muster-roll of society; something escaped from it by chance, and vain of standing aloof, untractable to its laws, and therefore believing himself beyond them. In his conversations with the Commodore he spoke in paradox, had systems out of the common scale, and theories of alembicated[14] refinement. An ideologist,[15 b] in the fullest sense of the word, in his philosophy he talked as one who believed that 'nothing *is*, but thinking makes it so:'[16] and occupied by an *ideal presence*, he affected to live distinct and independent / of all human interests. – The structure of his fine head was such as physiognomists assign to superior intellect;[17] and the precise arrangement of its glossy auburn curls left it difficult to decide whether its fanciful and fashionable possessor was more fop or philosopher, dandy or poet. His valet de chambre,[18] a Frenchman, presided with invariable punctuality at his toilette twice a-day, when the uncivil elements did not interfere with such arrangements; and the rest of his time was spent in musing, reading Spencer's 'Fairy Queen,' and 'State of Ireland,'[19] and occasionally conversing with the commander of the vessel, who seemed to inspire him with sentiments of curiosity and admiration, not usual to his ordinary habits of feeling. As he now stood beside him at the helm, or rather leaned in a recumbent attitude, with an half-closed book in his hand, his attention seemed not to be given to the beautiful coast scenery, which, en-/dowed with at least the charm of novelty, was now breaking on his view; for his up-turned glance, giving him the inspired air of one 'communing with the skies,'[20] seemed to pursue the gradual disappearance of the morning star,[21] as an object superiorly attractive in proportion as it was remote and fleeting. –After a long silence, mutually preserved, he withdrew his dazzled eyes from the reddening effulgence of the heavens, and addressed his companion, by observing:

'There is to me a singular attraction in the aspect of an unknown firmament, for it tells of distance from scenes, and objects long marked by sameness, and distinguished only by satiety.'

'It tells too,' replied the Commodore, 'of remoteness from objects, precious by interest or habit. The *cross of the south*,[22] first seen in tropical climates, draws tears to the eyes of the Spanish seaman, its image recalling remembrances of his distant country.' /

'*Remembrances of country*, however, are usually the finger-posts to ennui.[23] – One wears out every thing in one's own country before one leaves it; and, therefore, *it is* left. – Country! all countries are alike: little masses of earth and water; where some swarms of human ants are destined to creep through their span of ephemeral existence; coming, they know not whence; – going, they know not where.'

'These little masses of earth and water,' said the Commodore, 'are *therefore* precious and important to the ants that creep on them; and each little hill is dear to the swarm that inhabits it, as much from that very ignorance as from interest.'

After a short pause, Mr. De Vere resumed:

'Can you not credit then the existence of a creature placed by nature or circumstances beyond the ordinary pale of humanity, shaking off 'his poor / estate of man,'[24] scarcely looking upon that spot, called earth, with human eyes, nor herding with his species in human sympathy – one so organized, so worked on by events, and thwarted in feelings, so blasted in his bud of life, as to stand alone in creation, matchless, or at least unmatched, whose joys, whose woes, whose sentiments and passions, are not those of other men, but all his own, beyond the reach of affection, or the delusions of hope?'

'A being, thus constituted,' rejoined the Commodore, 'could not be man. He, who wants the appetites and passions common to all men, with the sympathies and affections that spring from them, is something better or worse, angel or dæmon, but he is not man.'

'You deny then the possibility of such an existence?

'Nay – madmen may fancy such a combination, poets feign it, or vain men / affect it; but it has no real existence in nature or society. Man is always man; and he who pretends to be *more*, is rarely placed by nature at the head of his species – he is in fact usually less.'

Before Mr. De Vere could reply, a question from a sailor interrupted the conversation, which was one of many held in the same tone and spirit. The Commodore was the next moment busied in giving orders for tacking.[25] He addressed his mate in pure Spanish, chided the French valet out of his way in good French, and fell foul of a lubberly[26] sailor in broad nautical English.

'There is somewhere,' said Mr. De Vere, turning over the pages of Spencer's Ireland, and resuming his conversation with the commander of the vessel, as he returned to his station at the helm – 'there is somewhere, through the quaint pages of Spencer, an admirable description of the natural advan-/tages of Ireland, which I cannot find.' 'Look around you,' answered the Commodore: 'you will find them here.'

'I prefer looking through the spectacles of books. I like the prismatic hues thrown by authorship upon places and facts.'

'Indeed! that is strange! but in viewing Ireland through Spencer's pages, you will see it, as children do an eclipse, through a smoked glass. He was one of those, whose policy it was to revile the country he preyed upon, to spoil, and then to vituperate. No Englishman can fairly estimate this island who comes not unshackled by his own interests. Spencer, the deputy of a deputy,[27] the secretary, whose servile flattery of the viceroy, his master, was rewarded with a principality (soon lost, indeed, but most unfairly won), is no author for impartiality to judge by; and when he stoops to eulogize the *'dreadless might'* / of his ferocious patron, Grey, one of Ireland's Herods,[28] when he defines power to be

'The right hand of Justice truly hight,'

however he may please as a poet, he is contemptible as an historian, and infamous as a politician.'

'Oh! as an historian or politician I give him up, because both characters are equally ridiculous: the politician always guided by prejudice and interest, the historian always immersed in ignorance and error. Time discovers and shames both: and thus it is with all that bears upon human facts. The imagination alone is always right; its visions are alone imperishable. The *Fairy Queen* of Spencer will thus survive, when his State of Ireland shall be wholly forgotten: and, for my own part, so much do I prefer the visions of *his* fancy to the historical relations of any period connected with the history of men, that I would go a thousand miles / to visit the ruins of his Irish *Kilcoleman*,*[29] where once

'He sat, as was his trade,

'Under the foot of Mole, that mountain hoar,'

Where – 'Allured by his pipe's delight,

'Whose pleasing sound y-shrilled far about;'[30]

the gallant Raleigh found him. But I am not sure that I would turn one point out of my way to tread upon the spot where legitimate despotism signed the

---

*   Originally the principality of the *Macarthies More*; afterwards the palatinate of the Fitzgeralds, Earls of Desmond; forfeited by them, and given to new spoliators, among whom was the thriftless adventurer Raleigh, who in Ireland (´) acted the part of a freebooter. The spoils which fell to the poet Spencer, as secretary to Lord Arthur Grey, (the 'Sir Artigall' of his dreary legend of that name) were three thousand acres of rich land in the County of Cork, with the beautiful Castle of Kilcoleman, the seat of the Earls of Desmond.

(´)   See Notes, at the end of this Volume.

fiat of its own destruction, and gave Magna Charta to an emancipated nation.
[31] / The delicious strains of Spencer are now fresh and true as when they were
first breathed; but where is the spirit that commanded and produced an English
Magna Charta?'

'Suspended, perhaps,' interrupted the Commodore, 'not extinct. For its
essence exists in the temperament of an Englishman. You must first give him
another position on the globe, or employ ages of misrule to change his national
character, before you can reconcile him to slavery – circumstances may lull him
in false security, or force him to temporary acquiescence; but no combination
can ensure his permanent obedience to unequivocal despotism.'[c]

The vessel at that moment touched the pier.

The Commodore had sprung upon land; and he stood for a moment on the
spot that had received the first pressure of his footstep. To judge by the darkling[32]
of his eye, and the motion of / his lip, some strong and powerful feeling occupied his mind; hut it was of brief duration. Emotions unconnected with action
seemed not made for him: by the tossing back of his head, he appeared to give
thought to the winds, and plunged into all the bustle and activity of the circumstances in which he was placed.

The Holyhead packet[33] was not yet visible; and the earliness of the hour left
the pier still in quietude. The land-waiter[34] had been called to go through the
necessary forms, and of him the Commodore asked some questions, with eager
curiosity, clearness, and rapidity of utterance, as if life were too short to suffer
one moment to pass by unoccupied, or uninstructed; then, as if impatient of
the drawling replies, anticipated the answers, and started new inquiries of local
reference. Meantime Mr. De Vere had landed; but wholly abstracted from the
noise and activity / that surrounded him, he stood, turning over the leaves of his
Spencer, while the valet was receiving parcels, portmanteaux, and port-folios,
from a sailor, who was flinging them on shore, and exclaiming, as he appropri-
ated or rejected each several article, '*C'est à nous*,' – '*ce n'est pas à nous*.' –[35] With
the exception of 'got dam,'[36] the Frenchman had not yet acquired a single word of
English. But with this small portion of the language, and his own very expressive
gesticulations, he had succeeded so well, as almost to think with Figaro,[37] that
this emphatic imprecation was the basis of the tongue; and that with it '*on ne
manque de rien, nulle part*.'[38]

'Will I step in for a jingle[39] for your honor?' demanded a voice, in the broad
languid drawling of the genuine patois of Dublin, addressing the full force of its
brogue[40] to the delicate ears of Mr. De Vere. 'Will I, plaze your honor, / step in,
Sir?' This question, several times repeated, at last obtained notice by its reitera-
tion. The young stranger raised his eyes for a moment to the face of him who
thus unceremoniously proffered his services, but he withdrew them again in disgust. The object of this ungracious glance, so little flattering in its expression, had

stood its inquiry with great coolness. He was leaning, and had been leaning since the dawn, against one of the posts of the pier, and had watched the approach of *Il Librador* idly and patiently for more than an hour, partly for the gratification of his curiosity, and partly in the hope of earning some trifle by going for a vehicle, or by carrying into the town some luggage for the passengers. There is scarcely any place so lonely, or hour so unseasonable, at which some one of these genuine lazzaroni[41] of the Irish metropolis may not be found lounging away time, between hope and idleness, / in the enjoyment of doing nothing, or the vague expectation of having something to do.

Miserably clad, disgustingly filthy, squalid, meagre, and famished, the petitioner for employment had yet humour in his eye, and observation in his countenance. Occasionally ready to assist, and always prompt to flatter, he did neither gratuitously. Taunt and invective seemed the natural expression of his habit; for though debasingly acquiescent to a destiny, which left him without motive for industry, in a country where industry is no refuge from distress, he yet preserved the vindictiveness of conscious degradation; and there was frequently a deep-seated sincerity in his curse, which was sometimes wanting to his purchased benediction. Idleness had become the custom of his necessity; and his wants were so few, that a trifling exertion would supply them. Yet he sought / early and late for employment; for he had probably wants more urgent than his own to satisfy.

This unfortunate representative of his class had hitherto lolled on the pier, a listless spectator of the scene, which was going forward, muttering at intervals a shrewd observation, laughing deridingly as he threw his eyes over the French valet, whose foreign air and dress were peculiarly notable; and again composing his sharp features into a look of respectful deference, as he reiterated his question to him, whom he supposed the master. – 'Will I step in for a jingle, your honor? will I, Sir?' 'Step in!' at last repeated Mr. De Vere, struck perhaps by the calm steady perseverance of his intrusion – 'step in where, friend?' 'Step into Dublin, plaze your honor, for a jingle, Sir, or a hackney.'[42]

'Is Dublin so near then?'

'It is, plaze your honor, handy bye,[43] / Sir, quite convanient: yez won't miss me, your honor, till I bees back wid ye.'

'If Dublin is so near,' said Mr. De Vere, closing his book, and addressing the Commodore, who now, with his rapid step, approached him, after having given his orders to his mate and men – 'if Dublin is so near, I should prefer walking, to trusting to any filthy vehicle we may be able to procure at this unseasonable hour.'

'I meant to propose it,' was the reply; and the active animated speaker, taking a rich pelisse[44] from his mate, which he drew over his ship dress, and exchanging his cap for a round hat, he gave some additional orders in Spanish, and desired the sailor, who stood beside him, with a large valise on his shoulder, and writing case in his hand, to follow him to Dublin. The two gentlemen then proceeded, arm in arm, to town, furnished by the officers of the customs with a card of one of the many hotels / which now succeed in the patrician streets of Dublin to the mansions of the banished nobility.[45]

Mr. De Vere, to whom the vulgar exertions of every-day life were all unknown, and even unguessed at, had left every thing to a valet, as helpless as himself. For the first time since he had come into his master's service, he was deprived of the assistance of a certain Portuguese laquais,[46] one who spoke all languages, performed all services, and united all the intrigue, roguery, and ingenuity of the Pedrillos and Lazarillos of the Spanish comedy.[47] This man had been dismissed for mal-practices, at the moment his master was leaving the port of Lisbon for that of Plymouth; and since that period the Frenchman had acted without deputy or interpreter. But as almost the whole of the interval had been passed at sea (for his master had remained but a few hours at Plymouth), he had but slightly felt the in- /convenience. Now, however, left to act, not only for his master, but for himself, he remained, standing on the pier, in all the embarrass of endless books, parcels, and the splendid *necessaire* of the portable toilette. [48] He had alternately taken up and laid down a valise, a dressing box, and a pocket edition of Zamora's Spanish Plays;[49] accompanying each movement with a 'sacre,' '*diantre*,' or '*Peste de moname*,'[50] slowly rolled forth from between his closed teeth; when the English sailor, jerking his own load on his shoulders, exclaimed, 'come, come, mounseer, know your own mind; either wait till we sends a coach for you and your trumpery, or get some-un to help you.'

'Shure I'll carry in them portmantles to town for you, mounseer, and the leather box, to boot, for a trifle,' observed the Irishman; who, disappointed in the commission he had sought, had remained motionless and silent, till the hope of / his services being again accepted suggested itself; and he repeated his proposal three several times, each louder than the other, as if the louder he vociferated, the better chance he had of being understood by the foreigner.

'Do you hear me now, mounseer?' he screamed close in the Frenchman's ear; who, stamping his feet with anger, exclaimed, 'Paix! paix!'[51]

'Pay, pay,' reiterated the Irishman. 'I'll engage you will, dear, and well.' Then, without further ceremony, hoisting the valise on his shoulders, taking a port folio under his arm, and carrying the dressing box by its handle, he nodded his head to the parcel of books, which were inclosed in a leather strap, observed, 'now, mounseer, I'll trouble you just to take them bits of books in your daddle;[52] and what would ail us, but we'd take in th' other trifles of things betwixt us aisy enough, plaze God; I'll engage we will. So now, my lad,' (address-/ing the sailor) 'follow me, and I'll shew you the road.'

The Frenchman comprehended the arrangements of the Irishman better than his language, grinned applause, muttered a good humoured 'got dam,' in token of approbation, and taking up the books, these three singular representatives of the three nations proceeded towards Dublin, following close on the steps of the gentlemen, who had inquired their route, and were some paces in advance.

The Irish lounger,[53] no lounger now, stepped on lightly with his burthen, in that short quick trot, with which the lower Irish frequently perform journies from one extremity of the kingdom to the other, bare-footed and bare-legged. The sailor and the Frenchman, with an appearance much more alert, and burthens infinitely lighter, scarcely kept pace with him, and obliged him frequently to stop, while he as frequently / addressed them with a sort of sly indirect curiosity, which ingeniously sought its gratification, without any obvious efforts to obtain it.

'I'll engage, mounseer,' he observed, first attacking the Frenchman, 'yez were never in ould Ireland afore, far as you've travelled; and yez

'May travel the wide world all over,
And sail from France to Balin-robe,'[54]

as the song says, afore ye'll see the likes of it again, any way.' 'Bon, bon,' returned the Frenchman, supposing that he communicated the joyful intelligence of their speedy arrival, 'Bon, j'en suis charmé.'[55]

'Why then it will *charmy* ye more every step ye take, for there isn't her match, by say, or land, with her beautiful eye, there, like a unicorn's, in the front of her forehead;* and her Hill of / Hoath,[56] like a mole on her cheek; and see there forenent yez, acrass the bay, there, there's the sheds of Clontarf, and the green groves of Marino, the great Earl of Marlemont's sate,[57] and ould Ballybough, the creatur! to the fore this day as when Bryan Bŏrugh lost his crown, and his harp on it, (the sowl), in the Musaum of Trinity.†[58]

'Comment donc!'[59] demanded the Frenchman, denoting his ignorance of this detailed description by the perplexity of his looks. 'Och bother,' returned the Irishman, out of all patience at what appeared to him obstinate stupidity.

'Bodere, bodere,' reiterated the Frenchman, indignant at what he saw / was intended for insult. 'Comment donc bodere gueux, que tu es!'[60]

'*Cut away* yourself,' replied the Irishman, laughing good humouredly, 'or troth, you'll be in too late for the fair, honey!'

The Frenchman, supposing that these words, and the conciliating laugh which accompanied them, indicated an apology, took off his hat with great politeness, and accepted the fancied excuses, with 'mais voila, mon ami, qui est

---

*   Ireland's eye – a rock at the entrance of the bay.

†   A harp is shewn in the Museum of Trinity College, said to have belonged to the Irish Monarch, and found on the Plains of Clontarf, where he fought his last famous battle against the Danes, and lost his life.

bien.'[61] 'Och, your humble servant to command, mounseer,' returned the Irishman, dropping his load to make an imitative bow: 'troth, you do your dancing
master every justice, whoever he was.'

The English sailor, much amused by this interchange of civility in his two
companions, observed, 'aye, aye, sirs let the mounseers alone for bowing and
scraping, and the likes.[62] Never a dancing dog at Bartlemy fair[63] will beat them at
that, I'll warrant.' /

'Why then I'll engage,' replied the Irishman, 'that yellow, swarthy, portly[64]
gentleman there, your captain, wouldn't be a Frenchman, with his eligant surtout,[65] for all he has a Frenchified air about him.'

'What he! Lord help your heart, not he – no more a Frenchman nor I am,
lad.'

'Och! he'd be very sorry, I'll engage; though he has an outlandish look with
him, for all that.'

'Why, aye sure, because he comed from the Hindies, d'ye see; the West Hindies, – or Spanish America. – It's all one for that, come from where he will he's a
hearty true blue,[66] every bit of him.'

'And is yourself come all the ways with him, dear, from the Western Indies?'

'Not I. I was lying in dock, for it is not now all as one as formerly – all goes
by luck and fashion now – Some how, one hears no more of the Howes, / and
the Hothams, and the Nelsons, and the wooden walls of old England.[67] – The
jacket, the old true blue's worn out, Sir. So this here gem'man, who owns that
tight bit of timber, every splinter of her himself, it seems, put into our Plymouth
Sound, three weeks ago, bound from Demerara, and sent back his Spanish crew
in a Cadiz merchantman,[68] (excepting old Grim Groudy, the mate), and paid 'em
like a prince. So then he set sail for London, aloft on the mail;[69] and when he
came back, he manned this little vessel with a handful of us Plymouth boys, and
we heaved anchor six days agone for Ireland; and this I'll say for him, a better
commander never stepped on forecastle, or walked the quarter-deck.'

'See that now,' replied the Irishman, quietly, 'and has 'nt a mild look with
him, then, for all that; only mighty stern. He wouldn't be a slave driver from the
Western Indies, Sir, I suppose?' /

'What he! not he, bless the heart of him; no more nor I bees; not but he's
hard enough, sometimes, and hates a lubber as he hates poison; but goes our
halves in hard work.'[70]

'See that, now, Sir: och, he has a fine look with him, and mighty portly; and
has a great name upon him, if a body knew it, I'll engage.'

'Can't tell ye that though,' replied the sailor, 'because why, I don't know it
myself. They called 'n *the Don* at the King's Arms in Plymouth – the Spanish
Don,[71] though he speaks as good English as the best. And then, when one asks

a question of Grim Groudy, who knows all about him, he only answers one in his d – d lingo.'

'And that tall slinder young man, dear, with his head in the clouds, as if he'd snuff the moon, fairly, he's his comrade, I'll engage?'

'What, yon fair weather, fresh water bird there? Mounseer's master – Oh, / I knows nothing of he, nor Commodore, nor mate either, for the matter o'that; he's a bird of passage, lad, a God send,[72] d'y see. Why, just as we had given Edystone lighthouse[73] the go-bye, out comes old Jack Andrews's wherry, the Shark, rowing at the rate of ten knots an hour; and when it came alongside the Librador, yon spark, there, stands bolt upright, and begs a passage for his self and our mounseer, here to Ireland, parlavering[74] about no packets plying from Plymouth to Dublin, and being in haste to get there. So the Commodore has him hauled up, and gives him the state cabin; a cabin fit for an English admiral; and so they've gone on well enough, yard arm and yard arm, jawing together fore and aft,[75] first in one lingo, and then in another; and what with mounseer there, that has not a word of English to throw to a dog, and the Spanish mate, who has bare sufficient to work the ship, why the vessel's / like to the town of Babylon.[76] But what's most oddest, is, that for all mounseer and Grim Groudy's gibberishing it so with their own masters, shiver me if they understand one another a bit. Ha! ha! ha!'

'Why then,' returned the Irishman, 'it *is* mighty odd, and very remarkable; for if foreigners won't understand one another, who do they expect will, I wonder. – And so yez are all going to *put up* in Dublin? Why then yez are in great luck.'

'Luck! no such luck either; but needs must when the old one drives. Why, Sir, we have been pelted about this little basin of dirty water these five days, and last night were fairly driven up the Channel, blown to shivers, tattered to rags, and must now put into dock here, till all's made right and tight; and then we're under orders to weigh anchor with old Grim Groudy, and sail for Dungarvon.'[77]
/

'Troth, then, if yez will take a fool's advice, yez will stay where ye are; for yez may go farther and fare worse than stopping in Dublin; only may be, your business does'nt lie here, Sir.'

'Why, for business, I don't believe we have much business here; only just a voyage of pleasure. Why that's all the go, now. The agreeablest trip I ever made was with a young Irish lord to the Mediterranean, just for sport like; round the world for sport.'

'Why, then, it's pretty sport that gives a man the say-sickness. But it's ill winds blows nobody good; and only for it, sorrow bit of Ringsend[78] yez had seen this day, and here it is.'

The two gentlemen in advance had at this moment halted at the entrance of one of the most wretched suburbs that ever deformed or disgraced the metropolis of any country; and the Commodore, whose quick and often back- /glancing eye had long since discerned the reinforcement obtained to the party, by the addition of the lounger at the pier, now called, and desired him to lead the way. 'I will, plaze your honor,' he replied, trotting briskly on, while the wearied Frenchman '*toiled after him in vain*;'[79] and even the sailor made an exertion to keep pace with him. 'I'll only just step in, Sir, by your leave, to get my morning,'[80] for I hasn't broke my fast yet, Sir.'

'*Broke his fast!*' reiterated the Commodore, shrugging his shoulders, as he observed his newly constituted guide *step in* to a little shop, whose gaudy placard of '*licensed to sell spirituous liquors*' was further illustrated by a range of glasses on the counter, filled with whiskey. The guide tossed one off, observing to the dirty lazy-looking woman, who stood wiping a jug with her apron, 'I'll pay you when I come back, Mrs. Hurley, dear.' With this / assurance from her wretched, but well known customer, Mrs. Hurley appeared satisfied; aware, from experience, that, in this instance, punctuality was guaranteed by self-interest.

'Break his fast?' repeated the Commodore: 'what a mode of breaking fast!'

'As good as any,' replied Mr. De Vere: 'it all comes to the same thing in the end. Habit and circumstances determine the mode and means without our consent or will; and gin or glory

'Leads but to the grave.'[81]

The two travellers now followed their guide with difficulty through collected heaps of mud and filth. The very air they breathed was infected by noxious vapours, which the morning sun drew up from piles of putrid matter. The houses, between which they passed, were in ruins; the sashless windows were stuffed with straw; the unhinged / doors exposed the dark and dirty stairs, which led to dens, still more dun and foul. Here, if 'lonely misery retired to die,'[82] living wretchedness could scarcely find a shelter. Yet many an haggard face, many an attenuated form, marked by the squalor of indigence, and the harshness of vice, EVEN HERE evinced a crowded and superabundant population. The guide, who, as he proceeded through this disgusting suburb, saluted several among those whose idle curiosity had drawn them from their sties, betrayed a courtesy of manner curiously contrasted with his own appearance, and that of the persons he addressed. Every body was 'Sir,' or 'Madam;' and the children were either 'Miss,' or 'Master,' or were saluted with epithets of endearment and familiarity.

'Morrow, Dennis, dear, how is it with you?' 'Morrow, kindly, Mrs. Flanagan: I hope I see you well, / ma'am.' 'Oh, you're up with the day, Mr. Geratty. How's the woman that owns you?' 'Here's a fine morning, Miss Costello, God bless it: is your mother bravely,[83] miss?' 'Eh! Then Paddy, you little garlagh, why is'nt it after the cockles ye are the day, and the tide on the turn.'

While, however, he seemed occupied with '*an unwearied spirit of doing curtesies*,'[84] he occasionally threw his shrewd, but sunken eye, over the persons he was conducting; and faithfully translating the expression of the Commodore's looks, he observed:

'Och! it's a poor place, Sir, sure enough; and no poorer room-keepers, your honor, than the Ringsend's, God help 'em, not even in the vaults, Sir.'

'The vaults?'

'Och! yes, indeed, the vaults under the fine new streets, Sir, that is'nt built,[85] where there's nothing to pay; only in respect of being mighty moist. Wait a / taste,[86] your honor, till yez *get an*, Sir, and yez will see them swarm out in great style, the craturs!'

'*And sure it is a most beautiful and sweet country*,'[87] read aloud Mr. De Vere, who had now found out the passage he had hitherto vainly sought in Spencer, and was treading a clear pathway as they left the miserable outlets of Ringsend and Irishtown[88] behind them. '*A most beautiful and sweet country as any under heaven, being stored throughout with many goodly rivers, with all sorts of fish, most abundantly sprinkled with many very sweet islands, and goodly lakes, like little inland seas, that will carry even shippes upon their waters, adorned with goodly woods, even fit for building houses and shippes, so commodiously, as that if some princes in the world had them, they would soon hope to be lords of all the seas, and ere long, of all the world – also full of very good ports and havens, / opening into England, as inviting us to come into them, to see what excellent commodities that country can afford. Besides, the soyle itself, most fertile, fit to yield all kind of fruit that shall be committed there unto; and lastly, the heavens most mild, though some what more moist than the parts towards the west.*'

'So much for *the Natural State of Ireland*,' said the Commodore, as the peripatetic student closed his book, to which the guide had given a very humorous attention 'So much for the *natural* state. Behold the first groupings of its *social*, its political condition.' As he spoke, they entered one of those long-laid-out streets, whose houses, in the course of many years, have not advanced beyond the foundations. From the vaults, the thick smoke of burning straw or rubbish was emitted through holes, perforated in the pavement; while hordes of wretched and / filthy creatures crept from beneath the dark roofs of their earthy dwellings, to solicit the charity of those who passed above them. One from among the number, who had been less alert in picking up some scattered small change, flung among them by the gentlemen, continued to run beside them, begging for an 'halfpenny to buy bread.' It was a little shivering, half-naked girl, pretty, but filthy and emaciated. As the guide came up, she retreated, and a significant glance passed between them, which drove her at once back to her den; but not before she had picked up a silver sixpence flung after her.

'God bless your honor,' said the guide, in a tremulous voice: 'that's a greater charity than you think, Sir.'

'This is all very bad,' said Mr. De Vere, 'disgustingly bad. Short of actual offensive disgust, affecting the health and organs, I have, myself, / no positive objection to suburbian[89d] wretchedness. There is sometimes a sort of poetical misery in such scenes, very affective to contemplate; not altogether so coarse and squalid as Crabbe's Borough Scenery,[90] but a species of picturesque wretchedness, that has its merit – rags well draped, misery well chiselled, affording a study for the painter's pencil, or a model to the poet's eye.'

'But who,' asked the Commodore with emphasis, 'can see such wretchedness as this, with a *man's eye*, and not feel it with a *man's heart*. The mind starts beyond the mere impulse of sympathy here; it rushes at once from the *effect* to the *cause*. Indignation usurps the seat of pity, and the spirit rests upon those who have afflicted, not on those who suffer.'

'Yes, but even so, you go but half-way. All is evil in political institutes; because all is bad in moral, / as all is disgusting in physical nature. All realities are evil, and the whole system, as we know it, but a fortuitous combination of corrupting particles: the brightest specks, the most lucent points, but the shining glitter of putrescency, and even

'The brave o'erhanging firmament,
The majestic roof, fretted with golden fires,
A foul and pestilent congregation of vapours.'[91]

'This is Merrion Square,[92] plaze your honor,' interrupted the guide, coming forward, 'where the quality lives. And there's* Sir John's fountain,[93] your honor. So beautiful! and cost a power! and would'nt get lave to build a taste / of them, only he declared to God, and upon his honour, he never would allow a thimblefull of water to come out of them, in respect of a sup never going in. And there they are to this day, a great job, by Jagers;[94] why would'nt they?'

The gentlemen, in their way to their hotel, in Sackville Street,[95] now passed through that line of the Irish metropolis, which brings within the compass of a coup d'œil[96] some of the noblest public edifices and spacious streets to be found in the most leading cities of Europe. All, however, was still, silent, and void. The guide, walking parallel to the travellers, with his eye furtively glancing on them, evidently watched the effect which the beauty of his native city (a beauty of which he was singularly proud) made upon their minds: and when they had reached that imposing area, which includes so much of the architectural elegance and social bustle / of Dublin, the area flanked by its silent senate-house, and

---

*   Sir J., afterwards Lord de B –. It is curious to observe, that the lowest classes of the population of Dublin are perfectly acquainted with the *jobbing* systems, under which all public transactions are effected in that metropolis: they also discuss them with a mixture of humour and anger that is extremely characteristic.

commanded by its venerable university,[97] he paused, as if from weariness, leaned his burthen against the college ballustrade, and drew upon the attention of the strangers (who also voluntarily halted to look around them), by observing, as he pointed to the right, 'That's the ould parliament-house, Sir. Why, then, there was *grate* work going on there *oncet*, quiet and aisy as it stands now, the cratur! grate work shure enough! and there's the very lamp-post I climbed up the night of the UNION.[98] Och! then you'd think the *murther* of the world was in it; and so it was, shure enough, – that's of Ireland, your honor; God help her. And there we were, from light to light, and long after, watching, aye, and praying too, and grate pelting, shurely, when they came out, the thieves that sould us fairly. And troth, if we'd have known as much / as we know now, it isn't that a-way they'd have got off. And never throve from that hour, nor cared to cry 'the Freeman's,'*[99] and the parliament debates not in it, nor counsellor Grattan.[100] Och, the trade was ruined entirely; and from that day to this, never hawked the bit of paper, nor could raise a tinpenny, only just on *arrands*, long life to your honors; and that's what the *Union* has brought us to; and sorrow paper they need print at all, at all, now, only in respect of the paving board, and Counsellor Gallagher's iligant speeches.'[101e]

'And what use is made of that magnificent building?' asked Mr. De Vere, who stood gazing upon it with evident admiration.

'What use is it they make of it? your honor; Why then, sorrow a use in life, only a bank, Sir; the bank of / Ireland;[102] what less use could they make of it? And for all that,' added the guide, significantly, 'it cost a power to make it *what it is*.'

'It is a beautiful thing of its kind,' said De Vere, still gazing upon it, and rather apostrophizing the building than addressing his companion, who stood silent, and self-wrapped – 'Beautiful, even *now*, entire and perfect in all its parts, what will it be centuries hence, touched by the consecrating hand of time, when its columns shall lie prostrate, its pediments and architraves broken and moss-grown, when all around it is silence and desolation? Then haply some strife of elements may conduct the enterprising spirit of remote philosophy to these coasts; may cast some future Volney of the Ohiho or Susquchanah upon the shores of this little Palmyra,[103] and he may surmise and wonder, may dream his theories, and calculate his probabilities; and, bending over these ruins, see / the future in the past, and apostrophize the inevitable fate of existing empires.'

'Or some American freeman,' observed the Commodore, 'the descendant of some Irish exile, may voluntarily seek the bright green shores of his fathers, and, in this mouldering structure, behold the monument of their former degradation.'

---

*   One of the most spirited, popular, and best conducted papers in the empire.

'Why, then, long life to your honors,' added the guide, who, with the subtlety incidental to his class and country, drew ingenious, and sometimes exact conclusions, from very scanty premises, and who believed that the strangers were predicting the ruin of Ireland from the event of the Union (an event execrated by all the lower orders of the country). 'Why, then, long life to your honors, it's true for you, and was said long ago, that after the Union the grass would grow high in Dublin streets; and would this day, plaze God, only in respect of the paving-board, that be's ripping up the / streets, and laying down the streets, from June to January, just for the job, by Jagurs.

'Well, there is ould Trinity,' he continued, turning towards the college, as he again raised his load upon his shoulders: 'the boys that used to bate the world before them oncet with their fun and their larning, are now down, like the rest, – and does not know one of them myself now, barring Collagian Barrett.'[104]

'By the bye,' said Mr. De Vere, 'is not this Irish College Smart's 'Temple of Dulness,' in the eyes of whose learned doctors, Swift and Goldsmith could find no favour?[105] I have little respect myself for incorporated learning, or for literature and taste acquired by act of parliament.'

'Intellectual illumination,' replied the Commodore, 'like other things, would, perhaps, best find its maximum when independent of legislative interference. / There is an education belonging to the spirit of the age, and carried on by its influence, far beyond the rules of these worn-out monastic institutions.'

'Och! it's an *ould* place, shure enough,' said the guide, 'and least said about it is soonest mended. Now, plaze your honors, I'm finely rested, many thanks to yez, and so is mounseer too, and will attind you, and lave ould *Nosey* there to *put an;* for they've began to deck the lad, early as it is.'

As he spoke, he directed the observation of the gentlemen to the equestrian statue of King William the Third,[106] which two men were now busily engaged in decorating with orange and blue ribbons.* /

'What does it mean,' demanded Mr. –.[107]

'What does it mane? Why it manes to vex the papists sore, your honor shure that's the ascendency, Sir; only for it, and the likes of it, wouldn't we be this day hand and glove, orange and green:[108] sorrow one colour you'd know from the

---

*   This ludicrous and offensive spectacle is exhibited at the expense of the civil magistrate, on the anniversary of events connected with the triumph of the revolution party, and the downfall of the Jacobites. To the Catholics, who behold in this outward sign a token of their political annihilation, and an insulting arrogation of the supremacy of the minority over the majority, it is a source of heart-burnings, and an incentive to discord. As, however, its continued exhibition is a proof of narrow intellect and bad feeling in the individuals who persist in repeating it, the oppressed party would do well to turn the laugh against their enemies, by ridiculing the taste, and mocking the vanity which finds pleasure in thus disfiguring the statue.

other. Och! but that would not do – where would the ascendency be? – only *all Irishmen then.*'

The gentlemen at length reached their hotel, which might have been taken for, what it had once been, the splendid mansion of a resident nobleman, / but for the shew-board,[109] which designated its present public use and object.

The capital of Ireland, since the Union, has become a mere stage of passage to such of its great landholders as occasionally visit the kingdom for purposes of necessity. They consider this beautiful city only as a *pendant* to Holy-head;[110] and take up their temporary lodging to await the caprice of wind and tide, in those mansions where a few years ago they spent a large part of their great revenues, drawn from their native soil. The bill that defrays the expense of a dinner at an inn, thus acquits their debt to the country from which they derive their all, which they dislike to visit, and are impatient to quit*.[111 f] /

Several idle persons stood lounging about the door of the hotel. The only person whom they wished to see, the master, did not appear; and they had to wait some time before the head waiter could be found to tell them whether they could be accommodated: for what is called the *dead time* of the year, is usually that in which Ireland is most visited by curious strangers (who choose that period as the best for visiting Killarney and the Giant's Causeway),[112] and by necessitous absentees, who, driven to look for their rents, or to canvass their county, take that time for their penance, which they cannot well employ elsewhere, and make a snatch at Ireland in / the interval between the London and watering-place seasons.

While the gentlemen walked up and down the hall, with every symptom of impatience, the guide applied to the exhausted Frenchman for payment, who was now lying full length on a bench, uttering many exclamations of annoyance and fatigue. When he understood the meaning of the Irishman's extended hand, he gave him what he considered a sufficient reward for his services. But as this sum was barely what the Irishman expected, he returned it carelessly, with 'Here, mounseer! I'll make you a present of it.'

'Mais, comment donc, mon ami qu'est ce que c'est.'[113]

'What is it, *I say,* is it? Why then it's what I say, I wouldn't dirty my fingers with it.'

---

*   'It is very extraordinary that in this large and populous city (Dublin), there should be such an almost total want of good inns for the accommodation of travellers and strangers.' – *A Letter from Ireland, by J. Bush,* 1764.
Thirty years ago there was but one hotel in Dublin; nor was there occasion for more. The nobility and gentry came from their seats at once to their mansions in the capital. When, however, the seat of honourable ambition, and the means of raising a fortune and name were removed to another kingdom, it is natural that the rank and talent of the country should emigrate.

'Then,' said one of the waiters, impatient to get him out of the hall, and snatching the portmanteau out of his / hand, '*I say,* that if you won't take, that, I'd give you nothing.'

'Wouldn't you, Mr. Connolly?' he replied coolly. 'Why then, faith, it's often you gave us *that,* Mister Connolly, and will again, plaze God.'

The laugh which this observation excited in the bye-standers, raised Mr. Connolly's choler, and he now endeavoured to hustle the guide out of the hall; but he stood his ground firmly, exclaiming with great coolness. 'I wont go till I'm ped, Mr. Connolly; not a foot, Sir, nor wouldn't quit if your master was in it himself.'

The Commodore now came forward to learn the cause of the scuffle, and having heard both parties, he turned abruptly to the guide, and demanded, 'What employment are you fit for?'

'What employment am I fit for? Every employment in life, Sir, good or bad.' /

'Would you like to go into service?'

'Is it into *reglar service,* your honor? Och, then, I never favoured that much.'

'Will you go on board ship?'

'Is it on board ship, Sir?' (rubbing round his shoulders and smiling,) 'Och, plaze your honor, I oncet went a long voyage, Sir, and the say sickness didn't agree with me.'

'Well,' said the Commodore, impatiently, 'if there was one inclined to be of service to you, to enable you to get some more certain mode of subsistence than that you pursue, what line of life would you prefer?'

'Why, then, long life to your honor, I pray God, and if there *was* a gentleman would have the great kindness to *lind* me a trifle to get my rags out of pledge,[114] that I might go back to the trade nate and dacent, as my ould / father did afore me, I would chose, 'bove all the employments in life, Sir, to stand at the Post-Office[115] and cry the Freeman's Journal, plaze your honor.'

'And what sum will do this for him?' asked the Commodore of the head waiter, who now appeared.

'God bless you, Sir, a pound note would make his fortune; and I would be his banker, and see it laid out to advantage.'

The Commodore silently presented the pound note, and was moving away, when the guide following him a few steps, dropt on his knees, and seizing the skirts of his pelisse, remained for a moment struggling for utterance, while the tears stood in his hollow eyes. 'Should I return to Dublin,' observed the Commodore, touched perhaps by the silent emotion of feelings so prompt and ardent, so opposed to the poor man's former gay and jocose acuteness, 'should I return, I will enquire for you / here, and if I find you have given up *breaking your fast with whiskey*' –

'My fast, your honour, that's all for the whole day, Sir, mate or drink, and the rest goes – Plaze your honor, the little bit of a naked girl, at the vault, that's my child, Sir, and four of them – only dacency, your honour, and a bit of pride, and the childre, and the pound note, Sir; oh! it's too much goodness intirely.'

The Commodore drew back from his grasp, and motioning him to rise, added, 'In that case – four children you say.' He then gave another note, and walked rapidly away.

'God bless you, Sir,' said the waiter, who ran before, and conducted the gentlemen up stairs. 'You have made *one* poor man happy this morning, at all events.'

'You have had a Scena,'[116] observed Mr. De Vere, languidly.

'Almost,' he replied, with a deep / sigh. 'Absentee! yes, well may they be absentees that can. What is that degree of enjoyment and individual happiness, which a man may procure, who is liable every day to behold such misery as we have witnessed, within the last short hour; or who is led to reflect for a moment on the train of misrule, of the collision of interests, prejudices, and feelings, which have produced such a state of society in this fine country?'

This speech was pronounced after they had entered a handsome drawing-room, and while each took possession of a lounger.[117] The waiter then began a long string of apologies. 'Dressing-rooms would be got ready in a few minutes, as soon as the Marquis of Inchigeela and his son, Lord Dunmanaway, were gone; and his lordship's travelling carriage was at that moment at the door: but the house was so full; a number of persons from England arrived by the last packet; others about to de-/part for Holyhead;' and he added, in an *aside* whisper, 'the elderly gentlewoman would be off in a jiffy, as her pochay was ordered,[118] and she had only stepped into the best drawing-room to write a letter.' He then added aloud, that he would just run down himself and introduce the French valet to the French cook, store the gentlemen's things in the dressing-room, and order breakfast.

The waiter then shuffled off, impressed with an high opinion of the consequence of the strangers, from the petulance of the one and the haughty look of the other; and believing them to be well worth attending to, from the extraordinary liberality of the Commodore, who, by an act well adapted to Irish feelings, had bought golden opinions from all who had witnessed it.

The mention made by the waiter of the 'elderly gentlewoman,' was the first intimation the strangers received / of such a person being present. They now threw their eyes round the spacious room; and a figure, which answered to the description, appeared seated in one of its remote corners at a writing table. They turned their eyes instantly away, for a very fine map of Ireland hung on the wall, near to which they sat. The Commodore took it down, and began to trace his route with a pencil, while Mr. De Vere followed his track with his eye as he looked over his shoulder.

Meantime the gentlewoman resembled, as she sat, one of those wax-work figures, which, at once grotesque and natural, are coloured to the life, yet inanimate as death; for she remained, for a considerable time after the strangers had entered the room, with her eyes rivetted on their persons, and her pen suspended above the paper upon which she had been writing. There was an intensity in her fixed look that implied something more than mere idle curiosity. / In whatever manner their sudden appearance had affected her, they seemed to hold her senses in suspension; and many minutes had elapsed, and the strangers had travelled, on paper, over the whole province of Munster,[119] before she resumed, with a long drawn sigh, the occupation they had interrupted. In her person this *elderly gentlewoman* was low and somewhat bulky: her headdress was a tête,[120] with side curls, powdered, surmounted by a small high crowned beaver hat, laid flat upon the head. She wore a black crape veil, so fastened up in the centre as to expose a very red nose, and a very large pair of dark green spectacles; her chin was sunk in her cravat, whose long fringed ends belonged to other epochs of fashion than the present. The immense chitterling[121] of her habit shirt appeared through her single-breasted, long-waisted, brass-buttoned camblet-joseph.[122] Her whole appearance, though most risibly / singular, was such as would have been scarcely deemed extraordinary in the remote counties of Ireland twenty or thirty years back, when old fashions and old habits remained in full force among the provincial gentry, who preserved the faith, principles, and costume of their ancestors alike unchanged. Even still such figures are occasionally seen in the middle ranks of rural life, riding on a pillion[123] to mass on a holiday, or making one of a congregation of ten in some remote and solitary church, whose parish, though it bring a large revenue to its non-resident incumbent, may not consist of as many protestant families.[124]

The impatience of the travellers for the refreshment of the toilette and the breakfast table was now considerably abaited by the occupation which the map afforded them. The Commodore had traced with his pencil the great Munster road as far as Cashel; then diverged, / by cross ways, towards the Gaulty Mountains, to the towns of Doneraile and Buttevant.[125] From this point he was proceeding towards Kerry, when his companion interrupted him, by observing:

'I perceive we are proceeding by the same route, as far as Buttevant. I am going to the south, and shall halt at Kilcoleman, the reposoir,[126] where, in the course of my pilgrimage through this island of saints, my imagination will do homage to the memory of Spencer. If you have not any objection, I should like much to accompany you so far; but you will reject the proposal with the same frankness it is made, if it is the least *géne*[127] to you.'

'On the contrary, I shall accept it with pleasure, as far as Buttevant; but from thence my uncertain route, through a wild country, will be passed on horseback; and the business of an ardent research would leave me no time / for the enjoyment of your society, from which I have already derived so much. But,' he added, after an abrupt pause, and suddenly speaking in Spanish, 'you are ignorant of my name and situation. You may dislike this equivocal position, in which I am necessarily thrown; for it would not suit my views or my convenience to reveal either. To the title, however, of Commodore, given me by my crew, I have a right: for the rest, you must take me as I am, and upon trust.'

'I take you upon your own terms,' was the reply, 'and I adopt them as my own: to confess the truth, I like the mystery and romance of our connexion. It is foreign to the established forms of the world's calculated ties: and whether or not, when we part, we ever meet again, I shall look upon the accident which brought me acquainted with the commander of Il Librador as among the most pleasant events of my life. I am weary of the stale forms of what is / falsely called civilized society; and he who picks me up unknown, unnamed, in the middle of the ocean, receives me between sky and sea, a wanderer in the elements, gives me the rites of hospitality, communicates with me frankly, cherishes no suspicion, seeks no confidence, nor obtrudes any, connects himself, in my imagination, with a state of things, often dreamed of, but rarely realized. Ties, formed under such circumstances, are precious as they are rare; and by me, at least, are valued accordingly.'

'And I,' said the Commodore, with his splendid smile, brightening the sever-ity of his singular countenance, 'have just romance enough to enter into your feelings; for I once made a friendship, in swimming down the Oronoko,[128] which influenced the fortune and bent of my future life.'

They then agreed to leave Dublin in two hours; and Mr. De Vere asked / 'What do you do with your servant?' 'I have none but my Spanish mate, whom I leave to take the command of my vessel, when she is ready for sea.' 'Then I also will leave my ridiculous Frenchman behind me, till I arrive at my place of destination; a period 'still hanging in the stars.'[129] The master of this hotel will take care of him, I suppose, if well paid; as he would of my grey parrot, green monkey, or any other exotic animal I might consign to him. I have not the least idea, though, how I shall do without a servant; but the situation will be new, and so far good.'

Here the waiter entered, and enquired of the elderly gentlewoman, as if merely to make an excuse to get her out of the room, 'Have you any luggage, ma'am, to put up?' – To this question she replied angrily, and interrupting her reassumed letter, which, by the motion of her hand, appeared to consist of char-acters complex as the ancient *Ogham*,[130] '*Have* I any luggage! / *have* I? Then do you take me for a snail, why! with all my goods on my back?' The rich round Munster brogue in which this question was asked, the guttural accentation of the '*you*' and the '*why*' peculiar to that province, and the sharp key in which it was uttered, made the gentlemen start; while the impertinent waiter took no pains to conceal his ready laughter.

'You are mighty pert, Sir,' said the old lady, tossing a black wafer about her mouth, and sealing and soiling her ill-folded letter with it: she then gathered up her papers (some printed tracts which lay on the table), and corking her inkhorn, which she dropped into her capacious pocket, as a pebble falls into the bottom of a deep well, she lowered her veil, resumed a black silk rabbit-skin-lined cardinal cloak,[131] and waddling to the door, turned full round, and made a formal courtesy to the gentlemen: the gentlemen bowed, and she retired. /

The French valet had now prepared the apparatus for the toilette: but before they adjourned to their dressing rooms, the waiter returned, and presented a note, illegibly written upon a dirty card, which Mr. De Vere took between his finger and thumb, and read, first eagerly to himself, and then aloud, with a look of disgust, amounting almost to nausea: it ran as follows:

'Mistress Magillicuddy presents her respects, on her way to Munster, would make a third in a chay, as far as Tipperary town, if agreeable. N.B. No luggage to signify, foreby a portmantle and bandbox, also a magpie and cage, would hang outside, if not agreeable within: would prefer the gentlemen if *serious*: begs your acceptance of a religious tract, and am, gentlemen, Yours, &c.

Molly Magillicuddy.'

The waiter chuckled, and observed: 'The lady says she forgot to mention the bird and bandbox are to be taken up / in *Thomas Street*.'[132] Mr. De Vere tossed the note on the table, and went to his dressing room; and the Commodore, with more good breeding, or rather with more good nature, desired the waiter to say that previous arrangements obliged them to decline the honour intended them by Mrs. Magillicuddy.

This singular looking lady had come by the Holyhead packet the night before, and had ordered a chaise previous to the arrival of the gentlemen. – The freedom, with which they had discussed their route before her, had probably suggested the idea of economising her travelling expenses by joining them. She might also have had some more important views, than those which were prudently directed to their purses; for her enquiry as to their being 'serious' (a technical term in a particular new light,) indicated her calling;[133] and it was possible she believed herself the elected agent of salvation to them, as to many / others, the Krudner or Johanna South-cote[134] of some Munster village, to which she might now be returning, laden with sectarian tracts, and Irish snuff, bohea tea,[135] and intolerance.

When the waiter delivered a negative answer to her card, she shook her head, and said: 'In their blindness they know not what they reject why! but the sickle will go forth, and the harvest will yet be reaped.'[136]

She shortly after set off for Naas,[137] accusing the waiters of sauciness and extravagant charges, talking Irish with the driver, and lecturing the beggars on the sin of idleness. She accompanied her admonition with some small change; at the same time accounting selfishly for her donation, by observing, 'He that giveth to the poor *lendeth* to the Lord.[138] 'O! I engage,' said the waiter as she drove off, 'it's little you'd give, if you didn't expect it back with interest tenfold – and that's now what the likes of / her calls *charity!* It's the charity that begins at home, aye, and ends there too. Commend me to the gentleman above stairs that gave his two pound notes, and never canted nor preached about it. That's the real charity, long life to him!'

To this ejaculation an 'amen' was repeated by all present, who had witnessed the liberality of the Commodore, and heard the departing apostrophe of the 'elderly gentlewoman.' /

CHAPTER II.

Oh! quel homme superieur! quel grand genie, que ce Poco-curanto! Rien ne peut lui plaire.
VOLTAIRE.[139]

THE two distinguished strangers, whom chance had so singularly united, and who had mutually chosen, from caprice or prudence, to hang the veil of mystery over their respective situations, appeared to touch on the extremes of human character. But there was, notwithstanding, an obvious dove-tailing in their dissimilitudes; and their moral disagreements, like some musical discords, produced a combination more gracious than the utmost perfection of a complete and blended harmony could effect. The one seemed a brilliant illustration of physical and intellectual / energy, thrown into perpetual activity; the other a personification of moral abstraction, originating ingenious reveries, which, though sometimes founded in fact, were generally inapplicable in practice. The fortunes of life seemed to have formed the one, and to have spoiled the other. The one thought, sympathized, and acted; the other mused, dreamed, and was passive. Their first half-hour's communication, however, on board ship, was a prompt commutation of mutual good will. – Each felt he was associated with a gentleman; and in that confidence had suffered intimacy to grow with a rapidity disproportioned to its duration. But though opinions were freely discussed, and almost always opposed; though sentiments were broadly debated, and principles vehemently canvassed; yet in the many and long conversations, held during the silence of calm seas and of slumbering elements, by the midnight moon, or the day's prelusive dawn, no / circumstance of personal communication had ever passed between them: mutually in possession of each other's leading opinions, and features of character, they were ignorant of all else beside.

Both gentlemen spoke Spanish and French fluently; but the Commodore had a foreign pronunciation of some particular English words, which denoted him to have been long absent from the countries where English is the vernacular tongue. The reading of the younger stranger seemed stupendous. It included the classics, ancient and modern, with the whole belles lettres of European and oriental literature. The studies of the Commodore were evidently more confined to the exact sciences; and, with the exception of Shakespeare, Milton, and Ossian,[140] and of some old quaint English prose writers, the chroniclers of Ireland's hapless story, the Campions, Spencers, and Hanmers,[141] his course of English reading seemed cir-/cumscribed. The conversation of the one, therefore, was more elegant, ornamented, and detailed; that of the other more original, energetic, and concise. The one spoke in epic, the other in epigram. They had both travelled much, and far; the one, it should seem, from choice; the other from necessity: and the result from their conversation appeared to be that the one had stored his mind with images, the other strengthened his judgment by observations. The one had studied *forms,* the other *men.* The one had only increased his constitutional tendency to satiety and ennui, by the resources which, young as he was, he had already exhausted; the other had sharpened his appetite for enquiry by the experience he had obtained.[g] Such as they were, they were both evidently 'out of the common roll of men'[142] – and alike distinguished by personal and mental superiority. /

The Commodore had dressed, breakfasted, made the necessary arrangements for their journey to Munster, and gone abroad, before his fellow traveller had gotten half way through his toilette, even with the assistance of Monsieur, his valet. Mr. De Vere had indeed but just sat down to his coffee, and his 'Fairy Queen,' when the elder stranger returned, after an absence of near two hours.

'Have you seen much of Dublin?' asked the younger traveller, laying down his book.

'Yes, I believe I have been half through it.'

'What impression does it give you upon the whole?'

'Why, with its extremes of poverty and splendor, the wretchedness of a great part of its inhabitants, and the magnificence of its buildings, it is to me a Grecian temple turned into a lazzaretto.[143] One-third of its population are in an / actual state of pauperism: one-half of its trading streets exhibit as many bankrupt sales as open shops: the best houses are to be let, and the debtors' prisons are overflowing.'

'Have you, then, had time to visit the prisons?'

'Business brought me to me one: business with the high sheriff of a county, who has delivered himself up for the purpose of a *Whitewashing* under the insolvency act,[144] as *he* termed it.'

'Ha! ha! ha! an high sheriff in prison – that's singular enough!'

'Not so singular in Ireland; for two other high sheriffs were confined in the same room with him, and for the same purposes.'

'The laws must be well administered! But, doubtless, they are all *honorable men.*'

'They are *loyal* men, as my friend the sheriff told me, though under a little present difficulty.' /

'You have purchased a pocket telescope, I perceive.'

'Yes, and a little information from the intelligent optician from whom I bought it. I went into his shop as the tax-gatherer was carrying out of it several articles which he had seized for non-payment. The owner was looking on calmly, and to some observation of mine, he replied, "I have not the money, Sir: there's no use in talking: when government have got all, we shall be at rest: we cannot be worse." To my remark on the supposed tendency of the Union, so often vaunted in newspapers, and in debate, that it would bring English capital into Irish trade; he answered, "The effect of the Union is ruin to Ireland: since that epoch her debt has increased, her resources diminished, her taxes augmented, her manufactures languishing, her gentry self-exiled, her peasantry turbulent from distress, and her tradesmen, like myself, drained to / the last farthing, and sighing to remove to that country, where they will not be obliged to pay a large rent to the government, for leave to live; to America.*[145] But all cannot do this." – I note these observations as being curious from one of his class.'

'It is a pity,' said the younger stranger, 'that these Americans are so *baroque*,[146] for they are, politically speaking, a great people; they are, however, so prosperous, that they can never be interesting: they are beyond the reach of prose or verse: we may say of their national, as of Darby and Joan's conjugal felicity,

They eat, and drink, and sleep, – what then?

Why sleep, and drink, and eat again.'[147]

The waiter now entered, presented the bill, and announced that all was ready for their departure. The land-/lord, who in his communication with Mr. De Vere, on the subject of his valet, had decided at once that he was a man of rank and fashion, now attended, and did the honours of his house in the usual style of Irish hyperbole.

'Upon my credit, gentlemen, I'm heartily sorry we're losing the honour of your company so soon; and think I could make the place *plazing* to you, if you would do me the honour; on your return from the Lakes (for *supposes* it is *to them* you're going), and am sorry you make such a short stay, without seeing the Rotunda, and the College, and the Dublin-Society house, and the statues.'[148]

---

*   America is considered as the land of Canaan by the lower ranks of Irish: the peasantry emphatically call it '*the Land.*'

'Statues! what statues,' demanded the younger stranger, catching at the sound, and stopping short.

'The statues, Sir, at our society house, that's kept in the greatest style, and gets a *touch up*, whenever the place is painted. That's *by order*, as we say, in the society house.' – 'By what order?' was demanded, with a smile. – 'By / order of the committee of fine arts; and myself was one, until business came on me so thick, and took up my attention; and has a brother that *shews* at the exhibition every year, a great artist. Indeed, I think you'd be plazed, gentlemen, if you were to stop and see the exhibition this *saison*, and portrait No.2, full length of Mr. Roger O'Rafferty, of the Back-lane division auxiliary yeomanry corps,[149] in full regimentals, standing quite quiet, and a cannon going off in the Phanix;*[150] that's by my brother, Sir.' This detailed statement of the cognoscente landlord to prove the flourishing state of the arts in Ireland, the country which has given to the English school of painting a Barry, a Shee, and a Tresham,[151] seemed quite sufficient to satisfy / the curiosity of the strangers, who passed on, through files of beggars, to their carriage: they threw some silver among them, and hastily drew up the windows, to exclude the infected air, as they drove away.

'Pa!' said the finer gentleman of the two, 'this is breathing pestilence.'

'And witnessing its causes in all their most shocking details: look, what a splendid scene for such a grouping![152] what a noble street, and what a mendicant population!'

As they passed through the southern suburb, the Commodore demanded of the postillion the name and purposes of an immense building, on the opposite side the water.

'Is it that forenent us, plaze your honor, acrass the Liffy? Oh! that's the Royal Barracks;[153] and them there's the Richmond Barracks; and if your honour could see behind you, Sir, you'd see the Porto Bello barracks, and there afore you is Island bridge barracks, and the barracks in the town; and Musha,[154] / myself does not know the half o'them. You might travel in the county Dublin mountains, rising there on your lift, from barrack to barrack, and never get sight of inn, or house, man or baste, only sogers, Sir.'

'From this sample,' said the Commodore, addressing his companion, 'we might suppose the whole country to be one great fortress; as it was in Elizabeth's day, when the population was divided into the *English rebel* and the *Irish enemy*.[155] What an expense this army of occupation must prove to an impoverished country!'

'I have, myself,' returned Mr. De Vere, 'no objection to a military government: 'tis at least a picturesque legislation: it affords something to look at, and

---

*   The Phœnix Park near Dublin, the seat of reviews, and military evolutions. This beautiful
       tract, to which Lord Chesterfield gave its epithet of Phœnix, is also the scite of the Vice
       Regal Villa, and the residence of the chief official persons

to describe. I like military architecture, battlements and ramparts, watch-towers and bastions. The militare costume, too! the helm and hauberk, and warlike sounds

"Of trumpets loud, and clarions."[156]

'England is hastening fast to this, / but she will always want appropriate scenery.'

'And I trust an appropriate spirit too! Look at Turkey.'[157]

'Why, yes, there is something to *look at*. But next to a military, I should prefer an ecclesiastical government, the despotism of some dark bigotry, some religion

'Full of pomp and gold,

With devils to adore for deities;"[158]

Familiars and inquisitors for ministers of state, and auto-da-fes[159] for national festivals.'

'Spain, for example; for though your fertile imagination invent, as it may, sources of oppression and degradation to man, there are still governments in Europe to leave mere fable far behind.'

'Well, after all, call governments by what name you will, they all equally leave man as they find him, feeble and selfish.' /

'Yes, because he *is* MAN. But in following the natural order of things, you at least make him all he is capable of being. Nature is the great legislator. In creating man free, she commanded him to remain so; and re-action, sooner or later, follows the violation of this her first great edict.'

'This is Naas, your honour,' observed the postillion, addressing himself to the Commodore, at the end of more than an hour's silence, interrupted only by occasional questions, addressed to the driver, relative to the surrounding objects – 'and there is more barracks, Sir;' and he pointed to a handsome square building, in itself almost a town:[160] 'and there's the jail, Sir, an iligant fine building, and a croppy's head spiked on the top of it.[161] I'll engage,' he added, opening the door (for Naas was their first stage); – 'I'll engage he'll rue the day he saw Vinegar-hill,[162] any how, wherever he is, poor lad.' /

The Commodore, as he alighted, raised his eyes to the point at which the postillion's whip was directed, and beheld a human head, bleached and shining in the noon-day sun-beam. Such are the objects still exhibited in Ireland, as monuments of times of terror, to feed the vindictive spirit of an irritated people; announcing triumph to one party, and subjection to another. The Commodore turned away his eyes in disgust, and passed under the fine arch of a ruined monastery of Dominicans;[163] as if it were relief to his feelings to associate with less frightful images of death in its retired cemetery, than to behold them connected with such horrific associations, exposed in the high road of a public thoroughfare, a frightful land-mark for an unfortunate country.

The travellers proceeded on their journey towards the province of Munster, a province peculiarly interesting for its historical recollections, and for / those scenes, alternately wild and picturesque, which attract to its site the footsteps of taste and curiosity, and furnish to foreign artists so many combinations of scenic loveliness. Conversation had been frequently dropped and renewed; and the travellers had remained silent for some miles, when they overtook a chaise, from which Mrs. Magillicuddy formally saluted them. The elder stranger recognizing the green spectacles and chitterling (the most conspicuous parts of her figure) answered her salutation with a bow; the younger turned away his head in disgust.

'An ounce of civet would not sweeten my imagination,'[164] he observed, 'from the infection communicated to it by that horrible old Irishwoman. Shut up in this chaise with her and her magpie!! – Do you know, this image has haunted me ever since she made the frightful proposal.'

The smile of his companion indicated / his consciousness of this avowed prejudice; and the attention of the travellers became again engaged with the passing scene. The various objects which presented themselves to their view, both moral and physical, were seen by each through such mediums as their respective peculiarity of character, taste, and temperament, were likely to produce. The one, rapid in perception, instinctively just in inference, quick, curious, active, inquiring, directed the whole force of his acute, prompt observation, to the people and their localities, as both appeared upon the surface. He turned his eyes to the peasant's hut: it was the model of the '*mere Irishman's*' hovel, as it rose amidst scenes of desolation during the civil wars of Elizabeth's reign. It was the same described by William Lithgow, the Scotch pilgrim, the noted traveller of that remote day. '*A fabrick erected in a single frame of / smoke-torn straw, green, long-pricked turf, and rain-dropping wattles; where, in foul weather, its master can scarcely find a dry part to repose his sky-baptized head upon.*'[165]

He beheld the tenant of this miserable dwelling working on the roads, toiling in the ditches, labouring in the fields; with an expression of lifeless activity marking his exertions, the result of their deep-felt inadequacy: his gaunt athletic frame was meagre and fleshless, his colour livid, his features sharpened: his countenance, readily brightening into smiles of gaiety or derision, expressed the habitual influence of strong dark passions. The quick intelligence of his careless glances mingled with the lurking slyness of distrust, – the instinctive self-defence of conscious degradation. He beheld multitudes of half-naked children, the loveliness of their age disfigured by squalid want, and the filthy drapery of extreme / poverty, idle and joyless, loitering before the cabin door, or following in the train of a mendicant mother, whose partner in misery had gone to seek employment from the English harvest, where his hire would be paid with the smile of derision; and where *he* would be expected to excite laughter by his blunders, who might well command tears by his wretchedness.

In the proclaimed districts,[166] the misery of the peasant population was most conspicuous. For he to whom

'The world was no friend, nor the world's law,'[167]

might well set both at defiance. The forfeit of life could be deemed but a small penalty to him, who in preserving it 'sheweth a greater necessity he hath to live, than any pleasure he can have in living.'[168]

The few vehicles, public or private, observable on the high roads, the total absence of a respectable yeomanry, / marked the scantiness of a resident gentry, and the want of that independent class, 'a country's boast and pride.'[169] Yet many stately edifices, the monuments of ancient splendor or modern taste, rose along the way; the former in ruins, the latter almost invariably unfinished. The castle of the ancient chief, and the mansion of the existing landlord, were alike desolated and deserted. Town succeeding town, marked the influence and power of the great English palatines, who drew their wealth and luxury from a land, to which, like their forefathers, for generations back, they were strangers; and the name and arms of the English nobility, suspended over inns, emblazoned over court-houses, and fixed in the walls of churches, or shining above their altars, marked the extensive territories of these descendants of the undertakers, and grantees of the Elizabeths, the James's, and the Charles's.[170] The surface / of the country, as it appeared, contained the leading facts of its history, and those who ran might read. He who now read, studied not without a comment the text whose spirit and whose letter were mis-rule and oppression.

The young stranger saw with other eyes; and by the illusory lights of a sleepless imagination. But his philosophy, though cynical, was not the cynicism of experience; it was the satiety of early excited and promptly exhausted sensations. Man, with him, was every where as well off as he deserved to be, because no where did 'man delight'[171] *him*; while all references came home to his own enjoyment, and were appreciated as they extended or curtailed its sphere. He looked only to that which could gratify the dominant faculty of his existence; and while he found

'Nature wanted stuff,

To vie strange forms with fancy,'[172] /

he sought in the combinations of art, as formed under various epochs of society, for such objects and images as embodied events long passed, or consecrated, and preserved in memory and imagination only.

He had induced his companion to lengthen and diverge from their route by visiting the town of Kildare, once a city of historical and monkish importance, because *there*, his road-book told him, were still visible some remains of the 'Fire-house,' the Christian temple, where the nuns of St. Bridget performed the rites of the heathen priestesses of Vesta, and watched over the sacred flame, which the English bishop, Henri de Londres, afterwards sacrilegiously extinguished (2).[173] He found a little town, ruinous and wretched, with many symptoms of poverty, and few of antiquity; and he hurried from it in disappointment and dislike. He insisted on stopping the first night at Kilkenny, / for the purpose of viewing the feudal castle of the Butlers, and the splendid ruins of its abbies.[174] But, even here, imagination had got the start of fact; and, though a busy fancy peopled the silent aisles of St. Francis and St. John's with

'eremites and friars,

White, black, and grey, with all their trumpery;'[175]

though he garrisoned the ramparts with 'Irish kernes and galloglasses,'[176] imagination left possibility every where behind. Disappointment hung like a noxious vapour upon his steps; and he every where found reason, or sought it, to scoff at the folly and feebleness of man, who, under all stages of society, is the victim of blindness, beyond his power to dispel; alternately tyrant or slave, impostor or dupe, and neither by his own free will. But though he saw the evil, he neither felt for its effects, explored its cause, nor suggested its re-/medy; and the talents of this accomplished ideologist, neither calculated nor exerted to benefit mankind, confined their lustre to him, they lighted alike to evil or to good.

Views thus opposed, and sentiments thus contrasted, naturally begot frequent and long protracted discussions, as fresh objects afforded themes for observation or reflection; and the travellers had passed the boundaries of the frequently proclaimed county of Tipperary, without interruption to their debate, or any impediment to their journey (such as have been supposed the inevitable concomitants of Irish posting);[177] when the postillion, alighting to lead his horses over a bad step, startled them, by exclaiming aloud – 'Why, then, the curse of the divil on ye, Longford-pass,[178] I pray Jasus, for you've joulted the very life out of me, so you have:' then having desired his horses to '*get along out of that*,' he dropped / back, and laying his hand upon the carriage window, entered into conversation with the gentlemen, by strongly advising them to give up the *iday* of making Thurles their sleeping stage:[179] first, *becaise* it was the same to his employer whether they went a few miles one way or t'other; and, secondly, becaise that Thurles town would be full of th' army, in respect of changing quarters; two regiments marching to Cork and Kerry, to be sprinkled among the towns and mountain-barracks: and there will be grate biletting the night, and the inn taken up entirely with the officers; and what matter? Shure Holy-cross was but a *dony*[*180] bit further, and wouldn't make an hour's differ. There was a new opposition inn in the neighbourhood set up against Thurles, kept by the

---

*   *Dony*, small – so used by Spencer.

maister's cousin-germain,[181] Mr. / Dooly, where every thing was nate and clane, and quiet.

'Is Holy-cross a town?' demanded Mr. De Vere, caught by the religious romance of its name (3).[182]

'It is, your honor; that is, it is *not* a town, Sir, only a *township* and chapelry; and blessed ground every foot of it, and well may be. Is'nt there a grate big piece of the holy cross itself, the wood of life, buried in the fine ancient ould abbey there, that the travellers be coming to see far and near? And it's that, why, plaze your honors, the saying goes, that of all places in the world round, the devil (Christ save us!) daren't shew the track of his hoof near that township: and troth, gentlemen dear, it would be worth while to go ten mile round any time to see it, only in respect of the lovely fine tomb of th' ould king that's in it, my namesake, Carbrogh O'Brien, King of Limerick.[183] Which / road shall I take, Sir? There lies the turn to Thurles, and there to Holy-cross, your honor.'

'I think the quiet inn, the ruined abbey, and O'Brien's tomb, decide it,' said the Commodore.

'Unquestionably,' replied his companion; and the driver received his orders for Holy-cross. As he turned his horses' heads, a chaise passed before them, taking the Thurles road; and the spectacles, tête, and high crowned hat of Mrs. Magillicuddy, appeared above the magpie's cage, which was suspended at the side of one of the windows.

'Raison de plus,'[184] said Mr. De Vere, sinking back in the carriage. 'I would rather fall in with a legion of marching regiments than come in the way of that horrible old woman, and a renewal of her terrifying proposition.'

The Commodore smiled. He was amused to observe, that Mrs. Magillicuddy and her magpie had taken pos- /session of his companion's susceptible imagination; that the idea of an intimate association with her had become as much the *chimæra dire*[185] of his fancy, as her actual presence would have been the annoyance of his senses, and the destruction of his ease and comfort: he had more than once alluded to the dégout[i] of an atmosphere of Irish snuff and marrow pomatum,[186] to the uninviting images of spectacles and pocket handkerchiefs, pious tracts, and fusty bird-cages. The accident of her going the same rout, and her being enabled to keep pace with them, by their delay at Kildare and Kilkenny (for till the last stage they had travelled with four horses), were conjured into nothing else than a fatality; and even her innocent magpie was considered as an *oiseau de mauvais augure*.[187]

'You are certain,' said the younger traveller, addressing the driver, and pointing to the route taken by the old / lady's chaise, 'that *that* road leads to Thurles?'

'Shure and sartain, your honor, straight on forenent, and a turn in it to the lift that lades to the nunnery, Sir.'

'What nunnery? Are there nunneries in this country?'

'Is it nunneries, Sir? There is *plinty:* there is one there, off to the lift, between Thurles road and Holy-cross, is the convent of our Lady of the Annunciation:[188] they say, your honor, that in th' ould times there was subterranies under ground, between the nunnery and th' abbey of Holy-cross; and there was a story went about a grey abbot, and – troth it makes myself laugh, its so funny, only Father Murphy, Sir, says there no truth in it, and so I don't believe it, for the church knows best always, Sir.' – He now jumped upon the wooden bar, which served him as a seat, and giving his horses the whip, proceeded at a rapid pace. /

As the travellers approached the miserable little village of Holy-cross, the sun's last rays had withdrawn from the horizon in all the mild and melancholy gloom of an autumnal evening. The grey tints of the clouded atmosphere were reflected in shadows on bosom of the Suir, along whose banks arose the stately ruins of the abbey. The inn, recommended by the driver, the only inn, was a small house leading to the village; and bearing the sign of the Mitre and Crosier, as appropriate to its site.

The approach of a chaise was evidently no common event; for the landlord, his wife, a ragged old waiter, with a bare-footed girl (the bar-maid, house-maid, and kitchen-maid of the establishment), had stood at the door for some time, eagerly watching its approach. All were instantly in employment, carrying in the portmanteaux, conducting the travellers to their room, and knocking their heads together, in a confusion, increased by / their efforts to do the honours to such unusual guests. The travellers perceived that they were also the *only* guests; and they were not displeased by a circumstance which not only ensured their quietude, but their accommodation; for in Ireland, inns are good in proportion as they. are unfrequented, that is, as they are *not* patronized by some great man, whose servant or dependant obtains the TONTINE or principal hotel of the town,[189] which his former master rules; and adds to this situation some office under government, which renders him above his business as an innkeeper, and induces him to act with insolence when called upon in the capacity he despises.[j] The humble innkeeper of Holy-cross had recently fitted up a couple of bed-rooms in what had lately been a mere *Shebean* house, (4)[190] and dignified with the name of inn the little building which had been for half a century a noted baiting-place for foot / and horse travellers, and of such pious pilgrims as still came (and they were not few) to visit the shrine of the holy relic.

A few inquiries, and the ordering of a late dinner, took up a quarter of an hour; after which the travellers proceeded to visit the abbey. The twilight was thickening into darkness, but the air was fresh and balmy; and motion and activity were positive enjoyments to those who had for many hours suffered the cramping restraint and fatiguing dislocation of an Irish post-chaise.

The inn lay half a mile from the abbey, to which they passed over a bridge, thrown across the river Suir, and forming a communication between the village and the abbey grounds. The ruins covered a considerable tract, and were contrasted in their imposing magnitude by a few wretched hovels constructed out of their fragments. This consecrated pile is among the few in-/teresting monuments of antiquity now extant in that country, which, according to the statements of the biographer of St. Rumoldi,[191] once contained some of the most magnificent religious edifices of Europe.

Raised by the piety and power of an Irish provincial prince, Donagh Carbraigh O'Brien,[192] for monks of the Cistertian order, and consecrated to the holy cross, St. Mary, and St. Benedict, it owed its principal consequence to the relic of the cross incased in gold and precious stones, and given by Pope Paschal II. to Mac Morragh,[193] the predecessor of Carbragh. The charms of the beautiful architecture must, in days so rude, have contributed not a little to its fame; and the devotion paid to the relic it enshrined has been declared by an English minister*[194] to have been universal throughout the island. /

The strangers contemplated for a considerable time the broken mass of its dark exterior, and the high steeple, supported by beautiful gothic arches. They entered the broad nave, but, like the rest of the ruin, it was wrapt in one undistinguishing hue; and the majesty of darkness succeeded to the deep and misty forms of twilight.

'Darkness,' said the younger stranger, after a silence of some minutes, 'is decidedly the source of the true sublime.'[195]

'And light,' replied the Commodore, 'of beauty: *light* is *life*, the source of forms and motions: darkness is death: I abhor it.'

'And I love it. I love the uncertainty of this mysterious dimness (for instance), where every thing is guessed, and nothing known; where at every doubtful step,
"Solemn and slow the shadows blacker fall;
And all is awful listening gloom around."[196] /

A deep sigh, heard near and distinct, answered as he spoke.

'Did you sigh?' he asked quickly.

'No: did not you?' was the reply.

'Not I. Yet some one sighed most assuredly.'

''Tis the wind among the ruins,' said the Commodore, carelessly.

'No, the air is breathless. It was a human, perhaps a super-human inspiration.'

'That is *physically* impossible: respiration is organization: spirits have none. But do you believe in super-human agency?'

'I believe, and I deny nothing. – I resign myself passively to events, moral and physical, as they occur. This, I fancy, was the original intention of providence with respect to man; which made him dark, and left him so; the child of ignorance, and its victim.'

---

*   See Sir Henry Sidney's State Papers.

'Then why endow him with faculties, which impel him to enquiry, and / force him into action, which lead him to dispel his darkness, and rise above his nature?'

'Hush! there again! I am certain I heard the heavings of a short convulsive respiration. 'Tis most singular!'

'The place affects you. We will return, and view it by daylight.'

'No,' said Mr. De Vere, seating himself on a fragment of the ruin: 'this is to me positive enjoyment.'

As he spoke, the dispersion of a dense cloud, which had long scowled over the darkened landscape, and which now broke into fleecy vapour, displayed the broad bright moon, rising in splendour above the roofless ruin. A sheet of light fell upon the nave, which the strangers occupied, but left in shadow the lateral aisles, which formed a pillared arcade on either side. Parts of the ruin remained black and massive, while the shrine of the holy relic stood illuminated; and broken rays and silver / points glittered on the projected tracery of the arches and twisted pillars, which supported the canopy of the royal tomb.

The imagination of the younger traveller was busied in conjecturing which part of the building had been the choir, which the refectory, which the dormitory,[197] when the Commodore observed: 'Fanaticism raised these walls, and fanaticism destroyed them.*[198] Their foundation recalls a degraded epoch of the human mind, when bigotry bribed its way to heaven, and purchased salvation with the fruits of that violence and injustice which risked it. These monkish potentates, these sanctified violators / in all ages and regions, are alike contemptible – their holy alliances and system of spoliation – their building of churches and breaking of treaties, combine the vices of fraud and hypocrisy, and rob ambition of its glory, and majesty of its respect.'

'Still,' said De Vere, 'I like a religion of forms, a tangible religion, as I beheld it in Spain, where I was once half tempted to turn monk; a religion mingled with intrigue and credulity, passionate and pious, the ready agent of love and devotion.' He sighed profoundly, and asked: 'Is not this the twenty-fifth of August?'

'I believe so,' was the reply.

''Tis a curious coincidence: on this day, at this hour, seven years ago, my birth-day too, the day I came of age, being in Galicia in Spain, chance led me to the site of a Moorish ruin adjoining the cloisters of the church of the celebrated convent of Nuestra Senora de / las Angustias.†[199] I passed, musing on the course

---

*   What the holy rage of the first reformers left undone, Cromwell's soldiers completed. Even the monument of the Earl of Thomond, in Queen Elizabeth's time, erected in the Cathedral of the city of Limeric, could not escape their fury, though none in this country deserved more from England.
  Antiquities of Ireland.

†   Our Lady of Sorrow.

of things, from the fragments of Arabic taste, and Mahometan superstition, into
the temple of Christian rites. Vespers were just celebrated. A few stragglers, who
had remained after service, gradually disappeared. I was still examining monuments, gazing on pictures, and numbering columns, when darkness fell around
me: the different avenues of entrance were closed, all save one, which led to what
had once been a Moorish orangerie: this orangerie formed a part of the pleasure-
ground and cemetery of the adjoining convent. While I looked round for some
means of egress, and twilight rendered all objects dim and uncertain, sounds,
that seemed to come from heaven, met my ear: the next moment my eye fell
upon the minstrel. By the white veil and rosary, it was an unprofessed novice: she
was seated on the fragment of / a Moorish bath, leaning her cheek close to the
lute, from which she had drawn such enchanting harmony, as if she were child-
ishly, yet prettily, charmed with the sound herself had made.'

'It is pretty image altogether,' said his auditor, seating himself beside him,
among the ruins, 'and reminds me of a famous picture of Rosso Fiorentino, of a
seraph listening to its own lute.'[200]

'The resemblance was so great,' returned the narrator, 'that I had that design
copied on this box, with the little alteration of substituting the novice's veil for
the wing of the cherub, and the head of a lovely woman for that of a seraph.'

As he spoke, he drew from his pocket a superb gold box, surmounted with
the picture he had described, done in enamel. The moonlight fell full upon its
surface; and in the position in which the Commodore held it, it was distinctly /
visible. 'Is this head a portrait?' he demanded.

'Not exactly. It was done from the *idea* I gave the artist; an *idea* in every sense:
for though the form and outline of the fair original, her fairy stepping, her aërial
motions, became too soon well known, yet the features which that envious veil
concealed were never but

dimly seen, half shrouded, half revealed, pale in the moon's uncertain light,
dark under the shadows of the monumental cypress. In the stolen and dangerous
interviews which followed the first accidental meeting, amidst scenes of silence,
mystery, and death, that face was never

fully revealed. Oh! there was in that sweet, pure, and short lived communion, a fanciful and unearthly charm, which I have often since vainly sought. It
was associated with scenes impressive on the imagination: it was pure as a spirit's
love: no sordid view or selfish feeling polluted the bright spring of genuine / passion. I was loved for myself; nor knew I the name of my concealed mistress, save
that which the church had given her – the Sister Benedicta.'

'Then you wooed, and won this mysterious saint?' asked the Commodore,
impatiently.

'Wooed! yes; wooed, and weaned the soul of this consecrated being from her
heavenly spouse, "her spouse in vain;"[201] but my conquest stopped there. I pro-

posed to carry my young novice to South America; and in some of the Eden clifts of the cloud-embosomed Cordelliras[202] to lead with her that blessed life of free unfettered passion, which nature dictated to the first created pair. Pride, bigotry, which *she doubtless* dignified with the name of *virtue*, triumphed over love. We parted: I found her innocent, I left her so; I found her happy too, at least contented and deceived; and it is not long since I ordered a Spanish friend to raise a cenotaph to her memory, in the cemetery of her / convent, with this device – A lily fading beneath a sun-beam; and with this motto '*Sic me Phœbus amat.*'[203]

'You know then that she died, and think 'twas of a broken heart?' asked his auditor.

'I cannot doubt it; though I have never heard from the friend to whom I trusted my sad commission; and to tell you the truth, the conviction still haunts my imagination, with a melancholy force, that grows with what it feeds on.'

'Oh! your *imagination!*' repeated the Commodore, significantly, as he returned the box.

'Yes,' continued the narrator; 'and in sketching the story, which I have given to the world anonimously, the description of her death-bed scene almost drove me mad.'

A short wild laugh now rang through the ruins, as if some malignant fiend had formed a part of the audience, and / scoffed at the fantastic folly of human vanity, the short-lived influence of human passion.

The strangers both started, and remained for a moment silent and motionless.

'We have been overheard,' said the elder.

'I should say by nothing human.' replied his companion. 'Look round you: see, we are alone: all is now silence and solitude.'

'*Now*, perhaps, but not a moment back. – Look there, something is in motion.'

They both darted forward. The moon had sunk in clouds, the stars were few, the pavement broken, and their steps uncertain. Still the Commodore attained the object of his pursuit. It was an old mule grazing on the scanty herbage which sprang up among the ruins.

'This is a most ludicrous adven-/ture!' said the Commodore; 'and we had better terminate it by returning to our inn and our supper.'

The younger stranger still loitered, still mused: the elder drew his arm through his: they proceeded in silence; and though during their meal they talked of indifferent subjects, it was evident to the quick perception of the latter that the incident of the abbey had deeply affected the imagination of his fanciful companion; he, however, made no allusion to it, and

his silence corroborated an inference founded in fact.[k] /

CHAPTER III.

Rocks, caves, lakes, fens, bogs, dens,
And shades of death. All monstrous,
All prodigious things! –
                    MILTON.[204]

BUTTEVANT, the Bothon of Ecclesiastical books, the Kilnemullagh of Spencer,[205] immortalized by his residence in its neighbourhood,[1] was the last stage which the travellers had agreed to pass together; and whether a feeling of regret attended this conviction, or other causes secretly operated to protract their departure, they left Holy-cross at an hour comparatively late, to begin a journey of some distance through one of the wildest mountain tracts, and least frequented cross roads, in the province of Munster. /

Their next stage, however, was excellent: it was only to Cashel; and to judge from the group of sturdy fellows, who lurked about the door of the inn to which the travellers were driven, that town was not without its due portion of idlers – a natural circumstance in the capital of a grazing country. As the chaise stopped, the gentlemen were looking over their travelling map. They had marked out their route by the road-book, and had chosen the most picturesque, rather, perhaps, than the best line of progress; and in crossing the elevated chain of the *Galties,* they had selected the road by Gaul Bally (the town of the Gauls or Celts), with its monastic ruins, in preference to the glen of *Agherlow,*[206] a valley on the opposite side of the mountains, which would have lengthened their route, but would have presented a more beaten track, though in itself sufficiently wild and romantic. Whichever way they took, the driver assured them that they / would reach Buttevant by sunset, 'God willing, and barring accident.'

As they descended, therefore, from their carriage, they ordered a chaise and horses for Gaul Bally, to be ready against their return from the rock.*[207]

'Certainly, Sir,' said the landlord,† slightly touching his hat, and resuming his conversation with a man-of-business-looking person, who was talking to him at the door. 'Barney, a chaise on to Gaul Bally.'

Barney, having taken due time to consume a portion of tobacco, called out in his turn to a driver near him, 'Tim, honey, just call out a chay to Gaul-Bally.' / Tim, who was seated on the steps of a horse-post, playing with a large dog,

---

*   The rock of Cashel, the romantic scite of its cathedral.

†   As inns, in common with the royal caravanseras of the eastern apologue, are subject to a frequent change of masters, it is probable that some such revolution has occurred at the inn at Cashel since these events took place: at least, the author has no reason to charge its present occupants with incivility.

addressed himself to a blind beggar, with 'step into the yard, and tell Corney Doolin a chay's wanting to Gaul Bally.'

'What is the distance to Gaul-Bally?' asked the Commodore, who, as well as his fellow traveller, had observed the progress of these deputed orders with impatience and irritation.

'What is the distance to Gaul Bally?' returned the landlord with sangfroid,[208] as if he now first observed them, 'upon my word and reputation, Sir, I can't say – that is really, – Gaul Bally. Barney, can you answer these gentlemen?'

'Och, Sir, shure you don't post to Gaul Bally at all at all: there's no posting there, Sir, nor wasn't many a-year. If the gentlemen bes going to Doneraile or Buttevant, they'd best go the low road, and take the glen of Agherlow to Mitchels town.'[209]

'We are resolved not to take any / road but that we've fixed on; and I suppose we can have a chaise and horses to what stage and place we choose, no matter where, if we pay for them.'

This observation, made with haughtiness and petulance by Mr. De Vere, induced the landlord to uncover his head, and to reply: 'Certainly, Sir: if you indemnify me, Sir, I can let you have every accommodation in life; up to the top of Mangerton,[210] if you please; only there is no posting, I give you my word, gentlemen, on these cross roads in Munster:[211] that is, I don't send out my cattle by the mile; but you can have them by the *job*, or *day*, and welcome.'

'Why then, job or day,' said Barney, with a significant look at his master, 'if the chay goes by Gaul Bally, its on a low backed car[212] it will come back.'

'Shure enough,' said Tim, rubbing round his shoulders, 'and wouldn't care to be the driver, barring I was well ped, and left my *throath* behind me, specially / near Kilbalogue, the thieves' wood, down there, below.'

'I came that way in my gig from Kilfinnen,' said the man of business, 'and found it good enough, and two dragoons with me.'

'Och, then, it behoves you, and the likes of you, Mr. Fogarty,' said Tim, 'to look to that, Sir; for the times never ran so hard against the excise as now: in respect of bringing down the military, and the grate stillhunting, and fining the townlands to ruination.'[213]

'Will you take the chay on to Buttevant, gentlemen?' asked the innkeeper.

'To Buttevant, certainly – perhaps further,' replied the younger traveller.

'I don't think I could give it under seven or eight guineas a-day,' he returned, musing; 'but I'll let you know in a minute;' and he entered / the house, followed by Tim, Barney, and the exciseman, to hold a council.

'Eight guineas a-day! sorrow send it you, Mr. Collogon! – eight guineas! Dioul!!'

This apostrophe was made by a person who leaned against the back of the stranger's chaise. He was wrapped in a huge frize coat,[214] wore a slouched hat over a grey wig, and stood slashing a long cutting whip against the pavement. When, however, he perceived the travellers proceeded towards the rock of Cashel without noticing him, he followed them, touched his hat, and said, 'I'll drive your honors to Buttevant, and that to your hearts' contint, for half the money, and has as iligent a chay, and as nate a pair of mountain cattle, as any in Condon's country; and keeps myself, your honor, hard bye, convanient to Buttevant, near Kilcoleman, Sir, and runs my garans / on my own account, and came with a fare to Cashel the day before yesterday, and was waiting for a return, your honor, which would sarve me entirely, Sir.'

'Do you know the route well through the Galties?'

'Do I, is it, Sir? Och! may-be I don't! and would go it my lone blindfold from Galtimore to Misenhead; and from Knockmell down to the reeks in Killarney;[215] and that's a brave step, Sir.'

'I should like to disappoint that *nonchalant* host of the Star, and his imposing driver,' said the elder traveller.

'And this man residing near Kilcoleman,' said the younger, 'has a classical interest with me. I shall probably engage him while I reside in the neighbourhood of Spencer's fairy ground.'

The bargain was instantly made, and / the chaise ordered to be at the inn door in half an hour, the time assigned to visit King Cormac's chapel. Meantime, the master of the Kilcoleman chaise undertook to inform the host of the Star that his horses would not be wanting; and when the travellers returned from their antiquarian visit, they found all ready for their departure.

While the light luggage was removing into the new vehicle, the appearance of that vehicle, its horses, and driver, were a source of affected entertainment to the disappointed landlord and his satellites.

'Barney, that's a nate article of a chay,' observed Tim. 'Troth, I would not wonder if it was ould Cormac Mac Coleman's travelling landau, when he went the pilgrimage to Holy-cross.'[216]

'Faith, Tim, lad, you're not much out, I believe; for there's a crown on it, shure enough, which shews it belonged to th' ould kings of Munster, / any how, King Flann[217] or Brien Borru, may be.'

'Why then, for all that, Barney, I wisht I had all the chickens that ever was hatch'd in it. grand as it is. And look at the *garans*,* Sir; Och! but they're grate bastes, and warranted not to draw. I'll engage they'd rather die than run, and no ways skittish, that's certain, any way.'

The owner of this equipage, against which so many sarcasms were launched, was hitherto coolly rubbing down his horses with a whisp of straw; and singing, or rather humming,

---

* Poor hack horses.

'I am a rake and a rambling boy,
My lodging 'tis near Aughnaghcloy.'[218]
He now paused, however, to observe, 'The cattle's shurely not so fine as them
was shot in the mail, near Kilworth, Mr. Barney Heffernan, but they are good
mountain cattle, for all that, / and will take the gentlemen better through the
Galties, and safer too, than handsomer bastes, plase Jasus!'

The former part of this observation had caused a very obvious revulsion in
the colour of Mr. Heffernan's face, who, drawing some straws from between the
wheels of the chaise, said, in a conciliating voice, 'I'm glad to see you about the
world again, Owny – when did you set up driver?'

'A little after the tithe-proctor's business[219] in the murdering glen below, in
the county of Waterford,' replied *Owny*, significantly.

Barney Heffernan slunk away, and no further sarcasm was launched against
Owny's *set-out*,[220] which both the gentlemen stood for some minutes examining
with curiosity; the Commodore wiping with his handkerchief the dust from the
pannel on which the coronet, alluded to by one of the drivers, was visible, sur-
mounting a defaced crest and armo- /rial bearing. The chaise was indeed of a very
singular and antique build; low, angular, with a projecting roof. The large windows, which once perhaps entitled it to the appellation of a glass coach,[221] were
now partly filled up with wooden pannels; and through the rents of the coarse
check modern lining, remnants of crimson velvet, and rich, but thread-bare livery lace, spoke its former gentility. The travellers had proceeded some miles from
Cashel, in a silence which the younger seemed little inclined to break, when the
falling down of an old green silk blind roused him from his reverie.

'This curious old vehicle,' he observed, 'doubtless belonged to some noble
family. Did you perceive a baron's coronet on the side pannel, and a crest beneath
it?'

'Yes, a dexter arm, issuing out of a cloud, and holding a naked sword, all
proper,[222] with the motto, *Vigueur / de dessus*[223] – the cognizance and motto
of some Norman adventurer, who formerly ravaged this country, and who, like
more modern victors, took the sanction of heaven for their deeds of violence,
and believed, or affected to believe, that '*Dieu est toujours pour les gros bataillons.*'[224]

'It is the motto and crest of the Fitzadelm family, of the present Marquis of
Dunore, the representative of that family,' said De Vere.

A silence of a few minutes followed this observation, and the Commodore
then carelessly added – 'The Fitzadelms! a branch of the far-spreading Geraldines? Yes, they got their portion of this fair province by grant from Henry the
Second, to whom they were SEWERS, as the Ormond family were BUTLERS;
and shared with *Hamo de Valois, Philip of Worcester,* William *de Barri,* and other

Norman adventurers, the princely palatinate of the Macarthies / More, once chiefs or kings of Desmond.'[225]

'It is in the order of things,' said De Vere, coolly.

'Oh! exactly; the 'vigueur de dessus,' which may be translated *'might*, not *right*,' has been the same in all ages; but it is peculiar to the conquest of Ireland, to behold Henry the Second in his camp at Aquitain, distributing to his follow-ers principalities, out of a country he had never seen, a country still in possession of its rightful chiefs, and in which his enterprising marshal, Strongbow,[226] had then scarcely left the track of his footstep. It is curious also to behold the pope, consecrating this robbery, the Irish chieftains disdaining the Saxon king and the Roman pontif, defending, losing, recovering, and forfeiting again their ancient territories; and finally the English lords becoming Irish in feelings, character, and language, and / avenging the very injuries they had themselves inflicted, because they had become victims of the same barbarous policy by which their ancestors had been influenced.[m] The causes of Ireland's misfortunes are so deep seated, that every page in her history is a palliation of her faults, and the graver errors of the people will all be found in the misrule of her government.'

'Better governed, she would be more prosperous,' said the younger traveller, 'and less interesting and less amusing. As it is, she is 'melancholy and gentle-manlike,'[227] a thing to make one laugh and cry in a breath. Her history, turned into metre, would dramatize into a sort of tragi-comic melo-dram of mirth and misery, ferocity and fun, that would leave the pathetic grotesque of chrononho-tonthologus[228] far behind.'[n]

'Them is the Gaulties, plaze your / honor,' said the driver, 'among the clouds. There, Sir, not a mountain in the province will bate them, any how, let alone Mangerton.'

'They are, indeed, truly respectable mountains for this little island,' said the younger traveller, directing his glance to a range of bold romantic perpendicular acclivities, whose conic pinnacles were lost in the clouds, and whose dark stu-pendous range might have formed a natural and impregnable boundary between rival and contending states.

At the village of Gaul Bally they found only the ruins of some religious houses, a barrack, and a little Shebean house, where the driver stopped for a few minutes to refresh his horses and himself. They soon recommenced their moun-tain journey, doubling a formidable ridge, and ascending a gentle acclivity, while the driver, almost throwing the reins upon the horses' necks, sat with his arms folded, and recommenced / for the twentieth time since they had left Cashel,

'The groves of Blarney, they are so charming.'[229]

'This will never do,' said the Commodore, letting down the front glass. 'Why, my friend, your horses seem tired already.'

'They do, plaze your honor,' was the cool reply. 'And do you know the raison of that same, Sir? Why, then, it's becaise they're on level ground, Sir. Sorrow a thing else ails them. Och! the craturs are kind and lazy like myself, and quite untractable to a smooth level plain; but wait till yez gets up among the glens and precipices. It's then, Sir, you will see them bate the reglar posters, why! entirely; for they knows the ways of the place, and little fear for the chay being left in smithereens,*[230] on the top of a rock, there, or at the bottom of that hollow, down in the divil's glin to your lift, Sir.' /

'It's very evident,' said the Commodore, 'that this fellow is as *untractable* as his horses. There is a dogged indifference about him, a good-humoured pertinacity of manner, with which it would clearly be in vain to contend; it were best, therefore, to leave him to his song and his waywardness.'

'Oh! I hold no contention with travelling contingencies,' replied de Vere: 'through life, as through a journey, the *'Laissez-aller*[231]' is my device. Who would take the trouble of even WILLING, when a pebble under your chaise-wheel may set volition at nought. Who would contend with accidents and events, uncertain and incalculable as the elements on which they so often depend?'

'This is a fine road, your honors,' said the driver, breaking off his song abruptly, and applying his remark to a rude, rough, narrow acclivity, moss-grown and torrent-worn, and becoming every moment more difficult of ascent. /

'Balleagh-na-Tierna 'tis called, in respect of being cut across the side of the Galties by the TIERNA-DHU, that is the BLACK BARON, as they named him in his own country here below.'

'Black baron!' said De Vere: 'that sounds well among these wild scenes. Does the black baron live in these mountains, friend?'

'He does, Sir; that's he did, but he's dead, Sir, and doing bravely these twenty years and more, and so is his brother Tierna Ruadh, the red baron, that followed him; whose son is now the Marquis Dunore: devil set his foot after them all, for its little good ever they did the country yet, them Fitzadelms!' (5)[n]

The two travellers, as if moved by the same mechanical impulse, started, leaned forward, and then sunk back in the chaise – 'At least,' said the elder, 'it was doing good to cut a road through this wild region, friend.' /

'Sorrow much then, Sir, any how; in respect of never finishing it, no more nor that inn there, fornent you to the left.' Here the driver pointed to the ruins of some dreary walls, which added to the desolateness of the scene.

'This Balleagh, I heard tell, was to join the low road, and was made in a great hurry to have a short cut for the Lord Lieutenant and the quality that came down in oceans from Dublin to the stage plays at court Fitzadelm;[232] and the inn

---

*   Smithereens; i. e. fragments.

was to bait at; for, barring Lis-na-sleugh, sorrow baiting place in the Galties at all at all; and that was no place for quality to stop in.'

'What an heterogenous association of images!' said the Commodore: 'mountain regions and private theatricals! A poor Irish lord beginning a work fit for an emperor, and leaving it unfinished, a monument of his uncalculating extravagance, of that wildness and refinement, that uncivilized dissipation, / which characterized the provincial nobility of Ireland fifty years back, and arose from the degradation in which they were held.'

'Oh, its delicious!' replied De Vere. 'I should like to know how the descendant or representative of these noble Fitzadelms would feel, in thus accidentally hearing what we have now heard, and seeing what we see.'

'If he was a vain man, flattered and spoiled by fortune,' replied the Commodore, emphatically, 'he would feel deep mortification; but if he were' – he paused abruptly, and demanded of the driver: 'Does Court Fitzadelm lie in the neighbourhood of these mountains?'

'It does, Sir, fifteen miles off, in the valley, down below, between the Galties and *Gotroes,* and the Balli-Howries,[233] cribbed round with them and the beautiful Avon fiorne, the *fair water,* running under the castle bawn,[234] that's all / that's left of it, Sir. For shure after the Lord's death it was broken up into smithereens, and scarce a skreed*[235] of it left to the fore.'

'And who has carried it away?' asked De Vere.

'Why, Darby Crawley has, Sir, and his father before him, ould Pat; and has'nt left a taste, but what's in their own hands this day. And the chay, your honors driving in, shure it was from him; 'twas bought at the auction. Troth, and if the young lord that got the title, or his brother was in it, they'd be entirely amazed to see their crown and arms running the road this day, that's the Galties, Sir.'

To this observation the travellers made no rejoinder. The horses now toiled slowly and painfully up a road, which every moment became more steep and laborious. On either side, the mountain scenery opened into in-/creasing wildness and sublimity. Innumerable defiles boldly diverged to ascending regions, while altitudes still greater, blue, misty, and cloud-cap'd,[236] terminated these natural vistas. The ascent had now become to steep and dangerous, that the travellers had not only alighted, but were frequently obliged to assist in lifting the chaise over deep ruts, cut by the torrents, but which the driver simply, called '*sore bits.*'[237] He frequently assured them that a little further on, a small quarter of a mile, the lord's Balleagh† would come down upon the Cloghniagh-Cluain, the *lurking place of the noisy water*[238] (a torrent he affected every moment to hear)

---

*   Skreed, a rag or morsel.
†   Balleagh – a road or way.

and then they would be upon the *low* road, which would bring them on the *high* posting road to Doneraile and Buttevant.

Obliged to pin their faith upon a guide of whom they now began to en- / tertain some suspicion, the travellers beheld one small quarter of a mile succeed to another, and heard and lost repeatedly the fall of many dashing torrents, until, as they ascended among the romantic elevations of the Galties, they lost sight of the inconvenience and tediousness of their journey in their admiration of the scenery. They even permitted the horses to halt in a narrow glen, while they proceeded to examine regions, where nature reigned in all her wildest magnificence; and they ascended from one commanding altitude to another till the whole stupendous chain of mountains broke gradually upon them, spreading far and wide in bold fantastic forms, and in the utmost freedom of outline. As the travellers stood thus occupied at the point of a bold cliff, they suddenly perceived a shadow thrown from their precipitous station, intercepting the blood red beams of the now settling sun, and turning / quickly round, round, they observed a man so close to them, that by a single effort he might have hurled the incautious wanderers down the abyss, they had, a moment before, shuddered to contemplate. He had a bold, strongly defined, but light and flexible figure, not much set off by a ragged frize jacket: his neck was scarcely covered by a loosely tied red handkerchief. In his countenance there was a look of mingled carelessness and intrepidity, of gaiety and acuteness, which is so often discernible in the Irish physiognomy. His hat, worn gallantly on one side, his light arch blue eye and curly luxuriant hair, gave to his whole appearance something of rustic foppery, mingled with an hardy daringness, that was peculiarly characteristic. This unexpected apparition in a scene so lonely amazed without alarming the travellers. When the man asked, with a sort of triumphant laugh, 'Doesn't your honors know me then? Shure, a'nt / I your driver, Sirs, that drove you from Cashel in the Kilcoleman chay, below, in the hollow there.'

This information rather increased than lessened the surprise his appearance excited. 'Only,' he continued, 'that I threw off my *cotamore*,*[239] in regard of the heat; and wishing to climb the mountain after you, I changed my old wig and *caubeen*[240] for this bit of a straw hat, Sir, that I keeps under the chay sate for warm weather, why.'

'But with such a profusion of hair, why do you wear a wig?' asked the Commodore.

'Och! becaise, your honor, it was my ould father's before me, Sir, †[241] – God / rest him' – and he crossed himself devoutly.

---

*   Great coat. The cotaigh was the upper garment anciently.

†   This reason the author has often heard assigned by the young Irish for covering their natural locks with an old scratch wig. Fine hair, however, is a national beauty, and an

This mode of accounting for a disguise, more of air and manner, even than of dress, amused, but by no means satisfied the travellers; and secretly convinced that he had some motive for concealing his person in Cashel, they accompanied him in silence back to the spot where he had left the chaise and horses. As they descended the declivities, De Vere observed, 'This is what Shakespeare calls "a fine, gay, bold faced villain:"[242] I should like to know his object in bewildering us in these mountains.'

'If he has any,' replied Commodore, carelessly, 'it must soon discover itself.'

On reaching the hollow, they were surprised and mortified to find that the daylight, which still lingered in tints of purple and gold on the summits of the mountains, had faded away from their vallies. /

'Yez may step in now, gentlemen,' said the driver: 'we have a smooth piece afore us for half a mile, and then we turn into Cloghnaigh-Cluain, and will be on the top of Doneraile in no time.'

'We are quite aware *that* is utterly impossible,' said the Commodore, decisively, as he got into the chaise; 'but go on as rapidly as possible: we should not like to be benighted in these mountains; indeed, we are resolved not to be so.'

'Och! sorrow fear, your honor, any how, of that shure: isn't there an ilegant fine moon? and if the worst goes to the worst, is not there the mountain house *Lis-na-sleugh*, at the foot of the Galties, and the best of entertainment there for man and baste.'

'No,' replied the Commodore in the same tone of cool decision, 'we must reach Doneraile or Buttevant tonight, except we ourselves change our minds, as we proceed.' /

'Which we shall not do,' whispered his companion, 'and yet, perhaps shall be *necessitated* to take up our night's abode in this *mountain-house* he talks of.'

They had in the course of a quarter of an hour reached the long promised turn to Cloghnaigh-Cluain; but the road, though it was a rapid descent, far from improving, became every moment more impracticable, and the twilight more obscure. The driver, at last, after a violent jolt, which threatened dislocation to the joints of the crazy vehicle, suddenly stopped his horses, and coming up to the chaise window, asked, 'Yez would not have such a thing as a crooked nail about ye, plaze your honors?'

The Commodore replied in the negative, half laughingly, though with feelings of annoyance, arising partly from suspicion of the man's intentions, and partly from impatience of delay in in such a place, and at such a time. /

---

article of rustic commerce. The females exchange their tresses with pedlars for trinkets and ribbons.

'Why then, murther alive, what's this for?' exclaimed the driver, scratching his head: 'the fore wheel off, and not a bit of a nail for a linch pin; and the spring broke too, and not a taste of rope to tie it up with.'

'This *is* a pleasant adventure,' said the younger traveller, throwing himself back in the chaise; while the elder, jumping out, examined into the accident: the spring was broken, the wheel was off.

'This is no accident,' he said, turning abruptly to the driver: 'the linch pin of this wheel has been drawn out purposely.'

'It has, Sir?' he reiterated with simplicity. 'See that now! why then, I wonder who would be after doing that same; if it wouldn't be your honors, out of sport, Sir. But sorrow much matter, any how; I'd as soon drive your honors with three wheels as four, and did from Cork to Kilworth: – that's father Mur-/phy, Sir; and the wheel will just slip in the front of the chay, fair and aisy, I'll be bound.

'But that's not the worst of it,' he continued coolly, endeavouring to force the wheel into the chaise on one side, while Mr. De Vere jumped out at the other: 'we've taken the wrong turn, it seems, entirely; for that Cloghnaigh bates the world, in respect of contrariness; and when I thought we were in on it, isn't it here the "*wolf's track*," we've slipped into? Dioul!'

'You are to remember,' said the Commodore, while his companion was enjoying a rapid combination of every real, fancied, or possible danger, 'you told us you were well acquainted with the road.'

'And if I wasn't, your honor, how would I know that this is the *wolf's track*. Och! musha! the likes of this never happened me before. Ochone! Here's your purse, Sir, dear, dropped in the hay;' and he carelessly threw the / purse, weighty from containing some golden Spanish coin, into the traveller's hand: he then continued his lamentation over his mistake, at the same time endeavouring to thrust the fore wheel of the chaise through one of its doors. From his tone of voice, peculiarity of manner, and the carelessness with which he restored a purse, that in all probability would not have been missed, every suspicion of sinister intention was hushed in the mind of the Commodore. The younger traveller, however, saw only in the latter circumstance some *ruse* beyond the ordinary stratagem of a common robber; and whether he was to be enrolled among a band of Shanavests, or stripped and plundered for the benefit of the Caravats,[243] were circumstances debated in his mind, under the influence of many romantic associations appropriate to the scene and hour. Meantime, as the driver assured them, that though they had not taken the best or the / shortest road, they were still making their way out of the mountains, they continued to walk in advance of the chaise, without further reproach; while the driver, leading his horses, recommenced his song, which he only interrupted to point out a stone cross under the cliff, that he called the 'Hag's bed;'[244] and some other features in the scene, characteristic of its wildness; thus evincing that his boasted acquaintance with the mountains was not an unfounded vaunt.

With that sudden change of temperature incidental to mountain regions, the air had become intensely cold; and through the increasing darkness of the evening, they hailed with pleasure a long level ray of light, which assured them of their approximation to some human abode; perhaps a forge, where they might have their chaise wheel reinstated; and they suggested this possibility to the driver.

'A forge,' he replied, 'then that's / the great luck, for if there's a forge, ye can put the night over at *Lis-na-sleugh,* for there's not a forge in the Galties round, barring the forge of Lis-na-sleugh, where there's the best of fine entertainment, as I hear tell, that's if the chay can't be mended, and yez don't care to get on by moonlight to Buttevant, which yez may after all, plaze God.'

'Freedom of agency,' said the younger traveller, with a short laugh, 'that may sound very well in a metaphysical argument, but here! – we are all the slaves of circumstance, the puppets of events over which we have no control. Observe, we had pointed out Thurles and Tipperary for our stages; we went, we were *obliged to go,* to Holy-cross, and Cashel. We proposed, we *willed,* dining in Buttevant, – we are passing the evening, amidst the savage mountains of the Galties! And now, you may depend upon it, bon gré, malgré,[245] we shall be fated to stop at this Lis – something, some fortress of the / Shanavests or Caravats, Whiteboys or Threshers;[246] our boasted freedom of agency, all reduced to inevitable submission to the intrigues of this masquerading driver, who, by the bye, has again, you see, assumed his disguise.' – 'Evidently not to deceive us,' replied the Commodore.° As they proceeded, the light had frequently appeared and disappeared; but as their descent became less rapid, and they advanced more deeply into the valley, it assumed a more steady beam; and the outline of a small building became visible amidst a mass of darkly defined objects: as they approached they perceived it was a little sash window, which emitted the red light of a blazing turf fire; and a volume of white curling smoke, issuing from an aperture in the roof, stained the deep dark blue of the atmosphere with fleecy forms. The moon just shewed her edge above the horizon, and more strongly defined the position of the building, / which occupied part of a little plain, forming a point of termination to four cross roads, that branched off round the base of the mountains. Those they had crossed appeared to rise almost to the clouds behind them; and of the many waterfalls, which dashed from the neighbouring rocks, one fell close to the rear of the cottage, dwindling into a rill, and forming a little horse-pool in its front. A light under a shed at a short distance shewed some horses feeding. A bunch of mountain hether suspended over the door, but above all, a post-chaise drawn up before it, which seemed, by its position, to have recently arrived by one of the low roads, designated this wild and remote edifice as an inn. This idea was confirmed by a smart crack of the whip, with which the driver brought up his weary horses, and by his taking off his hat to the gentlemen, and exclaiming, with a courteous bow,

'Why then, long life to yez! yez are welcome to Lis-na-sleugh!' /

'So,' said De Vere, 'I thought so. This, however, is wizzard scenery, and one may compound for a little inconvenience, or even danger, to enjoy it.'

The approach of the carriage had brought out from the shed, which served as a stable, a lame beggar, who officiated as hostler, and a ragged boy, who appeared as the substitute for a waiter.

'Here baccah ma vourneen,'*[247] said the driver, who was now once more muffled in his cotamore, his wig, and old caubeen, 'take off them cattle for me, while I show the gentlemen into the place. Come, my gassoon,[248] lend me the rush,' and he snatched the light out of the boy's hand. 'This away, your honors; take care of the sow, Sir: there's a bit of a *strame,* Sir. Widow Gaffney, ma'am, where are you agrah? Oh, here's the mistress herself. I'll / trouble, ma'am, to look after the gentlemen, while I give a squint at th' other bastes.'

The hostess took the light from him, and he joined the driver of the other newly arrived chaise, who was adjourning from the house to the stable. The *Widow Gaffney,* with many smiles and courtesies, led the guests from the dark little stone passages which separated the kitchen, clouded with smoke, from another small room distinguished by its plank flooring; exclaiming, as she moved before them, 'Och! but your honors is welcome, Sirs. It's a sharp night to cross the mountains, and will have a sod kindled in the *chimbley,* Sirs, if yez are going stay past the cattle's taking their lock of hay, gintlemin.'

As she spoke, she lighted, or endeavoured to light, a miserable candle, which stood in a dirty brass candlestick on a shelf over the *'chimbley.'* While thus engaged, the yellow flickering / light fell full on her face, and threw her sharp, but handsome features, her deep sallow complexion, and black bright eyes, into strong relief. A red kerchief was tied round her head in the Munster fashion, and the rest of her tall, slight, boney form was hidden in shade.†

The strangers withdrew their eyes from the figure of the landlady, to the apartment into which she had ushered them. Its whitewashed walls were partially covered with those pious prints which are hawked about for sale in the remotest parts of Ireland. The history of many a saint, the sufferings of many a martyr, were here detailed in bright vermilion and yellow ochre; and angels and devils, hymns and homilies, were mingled promiscuously with the amatory history of '*Cooleendas,*' '*Croothenamœ,*'[249] the '*Connaught daisy,*'[250] the 'last dying speech of Captain Dreadnought,'[251] bloody and barbarous murders, and a favourite song, called '*Ma chere amie,*' as sung by *Mrs. Billington.*[252]

---

*   Baccah, a cripple. All lame and deformed beggars, are called baccahs in Ireland.

†   The old Irish *head-kerchief,* is almost universally worn by the female peasantry of Munster.

A deal table in the centre of the room was still covered with some little pewter vessels, and two glasses with wooden bottoms. The hearth was stuffed with withered heath; and the atmosphere of the room, from which all ventilation was excluded, breathed the fumes of whiskey. The younger traveller, holding his perfumed handkerchief to his nose, asked if there was no other apartment they could occupy, while their horses were feeding, and their chaise mended.

'Och! blessed Virgin,' said the hostess, wiping down the table with her apron, 'this is the contrariest day ever rose on me! Weeks we'd be, God help us, and not a chay, or sign of quality come the road; and now, becaise its / the fair of Kiltish, and the world's in on upon us, here's two po-chaises, and not a sowl to help me, only the baccah, and my own little garlagh of a boy.'

'We should be glad to go any where where there's a fire,' said the Commodore, 'the kitchin for instance.'

'Och! your honor, that would be a poor place for the likes of you; but if you would demean yourself to step into it, while I kindle a sod here, and ready the place, and takes down these brusheens. –'

As she now began to raise a very unpleasant dust by removing the bushes from the hearth, the gentlemen walked at once to the kitchen.

The little inn of Lis-na-sleugh, or *the house of the mountain,* was the genuine prototype of all such inns in the remote cross-roads, or mountain ways in Ireland; and the kitchen, as is usual in such places, was equally the receptacle of the guest and the beggar; of / those who could, and those who could not pay for a temporary shelter. The earthen floor of this hospitable apartment was undulating and broken: a low mud wall, with an aperture in it to see through, screened the fire-place from the door; and the capacious hearth, lined with a stone bench, afforded a comfortable retreat to the chilled or wearied traveller. It was now occupied by a haggard, worn-out looking person, who repeatedly drank from a noggin of water beside him. Above the bright clear fire of mountain turf, built upon the floor, hung suspended an immense iron cauldron, filled with potatoes, not boiling, but boiled and drying (5). In an angle of the kitchen, over a three-legged table, and a little pewter vessel filled with whiskey, sat two travellers; one of them, by the pack which lay at his feet, a pedlar; the other, ill-looking and poorly clad: both earnestly conversing in Irish. Beside / the fire-place, on an old settle, were seated two females: one with her long Irish frize cloak, and the hood drawn over her face, exhibited her warmly-mittened hands to the fire, towards which she was turned. The other, stately and erect, her round figure covered in an old fashioned travelling cloak, and her head enveloped in that curious *cöiffure* made and called after the head of a French carriage, and not many years back worn in Ireland under the name of a *calesh*.[253] From the superiority of their appearance, they were assigned by the strangers to the chaise, which stood at the door on their arrival, and seemed but just to have preceded them.

As the gentlemen stood before the fire conversing in Spanish on the incidents of their journey, calculating upon the probabilities of the future, and making observations on all that surrounded them, the widow having lighted / a fire in the best room, returned to await the dispersion of the smoke it occasioned. She leaned indolently over a table, with her hands wrapped in her apron, or as she called it, her *praskeen*, and cast a glance of curiosity, directed alternately at her guests, in anxious hope that they would call for some refreshment. None, however, was demanded until the entrance of Owney, the driver, broke the spell; for he addressed her with –

'You would'nt have such a thing as a *cuppan* * of parliament in the house, Mrs. Gaffney?'

'Och! then, if I would not have that, what would I have, Sir, when I *sould* the bed from under me to pay the license; and would be sorry to see the barony fined, after the murther we had in the mountains about ould Sulivan's still, last week, and the waylaying of / the exciseman, and two men and one soger kilt in the action. Since the attempt at a rescue made for the Rabragh,[254] never was known the likes in the province of Munster, many a day.'

Mrs. Gaffney was helping the driver to a little vessel of licensed whiskey, which he had termed a cuppan of parliament, when the ill-looking man, who sate tête-a-tête[255] with the pedlar, asked,

'What's gone of the Rabragh, I wonder?'

'Och! Sir, he's about the world again, I hear tell,' replied the landlady, 'though never saw him, 'bove all the boys in the county. They say, the Ban-Tierna† had him released from prison last assizes twelvemonth, and went herself to the judges at Tipperary, in regard of her being his foster-sister.'[256] /

'Long may she reign,' exclaimed the ill-looking man; 'for she's a fine woman, and the poor man's friend. – Here's, may she live a thousand years.' and he tossed off a glass of spirits.

'Amen,' said the driver, moving his hat reverentially as he pledged the toast, in a voice tremulous with emotion.

'I drink to her in water, wishing it was wine,' said the poor man in the chimney corner: 'for I come from the land where her forefathers reigned. Here's to the Countess of Clancare.'

'Why then, if this were the last drop I had in the world,' said the driver, drawing his hat over his face, as he advanced in the light, 'you shall go my halves in it;' and he presented what remained in his cuppan to the water-drinker, who swallowing it eagerly, observed,

---

*   Cuppan, a little cup – *Parliament* whiskey, that is, *licensed*.
†   *Ban-Tierna*, the *female chief*; literally, the woman of the chief, or *noblewoman*. This epithet is occasionally applied to female representatives of noble houses.

'That's the first bit or sup passed my lips the day, barring a dry potatoe / and a draught of water; and came all the ways from the barony of Dunkerron, district of Clancare in Kerry,[257] over bog and mountain, to sell my little bit of an hobby*[258] at the fair of Kittish, to pay the rent of the shed I break my heart under.'

'Why then, is that hobby with the saddle your's, Sir?' asked the driver.

'She is,' said the poor man, sighing, 'to my sorrow: and a finer bit of a baste for bog or mountain journey doesn't breathe, for all I'm carrying her back with me this night; and offered her for a thirty shilling Cork note and a pair of brogues, to a hawker this morning.'

'Why then, Sir, see here,' said the driver in a voice full of compassion. / 'If I had the money, myself, I'd take her off your hands the night, if it was only to hire her out by the job to travellers, and to *sarve* you into the bargain, God help you.'

'Then purchase her for me,' said the Commodore, who, with his companion, had stood listening to this local and desultory conversation, uttered in an accent so strange to their ears as not always to be comprehended. The bargain was soon struck, and the owner of the *hobby,* with eyes streaming with joy, and a tongue profuse in gratitude, received a small sum over the price he had demanded.

'I believe,' said the elder stranger, addressing him as he counted out his money, 'at least I have read or heard, that your barony of Dunkerron was famous for this small breed of horses?'

'And is so, your honor, to this day, and that's *all* it is famous for now, barring St. Crohan's cell, the patron / saint of the barony, hewn out of the solid rock with his own hands.'†[259]

The Commodore leant his head eagerly forward, and in a peculiar tone of voice, said, 'And under the hill of Kilcrohan there stands – there *did stand,* a small ancient building, commanding the bay of Kenmare, once a friary.'

'I know it well, your honor; the chapelry of Glinsky, the school-house of Terence Oge O'Leary, and is there to this hour, troth.'

'To *this* hour?' repeated the Commodore in emotion. 'That's the ruins of it, your honor. After measter O'Leary quit the place, nobody cared to take up / in it; and somehow, the times doesn't favour larning now in Kerry as formerly; and besides, there was an odd story went about the school-house. I disremember me

---

* The little hobbies of this country are the most proper to travel through it; and a man must abandon himself entirely to their guidance, which will answer much better than if one should strive to manage and direct their steps.

† *Smith's Kerry.* – In this hill Antiquarians assert that St. Kieran, the first bishop of Ossory, wrote his rule for monks. The stalactitical exudations of this romantic hermitage are held in great veneration by the country people, who carefully preserve them, in the belief that they derive many virtues from the sanctity of the place that produces them.

what now; and was a slip of a boy then, and went higher up into Clancare – that's twenty years ago, aye, faith, twenty-two years, since Terence Oge quit the place.'

'And more,' said the lame beggar, who was filling a sieve with some oats out of a sort of chest near the hearth. I've good right to remember it well, for I was the very man that brought the young lord, that would have been, from Court Fitzadelm to Terence Oge O'Leary's house, who was his foster father, and gave him all the learning he got, now, young gentleman.'

'Did you?' said the Commodore, seizing his upraised arm; then suddenly letting it drop, he asked in an altered tone, 'Did you send for a smith to look to our chaise? /

'I did, your honor, and is at it this moment; and troth, I didn't see that same chaise drive up the night with a dry eye; for,' he added, turning to the Kerry-man, 'it was in that very chaise, which my lord brought his elegant bride in, that I afterwards carried her son, after her death, down to Dunkerron to measter O'Leary's, from whence he never returned dead or alive.'

'That's the young lord, was drowned off the Bay of Kenmare, in his own bit of a *corragh*,[260] and they say haunts the chapelry of Glensky to this hour,' demanded the Kerryman.

'Och! to my heavy sorrow,' said the mendicant, dropping the vessel he was measuring the corn with, and leaning over the chest, 'that was a sore day for me, Sir, for if he was in it this hour, it isn't in this condition I'd be, ould and lame, poor and desolate, and so I tould Measter O'Leary last week, who dropt salt tears when he saw me.' /

'Last week!' reiterated the stranger; then, with a change of voice, he added, 'Were you in Kerry last week, in Dunkerron? I am travelling that way, and should like to know the state of the roads.'

'I was not, Sir, in Kerry, and never put my foot in it since I left the young gentleman there, that's the honourable De Montenay Fitzadelm.'

'You said you saw O'Leary there, I thought.'

'It was down in the Peninsula I saw Mr. Terence Oge O'Leary, your honor, and am but just come from it this day.'

'The Peninsula!' repeated the Commodore, 'where is that?'

'The Peninsula of Dunore, Sir, on the other side of the Boggra mountains, where the Marquis's castle is, on the sea-side, at the bottom of the country, a lovely fine place.'

'I suppose the castle is in ruins?' / observed Mr. De Vere, carelessly – 'I mean Dunore castle.'

'Not at all, your honor, but as good as the day it was built, every stone of it; aye, faith, and better: for sure it was getting ready two years back for the young mad Marquis; but the workmen have been stopped since he went beside himself: and it would have been his cousin that was drowned, only for the villainy of the world that banished the cratur to the wilds of Kerry, as Mr. O'Leary says, and no luck could follow them after that, great as they are now.'

'I remember that O'Leary when he was out of his mind himself,' said the landlady, 'and I a bit of a slip of a girl: he used to be wandering in the mountains here, and bothering the world with the MACARTHIES and the FITZADELMS, and looking for their ould castles, in lone places.'

'Och, then, he's brave and hearty now, Mrs. Gaffney,' returned the lame / hostler, 'and has a fine school in the preceptory of Monaster-ni-oriel. Many thanks to friar Dennis O'Sulivan, the superior; for it was he who took him up, and preached the devil out of him (for they say he was possessed), and set him down there, snug and aisy, in the friary; and allows him to let his own apartment to bathers that come to the salt wather,[261] when himself's not in it: and, troth, you wouldn't think, the day, he had put more than fifty years over his head, that's Mr. O'Leary, though he's sixty right out; for its thirty-four years since his wife got the nursing at Court Fitzadelm, and Terence was twenty-six good then, and a brave lump of a poor scholar, when he missed his vocation,* and married Soosheen O'Calaghan.'

'They say it was larning cracked his brain,' observed the landlady. /

'No, troth! But grief for the loss of his foster child; and to this day, when he isn't going on with his *Shanaos* of the Macarthies More,[262] its of him he bes talking, in spite of the Crawleys.' The mendicant hostler now raised the sieve of oats on his head, and hobbled back to the stables.

'Och! but it's a pity of him, the cratur,' said Mrs. Gaffney, whose evident love of gossipry was much gratified by the conversation which had accidentally arisen – 'poor and lame as he is now, a Baccah, begging his bit through the country, and betimes doing a turn here for us: why, then, he has seen great days formerly, and was whipper-in[263] to Lord Fitzadelm, that's the black baron, and often called in to sing "*the hunt of Kilruddery*"[264] for my lord and the quality in the great parlour after dinner; and at last lent him even his trifle of wages, and sold his bit of a place to raise money for him, and got / his lameness by being *thrown off* in his service; and there you are now, Fineen Mac Crehan, without a rag to kiver you, or a shed to lay your head under, or a bit of a bed to die on, or as much as would buy a pipe to wake you with, this night. Ah! then, nothing ever *thriv* with them Fitzadelms: they had the *black drop* in them, for all they were the portliest men in the country (though I never see them, barring in pictures), and to this day its a saying in the country, "comely and wicked like a Fitzadelm." Well, there's the last stick and stone of the court to be sold next week. We had orders to stick up the bill, Sirs, here, from Mr. Crawley's land-baily of Dunore, who passed through the mountains yesterday.'

---

*   Vocation – to the priesthood. To miss vocation, always means *to fall in love.*

'Then the devil set his foot after him wherever he goes, and that he may never come back, I pray Christ,' said the driver, as he drew his cotamore round him, and went forth to look after the equipage. /

To this pious adjuration a very general 'amen' was returned; while both the travellers, as if moved by the same impulse of curiosity, advanced to read the advertisement hung over the chimney, by the rush-light which was fastened in a cleft stick near it. This paper indicated that the old castle and mansion of Court Fitzadelm, beautifully situate in a valley, watered by the Avon Fienne, and sheltered by the Galties and Ballyhowry mountains, were to be put up for sale on a certain day, or might be purchased by private contract. The materials were strongly recommended to any gentleman who was building; and a few acres of meadow land, with the liberties of a certain portion of the salmon fishery on the Avon-Fienne, were to be sold or leased. References were to be made to Darby Crawley, Esq. Newtown, Mount Crawley-Dunore, or at his house, Merrion Square, Dublin.

'I should like to see this Court Fitzadelm,' said the Commodore, address- / ing Mr. De Vere in Spanish. – 'Perhaps I may be induced to purchase it. The fishery of a fine river is a strong inducement, and my future destiny I hope is to reside in this country.'

'I should like to see it also, and will accompany you. By its vicinity to the Ballyhowry mountains, it can't be far from Buttevant,' replied De Vere.

On enquiries made from the landlady, and partly answered by the ill-looking man at the three-legged table, they found that Court Fitzadelm lay due south of the Ballyhowry mountains. 'Then,' said the Commodore, 'I can take it on chemin faisant[265] to the peninsula of Dunore.'

'Dunore!' repeated the younger traveller: 'I thought you were proceeding to Kerry?'

'Not immediately,' was the careless reply; and the next moment the Commodore, observing that he would endeavour to expedite their journey, left / the house. De Vere meantime took out his Spencer, and threw himself upon the settle, in the place of the female in the frize cloak, to whom the landlady was serving out some milk in another part of the kitchen; when his neighbour in the calash, jerking the skirt of her riding cloak forward, which he had incautiously sat upon, observed – 'I'd trouble you to move off: you were not so ready to put your *comether**[266] on me, when you refused me making a third in the chay, why! from Dublin to Cashel.'

Startled at this half-remembered accent, De Vere raised his eyes fearfully, and under the yawning cavity of the calash beheld the red nose and green spectacles of Mrs. Magillicuddy. He sprung from his seat and left the house. 'For heaven's

---

*   '*Comether*' – officious intrusiveness.

sake,' he exclaimed, as with rapid strides he advanced to his fel-/low traveller, who stood talking near the door to the Baccah and the Kerry horse-dealer – 'for heaven's sake let us be off directly, *with or without* a wheel. - Who do you think one of the two females at the fire may be?'

'Not your night-mare,[267] I hope,' said the Commodore, smiling – 'not Mrs. Magillicuddy.'

'My night-mare, indeed!' he reiterated, shrugging his shoulders: 'this *is* being fairly hag-ridden.'[268]

'Magillicuddy!' repeated the driver of the first-arrived chaise, who was putting-to his horses. 'Is that the ould lady's name, your honor? Why, then, troth, she's a gentlewoman every taste of her, and pays finely; and for that same I bate your chay fairly, and got in half hour before yez.'

'Where did you start from,' asked Owny, coming forward.

'From Cashel; and came the low road; and wonders yez would take to / the mountains; only it's what I believe you lost your way, Sir,' he replied.

'And where are you going to now?' asked De Vere, evidently interested in the question.

'We are going on to one side of Doneraile, Sir: and if we can't make that before ten o'clock, we are to stop at the New Inn; for th' ould lady doesn't care to be on the road after the moon goes down, though from this to Doneraile is as beautiful as a bowling-green.'

'I think,' said Mr. De Vere, 'I should be well contented to remain here to-night if there was a chance of clean beds, or even of fresh hether: we could then proceed to Court Fitzadelm early to-morrow, instead of having to tread back our steps by going to Buttevant first.' This was addressed to the Commodore.

'Och, then, not better beds you'll get in the barony than at the little back- / room at Lis-na-sleugh,' observed Owny, who appeared to listen with attention; 'and I carried two gentlemen here who slept in them last week, and one of them a priest, that's Friar O'Sullivan, on his way to Cork.'

'Then we will endeavour to make our arrangements accordingly,' said De Vere, turning sharp round, and coming in contact with the whalebone of Mrs. Magillicuddy's calash; for she had stood for the last few minutes behind them.

'Why, then, man,' she exclaimed to her driver, 'will you lave off your gossip, and not keep us here till midnight, why!'

To this remonstrance, made in a most stentorian voice, the man replied by opening the chaise door, letting down the steps, and letting in the infirm Mrs. Magillicuddy and her more youthful attendant, who sprung lightly into the chaise after her: – they immediately drove away. /

'I told you,' said the younger traveller, 'we were fated to remain at this miserable little mountain inn.'

'The fatality lies in your prepossessions,' replied the Commodore, 'or if you will, in the *super-human influence* of Mrs. Magillicuddy; for it appears that your motions are retarded or accelerated, according to your conjunctions or opposition with that most repelling body. She rules the ascendant.'[269] P

'Well,' he replied, shrugging his shoulders,

'In her bright radiance and collateral heat,

May I be comforted – *not in her sphere*.'[270]

'And yet,' said the Commodore, 'she is a woman.'

'A woman! Sex hath but one age: that passed, there is neither man nor woman. Who would assign to such *a thing* as *that* a gender, with her lungs and her bulk, her natural defects and artificial disgusts, her Bardolph's nose,[271] and tower of horse hair.[272] A woman! / gracious heaven! compared to the creatures one has seen, to the beings one has fancied, who for a moment have flashed their radiance on one's dreary life path! and *this* a woman!q 'Tis altogether another species, made of other elements, and composed of other organs!'

As he thus stood 'chewing the cud of sweet and bitter fancies,'[273] in apostrophizing all that was lovely in the sex, and all that had ceased to be so, leaning against the door, his eyes fixed upon the silver-lined clouds, that passed in forms various and fantastic as his own thoughts, before the broad bright moon,r his more active, more vigilant fellow traveller, was occupied in providing for their night's accommodation. He had also enquired for the driver, to inform him of their new arrangements, and learned from the lame hostler, that he was gone behind the other chaise, as far as the smith's forge, for an iron pin, which was wanting to the compleat re-/instatement of the broken machinery of their own crazy carriage.

The circumstance of two such guests remaining for the night at Lis-na-sleugh, produced a business and bustle most unusual beneath its humble roof. *Shaneen*,* the boy, was employed in catching, killing, and plucking a fowl, which had (reckless of the fate that awaited it,) taken up its roost on the rafter of the kitchen. The baccah was occupied in preparing such a table equipage for supper as the house afforded; and the hostess herself gave her attention to the little bed-room.

This apartment, which communicated by a few steps with the parlour, contained two small, old fashioned bedsteads, with patch-work quilts, the accumulated fragments of half a century; and check curtains of transparent texture. Though poor and mean, it was cleanly and cheerful; and was just such a sleeping apartment as is to be found / in every inn in Ireland, that lies in a road but little frequented.

When the strangers returned to the house, from a short refreshing walk among the moonlight glens, the house was cleared of its guests, silent and

---

*   Shaneen – Little John – Jack.

tranquil. A clean cloth was spread upon the parlour table, the turf fire blazed brightly; and through there was no wine to be had, and they had not yet made up their palates to what Peter the Great called 'Irish wine,' yet the clear spring that gushed from the neighbouring rock was pure falernian[274] to thirsty and temperate travellers. The supper prepared by their cordial hostess, though homely, was all *friandise*[275] to appetites sharpened by the mountain air, and placed beyond the delicacy of fastidiousness by long fast.

Owny, who had returned from the forge, enquired carelessly 'if they had now the place to themselves, barring the gentlemen,' and being answered in the affirmative (for the three guests in / the kitchen, the horse-dealer, the pedlar and his companion, had all departed under favour of the moonlight), he immediately threw off his cotamore, caubeen,[276] and wig. Light, alert, and diligent, he now officiated as valet to the gentlemen, and as coadjutor to Mrs. Gaffney's establishment; and his services added considerably to the little sum of comfort and accommodation which the travellers could naturally expect, in this improved imitation of a Spanish Posada.[277]

Meantime the Irish *kead mille faltha**[278] shone in every eye, and beamed its welcome on the strangers. The obvious goodwill of all compensated for the deficiency of ability, but too obvious; and even the younger, and less easily satisfied guest, was led to observe of the little Shebean of *Lis-na-sleugh*, as the French Philosopher did of the world, 'si tout n-y est pas bien, tout est passable.[279] /

CHAPTER IV.

'This Eden, this demi-paradise
This dear dear land is now leased out
Like to a tenement, or pelting farm.'
                SHAKESPEARE.[280]

'What harmony is this?
Marvellous, sweet music;
Give us kind keepers, heaven.'
                IBID.[281]

'Were such things here as we do speak about? Or have we eaten of the insane root that takes the reason prisoner?'
                IBID.[282]

THERE is scarcely any cabaret[283] in the remote parts of Ireland, over whose door is exhibited the usual advertisement of 'good entertainment for man and beast,'

---

*   Hundred thousand welcomes.

where a tolerable breakfast may not be procured; the abundance and freshness of the milk, butter, and eggs usually compensating for the indifferent quality of that far-fetched and / vivifying herb, which the widow Gaffney assured her guests was 'iligant tay from Cork,' as they seated themselves at her breakfast table, after the refreshing repose of the night. Luckily they were just then in a temper of mind to take much upon faith, and to be pleased on very scanty premises. That, which under the influence of exhaustion and evening gloom, was deemed misadventure, to the renovated spirits of morning and sunshine was amusing incident merely, and stimulating variety. There was a novelty, a romantic singularity in their actual position, which lent it a peculiar charm (at least, to the younger traveller, to whom it was evident that whatever was *new* was *good*), while it was obvious to both, that even the wildest parts of Ireland afforded security to the *stranger's* wandering: for it is only the local, official oppressor who has any thing to fear from an ignorant and suffering population; a po-/pulation, which, strangers to the protection of the laws, fly for redress to that force, by which alone they and their ancestors have been governed for centuries.[5]

The travellers left the inn of Lis-na-sleugh, followed by the blessings of its inhabitants, excited by their liberality. Had the younger of them been capable of observing any thing, in which he was not himself personally concerned, he might have noticed that, previous to their departure, his mysterious companion had been engaged in a conference with the lame hostler, which lasted for a considerable time: for while Owny was putting-to the horses, and arranging the portmanteaux, the Commodore, with arms folded, brows compressed, and eyes full of eager listening curiosity, remained silently attentive to some narration, which seemed circumstantially detailed by the baccah. As they both stood under the shadow of an impending cliff, the bold figure of the / Commodore in deep shade, and darkly defined, the bending form of the cripple supported by his crutch, and tinged with the light of a straggling sunbeam, they seemed appropriate figures for the wild scenery that surrounded them. In this point of view they were only considered by the tasteful observer, who stood looking at them through his half-closed eyes, and who simply noted the effect of their picturesque grouping,[284] without one surmise as to its cause. – The mountains the travellers had crossed, and the glen, in which they had passed the night, soon receded from their view: their journey lay along a comparatively good road, among a long chain of hills, which fenced within their undulating boundaries many a lovely glen and romantic valley, brightening in the morning sunshine. Acclivity rose above acclivity, lifting their bleak bare heads to the clouds, in wild and savage magnificence – those to the west forming the boundaries of the / country of Kerry; those to the north and east, the Ballyhowry and Nagle mountains, inclosing the classical scenery of Spencer; his own *Mole*,[285] rising conspicuously above all.

In the bosom of this wild and fantastic region, after a journey of twelve miles, the valley of Glenfionne, or the *fair valley*, was announced by the driver; and the old woods and towers of Court Fitzadelm were discovered in the distance, crowning a rocky summit, which seemed to hang perpendicularly over the winding waters of the Avon Fionne. The demesne of this fine old seat was accessible by many mountain ravines from the south; but the design of its late lord, who had cut a road across a branch of the Galties, to facilitate and to shorten the way from Dubin, though inadequately executed, was judiciously conceived. On that side its situation was inaccessible, remote, and romantic. The extensive stone wall, which ran round the north of the de-/mesne, forming an opposite barrier to that made by the winding river, was in many places dismantled and broken down; and through its frequent breaches, it exhibited the result of that pernicious and exhausting system of farming resorted to in such places. The ci-devant agent, now the actual but absent master, had let out this beautiful demesne in what is called jobbing farms, whose tillage rarely extends beyond the growing of potatoes; for which purpose the ground is uncalculatingly burned, to produce one good crop to its temporary possessor. Here and there vestiges of wretched crops of grass and oats evinced the land utterly exhausted; and, in many places, it was abandoned to the wild growth of weeds and briars. Almost every where the old meadow and pasture grounds were covered with furze, broom, and rushes, which, though now yellow and rich to the eye, were still but '*unprofitably gay*.'[286] The subdivisions of petty property / were marked by rude meerings,[287] and each temporary tenant had secured his own rood[288] of ground with unplanted mounds, whose occasional gaps were stopped with brambles and heath bushes. This coarse and rude system of farming added much to the desolate and neglected aspect of a naturally lovely scene, which in its present state, formed an apt epitome of the abandoned dwellings of the Irish absentees.

The scanty and miserable population which appeared in the neighbourhood of the once princely Court Fitzadelm was appropriately wretched and neglected. From a few mud-built huts, raised against the park wall, occasionally issued a child or a pig, while the head of its squalid mistress appeared for a moment through the cloud of smoke which streamed from the door, and then suddenly retreated. The long and broken road which wound round the wall, seemed to lengthen as the travel-/lers proceeded; and they stopped to enquire the way to the nearest approach of a poor man who was driving a lamb with a straw rope round its leg. The man pointed to a winding in the road, and directed them to the ruined gates of the principal entrance: he then took up the wearied lamb on his shoulders, and proceeded sullenly on.

'The cratur!' said the driver, who was now walking beside his horses, as were also the gentlemen: 'God help him! he is now going all the way to Ballinispig fair with that bit of a lamb; eight good long miles, and may be it won't bring him over three tinpinnies.'

'There is,' said the Commodore, 'a mixture of indolence and laboriousness in these miserable people that is singular; they have neither the activity of savages nor the industry of civilization. They want energy for the one, and motive for the other.'

'What I should complain of in Ire-/land,' replied De Vere, 'is, that there is no rural life; no pastoral manners; no subjects for the Idyls of Theocritus, nor the Arcadia of Sannazaro.'[289]

'I would rather see it an appropriate subject for the Georgics of Virgil,[290] the native energy of the people practically applied to the natural resources of the land,' was the reply.[t]

They had now reached the entrance of what had been considered one of the most magnificent demesnes in Ireland, once forming part of the principality of the Macarthies, and successively passing by grants and forfeitures from them to the powerful Desmonds, and again to the favoured Fitzadelms. It was now the ill-managed possession of an attorney, who had held it partly on mortgage and partly by lease from the elder Baron Fitzadelm, designated in the country by the *soubriquet*[291] of the 'BLACK BARON.'

The eyes of both strangers seemed / equally anxious in their gaze, which was more expressive of obscure and faded recognition than of mere idle curiosity. A long range of iron gate presented itself to their view, much broken, the bars drawn out, and the tracery covered with rust. The massive stone pillars on either side, overgrown with lichens, still exhibited some vestiges of handsome sculpture: the capital of one was surmounted by an headless eagle; the other shewed the claw and part of the body of a gos-hawk, both natives of the surrounding mountains, and well imitated in black marble, drawn from their once worked quarries. Two lodges mouldered on either side into absolute ruin; and the intended improvement of a Grecian portico to one, never finished, was still obvious in the scattered fragments of friezes and entablatures[292] which lay choaked amidst heaps of nettles, furze-bushes, and long rye-grass. The broad approach was still / visibly marked out, though now moss-grown and green, winding through beautifully undulating but neglected grounds: and there was a kind of mimic forest, richly cloathing the sides of the elevated hights, which rose, like little mountains, from the southern shore of the river, deceiving the eye, and appearing the same luxuriant wood which had once bloomed there. It was now but the sprouting stumps succeeding to the lofty majesty of the full-grown oak, pine, and mountain ash, for which this country was once so celebrated.

Frequently and recently as the hatchet had been applied to the towering woods of Court Fitzadelm, a few clumps and clusters of very ancient and noble trees were still left standing; but the red marks impressed upon their brown barks evinced that they also were destined to immediate destruction.

While the travellers stood looking upon this fine, but melancholy scene, / the driver thrust his head through the broken bars of the gate, and directing his voice towards one of the ruined lodges, whence issued a feeble smoke, cried out, 'Alleen ma chree! Alleen deelish!'[293]

'Who do you call to?' asked the Commodore, impatiently endeavouring to open the gate.

'To little Ellen, plaze your honor, the daughter of the poor baccah at Lis-na-sleugh, who lives here with her ould granny, that kept the gates in both th'ould lords' time, and is bed-ridden now: that's as the baccah tould me last night, when I was axing him about the way. Alleen ma vourneen.'[294]

'Che shin,'* answered a shrill voice from within; and the next minute a figure, small, wild, and frightful, bounded over the plank laid before the lodge-door, and stood at the gate. To a few words addressed to her in Irish, she lent a timid but fixed attention; then / flew back to the lodge, and instantly returned with a large massive key, which she applied with extraordinary strength to the rusty lock; and the heavy gates opened slowly, to admit the unusual visitors.

'That's my caen-buy-deelish,'† said Owny, kindly patting a head, to whose thick and matted locks adhered some bearded thistles. The little portress laughed with all the wildness of fatuity; but shrunk, scared, and intimidated, as she snatched the offered remuneration from the Commodore's hand. Her countenance, however, exhibited rather the stupor of unawakened intellect, than a natural deficiency of intelligence.

'That's a poor *innocent*, your honor: the likes of them be always found in lonely places, like the ould court here; and brings luck with them / they say. But for all that she's a *natural*,[295] her father tells me she's the finest cat-hunter and bird-catcher in the barony round; and is quite *cute*[296] at gathering brushneens for the bit of fire, and catering[297] among the neighbours with the cruiskeen‡ and wallet[298] for her ould bed-ridden granny.'

To this account the Commodore made no reply, but shrugged his shoulders; and both gentlemen proceeded in silence through the demesne, while Owny entered the lodge to make some enquiries from the bed-ridden lodge-keeper relative to the house; whether it was to be seen, and who occupied it. The grounds were divided into little plots and job-farms, up to the door of the mansion, which stood on a rocky hight over the river. On the opposite shores ascended a range of well wooded acclivities, whose summits mingled with / the line of the hori-

---

*   Who's that.
†   My yellow-headed darling.
‡   A little pitcher.

zon. Of the original building nothing now remained but a square ivy-clad tower, called Desmond's castle, flanking a less imposing edifice, built by the Fitzadelms in the reign of James the First. This wing was in good preservation: but the modern façade, raised forty years back by Baron Fitzadelm, the Tierna-Dhu, was ruinous and mouldering. It had been built by contract, was rapidly got up for a particular purpose, and had been constructed with bad materials, most of which were not even yet paid for. The precipitous declivities which swept down from the rocky foundation of the house to the river had been cut into terrace gardens, a fashion still observable at the seats of the ancient nobility of Munster:[299] and it was melancholy to observe the stunted rose-tree, and other once-cultivated, but now degenerate shrubs and flowers, raising their heads amongst nettles and briers, and long / grass, and withered potatoe-stalks. Many fantastic little buildings were also seen mouldering on romantic sites along the river's undulating banks; some of shells, some of rock-work: [300] all alike monuments of the bad taste of the day in which they were raised, and of the wanton caprice of the persons who projected them.

'It was doubtless from a scene like this,' observed Mr. De Vere, plucking an half-perished rose, to which adhered the foliage of the deadly night-shade, 'that Spencer drew his poetical metaphor of the seeds of vice springing up amidst the scions of virtue:'

> 'And with their boughs the gentle plants did beat;
> But ever more some of the virtuous race
> Rose up inspired with heroic heat,
> That cropt the branches of their scient base,
> And with strong hand their fruitful rankness did deface.'[301]

'It is thus, perhaps,' returned the / Commodore, 'that the rightful heir of Court Fitzadelm would act, did he behold this place as we now see it.'

'No,' replied De Vere, flinging away together the rose and the nightshade. 'It is probable that the representative of the Fitzadelm family (for the unfortunate and insane Marquis of Dunore cannot be deemed such) would look upon this ancient seat of his ancestors, as I now view it, with a new feeling of contempt for the species to which he belongs; and with as little interest for the posterity that is to follow, as to the ancestry that preceded him, he would put it up to the hammer,[302] and fly to enjoy its price in happier regions and more genial climes.'

'He would, on the contrary, perhaps,' said the Commodore, with a vehemence tinctured with irrepressible indignation, 'endeavour to redeem the folly and negligence of his ancestors, wrest his paternal demesne from the / grasp of fraud, or re-purchase it from the gripe of sordidness; he would then raise its fallen towers, reclaim its neglected soil, cherish the miserable population, and expiate the violence and rapacity by which his distant fore-fathers obtained this still beautiful territory, by a constant and beneficial residence in the land whence he draws his support and existence.'

'You know but little of Calista,'[303] replied De Vere, smiling significantly – 'you know but little of Lord Adelm Fitzadelm.'

'Who is he?' asked the Commodore, quickly.

'Why, the only brother of the present Marquis of Dunore, heir presumptive of his title and possessions: not to know him would argue yourself unknown.'

'Oh true,' said the Commodore, with the tone of sudden recollection, 'I have heard of such a person.'

'I suppose so,' was the dry reply. /

Owny now joined them with the information that the house was to be seen,[304] and that it was inhabited by an old housekeeper, a follower of the Crawley family, nick-named Protestant Moll, the '*divil's* own saint,' one he had often heard of, but never seen, and so called in regard of her having once been a great Papist and a *Voteen*,* and having afterwards become a hedger, (that's a turn-coat), and was made a kiln-dried Protestant, by Miss Crawley, a great preacher, and sister to the Portrieve[305] of Dunore, Torney Crawley, Esq. a raal slave driver, that had many a poor man's sowl to answer for. While he spoke, he was vainly applying a stone to the folding doors of the great entrance (for the knocker was off), and at last went round to the rear of the building, in search of a more easy ingress. In a few minutes his head appeared through one of the front windows; and assuring the gentlemen he / would be down in a crack,[306] and open the hall door for them, he indulged himself in a momentary view of the surrounding scene. He soon, however, descended, and was heard unbarring the long-closed portals, which slowly opened to admit the strangers. A most capacious hall of black marble discovered on either side several doors, half pannelled; a superb, but dismantled staircase, in the centre, branched off into a corridor, which surrounded the hall, and appeared to lead to different apartments. The rafters had in many places fallen in; and the plaister of the still crumbling ceiling lay in heaps upon the floor.

This ruinous and melancholy appearance gave peculiar force to a motto in gold letters over the folding doors of a private theatre, which opened into the left side of the hall. The motto was 'Laugh while we can.'

'Laugh while we can!' repeated the Commodore, with a shrug, that was almost a shudder. /

'Oh, it's delicious,' observed De Vere, ironically, 'a thing to moralize a song withall.'

---

* Devotee.

'Why then, its little of *it* them gets now that put it up there, why! that's now, God help them, in a place where there's no laughing, but weeping, and wailing, and gnashing of teeth.'[307]

The strangers turned round at this unexpected address, but not unknown accent, and beheld Mrs. Magillicuddy close behind them.

'This is the housekeeper, who will shew your honors the place,' said Owny, and then retired to look after his horses. De Vere drew back many paces from the frightful phantom of his imagination. The Commodore stood surprised, and something amused at the effect which this sudden apparition produced on his companion. Mrs. Magillicuddy, whose face was partly wrapped up in a worsted stocking, and who was endeavouring to keep a brown paper / steeped in whiskey on her nose, looked at them for a moment through her large green spectacles, and addressed them both in a tone of great familiarity, observing,

'Well, who knows but we may meet in heaven yet; little chance as there seems for some of us now, why! for we've met often enough in this world any how, and may again when least expected. And its little yez thought when ye refused me a third in your chay to Tipperary, that I'd be shewing you Court Fitzadelm; and is as much mistress here as the lady, if she was in it, and will be till it fall into better hands, plaze God. Why then, yez had great luck, gentlemen, not to go in the chay from Dublin; for its in it, shure, I got one of my rheumatrix fits, all down the face and head of me. And it was the Lord's will, I should be overturned last night, coming here, and broke my nose, why! Well, what matter? Shure I'll / be worse afore I'm better; for whom the Lord loveth, he chasteneth.[308] Is my strength the strength of stone, or is my flesh of brass?[309] No, troth! And so this young man here tells me yez want to see the consarn. Why then, its a sad place now; a watch-tower in a wilderness.[310] And little ever I thought to see the likes of yez in it again, though many of your sort frequented it formerly.'

'Of *our* sort? Why what do you take us for?' asked the Commodore in some surprise, tinctured with seeming uneasiness.

'For two rakes of quality, dear, going about the innocent country, seeking whom yez may devour,[311] like the old one, why!'

The gentlemen both smiled; and even De Vere seemed not displeased at the definition given of his appearance by the formidable Mrs. Magillicuddy, alias '*Protestant Moll.*' Still, however, he hung back, and looked upon her with disgust and apprehension. /

'I understand,' said the Commodore, 'that this old mansion, with a few acres of the ancient demesne, is to be sold, and I wish to examine the premises, before I apply for the terms to Mr. Crawley, to whose seat I am now proceeding.' 'As to the house,' said Mrs. Magillicuddy, 'it is an house of clay now;' and she waddled before them towards the theatre, the door of which she threw open. '*An house of clay, whose foundation is in the dust, and which is crushed before the moth.*[312] *There!* – there's the *devil's tabernacle.'*

Curiosity now got the better of prejudice; and Mr. De Vere approached to examine this monument of former dissipation and refinement, in scenes so inappropriate to its site. Most of the decorations, and nearly all the seats and scenery, had been removed. But fragments of scarlet cloth remained upon a bench, which had not been taken away. A cut wood scene still occupied the stage; and some orna-/mental painting and gilding were visible on the ceiling and cornice.

'This was a box fitted up for the Lord Lieutenant,' said Mrs. Magillicuddy, seating herself on the solitary bench; 'and when the bishop's lady came here to see me, after my wonderful conversion (and it was Miss Crawley that delivered me from the workings of iniquity,) and found the Rev. Mr. Scare'um sitting with me in this very place, (for he came to visit this benighted district, and to take under his protection the perishing sinners of the hill country) says the bishop's lady to me, (for my conversion made a great noise, far and near.) No, says Mr. Scare'um to Miss Crawley, it is curious to see, says he, by what great strides Molly Magillicuddy has made her way out of Babylon.[313] Upon which, the bishop's lady remarked –.'

'I cannot stand this,' cried De Vere to the Commodore in Spanish. 'I will walk down to the river, while you ex-/amine the house, if you really think there is any thing worth seeing.'

Mrs. Magillicuddy now rose with surprising alertness, and observed: 'May be yez would like to see the ould family pictures which will go with the house, being worth nothing now, barring the frames, the best being gone.'

The *family pictures* seemed to counteract the effect of even Mrs. Magillicuddy's egotistical jargon, who seemed to trade upon the history of her conversion, and to suppose, with pious vanity, that it interested her auditors as much as herself. The gentlemen followed her up the hall, while she continued her recital with – 'So, as I was saying, the bishop's lady, thinking me a miracle of grace (though, lord help me, I was then but a babe in knowledge, never having listened hardly to Mr. Scare'um, nor lived with the *sarious*), she says to me, "Molly says she – " '

'This is a curious apartment,' inter-/rupted the Commodore, as he threw open the door of the room, which Mrs. Magillicuddy announced as the presence chamber.

'Aye, curish enough!' said she. 'Here it was that royal idolater, James the Second, held a court in his way through Munster,[314] and was attended by all the papist lords, the "RECUSANTS," as Miss Crawley tells me. Oh! she's a great scholar; and was here in her way to Dublin just afore I went to England for that legacy left me by the pious Mr. Scare'um two months ago – for the Fitzadelms,' she continued in her digressive way, 'was then *Romans* themselves; until, by abandoning the scarlet lady of Babylon, they secured their lands and rights;[315]

and the king, when he looked out at this window (called the king's casement ever since), started back, wondering much at the great hight of the house above the river.' /

She threw open the window as she spoke; and the precipitous declivity beneath seemed to justify the royal astonishment.*[316] But the strangers were little attracted by the bold and beautiful views without, nor by the fine friezes within, which were painted by the Franchinis, two Italian artists, who visited Ireland a century back, and were employed in ornamenting its noble mansions:[317] the few pictures, which mouldered in their tarnished frames, upon the oaken wainscot, seemed to fix their most earnest attention. They were surprised to find the greater number to be portraits of the most eminent characters of Charles the Second's court.

The beauties, the wits, and the war-/riors of that day, were in a large proportion Irish; and while the pictures of the Hamiltons, the Butlers, the Villarses, the Fitzgeralds, the Talbots, the Muskerries, the Taafes, the Dongons, and the Burkes, are sketched for immortality in the delightful Memoires de Grammont,[318] their less durable portraits by Lilly and Kneller have been copied ad infinitum†[319] in Ireland, and are still to be found in many of the deserted mansions of the long-absent great. Many of these faded representatives of all that was once lovely and animated lay upon the ground; and the dilletante traveller soon detected 'la plus jolie taille du / monde' of the coquettish Countess of Chesterfield,‡[320] stopping a broken window. 'La Muskerry§ faite comme la plupart des riches heritieres,'[321] skreening out the ungrated hearth of a capacious chimney-piece; while the fair Hamilton, 'grande et gracieuse dans les moindres de ses mouvemens,'[322] hung in a most maudlin state out of her frame; and 'la belle Stewart,'[323] lay undistinguished in a corner, with a 'la blonde Blague,' now literally 'plus jaune qu'un coing.'[324]

'And are these pictures to go with the rest of the premises?' asked the Commodore.

---

*   A similar apartment and window are shewn at *Lismore Castle*, one of the Duke of Devonshire's seats, as distinguished for its romantic beauty, as the inhabitants of its immediate neighbourhood are for their courtesy, elegance, and hospitality.

†   Some by Souillard, a French artist, brought to Ireland by Lord Muskerry, to paint his castle of Lixnaw, in Munster, after the cartoons of Raphael; others by Gandy, who came over with his patron, the great Duke of Ormond, and who seems to have furnished half the great houses in Munster with the royal harem; and many also by inferior and nameless artists.

‡   Lady Elizabeth Butler, daughter of the Duke of Ormond, and second wife of the Earl of Chesterfield: she died 1666.

§   Lady Margaret Burke, daughter and heiress of Ulic Burke, fifth Earl of Clanrickard, wife to Charles Lord Muskerry.

'Its little matter where they go,' returned Mrs. Magillicuddy, indignantly, / 'or if they went with them they liken:[325] – a parcel of rakes and harlots! as Miss Crawley tells me; they are paying for their scarlet and fine linen now, I warrant; *for they that plough iniquity, and sow wickedness, reap the same.*[326] Fie upon such shameless Jezebels![327] say I, who look full of nought but worldly vanity and fleshly ease.'

'Fleshly ease, indeed!' repeated De Vere, gazing earnestly upon the picture of the beautiful Duchess of Cleveland.*[328] 'There is something in the swimming eyes and thick lips of the / beauties of those times, a charming unidea'd sameness of physiognomy, that is now lost in the female face.'

'Mental cultivation most diversifies the countenance,' replied the Commodore. 'In barbarous nations there is but one physiognomy for a tribe: where there is little intellect, there can be but little variety of expression.'

'I hate intellect in women,' said De Vere; 'and what is most delicious in the harem of that happy satrap, Charles,[329] is, that they all look such pretty idiots, so fond and foolish, as if they were of that sect which once flourished in Spain, the Embevecidos, whose life and faith were made up of love.'[330]

'Love, indeed! love! when hearts were purchased with French ribbons; and perfumed gloves went on successful embassies to ladies' affections. Oh! trust me, your royal satraps have more of laziness than of love in their engagements; and nothing is further from / passion than their idle saunterings *'in ladies' chambers.'*

"Tis all abomination! all vanity and vexation of spirit!'[331] said Mrs. Magillicuddy, interrupting the Commodore, indignantly. 'I didn't think so once, God help me! For I walked in utter darkness[332] till I was thirty; and did not wrestle with the *ould* one till I was forty good. My conversion made a a great noise far and near. The bishop's lady came to me, and said –'

Mr. De Vere was again retreating, when the old woman hobbled to a door at the further end of the apartment, and throwing it open, said, 'There, that's the drawing-room;' then flinging herself upon a broken chair, the only article of furniture in the room, except an antique japanned chest, [333] she continued, pointing to two pictures – 'There, gentlemen, there are the pictures of the two brothers; that is *half* brothers by blood, but *whole* brothers in iniquity. /

I always took the dark one in robes to be the Prince of Orange, and the red-headed one to be the Pretender,[334] till Miss Crawley, when she came here for the *Indy* cabinet, informed me that they were the two last Lord Fitzadelms, the Dhu

---

*   Lady Barbara Villiers, daughter and heiress of William Villiers, Lord Grandison: she was a native of the scenes here described, and spent the innocent and early part of her life in her father's castle of Dromana, on the lovely banks of the black water. She was afterwards consigned to immortal infamy as the mistress of Charles the Second, under the titles of Countess of Castlemain and Duchess of Cleveland. Part of the summer of 1817 was delightfully spent by the author amidst these delicious scenes.

and the Ruadg, the black and the red. Well, that's all that remains of them now: the ould one had a fine lob[335] of them both. He that would have wrestled for their salvation was not walking this benighted country when they were in it; and so they were left to go to the devil their own way, why!'

During this charitable speech the eyes of the travellers were fixed upon the pictures, pointed out by their pious Cicerone.[336] The elder brother stood in his parliamentary robes, by a table, on which his coronet was placed: his countenance expressed haughtiness, something mingled with indecision; and traces of wild ill-regulated passions, contrasted with a look of feebleness and / dependence, gave indication of a mind endowed with some natural strength of character, but which had been spoiled by circumstances and education; as if the natural force, which might have gone to the strengthening of his intellect, served but to irritate his passions and temper. He was of a dark and saturnine complexion; but intemperance had so bloated his features, and impurpled his naturally sallow hue, that the beauty, for which he had once been celebrated, even the painter's art could scarcely recal. This picture was done, by the date, above thirty years back: the name of the artist was so obscure, and the execution so inferior, that it was probably the effort of some itinerant painter, who worked by the square foot.

The younger brother was a true Geraldine in colouring and feature; the light curled golden hair, the full blue eye, and fair complexion, which distinguish-/ed almost every branch of that illustrious family, particularly the southern Geraldines: but there was an expression of licentiousness and cunning mingled in the countenance of Gerald Fitzadelm, which belonged not to the physiognomy of his family: he had a foreign air, was habited in a Venetian domino,[337] and held a black mask so near his face, that he seemed but in the very act of removing it: the picture was dated Venice; the name of the artist was Italian; and a label hanging from it, with orders how it was to be laid in the case, which was placed near it, indicated that it was about to be removed. On the case, in large letters, was painted 'For the most noble the Marchioness Dowager of Dunore, Dunore Castle.'

'Aye,' said Mrs. Magillicuddy, reading this address, 'aye, to the Marchioness Dowager: well, careful as she is of the picture, its little she valued the reality, why! Its from her, they / say, the madness got into the Fitzadelm family. For till the Baron Gerald married that hoity-toity English woman, (though, as I'm tould, they were foolish enough, and wicked enough before) none of them was ever lunatic, until the two young lords, her sons, went mad lately.'

'What, *both* mad?' asked the Commodore; while his companion turned round, and fixed his eyes with a very singular expression on the narrator.

'Aye, Sir, both as mad as March hares: the eldest being mad by nature, and t'other chap, from pride, why! But shure the sins of the fathers must be visited on the childer, as Miss Crawley says; *affliction cometh not forth of the dust, nei-*

ther doth trouble come out of the ground,[338] why! There is the young Marquis in a
madhouse, and there is Lord Adelm Fitzadelm, his brother, wandering the world
wide, they say, looking for something, he does'nt know / what, like a prince in
a story book; while his mother, the ould policizing Marchioness, is setting him
up for the borough of Glannacrime, here. But, mark my words, she needn't trouble herself; it isn't himself will get it, with the Fitzadelm name, and the Dunore
interest to boot.'

'No?' said the younger traveller, for the first time addressing this formidable
person.

'No, Sir, its meat for his betters, why.'

'Indeed!' returned De Vere, with an ironical laugh; 'and who may they be
pray?'

'Counsellor Con is, dear,' said Mrs. Magillicuddy, coming up close to him,
with an air of confidential familiarity, while he retreated before her advances:
'that's Counsellor Conway Townsend Crawley nephew to Miss Crawley, and son
to the Portrieve of Dunore. Och! that's the young man will prosper, why! / Mark
my words, and you'll see them come to pass yet.'

This was said with an oracular nod of the head, and peculiar emphasis of
voice: but the countenance of Mrs. Magillicuddy gave no superadded force to
her prophetic words. It was indeed pretty well concealed by her broad brimmed
hat, her green spectacles, the worsted stocking bound round her rheumatic jaw,
and the wet brown paper, that covered her broken nose.[u] While this short dialogue was carrying on, the eyes of the Commodore were glancing rapidly from
the features of the late baron, to the face and figure of his young companion;
but when De Vere turned round to him, he abruptly averted them, and took
up a parchment label, which hung from one of the massive brass handles of the
antiquated japan chest: the inscription on it was curious, and ran as follows:
'This travelling chest was presented by his most / sacred Majesty Charles the
Second, to Barbara, Duchess of Cleveland, who bequeathed it at her death in
1691 to her kinswoman, the Lady Geraldine Fitzadelm: she married in 1701
Thomas, Marquis of Dunore, her uterine cousin;[339] and died, leaving issue an
only daughter, 1730.'

'I wonder this most valuable relic is suffered to remain here,' observed the
Commodore.

'Och,' said Mrs. Magillicuddy, who seemed all care and eye to every thing that
was said and looked, 'och, when every thing went to sixes and sevens, why! and
all was ruination, the Black Baron dying in a garret in Dublin, and his brother
that came to the title, abroad, it was little regard was paid to the likes of that. But
it is now to go by favour of Mr. Crawley, who owns all, to Dunore, as a present
to the Marchioness, whenever she comes over: there's the matting to pack it.
They say it was / in it, that was found the family tree, which proved the ruined

Fitzadelms to be the heirs in the female line, in default of male issue, to the title and estate of Dunore; and to this day there is some curious papers in it. Perhaps, gentlemen, yez would like to see them?'

'Oh very much!' was the instantaneous reply of both. Mrs. Magillicuddy now foraged to the very bottom of her capacious pockets for the keys, crying,

'Weary on them, for keys, they are always missing when wanting;' then suddenly recollecting she had hung them in a closet, she scuded off[340] to fetch them.

The strangers again turned their observation to the portraits of the Lords Fitzadelm: but Mrs. Magillicuddy had been scarcely more than two or three minutes gone, when a female voice, with all the flute-like sweetness of the tones of youth, breathed a few clear melodious notes on their ear, as if some skilful musician was running a prelusive / division,[341] with equal taste and judgment: but the sounds, prolonged for a minute or two, were as abruptly dropped as begun, and all was silence. The rude war-cry of the Fitzadelms, or the howl of the long extirpated Irish wolf,[342] would have excited less amazement in the minds of the auditors, than these sweet and most musical strains. By their expressive looks, they seemed almost to doubt their own senses; and they remained for a considerable time silent, and in the attitude of eager and expecting attention. Nearly a quarter of an hour thus elapsed, yet all remained silent.

'Did ever mortal mixture of earth's mould breathe forth such sweet enchanting harmony?'[343] asked De Vere, entranced.

'It seemed to come in a direct line from behind that fragment of tapestry,' observed the Commodore; and he immediately raised the remains of what / once had been a handsome specimen of the Gobelin manufacture.[344] It had, concealed, a small iron door, above which was written, 'Evidence chamber.' The strangers both looked alternately, and for a considerable time, through the spacious key-hole, and discovered a small rude chamber, dimly lighted by a loop-hole, and perfectly empty. After some time, they looked out of the window, which Mrs. Magillicuddy had called King James's, and found that this Evidence Chamber formed part of the original building called Desmond's tower. Their joint thought was to leap out of the window, and to examine this tower, which appeared to lie open, and to be partly in ruins. But the steepness of the rocks rendered such an attempt impossible.

The shortest and surest way to discover the mystery (for a mystery of the most romantic nature it was asserted to be by De Vere), was to make inquiries / of the old housekeeper relative to the songstress of these ruined towers. But Mrs. Magillicuddy, though twenty minutes had elapsed, had not returned; and when they went to seek her, to their amazement and consternation, they found the door locked or bolted, and beyond their power to open or force. De Vere threw himself on the broken chair lately occupied by the housekeeper, in an ecstasy of emotion; his companion, on the contrary, displeased, annoyed, and irritated, as much as astonished, sought round the room for some mode of egress, in impatience and perturbation. A door on one side opened into a dark closet: two windows opposite to the king's casement he tried with considerable strength; but they were nailed down. A third, more manageable, was opened with difficulty; for the pullies were broken. It was, however, opened, and supported by a broken picture-frame. It communicated with one / of the ruined terraces hanging over the river, and cut out of the rock. The hight, which was inconsiderable, was easily cleared; but the way to the front of the house was intricate, and not easily found. The narrow irregular path was choaked with briars, with the stumps of old trees recently cut down, and lying at full length, and with fragments of the original ruined building, which had fallen in abundance.

As they proceeded through the entangled screen of underwood and briers, they caught a view of a man seated in a cot (6), on the river near a salmon weir; whose curious construction, with the picturesque appearance of the patient fisherman himself, would at any other time have attracted their attention. It was now, however, chiefly given to their obstructed and difficult path-way, by which they at last reached the front of this irregular and stupendous mansion. /

To their increased amazement, they found the hall-door again barred up. Every mode of ingress seemed closed, as when they had first approached it. Their chaise and its driver had alike disappeared; and the little Kerry horse, with the Commodore's valise strapped on his back, was fastened to a tree, and stood peaceably grazing within the length of his bridle; while the portmanteau of De Vere was placed near it, on a clump of rock.

The travellers remained for a moment looking at each other in silence; till De Vere burst into a fit of laughter, nothing less than the ebullition of gaiety. It was almost hysterical, and the pure effect of over-excitement: when it had in some degree subsided, he said –

'So, this is indeed the delightful "land of faery," which Spencer has described, in which he wrote, in which he was inspired. – Here his Gloriana seems still to fling about her spells; and / new adventures appear in ready preparation for other Sir Calidores and Sir Tristrams,[345] than those of his creation.'

'Had we not better,' said the Commodore, who for the moment was stunned by the event, which, though not of superhuman agency, appeared in his mind scarcely less comprehensible; – 'had we not better go to the porter's lodge, and make some inquiries there?'

'Oh! certainly. But you must not be surprised if the lodge, the portress, and the idiot, are all vanished, together with Mrs. Magillicuddy, Mr. Owny, and the chaise and horses.'

The lodge, the portress, and the idiot, remained, however, as they left them. The old woman was seated upright in her wretched bed, with a red petticoat over her shoulders, and employed in knitting. To the repeated questions of the

travellers, she replied 'Nil gaeliga,' I have no English.* / Nor could either of them
obtain the least information from her. Either she did not, or would not understand them. The idiot, when they approached her, laughed and fled.

Hopeless of information, they walked back to the spot where the horse and
their light luggage had been left. They re-examined the exterior of the house;
they went round to the postern door by which the driver had entered, and which
with some difficulty they discovered: it was padlocked on the outside; and to
their repeated knocks the echoes of the sound alone were returned. There was
something peculiarly singular, and almost laughably pantomimic in this adventure, which amused, though almost provoked the Commodore; while it defied
conjecture to detect the cause of its occurrence. He had reason to believe that his
name, person, and very existence, were unknown in Ireland; yet the league of the
old woman and driver / could not be without object, nor the whole event without motive: it was evidently unconnected with any sordid or dishonest view. The
housekeeper had not been remunerated for her trouble, nor the driver for his
horses or attendance. Rapid in his silent cogitations, and quick in his decisions,
he at once determined that the object of this farcical embrogleo[346] was the fanciful and accomplished ideologist,[v] with whom he was accidentally connected;
and giving further conjecture to the winds, after a few minutes reverie, he proposed that they should hail the fisherman at the weir, engage him to convey the
younger traveller down the river, as near as he could to Doneraile or Buttevant:
for himself, as the day advanced, and time pressed, he determined to mount his
Kerry steed, and proceed by the mountain route, he had obtained from Owny,
to Dunore.

To all these arrangements De Vere / passively assented; and while the Commodore, with the activity of boyhood, bounded down the precipitous rocks to
beckon the fisherman towards the shore, his companion, with folded arms, and
eyes fixed upon vacuity, stood the image of one, in whom

> 'Function is smothered in surprise,
> And nothing is but what is not.'[347]

The events of his journey had combined themselves in his mind under the influence of the most morbid imagination, and the most inordinate amour-propre.[348]
His vanity and his fancy had worked out a series of associations and conjectures
most favourable to the character of both. Every event, every object, however
unimportant in itself, was by him wrought into a miracle, or meditated into a
mystery, through the medium of his singularly organized mind: 'from trifles,
light as air,'[349] he had the unhappy power of constructing fabrications of ideal
pain and pleasure, of flattering or / mortifying importance; which rendered

---

*   Literally, the language of the stranger.

him the victim of delusion, and covered the prosperous realities of his life with shadows, alike illusory and unsubstantial. The perverseness of his journey from Dublin, the counteraction of his intentions with respect to his route, the impish laugh in the ruins of Holy-cross, his unintentional visit to Court Fitzadelm, the invisible musician of the Evidence Chamber, his reiterated contact with the formidable Mrs. Magillicuddy, the youthful figure of the female associated with her at Lis-na-sleugh, the masquerading mystery of the driver, and, above all, the league evidently subsisting between the old woman and Owny, and their sudden disappearance from Court Fitzadelm, unremunerated for their respective services, all these incidents, so strange, so unexpected, combined themselves in his meditations, till he believed himself caught in a thraldom, like that, 'Dove in dolce / prigione Rinaldo stassi,'[350] the object of some deep-laid project, of some romantic design, in which there would be little to mortify his vanity or to disappoint his feelings. The scenes he now inhabited were to him all fairy-land, and he believed that the Armida was not far distant, whose

'Teneri sdegni, e placide e tranquille

Repulse, cari vezzi, et liete paci

Sorrizi, paroletti,'[351]

were to compensate to him for the disgusting agents she had employed in her service, and who had by no means 'done their spiriting gently.'[352]

He had resolved, in his own mind, to take up his residence in some town or village in the neighbourhood of the Court, and there await the issue of an adventure, of which he alone could be the object. Notwithstanding his very ardent admiration for his compagnon de voyage;[353] the personal distinction, and almost heroical cast of character and / physiognomy of the extraordinary stranger, it never once suggested itself that he also might have had some share in this extraordinary event. He was alone the hero of his own thoughts; and, with the hypochondriacal egotism of Rousseau, he believed himself an object of occupation, of amity or enmity to the whole world.[354]

This train of thought was, however, soon broken, by the return of the Commodore, followed by the fisherman, who took charge of his valise, and stowed it in his little boat. He had engaged to row the younger traveller down the river, to its confluence with the Avonbeg, which ran by Doneraile, and which was the oft celebrated Mulla of Spencer, where

'On each willow hung a muse's lyre.'[355]

But the curiosity and interest excited by Kilcoleman, the Mole, and the Mulla, were now absorbed in feelings of a profounder emotion; and his approximation / to the shrine of his pilgrimage no longer awakened transports in the mind of the fanciful pilgrim. As the travellers walked together to the river's side, the elder observed, 'I have been making inquiries from the fisherman; and it appears that an old woman, who had the epithet of *protestant Moll*, and kept the mansion, where there is nothing to tempt to depredation, has been dead for some weeks. The house is unoccupied, and the approach by which we entered is the least frequented, there being several others, all open: Mrs. Magillicuddy is, therefore, some Ariel "correspondent to command," of a concealed Prospero.'[356]

'Ariel!' reiterated De Vere; 'the foul witch Sycorax,[357] rather.' 'Now, plaze your honor,' said the boatman, as he drew up his boat close to a ruin, which he called the *battery*. With some difficulty De Vere was placed in the cot, which was one of the / smallest construction known by that name. The boatman, with his spoon-shaped paddle fixed against a jutting rock, for a *point d' appui*,[358] was pushing off from the muddy shore: the figure of the Commodore was thrown into muscular exertion, in endeavouring to assist, and the cot was just afloat, as he seized the extended hand of his unknown fellow-traveller.

'We part,' said De Vere, in a tone of emotion, 'almost as we met.'

'Almost,' replied the Commodore, returning the strong pressure of his hand, with a grasp still stronger, but in a tone not firmer.

'Farewell, farewell!' repeated De Vere, as the boat cleared the banks; and he moved his hat, with an air of almost affectionate respect, half repressed by habitual apathy.

'Farewell!' returned the Commodore, with a mingled expression of courteousness and cordiality, returning the salute. /

The little bark glided into the centre of the sunny stream. He whom it left behind in scenes so dreary ascended the point of a rock, which commanded the winding of the river: his eye pursued the cot, as its paddles threw up the sparkling waters, and as it appeared and disappeared amongst the projecting cliffs, or glided under the shady alders, which fringe the lovely shores of the Avon-Fionne. It soon became a black speck in the water, and finally disappeared in a bend of the river. The Commodore, with a short involuntary sigh, turned away his dazzled gaze. The gloomy, desolate demesne of Court Fitzadelm spread around him, – he the sole occupant. 'Alone!' he exclaimed aloud, – 'once more alone, and where?' He glanced eagerly, anxiously, almost wildly round him. His respiration was short: emotions, long repressed, seemed to find vent: he threw up his eyes to heaven, and clasped his hands, almost convul/sively: years and scenes of distance and remoteness passed, in thick coming visions, before his memory; then by a sudden effort of volition, as one

'Not framed, upon the torture of the mind
To lie in restless ecstasy,'[359]

he changed at once his mood of thought, and elevated position, and descending rapidly from the rock, sprung upon his horse, galloped towards the dismantled park wall, cleared it at a leap, and proceeded on his way to the Peninsula of Dunore.

Whatever was the mission of this mysterious visitant, to a country for which he evinced so deep an interest, he seemed to forbid time's anticipations of his views; and in all things, and upon all occasions, appeared habitually to act as one who thought

'The flighty purpose never is o'ertook,
Unless the deed go with it.'[360] /

CHAPTER V.

I never may believe these antique fables,
These fairy toys.
　　　　　Midsummer's Night's Dream. [361]

But I have cause to pry into this pedant.
　　　　　Taming of the Shrew. [362]

THE Commodore pursued his solitary way to the peninsula of Dunore with as much rapidity as the nature of his mountainous road would admit. He had enquired the route both from the baccah and the driver; and to their various, and not always accordant instructions, clearly arranged in his memory, he added his own judgment, and such information as he could occasionally glean from the passengers he accidentally met.*ˣ These, however, were few; / for as he proceeded among the mountains, by roads only passable during the autumn, the population was so scanty, that in the course of many miles, ambled over by his admirable little steed, he met only with three individuals; a boy carrying a couple of chickens for sale to a distant market, a woman with a few hanks of yarn, proceeding to the same rustic emporium, and a priest, bearing the viaticum[363] to a dying penitent, whose temptations to err, amid scenes of such privation, could not have been very numerous.

The priest courteously joined, and accompanied the lonely traveller on his route; and might have been deemed an acceptable Cicerone, in a region, which, however rude and savage, was not / wholly destitute of something like classic interest. In the dialect and accent of the province, intermingled with a few French and a few Latin words, he pointed out, here a Cromlech, and there a

---

*　In Ireland, it is extremely difficult, to learn either the way or the distance, in performing a journey by the cross-roads, or mountain paths. In remote places, it may be literally said, that 'the way lengthens as we go,' since every one, of whom inquiries are made, adds a mile or two to the original distance.

cairne,[364] a Danish fort, or a monastic ruin, and added such scraps of antiquarian tradition, as are to be found, even in the remotest places in Ireland; where the superstition of the people lends implicit faith to all that is marked by miracle, and their national vanity to all that is stamped with antiquity. The legend of St. Olan's cap was repeated, as a distant view was caught of St. Olan's abbey.[365] Its miraculous efficacy, still acknowledged by the peasantry, and the belief of its having returned of itself to the spot from whence it had been removed (though composed of an immense hollow stone), was circumstantially recorded. One of the defile castles of the great Macarthies, called The Fairy's Rock,[366] or Carig-na-Souky, was / pointed out, in the distance, on the summit of a cliff, which hung above the ravine it guarded. The ruins of St. Gobnate's church, rather guessed at than clearly distinguished, introduced the legend of that fair saint, with the episode of the history of the stone cross, still extant among its ruins, where a far-famed rood of the Virgin was once kept, and where still a stone, fixed near it, in the earth, exhibits the impression of many a penitent pilgrim's bended knee.[367] For the rest, the communicative and courteous priest gave the Commodore some excellent instructions as to his future route, and lamented that he had not taken a road, which, though more circuitous by nearly a day's journey, was far less intricate than the one he had chosen. This he asserted to be a bird's flight route from the north to the south of the county, a bridleway or car-track, cut, time immemorial, by the mountaineers, for the purposes / of rural economy, and communicating among the neighbouring districts.

At the conjunction of four of these mountain defiles, marked by a large stone cross, placed over a holy-well, hung with ragged offerings,[368] the priest departed, with a cordial benedicite[369] and a bow, learned in his French college, some thirty years before, and not yet forgotten in the wild scenes, where his laborious and ill-requited calling placed him.

The traveller, again left alone, proceeded by the direction of the priest to a little mountainous village, called the Town of the Beloved, in Irish, Bally-na-vourna. It was silent and solitary, and seemed to sleep in the noon-tide sunshine, as if placed there only to form a pretty feature in the romantic scenery. Its inhabitants were all abroad, getting in their scanty harvest in a neighbouring valley. When the Commodore, after resting and bating his horse at a little / public house, lost sight of its moss-covered roofs and curling smoke, no further vestige of human habitation cheered his sight for many hours. Meantime his road became every moment more rugged, wild, and difficult. The extraordinary instinct of the little animal upon which he was mounted, and which seemed as peculiarly organized for the region it occupied, as the camel for the desert, or the rein-deer for the snows of Lapland, excited an admiration not unmixed with gratitude and respect. The traveller, rather abandoning himself to its guidance, than attempting to direct its steps, fearlessly permitted it to climb among the rugged rocks, to skim over trembling bogs and sloughy morasses; and it still preserved its pleasant ambling pace, where other horses would have sunk knee-deep, and was able to proceed where they would have perished.

The sun was now hastening to its / goal; the few birds of prey which inhabit these elevated regions were returning to their eyries among the rocks. The traveller had still to seek the landmarks which the priest had described as designating his descent to the Peninsula of Dunore.[370] He indeed caught glimpses of the Atlantic ocean, through the interstices of the mountains; but the evening shadows were gathering in vapours beneath his feet, as he descended, and yet he approached not the mountain's base. That he had missed his way, and might be benighted in a region so desolate, had suggested itself as a possibility; and he alighted for the purpose of ascending an high cliff, which seemed to command a vast extent of prospect, to ascertain his exact position. As he was in the act of fastening his horse's bridle to the stump of a furze bush, sounds, measured and mechanical, met his ear, and spoke of human proximity: they came from a little glen, near whose / entrance he stood. A narrow bridleway, leading through a deep ravine, presented itself: on the summit of a stupendous rock, some fragments of a ruin were visible; and beneath, seated in a sort of dry dyke, appeared a man occupied in scraping away with a sharp flint the lichens and mosses which incrusted a large angular stone, in order to decypher an inscription which he was endeavouring to copy. The characters were Irish, and beneath appeared a translation, in not very pure Latin, intimating that 'NEAR TO THIS PLACE, AT THE CASTLE OF MACARTHY, THE STRANGER WILL RECEIVE AN HUNDRED THOUSAND WELCOMES.'*[371]

The person who was engaged in this antiquarian occupation was so intent upon his task, that the approach of the Commodore was unobserved; who stood / gazing upon him with a look of singular and marked expression, as if he too was penetrating through the veil of time, and gradually recalling traces, and deciphering lineaments, which its mouldering finger had touched with decay, but not wholly defaced. There was an emotion of tenderness softening his countenance, as he gazed, foreign to its habitual expression; and when, leaning forward, he read aloud the Latin, and added the comment of – 'I believe there is a false concord[372] in that sentence,' his full, deep voice, wanted its usual tone of firmness and decision.

As he spoke, the flint dropped from the hand of the solitary sage, and he remained for a moment, in the motionless position of surprise, tinctured with apprehension; as if some 'airy voice, that syllables men's names,'[373] had suddenly addressed his unexpecting ear. /

---

* A similar inscription was found in a ditch near the ruined castle of the Macswines in Munster.

The traveller saw the effect he had produced, and endeavoured to counteract its consequences, by assuming a careless and familiar tone.

'I beg your pardon,' he said, 'for this intrusion on your learned researches: I am a stranger in this country, and I fear have lost my way: I wish to reach the town of Dunore before nightfall, and you will render me a service in pointing out to me the nearest road.'

This speech, evidently, recalled courage and confidence in him to whom it was addressed; and he slowly arose, putting the flint into his pocket, a cork into the ink-horn pendent from his button hole, and fastening a roll of paper and a pen into the cord of his hat, while he repeated,

'A false concord! sure enough; a stranger in the country!' He was now on his feet: the Commodore stood opposite to him, with his back to the setting sun, his figure cutting darkly / against its brightness; his face and features in deep shadow. The yellow light of the illuminated horizon bronzed the grotesque figure of him on whom he gazed. This person was of a low and clumsy stature; but, though evidently passed the middle age of life, was still strong and hale: the deep crimson of health burned on his slightly furrowed cheek; and his countenance gave indications of mingled simplicity and acuteness. There was also a certain indescribable quaint, solemn, dogmatizing importance in his look, and a wandering wildness in his eye, which were curiously and strongly contrasted; while his costume added to the characteristic peculiarity of his person. A very small wig of goat's hair surmounted a few thick, bushy grey locks, which curled round his short neck, for his shirt collar was thrown open; and three coats of frize, of various colours, excluded, like the cloak of the fabulist, / both wind and sun.[374] As he now stood, affecting to button up these coats, one after the other, he was, in fact, earnestly engaged in endeavouring to make out the traveller's features, on which his eyes were intently fixed.

'It's long,' he at last observed, 'since your honor was in these parts.'

'I never have been in this district before,' was the reply.

'Haven't you, Sir? then I *renage*[375] my remark, and *requist* your honor's pardon. I'll shew you the way to Dunore, Sir. I'm going it every rood myself, and lives a donny taste beyont it.'

As he spoke, he shifted his position, with the intention of obtaining a better view of the stranger's face; but apparently, in order to draw forth a ragged colt from a rocky shed: the Commodore at the same moment shifted his, and led forward his Kerry steed.

'That's a reyal ASTURIONES,' observed his new companion, 'and comes of a / breed of jennets brought over by *us* from Spain, on our way from Phœnicia: they are named Hobillers by Paulus Jovius, and Automates by Tournefort: they

---

*   Renage, revoke, recall.

are of pace aisy, and in ambling wondrous swift. Its little the English Edward would have done at the siege of Calais, but for them same Irish Hoblers.[376] Not that we were beholden to the likes of them; having our war steeds and our chariots.

'Infrœnant alii currus aut corpora saltu
Subjiciant in equos.'—[377]

He was now mounted on the back of his own steed; and his eyes were turned with a fixed look on the Commodore's marked profile, who rode with his head somewhat averted beside him: the view he thus obtained was dim and uncertain; but still it seemed to fix his attention: there was, as he gazed, an uncertainty in his look; a something of slow, doubtful, vague recognition, as if the faint and indistinct / resemblance of some features, once known, crossed his apprehension; now lost, now caught; determined by a light, a shadow, a motion, and flitting as soon as seized. As they descended into the deepening twilight of the glen, the obscurity of half-forgotten traits thickened into darkness; the clue of association was lost, and the hitherto silent spectator withdrew his eyes, with the simple observation,

'I could swear upon my soul's savetie, that I had seen your honor afore, Sir: I disremembers me where, but that cometh of my memory, which faileth me for present things; forgetting by times that my own name is Terence Oge O'Leary, which is remarkable.'

'O'Leary!' re-echoed the Commodore, in a voice of almost boyish softness and extreme emotion.

'Who calls?' exclaimed O'Leary, wildly, and suddenly checking his horse: 'Who calls?' he repeated, turning full / round, and throwing his strained and wandering eye in every direction.

'It was I who repeated the name you announced to me, Mr. O'Leary,' said the Commodore, in an altered and careless tone.

'Was it your honor?' resumed O'Leary, after a pause, and a deep inspiration. 'I thought it sounded like a voice I sometimes hear close in my ear, Sir, when I am alone in the mountains. They tell me 'tis my *fetch*;*[378] but I have heard it these twenty years, and am to the fore still – its no fetch,' he added with a deep sigh: 'its only an ould remembrance.'

His head sunk upon his breast, and they proceeded in silence to the edge of the glen. It terminated abruptly in a sloping surface of rich and mossy turf, / beyond which the sea-bathed track of land; called the Peninsula of Dunore, spread at the mountain's foot, extending to the ocean, undulating with green slopes, intermingled with rocky elevations, and combining many views of

---

*   It is a common superstition in Ireland to believe that a mysterious voice heard in lonely places gives notice of approaching death – it is called a *fetch*.

maritime and inland scenery, eminently beautiful and romantic. The descent, however, was so steep, and so difficult from its smoothness, that the travellers alighted and led their horses.

'There forenent you lieth Dunore, as it is called *now*,' said O'Leary, with emphasis; 'one of the tongues of land on the coast of Munster, so named by one Mr. Camden, a Saxon churl.[379] But its true and ancient name is DANGANNY-CARTHY, the fastness of the Macarthies, the kings of the country round, of the Coriandri and the Desmondii, and blood relations to the Tyrian Hercules,[380] every mother's son of them.'

'Indeed! that is an illustrious descent!' /

'Troth, and deed: for was not Maleeh-Cartha, the King of Tyre, says ould Bochart,[381] which manes Malachi Macarthy; that's plain, I believe, any how: and defies Geraldus Cambrensis, Dr. Ledwich, and Sir Richard Musgrave, with ould Saxo Grammaticus to boot,[382] to deny *that*: and would have been kings of Desmond to this very hour, if *right* was afore *might*, and only for the enticing bates of the English to entrap them in their policies, their plots, and their complots – their playing fast and loose, their English earldoms and English patents, their grantees, and protectees, and governorships, until the Macarthies degendered[383] with the rest, from their ancestors, and never rose to great power from that day forth – that's Florence Macarthy I mane,[384] the FOGH-NA-GALL, the Englishman's hate,* elected to the style and authority of Macarthy More, 1599, even after he descended to be / made Earl Clancare, anno 1565, Elizab reginae six.'[385]

'Florence?' said the Commodore, dwelling with a peculiar expression on the name. 'Florence then is a name given both to the males and females of this illustrious family?'

'It is, plaze your honor, and comes from the Spanish name Florianus, which the Macarthies brought with them on their way from Scythia,[386] as also the O'SULLIVAN BEARS.'[387]

'It is an Italian name also; and one Florianus del Campo[388] has, I believe, written on this country,' said the Commodore.

'He has, Sir, *belied* the land, like the rest of them,' replied O'Leary.

'The Macarthies followed the fortunes of the house of Stuart, I believe, Mr. O'Leary; at least I have some where read so.'

'They did, Sir, to their great moan. Of all the regiments after the surrender / of Condé,[389] Macarthy's alone refused entering the Spanish service, till their colonel got his dismissal in France, from the ra'al King of Great Britain, France, and Ireland.'

'They have, however, since distinguished themselves in the service of Spain; and even in the popular cause of South America.'[390]

---

*　　The foe of the stranger.

'They have, Sir, and every where but at home, God help'em, for a raison they have.'

'Do any of the family now remain in this county?'

'None at all,' said O'Leary; and then, after a pause, added, 'barring the BHAN TIERNA, who isn't in it at this present.'

'Ha! I have heard that epithet, accompanied by blessings in the mountains of the Galties: to whom does it belong?'

'To whom does it belong, is it – why, to whom should it, but to the grate ould ancient Countess of Clancare, / anno 1565, Elizabethæ 6. – But sure, what signifies talking about them now. You may see it all in my Genealogical History of the Macarthy More, written in the Phœnician tongue, vulgo-vocato Irish; [391] it being more precise and copious than the English, and other barbarous dialects; also sharp and sententious, offering great occasion to quick apothegm and proper allusion; the only pure dialect remaining of the seventy-two languages of Babel, introduced into Ireland by Finiusa Tarsa, the son of Magog, King of Scythia, from his own seminary of Magh-Seanair, near Athens; [392] and is to this day the ould language, spoken by Hannibal, Hamilcar, Asdrubal, [393] and the Macarthies More of county Cork and Kerry, anciently Desmond – and taught in my seminary, in the ould preceptory of Monaster-ny-oriel, according to the Bethluisnion-na-Ogma, [394] with Latin and Greek, and other modern dialects.' /

'And yet,' said the Commodore, with an half-repressed smile, 'there are some sceptics of opinion that there has always existed a perfect identity between the Irish and the Anglo-Saxon; [395] that in fact the Irish received their ancient alphabet from the Britons; and that their pretensions to an eastern origin is a groundless notion, generated in ignorance, and idly cherished by a mistaken patriotism, which might be better directed.'

'Oh murther!" exclaimed O'Leary, clasping his hands: 'the thieves of the world!'

'O tribus Anticyris caput insanabile!' [396]

Then suddenly mounting his horse, with a look of mingled indignation and pity, directed at his unknown companion, he added, pointing to a road which wound down a woody hill, 'there's your way, Sir, to Dunore town. If you crass the river at Ballydab bridge, you can't miss it.' /

He was trotting off, muttering to himself some broken exclamations in Irish, when the Commodore, who also had resumed his horse, followed him, and said,

'In detailing the opinions of others, I do not give them to you, Mr. O'Leary, as my own: you are to observe, I speak not to dictate, but to learn.'

'Why then, Sir,' said O'Leary, soothed by this conciliatory observation, 'I'd be loath to see the likes of you, or any gentleman, enticed by them traitors of the world, who come as espials on the land, and go forth to defame it; for sorrow one of them English but hate Ireland in their hearts: and there's an ould saying in Irish, which manes, 'keep clear of an Englishman, for he is on the watch to deceive you.' I wouldn't give a testoon*[397] for the whole boiling of them, / troth, I wouldn't. The Irish not brought over by our Celtic Scythean ancestors! Bachal essu!†[398] they might as well take St. Patrick[399] from us, and deny that the potatoe is the plant of the soil.'

'I am afraid, Mr. O'Leary, they would go near to do both.'

'Oh! very well, Sir: I see you are one of them that would go ould Strabo on us, and Saxo Grammaticus, and Dr. Ledwich.'[400]

'Nay, I speak as one ignorant of the subject, and desirous to obtain information. If there were now, as formerly, such seminaries to study in as the school of Ross Alethri,‡†[401] or such sages to study under as those sought for by the learned Monk Ealfrith,[402] who came from Britain for that purpose, I should like to become his disciple.' /

'To say nothing,' said O'Leary, 'of Agelbert, bishop of the west Saxons, Alfred, king of Northumberland, and the blessed father Egbert, and the saintly brother Wigbert, who for the love of the celestial Isle, quit their kin and country, and retired to Ireland to study.'[403]

'But what cell,' asked the Commodore with emphasis, 'what preceptory, what academy is there now open to the lover of Irish antiquities, where learning and retirement could for an adequate compensation be obtained together, by a stranger who thirsts for both?'

'There is,' said O'Leary, after a short pause, and in a voice full of importance, as he drew up close to his companion – 'there is, plaze your honor, a place called the Monaster-ny-oriel; an old ruin, but a larned retreat. And if there *was* a gentleman, who, for the love of Ireland, would put up with homely fare, and be satisfied to be how-/sel'd with an old SENACHY, or genealogist,[404] why then –'

'O'Leary,' said the Commodore, laying his hand familiarly on his shoulder, and eagerly interrupting him, 'should you receive me as your guest and disciple, you will find me not difficult to accommodate: my ostensible business in this barony is with a certain Mr. Crawley, but –'

'With who?' asked O'Leary, recoiling in horror, 'with one Crawley, did you say?'

'With Mr. Crawley of Mount Crawley.'

'With *him*! the land pirate! then, Sir, you cannot housel with me, and so I wish you luck.'

With these words, O'Leary, spurring on his little nag, trotted abruptly down a craggy glen, and disappeared. The Commodore stood looking after him till he

---

*   An old Spanish coin, once current in Ireland.

†   The name of the celebrated staff of St. Patrick. An usual exclamation.

‡   The Field of Pilgrimage.

was out of sight, and marked the path he had taken. Then with a deep-/drawn inspiration, as one, who after some enforced restraint, breathes freely, and with a smile almost characterized by sadness, he bent his course towards the town of Dunore.

As the descent of the mountain softened into an undulating valley, the approach to this town became extremely picturesque. The conjunction of many mountain streams formed a considerable river, which flowed under the single arch of an antique bridge, covered with ivy, which stood at the entrance of a poor, but pretty village, announced by a turf carrier in answer to the Commodore's question, to be BALLYDAB.[405] A rude bleak mountain, which overshadowed this village, and projected into the sea, formed a bold head land. At the distance of two Irish miles, the road joined the high road from Cork and Dublin, and wound to the left of a group of new unfinished houses, the embryo of some rising town, haply in-/tended to eclipse the fading glory of the decaying and ancient village of Ballydab. Within a mile of Dunore, the road proceeded by the edge of the bay, at the head of which the town stood, and then appeared to wind along the coast. The town itself (once of note, and of historical interest), was approached by a stately avenue of trees. Its ancient, but well preserved castle, terminated its narrow street, and presented a striking feature in a scene now tinted by the silvery rays of a cloudless moon. The castle casements were lighted with a fairy illumination by its beams; and the rippling tide, tinged with the same colouring, gave a gentle motion to a few fishing vessels, which alone occupied a port, once of considerable trade with the opposite shores of Spain, Portugal, and Italy.

As the Commodore rode up the street, it was already still and noiseless, save the barking of a dog, which the echo / of the horse's feet had roused. Two lanterns in the front of two opposite houses marked the site of the rival inns. That to the right had a new and gaudy sign flaunting in the breeze; and, under a profusion of gilding, yellow ochre, and whitelead, was written THE NEW DUNORE ARMS.

The faded sign of its inferior competitor exhibited a dancing bear, scarcely distinguishable, under which was written, in large fresh black letters, This is the real ould Marquis of Dunore. The Commodore chose the real old Marquis; and a tolerable supper, and a clean bed, left him nothing to repent of his election. The next morning, fatigued by his mountain ride, he rose late; and was surprised to find upon his breakfast table a note, directed '*To his honour, the gentleman at the ould Bear, who arrived last night, these.*'

He opened and read as follows: – /

Right honorable,

According to the advisement of my better judgment, I herein complie with your *requist* this tyme, in regard of the lodgement in the Friar's room; videlicet[406] *Fra Denis* O'Sullivan, superior of the order, now in Portugal, via Cork, where he bides at this present writing, pending the visitation.[407] He being likely to put the autumn over in foreign parts, the place thereby being vaquent, the floor clean sanded, and the stone belted window giving on the sea-coast, ill befitting your honor howsomever, or your likes, being righte worthie of Dunore Castle, which is nothing to nobody, sithe your honor think it fit. Touchinge the pintion thereof, should your honor consent to housel with me, it shall be left to your honor's liberalities; the lucre of gain, but little weighing; and if there be juste cause of complaynte touchinge ye unruliness of my / scholars, or any rabblement on the part of them young but larned runagates, they shall, on your honor's so deposing before me, their plagosus Orbilius,[408] undergoe chastisement in due austeritie: so praying an answer forthwith,

I remaine,
With humble commendations,
Your honor's dutiful servant,
Terentius Oge O'leary.
*From my Preceptory,
Monaster-ny-Oriel.'*

Whatever might have caused this sudden revolution in the sentiments of Mr. O'Leary, it evidently excited much pleasure in the person in whose favour it had occurred; and on learning that one of O'Leary's academicians, or *'larned runagates,'* awaited an answer, he sent back a verbal one, intimating his intention of riding over immediately to the Preceptory of Monaster-ny-Oriel, after he had taken his breakfast.

On passing through the town, on his / way to O'Leary's, the Commodore was struck, not only with the antiquity, but with the Spanish character of its architecture. Many of the better sort of houses had stone balconies, with windows and door frames of dark marble. The church was dedicated to St. Jago de Compostello,[409] and was raised (as an inscription on the gate indicated) by Florence Macarthy, Earl of Clancare, on his return from a pilgrimage to Galicia: it was called in Irish the church of the vow, and was afterwards largely endowed by a company of Spanish merchants, who had settled in Dunore, in the reign of Elizabeth. It was afterwards the protestant parish church, and became much decayed and ruinous. A stone inscription over a little pot-house, with a rose, carved in relief, gave the following quaint information:

'At the rose is the beste wine.'

'Anno 1563.'[y]

The castle, raised on a rocky eleva-/tion, and looking down upon the town, had, in the course of centuries, lost nothing of its feudal character. Massive and heavy, this ancient edifice formed a perfect parallelogram, with five flankers: its battlements, beltings, and coignes, were of hewn stone; and its strength and magnitude were, as far back as Elizabeth, so formidable, that the queen was induced to think it too considerable

an hold to belong to any Irish subject; and the lords of the English council transmitted an order to stop the works, which the Macarthy More of that day was carrying on for its completion. Shortly after, the chief of that family, with many of its immediate branches, were placed under the ban of royal displeasure. Forfeitures and deaths followed: some took refuge in Spain, the usual retreat of the persecuted Irish, and some in the less distinguished castles of their ancestors.[z] The castle, town, and manor of Dunore, were given to / Hildebrand, first Viscount of Dunore, a connexion of the great Lord Boyle's, by grant of James the First. This English lord completed the ramparts, which, under his jurisdiction, were no longer causes of jealousy. He also planted the ancient bawn,[*410] made a stately avenue of trees from the town to its portals, and placed above the arch of its entrance, in letters cut in the stone, and still perfectly legible –

'God's Providence

Is my inheritance.'

He had also, like his great kinsman, Boyle, endeavoured to turn the ancient catholic town of *Dangan-na-Carthy* (now called Dunore, or the 'golden fort') into a protestant colony (7).[411] But / the inquisitorial zeal with which this attempt was pursued defeated its intent, and persecution produced fanaticism where it meant to effect conversion.[a] He had also expelled the friars of Monaster-ny-Oriel, one of the communities, which, like many others, still subsisting in Ireland, had never been suppressed, and devoted its revenue for the pin-money of his daughter-in-law;[†412] but still, from time to time, some of the order were found congregating among the ruins of the building, in obedience to the rules of the order, which forbid the entire dispersion of its members.

The first Viscount Dunore was the last of his family who had resided in the *inheritance* bestowed upon them by *God's providence*.[b] One of his descendants, William, second Earl of Dunore, had visited it in a tour to the / south, which he made during his vice-regency of Ireland. The present marquis, the eldest of two twin brothers, had early in life suffered his susceptible imagination to dwell on some affecting and curious relations of the ancient and actual state of Ireland. Impressions thus received, wrought on his mind with an influence proportioned to the unhappy malady which now first betrayed itself in many symptoms, of which his sympathy for Ireland, and his determination to reside in what he perpetually called 'his beautiful castle,' were deemed by his mother and friends among the strongest. With the uncalculating impetuosity of his disease,

---

*   The BAWN was an inclosed piece of ground, reserved for purposes of recreation and exercise, answering to the modern lawn. Swift's Hamilton's bawn was the remains of this Irish *verger*.

†   A similar act was committed by Boyle, Earl of Cork, and for the same purpose.

he had ordered immense sums of money to be expended in repairing and fitting what had become almost a ruin. Furniture, the most sumptuous and appropriate, had been sent from England; and even wine and plate had arrived, and been stowed in the long-unused cellars and buttery of / the castle. Its lord and suit were daily expected, when his disease declared itself so unequivocally, that the promising but unfortunate young nobleman was placed in close confinement. Two years had elapsed since that event, and his mother, the Marchioness Dowager of Dunore, his sole guardian, and in whom centred the whole interest and influence of the Dunore property, had recently proposed visiting the castle, in order to set up her second son, Lord Adelm, who was abroad,ᶜ to represent the neighbouring borough of Glannacrime; but on some representations from her agent, Mr. Crawley, and her lawyer, counsellor Conway Townsend Crawley, his son, she had suddenly given up the intention.

The castle, therefore, remained in statu quo,[413] antique, superb, and desolate, such as may be found in every province of Ireland; the ancient residence of Irish chiefs, the quondam[414] possession of / English lords of the pale,[415] the property of more recent patentees, the inheritance of English-Irish absentees, known only by name to the tenants they have never visited. The traveller paused a few moments before its walls, threw his eyes rapidly over the stately edifice, and then proceeded under its once fortified terrace, along the strand, to the monastic retreat of the learned O'Leary.

Monaster-ny-Oriel was one of those ecclesiastical ruins, in which the south of Ireland abounds; it was once of great extent, and was (in the terms of its charter) given to God and to St. John the Evangelist, by one of the chiefs of the Macarthy family. The windows and arches, still in preservation, were of beautiful gothic architecture, the walls of the choir remained, but it was roofless: and in the newly thatched chauntry[416] of the blessed Virgin O'Leary held his academy, literally imaging Shakespear's description of a pedant keep-/ing a school in a church.[417] A tower on the verge of the ruins (once a small house for novices), hanging over the coast, was now called the Friary of St. John, where the order of the Dominicans was still kept up:* it was also the tenement now at O'Leary's disposal, through the kindness of its absent proprietor. Every where among the ruins, the tombs of rival chiefs were visible through the wild shrubs and furze that half concealed them. Here a 'GLORIA DEO IN EXCELSIS,' was raised for an English BOYLE or PETTY; there a 'GISTE ICI. – DIEU DE SON AME AIT MERCI,' for some Norman de Barri, or de Grosse;[418] and above all rose the high grey stone, that in the ancient Irish character pointed to the resting-place of Conal Macar-

---

* There are many friaries in Ireland, thus preserved by the residence of one or two of the order, among the ruins of their ancient houses.

thy More,[419] the swift footed, reposing in the midst of those who had opposed, or those who had betrayed him. /

This scene, so solemn, even when tinged with the cheery lustre of the morning light, was most incongruously disturbed by the hum of confused and nasal murmurings, resembling the discord of an ill-tuned bag-pipe. The ear of the traveller seemed to recognize this sound, once, perhaps, well known to him; and directing his steps to the chauntry of the blessed Virgin, he perceived several students stretched upon the rank grass, before its high arched Saxon door-way: thus refreshing the picture of an Irish School, given by Campion in Queen Elizabeth's day. The ardent, but barefooted, disciple of the muses, *now*, as *then*, '*grovelling on the earth, their books at their noses, themselves lying prostrate; and so chaunting out their lessons piecemeal.*'[420]

The breaking up of the academy took place as the Commodore approached it: a bevy of rough-headed students, with books as ragged as their habiliments, / rushed forth at the sound of the horse's feet, and with hands shading their uncovered faces from the sun, stood gazing in earnest surprise at the unexpected visitant: last of this singular group, followed O'Leary himself, in learned dishabille:[421] 'his customary suit,'[422] an old great coat fastened with a wooden skewer at his breast, the sleeves hanging unoccupied, *Spanish-wise*, as he termed it; his wig laid aside, the shaven crown of his head resembling the clerical tonsure; a tattered Homer in one hand, and a slip of sallow in the other, with which he had been lately distributing some well-earned *pandies*[423] to his pupils: thus exhibiting, in appearance, and in the important expression of his countenance, an epitome of that order of persons once so numerous, and still far from extinct in Ireland, the hedge schoolmaster.[424] O'Leary was learned in the antiquities and genealogies of the great Irish families, as an anci-/ent* Senachy;[425] an order, of which he believed himself to be the sole representative, credulous of her fables, and jealous of her ancient glory; ardent in his feelings, fixed in his prejudices; hating the Bodei Sassoni or English churls, in proportion as he distrusted them; living only in the past, contemptuous of the / present, and hopeless of the future;

---

*   The Seanachaiahe˙ were antiquaries, genealogists, and historians; they recorded remarkable events, and preserved the genealogies of their patron, in a kind of poetical stanza.– Each province prince, or chief, had a senacha; and we will venture to conjecture, that in each province there was a repository, for the collections of the different Seanachaiahe belonging to it, with the care of which an Ollamh-le-Seanacha was charged: the ancient college of arms of Ulster is still maintained. *Walker's Hist. of Irish Bards.*

˙   The very common word, says Gen. Vallency, is peculiar to Ireland; It is, indeed, daily used in the corruption of *Shannos.* – Och! he has fine old *Shanaos*, or *old* talk is frequently applied to, and family history, &c.

Duald Mac Firbis, who was murdered at Dunslin in Sligo, A. D. 1670, closed the line of the hereditary antiquaries of that province, to whom it may be supposed that for one inspired ten thousand were possessed.[d]

all his national learning, and national vanity, were employed on his history of
the Macarthies More, to whom he deemed himself hereditary senachy, while
all his early associations and affections were occupied with the Fitzadelm family; to an heir of which he had not only been foster father, but, by a singular
chain of occurrences, tutor and host. Thus, there existed an incongruity between
his prejudices and his affections, that added to the natural incoherence of his
wild, unregulated, ideal character. He had as much Greek and Latin as generally
falls to the lot of the inferior Irish priesthood, an order to which he had been
originally destined: he spoke Irish, as his native tongue, with great fluency; and
English, with little variation, as it might have been spoken in the days of James
or Elizabeth; for English was with him acquired by study, at no early period of
life, and principally obtained from such books as came / within the black letter
plan[426] of his antiquarian pursuits.

'Words that wise Bacon and grave Raleigh spoke'[427]

were familiarly uttered by O'Leary, conned out of old English tracts, chronicles,
presidential instructions, copies of patents, memorials, discourses, and translated
remonstrances, from the Irish chiefs, of every date since the arrival of the English
in the island; and a few French words, not unusually heard among the old Irish
Catholics, the descendants of the faithful followers of the Stuarts, compleated
the stock of his philological riches.*[428] ᶜ/

O'Leary now advanced to meet his visitant with a countenance radiant with
the expression of complacency and satisfaction, not unmingled with pride and
importance, as he threw his eyes round on his numerous disciples. To one of
these the Commodore gave his horse; and drawing his hat over his eyes, as if to
shade them from the sun, he placed himself under the shadow of the Saxon arch,
observing,

'You see, Mr. O'Leary, I very eagerly avail myself of your invitation: but I fear
I have interrupted your learned avocation.'

---

*   Several of the obsolete terms of Shakespeare and Spenser are to be found in daily use
among the Catholics of Ireland. In the conversation of the higher orders, not unfrequently,

'A bold expressive phrase appears,
Bright through the rubbish of some hundred years.'

The strong line of demarcation drawn between the Catholic and Protestant gentry of the
country, and which renders them a distinct society, explains the fact. Both in their speech
and manners the latter are singularly attached to old modes; and they still preserve that
peculiar courteousness of address, which is now considered as almost exclusively to be
found in France.

'Not a taste, your honor, and am going to give my classes an holiday, in respect of the turf, Sir.ᶠ What do's yez all crowd round the gentlemen for? – Did never yez see a raal gentleman / afore? I'd trouble yez to consider yourselves as temporary. There's great scholars among them ragged runagates, your honor, poor as they look: for though in these degendered times you won't get the childre, as formerly, to talk the dead languages, afore they can spake, when, says Campion, they had Latin like a vulgar tongue, conning in their schools of leachcraft the aphorisms of Hippocrates, and the civil institutes of the faculties,[429] yet there are as fine scholars, and as good philosophers still, Sir, to be found in my seminary as in Trinity College, Dublin. – Now, step forward here, you Homers. 'Keklute meu Troes, kai Dardanoi, ed' epikouroi.'[430]

Half a dozen overgrown boys with bare heads and naked feet, hustled forward.

'Them's my first class, plaze your honor: sorrow one of them gassoons, but would throw you off a page of Homer into Irish while he'd be clamping a turf stack. – Come forward here, / Padreen Mahony, you little mitcher,[431] ye. – Have you no better courtesy than that, Padreen? Fie upon your manners. Then for all that, Sir, he's my head philosopher, and am getting him up for Maynooth.[432] Och! then I wouldn't axe better than to pit him against the provost of Trinity College this day, for all his ould small cloathes, Sir, the cratur! troth, he'd puzzle him, great as he is, aye, and bate him too; that's at the humanities, Sir. Padreen, my man, if the pig's sould at Dunore market to-morrow, tell your daddy dear, I'll expect the pintion. Is that your bow, Padreen, with your head under your arm like a roosting hen? Upon my word, I take shame for your manners. There, your honor, them's my *cordaries*,[433] the little Leprehauns,*[434] with their *cathah*† heads, and their burned / skins: I think your honor would be divarted to hear them *parsing* a chapter – Well now, dismiss, lads, jewel – off with yez, *extemplo*,[435] like a piper out of a tent; away with yez to the turf; and mind me well, ye Homers ye, I'll expect Hector and Andromach[436] to-morrow without fail: observe me well, I'll take no excuse for the *classics* barring the bog, in respect of the weather's being dry: dismiss, I say.' The learned disciples of this Irish sage, pulling down the front lock of their hair to designate the bow they would have made, if they had possessed hats to move, now scampered off, leaping over tomb-stones and clearing rocks; while O'Leary observed, shaking his head, and looking after them, 'Not one of them but is sharp witted, and has a ganius for poethry, if there was any encouragement for larning in these degendered times.'

Having now gratified his pedagogue pride, and excused the 'looped and win-/dowed raggedness' of his pupils by extolling that which passeth shew,[437] he

---

*   Leprehauns, one of the inferior order of Irish Demonology.

†   Cathah – curly, or matted.

now turned his whole attention on his guest, who stood shadowed by the deep arched door-case, waiting till the last of the boys had disappeared. O'Leary led the way before him into the interior of the chauntry, which was divided into the school-room, and his own abode; then laying down his Homer and ferule,[438] and shutting the door almost to the exclusion of the light, and wiping down a seat with his wig, which lay on the desk, and which he afterwards placed on his head, he respectfully motioned his visitor to be seated. A silence for a moment ensued; when O'Leary, fixing his eyes into a look of expressive significance, observed, in a low cautious tone:

'I axe your lordship's pardon for the great liberty I took in calling you, Sir, my lord; thinking it due discretion so to do before my scholars; in respect / of your intention of biding here *in casu incognito.*'[439]

'Indeed!' said the Commodore, starting on his feet: 'for whom then do you take me?'

'For who you are – noble by blood, by birth, and by descent; and though no Irishman, but of Norman breed, a true Geraldine. And though the Fitzadelms are nothing to me now, for I have shook the dust off my feet at their threshold, and threw my ould couran* over the head of the last of the race, that shall ever give my heart a beat, or my eye a tear, yet I'd be sorry that it was to say, that a branch of the ould tree wanted a sheltering place, when I, Terence Oge O'Leary, the last Irish fosterer of the family, had a shed to housel him under.'

'For whom, then,' repeated the Commodore, in a calmer tone than he / had before asked the question, 'for whom do you take me?'

'For Lord Adelm Fitzadelm,' replied O'Leary, with a respectful bow. 'The cadet of the twin sons of Gerald Baron Fitzadelm, commonly called the Red Baron, himself the cadet of the father of the son, and heir that would have been if –'

O'Leary paused: his voice faltered; and after a moment's silence, the Commodore observed,

'It is strange that you should take me for the Lord Fitzadelm. For what purpose should he come incognito into this neighbourhood?'

'For every purpose in life, your honor, and the best of purposes, to circumvent them land pirates, them plot-hunters, them trianglers![440] them – them *Crawley thieves.* Bachal Essu! only let me live to see that day, and then doesn't care how soon I'm carried feet foremost to the *berring* ground of / the pobble O'Leary,[441] near St. Crohan's County Kerry: for its little else is left for me now to live for but to die.'

---

*   An Irish shoe or brogue, made without heels.

'And for this strange tissue of improbability, what grounds have you, O'Leary? Why should Lord Fitzadelm come over in disguise to circumvent, as you call it, his mother's agent?'

'If you don't believe me, your honor,' interrupted O'Leary, losing the supposed identity of the person he was addressing in the incoherency of his always confused ideas, 'will you believe your own eyes, Sir; that's my Lord, I mane?'

He drew forth a letter from his pocket as he spoke and the Commodore took it to the little casement, and read as follows:

'A distinguished looking stranger will shortly present himself to the learned and sagacious Terence Oge O'Leary: should he propose himself as a tenant / for the Reverend Mr. O'Sullivan's vacant apartments, he will do well to accept him. Terence Oge O'Leary may have heard that Lord Adelm Fitzadelm will shortly be in the Peninsula of Dunore, to circumvent the machinations of the Crawley faction, and will there be incognito. None but the well-wishers of the Crawleys would refuse to assist Lord Adelm in a temporary concealment, necessary for the effecting of his laudable purposes.'

After a frequent and amazed perusal of this billet, the Commodore demanded how this strange letter reached O'Leary.

'I found it,' he replied, 'after the dawn of day.'

'Found it?'

'Aye, did I, troth, and marveled much to see it fixed in the latch of the outside door of the chauntry; and was mighty loath to break the *sale*,[g] and didn't, only just skimmed round it.' /

The Commodore, on examining the seal, found it bore the figure of a child, plucking the thorns from a rose, with the motto:

Sou utile ainda que Bricando.*[442]

'And have you no idea from whom this letter comes?' asked the Commodore, after another pause, and some evident perplexity of idea.

'I have, plaze your honor, that's your lordship, I mane; every iday in life, it comes from the good people: often they do the likes of that kind turn by their pets – that's the fairies, my Lord.'

'In this instance, however,' returned the Commodore, smiling, 'they have done you an ill turn; for if they mean to impress you with an idea that I am Lord Adelm Fitzadelm, they most certainly deceive you.'

'Oh! very well, Sir,' returned O'Leary, with a most obstinate look of incredulity, 'as your lordship willeth, / that's your honor, I mane, *now*, Sir, if its *Sir* you plase to be.'

'Supposing,' said the Commodore, 'that even it were Lord Adelm who sought concealment under your roof, surely you would not defeat his intentions,

---

*   I am useful in sportiveness.

by persisting in giving him a title, which would at once reveal his rank, or at least awaken suspicion.'

'Is it me! och! I'd be very sorry! and will be bound, I'll never call your lord-ship my lord, if you was in it till the day of judgment, only when we are alone, Sir, and nobody by, barring our two selves, and can pass you as a tinnant come to bathe in the salt water, Sir, and need never name your honor at all, Sir, only pass you for my lodger.'

'You will then *pass me* for what I am anxious to become, O'Leary; I will there-fore look at the apartment you mean me to occupy. You shall name your own terms; and I dare say you have some old dame, who is wont to / boil a chicken, and make coffee for Friar O'Sullivan, who would undertake –'

'Aye,' interrupted O'Leary, eagerly, 'and who can toss up an omelette, and fry a bit of fish on maigre days,[443] your honor, and was taught by Fra Denis himself, who has a mighty pretty taste that way. Och! I'll engage we'll *table* your honor well. Here, Moriagh ma chree, throw me the keys of the friary.'

As he spoke, O'Leary rapped at a little blind window in the wall, which was instantly opened, and discovered at once the interior of his kitchen, and an old woman employed in carding.[444] 'That's my *Girleen*,'[445] said O'Leary, taking a bunch of keys from her, and opening a door opposite to that which led from the road to the chauntry. The host and his new lodger proceeded across a sort of grass-grown court, surrounded by a range of cloister, still in high preserva-tion, and bent their steps towards the friary. An old, and ap-/parently very feeble eagle, with a leather collar round his leg, and fastened by a chain to a fragment of the ruin, attracted the stranger's attention. O'Leary paused also, clasped his hands, and sighed, exclaiming,

'You are not long for this world, my Cumhal honey, and leaves your bit of food for the sparrows, my poor bird, that daren't come near you oncet, my king of the mountains.'

'He looks very sick, and I think dying.'

'Oh! musha, the pity of him! He's ould and desolate like myself. Its twenty years and more since he came home to me in Dunkerron; and when he came in, with his looks all on fire, as he was wont after being out all day, Terence, my ould lad, says he, for that's a way he had of calling me, that's he that brought me the eagle, Sir, he that had the eye of the eagle, and the spirit of an eagle; Terence, my old lad, I / have brought you *another pet*, says he. Do you mind, your honor, marking the word *another*, and maning himself to be one, the sowl! Have you, my lord, says I, for though he was then left to perish by his own kin, and was sharing my bit and sup, in the wilds of Kerry, I always called him my lord, as he was, or would have been; and did so that day 'bove all others, for he had scarcely a skreed of his ould red jacket left on him; and called him my lord, in regard of the jacket. Have you, my lord, says I; and Terence, says he, you'll be kind to this eaglet, (and it was fluttering on his left arm, with its blue bill and golden eye) you will be kind to it for *my* sake, and I'll tell you why, Terence, says he, leaning his right arm on mine, and looking with his smile, his mother's smile in my face. The poor bird has been driven from its parent's nest, says he, I found it fluttering on a bare rock exposed and perishing. / For it is the nature of the eagle to chase away its young, when unable to supply its own wants. For want, Terence, says he, may overcome even a parent's love. The tears stood in his eyes as he spoke, for it was his own story, plaze your honor, and it wasn't with a dry cheek I heard him. And yet, says he, cheering up and placing the fine young eaglet on the ground, the eagle is a noble bird, Terence, and even this poor fellow may yet soar high; though it isn't under a parent's wing he'll imp his flight.[446] Them were his words if I was dying, and that was great speaking for a boy of twelve years old. But he had Homer and Ossian at his finger's ends, to say nothing of Don Bellianus of Greece, the seven wise maisters, and Plae racca na Rourke.'*[447]

While O'Leary was giving this history, the Commodore seem'd shaken by some / deep feeling, which, however, was unobserved by O'Leary, whose attention was wholly occupied in striving to make the bird feed, while he described its first appearance under his roof. At last, by a powerful effort, shaking off his emotion, and giving a firm and indifferent tone to his voice, the Commodore asked, 'of whom do you speak, O'Leary?'

'Of whom do I speak, your honor?' said O'Leary, raising his head loftily;

'it's of the Honorable de Montenay Fitzadelm I speak, that would have been Marquis of Dunore if he were in it the day, the only son and heir of Walter Baron Fitzadelm: it's of your father's nephew I speak, my lord,' said O'Leary, with inveteracy, and raising his voice, 'his only nephew, Sir; and such a nephew! and nothing to be got by it but a poor bit of a title in distant reversion! not a scrubal in money *at the time*, not a *cantred* of land *then*; it was / for a sound, a breath, he sowld his sowl. But the curses that fell that day –' added he, closing his hands, and grinding his teeth, while he still seemed to struggle with feelings, which were giving the vehemence of insanity to his voice and its wildness to his look; when the Commodore, taking off his hat, as if to give coolness to his fervid brow, fixed his eye on him. O'Leary tottered back a few steps: his colour faded, his countenance lost its expression of fierceness; he several times drew his hand across his eyes as if to clear their vision; then stood gazing in silence for many minutes on the face of the stranger, which he now first beheld fairly revealed.

'You do not wish that the crimes of the father should bring curses on his children, O'Leary,' said the Commodore, in a tranquil voice, 'if indeed the late Baron Fitzadelm has been guilty of crimes which merit execration?' /

---

*   The celebrated song of the Irish bard, humourously translated by Dean Swift.

O'Leary remained silent: his mind seemed in abeyance: every other sense was condensed in one: his lips moved, but he uttered no sound: he stood motionless, till his eyes, dazzled by the intensity of their gaze, obliged him to press his fingers on their aching lids.

'But,' continued the Commodore, putting on his hat, and losing much of the character of his face by concealing its finest features, 'but, O'Leary, if you persist in believing me to be Lord Adelm Fitzadelm, say, is the son a well-chosen confidant of his father's misdeeds? or if you cannot keep the secret of your own indignant feelings, how may I expect you will keep my secret? that is, supposing *I were* the Lord Adelm, *or any other person*, O'Leary, whose interest it is to keep their real name unknown till certain purposes be effected. The absence of discretion, O'Leary, may render even the zeal of affection abortive. But come, time / wears, and time is precious: I will leave the arrangement of the friary to your care: I must now away to Mr. Crawley's. My host of Dunore tells me that it will be difficult to obtain an interview with your powerful portrieve after twelve: you shall shew me the way to Mount Crawley, and we will talk of the great Macarthies More as we walk along, the descendants of the Tyrian Hercules, the powerful chiefs of Desmond.'

The spirits of O'Leary rallied at this watch-word of the imagination: he looked round as one suddenly awakened from some strange vision of the night, and mechanically followed the stranger across the chauntry into the cemetery of St. John's, where the boy, to whose care he had delivered his horse, was still leading it about. – 'Bring your master his hat,' said the Commodore, taking the reins of his horse. 'You shall walk a mile of the way with me, O'Leary, and then return to your busi-/ness, to which I must and am resolved not to be an hindrance.'

The boy returned with the hat, which O'Leary suffered him to put over his little wig, now all awry. Plunged once more in deep cogitation, he walked silently beside his new tenant, snatching at intervals an eager glance at his person, and then shaking his head, debating as it were some point within himself; and at last clasping his hands behind his back, and exclaiming aloud, as he paced on heavily – 'Sure kin may *liken** kin; and no marvel in *that*, any how: only it all lies in the upper part of the face: and that was his mother's. The dark eyes, Milesian born.[448] The great O'Sullivan Bear's daughter coming from the Luceni in Spain,[449] of Scythian origin, and died of a broken heart, in the *sorrowful chamber*, so called to this day, only fallen to ruin, why wouldn't she, the cratur! and her own child first turning / out to be Judy Laffan's; and then, when that wouldn't do, the country being well insensed†[450] to the contrary, reported to be dead, and taken from her: and an hard case it was, as she said to my wife on her death-bed,

---

*   Resemble
†   Aware, acquainted.

God rest her: for they'd all desarted the court, barring the bailiff's for the execution, laving her to die *with only the child's nurse to wet* her lips. '*And a hard case
it is to lose one child, Susheen,*' said she, as she gave the prayer-book that had the
certificate of Mr. De Montenay's birth and marriage in it, that's her own marriage
with my lord, thinking, God help her, that it might be of use to the child one day
(which it never will), and sending it to the friar Denis O'Sullivan Finn, her own
kinsman at Dunkerron, for my lady was a Catholic by birth, and –'

'O'Sullivan,' interrupted the Commodore, 'is still in Cork, I suppose; but the
book of course lost, if that were of any consequence *now*.' /

'He is in Cork, Sir, and will be till the visitation is over, and then will be in
Portugal; and the prayer-book's safe. I saw it with him the day he departed; but
what matter is it? Sure there is nothing to prove but that he was murthered fairly,
that's drowned by force, vi et armis. I never will believe that he sunk when his
boat was overturned. Is it he, that dived and swam like a duck? and often saw
him, when nobody would venture out, cut his way through the wild waves that
bate the grate Skelegs,[451] and his cot overset, and a thousand *ullalues*[452] raised
from the shore, and he rise like a barnacle from the waves, and gain the land, and
scale the *stone of pain*, as it's called, and reach the spindle, the pilgrim's last station, a bit of rock projecting over the raging sea, the storm bating wildly round
him. Och! that was a great sight. Above the world he looked, and above his own
lot,

'Auditque ruentes
Sub pedibus ventos et rauca tombrua calcat.'[453] /

'And *he* to be drowned on a fine, calm, moonlight night, when he went out to
chase the porpoises; for that was great sport to him; and to fight the sea calves in
the caves, under the headlands of Kerry; for he was never aisy but when he was
after the seals and the *say*-dogs,[454] that covered the rocks and slept in the sunshine, or else in the mountains; sometimes chasing the deer with their beautiful
spotted skins, or coming home with a string of curlews on his back, barring when
he was reading Homer and Ossian, and the Seven Wise Maisters.'[h]

He paused, and again looked earnestly in the Commodore's face; who, musing, rather than listening to this apostrophe of O'Leary, was walking on with
a slackened pace, the reins of his horse rolled round his folded arms, when he
suddenly asked –

'And where does Mr. O'Sullivan live in Cork?' /

'At the Franciscan Friary' said O'Leary: and then continued, with a deep
sigh, 'It's marvellous: and does'nt know where the likeness is with the hat on.
Only it's the Fitzadelm mouth, any how – why wouldn't it? and minds, me of the
Macarthies More, and Macarthies Reagh of Carberry, who were kin by blood as

by descent, marrying through other, ever more, and preserving the family mouth always.'

'Oh! by the bye,' said the Commodore, abruptly, and throwing off his air of abstraction, 'did not this district of Dunore belong anciently to the Macarthies?'

'Did it? Is it Dunore? – The Macarthies, kings of the Coriandri, of the ancient Desmonds, the whole province of Munster, *late tyranni!*[455] See there, plaze your honor, behind you; that's Dunore Castle, the Dangan-ni-Carthie, the ancient fortress of the Macarthies; / now an English pale castle, as I may say: and look there to your left, near the *say*, at the brow of ould Clotnotty-joy; do you see a fine ancient ould castle? Well, that's Castle M'Carthy, hanging over its *depindency*, the village of Ballydab, oncet a bishoprick and borough. The castle on a rock, an elliptical conoid, defended by a barbican to the right, and the hall underneath, where Donagh Macarthy held his last court-baron, and his tributaries resorted to him for suit and service, the pobble O'Keefe and the pobble O'Leary.'

'I see nothing but a small square building on the mountain's brow,' replied his companion, in vain straining his eyes to view the features of feudal strength described by O'Leary, who saw only in the *mind's eye*, who now with all the associations of memory and imagination awakened, and with his wonted incoherence, launched into his favourite theme, for the moment forgetful of every other. /

'There is the very gabbion[456] Florence Macarthy stood on, when he saw the cannon planted against his only son, then in the Lord President's power,[457] sending the warder word that they kept him as a fair mark to bestow their shot upon. But the constable returned answer, *the fear of the boy's life should not make them abandon their country and its cause.* Then the Lord President of Munster and his men intrenched themselves between the river here to the left, and the castle forenent you, and planted before it two demi-cannons, and one sacre. Then, Sir, begins the battery to play from the ramparts of the castle; and a breach is made, by a cave under the great hall, the English forcing the warder to the keep; the musketeers, followed by the halberdeers, making their way up the turret stairs, there to the left, the Irish pour down on them *heart* and *hand, hæretpede pes densus que viro vir*,[458] man to man, breast to breast.ⁱ Gal-readh-a /boe,* cries the Fitzadelms, who were in the English army below, encouraging their men that appeared on the ramparts above: Lambh-laidre-aboe,† shouts Macarthy More, from the postern, like a flame of fire, bearing down all before him; – the English retreat: the war-horn of the Macarthies is heard through the mountains; the Macarthies carry the day. Hurra! Hurra! Hurra!'

---

*   'The cause of the red stranger;' the war-cry of many of the Norman families in Ireland.

†   'The cause of the strong hand,' the war-cry of the Macarthies.

O'Leary was now waving his hat in the air triumphantly, and transported beyond the present moment, when 'the vile squeaking of a wry-necked fife,'[459] and the roll of a drum, broke the thread of his ideas; and to the fancied engagements of the Irish and English cohorts of Queen Elizabeth's day, the gallow-glasses of the Macarthies, and the bow-/men of St. Leger, succeeded the New-Town Mount Crawley supplementary auxiliary yeomanry legion, a corps newly raised by Mr. Crawley, which stepped along the pathway of a very narrow road it nearly occupied, to the tune of 'the Protestant Boys,'[460] that, on the appearance of O'Leary, was instantly changed to 'Croppies lie down.'[461] To judge by the appearance of this evidently new raised corps, their leader, like Falstaff, had

'Misused the king's press most d – mnably;'

and whether it were, or were not, made up of 'revolted tapsters,' and 'hostlers trade-fallen,'[462] its members presented a most unsoldier-like appearance. There gleamed, however, through their awkward gate, and clumsy carriage, a consciousness of superiority, perhaps, both religious and military, which gave the last finish of ridicule to their exhibition: take them altogether,

'No eye had seen such scarecrows.'[463] /

The manner in which they had hustled O'Leary off the pathway, the well-known tune, and its well-known meaning, operated like a spell upon his agitated mind: he stopped short, till they had marched by; and then, wholly disenchanted from his splendid dreams, the Irish Macarthies, and the Norman Fitzadelms, vanished from his thoughts, and a third epoch in the history of his country was recalled to his recollection: this little image of local power, and petty ascendency, changed the current of his ideas, and with a deep sigh he added, 'And now 'tis the reign of the Crawleys.'

'Then let us hasten to their court baron,'[464] returned the Commodore, smiling, 'or we may be too late for an audience, O'Leary.'

All the circumstances of the immediate moment now flashed full through the mental confusion of O'Leary. The anonymous letter, Lord Fitzadelm incognito, the circumventing, the *Crawley faction*, were incidents which rapidly arranged themselves in his imagination. Recovering his composure, his spirits, and his vindictiveness, he gradually assumed the shrewd, animated, and important look he had worn, ere traces of his former hallucination had been awakened by a supposed or real resemblance to the object, whose loss had, for a time, bereft him of reason:[j] the idea that the stranger was the brother of the Marquis of Dunore had now taken possession of his mind,[k] with all the pertinacity incidental to his former malady; and persuaded that the ruin of the *Crawley faction*, as he termed it, was at hand, he neither speculated, nor reasoned upon the probable means by which that event was to be consummated. His hatred of that family had its source in the strongest feelings, and most fixed prejudices of his nature; and, like the rest of his countrymen, of his own class, his revenge was proportionate to his / devotion and fidelity. A few words, dropped at intervals, made up the conversation during the rest of their walk; he spoke of the stranger looking older than he ought, of his being '*mighty tanned* by *foreign parts*;' he asked if Mr. Crawley had seen him when in London, which being answered in the negative, he expressed his fear that a family likeness might be traced; and his hope that TORNEY CRAWLEY would be caught by his lordship in all his glory; for this was one of his great days, when people came to him from all parts of the county for law, justice, and money.

'There is New-Town Mount Crawley, plaze your honor,' said O'Leary, pointing to a few slightly-built red brick houses: 'sorrow call there was, at all at all, for them slips of card buildings, only to crush the ancient city of Ballydab, handy by. And there's the new barracks and the mail-coach road that is / to be. Och! Musha, English barracks and a mail-coach road in Dangan-na-Carthy! When in Florence M'Carthy's time, the English sheriff daren't set his foot in the place, but the country round rose to oppose him; and all this now in respect of the jobs, and the patronage, and the protectees, taxing the country: and before that road is finished, which it never will, any a false oath will be sworn, and many a sowl lost, and many a poor man's cattle be driven; and for all that, I remember me the portrieve's father, ould Paddy Crawley, herd to M'Carthy, of Castle M'Carthy, there beyont, that's the late ould titular Earl of Clancare. And now, there's Mount Crawley, plaze your lordship, on the top of that green sod hill, once called the Thane's heap,* in regard of a Macarthy was slain there in an engagement between them and the Fitzadelms, about / taking a prey of cattle, that's when the Macarthies' greatness overshadowed all the southern chiefs; and they made that day an elegant retrait through the pass of Mashanaglass, there below, to their own castle, as will be seen in my genealogical history. Sorrow much the retrait of Xenophon[465] was in comparaisment to that of Mashanaglass: but now, Dioul! *its the reign of the* CRAWLEYS.'

At the gates of the principal entrance to Mount Crawley O'Leary took his leave, observing, that he had made a vow in the year of the rebellion never to cross the threshold of a Crawley, 'till they had no longer a threshold to *crass*, plaze your Lordship.' At the word 'Lordship,' the Commodore put his forefinger to his lips, and O'Leary, recovering himself, added, 'your honor I mane.' He then retreated, leaving him, whom he persisted in believing Lord Adelm, persuaded, that among his virtues, the 'excellent quality of dis-/cretion'[466] could not be numbered; and that this affectionate, but inconsiderate person, was the last to be trusted with

---

*   Cairne Tierna

a secret, in which his own strong and ungoverned feelings had an interest. He had in the course of his desultory and incoherent conversation betrayed circumstances detrimental to the family honour of the Fitzadelms, and which had long slept in oblivion; that Baron Fitzadelm had been reduced by his distress, and influenced by his brother, to conceal the existence of his son, in order to raise money on the little that was left of his estate; that he had afterwards yielded to the story suggested by his brother; that this unfortunate boy was not his son, but the substituted child of his first nurse, to whom O'Leary's wife had succeeded; that the boy had afterwards been sent to the wilds of Kerry, to his foster father, to be kept for some sinister purpose out of the way; that immediately after his / father's death he was drowned by accident (though some told a different tale); that the herald's office had for some years after the death of the father and son refused to grant Gerald Fitzadelm the title of Baron Fitzadelm: all these circumstances, once the common topic of conversation in the province, had now died away, with the greater part of the generation who had witnessed them; and the details were only known to the few persons interested in their occurrence, and still surviving: these were the superior of the friars of St. John's, the old baccah of Lis-na-sleugh, and, above all, the fosterer of the deserted and persecuted heir of Fitzadelm, Terence Oge O'Leary. /

NOTES.

Note (1) Page 16. – This may seem harsh language applied to the 'gallant *Raleigh*,' who had rendered himself so illustrious in many instances, but it is fully justified by his conduct during his residence in Ireland, where he was little better than the captain of licensed banditti – the following anecdote is one out of a hundred to be found in the Irish tracts of Queen Elizabeth's day, which illustrates the truth of this apparently severe assertion.

'Soon after this action, Captain Raleigh, afterwards *Sir Walter*, went from Cork to Dublin, to his patron, the Lord Grey, who, on the Seventh of September, was made lord deputy of Ireland, with a complaint against the Barrys, (themselves descendants of the English lords who accompanied Henry II. to Ireland) and the Condons, for assisting the rebels.' (These complaints were easily made, but rarely substantiated, and never inquired into) 'He *obtained a commission to seize on the castle of Barry's court*, and the rest of Lord Barry's Estate, (on / the strength of *this complaint*) and had some horse added to his company *to enable him to take possession of it*. But *Barry* having notice of it, set *Barry's court* on fire, and the seneschal of Imokilly placed an ambush at Moore Abbey, which the young Raleigh courageously attacked, defeated, and broke through, so that he arrived safely at Cork. While Raleigh lay in this city, he performed several pieces of service against the rebels,* amongst others, Zouch ordered him (Ra-/leigh) to take *Lord Roche* and his lady prisoners, and bring them to Cork, they being *suspected* of corresponding with the rebels – the seneschal of Imokilly, and David Barry, having notice of this design, assembled seven or eight hundred men to fall on Raleigh; either going or on his return. Raleigh quitting Cork, with about ninety men, at ten of the clock at night, marched towards Bally, twenty miles from Cork, the house of Lord Roche, a nobleman well-beloved in the country, and arrived there early in the morning. He marched up to the castle gate; whereupon the townsmen, to the number of five hundred, immediately took up arms. Raleigh having placed his men in order, took with him Michael Butler, James Fulford, Nicholas Wright, Arthur Berland, Henry Swane, and Pinkney Huish; and knocking at the gate, three or four of Lord Roche's gentlemen demanded the cause of their coming: to whom Raleigh answered, that he came to speak with their lord, which was agreed to, provided he would bring with him only two or three of his followers. However, the gate being opened, he and all the abovementioned persons entered the castle; and after he had seen / Lord Roche, and spoken to him, by degrees, and by different means, he drew in a considerable number of his men, whom he directed to guard the iron gate of the court lodge, and see that no man should pass in or out, and ordered others into the hall, with their arms ready. Lord Roche set the best face he could upon the matter, and *invited* the captain to dine with him. After dinner, Raleigh informed him that he had orders to carry him and his lady to Cork. Lord Roche began to excuse his going, and at length resolutely said that he neither *would* nor *could* go; but Raleigh *letting him know that if he refused he would be taken by force,* he found there was no remedy, and, therefore, he and his lady set out on *their journey,* in a most rainy and tempestuous night, and through a very rocky and dangerous way,

---

*   *The rebels* of those days were chiefly such men as *Lord Barry*, who, sooner than give up their families to massacre, and their property to plunder, set fire to their houses, and took shelter in woods and fastnesses, and their strong holds. With the exception of *Macarthy-More, O'Neil,* and *O'Donnel,* almost all the *rebels* of this day were of English origin, men who still inherited from their ancestors some recollection of *Magna-Charta.* They therefore resisted the effect of such *complaints as Captain Raleigh,* and either protected or burnt their castles, and were consequently 'Rebels.' The persecution of the illustrious family of the Fitzgeralds, in the persons of the celebrated Earl of Kildare, and the great Earl of Desmond, whose crime was being the richest subject in the empire, are too well known to need comment. The Earl of Desmond, in an advanced age, was *despoiled of all his property,* hunted with bloodhounds through the woods and mountains, and discovered in a miserable hut, warming himself over a few fagots. His pursuers seized him by the long grey hairs, and to his appeal, 'my friends, I am the old Earl of Desmond,' they replied in a very brief and decided manner – they cut off / his head. The chief perpetrator was rewarded by the government with a commission and a pension, but was afterwards hung for some less horrible atrocity. For an account of this truly romantic tragedy, see 'Smith's Cork.'

whereby many soldiers were severely hurt, and others lost their arms. As for *Lord Roche,* he acquitted himself honourably of the crimes he was charged with, and afterwards did good *service* against the Irish.'

Smith's Cork, vol. 2.

It is notable, that '*doing good service* against the *Irish,*' was becoming a *plunderer* in *his turn,* to avoid being plundered. It was thus the natives of the land were plunged into crime in self-defence, by the fatal policy which raised its power upon the demoralization of the people it / *persecuted and brutified*; and England now complains of the want of principle and *incivilization* of the Irish. The Irish, in their tern, may exclaim with Toney Lumpkin to his mother:

'*As you made me,* so you *have* me.'[1]

(2) Page 96. – Of the inextinguishable fire heretofore kept by the nuns of St. Bridget at Kildare, thus Giraldus Cambrensis. At Kildare, famous for St. Bridget, are many miracles worthy to be remembered, among which is St. Bridget's fire, which they call inextinguishable, not that it cannot be extinguished, but because the nuns and holy women, by a continual supply of materials, have preserved it alive for so many years since the time of that virgin: and though so great a quantity of wood has been consumed in it, yet no ashes remain, From hence that nunnery is commonly called the fire-house. But this fire was put out by Henry Loundres, Archbishop of Dublin, in the year 1220, says an anonymous author, of the order of predicants, who compendiously writ the Annals of Ireland, from the year of our Lord 1163 to 1314, wherein he lived.

(3) Page 100. – Abbey of the Holy-Cross, by the River Suire. This abbey was founded in / honour of the holy-cross, for Cistercians, by Donald O'Brian, King of Limerick, about the year 1169, or as others, in 1181. The possessions were confirmed by John, Lord of Ireland and Earl of Moreton, afterwards King of England. This abbey was afterward, in a general chapter, subjected by the Abbot of Clarevaux to the Abbey of Furness, in England.

(4) Page 105. – Shebean – literally a house of concealment. The term is applied from the circumstance of the spirits which are sold in these private pot-houses being unlicensed, and consequently concealed.

(5) Page 138. – 'To the proper names of the ancient Irish, sirnames were added, either from some action, some quality of the mind, colour or mark of the body, or from chance, or ironically. So Neal, King of Ireland, was called Vigialac, because he had taken nine hostages from the lesser kings, and had held them for some time in fetters. King Brian was called Boruma, because he had recovered from the people of Leinster a certain annual tribute so called. Cænfela was called the Wise. S. Barr, Finbarr, or White Barr. S. Comin, Fada, or Long, and Æd, the

Bearded Clerk, from his / long beard: like as among the Grecians, Seleucus III.
King of Syria, was called Ceraunus, that is thunder, from his precipitate temper.
Ptolomy VII. King of Egypt, Physcon, from his great belly, and (to omit others)
Ptolomy, the last save one, Auletes, from his great love to the bagpipe.' – WARE.

'I return to Ireland, where, it is to be noted, that the ancient Irish, besides these
sirnames, had also, after the ancient manner, their fathers' names superadded, as Der-
mot-mac-Cormac, Cormac-mac-Donel, Donel-mac-Tirdelvac.' – WARE.

Both these customs are still extant in Ireland; and even in the families of the
provincial gentry, persons of the same name are distinguished by the colour of
their complexions, hair, &c. &c.[n]

(*5) Page 161. – This Irish *Marmite* formerly, and even within these twenty
years, was open to any hand its plentiful contents might tempt. Now, however,
the potatoe has risen in value with the increase of wretchedness, and of that,
one meal a day is often with difficulty procured. In the summer of 1817, the
author being in the country, within twelve miles of Dublin, on a visit at the seat
of a person of rank, frequently observed that when the twelve o'clock bell rung
to send the labourers home to dinner, / they lay down in the dry ditches. On
inquiring into the cause of a circumstance so unusual, she was informed, both
by the peasants and their overseers, that being unable to procure more than one
meal of potatoes, (taken only with salt and water), they preferred having that
meal at night. Even this wretched supper is extremely scanty. Formerly *potatoes*
(always the principal, or rather exclusive food) were sufficiently abundant in the
poorest families. Now the father, or head of the family, is obliged to portion
them out with great precision, lest an excess to-day should produce want to-
morrow. Even in the neighbouring counties of the metropolis the unfortunate
wretches are seen searching the ditches for offals or cresses; and many, to the
author's knowledge, when she visited Munster in 1817, supported themselves by
living on cabbage stalks thrown out from the *great house* of which she was guest.
To such sufferers imprisonment or death can have but few terrors. In Dublin,
persons, male and female, have been known lately to commit small depredations
for the purpose of being sent to jail, where shelter, with bread and water, was
provided for them. Two young women, lately brought before a most respectable
police magistrate in Dublin, assigned the above reason for breaking windows. A
few days back, July 9th, 1818, *eight hundred* persons presented themselves to /
the Mendicity Society of Dublin, to obtain any labour that could be procured
them at the rate of sixpence per day. Such is the '*flourishing state of Ireland*,' so
often vaunted by English official visitors, who drive rapidly through the country,
and are sumptuously entertained by the *Irish officials*, from whom they learn the
little they return to describe.[o]

(6) Page 231. – The ancient Irish used wicker boats covered with ox hyde, called corraghs, upon the open sea. Upon lakes and rivers they used another kind of boat, called *cotta*, made of a hollow tree. Both these boats are still in general use in Ireland, under the name of corraghs and cots, but are chiefly to be found on the rivers in remote counties, and on the south and west sea-coast.

(7) Page 276. – 'I admit neither presbyter, papist, independent, nor, as our proclamation says, any other sort of fanatick, to plant here, but all good protestants.' – *Earl of Orrery's Letter to the Duke of Ormonde*, 1662.

END OF VOL. I.

FLORENCE MACARTHY:

An Irish Tale.

BY

LADY MORGAN,

AUTHOR OF 'FRANCE', 'O'DONNEL', &c.

Know thus far forth:
By accident most strange, bonntiful fortune,
Now, my dear lady, hath mine enemies
Brought to this shore: and by my prescience,
I find my zenith doth depend upon
A most auspicious star, whose influence,
If now I court not but omit, my fortunes
Will ever after droop. SHAKESPEARE.[1]

Les femmes ne sout pas trop d'humeur à pardonner de certaines injures, et quand elles se promettent le plaisir de la vengeance elles n'y vout pas de *main-morte.*
DE GRAMMONT.[2]

IN FOUR VOLUMES.

VOL. II.

LONDON:
PRINTED FOR HENRY COLBURN,
PUBLIC LIBRARY, CONDUIT STREET, HANOVER SQUARE.
1818.
B. CLARKE, Printer, Well Street, London. /

FLORENCE MACARTHY.

CHAPTER I.

Having both the keys
Of officer and office, set all hearts i'the state
To what tune pleased his ear.
TEMPEST.[3]

Rampant et mediocre, et l'on parvent à tout.
BEAUMARCHAIS.[4]

THE Commodore had insisted on O'Leary's riding back his horse, and left the arrangement of his future residence at the friary entirely to his direction. He then ascended alone the steep hill, which, bleak, bare, and fringed only by a few scanty and ill-thriven plantations, led to the new-raised mansion of Mount Crawley. The house was a large square, lantern-like build-/ing, all wyat windows[5] and green verandas, unsheltered and unadorned, save by a cumbrous Grecian portico, an evident afterthought of the architect, who seemed to have consulted rather the genius of the owner than the place; for all was expense without taste, and shew without comfort.

It was a levee[6] day with Mr. Crawley, who, from an open window of his office, usually transacted, at the same time, the opposite and multifarious business of agent, magistrate, county treasurer, land jobber,[7] road maker, landlord, and attorney-at-law, captain of the Dunore volunteers, and commandant of the New-Town Mount Crawley supplementary-auxiliary volunteer legion, which he had just raised, and clothed at the expense of the — *county*.[8]

At this window, the object of many an anxious eye, which had watched its opening from the day's earliest dawn, now stood Mr. Crawley, en robe de / chambre et bonnet de nuit;[9] his shaving box in one hand, and his shaving brush in the other, which was applied to his already half-lathered face. A clerk was seated writing at a table by his side, disputing and wrangling with the crowd of suit-

ors who occupied the gravel-walk in front of the window. On one side stood
a host of applicants, endeavouring to obtain his attention, to whom time was
as valueless as it usually is to their class in Ireland, and who had come from all
parts to solicit law, redress, protection, interference, work, alleviation, or a long
day, for rent they were wholly unable to pay: on the other side, and close to the
window, with hard features, and looks full of petty importance, were to be seen
jobbers, drivers,[10] land bailiffs, constables and overseers, surrounded by petitioning, whining, wretched cotters, spalpeans,[11] road makers, and labourers. In this
group also stood two resolute, determined-looking men, / manacled, and in custody. They had been taken up on the preceding night as *Padreen Gar's boys;* a real
or supposed association, less formidable to government, than to Mr. Crawley's
peace of mind; and serving him as the ground-work of many well-got-up plots,
as the preamble of many proposed bills, suggested by him to the Irish government, for multiplying dependants, increasing influence, and depressing, galling,
harassing, and insulting, the beggared and catholic peasantry: most facetiously
termed acts for preserving the public peace, or more properly (because susceptible of an equivocal application) *insurrection acts.*[12 a]

These men were now waiting to go through the form of an examination previous to their committal to the county jail, where, guilty or innocent, they were
perhaps destined to wear out their lives in misery, vice, and incarceration, under
a form of law, known only in / Ireland, called a Rule of Bail.[13] Under the portico, with a table and some refreshments set before them, sat a few of the more
substantial tenants of the Dunore estate, who had just paid in their rents. In the
front of the house were drawn up the Mount Crawley legion, regaling the ears of
this catholic multitude with the (alternately performed) tunes of 'the protestant
boys,' and 'croppies lie down:'[14] the only tunes their military band, a fifer and
drummer, had yet learned. A crowd of idle people stood a short distance outside
a little gate, which opened on the lawn; and among these, the candidate tenant
for Court Fitzadelm had placed himself out of the view of the *great man* of this
characteristic Irish scene.

Meantime, Jemmy Bryan, ci-devant driver,*[15] but now termed the right-/
hand man of Mr. Crawley, was endeavouring to establish order among some
persons, who, from curiosity, were led to examine the new scarlet frize jackets
and worsted plumage of the legion more closely than was deemed respectful to
the sacredness of their military calling. He was laying about his staff of office
pretty actively, with 'Quit, quit, I say. Will yez let his honor get a sight of his own
legion, and he going to man-yeuvre them?'

Mr. Crawley now placed himself en evidence[16] at his window, brandishing,
not his sword, but his razor; and holding his nose obliquely with his left hand,

---

*   See note (1) at the end of the volume.

he exclaimed authoritatively – 'Jemmy Brian, make an era for the legion to go through their involutions in. Rare rank, take close order: mighty well. Where are your regimental gaiters, Corporal Costello? Oh, now while I think of it, Sargeant Kelly, apropos to my corderoys, if you don't finish them the / night, I'll send to Dublin for a pair; and that's the way you sarve me for encouraging the manufactory of the country,[17] Mr. Kelly.'

'Plaze your honor, in regard of the New-Town Mount Crawley legion,' said Sarjeant Kelly (a tailor by trade), stepping up with a military salute to the window, and in apologetic look, indicating that his new vocation had 'raised his soul above buttons.'[18]

'Well, Mr. Sargeant Kelly, you must sarve the government first; but that's no raison nor rhyme either that I'm to want my small-clothes; and now fugle me those haroes through all them system of tictacs[19] I sent you down from Lord Rosbrin in a castle frank last week, his own tictacs for the Kil-Rosbrin corps from the secatary's office.'

'I shaul, your honor; that's eyes right and eyes left, Sir; and is eligant marchers at a quick step, plaze your honor, captain.' /

'Well then, Sarjeant Kelly, march me them through a little circuitous cut to Paddy Scanlan's potatoe ridge; but have a care of my meadow: do you mind, Sarjeant Kelly?'

'I shaul, Sir. Quick march,' cried the sergeant, while the protestant boys struck up, and the legion went shambling off in a contrary direction to that intended by Mr. Crawley, who, with that half of his face which was not covered with soapsuds, purple with rage, called after them:

'Come back here, you scampering sons of guns! Halt, I say, don't you see my invisible fence[20] there before your eyes, you buzzards, and goes headforemost rollicking over it? Halt, I say.'

Halt was now repeated by an hundred voices to the inattentive ears of the Mount Crawley heroes, who, stunned by the noise of the drum and fife, and delighted with their exhibition before their less consequential countrymen, / were deaf to the orders of their captain-commandant, and went, as he termed it, 'rollicking on,' till overtaken by Jemmy Bryan, who brought them back in confusion, while Mr. Crawley vociferated:

'Is it to Jericho ye are marching,[21] ye shambling thieves, flopping over my hay?'

'No, plaze your honor,' replied sergeant Kelly, 'only to Ballydab, captain, to be ready against the *'ruction*[22] at the fair, Sir, to keep the king's pace, according to your honor's orders and the young sheriff's, Sir.'

'And did I bid ye go without your new colours, worked for you on elegant orange silk by Miss Crawley, Sargeant Kelly?'

'You did nat, plaze your honor.'

'Then draw up in a square hollow,[23] according to Lord Rosbrin's tictacs, under the virandow of her room, and she'll hand them out to yez. Order a / trevailly[24] to be bate to give her notice.'

The sergeant drew up his men, the reveillée was beat, the window opened, and Miss Crawley, the maiden sister of the captain-commandant, appeared with a little flag at the viranda, which she lowered to Sergeant Kelly, observing, as she resigned it:

'In presenting to brave men the standard that is to lead them to victory or death –'

'Och, murther!' interrupted Mr. Crawley, stretching out of his own window, and looking up at his sister's with a look of humorous surprise.

'In presenting to brave men,' continued Miss Crawley, 'the standard which is to lead them to victory or to death, I feel myself placed in a situation out of my sphere, and inimical to my feelings, which are those of peace and good-will to all men. But Judith did not disdain an act of courage in her / country's cause;[25] nor should I have shrunk from a Judith's part had that Holofernes visited this devoted land, that great leviathan,[26] who has threatened to swallow us all up.'

The intimidated legion expressed by their looks how little they would have relished being swallowed up, while Mr. Crawley, between jest and earnest, and much amused by the unexpected eloquence of his sister, exclaimed:

'There! there's a haro in petticoats for you.'

'Go,' continued Miss Crawley, emphatically, 'and may heaven crown your arms with meekly-borne success!'

The 'go' of the redoutable Miss Crawley, the deputy lady of the manor, as her brother was the deputy lord, was as commanding to the Mount Crawley Legion as the 'march' of their sergeant, who now led them forth to Ballydab, full of their own superior influence, and the ascendency appertaining both to their / political and military relations; and animated also by a little whiskey, ordered by Mr. Crawley to *steep* their colours in, they proceeded to oppose prejudice and ignorance, armed with power, to prejudice and ignorance in subjection; and, most probably (as is the usual case upon such occasions in Ireland,) to breed and foment the disturbance they were sent to anticipate or to quell, by tunes, colours, and speeches, long devoted to popular execration.

Mr. Crawley dismissed himself and his legion together; his clerk took his place at the window, and he retired to finish the duties of the toilette, which his military avocations had interrupted. Not so Miss Crawley: she indeed had retired, but retired only to return to her viranda with a green watering-pot and a sort of shepherdess's hat, added to the quaker-like simplicity of her dress. Her quick eye had lighted upon the Commodore, who stood mingled but not / confounded with the plebeian crowd; and she now returned, under the plea of watering her geraniums, to follow up her reconnoitre,[27] with a tactical skill, better understood and practised than Lord Rosbrin's system by the New-Town Mount Crawley legion. Meantime, the Commodore, unconsciously 'biding the keen encounter of the eye,'[28] walked towards the portico, and demanded of a servant, who stood lounging at the door, if Mr. Crawley was at home. The servant said he would 'try;' and, after the delay of a few minutes, returned, not with a direct answer to the inquiry, but with, 'If you please to step in for a minute, I'll try if my master's at home, Sir. What name, Sir, shall I say?'

'My name is of no consequence: meerly say a gentleman, a stranger, requests the pleasure of seeing Mr. Crawley.'

'I shall Sir. Walk this way if you please, Sir.' /

The unknown visitor followed the liveried cicerone through two spacious and splendidly furnished rooms, where the windows, closely blinded, and the hearth closely skreened, accounted for the chill and fusty atmosphere which pervaded them, and spoke the truth, that fresh air and good fires were rarely admitted into rooms kept exclusively for shew, and occupied but three or four times in the year for purposes of display.[b] Two slovenly housemaids were uncovering the furniture of the drawing room; the butler was occupied in laying out a gorgeous sideboard of plate in the dining parlor; and the arrangements every where spoke preparations for a formal country dinner party, the epitome of all tedium, ennui, and competition.

In that official class of life in Ireland to which Mr. Crawley belonged, the acquisition of fortune, unpurchased by honest, prosperous industry, but accumulated by servile arts, political delin-/quency, and fraudulent intrigue, is usually too rapid to admit of a gradual acquaintance with every-day comforts, found equally among the first and middling classes of society. A place under government, suddenly obtained, uniting wealth to influence, strikes the roots of ostentation deep, before the want of comfort and accommodation is felt by those whose original position was destitute of both. In such establishments penury combines with display, discomfort with expense; and while a competition is excited with those, to whom splendor is an inheritance and a habit, the less obvious, but more enjoyable elegances of life, are wanting and neglected. Of this, the cold, fine, formal apartments of Mount Crawley, like the habits of life of its occupants, were striking proofs.

This suite, intended to be imposing, terminated in a little room, into which the footman ushered the Commodore, and / then went out by an opposite door. Though close, unaired, and slovenly, this apartment had an air of pretension about it, that marked it out the retreat of some slip-shod muse.[29] Soiled muslin draperies, vases of dead flowers, offensive to the sense they were meant to gratify, an unfinished drawing on an easel; of New-Town Mount Crawley, with Dulce Domum[30] written under it, together with much literary lumber, and traces of vulgar sentimentality in every direction, would have decided at once the vocation of its proprietor, if pious books, strewed upon the tables, and evangelical tracts covering the sophas, did not indicate another calling than that of the muse; for though here and there appeared much of the Sappho,[31] there was also much of the saint.[c] Piles of bibles, filling every corner, indicated that this coquettish boudoir, and holy oratory, belonged to one of those persons who give books where they should give bread, / and lavish dogmas and credenda to those who want the means of existence. The Commodore, in the impatience and ennui of idle waiting, took up one book after another. For though all were not sectarian and polemical, yet none were to his taste. This Olla Podrida[32] of sacred and profane literature consisted of namby-pamby verses, and religious calls;[33] sentimental letters and methodist tracts; short cuts to learning of every description; summary views and meagre abridgements, elegant extracts, 'Alphabetical Citations,' rhyming, biographical, geographical, scriptural, historical and astronomical dictionaries of every calibre. Here 'Philosophy, for the Use of the Ladies,' lay with 'the true Religion of a Gentlewoman;' 'the Wanderings of a Water Wagtail in the sixteenth century' with 'Sermonettinos or religious Bagatelles;' 'Shreds of Fancy, or literary Patchwork;' with 'an Alarm to the Unconverted;' 'Delicate Crimes, / or sin, sorrow, and sensibility,' a religious novel, with 'a Call to the unrepenting, or Milk for Babes, and strong Meat for Men;' a duodecimo 'Beauties of all the Poets, or Pocket Inspiration,' with 'the History of a Child who knew not the Lord before her fifth year, and who died converted to the true faith at seven.'[34] Controversial tracts upon all the new lights lay mingled with quarterly, monthly, and evangelical reviews, 'Elegant Extracts for the Flageolet,' 'Hints for the Tambourine and Triangle,' 'A Method for tuning the Harp without an ear,' 'Mnemonic Systems for learning Languages without study, and a mode of playing three Piano-fortes at once with two hands.'[35] 'This catalogue raisonée, or rather *dé raisonée*,[36] might be taken as epitomizing the perversion of human intellect, and as evincing the successful circulation of the folly, hypocrisy, and imposition of the day, no less than the shallowness, bad taste, / and pretension, of the presiding mistress of this sanctum sanctorum.[37]

The Commodore had just taken up, and was about to throw down, in its turn, an historical work for youth, in the title-page of which appeared 'Stories of the history of England, by Conway Townsend Crawley, Esq. Barrister-at-law, dedicated to her who 'taught his young idea how to shoot,'[38] to Anne Clotworthy Crawley, by her nephew:' but finding that this history of England omitted the trifling events of the Magna Charta and the revolution, as jacobinical,[39] and tending to teach the young idea how to shoot in a direction unfavourable to the orthodox dictation of the day, the circumstance amused him, and he sat down to glance his eye over its pages. They contained an abridgement of doctrines which he was yet ignorant had been broached in Great Britain, under the special protection of the constituted authorities (doctrines, which, if accredit-/ed, defeat the claims of the reigning family to the throne, and place its august members on a line with the mushroom kings of the by-gone day). He was thus occupied when the door opened, and entered, not as he expected, Mr. Crawley, but Mr. Crawley's sister, with her chapeau de bergere[40] in one hand, her watering pot in the other, a marked primitiveness in her dress, and a mincing, languid, affected air in her gate and address: she commenced with a little start of surprise, at finding her boudoir so occupied, then approached full of smiles, graces, and graciousness, or what she meant to be such: she begged the gentleman to be seated, let down the muslin blinds, to exclude, as she said, the too propitious kindness of Sol;[41] and then took her seat near the sopha she had pointed out to the stranger. Whatever impression his manly and distinguished figure had made upon Miss Crawley, as he was seen leaning over the paddock / gate, that impression was now improved into boundless and enthusiastic admiration, by the singularity of his fine countenance, the extreme ease of his address, that disengaged air, which the world only gives; and, above all, by a bow, whose foreign grace she placed at once to the account of supreme English bon ton.[42] It was Miss Crawley who had received the Commodore's message, who had told the footman that she would receive him, until her brother was at leisure to attend to his summons; and who now believed that she was doing the honours to some man of rank, bearing letters of introduction from the Marchioness of Dunore, or from some other person of distinction; whom, by her laborious exertion, she had placed on the list of those she called 'her kind great friends.' Such events occasionally happened; for the beautiful tract of Dunore, like that of Glengariff,[43] frequently tempts the visitors of Killarney / to go some miles out of their way, and to take the coast road, in order to view its romantic scenery en passant.[44 d]

Miss Crawley now opened the conversation, after a few side-long looks, and serpentine motions, with apologizing for her brother's absence, enumerating the variety of his official, political, and professional engagements, stating the coincidence of the assizes, and the Glannacrime election, as an additional cause for the hurry of business; and episodically introducing sketches of the family importance in general; her second brother being a sergeant-at-law;[45] her third a first commissioner; her eldest nephew being that year sheriff of the county; her next a major in the army, a peninsula hero, covered with orders;[46] and the amiable cadet,[47] she added, 'the Magnus Apollo[48] of the age and country, was a young barrister of great poetical, political, and diplomatic promise, her éléve,[49] / and, as the poet said, darling without end.'[50] Encouraged by the silent attention, and occasional inclination of the Commodore's head, Miss Crawley added to this information some slight notices of herself; and in apologizing for what she called '*the literary litter*' of her boudoir, she referred to habits, that had become second nature, and that required an almost regenerated spirit to be broken, a light, to make darkness visible, a superhuman intervention; she sighed, and then threw up her eyes, and then added with an air, half primitive, half dramatic,

'It was my good fortune, or should I not rather say my ill fortune, early in life to be distinguished by the celebrated Lady Clotworthy, of Bath, whose prize poems –'

Here the Commodore involuntarily took up his hat, and Miss Crawley suspecting that she was bestowing more of 'her tediousness' on him than might / suit with his previous arrangements, observed,

'I have obtruded this family sketch upon you, in the expectation of presenting you to the originals; for we hold a family congress here to-day; and whether your visit to Dunore be a pilgrimage of taste, or of mere amusement, my brother will be happy to do the honours of these romantic scenes in the absence of their lord, whom he represents.'

'My visit, madam, has not been destitute of the gratifications of taste; but it is not a pilgrimage made merely in pursuit of amusement; business of a more serious nature.'

The word 'serious'[51] fell like an electric spark upon the imagination of Miss Crawley; and the first self-created vision she had conjured up vanished before another of equal interest and importance; for she was now led to believe, that herself, and not her brother, was the object of this visit; that what she / had taken for temporal distinction, was 'the beauty of holiness,'[52] and that she saw before her, not, as she had supposed, a mere idle elegant English man of fashion, 'prominant ses ennuis,'[53] in the wilds of Munster,[e] but one of an higher calling, who might unite worldly elevation to that which is above the world's giving or taking away: some male Huntingdon, some imitative Wilberforce,[54] whom the odour of her new fangled sanctity had allured to the scenery of Dunore.[f]

Miss Crawley was of that undefined age which is occasionally found to vibrate between the folly and susceptibility of youth, and the despondence and experience of disappointed senility: that drowning age in which female celibacy catches at every straw held out by hope, or offered by vanity, and which, with the illusive chemistry of self-love, converts every circumstance of the day's ordinary routine into the / chance of that change so devoutly wished. She had long sighed for a fellow labourer in that cause, which, like all other causes tinctured with human leaven, is best carried on with the auxiliary of rank, fortune, or personal advantage.*[55] The object might now stand before her, her hour might have arrived, and the sudden hopes kindled by this visit (hopes always on the *qui vive*)[56], for a moment stunned and deprived her of her wonted, elegant, graceful, picturesque presence of mind. The half conscious gaze, which, (while all these deep but rapid ruminations crossed her mind), she fixed upon the Commodore's

---

*   'A saint in crape is twice a saint in lawn.'

face, crimsoned that face almost to the brow; Miss Crawley saw and caught the soft infection; it called a faint blush to her pale and sallow cheek: then inhaling the odour of the offensive flowers, that withered in a tawdry vase / on the table,[g] she repeated his words in a certain soft solemnity of voice: –

'A more serious nature! may I add my ardent wishes to my sanguine hopes, that whatever may be the purport of your visit here, success the most perfect may attend it.'

The Commodore bowed low, and even in some little confusion, but looked to the door for the momentarily expected entrance of Mr. Crawley:

'You may, perhaps, have known,' said Miss Crawley, 'the late celebrated Zachariah Scare'um, of pious memory.'

'I have heard of him,' replied the Commodore, with the conversion of the mysterious Mrs. Magillicuddy full in his memory, and again taking his hat.

'You have heard of him,' said Miss Crawley, 'of course: disciples of every sect have heard of him, though all do not agree with him. His gladiatorial wrestle with many of the ramifying and heterodox divergencies of the only true and infallible light has / gained him a worldly distinction, he craves not; his sturdy and zealous opposition to the Sublapsarians, the Baxterians, Necessarians, Antinomians, Sabalarians, Swedenbourgians, Independents, Universalists, Destructionists, Hutchinsonians, Millenarians, Shakers, Jumpers, Dunkers, Fifth-Monarchy men, and Muggletonions –'[57]

Here Miss Crawley's breath and the Commodore's patience failed together. She paused for inspiration, and he rose to interrupt this tirade of sectarian pedantry, by demanding if he had any chance of seeing Mr. Crawley that morning. With a look vibrating between doubt and disappointment, Miss Crawley rose and rang the bell; but to her inquiries for her brother, the answer, as she expected, was, that he had driven out in his curricle[58] to Glannacrime, and would not return till dinner.

'This is unfortunate,' said the Commodore; 'for I am obliged to leave Dunore early to-morrow morning.' /

Miss Crawley grew pale with disappointment. As saint or sinner, as a traveller of rank or a missionary of distinction, the stranger had equally obtained the most favourable prepossessions. There was a romantic cast in his countenance, an air of elevation diffused over his whole person, which answered to all her sentimental ideas of heroic beauty. There was also a mingled gravity and ardor in his look, which belong to the zealous in the true cause; and whatever led him to Mount Crawley, whatever his class or calling might be, Miss Crawley was certain that of that class or calling *he was at the head.*[h] Such guests were not always to be had in the country, such persons were rare every where; and to prevent the chance of this desirable acquisition escaping from the list of her 'kind great friends,' she politely and warmly pressed on him an invitation to dinner for that day: for presiding in her brother's house, who was a / widower, her privileges and immunities were unlimited; and she now pressed her invitation with the air of one who had a right to give it, and the ardor of one who had an interest in its being accepted.

This conviction at once struck on the apprehension of her quick-sighted guest, and uniting with the exigencies of his own situation and business, it at once decided him in yielding to solicitations, which, coming from a woman, even such a woman, he was not, perhaps, of a character to reject. With that peculiar frankness, which characterized his manners, after the pause and hesitation of a moment, he said,

'Well, Madam, I shall avail myself of your polite invitation. The few words I have to say to Mr. Crawley can be despatched over our coffee, and time, precious to both, may thus be spared.'

He now took his leave, and the bow / with which he departed finished the impression his first appearance had made. He had been gone near twenty minutes, and Miss Crawley still remained lounging on the sopha, in the attitude of one absorbed in a pleasant reverie; when suddenly recollecting she had neither asked the name or address of the person she had invited, and that he had not himself volunteered it, she rose and rung the bell to make some inquiries among the servants, when the arrival of two barouches and four,[59] with out-riders, called off for the present her attention. These handsome and shewy equipages contained nearly the whole of the family congress alluded to by Miss Crawley. The one contained Serjeant and Mrs. Crawley and their four daughters; and the other Mr. and Mrs. Commissioner Crawley, with a pretty daughter of the latter by a former marriage. The first were on their way to Killarney, and stopped by / special invitation for a few days at Mr. Crawley's. The latter had come to take possession of an estate purchased for him by his eldest brother, the attorney, in the neighbourhood of Dunore; whence they were to proceed on a visit to the bishop of the diocese.

If ever there was a period in the history of a country when it might be said, that

'Crime gave wealth, and wealth gave impudence,'[60]

it was that period in the history of Ireland, when rebellion, excited for the purpose of effecting a ruinous union, called forth all the worst passions of humanity, and armed petty power with the rod of extermination;[61] placing torture at the disposal of personal vindictiveness, and making falsehood, treachery, and corruption, the stepping-stones to power, office, and emolument.[i]

The wealth, influence, and importance of the Crawley family took their / date from that memorable and frightful epoch in the tragedy of Irish history, which produced both moral and political ruin to a long-devoted country, under every form of degradation; of which civilized society is susceptible. Previous to that period the three brothers had remained buried in the obscurity which belonged to their social and intellectual mediocrity. The eldest, Darby Crawley, the country attorney, found his highest dignity in being the factotum of the two Barons Fitzadelm, the agent of their embarrassed property, on which he lent them money saved by his father in their service, until the little that remained of the estate fell into his hands. Through the interest of his employer he had been put into the commission of the peace. The year 1798 found him a magistrate, and fortune and his *merits* had done the rest.

The second brother, whose gravity was mistaken for ability by his father, / (the illiterate land-bailiff of the Fitzadelms) was made a gentleman by the patent of a college education, and the legal degree of barrister-at-law. He had plied in the courts with an empty green bag,[62] and more empty head, year after year, with fruitless vigilance, till his energy in the melancholy prosecutions, produced by the rebellion, obtained him notice, patronage, place, and a silk gown.[63]

The third brother, at once pompous and officious, servile and oppressive, formed alike to tyrannize or cringe, had been placed a clerk in a government office; where, by his pliancy and industry, he made himself useful to a personage of shallow endowment and official importance, whose political views and flimsy attainments rendered agents thus qualified necessary to his purposes. The dull but zealous commissioner, who could not be daunted, because he could not feel, was deemed / a proper person to represent a government borough in the Union parliament;[64] and having effected 'this most filthy bargain,'[65] was rewarded with the place of first commissioner of a particular board, one of those boards instituted and perpetuated for the purpose of paying such debts to such creditors as the members of the Crawley family.

Mr. Commissioner, like his elder brothers, characteristically represented the BUREAUCRATIE, or office tyranny,[66] by which Ireland has been so long governed; whose members, arrogating to themselves exclusively the virtue of loyalty, and boldly assuming its insignia and device, have become formidable and oppressive to all who thwart their career, question their title to this unfounded assumption, or insinuate that their loyalty lies more in their places than their principles. The basis of fortunes being thus broadly laid, industry and zeal were not wanting to these *wise / men of Gotham*,[67] for raising the superstructure to the imposing elevation which it now exhibited.[j] The elder brother, Darby, was inferior in acquirements and destitute of that education which his father's increasing prosperity had enabled him to bestow upon his younger sons; his success, however, was equal to their's, and his places and avocations were still more numerous. He had been a crown-solicitor,[68] at a moment when that place was the most inordinately lucrative: he was treasurer of a county; and he united to these trust-worthy situations those three capacities, whose unity is named in the country parts of Ireland, 'the tripple tyranny of the land:' he was agent to an absentee nobleman, an active magistrate, and captain of a yeomanry corps.

As agent, he kept off the landlord by misrepresentations of the political and local state of the country, and worried the tenants, by obliging them to labour / for his own personal benefit. They drew his turf, mowed his meadows, fenced his fields, thatched his out-houses, grazed his hunters, and contributed their poultry to his table: for, in the absence of their natural protectors, they felt themselves thrown for favours and redress upon the mercy of one, whose indulgencies and whose justice could alone be purchased by such bribes.

As a magistrate, and the representative of his employer, he got up grand juries, domineered at the sessions, corresponded with the state secretaries, became an organ of intelligence to the great officers of the Irish government, and obtained the name of the most loyal man in his county.

As captain of yeomanry, he clubbed his own tenants, and labourers of the dominant persuasion, made his returns full to the government, distributed the money ad libitum,[69] pocketed the surplus, kept the neighbourhood in terror, / and apprehended, and committed to prison, whom he pleased, with more regard to prejudice and private feeling than to justice, or the public peace; for he was a man of constitutional timidity, and believing himself an object of popular execration, he acted as if he was its victim.

Though in his magnificent house in Dublin, and his seat at Mount Crawley, he received and entertained persons of the first distinction, the society he frequented, the circle in which he moved, had produced no influence on his mind or manners. The stubborn, intractable, incorrigible vulgarity which distinguished both, was accompanied by a sort of low native humour, which gave a peculiar expression to his shrewd leering eye, and screwed up puckered mouth. But though all refinement, all mental illumination were placed beyond his possibility of acquirement, he had still that species of natural sagacity, that / subtilty of littleness, which, operating like instinct in small circles, attains to a precision proportionate to its circumscription; and which has been so well styled by Bacon, 'left-handed wisdom'[70] – he possessed, too, a certain cheerfulness of temperament, a constitutional hilarity, which hid out the darker qualities of his character, and rendered even the contempt he inspired free from the asperity of fixed aversion.[l] The laughter he excited blinded many to the injuries he had committed; his blunders and humour kept his designs out of sight; and his ridicules were so prominent, and stood so broadly on the surface, that if they did not conceal his vices, they gave even to his arts the air of simplicity.

At the period when the genius and worth of Ireland, combining with all that remained of public spirit, stood forward in the cause of its independence,*[71] /

---

*   In the year 1782.

when the Irish parliament, and the Irish law courts, shone with a splendour, soon eclipsed, but never surpassed; it was the fashion of the ruling party to turn loose upon the scene of legal or senatorial action some ruffianly humourist, to pick from the herd of briefless barristers some professional buffoon, whose vulgarity might over-bear, and whose unfeeling impudence might elude the wit and the argument it could neither vanquish nor refute. Low humour, coarseness that passed the bounds of decency, blunders that bordered on fatuity, sometimes the genuine products of intellectual confusion, more commonly the results of a long-sighted affectation, whatever, in short, could divert public attention from public interests, replace gravity by laughter, stamp talent with opprobrium, and mark patriotism for proscription,[k] was then put in requisition,[l] along with the many other debasing schemes, for vitiating public taste, cor-/rupting principles, blunting feelings, and subduing the spirit of a regenerating and awakening people.

In this school, and at this period, Darby Crawley, then a clerk in an attorney's office, had studied deeply. He estimated every thing by its success. Genius and patriotism, or, according to his own accentuation, *ganius* and *pathretism,* with him meant *folly* and *disloyalty.* But while his experience taught him the danger of possessing the one, or of cherishing the other, he had an high and reverential approbation for *purchased* acquirements, for that education which wealth can obtain. Education had made gentlemen of his brothers; education had made a fine lady of his sister; education had made his sons wiser than their father; and *want* of education had left himself upon the last degree of the family scale whom nature had allotted to the first. To supply his early deficiencies, he became therefore a close / copyist of the sentimental jargon and foreign slip slop[72] of his sister; and even attempted the fluent verbosity and college pedantry of his youngest and most admired son. But the double treachery of a bad memory and a false ear plunged him into inaccuracies and mistakes, which the reprehension of those two leading members of his family was in vain applied to correct.

It was, however, curious to observe his natural sagacity, and the intuitive ability of his low, creeping, sordid, self-interest occasionally assuming their superiority over the flimsy attainments of his brothers and children; whose accomplishments he was wont to admire, and who, in return, while they reverenced his success in life, and availed themselves of its advantage, blushed, and looked down on the ignorance and vulgarity by which it was accompanied.

A wet evening in the country, during the long vacation,[73] would frequently / afford him an opportunity of displaying his intuitive views of advancement in life, for the benefit of those who stood indebted to education alone for their distinctions. Then, released from the necessity of representation, and indulging to its full extent his natural vulgarity, seated over what he called his 'sup of hot,' or a tumbler of punch, he might truly be said to be in his element. Then, surrounded by his family, his sister presiding at the tea-table, his three sons lounging in different parts of the room, his intellect quickened by his potations, his feelings softened into maudlin tenderness, his eyes half closed, his punch half drank, his hands half clasped, and his thumbs in twirling motion, giving loose alike to prospect and to retrospect, thinking over what his family had been, and what they might still be,[m] he would begin his customary exhortations to his sons. These domestic lectures usually commenced with / drinking their health to call their attention; then reproving, then advising, and at last becoming pathetic as he grew fuddled, he usually concluded with his own death and the family ruin, which must ensue if his advice was neglected and forgotten. – 'Tim, Con, Thady, your healths; Anne Clotworthy, my sarvice to you: well then, Clotty dear, will never you send away that *water bewitched?* It's little the tay ever your mother drank at your age, though she got to be the taydrinkingist sowl in the barony before she died, poor woman. Why then, Tim, dear, have you nothing to do but to lie stretched on the broad of your back along my new hair-bottoms,[74] with your arm dangling down, and surprising them innocent animals of flies on the carpet that's strewn with their corpses: upon my word, Tim, it would be fitter for you to be raiding the '*Hints for a Magistrate,*' or '*Mach Nally's Justice of Pace*;'[75] you that will be in the / commission, and high sheriff of the county, by promise since the Union. I wonder, Tim, but you'd send them game to the bishop you brought home last night, instead of giving them to your crony, the surveyor; – and the bishop, brother to a minister! and he that likes a bit of grouse above the world. There is nothing better bestowed than that which we give to them that want nothing; mind my words, Tim. Why then, captain, I wish you'd quit with your rattan[76] against my iligant Northumberland table,[77] and get off it intirely. What use is the chairs but to sit on; and if you had gone, as I bid you, to make your compliments to the general of the district the day, you wouldn't be playing your devil's tattoo and spoiling my Northumberland. I've often told you the general might make a man of you with the Duke of York: is it by whistling and rapping my stick against the table for / the length of a wet evening that *I* got on in the world? No; but night and day, wet or dry, summer or winter, watching the main chance, Thady; and when I hadn't as much as 'cuddy would you taste,'[78] for myself, I had still always a bit of a *dewshure*[79] for the great, a Wicklow pebble, or a lump of Irish diamond, or an hundred of Puldoody oysters, or a cask of Waterford sprats, or some sort of a pretty *bougie*[80] for my friends.'

'Bijou,' interrupted Miss Crawley.

'Well, bijou then; but *apropos* de *bot,*[81] Thady, in regard of your flopping fat Miss O'Flaherty of Dunore on your fine mare, and riding her round the country, when you couldn't plaze the gineral's lady more than giving her that very mare, which only just lies here doing nothing at all but ating my hay and corn, while you are with you regiment eleven months in the year; for the great likes a present, every man jack of / them; and fat Miss O'Flaherty's a papist, and was a marked man in the rebellion, that's her father; and her brother this day in America: and is it by lending a mare to fat Miss O'Flaherty I got your ensigncy from the secatary of war, and made a captain of you, over the heads of them might be your father? No, faith, it was the Puldoodies that did it, and being a good friend to government through thick and thin. What is it you're writing there in them short lines, Conway Townsend? Is it rhymes? Why then, I wish you'd lave off with your *poethry* and your *ganius:* mind my words, Con, dear, your ganius will play you a dirty trick yet; for sorrow good *ganius* ever did for man or baste. What was it brought the country into jeopardy, and *bull-veasied*[82] the governin the year 82? – Why, ganius. What was it that set the world wild with the Irish volunteers, the free trade, and the catholic bill,[83] and counsellor Curran,[84] / and ould Lord Charlemont, with his statues, and his pictures, and his popularity;[85] and Mr. Grattan, and his *people,* and Irish eloquence,[86] and the Irish aristocracy; – why, wasn't it *ganius?* Och! Sir, times is changed since then, since a man should talk eloquence and pathretism, and all that Gally-my-jaw,[87] as the French call it, to get on in the world.'

'Galimathias,' lisped Miss Crawley.

'Well, Gally-matchaw, then, – and not all as one as *now,* Con, when a man has only to follow his nose, and walk into place or pension, just by sticking to the main-chance. Och, Sir, the Irish bar (1) is another thing since them days. Tell me, Con, dear, is it *independence* will get you a silk gown? Will *genius* make you first counsel to the commissioners, with your eight thousand a-year for doing nothing at all at all? Will it make you a *deputy remembrancer,*[88] with your nate four thousand, which is the *true* remembrancer. Or would / ganius, poethry, and pathretism, with the aristocracy at their head (that is barring the Union lords), get you at this moment to be one of the *thirty-one* county sessions chairmen, all made since the year eighty-nine, for the encouragement of the rising young barristers; or even a magistrate of police, or a seneschal of the Dublin liberties,[89] or a missionary to explore disturbed districts! Troth and faith, they wouldn't. And could do more this day myself for you than the whole boiling[90] of them, in respect to pushing you up the stick, Con, at the bar; that's if you'll lave off bothering us with your poethry. For see here, the thing's as plain as *pais* (peas). – Sure, there's spectacles for all ages, as well as wigs and gowns. Thanks to him that served the country well when he was in it, and does to this day, for all he butters them up with the Catholic question, and votes, with his tongue in his cheek, with the opposition, about it; and it's only for / him the Crawleys wouldn't be where they are the day. And there's a little bone-bush[91] in store for you all round, if you will just be aisy and mind your hits, and drive on the ball when it comes to you, and be ready for your turn. For there is two hundred of yez, great and small, ould and young, walking the hall, with your wigs and your bags, and there is three hundred places to divide among yez – make money of that, Con; and not one of you but may be a loyal man, and an enfant trouvé[92] of government, as the French say, if he plazes.'

'Enfant cheri,' interrupted Miss Crawley.

'Well, enfant cherry, if yez will just mind your P's and Q's;[93] and so now you know the ways of the place; there's neither twining nor turning, but straight forward. So let's have no more of your rhymes and your ganius, and your satirical perigrams, Counsellor Con.' /

'Epigrams, my dear Darby.'

'Well, *epigrams,* then; but –'

'Can't you mind what I *think,* and *not what I say;* for you're not beholden to them, Con, with your college education, and your speaking French like a Nabob.[94] Now, just ask yourself, is the chief baron a ganius? or the counsel to the commissioners a ganius? Or was it poethry made a serjeant of your uncle? – No; but wigging*[95] all the chancellors that ever were created, and offering to kick a Catholic barrister, which he didn't after all, for a raison he had; – but the will, Sir, was taken for the deed. So come to your tay, Con, and be aisy with your poethry. Well boys, dear, I'll see the day yet, when I'm dead and buried, God help me, and in my new *moleseum* in Dunore church, when my words will come to pass, and you will be thinking of your / ould father Darby Crawley, when some of yez may have titles, which, if ever there comes about another rebellion, as I expect there will, plaze God, – but that's neither here nor there, – only, just as I was saying, when I am dead and buried, and[n] Clotty there places an epithet[96] over me, from his affectionate sister, and the pew hung with black, like the Dunores, I'll see my words come to pass, and you'll remember your poor father, that worked night and day to make gentlemen and loyal men of you; for we must all die, boys, honey, great as we are. *Momenti mori,*[97] as the tomb-stone says, and the yeomanry corps fire over us, the Lord help us! for dirt we are, and to dirt we must return;[98] the Crawleys like the rest.'

As this compound idea of death and supremacy rounded off the admonitory peroration of Mr. Crawley, snuff and punch had usually wound up his whining sensibility to its utmost excitement, and / the tears which he shed for his own death were commonly followed by that profound sleep which images it.

On the three hopeful disciples of this worldly doctrine, though its letter made but little impression, its spirit sunk deep; and the characters of the three younger Messrs. Crawley, were but modifications in various degrees, and proportions, of those qualities, which combined in those of the three elders. Timothy Harcourt,

---

* Ear-wigging, *i. e.* whispering.

the high sheriff, the true representative of that class, contemptuously designated by the peasantry 'the Squiranty,' was dull, over-bearing, vulgar, and profligate; at the head of a party association in the country, gambling deeply at the clubs in Dublin, he every where assumed airs of importance on the strength of the family relations with the government, and affected a fashionable libertinism in his morals, with a violent outcry in favour of *church and state*. Still, however, he preferred a cock-fight at Dunore, or a ca-/rousal at the Dunore Arms with his friends, the port surveyor,[99] and the subsheriff, to the higher class of society, which he occasionally commanded, but never enjoyed. The lower classes, whom he oppressed, hated him to abhorrence; the middle classes in the country feared and avoided him; and the higher circles won his money, and admitted him to their drinking parties, where his intemperance passed for joviality, and his vulgarity for humour.

Major Thadeus Windham Crawley, (for it is the fashion among the Crawley class in Ireland to tack the names of viceroys and secretaries to their baptismal appellations)[100] called himself a dasher;[101] and was a fair illustration of that term, as applied in Ireland. He was handsome, good-humoured, vulgar, and self-sufficient. He had seen a little service in America, a good deal in the peninsula;[102] and though his residence in other countries had cleared away many / of his local prejudices and littlenesses, it had added little to the stock of his original ideas, and took nothing from the purity of his original brogue. His phrases were all broadly idiomatical; his conversation enriched with regimental technicalities and Irish slang; and when he had talked of BIVOUACKING and WIGWAMS, of making the *ould one* come *down with the pipeclay*,[103] sung *'I am the man for the leedies,'*[104] and described the prince RAGENT's levee, (commencing every phrase with 'I'll give you my honor),' he had gone through the whole *menage*[105] of his intellectual capabilities. The rest of his existence was made up with whistling, humming, drawing up his cravat, to make a sensation on the appearance of a stranger, reading the army-list, and beating his rattan against his father's Northumberland table.

The character of the barrister, Conway Townsend Crawley,[106] the Magnus / Apollo of his aunt, and usually called Counsellor Con, by his father, seemed to have its foundation more particularly in temperament, and to be of a more definite and distinct class, as well as of a plus haute volée,[107] than his brothers. It was obvious that both its merits and its defects originated in physical infirmity beyond his control. Called by his father his posthumous son, because his mother died in giving him life, his inauspicious birth seemed to have entailed upon him a bilious saturnine constitution. Even his talent, if talent it might be called, was but the result of disease. No 'overflowing of the pancreatic juices'[108] had influenced the system of Conway Crawley, even in that age when the blood is balm. The dark bile, which from childhood sallowed his cheek, dimm'd his eye, and tinged the spirits of youth with the causticity of age, continued, through adolescence and manhood, to communicate its bitterness / to all his views; turning his words to sarcasm, his ink to gall, and his pen to a stiletto; and combining with an education, whose object was pretension, and whose principle was arrogance, it made him at once a thing fearful and pitiable, at war with its species and itself, ready to crush on the verge of the tomb, as to sting in the cradle, and leading his overweening ambition to pursue its object by ways, dark and hidden, safe from the penalty of crime, and exposed only to the obloquy which he laughed to scorn; for opinion has no punishment for the base.

If ever there was a man formed alike by nature and education to betray the land that gave him birth, and to act openly as the pander of political corruption, or secretly as the agent of defamation, who would stoop to seek his fortune by effecting the fall of a frail woman, or would strive to advance it by stabbing the character of an honest one, / who would crush aspiring merit behind the ambuscade of anonymous security, while he came forward openly in the defence of that vileness which rank sanctified and influence protected, that man was Conway Crawley. He was yet young; but belonging to the day and the country in which he first raised his hiss, and shed his venom, success already beckoned him, through the distant vista, towards her, with a smile of encouragement and a leer of contempt. Prompt, pert, and shameless, he had already, both at the bar and in society, evinced a well-managed talent for display and for evasion, a fluency that bore down where it could not convince, and an insolence which humility could not soften, nor power brow-beat. Lampoons, which he solemnly denied, had been brought home to him, and obtained a sort of local notoriety, while they evinced talents which were to pave their way to distinctions more solid, by means / more ingeniously despicable than he had as yet been called on to exercise. While in every pursuit

'*wisely shunning* the broad way and the green,'[109] his paths were paths of darkness; and had he been found guilty of one good, one generous action, he would 'have blushed to find it fame.'[110] It was by another species of reputation that the gates of promotion and wealth were to be opened to the ambition of Conway Townsend Crawley.

He was now going the Munster circuit,[111] and took his father's house in his way between two assize towns. He did, however, but little in his profession, notwithstanding that his father had procured him several crown prosecutions, and had made him counsel to two boards. His views were higher than thus creeping through professional places, offices, and sinecures, such as are now reserved for the Irish bar. He was deeply interested in the Glanna-/crime election, and was law-agent for the absent candidate, Lord Adelm Fitzadelm, whom he had never seen, but whose character he particularly disliked. To his mother, the dowager marchioness, he was personally known; and to her, while at the Temple, he had paid most obsequious attention. His fluency, his light literature, poetical scraps, and critical discussions, had passed upon this capricious and powerful woman of fashion for talent, wit, and erudition: for pretension in this, as in every other instance, succeeded when it amalgamated with all the well-whipped froth of courtly sense.

At the head of the females of the Crawley genius,° with all the characteristics of the family, stood Miss Anne Clotworthy Crawley; *Anne,* after her humble mother, Nancy Malone, a broguemaker's daughter of Doneraile; and Clotworthy, from a certain Lady Clotworthy, who distributed poetical prizes / at Bath, and to whom Miss Crawley had rendered herself dulcis et utilis[112] during a six months' residence in that city; when, at a late period in life for such purposes, she had gone to finish her education. Her first simple name she had received at her christening, in the steward's room at Court Fitzadelm, forty-five years back; the second she had adopted at her confirmation at Bath twenty years after. This mature renaming she called her 'sentimental regeneration;' and she heard with horror a name so distinguished, so dear to the Muses, at least to the Bath muses, as Clotworthy, curtailed by the fraternal familiarity of her brother Darby into the endearing, but ill-sounding diminutive, of *Clotty.* Against this abbreviation Miss Crawley had vainly remonstrated: it had seized both the imagination and the affections of her brother; and with this good-humoured, but choleric relation, she dared only to go cer-/tain lengths. Placed at the head of his sumptuous establishment, her alternative was living in a boarding-house, on a legacy left by Lady Clotworthy; for as a resident in the house of her brother, the serjeant, or in that of the commissioner, her two sisters-in-law had shut the door against her. To live with the great, to be noticed by the great, to influence and render herself necessary to the great, was the ambition and object of Miss Crawley's existence. For this purpose she took the only paths open to her, pretension and flattery; pretension arising out of a few flimsy, shallow, common-place acquirements, the produce of every vulgar boarding-school, – and flattery, as consonant to the groveling time-serving spirit of her family, and to the smooth, silky, insinuating, serpentizing temper of her own character. At once feeble and vain, deficient and ambitious, her original endowments were below mediocrity, and / her stock of literary and sentimental ideas, like the contents of her boudoir and library, was made up of scraps and fragments: her étalage de sensibilierie[113] was gleaned from a class of sentimental novels, now gone by, whose heroines

'Died of a rose in aromatic pain,'[114] p

her critical judgments were borrowed from reviews, journals, and the oft-copied opinions of orthodox authority; and her musical talents, on which she piqued herself, consisted of a few got-up songs, sung in such tune as it pleased heaven, in two airs on the harp, one on the Spanish guitar, and four waltzes, with one bass on the piano-forte. To these higher endowments she united other little 'useful uselessnesses,' which enabled her to supply the wants of her great friends, which she herself first created. Cloth fruit and filligree baskets, daubed velvet and paper card-racks,[115] French mottoes and English devices, / with all the industrious arts which bad taste supplies to unoccupied mediocrity, were devoted to the drawing-rooms and boudoirs of the great and shallow persons who admitted her as their inmate. With that cunning which invariably belongs to intellectual inferiority, she rapidly obtained the secret of a dominant weakness or a master-passion; and she administered to both with an address worthy of higher views and better objects. She had little valueless appropriate offerings for every one: and from an evangelical tract, or a society bible, down to sugar sweetmeats or paper dolls, her adroitness administered, (and cheaply administered) to the passions, prejudices, and infirmities of all ages, characters, and classes. There were instances, however, where even flattery failed; and there Miss Crawley sought the *dernier resort*[116] of bold, pushing, presumptuous intrusion, which no delicacy checked, no pride restrained. Many a / coronetted dame has felt the pressure of Miss Crawley's arm on her's in public, with the half-stifled swell of provoked indignation; mortified at her own good-natured weakness, which could not resist the impudent request of protection made in the whining tone of humble supplication.

With all this Miss Crawley *got on;* and though admired but by few, laughed at by many, and progressively found out by all, she contrived to obtain a place in society which modest genius could scarcely hope for, and proud independence would scornfully reject. Her success, like that of her nephews, was the triumph of pretension; it belonged to the day, and the circle, and the family in which she lived.

During the first thirty-five years of Miss Crawley's life, she had professed herself devoted to friendship and the muse; but she by no means suited the action to the word. Other altars than / those of Minerva[117] had received her adoration, and she had long coquetted from the bench in her brother, the attorney's office, to the bench of the Common Pleas, and Exchequer,[118] until a platonic engagement and sentimental correspondence, with a certain Counsellor O'Rafferty, induced her to render her legal flirtations 'moins bannales.'[119]

This correspondence, fed by the tenderest hopes, did not prevent other views from being cultivated. Rank was her object, but in failure of her vaulting ambition, which might o'erleap itself,[120] Counsellor O'Rafferty, whom she called the 'soft green of her soul,'[121] was kept in quiet reserve, until Counsellor O'Rafferty, unexpectedly elevated to the bench,[122] pronounced a verdict so little favourable to Miss Crawley's pending cause, that she saw herself at forty the victim of a too-confiding heart, and found

'What dust we doat on when 'tis man we love.'[123] /

The delicate line which is said to divide coquetry from devotion was now broken; and an introduction at this period to some *serious* ladies of rank, who, in Dublin, preside over faith and tent-stitch,[124] and dictate creeds while they cut out shirts, for the benefit of poor sempstresses and expected converts, together with the influence of an itinerant evangelical preacher, the celebrated Zachariah Scare'um, awakened her to a vocation, which induced her to give to heaven all that had once been Counsellor O'Rafferty's. Still, however, she coquetted with religion, as she had done with the bar, to *agacer*[125] many a sturdy polemic, as she had done many a promising lawyer. She had ran in rapid succession through all the shades of the sectarian prism, successively reflecting old lights, new lights, broad lights, and twilights, until finally deciding that she should never stand in her own light, she brought her love of / rank, power, and ascendency, to quadrate with her religious system, and settled down into an high church methodist.

The former fantastic frippery of her dress was changed into that coquettish simplicity, adopted by ladies who advertize to the world their inward superiority, by the outward and visible signs of the toilette; who pin up their creed with their top knot, indicate their piety by the cut of their bonnet, and who look upon the bright hues and rich tints of heaven and nature as symptoms of sin and badges of iniquity; but who nevertheless bestow upon their ostentatious reserve of costume a care, a precision, a singularity which attracts the eye to their studied appearance, and might put the recherché[126] taste of a finished Parisian milliner to the blush of inferiority.

At the head of these pious petite maitresses[127] stood Miss Crawley, emi-/nently primitive in all the exterior forms of her calling; looking upon celestial rosy red with eyes averse, doubting the faith that pranked itself in azure, – 'Heaven's own proper dye,'[128] giving yellow to the devil, and placing coquelicot[129] beyond the pale of salvation; while her own greys, fawns, puces, and snuff colours, 'breathing a browner horror'[130] over her swarthy complexion, were chosen with all the delicacy and selection which belong to the studied *faste*[131] of the sectarian wardrobe.

But, though dead to colours, Miss Crawley was not insensible to forms. The person of the stranger guest had taken possession of her evangelical imagination. There seemed to her a mystery in his visit; and she foresaw in her vanity, her visionary idleness, and wordly romance, a conquest or a convert, a partner in her labours, or at least another distinguished name in her list of noble and literary friends. She / was, therefore, prepared to prepossess her family, who were now all assembled at Mr. Crawley's, in his favour; but the late arrival of the men from the assizes left only time for family salutations and greetings, when the Commodore was present to make his own impressions in propriâ personâ.[132] q

Mrs. Serjeant, and Mrs. Commissioner Crawley, were less marked by peculiarity than their sister-in-law, at whom they laughed, – not in contempt, but in envy: for they gave her credit for all she assumed, and hated her for her success as much as if she had merited it. Mrs. Serjeant Crawley, half Irish, half East Indian, with the hue of one country and the brogue of the other, prided herself upon the fortune she brought her husband, the size of her house, and the accomplishments of her four exhibiting daughters. To these grounds of self-satisfaction she added the honour and eternal boast of / her intimacy with Lady Kilgobbin, an old lady of rank and pretension, who had been left a solitary straggler on the Irish red bench,[133] after the dispersion of the nobility by the union. Pew-fellow, card-player, and news-monger in ordinary to Lady Kilgobbin, Lady Kilgobbin was with Mrs. Serjeant the beginning and the end of all things. With Mrs. Commissioner Crawley, on the contrary, the Lady Lieutenant was the alpha and omega[134] of special reference. Her life had however furnished her with other sources of pride. She had once been the young widow of an old bishop; and when, with an unprovided daughter, and a portion of an hundred a year, she accepted the hand of the court-favoured commissioner, she had endeavoured to perpetuate the recollection of her former rank and connexion by perpetual references to the memory of her *dear late lord*. Cold, arrogant, and supercilious, she mistook / a dogmatizing spirit for cleverness, affected to despise accomplishments, because she was too indifferent and too negligent of her daughter to give her any, and fancied herself a woman of fashion because people of rank came to her expensive parties, but who laughed at her for the pains she took to induce their visits.

It was impossible for any daughter to be less like her mother, or less like the daughter of a bishop, than Miss Kate Lesley. Her education had been founded by the maid, who had taught her to read, and finished by the footman, with whom she giggled at the carriage window, while her precise mother was paying morning visits. Not yet *come out*,[135] she was fat, fair, slovenly, and fifteen, with her sleeves hanging off her shoulders, her comb out of her hair, and her slipshod shoes off her feet. In every thing a striking contrast to the four wousky-looking,[136] slight, sal-/low, overdressed Miss Crawleys, who had been presented at the Irish court, went to parties, and played, sung, and waltzed, for any one who had the kindness to listen, or the benevolence to look at them. /

CHAPTER II.

What hempen homespun knaves have we swaggering here?

SHAKESPEARE.[137]

He gives the bastinado with his tongue:
Our *ears are cudgelled with it*.

IBID.[138]

I abhor such phantastic phantasms – such unsociable and point device companions – such rackers of orthography.

Ibid.[139] r

In addition to the Crawley family, which a six o'clock dinner-bell assembled at Mount Crawley, were a few guests supplied by the situation of the country, and the circumstances of the neighbourhood. They consisted of two barristers, friends, and (in their respective ways) *toadies* of the young counsellor: two protectees of Mr. Crawley senior, bearing the official dignities of sub-/sheriff and port surveyor; two country gentlemen, tenants of the Marquis of Dunore, (the one of an ancient Catholic, the other of a respectable Protestant family):[s] and the brigade-major of the district, who, from his strict adherence to the prudent rule of never dancing with the daughter where he had not dined with the father, had obtained from the wits of Dunore, the sobriquet of the 'cut-mutton-jig-major.'

Of the two barristers, the elder was one of that class termed in London Old Bailey counsel.[140] He piqued himself principally upon the vulgarity of his humour, and the coarseness of his address; wore a coat well powdered and ill brushed; and laughed at the legal coxcombs, who sought to get rid of the dust of the courts, before they sat down to a circuit dinner. He might, however, be said rather to entertain the bar than to practise at it; and to pick up on the circuit more jokes than / briefs. He was now a sort of hanger-on – a *proneur titré*[141] of Mr. Conway Crawley, and was always contented to swallow the insolent superiority of the son, so long as he was permitted to swallow with it the claret of the father. The other barrister, more timid and more gentleman-like, followed in the track of the young legal Bobadil[142] from genuine admiration, and with a firm resolve to adopt his course, and to trace his steps to promotion, whatever path he might take, indolently reposed on his higher genius for his own future fortunes, and catered applause for talents he emulated, the jackall of another's vanity.

The two country gentlemen were simply country gentlemen, such as they are found in Munster. Gay, cordial, courteous, hospitable at home, and convivial abroad; but a little out of their natural element in Mr. Crawley's circle, where the business of signing / leases alone had detained them. The sub-sheriff and surveyor owed every thing to the Crawley interest; and full of gratitude for favours *yet to come,* they looked up to Mr. Crawley, of Mount Crawley, with a deference evinced, in proportion to their expectations. The applause which this gentleman usually extorted from both, by a significant wink of the eye, whenever he chose to be witty, or was inclined to be humorous, was generally paid by the sub-sheriff in the formula of 'That's nate;'[143] which the surveyor constantly confirmed by the echo of 'Mighty nate!'

Such were the party assembled in the best drawing-room of Mount Crawley; when the commissioner observing, that no verbal announce of dinner followed the summons of the bell, turned to Mr. Crawley impatiently, and asked,

'Who do we wait for? – Do you expect any one to dinner, Darby?'

'Not a Christian,' returned Mr. / Crawley. 'Thady, dear, give the bell a touch, and bid them dish.'

'You forget, brother Crawley,' said his sister anxiously, 'that I told you, if you would have listened to me, or to any one but Jemmy Bryan, when you came home, that I had asked a gentleman to dinner, a very distinguished person, that called on you this morning, after you were gone to Glannacrime.'

'Oh, very well, he'll be here while dinner's dishing, I'll engage. – Did he lave his name?'

'I cannot tell you his name,' said Miss Crawley, with a smile, 'because I really forgot to ask it. '*But what's in a name?*' as Romeo says.[144] This I however can tell you: he is not only the most distinguished, but the most poetical-looking person, as dear Lady Clotworthy would have said.'

'You know, Anne Clotworthy, I am always rather a *stiptic*[145] to your descriptions,' said Mr. Crawley, winking / to the sub-sheriff, 'ever since you tould me that that methodist preacher, who came to us on a visit of two days, and staid three months, *was an angel without wings*. He was without wings sure enough, but it was a scare-crow without wings he was the very moral of.'

'That's nate!' said the sub-sheriff.

'Mighty nate!' replied the surveyor.

'When I spoke of the angelic properties of the Reverend Jeremiah Judd, I alluded to the inward man, and I was induced to day to believe, for a moment, that this gentleman had brought letters from him; but though he avowed that his mission into this country was of a serious nature –'

'Then I'll tell you once for all, Miss Crawley,' interrupted her brother in a passion, 'I will not have my house made a magdalen asylum[146] to a parcel of canting methodistical thieves, who are of no use but to set aside the simple *lethargy*[147] of the church service, and to / substitute the errors of the Presbyterians for those of the established faith. With your missions and missionaries, conversions and perversions, have you left me a tinpenny in my pocket to give to my own poor in New-Town Mount Crawley? And pray, what's gone of my one pound note that went to make Christians of the black negroes? Never saw a single sowl of them set foot in a church yet, barring Mrs. Casey's little black boy, that carries her prayer-book to early service. And I'd trouble you for my eleven and fourpence halfpenny,' Miss Crawley, that you made me give to get King Pomarre, of the Otaheitee islands,[148] to let himself be baptized; though faith I believe it was king of the Mummers, that's king of the *hummers*[149] he was? And 'bove all, where's my sixteen and three-pence, carried off by your '*angel without wings*,' for, 'lighting up the *dark* villages;' and my elegant *surtout,* that was stolen out of the hall in Merrion Square, by your / converted Jew, that was waiting for your '*Guide to the*

Land of Promise.' I wish you had given the Devil his *Jew* (due), and left me my great coat; that's all, Miss Crawley.'

'That's nate!' cried the sub-sheriff, looking to the surveyor.

'Mighty nate!' echoed the surveyor, nodding his head, while Mr. Crawley, who had punned himself into good humour, as the man in the Guardian punned himself out of a fever,[150] and who observed the rest of the party much amused at this attack upon the evangelical and dictatorial Miss Crawley, continued, in a milder tone,

'Now, Clotty, dear, I tould you before that I never would let one of your *angels without wings* roost in my house to the day of my death, since Mr. Judd's visitation, who did nothing but preach and ate from morning to night, frightening the life out of me, and abusing the cook. I'd rather see / the Devil come into my house than a methodist preacher. Lord forgive me! and thinks when there's a religion by law established, which qualifies a man for every place in the state, it may serve our turn as well as our betters. If this gentleman then is one of the sarious, one of your missionaries –'

'Here he is, to speak for himself; here at least is one of the Dunore hack chaises[151] driving up the approach, so I'll ring for dinner,' observed the commissioner.

'Oh! a hack chaise,' said his wife superciliously, and letting fall her spyglass.

'Is it a *hack* chaise?' asked Miss Crawley in a tone of mortification; but before any other observation could be made, the door was opened, and the stranger, unannounced, appeared. He was in full dress; and the air with which he entered the room, and walked to the place occupied by Miss Crawley, was / marked by a certain disengaged freedom, beyond what is merely acquired in society – the ease of conscious, careless superiority. While he stood paying his respects, and offering apologies for his late arrival to Miss Crawley, every countenance in the room had changed its expression. Some who had risen even forgot to sit down; others eyed him with curiosity: the four Miss Crawleys paused for a moment in their flirtation with the barristers and brigade-major; and Miss Kate Lesley left her shoe in the middle of the room, where it had been thrown by Major Crawley, whose manual gallantries she had in vain resisted, with 'Quit now! behave, Thady Windham, or I will complain to your aunt – I will upon my honor;' to which the major only replied by twitching off her slip-shod shoe, and reiterating: ''Pon your honor!' The two Mesdames Crawley looked mortified at their demi-toilette,[152] assumed for a family / dinner; and Miss Crawley's countenance was radiant with triumph, in spite of the Dunore hack chaise.

Mr. Crawley, who loved company, when he was prepared for it, who liked his plate to be seen, when he took the trouble of displaying it, whose favourite aphorism on a company-day was, if there's enough for ten there's enough for twelve, and who now felt satisfied that his guest was not a methodist, from the manner in which he had sprung from the chaise into the portico, with, the light bound of an impatient schoolboy,[u] advanced to receive him with his wonted overcharged civility; but when that guest appeared, his head uncovered, and his face turned full to the light, he staggered back a few steps, and stood gazing on a form and countenance, that seemed to burst upon his view, like some half-forgotten image of an unpleasant dream. After a minute's silent pause, he took his youngest son's arm, / who stood turning over the leaves of the Review, and glancing a furtive look at the stranger, drew him into the open veranda, with the manner of one 'perplexed in the extreme.'[153]

'Con, dear,' said he, 'can you give a guess who that chap is, or what he is, or what brings him here at all?'

'I am sure I have not the least idea, Sir,' replied his son. 'I don't think his name was announced; but I suppose you will soon know his business. He seems a confident presuming-looking coxcomb enough; most likely a recruiting officer, or a maudlin traveller to the lakes, who will eat your dinners, and put us all into his book, in return for your hospitality.'

'I don't care where he puts us, if he's *only* a ganius,' said Mr. Crawley, evidently relieved by this suggestion. 'If I was sure of that, Con –' he paused, and then added, 'It struck me just at the first glance that – but what does / that prove? Sure they say that I am the very moral of Paddy Duigenan[154] about the corner of the mouth and the eye, and is no more to him, either in kith, kin, or relationship, than the lord chancellor, only just play-fellows, when slips of boys together, and great cronies.'

'Does this person resemble any one you know?' asked young Crawley.

'Does he? Why – but it was before your time; – and knows now that I'm entirely mistaken, only the first look, for it's quite clean impossible.'[v]

'Dinner is announced, Sir,' said the surveyor; 'and Mrs. Commissioner Crawley is waiting for you to hand her down, Sir.'

Ceremony, with all its laws of precedence, is the *cheval de bataille*[155] of the demi-officials of Ireland. Every guest in Mr. Crawley's drawing-room knew his place, while the Commodore alone, accustomed to the manners of foreign / countries, where the circle of private salons, neutralizes all rank, offered his arm to Miss Crawley, because he stood next her; but she gently resisted the offer, and the procession began. Mr. Crawley led out Mrs. Commissioner Crawley, Mr. Commissioner led out Mrs. Serjeant, Mr. Serjeant escorted the elder Miss Crawley, Miss Lesley, as a bishop's daughter, claimed the *pas*[156] of the four Miss Crawleys, and was ushered by the high sheriff; the four Miss Crawleys were divided amongst the lawyers, the brigade-major and their cousins; Counsellor Con followed alone, proudly pre-eminent, and took his place at the foot of the table; the sub-sheriff and surveyor bowed each other out, with pompous solemnity; the stranger and the two country gentlemen, having '*done the state no service*,[157] and being without any precise *état*[158] in this official hierarchy, were left to arrange their precedence as they might; and they / followed last in the train which proceeded to the dining-room.

The tables of these demi-officials are distinguished by a sumptuousness, a luxury, an extravagance, almost unknown, except to the highest ranks of other countries. Apparently abiding by the maxim of 'let us eat and be merry, for to-morrow we die,'[159] their device is frequently illustrated by the event. Commissioners of enquiry, suddenly start up with their inquisitorial researches into exorbitant fees, overcharges, bribes, &c. &c. and by a stroke of their pen, convert these chambers of festivity into houses of mourning; while the government, which winks for a necessary time at their malversations,[160] suddenly pounces on their enormities, as an excuse for displacing them, to make room for newer candidates for loyalty and places, where the 'last fool's as welcome as the former,'[161] and each serves, rules, and is ruined in his turn.[w] /

The dinner-table of Mr. Darby Crawley, attorney-at-law, differed in nothing from that of the Lord-Chancellor of Ireland, except in the polish of him that presided over it. Services and réléves[162] succeeded each other in due alternation. The soup, fish, and patés, were swallowed in solemn silence; but when the first flush of appetite subsided, champaign circled, burgundy went round, old hock was recommended, and every one talked across the table, round the table, and from the top to the bottom of the table: for the quietude and reserve of a bon-ton dinner table has not yet been acquired by the pseudo-grandees of the desk-aristocracy, who imitate the great in nothing but what money can procure.[x]

Mr. Crawley, who had raised his eyes to the stranger's face between every spoonful of his soup, questioned him with great civility, but with great hesitation, on his opinion of the coun-/try; and, by degrees, yielded up his uneasy, vague, and undefinable sensations of perplexity, to the influence of the frank replies of his nameless guest, and to the exhilaration of his own sparkling champagne and burgundy. Thus restored to his ease, convivial, talkative, and ridiculous as usual, he mentally observed, as he helped himself to mock turtle, his favourite dish, 'I wonder what the devil came over me, making a Judy Fitzsimmons of myself[163] about nothing at all – and all for a look, which is no proof; how could it?'

Thus finally chasing the unpleasant impressions, (whatever they might be) from his mind, he gave up his attention to a series of bad jokes arid circuit anecdotes, '*mille fois repetês*,'[164] and now told, with a broad, vulgar, slang humour, by young Crawley's elder friend, Counsellor Mulligan. This facetious barrister having just finished a good story, of which Judge Aubrey and Baron Boulter (the / judges then on circuit) were the heroes, he observed, turning to Mr. Crawley,

'By the bye, Sir, Judge Aubrey has let out the Rabragh, whom you put up last summer, and whom Baron Boulter left in Tipperary jail, under rule of bail.'

'So I hear,' said Mr. Crawley; 'but *bathershin* (as the Irish say), mind my words, Counsellor Mulligan, I'll have the Rabragh where he won't so easily get lave of absence; that's with due deference for Judge Aubrey: and has good reason to know (though nothing has been brought against him yet) he's at the bottom of every thing in this country, Padreen Gar's boys, and all.'

'Have you seen Conway's 'Familiar Epistle to a Jacobin Judge,' written on that occasion? By jove, 'tis the best hit that ever was made, and has set the judge wild, they say.'

'No, I have not, Counsellor Mulligan, nor doesn't care if I never see a / scrap of his poethry again while I live; and wishes he would lave off with his hits.'

'Me!' said Conway, tossing off a glass of liquor (for the dessert was now on the table.) 'Upon my honor, I didn't write that lampoon, which was circulated at Cork, if you mean that.' And he felt as he spoke for the manuscript in his pocket. 'I don't know how it is,' he added, conceitedly, 'but every wicked thing is laid at my door.'

'Every witty thing is,' said the timid young barrister, with a smile.

'Well! that comes to the same thing. I had just the same fatal preeminence when I was at the Temple.[165] All the foundling genius of the inns of court was placed to my account.'

'I wish,' said! Mr. Crawley, flinging an apple skin violently from him, 'there never was a ganius in the world. – What use in them? What good did ever one of them do? No, / but great harm; and when a man is rared at college, and has read the classics and the college course, what call has he to ganius after that?'

'I doubt, however, my dear Darby,' said the serjeant, projecting an immense pair of bushy black eyebrows, in which lay all his reputation, and over which he exercised a singular power of contraction and expansion. – 'I doubt that we should have had the classics to read in college, if there had not been authors, and what are called men of genius, to write them.'

'You are quite right, William,' said his brother, the commissioner, speaking with the authority of one who presided at *a board;* for if we must have books to read, there must be authors to write them, that's certain.'

'*C'est clair!*[166] said Conway Crawley, in a tone of ridicule (frequently directed at his uncles), and a smile of intelligence at his aunt, who had hitherto vainly / endeavoured to draw the Commodore into conversation across the table.

'*C'est clair* indeed!' repeated Miss Crawley, with an affected laugh.

'See Clare,'[167] reiterated Mr. Crawley senior, angrily: 'well, and see Clare, and see Lyttleton upon Coke,[168] and see all the great crown lawyers that ever wrote, and see if ever one of them wrote a line of poethry. Chancellor Clare hadn't as much ganius for poethry as my foot, and if he had, would have been ashamed to own it.'

'I am not now,' said Miss Crawley, delighted with the turn conversation was taking, 'as once, an advocate for the *idle visions of the brain.*[169] But still I think no chancellor need have been ashamed of producing such poetry as Watt's Hymns, [170] nor do I see why Themis and Apollo should not have their *liaisons.*'[171]

'I am afraid, aunt,' said Conway, 'that as my father supposes, they / would be *liaisons dangereuses.*'[172] – Blackstone, however, was a poet.'[173]

'Yes,' said Miss Crawley, 'and it was a private traditional anecdote of Shenstone in the Clotworthy family, (for Lady Clotworthy was his relation,) that the sweet bard of the Leasowes was intended for the English bar;[174] and surely had he sat upon the wool-sack,[175] he would not have denied being the author of that sweetly moral, and simply pastoral eclogue, –'

> 'I have found out a gift for my fair,
> I have found where the wood-pigeon breeds.'[176]

'Oh, dacency! Miss Crawley,' interrupted her brother Darby, winking at the sub-sheriff, while the ladies smiled, and Miss Crawley placing the smile to the right account, triumphantly went on, –

> 'But let me that plunder forbear,
> She will say 'tis a barbarous deed.'

'Sorrow harm I see in robbing a bird's nest, Sir,' said the sub-sheriff, addressing his critique to Mr. Crawley, / in conformity to his patron's very humorous look at the moment –

> 'For he ne'er can be true she'll aver,
> Who could rob a poor bird of his young.'

'Oh! a most lame and impotent conclusion, my good aunt. But for heaven's sake give us no more of that *fadaise,*'[177] said Conway Crawley – 'that gone-by *trash,* which is worthy of the Della Cruscan school,[178] only that it's still more insipid, and would scarcely furnish my friend of the Baviad and Mœviad[179] a peg to hang a note on.'

'But your friend of the Baviad, my dear Conway, got out of all keeping, when he called Anna Matilda 'a wretched woman,'[180] and other hard names, especially as it was known in the literary circles of Bath and Litchfield that Anna Matilda was dear Lady Clotworthy.'

'Lady Clotworthy! not a bit,' reiterated Conway Crawley. 'Anna Matilda was neither more nor less than / that *enfant gaté* of a particular set, Mrs. Cowley, [181] the author of that tissue of all nonsense and absurdity, the Belle's Stratagem.'[182]

'The Belle's Stratagem!' said Mrs. Commissioner – 'Why the Lady Lieutenant bespoke it this winter. It was played by command; and I had seats in the next box to her.'

'And I,' said Mrs. Serjeant, 'had a row in Lady Kilgobbin's 'box for the girls and myself, and we thought it a charming comedy, so much fashionable life in it. And Letitia Hardy so *talented*, as Lady Kilgobbin said, and sung, and waltz'd, so delightfully.'

'It certainly *is* a very amusing comedy,' said the Commissioner authoritatively.

'Very amusing,' said the serjeant, with his eyebrows.

'The Belle's Stratagem,' said young Crawley, with cool insolence of look and tone, and folding his arms upon the / table, 'is, what I have asserted it to be, a tissue of nonsense and absurdity. I repeat the words –, 'tis more, 'tis a crying sin against good taste, good sense, good manners, and good morals. It's very title justifies every word of my assertion. The Belle's Stratagem! observe – Belle, a foolish French term for a young woman, according to Johnson, and so used by Pope, in his namby-pamby poem, of the Rape of the Lock.[183] Stratagem, too, a term derived from the Greek, etymologically meaning an artifice, *or ruse de guerre*,[184] a device, trick, imposition. The trick of a young woman, to take in a young man of fortune. A notable play for mothers to take their daughters to, truly!'

'I wonder, my dear,' said the serjeant, with an unusual projection of the eyebrows, 'you should take the girls to such a thing.'

'Lady Kilgobbin,' – interrupted Mrs. Crawley; but their nephew interrupting / both, and bearing down all before him, poured forth a torrent of hypercriticism, imposing in proportion to its shallowness; refining away the merits, exaggerating the faults, mis-quoting, misrepresenting, and mis-judging, one of the most elegant and popular comedies on the English stage; until all those, who had given it their unequivocal approbation a few minutes before, endeavoured to expiate their former, hasty, but independent judgments, by approving, seconding, and adopting, that of this formidable Zoilus[185] of the Crawley family.

During this tedious, but fluent tirade of pedantic critical jargon, Miss Crawley sat transported; and only fearful that a conversation should cease, in which she and her élève were alone, of all the race of Crawleys, calculated to shine, she endeavoured to keep up the ball, while the nephew paused to take his claret.

To force the stranger into the lists, / she asked him across the table: 'May I beg to know what is your opinion of the English poets in general?'

This sweeping question startled the Commodore into a sudden and abrupt ejaculation of 'Madam!' Every one smiled; Mr. Crawley winked at the surveyor; and Miss Crawley, with her former suspicions of the stranger's vocation, revived by his silence and gravity, and by the little part he had taken in a conversation, hitherto unworthy of the 'elect of the Lord,' added with. a demure and primitive air, 'Your poetical studies are, perhaps, from necessity, far from general, but Milton's divine poem of the Paradise Lost may have come under your observation, and stood the test of your critical acumen; if –'

'The term *divine,* my dear aunt;' interrupted the 'never ending, still begin-ning'[186] nephew, 'is rather strong to be applied to any uninspired writer; and most of all to such a poet, and such / a poem as Milton, and his Paradise Lost. I don't, however, mean to say – pray hear me out, Madam, – that Milton was not a poet, and a good poet, but I must add, that he was a most profane writer, and a most sacrilegious parodist. Nay, grant me your patience one moment.'

'I only mean to say, in my own exculpation, Conway Townsend, that the term divine, as applied to Milton, does not originate with me; that others of higher authority –'

'Oh, yes, I know Ma'am what you would say: and it is very true, that within the last century Milton has enjoyed a most preposterous fame, a most exagger-ated, unmerited celebrity; a fame wholly denied to him by his cotemporaries, the best judges; for, after all, the *trash* that is talked about posterity, the true reputa-tion is cotemporary reputation, tangible fame, fame that one can lay one's finger on, that one can touch.' /

'Devil a bit, Counsellor Con; but I give you credit for that,' said his father, cracking a nut between his teeth: 'touch and go, Sir, that's the ra'al fame for my money. Sub, hand up the port, and put the church in the middle of the parish: *ergo,*[187] the salt-cellar: I always take my nuts cum grano salis, as the French say.'[188]

'But,' continued young Crawley, 'even the fame which posterity, that is, which the last century have bestowed on Milton, cannot be called legitimate fame. It is his political principles, that harmonize with the revolutionary systems of the last fifty years,[189] which have given to the sturdy jacobin the fame that is supposed to be extorted by the poet, a poet, by-the-bye, who has taken the devil for his hero, –'

'The Lord bless us!' said Mr. Crawley, throwing down his nut-shells in pious horror.

'Hell for his principle scene of ac-/tion, and rebellion for his theme,' contin-ued young Crawley.

'Why then, who is he at all?' asked his father with vehemence. 'Will nobody tell me?'

'And of this I am certain, that had he published his Paradise Lost in the pre-sent day, there is not one genuine English review that would not have denounced him for an impious parodist, and condemned him, *out of his own words,* as pro-fane, jacobinical, indecent, and immoral.'

Every body shook their heads, though nobody knew why; while Mr. Craw-ley, stealing a timid suspicious look at the stranger, and then turning to his sister, observed:

'I'll trouble you, Miss Crawley, not to mention that man, whoever he is, any more at my table. How do I know but every word of the conversation may be reported at the castle, and the secatary think I'm hand and glove with him.' /

'It is curious,' continued Conway, not even hearing his father, and borne away by the shallow rapidity of his own exhaustless volubility, 'it is curious to observe Milton's hatred of kings breaking out in some of his most poetical effusions. Thus, in his famous simile:

> 'As when the sun new risen
> Looks through the horizontal misty air
> Shorn of its beams; or from behind the moon
> In dim eclipse, disastrous twilight sheds
> On half the nations, and with fear of change
> Perplexes monarchs.'[190]

'Perplex a monarch!' exclaimed Mr. Crawley, inarticulate from vehemence. 'Och! the thief of the world! Why, then, Con, where was the Suspendeas Corpus Act? Where was the law of libel?[191] What was the attorney-general about?

'The fact is,' said young Crawley, taking snuff, and pushing on the box, 'that, notwithstanding the legitimate prince was then but recently seated on / his throne, and the reins of government still hung loose, this very passage nearly caused the suppression of the book by the royal licenser, and Milton and his Paradise Lost would then have been condemned to eternal oblivion (we cannot say unjustly), and sacrificed to the insulted majesty of the house of Stuart.'[192]

'Better,' exclaimed the Commodore, with a sudden explosion of fiery indignation, that resembled the brilliant bursting of a sky-rocket, 'better that the whole line of Stuarts, and the memory of that feeble, worthless, and despotic family, should be given to eternal oblivion, than that one bright effusion of the genius of Milton should be lost to the great nation, whose intellectual glory it has raised above that of all modern people. Any land might have produced the Stuarts; and one land, blushing to own them for her sons, twice drove them from her shores,[193] a false and feeble race, whom Milton / would not flatter, and Sydney could not save.'

A dead silence followed this animated burst of uncontrollable feeling. All were struck, as much by the manner as by the matter of the unexpected apostrophe, from one, whose silence, in spite of the personal distinction which had at first been so opposing, had given a general impression of dulness and inefficiency. But if all were startled, old Crawley was confounded. His son, darkling with ire and irritation, sat for a moment silent as the rest; while his father, whose native cowardice had taken the alarm, doubted whether a French spy, a government informer, or an Irish rebel, now sat at his table. He was even half inclined to send out an ukase[194] to Jemmy Bryan and his myrmidons[195] to hold themselves in readiness; but he first resolved, before he took any decided step, to give a toast as a *pierre de touche*[196] of the stranger's political / creed, a toast which he considered as the watch-word of his own dominant party. Passing, therefore, his hand over his face, so as to give a significant wink to his youngest son, unseen by the rest of the company, he exclaimed:

'Come, Counsellor Con, fill the gentleman's glass next you. I don't mane to give you an hint, Ladies, but before you go, you must all join in a toast, which I believe no one will refuse to drink in this house; this is, Sir,' (nodding to the Commodore,) '*the glorious and immortal –*'

'The glorious and immortal what, Sir?' asked his guest, putting a little wine in his glass.

'Why, the glorious and immortal memory;[197] every loyal man knows that.'

'I hope I shall not forfeit my claim to that designation, by confessing I have yet to learn whose happy memory has merited these distinguished epithets.'

Mr. Crawley pulled down his little / *Beresford bob*,[198] as he called his wig: he was not prepared to answer such an unexpected question; and his son, seeing his perplexity, promptly came to his relief, observing coldly and superciliously to the stranger, 'My father, Sir, gives a toast, which in Ireland at least requires no explanation; he gives the glorious and immortal memory of William the Third.'

'I drink it; with all my soul,' said the Commodore with animation, filling first his own glass to the brim, and then that of the poor catholic gentleman, who sat next him, and to whom 'the glorious and immortal' was the memory of the overthrow of his religion, the ruin of the fortunes, and the hopes of his family. 'The memory of William of Nassau,' continued the stranger,' should find its monument in the breast of every true lover of British freedom: it is the memory of a great captain, chosen by a, great nation, to lead it forth in the defence / of its natural rights and dear-bought constitution, and to drive from the violated sanctuary of their laws that despotic bigot,[199] whose feebleness and corruption had forced a, loyal people into the hazardous experience of revolution: with such recollections, I drink,' and he arose as he spoke, 'to the glorious memory of William the Third.'

This was so new an exposition of the revered text of 'the glorious and immortal,' that Mr. Crawley senior was not the only person present whom it puzzled. With this party of placemen, 'the glorious and immortal' had but one signification; it was the watch-word of their own influence, the cry of their own petty, but powerful ascendency: and these genuine Tories, these advocates of their own arbitrary power, had been all their lives giving the Whiggish toast, without an idea attached to it, save the subjection of the catholic population, an unequal distribution of / rights, and the supremacy of a narrow, bigotted, and impolitic intolerance; coupled, therefore, with the terms 'glorious constitution,' and an 'emancipated people,' it produced a dead silence: even the '*imperturbable*,' the overbearing and insolent Conway, was at a loss how to attack a definition which his reading told him was just and true; he sat, therefore, pulling grape after grape from his bunch, as if he had not thought the stranger's remark worth replying to, and only noticing it by a supercilious sneer; while Miss Crawley observing his annoyance, and now^y wholly thrown out as to her former opinions of the stranger, came to her nephew's relief by observing, 'Well, before I go, I must express my regret that a few literary remarks thrown out at random should have led to any thing like political discussion; and in my own defence must say, that the eulogium I ventured to / pass on Milton was wholly confined to his poetry; for I believe, whatever may have been his principles as a politician, he is, undeniably, a good poet.'

'He has written a good poem of the second order,' said young Crawley, rallying, 'for strictly speaking, the Paradise Lost is not an epic; and in a moral point of view, there is not one maxim of prudence or conduct to be drawn from it. Besides, one-half of his poetical beauties are downright plagiarisms from the ancients, in whose snow I can track him at every step.

Thus:

> 'As when heaven's fire has scath'd the forest oak,'
> happens to be a cento made up from Homer and Virgil;[200] and again,
> 'Thrice he essay'd to speak, &c.'
> is Ovid's 'Ter conata loqui et ter vox faucibus hæsit.'[201] /

'So much for the bright effusions of this republican genius. This, Sir, however,' and he turned to the stranger with a triumphant sneer, 'may appear flat heresy to you, and a new reading of your favourite author.'

'New! not at all,' returned the Commodore, carelessly: 'I have read every word of it long since, in the dull forgeries of that convicted impostor, Lauder; but since the ingenious detection of Douglas,[202] I had imagined that Milton's plagiarisms had been at rest, or remembered only as warnings against literary credulity.'

'Shall we go, Mrs. Crawley?' asked Miss Crawley, rising and colouring, while the complexion of her nephew deepened in its sallow hue, and became dark with ire and mortification. He was wholly unprepared for the detection of his gotten-up criticisms, even before an audience so insignificant. This singular stranger, who sat a nameless guest / at his father's table, with his bursts of light and involutions of darkness, his habitual reserve and silence, and his occasional involuntary explosions of mind, seemed to hover like an incubus over the vision of his self-importance. Always the centre of his own circle, he was alike unused to opposition or superiority, and from this moment the stranger became the object of that strenuous, inveterate, and unappeasable enmity, which springs from the wounded self-love of a vain man.

The retreat of the ladies, the removal of the great table, and the placing of a smaller one, the preparations for whiskey punch (asked for by the sub-sheriff and surveyor, and eminently enjoyed by Mr. Crawley, who confessed himself no *accoucheur*[203] in wine), with the change of seats incidental to the separation of the sexes after dinner, occupied a considerable time; and the Commodore / was on the point of taking advantage of his seat next Mr. Crawley, to mention to him the business which had brought him to Mount Crawley, when he was interrupted by the entrance of a servant, bearing a letter to the master of the house.

'A coronet sale,' (seal) said Mr. Crawley, wiping his spectacles: 'The Dunore crest, the Marchioness's hand. James, come back here – Who brought this letter; it isn't a post one,[204] sure?'

'It is not, Sir; it came by express; a castle express. The dragoon is just gone down to the horse-barrack.'

'A castle express!' said: Mr. Crawley, opening the letter with trepidation, while his son Conway took his seat at the back of his chair.

'Hem! Emily Dunore – Dublin Castle, August 25,' read aloud Mr. Crawley, glancing his eye over the page to the signature and address; then rising, / he retired to a remote table with his son, in evident perturbation. After the perusal of the letter, and a few moments conference, the father and son rejoined the party.

'Here is good news,' said young Crawley, with affected gaiety, while his father remained silent.

'Lady Dunore is arrived in Dublin, and is coming to Dunore Castle immediately. She is merely recruiting from the fatigues of her voyage, with her friends the vice-regals, and then sets off with a large party.'

'Come, Sir,' addressing his dejected father, 'we'll drink to her ladyship's speedy and safe arrival.'

The toast went round, and many comments were made on the effects of this event. The Protestant country gentlemen observed,

'This will give an helping hand to the election. The presence of Lady Dunore on the spot will be of infinite / service to her son's cause at Glannacrime.'

'It will be of service,' said young Crawley.

'Why I thought she had given up all thoughts of coming to Ireland,' said the commissioner: 'I heard Lord Rosbrin say so in Dublin.'

'And so she had,' said old Crawley, with uncontrolable irritation, 'but you might as well fix th' ould weathercock on the top of Dunore Courthouse.'

'The residence of the Dunore family, even for a short time, will do great good,' said the catholic gentleman.

'Great!' said young Crawley, filling his father's glass, and giving the health of the absent candidate Lord Adelm Fitzadelm.

'I wonder,' said the catholic gentleman, 'since the Fitzadelms have come in for the Dunore property, that / they haven't tried to re-purchase the old house and grounds of Court Fitzadelm.'

'Apropos, Mr. Crawley,' said the stranger in a low tone of voice. 'It is time that I should apologize for my intrusion on your hospitality, by accounting for it. I am desirous to become a purchaser of Court Fitzadelm; for that purpose I came to Mount Crawley, and being obliged to leave Dunore to-morrow morning on urgent business, I availed myself of Miss Crawley's polite invitation, in order to obtain an audience from you. The time, I am aware, is an awkward one for business: all I can now expect to learn is, what may be my chance, and on what terms?'

'I believe, Sir,' interrupted young Crawley, 'you stand so engaged with Mr. Skerrett of Inchigeela, that you cannot open any new engagement.'

'Mr. Skerrett!' said the old man, / rousing himself, 'to be sure I can't. And may I presume to ask, Sir, is it to take back, that is, to purchase, I mane, Court Fitzadelm, that brought you into this country?'

'Not exactly, Sir. My wish of taking Court Fitzadelm is merely accidental. I saw it advertised, liked the description, visited the grounds on my way hither, and liked them still better. I resolved to purchase if I could, and waited on you for that purpose.'

Old Crawley passed his hand across his forehead, first looked at his son, and then at the stranger; then he added:

'And you mane to return to this country, Sir?'

'My hope of arranging matters with you will be a strong inducement for my doing so.'

'Then, Sir,' said old Crawley, eagerly catching at his word, 'you need not give yourself the trouble. The place / is all as one as sowld to Mr. Skerrett, an ould acquaintance, and a residenter in the country; and of course I would give a neighbour the preference over a stranger, an entire stranger.'

'It is very natural, Sir,' said the Commodore. 'Am I to consider this answer as definitive?'

'Certainly, Sir,' returned Conway Crawley. 'The concerns of Court Fitzadelm are, in fact, disposed of.'

The stranger paused for a moment, then took a polite leave of Mr. Crawley, and departed. /

CHAPTER III.

For now enforst a farre unfitten taske,
  – – to change mine oaten reeds,
   And sing of knights' and ladies' gentle deeds,
Whose praises, having slept in silence long,
Me – all too meane, the sacred muse areeds,
To blazon far.
       SPENCER.[205]

THE intended visit of the Dunore family to the ancient and long uninhabited castle of their ancestors was of too general importance to the district and neighbourhood, not to excite sensation and awaken interest. Mr. Crawley had made no formal announce of the important circumstance, but the arrival of a maitre d'hotel[206] and a French cook at the castle gave sufficient indication of the event. These *chefs du menage*[207] were daily followed by squadrons of non-commissioned officers in the capa-/city of footmen, stable grooms, and grooms of the chamber, with light, and heavy baggage, and all the artillery of luxury, comfort, and splendor, which follow in the train of the great, the opulent, and the sumptuous.

The Marchioness of Dunore was all *this* in its fullest extent; and she now visited the domains of her son (whom she represented) with a, spirit as imperially extravagant, as accompanied the fair autocrat of the north,[208] in her journies to her ancient city of Moscow; the means alone fell short in the ratio of the states of Dunore to the empire of all the Russias. The arrival of her ladyship was, however, to the full, of as much consequence to the inhabitants of the barony, as that of the great Catherine to the expecting Muscovites. The higher ranks looked forward to festivals at the castle, and balls at the court-house, election dinners, and canvassing parties without end. Mothers / turned their eyes on Lord Adelm Fitzadelm; who, as it was reported, would join his mother from the continent. Daughters were not very averse from the same splendid speculation; and with whom Lord Adelm would dance *(the member's daughter not being in the country)* was a subject of endless discussion.[z]

The lower orders were equally interested in an event, which awakened that train of idle hopes, to which the discontented are always victims. Protection, interference, and redress, were expected by those, who, looking to all good, under the forms of *backing, seconding,* and *favouring,* make no reference to justice, and have no idea of rights; – of rights violated in their own persons; and, according to the laws of re-action, by them in their turn violated on the persons of others.[a] To appeal from the powerful Crawleys to the powerful masters of those Crawleys, / was a favourite scheme with many, and in some nurtured and encouraged, by one who held a peculiar influence over all. This important agent was *Terence Oge O'Leary.*

The lower Irish entertain a respect, bordering on infatuation, for what they call learning; and much of this respect centres in their rustic schoolmasters, the depositaries of their national and traditionary lore. The influence of this order of men was deemed so formidable during the most unhappy period of the Irish rebellion, that they became objects of peculiar suspicion; not to the government, but to the petty magistrates, to whom the government had given such frightful and unqualified power, that ignorance, cruelty, and personal vindictiveness, were

armed all over the kingdom, and corporal punishments were inflicted with a bar-
barity which exceeded the horrors of the rack and the wheel. O'Leary, on whom
/ the fever of insanity was then still preying, had thrown out many incoherent
aspersions against the Crawleys, having the death of the young Lord Fitzadelm
for their chief point of reference. A note in Latin and Irish, found in his pocket,
which Mr. Crawley could not read, served as a sufficient pretext for accusation,
at a time, when a magistrate asserted to the Irish House of Commons 'that it
was necessary to whip many persons, of whose guilt he had *secret information,*
from persons *whose names he could not publicly disclose.*'[209] Under such a system,
O'Leary had been sentenced to the lash. To his plea of innocence Mr. Crawley
replied, 'What, you rebelly rascal, dare you speak after sentence?' (*)[210]

The sentence was put in force; it prolonged and increased his mental irritation; but it elevated him to the honours / of martydom, in the estimation of
his sympathizing compatriots; which, added to the benevolence of his character,
and the supposed profundity of his erudition, gave to the feelings he inspired
something of tenderness and deference, mixed with veneration. The hopes,
therefore, which the return of the Dunore family awakened among their tenantry and dependants were confirmed by the vague, mysterious declaration of
the oracular O'Leary, who continued to repeat every where, that 'the fall of
the Crawleys was *handy bye,* that the reign of the land pirates was nearly over,
and that the red arm of the Fitzadelms would stretch forth once more over the
land, or perhaps join that of the Macarthies More, as the Geraldines and Butlers
had once done. (2) These mystic ravings were considered as Delphic oracles;[211]
and sunset brought many a votarist to O'Leary's cell of Monaster-ny-Oriel, to
consult on points concern- /ing the validity of leases granted them under the
Crawley regime:[b] meantime O'Leary was himself convinced that his guest was
no other than Lord Adelm Fitzadelm, whose incognito arrival had preceded
his mother's by a few days, and whose resemblance to his unfortunate cousin
had already awakened his affections and devotional interest. This 'noble espiall,'
(as he termed his guest) upon the tricks and puppet-shew state of the Crawleys, which he likened to king Solomon's court in the *fringes,* (3)[212] had slept but
one night at the friary, and had left Dunore the next morning for Cork, with
the promise of returning in a few days; and took with him a '*missive,*' from the
pedagogue of the preceptory to Friar O'Sulivan: 'touching, plaze your lordship,
that is honor I mane,' said O'Leary, 'the Ogygia of the great O'Flaherty, and
the Histoire d'Ireland, by Abbe' O'Gaghegan,[213] which Fra Denis will dispatch /
forthwith to me, by the Dunore carrier.'

'I will bring them back myself to you, O'Leary,' said the Commodore, as he
mounted his Kerry steed.

---

*　　Facts.

'That's too great honour entirely, my lord, and reminds me of the goodness of him whom you liken, who carried Ware's Antiquities, and Lynche's Cambrensis Eversus,[214] from Dingle town to St. Crohans for me, on one shoulder; and a string of curlews, and his little ould gun, the jewel of the world! on the other; for they were of great value to me then, that's the curlews, and helped to pay the rint; the ould saying being true,

> 'A curlew, be she white or black,
> Carries twelve-pence on her back.'[215]

The stranger departed. O'Leary's doubts as to the purport of this journey, which were, like all his thoughts, confused and wild, became suddenly cleared up by the report of the expected / arrival of Lady Dunore; for it was natural that Lord Adelm should go to Cork to meet his mother, and to return with her to Dunore, and then discomfit the Crawley faction, whom he had seen *in all their glory.*[216] Of the result of the Commodore's visit to Mount Crawley; as of its pretext, O'Leary remained ignorant, for he had made no communication to him; arid the respectful deference of the Fitzadelm fosterer, checked the suggestions of a vague, but ardent curiosity.

But if the population of the barony of Dunore looked forward with various views of interest to the arrival of the chiefs of the territory, the Crawleys who had so long and powerfully governed it in their absence, felt little pleasure from the circumstance. They 'wanted no change;' and the irritation of old Crawley's spirit could scarcely subdue itself; from the moment he had received Lady Dunore's letter, or suffer him / to listen to the prudent suggestions of his youngest son,

'His bosom's counsellor, and better self.'[217]

It was in vain that Conway enforced the necessity of *representation,* of fitting his conduct to *existing circumstances,* and meeting exigencies with *applicable expediency.* To all this primmer jargon[c] of the young diplomatic apprentice old Crawley only replied with an ominous shake of the head, and, the observation of – 'And the Glannacrime business going on so *iligant;* and that rebelly thief, O'Leary, drinking the downfall of the Crawleys at the Dunore Arms, as Jemmy Bryan tells me, who was on the look out; and that stranger whom Miss Crawley flopped down on us at dinner, the other day, lodging for a night at the friary, and then *exeunt manent,*[218] before Jemmy could make out a tittle about him. But what signifies talking now; 'on time's uncertain date, eternal hours / depend,' as the dial-plate on the new clock says;[219] and so send to Cork for coloured lamps to light up Mount Crawley, for the town of Dunore is going to illuminate, and wouldn't be behind hand with it.'

'On the contrary, Sir,' replied his son, 'we should be *before-hand,* and light up New-Town Mount Crawley, and order your new corps under arms immediately.'

'And a *few*-de-joy,'[220]cried old Crawley, cheering up; for his new corps was the master-passion of his present existence; and his son well knew the chord by which his relaxed spirits could be restored to their habitual tension.

Miss Crawley, who was not very deep in the family politics, was the only member of the house of Crawley to whom the arrival of the noble Marchioness and her fashionable party gave any pleasure. Lady Dunore had said, in that fatal letter which announced her / intentions, that she meant 'to instal the always obliging Miss Crawley (for whose prettily painted skreens she returned a thousand thanks) as DAME DU PALAIS,[221] or mistress of the ceremonies at Dunore Castle, where she would herself be necessarily the greatest stranger.'

From this distinguished promotion, Miss Crawley saw a train of delightful consequences, all big with influence, benefit, and importance. She would preside over the ingress and egress of the castle, exclude or admit whom she pleased, blacken and whiten according to her own personal feelings, towards the favourers or thwarters of her vanity and pretension. She would have the Dunore patronage and the Dunore purse for her 'subscription, cheap, charitable repository in Dublin,' where piety and patch-work were sold together, for her evangelical school at New-Town Mount Crawley, which stood equally opposed to the protestant and catholic schools at / Dunore, and for her 'society for disseminating cheap tracts,' got up for the especial diffusion of intolerance, and sowing of division among the families of the credulous and unenlightened: but most of all, and best of all, she would have the opportunity of converting, saving, and *governing* the gay, dissipated, and worldly, but *most noble* Emily Augusta, Marchioness of Dunore; of accompanying her back to London, and founding and presiding over religious conversaziones[222] at Dunore House; herself the star of attraction to parliamentary saints and borough-mongering devotées;[223] out-rivalling Madamoiselle Espinasse,[224] who drew from *her* noble patroness the disciples of a very different sect, and, in the end, became chief, where she had *debutée*[225] as follower.[d]

The evening destined for the arrival of Lady Dunore at last approached; not 'like a pilgrim clad in sober grey,'[226] but like a flaunting dame, 'in flame-/coloured taffetas.'[227] It was one of those rich, red, autumnal evenings which, in Ireland, make the sole, the short indemnification, for eleven months of rain and vapour. For miles along the road which led to the town of Dunore, and which wound under the brow of hills, that were almost mountains, the expectation of her cavalcade crowded the acclivities with a long-waiting populace; and when her barouche, followed by two travelling carriages and out-riders, appeared, leaving the high road from Cork, and turning down Mr. Crawley's new made mail-coach road, which passed by Dunore, the old war-cry of the Fitzadelm family rendered the air vocal, and '*Gal-ruadghaboo*,' shouted from a thousand voices, was followed by the descent of a multitude, who, with countenances and gestures as wild as their cry; swept down the sides of the hills, threw up their hats and shelelaghs[228] in the air, surround-/ed the carriage, and attempted to unharness the horses for the purpose of drawing the barouche, as a token of devotion and willing hereditary servitude to the long-absent Fitzadelm family.

Lady Dunore (who had never before visited Ireland), with two gentlemen and one lady, occupied the barouche. Rather agitated than frightened, she gave way to a strong hysterical affection. Her journey to Dunore, like her journey through life, had been subject to sudden alternations of excitement and lassitude, of emotions as opposite as their causes were inadequate. She had wept and laughed in a successive series since she had left Dublin, alternately amused and frightened as the sun shone or the clouds loured: she now wept and laughed together; and would have screamed had there been any chance of her screams becoming audible, but that was impossible. The cry of the '*Irishry Mere*,' and the wrangling of the '*Eng- /lish by blood*' (for Lady Dunore's sturdy English coachman and out-riders protested against the carriage being drawn with *suggans*)* gave her Ladyship no chance for a successful exhibition of powerful emotion; she therefore concealed her face on Lady Georgina Vivian's shoulder, the lady who sat next her, and who, infinitely more intimidated, expressed her fears only by a death-like paleness and a quickened respiration.

Meantime, one of the two gentlemen who occupied the back seat in the barouche, Lord Frederick Eversham, not particularly affected by the alarms of either lady, which he saw were perfectly without cause, endeavoured to dispel them by diverting their attention, and indulging his own peculiar humour. Standing upright in the barouche, he waved his hat, joined the Irish cry, and addressed the multitude with the same / air of mingled drollery and affectation he was wont to assume in a circle at Almacks.[229]

'I believe,' he said, 'I have the honour of addressing the respectable population of Dunore.'

An ill-favoured, but intelligent looking man, who was walking with his hand on the carriage door, and who was the identical travelling companion of the pedlar at Lis-na-sleugh, replied –

'We are the Dunore boys, plaze your honor, up the mountains, come down to welcome home the Marchioness.'

'Then if you please, I will consider you as the organ of that august body, and beg to know the name of so enlightened a representative,' replied Lord Frederick.

'Is it what name I have *upon* me, your honor? I'm called Padreen Gar, for want of a better, Sir. / Is yourself the young Lord, plaze your honor, the Marquis's brother, Sir?'

---

*   Straw ropes.

'I am *a* young Lord, my friend, and *a* Marquis's brother; but not Lord Fitzadelm, if you mean that.'

'It's what I mane shure enough, long life to your Lordship's honor. And is the Marchioness in it, Sir, if you plaze?'

Lord Frederick now gently drew forward. Lady Dunore, who from fits of crying was now convulsed with fits of laughter:

'This, gentlemen,' he said, 'is your liege chieftainess, the Marchioness of Dunore, the mother of your absent chief, and this fair lady,' (drawing forward in her turn the still intimidated Lady Georgina) 'is a noble Saxon dame, come among you to encourage your native manufactures. See, gentlemen, she wears an Irish tabinet pellisse! *que voulez vous?*[230] Here too is, the celebrated Mr. Pottenger, the *Balthassar, / Castiglione,* or complete courtier,[231] of the Dublin Court, alias, the *ca-astle.* He could make you a bow would astonish you, gentlemen, if he had but room. The delicate task now remains of speaking of myself. I am – I am very sorry for it – a young English lord of the pale,[232] or, perhaps, more properly speaking, and as you must observe, a *pale young English lord.* I would have been Irish, gentlemen, if I had been consulted, but, *c'est un affaire arrangé,*[233] and there's no more to be said on the subject. If you have any interest in a name, not purely Milesian,[234] mine is Eversham, and I have the honour to be in the service of the Irish Lord-Lieutenant, who shortly means to visit this oppressed barony, to redress all your grievances, grant all your petitions, banish proctors, suppress tithes, to permit every man to distill his own *poteen,*[235] and every woman to drink it; – that is, if she pleases: for liberty, gentlemen, liberty is to be the order of / the day; so, ERIN GO BRACH![236] Ireland for ever!'

'*Erin go brach!*' and '*Ireland for ever!*' now rent the air, with a thousand '*long lives*' and '*successes*' to his Lordship's honor, and the Marchioness of Dunore. For though not one word of Lord Frederick's mock address had been understood, even by those who could speak English, and they were the minority, yet the exquisite good humour and gaiety of the speaker had their due effects upon the spirits, alive to every impression of kindness and pleasantry. The joyousness, however, that beamed in every wild countenance, and betrayed itself in every forcible gesture, was soon dispelled; for the sound of a drum and fife was heard at a distance, and in a few minutes Mr. Crawley, accompanied by his sons, (the two elder and himself in full uniform), and riding at the head of the Dunore yeomanry cavalry, ap-/proached the carriages at a gallop, scattering on every side the bare-footed crowd, which climbed up the mountain's acclivities, and left the captain-commandant and his troop in full possession of the field. They still, however, continued their route along the ridge of the hills, parallel to the cavalcade, where they rolled along like a mass of dark vapour, borne by the evening breeze.

'By Confucius,' (exclaimed Lord Frederick, as the Crawleys and their troop approached), 'here is the whole armed militia of the celestial empire, led on by the chief mandarin of the province, [237] issuing forth to meet us on our imperial progress, with gongs beating, and colours flying. This is too much! *c'est à mourir de rire!* [238]

'It is altogether too delightful, too odd,' said Lady Dunore, in an ecstasy, who, a few minutes before, with sobs of terror, had pronounced it, 'too frightful, / too barbarous.' 'Oh, my dear Mr. Crawley, how do you do? This is so very kind of you, so very attentive!' She gave him her hand, which he took off his hat to kiss, and turned aside her head, not to conceal her laugh, but to indulge it. She then recognized Mr. Conway Townsend Crawley, begged to be presented to his brothers, enquired with the utmost appearance of affection for Miss Crawley, spoke with vehemence of the warm feelings of the kind-hearted poor Irish, introduced the Crawleys to her travelling companions, and, meeting Lord Frederick's eye, who was alternately gazing on Mr. Crawley and his sons through his glass, [239] was again seized with a violent fit of laughter, as suddenly checked by a speech from Mr. Crawley to some of the peasantry, who still lingered round the carriages.

'I suppose, my lads,' he observed, by no means pleased with her ladyship's commendations of the warm-hearted / poor Irish: – 'I suppose there is not one of yez but knows that your district is proclaimed, [240] and that not a man Jack among you but is liable to be shot dead if he's found out of his cabin at nine o'clock.'

'The district proclaimed!' repeated Lady Dunore, in a voice of surprise and emotion.

'Shot for being out of their cabins at nine o'clock!' re-echoed Lord Frederick, with a transient gravity.

'Oh, yes, my lord, one wouldn't sleep alive in our beds only for it. Not one among them about the carriage there,' he added, in a low confidential tone, 'but is a murderer twenty times over and over.'

Lady Dunore sunk back in the carriage, and in a voice half inarticulate, said, 'I wish, sweet love, we were safe back in England.'

'I wish we were,' replied Lady / Georgina, returning the pressure of her friend's hand; while Lord Frederick, who had been the chief cause of the two ladies visiting Ireland, and who felt himself thus indirectly reproached, endeavoured to turn the object of their fears into ridicule; and, pointing to Mount Crawley, which now blazed with lights on the top of its high dark hill, he exclaimed,

'By all that's luminous, the feast of lanterns! [241] the interior of the celestial empire in a blaze!'

'I fancy, Lord Frederick, 'tis an illuminated air-balloon,' said Mr. Pottinger. 'We sent up one from the Castle-yard on the occasion of the Jubilee. [242] The

Lord-Lieutenant walked that night about the town, accompanied *only* by one aid-de-camp, and one orderly. I had the honour of driving through the streets in one of the vice-regal carriages with the dear little vice-regal children.' /

'Memorable events, my Potty!' returned Lord Frederick, solemnly.

'But, Mr. Crawley, pray explain to us the device of that very brilliant object on the top of yonder hill: is it a temporary edifice?'

'No, my lord, it is nat; it is perennial: for it's my own sate of Mount Crawley; and that part which is lighted up with coloured lamps and transparencies,[243] in honour of her ladyship's arrival, is my Grecian *vesbitule* or portico[244] supported by *cantharides*.[245] It's quite a gem, a perfect *bougie*,[246] in respect of the architecture, I'm tould.'

A general burst of half-smothered laughter followed this speech; but Mr. Crawley, wholly occupied with his own description and importance, continued –

'That painting in the front is done by Miss Crawley, and is an *aregorical*[247] device of Lady Dunore, in the character of the horn of plenty, throwing down pace and prosperity on her people. / To the lift is the great Wellington, bating the world before him, with a retrospective view of Nelson's pillar: [248] and on the right the Ragent's plume;[249] and the British lion there, like a little dog, trampling down upon Boney-part.'

'Crawley, Crawley, thou art mine,

'Crawley, Crawley, I am thine,'[250]

murmured Lord Frederick, in a voice of unrepressed ecstasy. 'To live without thee is impossible! to live with thee is death!' and he wiped the tears from his eyes; while Lady Dunore, no longer taking pains to conceal her risibility, said, in a sobbing voice,

'But, my dear Mr. Crawley, if you really live on the top of that mountain, how am I ever to visit you? You might as well expect to get my horses up Mount St. Gothard, or Sierra Leone.'[251]

'Why, Lady Dunore, though Mount Crawley looks mighty high, seen here / from the bottom, yet when you are close up to it, 'tis nothing at all of a hill; besides, my new approach from Dunore Town, *if any thing*, has an *incline downwards*.'

Lady Dunore, whose hysterical affection had recently taken a tone of risibility, wholly beyond her own control, now absolutely screamed with laughter; while the civil Mr. Pottinger, full of the *respectability* of the Crawley family, and of the excellence of Mr. Crawley's dinners, of which he had often partaken, observed, in a low voice,

'I assure your ladyship, for all his lapsus linguæ,[252] Mr. Crawley of Merrion Square is a most worthy gentleman, and a peculiarly loyal man. He is asked to the private dinners at the castle very frequently, and is a prime favourite with the secretary.'

'You don't really pretend, Mr. Pottinger,' said Lady Dunore, half haugh-/tily, half laughing, 'to tell me *who,* or *what* Mr. Crawley is? He happens to have been the man-of-business-person of my son's family these forty years: he is an excellent creature, to whom we are much indebted; only' (she added laughing violently, and speaking with difficulty,) 'I had half forgotten his slip-slop;[253] and never having seen him *sur son terrein,*[254] I find him too delicious, and I do not think I shall be able to live without him a day.'

'A day!' exclaimed Lord Frederick – 'an hour, a minute. Life I see will now be insupportable, parted from Ching-Foo-Crawley of the yellow button![255] He is mine henceforth, *par tous les dieux!*'[256]

During this short dialogue, young Crawley was urging his father to with-draw from the side of Lady Dunore's carriage, and permit the party to proceed at a more rapid rate, while he took his place himself, and entered into con-/versation with the marchioness. He had seen with the sensitive quickness of self-love, always on the watch to sustain its own consequence, that the blunders and vulgarity of his father, while they were admirably adapted to amuse the idleness, and feed the love of the ludicrous, incidental to the class with which he was now associated, were likewise throwing, by reflection, a shade of ridicule upon the whole family; and having succeeded in removing him, he endeavoured to efface the impression of old Crawley's folly by his own intellectual superiority, and his knowledge of persons, whose acquaintance in London were calculated to increase his own consequence. He inquired for ministers, and men high in office, whom he had met at Dunore House, asking for them by their names, and omit-ting their titles. He told Mr. Pottinger, that he had been made *devilish* ill by their friend the Irish secretary's *bad claret,* / quoted some lines to the rising moon, compared the present state of the southern counties to a slumbering volcano, and then turned the conversation to the Glannacrime election, to speak of the three hundred freeholders of his father and his uncle the commissioner, (who had lately purchased an estate in the county,) all registered in time for the benefit of Lord Adelm, whose absence as yet had produced no ill effect.

'There was no doubt,' he added, 'that his own, and, his father's strenuous exer-tions, and the influence which his family's *personal* and *estated interest,* carried, would ensure success. The hour of attack was approaching, and he was impatient for its arrival, for it would not fail to be the hour of triumph.'

All this *succeeded* with Lady Dunore: it did not wholly fail with her friend Lady Georgina: it produced a whispered remark from Mr. Pottinger, that / young Crawley was a most *talented* fellow, and a particular friend of the secretary.

On the mind of Lord Frederick it impressed the conviction that he was vulgar and presuming; for vulgarity and presumption were qualities readily discernible by the man of fashion and high birth, even though pedantry and affectation might escape him.

The splendid cavalcade at last arrived before the turretted gates of the castle of Dunore; and as the carriages rolled over the pavement of the gloomy court, and the tenants of the old rookery in the rear of the castle screamed their disapprobation of the unusual intrusion, Lady Dunore's susceptible spirits again sunk from their high-wound pitch.

'God send us safe out of this wild country,' said her ladyship, with a deep sigh.

'Amen,' said young Crawley most emphatically. /

'Amen,' repeated Lord Frederick, most theatrically; adding,

'The raven himself is hoarse,

That croaks the fatal entrance of Duncan

Under my battlements.'[257]

'Good heavens,' exclaimed Lady Dunore, 'how can you, Lord Frederick! *you* too, who were in part the cause of bringing me here, with your ridiculous accounts of the "celestial empire," and your "chop mandarins,"[258] that made me die with laughter in London, but are a monstrous dull set out, here!'

The carriages stopped before the last gate; and the lights flashed full upon '*God's providence is my inheritance.*'[259] Lord Frederick read aloud the inscription with solemn emphasis: the ladies alighted, and Miss Crawley appeared in the centre of the dark oak hall, to welcome them to the castle, and to avail herself at once of the immunity which had elevated her to the enviable station of *Dame du Palais*. /

Lady Dunore, who had seen her twice in London, and had received an hundred pretty notes and paper presents from her, was, notwithstanding this basis of intimacy, on the point of addressing her as the housekeeper, when Conway Crawley, anticipating, perhaps, the probable mistake, stepped up to obviate it, by presenting his aunt in form, as one 'equally willing and capable of being useful to her ladyship, in a place where all *must* be to her new and strange.' The sliding, smiling, devoted, and reverential manner of Miss Crawley, all homage, zeal, and humility, decided at once a strong prepossession in her favour; and Lady Dunore, familiarly taking her arm, as the party proceeded to the saloon, left the rest to follow as they might, observed,

'My dear Miss Crawley, I must throw myself entirely on your kindness. I am afraid I shall be monstrous unpo-/pular here: I do not at all know what is to be done with your Irish folk: you understand I am expiring to be popular, and get Fitzadelm his election; I suppose there is nothing, absolutely nothing, in this old castle. Poor Dunore, I believe, only sent over a table service for a petit couvert,[260] and the batterie de cuisine;[261] but you can borrow plate any where, can't you, my dear Miss Crawley, for our election dinners? And then we must have cups and saucers, and cut glass and things for the country ladies. Somebody told me they are very particular in Ireland about those sort of machines. I am the plainest person in the world myself. I don't care in the least if I eat off yellow delf:[262] I can put up with any thing, only let me have plenty of lamps and loungers.[263] But, oh! the misery of these chairs, where one must sit bolt upright! This is all poor Dunore's doing, when he would have every thing Gothic.[264] Georgy, love, we shall / get the lumbago. By the bye, my dear Miss Crawley, have you any doctors, or things of that kind here? I take it for granted you know that we must put up with every sort of misery and inconvenience; but I am myself equal to any thing. Heavens! here's an old French parquet, and no carpet. Good God! is it possible to image such a thing in the nineteenth century! My dear Miss Crawley, do make me out something to put under my feet. I don't care the very least in the world what it is; a bit of Turkey carpet, or a Merino wool rug, or a bear skin, or any thing that is soft and warm you know: Heneage, will you just inquire for a couvre-pied,[265] that is lying loose somewhere in the carriage; or one of my doe-skin travelling blankets: any thing, no matter what. You know I don't care in the least, provided I have something under my feet.'

Mr. Heneage arose to obey, but the / announce of dinner, ordered by Lady Dunore to be ready at nine o'clock, obliged the party to retire, and make some change in their dress, before they sat down to table: meantime the Crawleys took their leave, though pressed to stay by Lady Dunore; but they pleaded in excuse the disturbed state of the country, and the danger of being out after nine: Lady Dunore only replied, with a deep sigh; and when Miss Crawley's carriage was announced, she observed,

'Well, I hope you will muster as strong about me as possible, and remember you all dine here to-morrow: and Miss Crawley, you will come over early in the morning. You know I am altogether in terra incognita.'[266]

Miss Crawley readily complied with this summons; hinting, however, that she was just then occupied with a family party, who would remain a day or two at Mount Crawley, and thus / getting her two younger brothers' families included in the dinner invitation already given.

The cognizance and device assigned to Lady Dunore, by the fanciful gallantry of Lord Frederick, was a branch of the orange tree in fruit and flower, with the motto *Le fruit ne fait pas tomber la fleure;*[267] and her fine person, even at forty-five, was an illustration of the emblem. Time indeed had faded some tints, and effaced some lineaments of loveliness, which no care, no art, could rescue from his touch; yet still she had preserved her claims to personal admiration, which were not suffered to lie idle for want of being asserted. – But if Lady Dunore's personal charms had slightly suffered from the effects of years, her character had submitted so little to their influence, that she preserved to senility all the incoherence and unregulated feeling which had distinguished her youth; and was still as / fresh in folly and inexperience, as when at the age of eighteen she had eloped from a window by a ladder of ropes, though the hall door was free of egress, to marry the Honourable Gerald Fitzadelm, the insolvent and younger brother of a ruined Irish peer. The beautiful person and insinuating manners of Mr. Fitzadelm might have had their due influence; but the circumstance which had decided the sole heiress of eighteen thousand a-year to elope with one, alike lost to character and fortune, was, that her father, the old eccentric Earl of L. had declared he would rather give his only daughter to an English highwayman than to an Irish peer. Two days after, Lady Emily de Vere was on her way to Scotland, with the last Irishman, or rather the last man, that a prudent father would wish to become the husband of his daughter.[e]

Brought up in boundless indul-/gence, free as the winds, which she resembled in violence and instability, compliance had become to her satiety, and opposition enjoyment. The *besoin de sentir*[268] was her disease; and excitement, whether a pleasure or pain, was necessary to her existence. Habit and time increased the demand for a variable series of sensations; and her wanton opposition to her father's will was the brief abstract of her subsequent life.

The Earl of L. had married an Irish lady of singular beauty and attraction. His violence bordering on insanity, his eccentricity and humour drove her to despondency, and then to error. She was frail, divorced, remarried to the object of her imprudent passion, an Irishman, and intailed for ever after the hatred of her first husband upon a country he had never visited. The prejudices of Lord L. were passions; his passions had the durability of principles. He vowed / never to see his daughter, and he died with his vow unbroken, leaving a singular will of a few lines, in which he bequeathed to her his whole fortune, with the proviso that she should neither touch principal nor interest during her husband's life. At her death it was to go to her second child; and from him, if he died without issue, to a remote connexion.[f]

Love had no share in the union of Lord Fitzadelm with the self-willed heiress of the house of L. and cupidity, thus disappointed, retaliated its mortification on its imprudent victim. Lady Emily, in all the humiliating privations of indigent rank, and all the vicissitudes of a gamester's fortunes, led a life more consonant to her unregulated character than favourable to her happiness. The remote chance of a succession to the Dunore property and title enabled Lord Fitzadelm to raise money from credulous usury; and with / such sums, the emoluments of a sinecure place under government, and occasional successes at the gaming-table,[g] they were enabled to support an existence, which frequently touched upon the extremes of fortune, sometimes endured in a prison, sometimes enjoyed in a palace,[h] until a bankrupt credit in England drove them, after a struggle of fifteen years, into an economical retreat in Italy. The ravages of an hereditary disease in the elder branch of the house of Fitzadelm, gradually brought her husband nearer to the goal of his long-cherished hopes. The succession was the die upon which Lord Fitzadelm had staked his fraternal feelings, his honour, and almost his life; and when he was upon the point of obtaining the object of sacrifices, never to be remunerated by any worldly good, death snatched him from its enjoyment. The old Marquis of Dunore, his remote kinsman, having followed his son and his grandsons to / the grave, survived his ambitious heir, Baron Gerald Fitzadelm, by some years.

By her husband's death, Lady Emily was at last relieved from a precarious existence, and restored to that immense fortune, of which the continuance of his life had so long deprived her.

At the head of this princely property, and mother to the heir presumptive of the Marquis of Dunore, she beheld herself possessed of the disposal of three voices in the senate, at a moment when even the echo of a voice had its price, when the British House of Commons was considered by the ministry as a market where the barter of independence was openly to be carried on. To this actual interest, Lady Emily added the chance of an influence over the political opinions of her son and his boroughs; and she became at once an object of anxious solicitude to ministerial intrigue and political cupidity. One member of the cabinet proposed marrying her on the / death of his wife, whose life was limited to a fixed day by her physicians; another solicited her for his brother, and a third had a daughter for her eldest son, and a niece for her youngest, in whom her boroughs would vest at her death. Thus suddenly raised to the summit of political consideration, she found no difficulty, on her son's succession to the marquisate, in obtaining for herself and younger child the rank of a marquis's wife and son. Thus equally high in the gay and diplomatic circles, she became queen at arms in the world of fashion, presided despotically over its heraldry, bestowed or rejected claims to notoriety at pleasure, and was at the head of that small exclusive class of women, who, in London, hold in their own hands the keys of the paradise of vogue, and give or withdraw the patent of bon-ton, as whim, taste, passion, or prejudice decide.

Power and influence, while they in-/creased all the virulent and domineering qualities of her natural character, were not calculated to satisfy that craving for excitement which the vicissitudes of her former life had contributed to beget. In the midst of boundless prosperity she became therefore a hunter after afflictions, and was a *woe-fancier,* as she had been a borough and a china fancier, from mere caprice. She had passed her days in a sort of intermittent fever; and when intervals of rational conduct did occur, they were but pauses of exhaustion between the paroxysms of her disease. Her language and her character became alike volcanic: all was eruption and explosion, or darkness and silence; she felt and acted *par accés;*[269] her laugh was a convulsion, her tears hysterics; and her property and her affairs, partaking of the disorder of her character, set regularity so far at defiance, that her stewards and agents, like harlequin in the comedy,[270] had usually their orders in / one pocket, and their counter-orders in the other.[i]

While the ministers succeeded to their fullest desire with the mother, who gave them up her votes, and talked more nonsense in their favour *out* of the house than their most approved and long-winded disciples could deliver within its walls,[j] the sons (who were assailed, even before they were of age, by all the undermining arts which power exerts to seduce where it cannot convince, and to attain by numbers what it wants in efficiency) were found wholly untractable. Self-willed and perverse as their mother, their obliquity had taken another direction: they laughed at her politics, and held those from whom she received them in utter contempt. It was curious also to observe the family temperament breaking out in a third generation; and what had been violence, bordering on insanity, in the grandfather, exaggeration of feeling, even to / childishness in the mother, terminating in absolute madness in the elder son, and betraying itself in the younger in a brilliancy but eccentricity of genius that was tinctured by all the wildness, oddity, and irregularity of the family infliction. The young Lord Dunore had not long enjoyed his new honours, when it was found necessary to put him under strict confinement; and his mother had the interest to get herself appointed his representative and sole guardian.

Lord Adelm Fitzadelm, the object of all her solicitude, and of whatever she possessed of maternal affection, still held his supremacy by his opposition to her will. Dependent during his life upon her bounty, he turned even his dependence into a tyranny. His extravagant demands upon her purse gave occasion for that resistance and complaint which now formed the principal good of her too prosperous existence. His opposition to all her political ambition / in his favour, his refusing a seat in the house, and an office at court, were sources of eternal reproach, increasing her artificial stock of

'Unheedful passions, and unfruitful woes;'[271]

and while his frequent absences from England, his eccentricities, and his extravagance, afforded her a constant supply of delightful misery, he became necessary to her existence in proportion as he tormented it: and had he been more amenable to her will, he would have been less dear to her affections.

Lord Adelm Fitzadelm, who went wrong by system, and right by impulse, wanted only the spur of necessity to have become super-eminent in whatever direction his talent might have taken. But fortune had spoiled all that would have been a counter-balance to a morbid temperament. Without occupation, contemning the strenuous idleness of official, inefficiency, as he / despised the political system which might have devoted him to it, he gave himself up without reluctance to his natural disposition. Indolent and meditative, at once subtle and fanciful, he possessed the acuteness and querulousness of melancholy, without its causes. The victim of a metaphysical hypochondriasis, he indulged in every species of eccentricity, and was gratified by the singular reputation it acquired for him, where dulness and apathy, mediocrity and moderation, formed the prevailing characteristics of his less gifted cotemporaries. Vain and capricious, but high-spirited and liberal, the shadows of his faults, like those of evening, fell with a breadth disproportionate to the objects which projected them, and were spread far and wide before the world's gaze; while his merits, like the rays of light collected on a focus, were circumscribed within the narrow circle of intimacy, where / they burned brightly in proportion to their concentration. He had made the world the confidant of his errors, and was almost jealous of the friend who acknowledged that he had discovered his virtues.

Lord Adelm was in Portugal in the pursuit of some object of dominant caprice, when a communication was made to the Marchioness of Dunore through Mr. Crawley, from the loyal corporation of Glannacrime, of their wish that she should set up her youngest son for that borough, on the demise of their last member, and in opposition to the family of O'Mahonney, notorious whigs, and supported by the independent interest. Lady Dunore, by the advice of her ministerial friends, acceded to this request, and while her uconscious son was wooing the muse of Camoens, in the shades of Coimbra,[272] she determined to have him placed in nomination for the vacant borough. Thus / would he have been kidnapped into the representation of this borough (for his mother preserved a profound silence on the subject, and kept it out of the English papers), but for a letter he received, containing a few lines, without name or date, but with an English postmark, which informed him of the whole intrigue. This letter had nothing singular about it but the motto of the seal, which was Portuguese, and was '*Sou utile ainda que briccando.*'*[273]

The friends or acquaintances of the Marchioness of Dunore were composed of such persons as are usually found following the great to their temporary retreats, from what is designated *the world;* and were picked up by accident, chosen by caprice, or tolerated from necessity. Her dear friend and quondam[274] rival (selon les régles),[275] Lady Georgina Vivian, was a person of high rank and moderate fortune, one of the supreme / exclusives of the supreme bon-ton. With a character vibrating between sentiment and libertinism, refined in her manners, free in her conduct, she had already replaced the bloom of youth by the complaisance of experience, and secured an ascendency over the *amour-propre* of her male friends, which brighter charms in vain disputed. Acting with desperation against the world's rules, she obtained by her address its suffrages and sanction; and with an air

* I am useful even when sportive.

'silent and soft as saints removed to heaven,'[276]
she had the courage to venture beyond those barriers of discretion, which others of freer deportment trembled to approach.

The character and appearance of Lady Georgina formed opposite extremes. Her conversation was a murmur, her look simplicity, her manner naïveté. She coquetted through a series of attitudes with her lovely children, / and talked of poor dear Vivian, whom she had left at home in the gout, with a tone so tender, that it was difficult to decide how so fond a mother and so devoted a wife could live without the objects of her affection. A letter received by her ladyship from Lord Frederick Eversham, who, on his recent return to England, had been appointed first aid-de-camp to the Irish Lord-Lieutenant, had been shewn by her to Lady Dunore. This letter contained a most overcharged and ludicrous description of the country, from which Lord Frederick derived a salary, very acceptable to the younger brother of one of the poorest dukes in Great Britain. But most of all, his descriptive ridicule rested upon the little court of which he formed a part, and on the government, out of whose arrangements his sinecure originated. He had visited many courts; was familiar with princes, and known to monarchs; he / had fought in the field with emperors, and done the honours for sovereigns: a court without a government, a representative of majesty without power, patronage, or influence, seemed therefore to him an incongruous combination; while the solemn trifling formalities, in which he was himself officially involved, afforded him endless amusement. The whole recalled to him something he had heard or read of the formal puerilities which distinguish the government and court of China; and from the moment he discovered the similitude, Ireland was to him the *celestial* empire, the castle of Dublin,* TIEN SING, or the HEAVENLY SPOT;[277] and secretaries, chiefs, and subs, aides-de-camp, and officers of the household, were *chop-mandarins* of every coloured button in the prismatic scale. /

The letter of Lord Frederick, which promised amusement, the epistles of the Crawleys, which threatened dangers, a dead season, hatred of watering places, an offer from Lady Emily to accompany her friend, a promise from Lord Frederick to compose a party, *faite à ravir*[278] for Dunore Castle, combined to fix the wavering intentions of Lady Dunore. She had a few weeks before given up all idea of attending the election; and her new orders, issued with the promptitude of lightning, and executed with equal celerity, enabled her to reach Dublin before she could find leisure to inform Mr. Crawley that she had changed her mind, and meant to visit Ireland.

---

*   The castle is the residence of the Lord-Lieutenant. From this 'heavenly spot,' all that is good and great is supposed to emanate.

The party promised by Lord Frederick to dissipate the ennui of Lady Dunore, consisted of Mr. Heneage, a young Englishman of fashion, and brother aid-de-camp, and a *Mister* Pottinger, whom Lord Frederick had de-/scribed in his letter as 'the Baldassar Castiglione, the *Cortegiano* of the Irish court,[279] the very representative of its insignificance, formality, and obsequiousness to all the powers that be.' To call forth the results of these qualities had indeed been the principal amusement of Lord Frederick's life, since his arrival in Ireland; while Mr. Pottinger, proud of being distinguished by any great man, looked up to the brother of a duke with a deference, which no consciousness of Lord Frederick's ridicule ever disturbed.

During nine months of the year there is nothing to do at the Irish court; and the office of viceroy, which costs the country near sixty thousand pounds per annum, would be a mere sinecure, but for the necessity of giving half a dozen dinners, and half a dozen balls during the short season of the Dublin winter. Mr. Pottinger and the aid-de-camps were therefore readily spared from *the / park*;[280] and, invited by Lady Dunore, through Lord Frederick, they were charmed to accompany her ladyship to the south of Ireland.[k]

Mr. Heneage was of the rising order of *dull dandies:* he had just sufficient volition to choose his calling, and sufficient energy to iron the cravat that indicated it: he spoke little, because he had nothing to say, and would have spoken less, had it been possible in the necessary intercourse of life to use fewer words; for he believed, that to be truly fine, one should not speak at all. His dandy aphorism was, that every lady should be her own link-boy; and his dandy system was to suffer her to be so. In Dublin he looked down upon the dawning dandyism of the aspiring natives; and in Dublin, as in London, he looked *up* to Lord Frederick Eversham, as the *arbiter elegantiarum*[281] of that system, of which his own particular sect was but a subaltern / branch, suited to inferior spirits, and accommodated to their subordinate capacities.[l] Lord Frederick, though a *young* man, was a *dowager* dandy, and among the original founders of that now degenerate and declining order. Great tact, savoir vivre[282] and humour had distinguished his early probation; when to be a dandy it was requisite to be something more than a coxcomb. Two years residence at Paris (where, as a prisoner of war on parole, he had been the *delices*[283] of every fashionable circle) had confirmed him a *merveilleux*;[284] and he now so pleasantly mingled the fopperies of his home vocation and foreign calling, that it was difficult to say, whether ST. JAMES'S STREET, or the CHAUSSÉE D'ANTIN,[285] had the fairest claim to his peculiarities: he had fought *against* France with a spirit and desperation that would have raised trophies to his fame, had he been a military chief, instead of a subaltern; but he / loved her gaiety, her graces, and her language, with a passion that bordered upon prejudice. He had just returned from his delightful imprisonment, exclaiming with Petrarch, 'I am free – but I am wretched;'[286] and was too much embued with the spirit and grace of French foppery, not to contrast it with the dulness, silence, reserve, and coxcomical pedantry of the new sect of dandies, that had sprung up in his, absence: for the rest,[m] Lord Frederick was one

'Whom folly pleases, and whose follies please,'[287]

who almost dignified vanity, and rendered affectation supportable by the good sense and good feeling, which, in spite of his efforts to conceal both, formed the basis of his character. In gallantry, '*aimer en courant*'[288] was his device; and it was literally *en courant* from Dover to Dublin, (where / his new appointment awaited him,) that he dropped into the opera, saw Lady Emily Vivian in Lady Dunore's box, found or fancied in her what he called 'the *delicious laissez aller*[289] ease of a charming French woman;' and after a few days devoted *aux petit soins*,[290] left London in love and in despair: in Dublin he viewed every thing in a distorted point of view, and wrote that pleasant and ludicrous letter to Lady Emily, complaining of his exile to the CELESTIAL EMPIRE, and describing the ceremonies of the *yellow skreen,* and castle Ko-tou,[291] which had finally effected the existing arrangements at the castle of Dunore.[n]

Lord Rosbrin, who did not arrive with this party, '*faite à ravir*,' but who was to join it from his seat in the neighbourhood, was a foolish-looking young man, whose vacant countenance seemed to beg Macbeth's question of

'Where got'st thou that goose look?'[292] /

He was born and educated in England: his vast property lay in the south of Ireland; and his first visit to that country was for the purpose of enlisting himself into the service of the Kilkenny theatricals,[293] where his rank not obtaining for him a high cast of parts, he was contented to exhibit himself as one of Macheath's gang,[294] and to appear in the character of mutes, senators, generals, and '*others.*'

The intellectual capabilities of Lord Rosbrin went further towards overturning the doctrine of innate ideas than all Locke has written on the subject;[295] without, however, affording much testimony in favour of *ideas acquired* – His mind was a tablet, upon which memory, the genius of fools, had made some traces; and upon this stock of tagrag recollections, collected from playbooks, he had traded through life, without anyone calling into question his property in the possession. Vain, in / proportion as he was weak, his dramatic vocation had arisen from the applause bestowed upon his recitations, when a child, a noble infant Roscius,[296] and the blue and silver draperies in which he had played Ariel[297] at a private theatre, decided his calling for life: from that moment, to him all the world was a stage,

'And all the men and women merely players.'[298]

His mind was stored with theatrical associations, stage properties, and stage anecdotes; scraps of Shakespeare, and silver spangles, with prologues, epilogues, tags, and clap-traps,[299] daggers, cups, and processions,

'Peers, heralds, bishops, ermine, gold and lawn,'[300]

leaving him little better than a walking prompter's book. While Lord Rosbrin only ambitioned the first cast of parts in the theatre he was building at Kil-/
rosbrin, he looked down upon all senates, but that in Othello; and prefering the
potent, grave, and reverend signors of Venice, to the potent, grave, and reverend
signors of St Stephen's: [301] he threw his Irish boroughs into the hands of a political stock-jobber, who dabbled so successfully for him in the funds of ministerial
influence, that from a mere Irish baronet, he in a few years became baron, viscount, and Earl of Rosbrin of Kilrosbrin in Ireland, and Mount Wareham in
England.

To meet this party, Lady Dunore had sent from Dublin a most pressing
invitation to her maternal uncle, the Right Honorable Hyacinth Daly, of Daly's
Court, in the province of Connaught; who obeyed the summons with such
alacrity, that he was seated at his niece's toilette the day after her arrival at the
castle. He loved her for her mother's sake, whose frailty and misfortunes had
substituted pity for the / resentment which had risked his life in a duel with her
betrayer. Mr. Daly, now in his 70th year, of an ancient Irish family, which, for
two centuries, had represented their native county, a privy-councillor of forty
years standing, and one of the small minority which went out on the occasion
of the Union,[302] was in person, character, and manners, a genuine epitome of
the ancient Irish gentleman. He preserved, even at his advanced age, that species
of chivalrous gallantry in his manners, which not long since distinguished the
gentry of the country, and which sent them forth to foreign courts, the most
accomplished cavaliers of their day, or as a monarch, who was himself a fine gentleman, named them, '*the finest gentlemen in Europe.*'[303]Time, which had shed
its snows on the venerable head of Hyacinth Daly, had not 'thinned his flowing
hair,'[304] which he still wore dressed with infinite care, and precisely as he / had
worn it forty-four years before, when he first took his place in the Irish House of
Commons. This luxuriant cöiffure raised itself above a forehead unfurrowed and
fair as the brow of youth, and strongly contrasted with eyes and eyebrows, dark,
and unchanged in hue or lustre. The beautiful person of Mr. Daly, and it was
genuine Irish beauty, had, like his spirits, retained much of its freshness and vigour; and nothing seemed changed by time, but those hopes, with which he had
entered life, and which had the independence of his country for their object.°

Mr. Daly had distinguished himself in the House of Commons, in the memorable year 1782, when Ireland for a moment was a nation, and had kept his
noble mansion in Dublin until the Union: then, having followed the liberties
of his country from their cradle to their tomb, he retired for ever from the scene
of their ruin; spent his winter / in London, and his summer at Daly's Court,
and never saw the capital, but to pass through it for the purpose of crossing the
Channel. His mansion in Dublin, now a barrack, had been open to all the rank,
talent, and worth of the land. There all that has been flatteringly said of the

genius, spirit, and gaiety of the Irish character, was realized in its circles: there he had lived with the Charlemonts, the Burghs, the Grattans, the Currans, the Floods:[305] there many a beauty, who had afterwards added splendor to the galaxy of British loveliness, had imped her wing for conquest; the Gunning, Munroe, or Birmingham,[306] of her day. – With such recollections, brightening as they passed through his memory, Mr. Daly was little fitted to sit down in the fallen capital of his country, under the overshadowing supremacy of cold formal boy politicians, who bring nothing into the land for all they take out of it; and of official clerks, / who, like ill-thriven weeds, impoverish the soil, out of whose waste they have sprung. Mr. Daly's arguments in favour of absenteeship were many and ingenious; and it is melancholy to add, that they were not only founded in truth, but in genuine and indignant patriotism.[P] /

CHAPTER IV.

La noblesse, de soi, est bonne; c'est une chose considerable assurement: mais elle est accompagnée de tant de mauvaises circonstances, qu'il est tres bon de ne pas *s'y frotter*. –
GEORGE DANDIN.[307]

THE time, thoughts, and feelings of Lady Dunore, on the day after her arrival, were wholly engrossed by the three leading members of the Crawley family, whom she had received in her dressing-room after breakfast.

The elder Crawley overwhelmed her with manorial business, plunged her in all the endless details of rents and roads, leases and fines; bills, parchments, and accounts; till her eyes were dazzled with figures, and her head ran round with fatigue. The business, upon which she had at first entered with eagerness, as being new, and out of her / way, became intolerably wearisome, and insupportably disgusting in its progress. Throwing from her therefore a pile of papers, with which Mr. Crawley had heaped her table, she exclaimed in a tone of exhaustion,

'There, Mr. Crawley, I can hold out no longer; pray remove these horrors from my sight, if you wish me to live. You are the best judge of what is for my son's interest. You have always been active in our service. Only we want money to carry on the war, observe; for you Irish are always dreadfully in arrears, at least so our English agent tells me; and in fact, Mr. Crawley, we must get our rents better paid. For the rest, if you wish me to remain among you another week, never overwhelm me again in this way. I would rather,' she added, gradually working herself into a fever of annoyance, 'I would rather be mistress of an Irish cabin, and live upon your Irish potatoes / and butter-milk, than submit to this, Mr. Crawley; and if *this* is the tax upon Irish property, give me back the '*far niente*'[308] of my Italian indigence, where, when one enjoyed the climate, one enjoyed every thing; and when time, patience, temper, pleasure, and health, were not sacrificed for leave to live in a melancholy old castle, on a savage seacoast, at the head of a beggarly town, amidst clouds and storms, and among people, who, as Mr. Conway says, even when quiet, may be compared to a slumbering volcano.'

Old Crawley, with a mingled look of obsequiousness and humour, thus attaining his point, swept up all his papers and parchments into his green bag, and was succeeded by the law agent for the election, who, in his turn, poured forth a tirade of invectives against the whiggish O'Mahonneys, whom he represented as sturdy opponents of the present order of things, and as inflaming the minds of the / people for their own private ends. He spoke of strengthening the hands of her ladyship's ministerial friends, talked jocosely of '*we the corruptionists*,' paraded, with great pomp of words; his electioneering schemes, detailed his wonderful successes, and went through a general account of the large sums which had already been lavished in the prosecution of the cause.

To this specimen of his business talents, he contrived to mingle some smart jokes, and good points, drew forth his '*little equipage of wit*,'[309] dealt largely in quotations, poetical and French scraps, and rounded off his peroration with a well-timed, well placed, and well-received flattery, offered to the rank, political importance, and even personal attraction, of his noble patroness.

'Well,' interrupted Lady Dunore, yawning, as he attempted to return to some detail of the freeholders lately / registered; 'well, for the present that will do, Mr. Conway, but spare me the *refrain* of the *eternal* election. You have managed so well that I think we may promise ourselves a dull kind of success enough. It would set one wild if Fitzadelm should come over and spoil all though, and refuse the borough, after so much money has been spent upon it.' And she added, with a look that indicated it would *not* be an unpleasant thing if he did, 'but there is no chance of that, and so things will go on sleepily enough; and I don't think I need go to catch one of your Irish typhuses, that you describe so frightfully, by personally canvassing your greasy corporation people of Glannacrime. So I leave it all to you, Mr. Conway, only just don't let us say any more upon the subject now. But, oh dear, Miss Crawley, what pretty thing are you making out of that scrap of *couleur-de-rose*[310] *note paper?* Couleur-de-rose is such / a relief to the eye after yellow parchments.'

'It is an invisible fly-trap, Madam, to catch the little epicures who come to feast upon hands, which, as Cleopatra says, 'kings have lipped,'[311] replied Miss Crawley with an insinuating smile.

Miss Crawley, with scissars and cut-paper, now succeeded in her turn to her brother and nephew: but pink paper, like yellow parchments, and flytraps, as well as elections, were soon destined rapidly to wear out the attention of Lady Dunore; and Miss Crawley had recourse to the castle, of which she voted herself the Cicerone, to revive her flagging interest, and to engross her ladyship to herself for the rest of the day. In the course of two hours they had mounted to the highest turret, descended into the deepest dungeon, penetrated the darkest closet, stood exposed upon the rudest battlement, talked of ghosts and rebels, balls and / insurrections, marked out alterations and improvements, ramparts to be thrown down, and verandas to be raised, swans to be procured, and ponds to be cut for them, the sea to be banked out, and rivers to be turned in, families to be excluded, and families to be admitted; with some discussions upon evangelical schools, some quotations from evangelical tracts, and many, very many, soft, insinuating, penetrating compliments from the diplomatic Miss Crawley on the reform, which the power, influence, rank, talents, and virtues, of Lady Dunore might effect in a dark, unfortunate, and bewildered people.

Reform, with Lady Dunore, meant change; change was always delightful; and for the present so was Miss Crawley, who indicated its possibility, and who had already awakened so strong a prepossession in her intended neophyte, that Lady Dunore would not part with / her, to return to Mount Crawley to dress for dinner, till she had promised, that as soon as her family visitors should leave her, she would come and take up her residence at Dunore. The male Crawleys had fatigued with their facts, the *female* had amused with her speculations; both served their own purposes, while they played with her feebleness and caprice: and as Miss Crawley drove off from the castle in her jaunting car,[312] she mentally exclaimed, with triumph, '*Dame du Palais indeed!* and *now* let Lady Clancare look to it.'

The fashionable guests at Dunore Castle had not met till the idle half-hour before dinner assembled them in the saloon, into which they straggled one by one. Mr. Pottinger was engaged with Debret's Peerage,[313] Mr. Heneage with his cravat, and Lady Georgina in winding gold thread from an ivory reel, held by Lord Frederick, who lay lounging beside her on an ottoman, when the / whole house of Crawley, male and female, were announced en masse,[314] and made their entrée[315] together. The men were in inky suits of professional black, save the major, who was all scarlet and *orders*.[q] The ladies were covered with Honiton lace,[316] and Irish diamonds. The four tawny Miss Crawleys were beflounced and befurbelowed, knee deep; and Miss Leslie dragged up her gown on her fat white shoulders, as she entered, with a look of innocent effrontery that might put even fashionable ease to the blush of inferiority.

This '*incursion of the Kalmucks,*'[317] as, Lord Frederick termed it, seemed to afford him strong motives for amazement and delight. He dropped the ivory reel, seized his glass,[318] and murmured his observations to Lady Georgina, who seemed no less amused than himself, while, according to precedence, precise and formal, they passed up to the top of the room, where Mr. Pot-/tinger, with his old habits of ceremony, stood receiving them in the absence of Lady Dunore, the Lady-Lieutenant of the hour. The eldest Miss Crawley, who had for the day amalgamated her high-church Methodist costume, with the pastoral simplicity of a white chip hat[319] and primrose ribbands (a sacrifice to the genius of the place where she now found herself),[r] was the first, as proudly pre-eminent in ridicule, to attract his attention; and he asked Lady Georgina, whose spy-glass followed the direction of his own:

'Now, in pity, who is that *Bergere derangée*,[320] so withered and so wild in her attire? – the oldest piece of mortality, surely, that ever took shelter under a white chip hat! *Cela a cent ans sonnés!*[321] not an hour less! and then the matron, with the green necklace and the green eyes, set apparently by the same hand. And those four little 'tawny tight ones,'[322] and the fat pretty rolly polly / soul, with the brogue in her shoulders! *c'est impayable.*[323] But here comes *Ching-foo* Crawley, of the yellow button, at the head of the Chop Mandarins of the interior. I must go and do Ko-tou,[324] and renew my acquaintance with him. No, the whole celestial empire furnishes nothing like my Ching-foo Crawley.'

While Lord Frederick, with great cordiality, returned the familiar pressure of Mr. Crawley's two hands, who, as he afterwards expressed it to Lady Georgina, was an '*embrasseur impitoyable*,'[325] Lady Dunore entered, leaning upon her uncle's arm, flushed and animated by the bustle and excitement of the morning, and by the arrival of her venerable relation, who was the most welcome of all her guests, because he was *the last*. She received the whole Crawley congress, to many of whom she was a stranger, with an air, imposing from its decided, but carelessly betrayed, consciousness of high superiority; and / which was the more marked, by the exaggerated condescension of her manner and over-wrought cordiality, a cordiality, which, though eminently conciliating, was any thing but familiar.

When the first salutations were over, the Crawley phalanx, 'taking close order,'[326] ranged into a formal circle, and seated themselves in a row with the regularity of nine-pins, looked as if they were incorporated with their chairs, and remained silent, motionless, and under evident restraint. The women, when called on by Lady Dunore, minced their Irish accent, and spoke in monosyllables to conceal it: the men for the moment were struck dumb by the appearance of the 'great Daly of Daly's Court,' who was out of their *cast* and *class,* and whom they had never seen at *the castle dinners*. The intermitting fever of Lady Dunore now seized upon her imagination, as she contemplated the group of which she was the restless / centre. The Crawley *circle* was a circle she never could break; the Crawley *dulness* was a dulness she never could dissipate; and while she fluttered and floundered, as if under some spell, she in vain endeavoured to dissolve all restlessness, motion, and ennui. Lord Frederick, seated by Lady Georgina, followed her motions with transport, and whispered to her as she hovered near him:

'*Marquise de mon ame,*[327] that circle is your death-warrant. You die the death of the bored: this day, this fatal day, *je vous en repond, bel idol mio*.[328] Look! 'tis the hieroglyphical circle of eternity! the serpent with his tail in his mouth![329]

an image of the durability of the celestial empire! and the reign of the Crawley manderins and manderinas, without beginning or end!'

'I won't wait another minute for Rosbrin,' said the marchioness, reddening to the eyes, and pulling the bell / with a violence that left its cord in her hands. 'I will have dinner directly.'

'Wait for Rosbrin!' repeated Mr. Daly: 'no, to be sure; nobody waits for Rosbrin. His movements are more likely to be regulated by a prompt-book than a time-keeper; for while your soup cools at Dunore, he is probably 'supping, full of horrors,' at Macbeth's banquet, or flinging a shoulder of mutton at Catherine's head,³³⁰ while your venison drops from the spit.'

Dinner was now ordered; and its announce broke the spell of Lady Dunore's torment, by breaking up the Crawley circle; – the consequence she had contemplated in hurrying the event which she believed could alone effect it.ˢ

Of all the members of the Crawley family, old Darby, though lowest in professional rank, was the person most at ease with respect to himself and the circle in which accident might place / him. There was a proud consciousness of native humour about him, which, if it did not enable him to distinguish between being laughed *with*, or laughed *at*, led him to risk himself in all situations; for, save where his worldly interests were concerned, there was an obtuse, inveterate, untractable dulness about him, which left him the most unguarded mark the point of ridicule could aim at. The distinguished attention paid by the marchioness to his family, the desire to SHEW OFF before Mr. Daly, and to evince to him the intimacy in which he stood with the Dunore family, now led him to the assumption of a more than ordinary ease and familiarity; and before the marchioness had finished her soup, he addressed her, with –

'If I'm not entirely mistaken, the last time I had the honour of *téte-à-téte*-ing³³¹ your ladyship in a glass of wine, as the French say, it was at your sweet little / villa of *Sans-six-sous*,³³² near London: and I should he proud if you would allow me the honour of commemorating that pleasure now. I remember some charming Madeira you had at *Sans-six-sous*. What wine does your ladyship choose, Madam?' and he looked in vain for the wine glaciers of solid silver, which heated rather than cooled the wines of his own table. Miss Crawley had equally in vain whispered 'Sans-souci' during this speech, while Lord Frederick, laying down his spoon with a look little short of ecstasy, called the attention of Lady Dunore, who was debating with Mr. Daly the probability of Lord Rosbrin's arrival, by saying,

'Lady Dunore, Mr. Crawley is addressing some little *reminiscence* to your unattending ear, about *Sans-six-sous*, your villa near London.'

'I am after requesting your ladyship to drink wine with me,' added Mr. Crawley. /

'Oh, willingly! but I don't drink wine at dinner. I am upon a regimen[333] just now: but I'll take *soda water* to your wine, Mr. Crawley, with all my heart.'

This was an innovation in Mr. Crawley's idea of good-breeding, which threw him entirely off his centre. In his circle, ladies never refused to take wine, whether they wished for it or no: and the circumstance of no wine being upon the table added to his confusion; when the butler stepping up, and asking what wine he chose, relieved his perplexity, and he answered, 'Port, if you plaze;' adding, 'If your ladyship is upon a *regiment*, I should be sorry to make you give up your proscription.[334] So I shall have the honour to drink your ladyship's health, *solus cum solo.*'[335]

'Thank you, thank you, Mr. Crawley,' said Lady Dunore, laughing unresistingly, while Lord Frederick, wholly / foregoing his soup, ecstasised over the richer feast presented him by Ching-foo Crawley, of the yellow button. Meantime Mr. Crawley repeatedly sipped from his glass with a great variety of expression in his countenance, each indicating disappointment; till at last he bent forward, and with a face of great importance, said,

'Pray, my lady, who do you dale with?'

'Who do I deal with, Mr. Crawley?'

'Yes, Madam: I'd just be glad to know the name of your ladyship's wine merchant, that's all.'

'I believe that wine was sent in, two years back by poor Lord Dunore. Is it not so, Robertson?'

'Yes, my lady.'

'Why then, whoever he is, he does not use you well,' returned Crawley, significantly. /

'Why, what is the matter? Is the wine bad? Pray taste that wine for me, Mr. Daly.'

Mr. Daly having put the glass to his lips exclaimed, with a look of nausea, 'By jove, 'tis catsup.'[336]

'I give you my honour,' said Crawley, coolly. 'I thought it was no great things, no more than the mare that ran for the whiskey; but didn't care to be the first to find fault; for every one to their taste; and I didn't know what might have been the *bon mot*[337] of London in the present day.'

'Oh, but you Irishmen are such judges of wine,' said Lady Dunore, smiling, 'I suppose it is very difficult to please you.'

'We were,' said Mr. Daly, 'before the introduction of that coarse, vulgar beverage, *port*, at our tables, which the severe taxation at present obliges us to drink. In my time, every gentleman / imported his own claret, which he drank out of the wood;[338] and they tapped a hogshead of French wine as we now broach a barrel of small-beer. I remember when I first prohibited wine at the second table at Daly's Court, it caused a mutiny; and I was obliged to promote the livery servants to the steward's room; and discharge the upper servants, who would not consent to drink punch after dinner. But if our present draining system of taxation continues, I must soon come to whiskey punch myself; for we poor private gentlemen, who have nothing but our estates to live on, which, like the country, are daily losing in their intrinsic value, must give up our habits before the means of supporting them give us up; and so make a virtue of necessity.'[t]

'It is however to that very taxation,' said young Crawley, pertly, 'together with other measures of equal wisdom of / his Majesty's ministers, that *we* owe *our* present prosperity.'

'Exactly,' said Mr. Daly, dryly.

'Exactly,' in an emphatic tone, reiterated every member of the Crawley family; while the commissioner made a speech upon the flourishing state of the revenue, and concluded with asking Lady Georgina to take wine. Lady Dunore taking the hint of drinking wine, whispered Lord Frederick–

'Now pray do the honours, and help me on, or I shall never hold out.'

'No, no – now, pray,' said Lord Frederick, 'it is not in my way. Heneage always drinks wine with the young ladies at the castle, as youngest
aid-de-camp.'

Mr. Heneage, thus called on, pointed his spy-glass round the table to observe who was worthy of the distinction, and at last sent the butler to Miss Leslie, who sat within two of him; and then lean-/ing back in his chair, and suffering his own man to fill his glass, instead of bending forward to meet the accustomed inclination of the head of the fair person he had challenged, he simply asked the servant, 'Wilkie, does she bow?' and being answered in the affirmative by his cup-bearer, he drew his chin within his impregnable citadel of starched muslin, and again gave up his attention to his Bechamelle.[339] The first course was still removing, when the attention of the whole company was attracted to the windows by a curious sort of vehicle – a chaise-marine,[340] covered with a canvass awning, gaudily painted with dramatic trophies, cups, daggers, and masks, surmounted by a scarlet flag, and drawn by four horses, with bells and shewy harness, driven by two boys, in English waggoners' frocks, and straw hats with green ribbands, resembling the carter's, formerly produced on the stage in Love in a Village.[341] /

'Good heavens!' exclaimed the startled, and therefore delighted Lady Dunore, 'what is that?'

Every body rose from their seats, and Mr. Daly observed,

'That! that's Lord Rosbrin's thespian car, as he calls it, which he brings
every where with him in Ireland, and which is freighted with theatrical paraphernalia.'

'Is he so stage-struck as that?' asked Lady Dunore of her uncle.

'He asserts that he is so, upon political and national principles. Haven't you heard of his new system of civilizing Ireland, by establishing dramatic encampments, and opening private theatres in the remote counties, as we found schools, drain bogs, or cut roads through the mountains, for the public good?'

'Do you know, that I think his scheme excellent,' said Lady Dunore,

who, like the maitresse du tripot of Scarron, '*aimoit la comedie plus que / sermon ou Vêpres*,'[342] 'and I promise you he shall have my hearty concurrence. I will have one of the turrets turned into a theatre immediately.

A chariot and four, with out-riders, now passed the windows.

'Here is Rosbrin himself,' said Mr. Daly; and at Lady Dunore's desire he went forth to receive his grand-nephew. Lord Rosbrin soon appeared, following his venerable kinsman, on whose countenance a good-humoured ridicule was visibly marked. His lordship had made his toilette at the last stage, and presented himself to the delighted and astonished eyes of the Crawley ladies in the singular and elegant costume of an

Austrian chasseur:[343] u his belt, studded with mock stones, his embroidered pelisse, his yellow boots, and waving plumage, produced all the sensation he expected on those who had never seen him before, and even on those who had. After a moment's pause, he advanced; and having paid his respects to Lady / Dunore with a theatrical air, he turned alternately to Lord Frederick and Mr. Heneage, giving a hand to each, with 'Great Glamis! Worthy Cawdor!'[344] then bowing round the table, solemnly pronounced – 'Now good digestion wait on appetite, and health on both,'[345] and took his place by his fair hostess and cousin.

'You seem out of spirits, Rosbrin,' said Lady Dunore, observing the short incoherent answers he gave to some questions put to him by some of the company.

'I care not for my spirits,' he answered in the words of Celia, 'if my legs were not weary.[346] But I pray you bear with me, gentle coz.'

'Bear with you! Why what is the matter?' asked Mr. Daly.

'Nay, mine uncle Clarence, nothing of moment; but I have been fagging to death to get my theatre up at Kil-Rosbrin against November. We open with Macbeth; an amazing strong cast: / great tragedy forces. I mean to play Lady Macbeth myself. Mrs. Siddons[347] is to lend me her old point,[348] the finest, the only original point in the world: were it mine I would not exchange it for '*one entire and perfect crysolite*.'[349] Apropos of the Siddons' dynasty. I dined in *private* with Kemble the other day:[350] mark me 'good man delver:' you will hear of an event in the dramatic world will '*scatter wild amazement round*.'[351] Let Drury look to it: there's '*something rotten in the state of Denmark*.'[352] I shall allude to it in my opening prologue.'

'By-the-bye, I am enchanted with your theatrical scheme, Rosbrin,' said his fair cousin, 'and mean to visit you as soon as you open the campaign.'

'*That will be ere set of sun*,' replied Lord Rosbrin; 'that is, I mean by November, in order to follow close upon the Kilkenny plays. Their '*funeral baked meats will coldly furnish / forth our marriage feast;*' for some of their principal performers join us: and the Lord and Lady-Lieutenant, with all their suit, will attend '*on our solemnities:*' aye, '*we'll make the welkin dance:*' we'll '*raise the night owl in a catch, shall draw three souls out of one weaver.*'[353]

'Out of *one* waver!' repeated Darby Crawley, who looked up with great deference to the rank of Lord Rosbrin, though quite at a loss to discover whether his strange phraseology was supreme fashion or absolute nonsense.

'But you don't really mean that?' said Lord Frederick in a tone of vexation. 'You don't absolutely mean that the *castle people* are coming to you in November?'

'*Take this from this*,' said Lord Rosbrin, pointing to his head and shoulders, 'if this be otherwise; 'tis truth, '*if truth were ever pregnant
made by circumstance.*'[354] /

'What! do you really mean that they come down in their *public* capacity, with little pages and lank aid-de-camps, busy chamberlains and sinecure controllers, fat battle-axes and battered kettle-drums, with the eternal '*God save the King*, and *Patrick's Day*, and *Patrick's Hall,*'[355] and the whole set out of the *ca-astle?*'

'*All*,' said Lord Rosbrin, in a tone of absence, and going over in his mind the business of the stage for the performance of Henry the Fourth;[356] 'all, sheriff, vintner; chamberlains, drawers, two carriers, travellers, and attendants, with the sign of the Boar's Head for East-cheap.'

'The Lord bless us!' exclaimed old Crawley, much astonished at this travelling equipage; while Mr. Pottinger, dropping his knife and fork, and rubbing his hands, was about to set both gentlemen right by describing the *real* arrangements of the vice-regal tour, as / they occurred to his memory, with all necessary dates, places, names, &c., when he was stopped short by Lady Dunore addressing Lord Frederick:

'By the bye, Lord Frederick, how does Lady B. get on in her new office? Doesn't it bore her to death, that kind of representation? It must be entirely out of her way, poor dear!'

'Why it does, I believe, *tant soit peu*;[357] but, upon the whole, she gets on pretty fairly. For ten months in the year, she lives at that bel respiro,[358] the *Phaynix*, where she rears little pigs, sows mignionette seed, talks of her liver, and drinks chamomile tea.'

'Yes, yes. I know all her *façons à la ordinaire*[359] well enough. But I mean as *Lady-Lieutenant!* – Is not that the Irish phrase for your *viceroy's wife*? How does she manage?'

'Oh! as she can; like the rest of them, I believe; ask my *Potty*; he is the law and the prophet on these / points. But, on the whole, she *cuts* when she can,

keeps clear of the Kalmucks (except on the regular Ko-tou days, when the yellow skreen is exhibited), and lives *toute comme une*
autre.'[360]

Mr. Pottinger opened his eyes. This was flat profanation of a subject sacred to his imagination; and he would have opened his mouth, but that Lady Dunore went on, while her careless manner of talking of the Lady-Lieutenant and the castle astonished and almost mortified the Crawley mandarins as much as Mr. Pottinger.

'But then, you know, Lord Frederick,' continued the marchioness, 'poor dear Lady B. is such a dowager dowdy, and so very little *en evidence*[361] in the world. It's very odd, but she never could get on, *par example*;[362] I don't know why, except, I believe, that she fevers one so, and fusses and fidgets, and that sort of thing, when / she is taken in for a squeeze.[363] For as to an exclusive thing, she is quite *hors du combat*;[364] and then she talks so of herself, and her liver, and things. In short, I can't conceive Lady B – *en grande ceremonie*;[365 v] besides, she dresses so ill. I used to think she spoiled the look of my *opera-supper*: didn't you, Georgy, love?'

'Her excellency,' said Mr. Pottinger, solemnly, and endeavouring to get in a word, 'goes through the necessary forms of drawing-rooms and birth-days[366] with peculiar grace and dignity; and –'

'And kisses all the Mrs. *Maguffins* and Mrs. O'Gallaghers, *à toute entrance*,'[367] interrupted Lord Frederick. 'Then she simpers, bobs under a canopy, and she walks in and walks out to 'God save the King,' with a white wand, and an usher at the end of it; then struts forth Lord B –, bored to death with '*Son nez en l'air*,'[368] and his heart / under the ribs of his South-Downs,[369] and followed by Grizzle, Noodle, Doodle,[370] Foodle, and 'others,' while we English all walk after, like '*chickens, come cluck*,'[371] – to slow music, by Jove! Only think of *my moving* to slow music! *Voyez vous*?[372] like a mute in a play. But the fun of all fun is my Potty's face upon these high solemnities. Ha! ha! ha!'

Here the image of the court, of which he was so distinguished a member, became too ludicrous for the risible faculties of the noble aid-de-camp, and amidst bursts of hearty laughter, in which he was joined by such members of the company as did not consider the Irish court to be the TIEN SING, the, 'heavenly spot,' he continued to repeat, 'Moving to slow music, by Jove! That's the fun!'

The lengthening faces of the Crawleys and Mr. Pottinger induced Mr. Daly to call to order; and Lady Dunore / taking the hint, arose, and left the gentlemen to Lord Frederick's further details *of the celestial empire*. – She conducted the ladies to the drawing-room, and then left them, desiring Miss Crawley to be *her lady-lieutenant*, and call for coffee when they wished it. The two friends ascended the stairs together, on their way to their respective dressing-rooms, where each was in the habit of taking a *siesta*[373] between dinner and tea. Lady Georgina observed, in her fondling way,

'These people bore you to death, sweet love.'

'No, dearest,' yawned Lady Dunore.

'But,' continued Lady Georgina, yawning in turn, 'they are very good sort of people, I dare say, *Ma Belle*.'[374]

'Yes, I dare say they are, *mignonne*;[375] but they need not sit in a circle for all that. You have no idea the effect a / *circle* has on me, Georgy love, – it kills me.'

At this moment, her own woman passing, she said, 'Do let some of the footmen go into the drawing-room, and place the chairs back to back; and take the tables and things from the walls, and throw all into the middle of the room, and send coffee to Lady Georgina's dressing-room, and call me when the gentlemen come out.'

'By, bye,'[376] dearest,' said Lady Georgina, kissing first one cheek, and then the other.

'Day, day, love,'[377] said the marchioness, pressing her lips to her friend's fair forehead; and she added 'I'll try and dose away the Crawley stupor, till the men come out.'

More than an hour elapsed, before the marchioness joined her guests: tea was serving as she entered. Lord Frederick, Mr. Daly, and Lady Georgina, occupied an ottoman on one side / of the fire-place; and the whole race of Crawley formed from that point a semi-circle, which reached to the other. The marchioness started back, and then raised a desponding look; but took the seat offered her by Mr. Pottinger. A dead silence ensued, interrupted first by the young counsellor, who had been upon some political subject when the lady entered the room, which he again resumed. His brothers, meantime, remained silent and stupified; the high sheriff not venturing a single observation, and the major becoming absolutely confounded, after having made an unsuccessful effort at wig-warns and bivouacs, 'the Peninsula,' and 'the Raygent's levy.'

'There,' said Lord Frederick, raising his glass to Lady Dunore's face, 'there's a bored marchioness; this is a *coup de grace*:[378] let her survive it, if she can. Mr. Po –tinger,' he exclaimed aloud, 'will you sing a / comical song, or tell a story, my Potty –.'

'*That antique song*,' interrupted Lord Rosbrin: '*we've had last night*,' '*Music hath charms*'[379] Mr. Pottinger! or give us '*Let us the cannikin clink*,' or '*Troll us a catch*;'[380] and he ran over the keys of the piano-forte as he spoke. At the word *music*, Mrs. Serjeant, and the four Miss Serjeant Crawleys, were thrown into a state of gentle agitation. Mrs. Crawley's life had been passed in running about with her accomplished daughters, from one musical system-monger to another; and the many hours a day they practised, the various methods they had adopted, the public exhibitions in which they had assisted, and the effect they had produced *at Lady Kilgobbin's parties*, were the eternal themes of her conversation. Although she had not before opened her lips, (overawed by the fashionable *non chalance*[381] of the two great ladies); yet / now, animated by maternal vanity, she ventured to observe that 'music was a charming *talent,*' inquired '*who made the piano-forte*' that stood in the centre of the room, and asked if it '*was in tune:*' the hint was immediately taken by the dowager Miss Crawley, always on the alert to puff off the family acquirements; and it followed, of course, that the Misses Crawley were asked to perform, at the sly suggestion from their aunt, 'that they were charming musicians, taught in Dublin, and *finished* at Bath!'

'Oh then,' said Lady Dunore, starting up, 'for heaven's sake, let us have music, let us have any thing;' and scattering about the chairs from whence the Crawleys, on the impulsion given by this mainspring of all motion, had risen, she begged the young ladies would try something. The young ladies unprepared, indeed, but never unwilling to exhibit, went to the instrument; / while Lord Rosbrin, turning to Darby Crawley, asked him from the Tempest, '*Did you ever hear the tune of our catch played by the picture of nobody?*'[382]

'Why then, I can't charge my memory that I ever did,' replied old Crawley, gravely.

'Music,' continued Lord Rosbrin, taking hold of Mr. Crawley's button, '*was ordained (was it not?) to refresh the mind of man after his studies.*'[383]

'To be sure it was, my Lord!' replied Crawley flattered at this reference; 'and when my son Conway was going through his college course, he was *ingenuous*[384] at the flute, being always given to *sedentary* habits.'

'*Here then we'll sit; and let the sound of music come upon our ears,*'[385] said Lord Rosbrin; and he handed Mr. Crawley a chair.

Meanwhile the four, Miss Crawleys laid by their gloves and fans, and ar- / ranged themselves round the instrument. Two sat down to the pianoforte; one stood on the right of the keys to get in one hand, to play the extreme treble, according to a new system of playing with five hands upon one piano-forte; and the other two prepared their voices by gentle *hems*! to sing a duct to this multifarious accompaniment. They now began. '*Away with melancholy,*'[386] which they sang with such sad faces, arid tuneless voices, that it made everyone melancholy to hear them; until the *alto*[387] Miss Crawley, who had never before played out of her musical stocks, went rambling with her emancipated hand over the instrument, like a colt released from harness, to the utter confusion of her sisters, vocal and instrumental, and to the consternation and agony of her mother and aunt, she suddenly burst into tears, and cried out that 'she could not play without her cheiroplast.'[388] /

Lady Dunore, equally delighted with tears and laughter, exclaimed,

'Poor little thing! what is the matter? what is her cheiroplast? can my maid make it? There is nobody so ingenious as Dorette: what is it like?'

Miss Crawley endeavoured to explain what a cheiroplast was, for Mrs. Serjeant was utterly confounded at seeing the labour of years thus overthrown in a moment, and in such a moment. The young ladies now arose, pulling up their gloves and seizing their fans, in becoming emotion, while Mr. Crawley, to, relieve the general confusion of the family, took fat Miss Leslie by the hand, and said,

'Come Miss Leslie, honey, give us a touch on the piano; a song or a country dance in your own sprightly way. She has a sweet little voice. I give you my honour, Lord Rosbrin, and would rather hear her than all the *bravado*[389] singing and Italian haberdashery in the / world. Kate, my dear, this is the Earl of Rosbrin.'

'Kate,' said Lord Rosbrin, taking her hand on this presentation, and instantly transformed into Petruchio,[390] '*the prettiest Kate in Christendom, Kate of Kate Hall, my super-dainty Kate, for dainties are all cates; and therefore, Kate, take this of me, Kate of my consolation:*' and he kissed her hand as he placed her at the piano-forte, while Kate of Kate Hall, blushing more from triumph than shame, drew up her frock upon her naked shoulders, and, without further preface, began to sing, 'My Henry is gone.'[391] Her song ended, was encored by Lord Rosbrin, applauded by Lady Dunore, bravoed by Lord Frederick, and epilogued by Darby Crawley, who, with a humorous wink at the gentlemen, said,

'The devil is in them *Henrys!* I never knew one of them would stay with a girl yet.' /

To Lady Dunore's horror, the Crawleys were now all returning to their chairs and their circle, when, to her infinite joy, their carriages were announced, and she bowed them out with as much pleasure as she had bowed them in: observing to Miss Crawley, as she came up to wish her good night –

'When you get rid of your friends remember your promise; and pray get rid of them soon.'

She then threw herself on a cushion at Lady Georgina's feet, and laying her head on her lap, uttered a pious 'Thank heaven!'

'Oh! don't think you are *quitte pour la peur*,'[392] said Lord Frederick, 'The Crawleys are *your's au revoir*.[393] In the mean time let us call for the brag table.'[394]

Cards were now brought in; and in the vicissitudes of a game, in which Mr. Daly and Lord Frederick played desperately high, she forgot the Craw-/leys, dull and clever, and their spell-bound circle, which, for want of some greater source of annoyance, had become the phantom of her easily excitable imagination, and propensity to annoyance, real or fancied.[w] /

CHAPTER V.

'Citizens! your voices!'[395]
'Cruel are the times when we are traitors
To ourselves – when we hold rumour
From what we fear – yet know not what we fear;
But float upon a wild and violent sea,
Each way –'
                    SHAKESPEARE.[396][x]

CIVILIZATION and social happiness, among the ancients, may be considered as having been almost stationary. The refined philosophy and elegant accomplishments of the Greeks, the vigour of volition and hardihood of enterprise of the Romans, contributed little towards the permanent prosperity of the species; for mankind remained, nearly as in a state of nature, divided into two classes; the strong and the free, and the feeble and the enslaved. /

In the woods of Germany[397] were laid the foundations of a combination, which, favoured by accident, and nurtured by the co-operation of many causes, has given a new impetus to society, and has effected a substantial improvement in the human condition, equivalent almost to a second creation.

The principle of representative government, founded in the positive equality of all men before the law, by raising the importance of the people, has given activity to their industry, combination to their efforts, illumination to their intellect, and integrity to their morals. The security of property, and the sacredness of person, by elevating individuals in their own estimation, has inspired in them a reverence for the opinion of others; and while they place the mere man beyond the physical sufferings, they raise him above the moral turpitude and groveling vices of slavery and subjection. /

The connexion between virtue, happiness, and liberty, is inseparable; and that insatiable lust of power, which had so repeatedly been foiled in its direct efforts against popular rights in these kingdoms, has more fatally succeeded, by sapping and undermining the foundations upon which they repose. A well organized system of corruption, commenced even before the reign of George the First, has been perseveringly directed to overthrow the constitution, by demoralizing the subject; and has rendered the luxury of commercial prosperity an unperceived agent of political degradation. This system, which in England was at first cherished in silence, and propagated in darkness, has from the beginning been openly and unblushingly pursued, and unresistingly admitted, amidst the dispiriting factions, and debilitating dissensions, which have constantly agitated the sister island.[y]

Centuries of cruelty, and injustice of / misrule, and military violence, had not subdued the spirit of the people of Ireland, a spirit which might be said to belong almost to their temperament; and other means were resorted to, in order to quench a fire, which direct oppression could not extinguish. Their parliament, filled with men selected by the English government, and separated in feelings and in interests from the people, it affected to represent, set the country up to sale, and concluded their '*most filthy bargain*,'[398] on the ruin and degradation of the land.

By this act of political suicide, which banished at a blow the entire rank, illumination, and wealth of the kingdom, and left the manufactures to pine without encouragement, and the soil to exhaust itself under an inadequate and unthrifty cultivation, the political and legislative interests of the people were entrusted to a foreign and a rival senate of five hundred and fifty-eight / members, diluted indeed by one hundred Irishmen, the representatives for the most part of the English ministry, and the dominant religious faction, and all exposed to the dissipations of a luxurious and expensive capital, impelled by an almost pardonable vanity to exceed their incomes, and thus thrown by their necessities at the feet of power, and insensibly imbued with the feelings, the prejudices, and the opinions, of those with whom they are sent to associate.[z]

Among what are vulgarly called the *pot-walluping*[399] boroughs of Ireland,[a] Glannacrime stood conspicuous for its corruption and servility to the dominant power of the day, whatever that power might be. Mr. Crawley assured Lady Dunore that the corporation was at her devotion, and that any effort on her part would be but a work of supererogation. This assurance, so often reiterated, had wholly lulled that interest and solicitude / which the chance of a strongly contested election could alone have maintained alive in her capricious mind; and in a few days the event would have become wholly indifferent to her, if not quite obliterated from her memory, but for the open and candid declaration of Mr. Daly, that whatever interest he possessed, or could make in Glannacrime, should be exerted against his grand nephew, and in favour of Mr. O'Mahonney.

This determination, far from annoying Lady Dunore, revived all her faded electioneering ambition; she found the unbiased independent intentions of her uncle as he stood opposed to his own kinsman, and in favour of a stranger whom he had never seen, new, extraordinary, and therefore *charming*; and she even proposed that they should both set forth in the same barouche to canvass on their different sides, and that each should try a tour de force[400] with the / other.[b] To this Mr. Daly objected, as giving a ludicrous air to the business; but when he mentioned that he should ride over to Glannacrime for the purpose of trying his interest, Lady Dunore then ordered her carriage with the same intention; and while he took one road on horseback, she, attended by Lady Georgina and the two Mr. Crawleys, took the other in an open barouche.

With the successful electioneering talents of the celebrated and lovely Duchess of D. full in her imagination, (for she had read an account of the famous

Westminster election[401] in an old magazine on the night before), Lady Dunore, all life, spirit, and expectation, performed the first three miles of her journey with a restless and eager impatience to commence her canvass; and insisted that she should stop at the first freeholder's residence, of whose vote there was any doubt. /

'We are now,' said young Crawley, with a significant look at his father, 'within a few paces of the residence of a genuine Irish freeholder, who is as yet undetermined between the contending interests of Fitzadelm and O'Mahonney. Shall I pull the check-string,[402] Lady Dunore?'

'Oh, by all means in the world,' said the marchioness eagerly, and arranging the becoming gossimer shade of her Brussels lace veil, while she asked Lady Georgina, 'am I *blue*, Georgy, love, perfectly *blue*, with this north-east blast?'

'On the contrary, sweet love,' replied *'Georgy, love,'* drawing down her own veil, never wholly raised in broad day-light, 'you are absolutely

petrie des lis et des roses.'[403]

The coachman was now ordered to turn to the left, while young Crawley observed: /

'It is a narrow rough road; but I think your ladyship's springs are equal to it.'

'I'll venture my springs,' returned Lady Dunore, gaily: 'never mind the springs, Mr. Conway.'

The barouche now wound along the rutted road of a little valley. On either side peat mixed with rushes seemed the only produce of a soil almost beyond the reach of cultivation. The few patches of grass which were discernible were of a brown and stunted growth. As the carriage came in front of a small dunghill, which usually forms the first *vallum*[404] to the residence of an Irish peasant, Mr. Crawley pulled the check-string. A hut or cabin rose behind in all the irregularity of architecture which the most extravagant lover of the picturesque could desire.[405] The cabin itself was built of rounded stones, which, like the edifice in the Fairy Queen, were

'Cunningly and without mortar laid.'[406] /

The door was removed from the door-case, and laid cross ways, to keep in the children and the pigs: on each side were two holes, both partially stopped up, the one with an old hat, the other with straw. Another aperture in the roof, near the gable end, was surmounted by a broken pitcher, being a refinement upon the mere hole in the roof, and intended to exhibit an improvement little known in the peasant architecture of Ireland – a chimney. The roof of this curious, but not singular building, luxuriated in a variety of vegetation, being composed of potatoe stalks and grass sods, it sent forth vigorous shoots, and bloomed amidst the surrounding sterility.

'What is this? Why do we stop here? Can't we proceed?' asked Lady Dunore, impatiently.

'Certainly,' said young Crawley, 'but your ladyship would of course like to see and speak to the masters of this freehold.' /

'Freehold!' repeated Lady Dunore faintly, and holding her eau de luce to her nose, as the mid day sun drew up the putrescent vapour of a flax pit,[407] and as every gush of smoke which burst from the hut, and rolled over the open carriage, came fraught with the stench of the cabin's pestilential atmosphere. Two little half-naked and bloated children, who were plucking up some dead brambles for firing, raised their eyes in stupid wonder on the carriage, and then ran into the cabin, with looks of consternation. The next moment they returned with a group, consisting of two smaller children, followed by a man and woman, the father and mother of this ill thriven brood. The man, like the southern peasantry of Ireland, many of whom are descended from a Spanish colony, was dark, meagre, and of a countenance marked by strong lineaments. His clothes were a patchwork of every colour. His worn-out / brogues were stuffed with straw. His beard half an inch in length; his long black hair clotted and overshadowing his eyes, indicated the neglect of hopeless and irremediable poverty. The woman, who came forward wiping her mouth, (for they had been at their customary meal of potatoes and salt), inquired in a whining voice and broken English, 'what was their honour's will.'

Barefooted and bare-legged, her eyes bleared with smoke, her form attenuated by insufficient diet, her complexion bronzed by exposure to the inclemencies of the weather, her dress in shreds, she still had a cheerfulness of manner that seemed ill assorted to her situation.

Such in general is the family, and such the dwelling of the Irish forty-shilling freeholder;[408] a class which is daily multiplied, to the ruin of agriculture and the misery of the population, according to the exigencies and interests of in-/triguing landlords.[c] Old Crawley, who was perfectly aware of his son's manouvre, and who had sat silently enjoying the disappointment, surprise, and disgust of his patroness, now exclaimed, in the usual tone of familiarity with which he addressed the lower orders, from whom, in manner and language, he was so little removed,

'Morrow, Denis Regan: how is it with you, man?'

'Musha! long life to your honor, I'm brave and hearty, Sir; and hope you're well, Mr. Crawley, dear.'

'And how is the woman that owns you, Denis? How are you, Judy?'

Judy dropped a courtesy to the ground. 'Well, I thank your honor's asking, praise to God, amen, and am glad to see you looking so beautiful, Mr. Crawley, Sir.'

'We are come for your vote and interest, Denis, for the approaching election; and while I think of it, I have / ordered *bog leave*[409 d] for you from the bailiff.'

'Och, to be sure, and why wouldn't you have it, Sir, to be sure, only Mr. O'Mahonney, Sir, has.'

'And here's Lady Dunore come to solicit your vote in favour of her son Lord Fitzadelm,' interrupted old Crawley.

'See that now! and shall have it, Sir, if it was worth thousands, any friend of your honor's or the young counsellor's, Sir, long life to yez; and hopes my lady will spake for us to your honor, Sir, about the trifle of rint, and times going hard.'

A dead silence now ensued; the Crawleys purposely making an opening for Lady Dunore to exert that electioneering talent, of which she had so frequently boasted during the ride; but, with her handkerchief stuffed in her mouth, and her look divided between curiosity and disgust, she remained sunk in the back of the carriage. /

'Would your ladyship wish to alight?' asked young Crawley.

'Alight! why the road is ankle deep. Pray let us get out of this shocking spot,' said Lady Dunore, with a countenance of nausea.

'I am afraid, however, your ladyship must alight, for this road is terminated by a bog; and there will be some difficulty, if not danger, in turning the carriage in this narrow spot.'

'Good God! how could you bring us into such a scrape, Mr. Conway Crawley?' asked Lady Dunore, angrily.

'Madam,' he replied, in affected consternation, 'I hope I did not mistake your ladyship's order. I thought it was your wish to stop at the door of the first freeholder, who –'

'Yes, yes, but I could not for a moment suppose that *this* wretched place, these wretched persons – in short, if I stay a moment here, I shall catch / a typhus fever, or be suffocated by the stench. Thompson, why don't you turn instantly? Do you hear me?'

'Yes, my lady, I'll try; but this is a bad bit of ground to turn in.'

Aware, from experience, that his lady's orders were indisputable, however difficult they might be in execution, Thompson endeavoured to turn; but the horses, frightened by the sudden flutter and flight of a flock of geese, near the cabin door, became quite unmanageable, resisted rein and whip, and ran off with a velocity neither to be checked nor overtaken. The Regan family set up the usual Irish cry, 'Millia murthur;'[410] while young Crawley, coolly looking after the flying vehicle, indulged in a smile, which there was no one to witness; meantime the coachman, with the utmost skill and effort, could not restrain the horses' speed,

and every moment threatened destruction to the springs and wheels of the car-/
riage, and fracture or dislocation to the limbs of its occupants; when a peasant,
who was clamping turf in the bog, sprang forward, seized the reins of the leaders,
and with no less skill than strength, not only succeeded in stopping the horses,
but assisted the coachman in turning the carriage.

Lady Dunore and Lady Georgina, recovered from their fright, were loud in
exclamations of gratitude and admiration to their deliverer, who had refused
their proffered liberality, and who, in answer to their inquiries as to his name,
replied coldly, 'Plaze your honor, my lady, its but a bad name. I'm PADREEN
GAR, Madam, the boy that welcomed your ladyship home when we comed
down from the mountains to meet yez.'

'It's by no means a bad name,' said Lady Dunore, 'and I shall take care not to
forget it, Mr. Gore.'

The Crawleys smiled significantly; / and Lady Dunore, offended by looks
which had not escaped her, ordered her coachman to drive back to Dunore,
conversed in *Italian* with Lady Georgina the whole way, preserving a dignified
silence towards the Messieurs Crawley, who had 'smiled in such a sort'⁴¹¹ as to
throw an air of independence on their own opinions, which on the subject of
Padreen Gar evidently differed from those of her ladyship.ᵉ Thus placed under
the ban of her temporary displeasure, they received all its symptoms with the
enduring complacency of persons whose patient servility can abide the stormy
brow of greatness, in the certain expectation of the harvest of its returning sunshine.

A few days had succeeded to that on which the unruly horses had formed
a sort of adventure, in an existence already deemed monotonous by the lady of
the castle. Lady Dunore, who generally took up an opinion out of opposition, /
and supported it out of obstinacy, praising in spite, and approving in malice, had
dwelt with a duration unusual to her instability, on the gallantry of Padreen Gar,
whom she persisted in calling Mr. Gore.

Erected into an hero, the object of many of Mr. Crawley's plots and fears now
disputed even the influence of Miss Crawley herself, who, since the departure
of her friends, had become a resident in Dunore Castle; and she still held her
precarious tenure by the tie of adulation, which her sex rendered unsuspicious,
and her sectarian zeal sanctified. Lady Dunore now expressed her intention of
becoming a frequent visitant to a country which produced such a fine race of
peasantry as Padreen Gar, alias *Mr.* Gore; and time and circumstance had not yet
worn out her prepossession (which, however, produced no benefit to its object),
when a letter reached her hands, that broke up the spell of her / partiality, while
it furnished new motive for action, and agitation to her feverish existence. This
letter was one of those productions so frequently circulated in Ireland, among
the timid and the credulous, to excite suspicion, awaken distrust, and give occa-

sion for those efforts of coercion and resistance which usually produce the very events they are adopted to suppress. It was something between a threat and a warning. It talked of the black flag of rebellion being speedily unfurled, of meditated assassinations, and intended massacres, of an hatred to English residents, and Protestant ascendency advocates; of the noxious seeds of sedition being deeply sown in the breasts of the credulous and the poor; and of a probable and immediate attack upon the castle of Dunore by *Padreen Gar's boys*, who were to assemble for a moonlight parade on St. Gobnate's eve, near the holy-well of Ballydab,[412] to plan this / siege for the following night. To this was added, that Padreen Gar, accompanied by his boys, who were concealed in the pits of the bog, had intended to surprise her carriage on the day of her proposed visit to Glannacrime, but were prevented by the presence of the two Crawleys, and that an artful rescue was substituted for the meditated attack.

To this letter Lady Dunore gave implicit credence, merely because she wished it to be true. The threatened danger relieved the torpor of her feelings, gave play to her wild imagination, and afforded ample occupation to her laborious idleness. Mr. Crawley and his son were on business with her when this letter arrived by the post, and bearing the office-mark of a neighbouring town: its contents were of course instantly communicated to them; but instead of urging her immediate departure, as they expected, it furnished / her with additional reasons for remaining. To her expressions of horror at the state of the country, and the ingratitude of a people for whom she had roasted an ox, young Crawley replied, that of all this he could have informed her before, even when her predilections for Padreen Gar ran highest; but that he feared to frighten her away from the country, when it was his and his father's wish, rather perhaps than her ladyship's interest, that she should remain forever.

Measures for meeting the evil were now discussed. Secrecy and concealment from all the guests at the castle were strongly recommended; and Lady Dunore '*qui aimoit terriblement les enigmes*,'[413] readily yielded her assent to this necessity. The object of the Messieurs Crawley was, as they declared, that Lady Dunore should judge for herself of the state of the country, and of the people: for this purpose, the band / of ruffians, with the principal incendiary, should be surprised and seized on the eve of St. Gobnate, and brought to the castle, on their way to Dunore jail. A sort of little star-chamber,[414] or secret committee, should sit to take their examinations in presence of her ladyship, where their appearance and countenances, as well as their confessions, should testify against them.[f] To all this Lady Dunore acceded, delighted to be surrounded by rebels and ruffians. To hold a sort of presidential court, or special commission, in her own castle, was an event consonant with her feelings; and while the Crawleys believed they were awakening her timidity and distrust, they were, in fact, flattering the dormant qualities of her being. Their low cunning aimed only at the feebleness of the human character, but were ignorant of the varieties of which that character is susceptible: and accustomed to work with no other tools than terror and / intimidation, they used them with an universal and indiscriminate application, and mistook the credulity of Lady Dunore for a timidity foreign to her temperament and disposition.

The eve of St. Gobnate was still distant by some days; and in the anxious interval, the Crawleys regained their former influence over the Lady of the castle, and were frequently closeted with her for hours, to the exclusion not only of the numerous visitors who called to pay their respects, but even of her domesticated guests, who were left to amuse themselves as they might. While the Crawleys thus engrossed her society, they directed the channel of her thoughts, and worked powerfully on her imagination. Exparte[415] statements of the events of the unhappy rebellion of 1798 were added to the raked-up horrors of the more dreadful 1641.[416] Mr. Conway Crawley, sometimes, read his way to her favours through murders / and massacres, while his aunt cut her's through paper screens and watch papers;[417] and while trophies, devices, and card-racks, multiplied in her boudoir, the siege of Drogheda, by the Dean of Ardagh,* was dipped into; the history of the Irish rebellion was commented upon; and the not less prejudiced work of Sir Richard Musgrave[418] read almost entirely[g] – thus combining the frivolous and the sanguinary, to occupy her mind, and to work upon her feelings.

Meantime the rumour of an insurrection had been spread through the town of Dunore, and had reached the steward's room and servants' hall of the castle; whence it ascended to the drawing-room, where some laughed and / some trembled at it. Although Lady Dunore and the Crawleys preserved a profound silence on the subject, it was understood that a party of the New Town Mount Crawley supplementary auxiliary legion occupied the flank towers of the castle every night after sun-set. Expresses had been forwarded to Dublin, and many of the English servants had applied for leave to return to their native country. What, however, had spread the greatest consternation in the neighbourhood, was, that Terence Oge O'Leary's house had been entered by constables, his papers seized,

---

*　In this work, the dean asserts that the papist rebels were protected by charms, that a naked rebel, fired at by many bullets, remained uninjured, the balls only making marks. 'Of this many eyes were witnesses, one of which of good trust hath repeated it to me.' – This is deemed a work of great authority; and most of the accounts of that unhappy event are taken from it.

and officers of justice stationed to arrest any persons found lurking about the cemetery of the Monaster-ny-oriel. O'Leary himself escaped by being absent on some of his usual antiquarian researches.

On that day, observed in the country as the feast of Saint Gobnate, Lady Dunore descended earlier than usual into the breakfast-room, her cheek / flushed, and her eye wandering: she was also dressed in black, as was usual with her when under the influence of grief or anxiety. She spoke little, and refused to breakfast, alleging that she had been drinking gunpowder-tea[419] since daylight. She was restless and unquiet, appeared and disappeared like a phantom, despatched note after note to Mr. Crawley, and seemed so agitated by ill suppressed emotions, that Lord Frederick, who was sipping his caffé au lait,[420] and reading a French novel, at last inquired of her, in his usual tone of affectation, 'Mais qu'est ce qu'il y a donc, belle Chatelaine?'[421] What is the matter, my marchioness. Are the reports we have heard of incipient rebellion in the celestial empire really true, or are they only got up by the chop-mandarins for their own special purposes? I dare say that *professeur de bavardise*,[422] Duke Conway Townsend Crawley, of the peacock's feather,[423] is at the bottom of all / this; or that my own ching-foo, of the yellow button, is amusing himself with a plot, like the honest gentleman that got his own effigy shot at,[424] to alarm the sleeping sensibility of the lenient government people at the castle.* Now pray speak: Are we to be roasted a la mode Irelandaise before a slow fire, like so many chesnuts, or spitted like the children in the *old* rebellion, like so many snipes[425] – Voyons donc!'[426]

Here Lord Frederick was interrupted by the loud stamping of feet outside the door, which was suddenly burst open, and Lord Rosbrin, in his black velvet Hamlet suit, which he had been trying on before he dressed, with wild looks and wilder voice, rushed in, crying out –

'Oh! horror, horror, horror, tongue nor heart
Cannot conceive nor name thee!'[427] /

Lady Dunore shrieked. Lord Frederick laughed to hysterics, and Messrs. Heneage and Pottinger stood aghast. Mr. Daly, who had been hitherto quietly reading the English papers, now started up astonished, exclaiming with vivacity:

'Why, are you all mad! what is the matter? Rosbrin, see, you have frightened the ladies to death. What *is* the matter?'

'*What is the matter?*' reiterated Lord Rosbrin, seizing the well remembered lines of Macduff, 'why confusion is the matter.'

'Confusion has made his master-piece.
Most *sacrilegious murder* hath broke ope
The Temple, and stolen thence –'[428]

'*Murder!*' said Mr. Daly, shuddering.

---

*   Fact – the ingenious party was a magistrate, and pooh pudor,[h] a clergyman.

'Stolen! stolen what?' interrupted Lord Frederick, becoming suddenly serious.

Lady Dunore, now believing that there was reason for her fears, continued / to scream louder than before; and Lord Rosbrin, pointing to a letter he held in his hand, observed, with a little paraphrase in his citation,

'Approach this letter, and destroy your sight

With a new gorgon.' [429]

'Who is it from?' said Mr. Daly, snatching the letter, and searching for his spectacles.

'Who from?' continued Lord Rosbrin, pacing up and down the room with frantic, but with theatrical gestures. 'Tis from the deputy prompter of Covent Garden Theatre.

'Oh! insupportable, oh heavy hour!

It should be now an huge eclipse o'the sun;' [430]

for oh! my friends, Mrs. Siddons's point lace, Mrs. Siddons's lace, alas! *she has no lace*! but her point lace that WAS, and that *I* should have worn is stolen / away from her dressing-room at the theatre; all, all gone!

'Nor left a wreck behind.' [431]

'So,' said Mr. Daly, much provoked, and resuming his newspaper, 'so, as Moliere says of his capricious lady, 'ou fait la sottise et nous sommes les sots.' [432]

Meantime, Lord Frederick rolled in convulsions of laughter; Mr. Pottinger and the ladies dried their humid eyes; and Mr. Heneage, smelling a flowerbox in the, window, observed, 'the mignionette harvest had been vastly abundant this year.' [433]

A servant at this moment entered, and presented a letter to Lady Dunore, which she took with trepidation, but as she read it, her clouded countenance brightened into smiles, and ere she finished it, she said –

'No, never was there so fortunate an event. The circuit judges dine here / to-day, and will be present at the trial. Well, after all I must say, there is nothing like Ireland, where one is kept in a constant state of emotion and occupation.'

'Trial! what trial?' demanded Mr. Daly in astonishment.

'Why the fact is, my dear uncle,' said Lady Dunore, no longer deeming it necessary to keep a secret, which was beginning to be *a charge* — 'the fact is, the castle of Dunore was to have been attacked this very night, on the feast of St. Gobnate, but for the timely prudence of the two Mr. Crawleys, who had discovered the plot, and have hitherto concealed their knowledge of it, from political motives. They have succeeded this morning in surprising and seizing that ferocious and lawless banditti called Padreen Gar's boys; and I am this moment expecting their arrival at the castle, escorted by a party of military, on their way to the jail. We / meant to have kept all this quiet, for fear of frightening Georgy, love, and alarming you all. But now that the judges and things are coming to the castle to dine,' she continued in a fever of delightful agitation, walking up and down the room, and fanning herself with a hand-screen, [434] 'now we shall have a regular imposing, and I dare say amazingly amusing trial.'

'Oh! a regular *special commission*,' said Mr. Daly, with ironical seriousness. 'An inquest held on a parcel of shanavests and caravats must be rare sport for ladies. [435] But who are the charming judges, who come so appropriately to preside in your ladyship's court, and to assist in getting up a scene for our private amusement, at the expense of the public character of the county?'

'Oh! I know nothing in the world about them,' said Lady Dunore, 'only they are judges of some kind or other, who are on circuit, and who have invited / themselves here. Mr. Crawley will be enchanted at this; it will save him trouble. Here is their letter: pray read it aloud,' and she tossed it to Mr. Daly, who read it aloud, as follows –

'Baron Boulter presents his respectful compliments to the Marchioness of Dunore; he purposes, with his brother judge, Mr. Justice Aubrey, having the honour of paying his respects at Dunore Castle this day, between his breakfast and sleeping stage, on his way from circuit to Dublin, when Baron B. will be happy to become the bearer of any commands her ladyship may have for the metropolis.'

'The wretched accommodations,' observed Mr. Daly, 'at Bally-na-scroggen, have, I suppose, induced Baron Boulter, who is a man of the world, and a true disciple of the savoir vivre, to claim your ladyship's hospitality. But I know not what argument has pre-/vailed on his excellent, but *not always very accommodating*, brother judge, for once to agree in his decisions.'

'O, it is no matter what brings them here provided they come, There never was such luck,' continued Lady Dunore, fluttering about the room: 'we shall have quite a regular *special commission*, as you say, my dear uncle: I hope though they will not hang many of these wretches. You have no idea how I hate to have people hanged:' and she added, wiping away her now fast coming tears – 'If I heard sentence pronounced on a great many at *once*, and the clanking *of chains*, and the condemning cap, [436] and things –'

'By-the-bye,' interrupted Lord Frederick, 'apropos to *hanging*, isn't Baron Boulter the facetious hanging *judge* who makes us all die laughing at the castle dinners with his bon-mots?'

'He is thought to be a *leetle* severe,' / said Mr. Pottinger, 'but he is zealous for government, and is perhaps the best punster on the bench; that is I believe admitted on all sides.'

'An high judicial qualification, my Potty,' returned Lord Frederick, gravely.

'But should we not have something of a court for them?' asked Lady Dunore. 'Good heavens! how unlucky Miss Crawley should not have returned yet from her evangelical school at New Town Mount Crawley; she would have cut me out a court; got me up a court, I mean, or something in that way, in a minute, some-thing that would produce a striking effect, something scenic you know.'

'Scenic! a striking effect! a *good stage effect!* exclaimed Lord Rosbrin. 'Leave that to me, my gentle coz, my pretty coz. I have all the requisite properties with me, *maces* and halberds, senators' wigs, ermine, and all.'

'We must have the packing cases re- /moved out of the hall,' continued Lady Dunore, 'and tables, and pens, and ink, and things you know; for if we are to give the thing an air of a regular trial, we may as well do it handsomely.'

'Trial!' repeated Lord Rosbrin, 'I have the Covent Garden' promptbook, with the *Merchant of Venice trial*,[437] in my pocket; here it is.'

Lord Rosbrin now pulled out a ragged book, with all the business of the stage laid down, and Lady Dunore continued:

'Do then, dear Rosbrin, get things in order, you understand these matters so well: I'll ring the bell for the servants to attend you.'

Lord Rosbrin caught her arm.

'Leave every thing to me, my fair coz. Scene a hall.'

'I think I could assist you,' said Mr. Pottinger.

'We shall want,' interrupted Lord / Rosbrin, stopping his mouth, 'trumpets, marshal's staff, two aldermen, Archbishop of Canterbury, Duchess of Norfolk, godmother. No, hang it, that's the christening in Henry the Eighth. [438] Here is the trial scene – trumpets and cornets; two vergers, with short wands; scribes in habits of doctors. Well, only leave it to me. Come, Pottinger, you shall act as scribe or verger, or property boy. *What's in a name?* [439]

The peer and Mr. Pottinger left the room together, followed by Lady Dunore, who was all emotion and gratification, while Mr. Daly and Lord Fred-erick laughed without restraint; and Lady Georgina said, 'that poor thing will wear herself out with her strong feelings. There never was such a quick irritable sensibility as her's.'

'Oh, she is delicious!' said Lord Frederick, 'taken in small and distant doses. But it were as well to live in a / tornado as occupy the same house with her vol-canoship for two months together.'

'I have never seen her thus extravagant before,' said Mr. Daly, in a tone of mortification. 'I confess I lose all patience when I see her the dupe of these Craw-ley plots, or rather of her own caprice and whim, and of that insatiable thirst for scenes and sensations that has made the torment and the enjoyment of her life. I would not wonder if she has worried poor Dunore out of his reason, and been the cause of all the eccentricity of that other froward but clever boy, whom she has induced to forego his independent principles, and set up for this corrupt saleable Crawley· borough. And yet I love her for her mother's sake; for she was an angel, – at least before ill usage had –'

He paused abruptly, sighed, and resumed his newspaper; while Lord Fre-/derick whispered Lady Georgina – 'A *fallen one.*'

Within the ensuing hour the judges Boulter and Aubrey arrived at the castle, were announced, and received in the saloon, as old acquaintances, by Mr. Daly.

The Right Honorable Baron Boulter was a collateral descendant of the celebrated English ecclesiastic of that name, who, under the title of *primate of Ireland*, governed the land with a crozier of iron.[440]

Bishop Boulter, in his celebrated letters, has divided Ireland into a population of his own party, and the natives; or, as he termed them, *we of the English nation*, and the *poor Irish.*[441] His grace added to this curious classification a maxim, that '*Ireland is only to be governed by being divided* (4),[442] and a counsel, urging the necessity for employing spies and informers as proper agents of / government, and worthy of being remunerated and recompensed even unto the third and fourth generation.

The inheritance of this family creed was the sole succession of Baron Boulter, himself the *younger* son, of a *younger* brother; for little was added to it but a *rattle and bells*,[443] bequeathed him in his infancy by his grand-aunt, Mrs. Barbara Boulter, which the Baron ever afterwards preserved; and which, even on the bench, he was wont to play with gaily enough, when forensic dulness made claims on his patience, or the pauses of business left leisure for innocent amusement.

Baron Boulter had nothing of the saturnine and irascible spirit of his great political predecessor the primate. He was of a cheerful sanguine temperament; possessed an evenness of temper that usually supplies the absence of sensibility; and, any where *but in Ire-/land*, might have been as respectable in his public character as he was pleasant and courteous in his social deportment. But he had come forward at a period when the maxims of the Irish government, in every department, tended to national debasement; and, like other aspiring barristers, weary of hawking a bag, light as his own spirits, and vacant as his heart, he submitted to the necessary probation of political corruption, graduated with success, and rose to professional eminence by a facetiousness that amused, and a severity that horrified.[i]

The rebellion was the great scene of action for such qualities; and to that period, like many others of his professional cotemporaries, he stood indebted for his pre-eminence. The means of his rising, became the habit of his character, and he continued to joke and to condemn with a gaiety and contempt / for human life which belonged to his temperament, and which served to uphold the reputation of his loyalty.

No one trifled away liberty with more grace, or pronounced sentence with more humour than Baron Boulter; and the culprit whom *he* jested to the gallows, had his love of wit borne any proportion to his fear of death, must almost have been reconciled to his fate by the gaité du cour[444j] that sealed his destiny.

His professional interests, and political principles aside, which in Ireland are always closely connected, Baron Boulter was fair judging and clear-sighted; he came at results with the prompt but unlogical process of a woman's perceptions; but living always on one spot, within a narrow circle, his knowledge of human nature went no further than the sphere of his action, and his philosophy was as local as his jokes; he could flatter an *Irish* chancellor, adulate an *Irish* / *viceroy*, amuse the priggish dullness of an Irish secretary, joke *with*, or sift *to* the very bottom of evasion and circumlocution, an Irish *peasant*, while he gaily laughed *with*, and secretly laughed *at all*. Still his human nature was always *Irish* nature; and though, as far as his experience went, his premises were just, yet they were confined, narrow, and home directed: for the rest, social in habits, of amiable address, and pleasant humour, he was sought for by the great, whom he amused; and feared by the poor, whom he – hung.

Judge Aubrey was in character a melange of those temperaments which produce a quick and irritable sensibility, a prompt uncalculating sympathy, and a warm, deep-seated, violent indignation; qualities which form so broad a basis for human excellence, while they unfit it for a patient endurance of baseness, meanness, and cupidity. These were powerfully worked on, and hourly / called into action, by the political situation of a country, which he loved with all the fervour of an ancient Roman;[445] and by the systematic degradation of a profession, he venerated as the guardian of human rights: his bile and his experience increased together; the hopes of the patriot, and the health of the man, suffered in equal proportion; and the social simplicity and playful gaiety, which formed the charm of his domestic hearth, from which the world was shut out, deserted him in that public tribunal, where the liberty he worshipped was sacrificed, and the profession he revered was debased.

Ireland, his native country, was his object: he had upheld her cause in the senate, until her independence had breathed its last gasp; and he retired from the scene of her ruin with a minority that might be deemed 'glorious,' in every sense of the word. Ireland was still his object; and the lowliest of / his children found redemption from his mercy, solace in his commiseration, and relief from his liberality. From the bench he expounded the causes of their crimes, while he lamented their effects: he taught while he judged, he wept when he condemned.

From the period of the Union, Judge Aubrey had retired from what is called the world, from the bustling walks of life, and from the giddy round of fashionable circles: living for, and with a few, he had for many years made no progress in the successive modes and jargons of succeeding fashions; and it was in part to this circumstance that he owed much of that peculiar freshness of character, and something of that austerity of manner, which the friction of society is so apt to efface. This well-preserved individuality was set off by a peculiar manner, idiom, and phrase, which, as well as his broad accent, were genuinely Irish. To profound classical / reading, and considerable scientific acquirement, he added an unpretending simplicity, which is inseparably connected with the highest order of talent, though so often falsely attributed to mediocrity and ignorance.

Such were the two high judicial characters, who, now linked in a professional yoke, drew as different ways as untrained colts in the same harness. Since the commencement of their circuit, they had never agreed upon any one point, except the expediency of trying the French chef de cuisine[446] of the Marchioness of Dunore, instead of relying on the gastronomic talents of Judy Mulligan of the Cat and Bagpipes in the neighbouring town of Bally-scroggin. /

NOTES.

Note (*) Page 5. – The driver is generally a peasant's son, taken from the spade, and hired at a salary of five or six pounds a-year. His occupation is to drive or distrain cattle, sheep, and other stock of the backward tenants; to cart and sell without mercy; to threaten and importune for money, and to be the most formidable of all animals to the poor. These men are frequently the objects of popular vengeance, and are devoted to death, with the tythe proctor, the police constable, &c. &c. He is ever the ready instrument of oppression; whether to take a blunderbuss, or to take an oath; to serve a law process for the tything parson, the tax gatherer, or the absentee landlord; or, in short, to bear the whole risk and odium of executing the sentence of harsh laws ill their fullest and most oppressive severity. Like the robber of the desert, his hand is against every one, and every one's hand is against him. Thus there subsists a constant action and re-action, alike subversive of the public peace, and of the public morals; / oppression and inhumanity sanctioned by law; and violence and bloodshed in opposition to it. Those in power must inevitably designate the peasant's resistance to the driver as outrageous murder, as crime of the blackest dye; but nature, deep within the bosom of an oppressed and starving population, acknowledges [sic] it a necessitated self-defence, or a just retaliation.[k]

Page 48. – Places of emolument, rank, precedence, and profit, enjoyed by and distributable amongst the Irish bar, April 22, 1818, [447]viz.

Lord Chancellor (salary encreased since 1789)	{1}	15,000*l.* for self and servants.
Master of the Rolls (ditto)	1	5,000*l.* ditto
Judges of the Law Courts (ditto)	{12}	from 8,000*l.* to 4,000*l.* each.

Masters in Chancery	4	3 to 4,000*l.* each.
Deputy Remembrancer of the Exchequer	{1}	same.
Attorney General	1	about 10,000*l.*
Solicitor General	1	5,000*l.*
King's Serjeants	{3}	rank, precedence, and profit
King's Counsel (formerly but 20) present number	{37}	same.
Judge of the Prerogative Court	1	1,800*l.*
Consistorial Court	1	600*l.*
Carried forward	63 /	

Brought up ... 63

Master of the Faculties under the Archbishop of Armagh	{1}	500*l.*
Judge of the Admiralty Court	1	1,200*l.*
Sarrogates in ditto	2	200*l.* each.
Recorder of Dublin City	1	1,200*l.*
Chairman of the City of Dublin Sessions	{1}	1,200*l.*
Chairmen of Thirty-one County Sessions (since 1789)	{31}	400 to 800*l.* each.
Counsel to Revenue Commissioners	2	6,000*l.* and 8,000*l.*
Ditto to Masters in Chancery	4	200*l.* each.
Ditto to Deputy Remembrancer	1	300*l.*
Ditto to Attorney General, opening and signing pleadings	{1}	400*l.*
Ditto to ditto in Extents and Custodians, &c.	{2}	300*l.* each.
Ditto to ditto in Six Circuits, in Still Fines, &c. (since 1789)	{6}	200*l.* each.
Ditto to ditto in Six Circuits in Crown Prosecutions (ditto)	{30}	200*l.* each.
Ditto to Dublin Castle (ditto)	{1}	1,000*l.* by Townsend.
Ditto to Commissioners of Wide Streets (ditto)	{1}	1,500*l.*
Ditto to Barrack Board	1	worth 300*l.*

Ditto to Ordnance ditto	1	ditto 200*l*.
Ditto to Linen ditto	1	ditto 200*l*.
Ditto to Bank of Ireland on Six Circuits (ditto)	{6}	100*l*. each.
Ditto to Post Office on Six Circuits (ditto)	{6}	100*l*. each.
Carried forward	163 /	

Brought up.... 163

Counsel to Paving Board (since 1789).	{1}	200*l*.
Ditto to Dublin Police (ditto)	1	200*l*.
Commissioners of Bankruptcy	25	200 to 600*l*. each.
Ditto of Public Records (since 1789)	4	400*l*. each.
Ditto of Inquiry into Fees, &c. (ditto)	{5}	1,200*l*. each.
Lay Vicars General of Dioceses	12	100*l*. each.
Dublin Police Barristers (since 1789)	6	500*l*. each.
Commissioners of Appeal	5	800*l*. each.
Commissioners of Accounts and their Secretary	{6}	800*l*. each.
Directors of Inland Navigation	4	1,000*l*. each.
King's Inns Treasurer (since 1789)	1	500*l*.
Ditto Librarian (ditto)	1	300*l*.
Cursitor Baron of Exchequer	1	200*l*.
Cursitor of Chancery	1	400*l*.
Examiners in Chancery	2	500*l*. each.
King's Advocate General	1	300*l*.
Commissioners in Lunatic Cases	2	200*l*. each.
Secretary to Commissioners of Charities (since 1789)	{1}	400*l*.
Accountant General of Chancery.	1	800*l*.
Ditto ditto Exchequer.	1	800*l*.
Seneschal of Dublin Liberties, Doners, St. Sepulchres, St. Patricks, &c.	{5}	100 to 200*l*. each.
Colonial Situations in Ceylon, Canada, Grenada, Prince of Wales's Island, &c.	{10}	worth 500*l*. to 5,000*l*. each.
Carried forward	259 /	

Brought up 259

Missionaries to explore the State of disturbed Districts, &c.	{2}	300 guineas each visit, (T. Prendergest and Edward O'Grady, &c.
Recorders of Cities and Towns, about.	{21}	100 to 800*l*. each.
Other Places, Sinecures, Pensions, &c. dispersed according to Services and Influence, about.	{18}	
	300	

Among two hundred barristers, besides about fifty more remaining unplaced.[1]
(2) Page 125. – The Butlers and Fitzgeralds had been powerful rivals and enemies from the time of their arrival in Ireland with Henry II. The anecdote is well

known of the Earl of Desmond being taken prisoner by the Earl of Ormonde, and borne off wounded on the shoulders of the Ormonde followers, returned in answer to the taunting question of 'where now is the great Lord Desmond?' 'Still on the necks of Butlers.'

When a temporary reconciliation was effected between these powerful chiefs, a hole was cut in the door of the chauntry of St. Patrick's / church, that they might shake hands *through it* to *prevent accidents*: this hole, with a piece of board nailed over it, was shewn not long since at St. Patrick's, and may still exist.[m]

(3) Page 126. – The '*Fringes*' was a procession of *the trades and corporations*, performed in Ireland on *Corpus Christi* day, even within the author's recollection. King Solomon, Queen Sheba, with Vulcan, Venus, and Cupid, were leading personages upon this occasion. The ceremony was the remains of an old Roman Catholic superstition. Something in the same way is still celebrated in Shrewsbury, or at least was a very few years back.

Page 211. – The private theatricals, held annually at Kilkenny, assemble whatever Ireland still retains of rank, fashion, talent, and taste. There party loses its asperity, sect its distinction, and prejudice its bitterness. *Bye-laws* and *military laws* are there forgotten, and the laws of this amiable institution, like those of nature, are governed by harmony only.

(4) Page 268. – The system of governing Ireland by *dividing* it, is of very ancient origin. The following is an historical anecdote in proof. / Anno 1278, there arose civil wars, no better than rebellion, between M'Dermott de Moylaoge and Cathyeer O'Connor, King of Connaught, where there was great slaughter and bloodshed on both sides, and the King of Connaught slain. Raphael Holinshed, in his Irish Collection, thinketh that there were slain at that tyme above two thousand persons. The King of England hearing thereoff, wae mightily displeased with the Lord Justice, and sent for him into England to yielde reason *why he would* permit such shameful enormities under his government. Robert Ufford substituted R. Fulbert as before, and satisfied the king that all was not true that he was charged withal; and for further contentment yielded this reason: *that in policy he thought it expedient to wink* at one knave cutting off another, as that would save the King's coffers, and purchase peace to the land by extermination. *Whereat the King smiled, and bade him return to Ireland!!* – WARE.

The spirit of the *law*, and the policy with which Ireland has been since governed, is contained in this passage.[n] /

FLORENCE MACARTHY:

An Irish Tale

BY

LADY MORGAN,

AUTHOR OF 'FRANCE,' 'O'DONNEL,' &c.

Know thus far forth:
By accident most strange, bountiful fortune,
Now, my dear lady, hath mine enemies
Brought to this shore: and by my prescience,
I find my zenith doth depend upon
A most auspicious star, whose influence,
If now I court not but omit, my fortunes
Will ever after droop. SHAKESPEARE.[1]
Les femmes ne sont pas trop d'humeur à pardonner de certaines injures, et
quand elles se promettent le plaisir de le vengeance elles n'y vout pas de *main-*
morte.
DE GRAMMONT.[2]

IN FOUR VOLUMES.

VOL. III.

LONDON:
PRINTED FOR HENRY COLBURN,
PUBLIC LIBRARY, CONDUIT STREET, HANOVER SQUARE.
1818.
B. CLARKE, Printer, Well Street, London.

FLORENCE MACARTHY.

CHAPTER I.

'The council shall hear it – It is a riot.'[3]
– 'Sir Hugh, persuade me not – I will make
a star-chamber matter of it.'[4]
'To vouch this is no proof!
Without more certain and more overt test
Than these thin habits, and poor likelihoods of
modern seeming, do prefer against him.'

SHAKESPEARE.[5a]

LADY DUNORE, who, like sister Anne in Bluebeard, was stationed on the top of one of the castle turrets,[6] alternately watched the approach of the expected prisoners in one direction, and that of their accusers and judges, Mr. Crawley and son, in another.[b] /

She was now summoned on the arrival of Baron Boulter and Judge Aubrey to the breakfast parlour.[c] Already from her watch-tower she had seen a crowd of persons wandering among the hills, and the glitter of arms flashing in the sun-shine. Her ardent imagination magnified the New-Town cavalry corps, and half a dozen peasants, into a prodigious military force, and a formidable band of rebels; and she rushed into the apartment where the two judges were quietly taking a bouillon[7d] after their long morning's ride; and with eyes flashing, and cheeks suffused, welcomed them in evident agitation to the castle. She expressed her gratitude to Baron Boulter in exaggerated terms for a visit so kindly volunteered; and uttered a fervent hope that their presence would give importance to an event in which many lives were concerned. She then abruptly ended with the question of – /

'But which of you, my lords, is the hanging judge?'

This question, which startled the judges, confused Mr. Daly, and threw Lord Frederick into agonies (lest in her delirious ravings she should cite him as

– 199 –

authority for this judicial sobriquet), produced a short silence, until Mr. Daly coming to the relief of the party, observed,

'My dear lords, I must account for this agitation of my niece, Lady Dunore, by informing you that her mind and feelings have been worked on by some representations of the state of this province not perfectly correct. Her agent and confidential person, Mr. Crawley, is a timid man; and it is but fair to say, that I believe he is frequently the dupe of his own fears. But he also belongs to a certain party, who, under the guise of inordinate and exclusive loyalty, act in defiance of the law / of the land, are lawless by the concurrence, or at least the countenance of those in authority, and may be said, in the language of a celebrated orator, to be 'opposed to *rule* by act of parliament.'[8] Among such persons, it is a favourite system of tactics to create false alarms, and then to engraft strong measures upon the fears they have awakened. I have some reason to think my niece is at this moment the victim of this wretched and hacknied policy, and that the attack on her castle, and the smothered insurrection with which she has been anonymously threatened, are the phantoms, I will not say the creations, of Mr. Crawley's brain.'

Lady Dunore, mortified and disappointed by a speech that threw her out of a sphere of action, to which all her fancies and feelings were made up, was beginning an expostulation with her uncle, when Baron Boulter interrupted / her by observing that 'the Irish were a very fine people, and a very handsome people. But that it was most certain a little occasional hanging, just now and then, did them no harm: and though they might not, in the present instance, be so deeply implicated in rebellious practices, as the loyal and vigilant prudence of his worthy friend, Darby Crawley, suggested, yet a little timely caution, and wholesome severity, rarely came amiss; that he would willingly lend his aid in examining into the circumstances of the case, and endeavour to dissipate her ladyship's fears by exploring their cause.'

'The people of Ireland,' said Judge Aubrey, in a tone between sullenness and indignation, 'are like the people of other nations, pretty much what their government has made them. They are factious, because they are wretched; and it is the fashion of the day to give to / their local disturbances, to their resistance to the collections of the tithes, they are unable to pay, to their murmurs against the taxes, which have reduced the country to ruin, and even to their personal and often barbarous conflicts among each other, the names of insurrection and rebellion. Mr. Crawley, Madam, is an old alarmist, and your ladyship is, I perceive, new to the modes by which affairs in this country are carried on.'

'But when an armed force is at our gates,' said Lady Dunore, in a tone of irritation and impatience, 'when letters reach my hands, Judge Aubrey, which inform us that.....'

'The charge is prepared, the lawyers are met,
The judges arrayed, a terrible sight,'[9]

interrupted Lord Rosbrin, as he burst into the room, with a billiard cue in his hand for a wand.[10] /

'Every thing is ready,' he observed: 'the court waits, the prisoners are arrived, and the counsel will be here in a few moments.'

'We have endeavoured to make things comfortable for you, Baron,' said Lady Dunore, putting her arm through Baron Boulter's, and hurrying him towards the hall, where she was followed by Judge Aubrey, Mr. Daly, Lord Frederick, Mr. Heneage, Mr. Pottinger, and Lady Georgina.

'There,' said Lord Rosbrin, presenting two arm chairs to the judges, placed at the head of the hall, before a table covered with heavy volumes, 'there, my lords, that is the awful seat of judgment. Here, Lady Georgina, this is your place, and your's, Eversham and Heneage: you are the special jury. You see we have a fine gallery, a charming audience,' and he pointed to the corridore, which ran / round the hall, and which was filled with valets-de-chambre, ladies' maids, with the inferior branches of the Dunore household; 'and,' he added, fixing some chairs and a table to the left, 'this is the place for the counsel for the crown, the learned Crawleys, 'very Daniels;'[11] and the prisoners, you see my lords, occupy the lower part of the hall, the back-ground or portion filled up with guards, officers, mutes, and others: and the solitary female prisoner, the Queen Catherine of the trial,[12] though in a rug cloak,[13] is placed, in delicacy to her sex, in the shade of this recess and painted window.'

Every thing was, indeed, in the order which Lord Rosbrin had described.

The prisoners occupied the foot of the hall. The New-Town Mount Crawley corps filled the portico. A woman, in a coarse grey cloak, and straw bonnet, drawn over her face, was seated in the / recess of the Gothic window; and the rest of the party were disposed of according to Lord Rosbrin's idea of the stage business of the trial in the Merchant of Venice.

On the countenance of Baron Boulter was painted an expression of great humour, as of one ready to be amused, as to amuse. Judge Aubrey was, on the contrary, sullenly looking over a volume of Hogarth,[14] which lay before him on the table; and evidently out of patience and out of temper with the absurdity of the passing scene. Lady Dunore was fluttering about from place to place, and from person to person, in hysterical emotion, tears in her eyes, and smiles upon her lips; and Lord Rosbrin was beginning a speech from the trial of Queen Catherine, and had, in the legal phrase, got on his legs, when Mr. Crawley, his son, and sister, followed by his clerk, Jemmy Bryan, / carrying a green bag, appeared pushing through the crowd, which filled the bottom of the spacious hall.

'Oh! I am glad you are come,' said Lady Dunore, speaking to them from her *jury-box*. 'Are you not enchanted at the turn things have taken? Only conceive, what luck! Baron Boulter and Judge Aubrey so kindly consenting to be present at our little *special commission.* Rosbrin, pray shew the Mr. Crawleys their place. Miss Crawley, I'll make room for you here: we must put you on the jury.'

The Crawleys for a moment remained motionless. To their utter amazement, the whimsicality and extravagance of Lady Dunore had overturned all their long and ingeniously concerted plans. Instead of their snug star-chamber trial, they now stood confronted before the judges of the land, in the presence of a large assembly; while the examinations / of the prisoners, which they meant to turn to the account of terror, would now be taken out of their hand, and be made a jest of by the Baron, or be conducted in such a way by Judge Aubrey as would betray the inadequacy of the charges upon which their wild-looking prisoners were to be committed.

There was, also, in the scene before them, a *melange* of the ludicrous and the serious, which at once struck upon the sensitive apprehension of young Crawley; but armed in that mail of brass and heart of adamant,[15] which were to form the bases of his future fortunes, he came almost instantly to his father's relief; and whispering him a few words, which included reliance on their kind friend, Baron Boulter, and the necessity of courage and presence of mind, he suffered himself to be led by Lord Rosbrin to the place assigned him.^e

Meantime, the clerk spread the table / with depositions against the prisoners. Old Crawley seated himself before it, and Lord Rosbrin, flourishing about, with theatrical solemnity, exclaimed:

'Now then proceed in justice, which shall have due course.

Produce the prisoners. Silence.

Read the indictments.'[16]

The clerk put on his spectacles, and cleared his voice; while Baron Boulter, endowed with a pliancy of mind which permits the pursuit of many objects at the same moment, and who was in the habit of despatching an epigram, and a warrant, of giving judgment and an invitation to dinner in the same breath, now called for pen, ink, and paper, that he might answer a few letters, and listen to the examinations '*without loss of time or hindrance of business.*'[17]

Judge Aubrey, throwing aside his / book, observed, 'Since I take my seat here in the quality of a magistrate, at the desire of the Marchioness of Dunore, I beg that if there are any depositions to be made against these men, who appear to be under a double guard, civil and military, they may be gone through forthwith.'

'My lord,' said Conway Crawley, getting on his legs, with the air of a counsel opening some important cause, 'my lord, before we proceed to read the depositions against these unfortunate men, I shall beg leave to state the case as it appears to me, and to give a slight sketch of the actual situation of this barony.'

'Sir,' interrupted the judge, 'I won't hear you. You can tell me nothing of this country that I do not already know. I have neither time nor health to listen to idle declamation, and ten times "told tales."'[18] /

'My lord, I must observe,' continued young Crawley, petulantly, 'that among the virtues of a judge, patience is the most necessary; and Lord Mansfield,[19] my lord, obtained more credit for that virtue, than for all his other judicial merits combined.'

'Then, Sir, my Lord Mansfield never was obliged to listen to you,' replied the judge, coldly.

A universal smile followed this observation, which was made with a sort of sullen naïveté, that gave it great effect: while old Crawley, trembling at the audacity of his son, whispered him,

'*Aisy* now! *aisy*, Con, dear: troth you'll put your foot in it, if you let your janius get the better of you this way.'

The clerk now read the depositions in a nasal tone, and drawling brogue, which gave infinite amusement to the / fashionable part of the audience; and at last got through the sundry charges against Padreen Gar, Dennis Tully, Shamus Joy, Dan Brogan, Teague Mac Mahon, Owny Sullivan, and others, who came under the denomination of 'PADREEN GAR'S BOYS.'

They stood accused of feloniously assembling for purposes of rebellion, and breach of the king's peace, at Saint Gobnate's well, under the pretence of celebrating the feast of that saint; and of acting under the influence of Terence Oge O'Leary (who had absconded, and whose papers, being seized), betrayed a regular plan of insurrection, aided by several catholic gentlemen of the country, in correspondence with Spain and France.

Baron Boulter now folding his letter, called for a lighted candle and sealing-wax, and addressing the prisoners, said, /

'My honest friends, it appears to me, from the depositions which have been just set forth, that you all have incurred the chance of being hanged; an event that must, in all probability, have taken place at one time or other of your lives: and I dare say you will agree with me, my honest friends, that whether a little sooner, or a little later, is a matter of but trifling importance. (I'll trouble you, Sir, to snuff the candle.) You see, my friends, I wish to do *nothing in the dark*, and am endeavouring to throw *every possible light upon* your case. There now, is my young and clever friend, Mr. Conway Townsend Crawley, smiling at me; and my old friend Mr. Crawley, his venerable father, smiling also. The Crawleys, gentlemen, are good-humoured men, and cheerful men. I am, myself, a good-humoured man; and in that point, at least, I resemble Lord / Mansfield. And now, my friends, with such active magistrates and loyal men as the Mister Crawleys among you, the one an high sheriff, the other an high treasurer; the one a sitting barrister, and another a serjeant, (not, however, I trust *a permanent serjeant*); with such enlightened guardians of the law, to keep you quiet, and put you up, and put you down, it is singular that you should meet at Saint Gobnate's well, for the purposes of sedition and rebellion. For Mr. Crawley, Sen.

may be justly styled the grand conservator of the peace of Ballydab; and with his worthy sons, I must say, forms an *aula regis*,[20] (a term, by-the-bye, borrowed from the Norman law, as you well know, my honest friends, none better). (I'll trouble you, Sir, for a little black wax.) As for Counsellor Conway Crawley, I look upon him as the very repertorium[21] of the laws; one / who has read every thing; Burn's Justice, Blackstone's Commentaries, the Registrum Brevium, and Paley's Evidences;[22] deep read in the Saxon law, the Norman law, the Brehon law, and the game law[23] – apropos to *game laws*! Would you, Mr. Footman, step out to my servant, and tell him to take the grouse out of the gun case, and present them to the cook, with Baron Boulter's very best compliments? But, my honest friends, the point to establish is this – were you de facto[24] at Saint Gobnate's well for the purposes of sedition? Can you prove that you were not? I address myself in particular to you, Mr. Padreen Gar, as chief of this conspiracy: were you at Saint Gobnate's well this morning? and for what purpose?'

'Is it for what purpose, my lord?' said Padreen Gar, advancing intrepidly into the centre of the hall, and display-/ing a bold and careless countenance. 'Is it, what brought me there, Sir? Sure your lordship knows right well, what would be bringing a poor man to the holy well, plaze your lordship's honor, Sir; isn't it his *dewotion,* my lord? what else, Sir. And has been going to the well an hundred years, and more, my lord – troth we have.'

'Will you make affidavit of that, Mr. Padreen Gar?'

'I will, plaze your lordship.'

'Then, Mr. Padreen, I can only say, that a pitcher that goes *so often to the well is liable to come home broken at last*,[25] which I think I shall be able to prove to you before I have done. But who is that in the red shanavest? (I believe that is good Irish for a waistcoat, as some of you know, my friends, to your cost;) he who is seeking my attention, as I judge by his expressive countenance.' /

'Its Barney Tully, as sould your honor a *harse*, my lord, last sizes;[26] long life to your lordship,' said a slight, meagre, but alert person, stepping before Padreen Gar, and displaying a countenance of sly and intelligent expression.

'So, Mr. Tully, how do you do, my equestrian friend? Now, Mr. Barney Tully, though I have too much respect for your name and calling to wish to pry into *Tully's offices*,[27] I must nevertheless institute an enquiry into the cause of your appearing at St. Gobnate's well?'

'Och! plaze your honor, I'll prove an alibi, my lord; for upon oath this day, 'bove all days of the year, I was working on Mr. Crawley's new road, when I was seen and taken at St. Gobnate's well, Sir.'

'Then, Tullus Aufidius,[28] it is very plain you are of that class in Irish zoo-/ logy, so puzzling to other naturalists, called *the bird that can be in two places at once.*'

'I am, Sir,' replied Barney, smiling archly; 'sure enough an Irish bird, egg and feather; and so was my father before me, my lord.'

'We have nothing to do with your father, my honest friend Tully, because we do not want in this instance to *kill two* birds with one stone; and prefer in all instances a bird in the hand to two in the bush. Now, my friend in the *carawat*,[29] what is your name?' addressing a foolish-looking person with a red handkerchief tightened round his neck, almost to strangling.

'I'm called Teague MAC MAHON, plaze your lordship.'

'You could not be called by a better name, Mr. Mac Mahon, if your father was as anxious as Tristram Shandy's to give you a *lucky one*.'[30] /

'Long life to your lordship, and God bless you, Sir.'

'But, Mr. Mac Mahon, with *such* a name, I cannot well understand how you should be guilty of such disloyal practices, as to join Padreen Gar's rebellious band, at that site of all insubordination, St. Gobnate's well.'

'Why then, see here, plaze your lordship,' said Teague Mac Mahon, waving his hand, and speaking with great emphasis, 'I should never gone near the well, and had no occasion, only in regard to my taste of bacon, which was stolen dishonestly from me, plaze your honor.'

'Then you are one of those improvident persons, Mr. Mac Mahon, who have not the art of saving your bacon.'[31]

'Sure, I did *save* it,*[32] plaze your honor, and saved it well, and hung it up in / the chimbley, and quartered it in three halves, my lord; and was to give a small half to Darby Hoolegan, in lieu of two pecks of *male*, (meal) and an hundred of nails for my brogues: and while I was at mass, what should he do, but comes in, and skelps[33] off with the biggest half, and leaves me only a donny taste; and so I went after him to St. Gobnate's, where I was taken up, Sir, only for looking after the remains of my bacon.'

'The truth then is out, Mr. Mac Mahon; you went in search of a man, who had the boldness to *make an abridgement of Bacon*.'[34]

'Och Musha! that's it; long life to your lordship,' said Teague, triumphantly.

'I hope, however, Mr. Mac Mahon, that your friend had the *taste* to *preserve* all the *attic salt*.'[35]

'Och! plaze your honor, it was well / *salted* and *smoked* too before he took a taste of it.'

'Then, Mr. Mac Mahon, I *must* say, that had you but *smoked your friend* as you have *smoked your bacon*,[36] you would not now be the victim of your credulity, nor brought before me on suspicion of high treason.'

'My lord, my lord,' interrupted Judge Aubrey, with an air of irrepressible, impatience, 'I beg your pardon, but though I believe this mockery of justice is

---

*   i. e. *Cure* it, *salt* it. – An Hibernicism.

got up simply for the amusement of this distinguished circle, yet I cannot witness or assist in carrying on a farce, which may in the end be pregnant with evil to the persons who stand in custody before us. The depositions are a tissue of absurdity and nonsense: and though magistrates can in this country deprive persons of their liberty upon grounds quite as slight, yet I am not quite certain that the warrant upon / which they have been arrested, is a legal instrument. Show me your warrant, constable. – Yes, it is, as I suspected, a vague mittimus;[37] a contrivance of certain active magistrates, to get obnoxious persons into their power, and by which they baffle the protection of the laws, omitting to state any name, day, or place, or particular of the offences. Nothing, therefore, remains but to discharge these poor men, and send them to their work.'

'My learned brother,' said the baron, with much pleasantry of manner, ''tis not for you or me to bring in the verdict: we must refer it to the jury; and I believe a *fairer* jury never sat. What say you, ladies! guilty or not guilty?'

'*Not guilty* upon my honor,' cried Lady Georgina, joined by all the patrician voices present; while Lady Dunore, as much amused by the turn the / mock trial was taking, as she had been agitated by its probable issue, cried out louder than them all, 'Oh not guilty, not guilty.'

The judges now arose; and Judge Aubrey was about to address the prisoners, and to dismiss them with an admonition, when young Crawley starting forward, exclaimed with vehemence –

'Stay, my lord, before you again turn these lawless men loose upon this unfortunate district, whom your lordship must be aware have had no examination whatever, I beg to be heard for a few minutes. Your lordship has called the depositions made by sundry respectable persons a *tissue of nonsense and absurdity*; but we know how easy it is to despise the dawnings of *all* insurrections; we have learned also how dangerous it is to do so. The ravings of the first few followers of Cromwell at Huntingdon, a scuffle / for apples by Massaniello at Naples, and the dissensions of the Poissards at Paris,[38] however contemptible in their origin, were yet the *commencement and causes* of the mighty and terrific revolutions which followed. But, my lords, I will, I think, convince you that the seeds of rebellion have taken a deeper root in this province than in the breasts of a few barbarous peasants; that foreign incendiaries are at work to undermine the good will that subsists between Ireland and the parent country; and that intrigues are now carried on between France, Spain, and some of the Catholic gentlemen of this country, through the medium of an old offender, who was deeply implicated in the rebellion, a sort of pedagogue, named Terence Oge O'Leary.'

'Good God!' exclaimed Lady Dunore, plunged into a new series of emo-/ tions, 'how extraordinary! only conceive! French agents in this remote spot! Go on, Mr. Conway, pray go on.'

'Last night,' continued young Crawley, with renewed spirit, 'a search warrant was procured for examining O'Leary's papers; and as he was not at home, his desk was opened, and some curious plans of the intended rebellion came to light, which were forwarded by a military express to the castle after I had taken copies of them. Here,' continued young Crawley, triumphantly taking up paper after paper out of his father's *green bag,* 'here is first a list of the ancient families of this province, whose descendants, labourers in my father's grounds and her lady-ship's, will be doubtlessly proved one of these days to be lords of the soil. Here is a fragment relative to the late Florence Ma-/carthy, a drunken old dotard, who lived in this neighbourhood, and was called the titular Earl of Clancare, which is curious, for it proves that he has long been considered as the true lord of this district, and was secretly acknowledged such by his own party, which includes all the disloyal people in the country; for this paper states the following fact, in the quaint old language, still used by the Catholic gentry, and particularly affected by Terence Oge O'Leary: – that 'Florence Macarthy, by consent of all the popish bishops, deacons, jesuits, friars, and all the Irish nobilities assembled, was cre-ated Macarthy More, using in creation all the rites and ceremonies customary to the ancient Irish, being joined by all the nobility and noblesse of the province: – viz. the Na Donnells-Ferrars, the Offaleys, O'Sulivans-Beare, and Moriarty M 'Teague,' (names, / my lord, better known in the flourishing city of Ballydab than in the Red Book or Debrett's Peerage).[39] It is with regret, also, I add – that among these provincial noblesse are inscribed the names of the knights of Kerry and Glynn,[40] the white knight, and the knight of the valley, and, in short, many members of the Fitzgerald family. But what is most curious of all is the following letter from a Spanish priest, on whom it seems the archbishoprick of Dublin has already been bestowed. This letter, without date, is addressed to the late Florence Macarthy, of Ballydab, by the style and title of the *Most Excellente Earl Florence Macarthy, of Clancare,* and is well worth attending to.'

'Oh! let us have the archbishop's letter by all means,' said Lady Dunore. 'Only think, Georgy, love, of giving away an archbishoprick: it is quite / too amusing. Pray go on, Mr. Conway.'

Mr. Conway cleared his voice, and read as follows:

'My good Earl,

'God is my witness, that after my arrival in Ireland, having knowledge of your lordship's valour and learning (his valour, Lady Dunore, was leading the Bal-lydab boys some thirty years back in a contest with the Glannacrimes), I had an extreme desire to see and to communicate, and to confer with so principal a personage; but the length of the way would not permit me. I am now departing into Spain, with grief that I had not visited those parts; but I hope shortly to return to this kingdom, and to give you entire satisfaction: and be assured that I will perform with his majesty what a brother ought to do, that he should send from Spain; because by / letter I cannot speak any more; I leave the rest till sight. The Lord have your lordship in his keeping, according to my desire,

YO MATEO,

Arcobispo de Dublin.' *[41]

'Now, my lords and Lady Dunore, whether *his majesty*, here alluded to, be Bonaparte or King Joseph,[42] it is evident that the late Mr. Macarthy kept up a secret correspondence with the enemies of the country; and it is also pretty certain that this '*yo Mateo*' has fulfilled *his* promise of returning to communicate viva voce,[43] what he dared not write. He has been for more than a week back lurking in this neighbourhood, and even had the audacity to present himself in my father's house on false pretences. He is now under escort / on his way to Dublin; and his coadjutor and host, the successor of Mr. Macarthy in treason, has absconded. But there is no doubt, the vigilant police of the country will ferret him out of his hiding den.'

The detail thus given by Conway Crawley, with an impressive earnestness of manner, the documents he produced, the singular circumstances he developed, excited a very striking emotion in the English part of his auditory. A pause of a moment ensued.

Old Crawley pulled down his wig, and stole a sly glance of satisfaction at Judge Aubrey. Miss Crawley, who for the first time learned that her saintly hero was a French or Spanish spy, grew pale. Baron Boulter left an epigram unfinished, and began to lend a serious attention; while Lady Dunore exhausted herself in reiterated exclamations of amazement and consternation. /

'Only conceive, Georgy, love, a *real* Spanish monk, an incendiary too; good heavens! how extraordinary! Do you know I would not for the world miss seeing yo Mateo. But pray go on.'

'I believe there is little more to be added, Madam. The principal facts are before your ladyship and the judges; and your lordship,' added young Crawley, insolently turning to Judge Aubrey, 'may now conceive the propriety of our not dismissing these men, at least till we are in possession of the principals and leaders.'

'I see no more reason than ever for detaining them,' returned Judge Aubrey. 'But I hope, Mr. Crawley, the documents, whose copies you have had the trouble to make and to read, have not actually been sent off to the chief secretary's office by military express.'

'They are, I hope, by this time nearly in his possession,' returned / Conway Crawley, in a tone of great elation.

'I am sorry for it,' said Judge Aubrey, coolly, 'very sorry, Mr. Crawley; for as far as my black-letter Irish studies go, and if my memory does not wholly fail me, you have copied verbatim some extracts from the Pacata Hibernia of Robin

---

*   I, Matthew, Archbishop of Dublin.

Carew;[44] and you have transmitted to government a faithful account of the insurrection, of the celebrated Florence Macarthy, in the reign of Queen Elizabeth.'[45]

A burst of laughter, in which all joined, save the Crawleys, followed this observation, while a voice in the distance cried out –

'To be sure he has, sorrow lie there is in that.'

The next moment, O'Leary, bustling through the crowd, his cotamore slung over his shoulder, his wig awry, and his ferule in his hand, presented himself / in the centre of the hall. His appearance excited considerable amusement, for having bowed formally to Lady Dunore, with a tone of uncontrolable irritation, he turned upon young Crawley, exclaiming –

'I'll trouble you for my documents, Counsellor Con; my heads, and tails, and perorations; my notes, and minutes, and *memories*, for my genealogical history of the great Macarthy family, written in the Phœnician language, vulgo-vocato Irish. What call had you to them at all? Dioul! What right had you to break open my box, and I not in it, and to purloin my codices? And what dirty lucre did you expect by it, Counsellor? If it wasn't out of fear that I'd tell to the world that your ould grandfather, Paddy Crawley, took some of the property of the late Earl of Clancare, in trust for him during the *painals*, (penals)[46] Sir, / and refused to restore it after the *repail*; which was the first step he got in the world: and troth, a dirty step it was. Now answer me that, Counsellor Con, before the English *noblesse* here present.'

'I believe, Mr. Conway Crawley,' said Judge Aubrey, significantly, 'we *may* dismiss all these persons now.'

Every body arose and came forward, *good-naturedly* amused with the consternation of him whose pretension and insolence had been equally entertaining and imposing a few minutes before. Old Crawley almost buried his head in his *green bag*; but Conway, though confused, still unsubdued, came forward, and addressing Lady Dunore, who was now laughing with Lord Frederick and Lady Georgina, he said, 'I must request your lordship's attention and patience one minute more.'

'Oh! by all means,' said Lady / Dunore, fluttering back to her place. 'I don't care in the least if this trial goes on for ever. I never was so agitated and so amused in all my life; now, pray all sit down. My dear Judge Aubrey, pray resume your seat.'

'All that your ladyship has heard,' continued Conway, 'is mere invention, mere subterfuge. – Baron Boulter, better than any other, must be aware that it is so; since his lordship, as senior circuit judge, has granted a bench warrant to my father to take up the incognito Spanish priest, upon such information as his lordship certainly deemed sufficient.'

'I certainly granted a warrant a few days back,' said Baron Boulter, with a look of mortification, 'on informations sworn by one Mr. James Bryan, who holds some place in Mr. Crawley's office, for the purpose of apprehending a very suspicious character; who, with- /out any visible business, or means of livelihood, has for some time been lurking about this neighbourhood.'

This confession produced a visible change in the opinion of all present; while an expression of half-suppressed emotion distorted the countenance of old Crawley; and he muttered, in acrimonious tone, to his son –

'You have made a pretty kettle of fish of it, now. What the devil business had you to mention that stranger at all at all. Couldn't you let him go quietly on to jail. Troth, your *janius* will get you muzzled yet, great a scholar as you are, Counsellor Con.'

The silence which Baron Boulter's confession had produced was now suddenly interrupted by a noise in the portico. The crowd which still lingered there gave way, with a spontaneous and respectful motion; and a person of singular and splendid appearance ad-/vanced boldly up the hall, followed by two officers of justice. He approached the table where the judges sat, removing his hat with one hand, and leaning the other on a pile of books, with an air disengaged and imposing; and in a voice full, clear, and rapid, he said –

'I beg to present myself to Baron Boulter.'

Mute astonishment trembled upon every lip. Wonder and admiration animated every eye. All was breathless eager suspense; but O'Leary alone moved, and placed himself near the object of attraction, with a look, in which wildness and triumph disputed pre-eminence.

Baron Boulter was the first to recover presence of mind, and he replied, '*My* name, Sir, is Boulter, and I have the honour to hold his majesty's commission, as Baron of the Exchequer.[47] I can only add, Sir, that I shall be / happy to make the acquaintance of so handsome a man, and so fine a gentleman: pray be seated.'

The stranger put back the chair presented to him.

'My lord,' he said, 'I am a prisoner. On my arrival in this district this morning, and in my way to my lodging, at the dwelling of this person, Terence Oge O'Leary, I was arrested on a bench warrant of your lordship's, on informations sworn by a notorious informer, who was condemned for perjury some years back, and was saved under an indemnity act procured by his employer, Mr. Crawley. I shall obey your warrant, my lord, if you acknowledge your signature. But in the presence of this assembly, I deny that you have any authority to order the arrest of any man, either of your own free motion, or on such information as that upon which I am now a prisoner. It / is to you, therefore, my lord, I shall look for responsibility.'

'You will do what you please, Sir,' said Baron Boulter, firmly and coldly. 'The law lies open to all men.'

'And we, my lord,' interrupted young Crawley, trembling with rage and mortification, while his father, pale and silent, sat with his eyes bent upon the stranger, 'and we, my lord, shall find precedents enough *in this country* to defend us.'

'*In this country!*' interrupted the stranger in a loud and indignant voice. 'Has this country, then, a set of bye-laws of its own, to answer the purposes of particular individuals? Are not the *laws of England the laws of Ireland*?'

'Officers, do your duty,' said young Crawley, authoritatively, and almost incoherent with stifled rage.

'I shall accompany *your officers*,' / returned the stranger, coolly; 'and I have to thank *them* for their indulgence, which has confronted me with Baron Boulter. His lordship, I doubt not, has been imposed upon; but for the rest, I am aware that no man shall be imprisoned but upon the lawful judgment of his equals, or by the law of the land. This is the charter; by this I shall abide.' Then dropping his extended arm, his countenance lost all the sternness by which it had been energized; and bowing gracefully and low to the ladies, he added, 'I trust, in a moment of exigency like this, I shall be forgiven, if I have violated the laws of ceremony, in asserting those of justice: and I offer a thousand apologies to the Marchioness of Dunore, and her distinguished circle, for this unseasonable intrusion.'

He then bowed slightly round, to the judges respectfully, and dropped / back between the officers of justice; while Lady Dunore, in a fever of admiration, and O'Leary in the delirium of strong emotion, both approached him as he retired; but the deep stern voice of Judge Aubrey arrested his steps.

'Stay, Sir, you are I apprehend a stranger in this country?'

'I am, my lord, an utter stranger.'

'You have then, Sir, a prescriptive right to courtesy and protection, in a land where the name of stranger is still held sacred. I have no doubt my learned brother has been imposed on. His confidence in Mr. Crawley's zealous loyalty, and the hurry of business, may have urged him to give a warrant which I pronounce to be illegal, as given upon the testimony of a convicted perjurer.'

'You cannot prove it, Judge Aubrey,' exclaimed young Crawley, vehe-/mently. 'You would set aside all judicial privilege, all *propter dignitatem*,[48] of the bench.'

'Sir,' said the judge, 'these ebullitions of a mind, fraught by self-interest with arbitrary notions, are not worthy of reply. The dignity of the judicial station can only be degraded by him who holds it. I beg your pardon, Sir,' he added hastily, and turning to the stranger, 'I fear I have detained you; but I would impress upon your mind, that the judges of the land are the natural guardians of the oppressed; and I would suggest to you, that by giving bail, you will be spared the annoyance and inconvenience of a temporary imprisonment.'

'My lord,' said the prisoner, 'I thank you for this mark of consideration. But I have already said that I am an utter stranger here; where then / should I seek for bail? Who is there that would hold himself responsible for a *stranger?*'

'I will,' exclaimed a voice from a distance; and the next moment the hand of a young and very noble looking person was clasped in that of the stranger.

'And pray, who are you, Sir?' demanded young Crawley, stepping forward with a tone and demeanour of the pertest effrontery.

'I am,' said the party interrogated, throwing his eyes haughtily over his questionist, 'I am Lord Adelm Fitzadelm: pray who are you?'

The elder stranger started back with astonishment, while among the general bursts of exclamation, which rang through the hall, the shrieks of Lady Dunore were predominantly audible. She threw herself into her son's arms, / as much transported by the theatrical scene of his unexpected appearance, as if she had not, for months, intrigued his absence. She wept and laughed with hysterical alternation; presenting him to those he already knew, and to those he had never seen before. Then turning to the stranger, she addressed him as Don Yo Mateo, Archbishop of Dublin, asked a thousand pardons, welcomed him to Dunore, and went on repeating, 'was there ever any thing so charming! any thing so delightful! This is Ireland *par exemple!*[49] Delightful Ireland, where one is never safe and never *ennuyée*[50] for a single moment!'

Meantime the hall was cleared: the company at the castle, Lord Adelm, his friend, the officers of justice, and O'Leary, were nearly all that remained. The latter stood in the back-ground transfixed and pale, a monument of con-/sternation, and motionless as death, save that his quick glancing eyes turned alternately from Lord Adelm to his guest, and from his guest to Lord Adelm.

'But who *is* your friend?' asked Lady Dunore eagerly, and interrupting Lord Adelm's details of his journey, and pointing to the stranger, who stood talking to Judge Aubrey, 'Is he a *real* Spanish monk? Sure you are not implicated in this rebellion, which is found out to be no rebellion at all.'

These questions were repeated by every eye, if not by every tongue.

'Allow me to present my mother to you,' said Lord Adelm, taking the stranger's hand, 'the Marchioness of Dunore. General Fitzwalter, of South America, that brave Guerilla chief, whose life and fortune have been devoted to South American independence. / He is doubtless already known to you by fame, as he is in the Terra Firma,[51] by the glorious sobriquet of the Librador.'

Something like amazement was depicted in the countenance of the stranger, while he went through the forms of presentation, and listened to this detail of himself.

Lord Adelm continued uninterrupted: 'I do not believe, however, that my friend aspires to the double influence of the crosier and the sword. If, at least, he ambitions the Archbishoprick of Dublin, in the course of our travelling companionship (for we came to this country together), he has not made me his confidant.'

'Travelling companionship!' muttered old Crawley, with a look of alarm, while Lady Dunore reiterated welcomes and exclamations of delight, surprise, and wonder. /

The question of bail was then resumed; and a form being prepared, Lord Fitzadelm signed the paper: but this was not sufficient, as the instrument required two securities.

'Oh!' cried Lady Dunore, gaily, 'I'll be bail for the *archbishop*, that is, for the general: give me the pen – only think how odd! and you, Georgy, shall be another.'

Young Crawley, however, gravely demonstrated the illegality of her tender, and stated that female bail was not usual.

'Well, well, Mr. Conway Crawley, you happen to be monstrously unaccommodating to-day, and very tiresome,' interrupted Lady Dunore, 'but I suppose it must be so. Then do you, Mr. Crawley, if you please, sign for me. I imagine that will do as well. – I mean *Crawley pere*.'[52]

The tone and manner in which this / request was given were too peremptory to be resisted; and old Crawley, to his own amazement and consternation, became bail for the person whose arrest had taken place at his own instance, while he mentally observed, 'Well, this *bates Banacher* any how.'*[53]

Young Crawley in the meantime had left the table, and was engaged in earnest conversation with his aunt apart.

Baron Boulter was profuse in his apologies, spoke with some harshness of the two Crawleys for being led away by *over* loyalty, offered to discharge the warrant altogether, and asked the general on a visit to his house whenever he should come to Dublin.

To the discharge of the warrant, General Fitzwalter firmly objected: the / transaction, he observed, must be followed to its consequences. To the proffered hospitality he returned a polite answer, as general in its terms as the proposition to which it replied.

Judge Aubrey sat still, in silent triumph; the ladies' eyes were all turned on the Guerilla chief; and Lord Rosbrin, seeing every thing in a dramatic point of view, talked of situations, incidents, and clap-traps.

Lord Fitzadelm now came forward, and, seconded by his mother, pressed General Fitzwalter, with earnest solicitation, to make Dunore castle his residence while he remained in the country; but before he could reply, the attention of all was suddenly attracted to the recess of the painted window, by one of the bailiffs observing to Mr. Crawley,

---

*   A common Irish expression, applied to the doing of an extraordinary thing.

'Now, what am I to do with that faymale prisoner in the hall window, plaze your honor, that we took up ac-/cording to order, Mr. Crawley, going into Ter-ence Oge's a little bit ago, and wouldn't tell her name, Sir, nor shew her face, only just axed lave, Sir, to send a bit of a message to Castle Macarthy, Sir, to the Bhan Tierna, by a bit of a gassoon, Sir, and is cooped up there forenent you, Mr. Crawley?'

'You may do with her what you plaze, Larry Costello,' replied Mr. Crawley, in a dejected and absent tone, and still under the influence of profound chagrin, amazement, and alarm, which were all depicted in his countenance.

Larry Costello *plazed* to let out the prisoner from the dock where Lord Rosbrin had placed her, and to give her her liberty; when Lord Frederick, inter-fering, said, 'By Jupiter, this lady rebel has as good a right to a fair trial by jury as the rest; and I vote that we take our seats, and impannel[54] forthwith / for the cause of this *Pucelle de Bally-dab*.'[55]

'Oh! by all means in the world,' said Lady Dunore, unsatiated by scenes, sensations, and surprises: 'we must hear the *Pucelle de Ballydab*;' and she took her son's arm, who seemed satisfactorily to have accounted for his arrival; for to whatever he had said, she replied – 'You are quite right – exactly – certainly. I am delighted to see you here.'

The party now drew up in a circle, without resuming their seats, while the poor woman, apparently intimidated, and wishing to conceal herself, was led forward for examination by Larry Costello, who endeavoured to encourage her, by repeating: – 'Hold up your head now, honey. Sure there's money bid for you. If the Bhan Tierna will stand up for you, sorrow thing you have to fear ma'am. I'll engage she'll carry / you through, and well. Only just, sure, if you don't shew your face, their lordships will not see it agrah.'

Larry Costello, who was as easy in the presence of his superiors as the lower Irish usually are, with very little ceremony now pulled back her grey hood, and the straw bonnet it covered fell to the ground, discovering, not the coarse fea-tures of an Irish peasant, but such a head and such a countenance as might have belonged to that

'Rare Egyptian, the serpent of old Nile.'[56]

The immediate expression, however, of this singular countenance was confu-sion; but though the eyes were rivetted to the earth, and a colour, changeful as thought, indicated the excess of bashful womanly embarrassment, yet the acute smile, that for a moment gleamed and vanished, and a certain air of mockery and shrewdness, which seemed the na-/tural involuntary expression of the irregular but pretty features, combined to present a model for one of those happy pic-tures of gypsy beauty, where 'fancy outworks nature,'[57] and which mingles with the admiration, its equivocal charms attracting from the spectator something of fear, if not of distrust. Amazement universally, and almost audibly expressed, followed the sudden apparition of this unexpected vision.

'The BHAN TIERNA! by the powers,' exclaimed Larry Costello, in consternation, and respectfully withdrawing from the prisoner's side.

'LAMBH LAIDAR ABOO!' shouted O'Leary, throwing up his wig instead of his hat in an ecstasy of triumph.

'Lady Clancare!' cried Judge Aubrey, coming forward, and taking her hand with an air of kindness and protection.

'Lady who?' said the marchioness. /

'Lady Clancare did you say? Good heavens! it cannot – it is – My dear charming, odd, out of the way Lady Clancare, I have no words to express my delight. To meet you here, of all places in the world! a prisoner too! a rebel chieftainess perhaps! Oh! it's quite too good! Isn't it Georgy, love? One never meets with such things in London. But where are you come from? How fat you are grown! Why did you disappear so suddenly, when you had obtained such a *grand succés*[58] in London? Do you know, people said all sorts of odd things of you? No one could make you out in the least; and your pretty, pretty tales, and stories, and things. – How tanned you are! – how well you look! – Georgy, love, don't you know Lady Clancare, who made the *frais*[59] of my two last assemblies? And my forgetting you too, dear Lady Clancare, so completely, when you were out of sight, it's so very odd, arn't it / Georgy; but one forgets every thing in London, except what one sees every day.'

To this *Georgy* assented, at the same time renewing a very slight acquaintance with Lady Clancare, formed at Lady Dunore's parties in Town.

While the ceremonies of recognition, and the multiplicity of Lady Dunore's questions, afforded to the young Irish peeress a moment of self-collection, her spirits rallied; but still, as she threw round her eyes, there was an air of '*tongue-tied simplicity*'[60] in her eloquent silence, which, contrasting with the expressive character of her countenance, produced, what Lord Rosbrin called, '*a fine dramatic effect.*' For

'Having lost her breath, she spoke and panted,
That she did make defect perfection,
And breathless, power breathed forth.'[61, f]

Her emotion seemed something be-/yond the natural confusion incidental to her actual position, and she turned her eyes with a glance of supplication on Lady Dunore, as if soliciting her interposition, to withdraw her from a situation where every look was turned on her; where she formed the centre of a circle evidently animated by idle curiosity and amused amazement. Lady Dunore, flattered by the claim made on her protection, and understanding it, drew her a little on one side, listened, smiled, laughed aloud at some detail which Lady Clancare related in a low murmuring voice, and with a countenance varying, animated, and humourous; while to the conclusion of her relation, whatever it had been, Lady Dunore, gently leading her back to the group, replied,

'Don't make the least apology. Oh! no, its better as it is, a thousand times. This impromptu is worth an hun-/dred formal premeditated visits; besides, all this never could happen but in Ireland. It was so kind in you, to suffer yourself to be taken prisoner too -- you are always so amusing. But who are you, my dear creature, for I forgot to ask you when in London? You know Georgy, love, one doesn't want to know who people are in London, especially LIONS.[62] But are you really Irish, my dear Lady Clancare?'

'Irish!' exclaimed O'Leary, with a burst of emotion beyond all power of control; and darting forward, 'aye, troth is she *Irish,* body and soul. Irish, by birth, by blood, and by descent. Irish every inch of her, heart and hand, life and land! and though the mother that bore her was *Iberian* born, Bachal Essu! she was Milesian, like herself, descended from the Tyrian Hercules:[63] and there she stands, the darling of the world, with the best blood / of Spain and Ireland flowing through her veins. A true Irish woman, that loves her country, and lives in it; long life to her! and an ancient ould countess to boot, in her own right, Anno 1565, Elizabeth, Reginæ 6; the lineal heir of Florence Macarthy More, the *fogh na galla,* and King of the Desmondi, to this blessed hour.'

A smile played over the countenance of Lady Clancare, who retreated a few steps, as this address again brought every eye on her, and again covered her with confusion.

'And who are YOU? you delightful creature,' cried Lady Dunore, walking round O'Leary with her glass to her eye, and more than sharing in the general surprise and amusement occasioned by his sudden appearance and speech.

'Who am I, Madam, is it?' said O'Leary, firmly, but respectfully: 'I / am Terence Oge O'Leary, plaze your ladyship, of the Pobble O'Learys, of Clancare, county Kerry, anciently Cair-Reight, from Ciar-na-Luochra-Macarthy, who was King of Munster, Anno Mundi, 1525, Noah Rex.[64] and am tributary and seneachy, or genealogist to the Macarthys, before the English was heard of, Anno Domini, 1166, Hen. secundus Rex;[65] and defies Johannes Major Scotus, and Measter Camden, Dr. Ledwitch, and Sir Richard Musgrave,[66] to deny that, any how, the thieves of the world! with ould Saxo Grammaticus[67] to back them; and am, at the present speaking, a poor Irish schoolmaster, *Ludi Magister,*[68] of Monaster-ny-Oriel; and lastly, plaze your ladyship, Madam, I am a servitor in the great Norman family of the Fitzadelms, being fosterer, (his voice faltered) – fosterer, Madam, of him, who, though he now lies low in the ocean, / with none but myself, and the winds of heaven to moan over him, yet, if he had his right, would now be reigning here in this very castle; I mean the –'

Here General Fitzwalter advanced in front of O'Leary, leaning on Lord Fitzadelm's arm. O'Leary started back: his voice dropped, his colour changed, and he paused abruptly. The general took his place, from which he had involuntarily retreated; and some low whispered words from Lady Clancare to the marchioness, who had, during O'Leary's speech, drawn the arm of the Irish peeress through her own, now wholly diverted her attention from the *last* of those *dramatis personæ*,[69] which the happy events of this eventful day had brought upon the stage.

Withdrawing from the circle, the two ladies, in earnest conversation, moved towards the portico, followed by / every eye. The appearance of Lady Clancare produced an instantaneous effect upon the crowd assembled at the gates.

The report had gone abroad, that the idol of popular feeling had been taken prisoner by Mr. Crawley, and brought to Dunore castle. Hundreds of wild, but strong affectioned persons, had gathered for her protection and rescue. Thousands were at her service; but her appearance, leaning on Lady Dunore's arm, lulled every fear for her safety. Cries of BHAN TIERNA GO BRACH! rent the air; and when both ladies sprung into a little cabriolet,[70] drawn by mules, (the carriage of Lady Clancare, which had just arrived,) the name of the Marchioness of Dunore, mingled with these more national sounds, and '*long lives*,' and 'long reigns,' were liberally distributed to both ladies.

The guests of the castle had now ad-/vanced into the portico to witness this singular scene. Lady Clancare had taken the reins; and while Lady Dunore drew her cashmir[71] over her head and round her shoulders, her new friend turned her extraordinary countenance on the group in the portico; and with a mingled expression of extreme slyness and humour, she threw round her dark eyes. They met alternately the looks of all present; till at last fixing their glances, charged with a malicious gaiety, something between triumph and derision, on old Crawley, she kissed her little whip in salutation to all, and drove off with the lady of the castle, both laughing loud and violently.

There was in all this little transaction a something that gave a poetical image of an enchantress, whose struggles with a rival *Ogre* finally prevail and Lady Clancare looked as the *Tita-/nia* might be supposed to look, when, on Oberon's begging from her the

'Little changeling boy to be his Henchman,'

she replies in the triumph of conscious possession, 'not for thy fairy kingdom!'[72] The possession of Lady Dunore seemed to her desirable as the changeling boy to the fairy king.

With the departure of the two chieftainesses, English and Irish, the rest of the company, somewhat fatigued, and infinitely amused by the events of the morning, withdrew and dispersed, except the members of the Crawley family, who still remained in the hall, congregated in close conference.

'The game's up,' said old Crawley, with his eyes fixed on the spot where the phantom of Lady Clancare still floated before him, bearing off the marchioness: 'she has got her now,' he / continued. 'That's the way she took my *lunatic* from me, whom I'd have had to this day, only for her, and the management of his estate. That's the way too she let loose the Rabragh on the world, with the help of Judge Aubrey, just the ditto of herself. Well, the devil is not able for her, Christ pardon me; and believe after all she is the devil *ingarnet*, if the truth was known.'

'This is no place for idle talking,' said young Crawley, at last himself overpowered by the contentions of the day. 'Follow me to my aunt's room: you see Lord Rosbrin is still in the portico – your discomfiture may be observed.' He then left the hall, with his silence-stricken aunt on one arm, and his green bag under the other. Old Crawley, after a moment's pause, was preparing, with a deep sigh, to obey the authoritative commands of his son, / when Lord Rosbrin, entering the hall, arrested his steps, with a solemn beckoning of his finger, and exclaiming with a significant air –

'*My gentle Puck, come hither*.'[73]

Crawley involuntarily obeyed the summons, though by no means liking the *nom de caresse*[74] which accompanied it.

'Say, *my fat lad of the castle*,[75] continued Lord Rosbrin, 'rememberest thou aught in scenic effect more striking than that last dramatic incident; I mean the old woman transformed suddenly into a *Roxalana,* or an Urganda in the burletta of Cymon? Does it not beat the skreen scene in the School for Scandal,[76] hollow?'

'*Hollow*,' replied old Crawley, endeavouring to extricate his button from Lord Rosbrin's grasp.

'Rememberest thou,' proceeded Lord Rosbrin, emphatically, '*remem- /berest thou, since once I sat upon a promontory, and heard a mermaid, on a dolphin's back, uttering such dulcet and harmonious breath, that the rude sea grew civil at her song?*'[77]

'Why, then, upon my credit, I can't say I do,' returned Crawley, with another impatient effort at release.

'*That very time*,' continued the peer, '*I saw – thou could'st not – flying between the cold moon and the earth –*'[78]

At the word *moon,* a sudden conviction of the young lord's lunacy struck on Crawley's mind; and bursting away, and leaving his button in Lord Rosbrin's grasp, he muttered, as he went along, 'Devil a bit; but I believe it is full moon with you all, men, women, and children, the Lord save us!'

Lord Rosbrin, looking after him, uttered a *stage laugh,* and crying, 'A / fool, a fool, a motley fool!'[79] retired to his dressing-room, to clean some silver spangles, and cut out foil for his coronation dress in Lady Macbeth./

CHAPTER II.

'Lovers and madmen have such seething brains,
Such shaping fantasies, that apprehend
More than cool reason comprehends.'
SHAKESPEARE.[80]

'What! shall quips and sentences, and these paper bullets of the brain, drive a man
from the career of his humours?'
IDEM.[81] g

WHILE the guests of the castle dispersed in different directions, Lord Adelm
and General Fitzwalter proceeded arm in arm together across the castle court to
a sort of terrace, once a rampart, which gave on the sea.

This rampart opened by a door upon the strand; and Lord Adelm, proposing
/ that they should direct their steps beyond the reach of intrusion or observation,
was endeavouring to draw back the rusty bolt, and obtain egress, when O'Leary,
with his hat squeezed between his hands, and his countenance distorted by agitation, caught the general's eye, as he followed him at a short distance.

'What is the matter?' asked the general, turning back on his steps, and meeting the approach of his host.

'The matter, my lord! that's your honor, I mane *now* gineral, Sir, any how.
Nothing is the matter, gineral, only great times, and great luck, Sir! and the
young lord, the very *moral* of the honourable Gerald, his father: and the Crawley
pirates foiled, Sir, for oncet: and I'd only crave a word with your honor, gineral,
since it's a great gineral you are, Sir, and was a great gineral in the family an hundred years / back and more – that's the ould Brigadier, anno 1698, in armour this
day at Court Fitzadelm, only no frame – but stopping a chimbley. And it's what
I'd just make bould to ax your honor, and never will trouble you more, Sir, plaze
Jasus! if you arn't the young lord that's laning over the battlement, waiting for
you, gineral? that is Lord Fitzadelm, Sir?'

'O'Leary,' said General Fitzwalter, in a soothing voice, 'O'Leary, put on your
hat, and go home. My good O'Leary, I shall shortly follow you to the Friary to
dress, and you may bespeak me a chaise to bring me here to dinner. And, above
all, O'Leary' (and he patted his hand on his shoulder as he spoke, his voice softening into a tone of great affection), 'take care of the health and life of a person
who is very dear – that is very *necessary* to me, O'Leary.' /

'And who is that?' said O'Leary, eagerly. 'Is it th' aigle, gineral? Sure he's dead,
Sir. Poor Cumhal's dead at last, your honor;' and the tears dropped large and fast
from his eyes, but they fell not all for Cumhal.

The tone of the general's voice, and the pressure of his hand, had been too much for the state of exaltation in which the events of the morning had left him; and the death of his old companion furnished him with an excuse for weeping, which relieved his heart, weighed down with oppression.

'Dead!' repeated the general: 'poor old Cumhal!' – he sighed and added, absently, 'it was much such an evening as this, and such a coast too: poor Cumhal – dead!'

'Och! you need not moan him, gineral,' said O'Leary, reproachfully; 'he's better provided for nor them he's left behind him, Sir. For shure, he / wasn't shook off like a wither'd leaf from a young green tree, and rejected by him, that was reared on his milk, that's my wife's milk, Sir. And thought, troth, we'd break our hearts the day he was weaned; and we sent back to St. Crohan's; and wasn't long till he followed us there, *Nolens Volens*,[82] and –'

'You are much altered since we *met*, since we *first* met in the mountains, O'Leary,' interrupted the general, as he fixed his eyes on a countenance, where the perpetual conflict of revived feelings, vague doubts, and uncertain hopes, had made great ravages: 'you are not well, my dear O'Leary.'

'That's it, plaze your honor, I am not well, surely, Sir,' said O'Leary, eagerly, 'and thinks betimes that it's the lycanthropia I have got, which Maister Camden saith was common to the ancient Irish,*[83 h] and affirmeth that / melancholie persons of this sort have pale faces, soaked and hollow eyes, with a weak sight, and never shedding one tear to the view of the world – only now, Sir, for Cumhal, the poor bird.'[i]

'We will talk this matter over to night, O'Leary,' said the general, answering the impatient beckon of Lord Adelm's hand; 'or to-morrow, or at no distant period: and you *shall* be well again, O'Leary, and be gay and contented as I first found you in the midst of your learned disciples; and you shall change your scene too: you shall travel with me to other countries; and then you will return to Ireland, and finish your genealogical history of the Macarthies, and dedicate it to that very '*ancient old Countess of Clancare*,' in whose favour you were so eloquent to day; and by all means get her picture if you can, for your title page: I promise you it will sell your book.'

With these words, gaily pronounced, / he left him whom they had cheered, before he had time to reply; and joining the impatient Lord Adelm, they proceeded along the shore together.

There was a magic in the name of the Macarthies that operated like a spell upon the ideas and feelings of O'Leary, and drew him from the remembrance of his own griefs. General Fitzwalter had probably discovered this, for he often had recourse to it in moments when the wandering mind of the schoolmaster be

---

*   The disease of the wolf – a malady attributed to the ancient Irish.

came immersed in recollections which were the sources of his hallucination.[j] It now had its wonted effect; and O'Leary, as he left the castle gates, with his usual short heavy step, and his hands clasped behind his back, murmured to himself: –

'My *genealogical history of the Macarthies,* in troth; and never tould me a word since he came of the Ogygia of the great O'Flaherty, nor the Histoire / d'Irelande, by Abbé O'Gaghehan:[84] how could he, and he in jeopardy of the Crawleys? And my codices sent to the Lord-Deputy, that's the Lord-Lieutenant;[85] and troth, I think they'll astonish him. And the Bhan Tierna, after all, at the castle of them Dunores, after keeping out of their way, and then circumventing the Crawleys: aye, *'still on the necks of the Butlers,'* Dioul! and carrying off the great lady to herself, when it's what she couldn't help appearing before her; and letting herself be taken, and turning bad to good, always after her ould fashion. A Macarthy in the halls of the Fitzadelms: Bachal Essu! Wonders will never cease!

"Turne quod optanti divum promittere nemo
Auderet, volvenda dies en attulit ultro."[86]

And to see her standing in the midst of them Boddie Sassoni, just like a young scion of an old oak on the Boggras, flou-/rishing lonely and green among the scraws[87] and briars that have sprung up in a night saison, like mushrooms.'

While O'Leary was thus soliloquizing his way to the DUNORE ARMS, where a crowd was assembled, relating and listening to the extraordinary events that had taken place at the castle, the two adventurous fellow travellers were pursuing their walk up and down the sea-shore. Lord Adelm Fitzadelm, occupied with himself and his own views, as those usually are who have long engrossed the world's attention, and have become the spoiled children of society, was eager to pour the confidences of his self-love into his companion's patient ear; and taking his arm, as they passed through the postern gate, he entered at once upon the history of his feelings and of his life since they had parted at Court Fitzadelm.

'I am ordinarily but little influenced,' / he observed, 'by the ebb and flow of joy or sadness, which govern the capricious tide of human affections in the everyday children of the world: yet *I am* glad, sincerely glad to see you here; glad that it may be in my power to return some part of the hospitable rites which, as a stranger, I received at your hands; and happy that my timely presence has been the means of saving you from at least a *temporary* inconvenience, and rescuing you from some intrigue of my mother's friends, the Crawleys, which might have involved you in transient vexations, though eventually they must have fallen of themselves into insignificance.'

'I am not quite so certain of that,' returned General Fitzwalter: 'had they succeeded in shutting me up at the present moment, they might have crossed me in pursuits, to myself, at least, big with importance. They might have / succeeded in throwing suspicion on my character, which, at a future moment, might have invalidated my testimony, when all but honour will be at stake. Their motives of action are, however, still a mystery.'

'To me it seems impossible,' replied Lord Adelm, 'that you could come into the sphere of intrigue of these reptiles. There is a sort of poetical elevation in your character, your profession, or rather your vocation, that places you so far out of the reach of the meddling little faction of an Irish district.[k] The admiral of the gallant fleet of Martingaria, the general in chief of the guerrilla troops of the mighty Cordilleras,[88] a warrior, a patriot, in a word, YOU in the power of the Crawleys! This is a solecism not easily understood! and

"Comes not within the prospect of belief.'"[89]

'You measure my character by the / elevation of the great regions in which it was developed; and associate me personally with the glorious cause in which I was involved. But how came you by these facts? Where did you learn that the Commodore of the LIBRADOR had once commanded the little fleet of Martingaria, or had been distinguished by an higher command among the cloud-embosomed Cordilleras?'

'Where?' repeated Lord Adelm, with animation, 'and how? Why may not I have my Egeria or my dæmon,[90] as well as another? for if I obtained not my information through super-human agency, faith, I know not how I got it, or *came by it.*'

'You speak enigmas.'

'I have lived in them of late.'

'And the sphinx[91] who has presided over them is still, I suppose, Mrs. Magillicuddy,' said Fitzwalter, ironically.

'Not exactly,' replied Lord Adelm, dryly, 'except Mrs. Magillicuddy be / a sort of *petite maitresse*-sphinx,[92] fanciful and elegant as she is mysterious and powerful: one, for example, who traces 'thoughts that breathe, and words that burn,'[93] upon paper, that blushes roses and smells of them; one who takes for her device, *love depriving flowers of their thorns,* and for her motto, '*Sou utile ainda que Briccando.*'[94]

The general started; and Lord Adelm, producing a small embroidered letter-case, took from it three billets, written on rose-coloured paper, and literally breathing odours. The seal and motto, to which he pointed, were no strangers to the general's eyes.

'I might,' he continued, 'shew you the contents of these billets; for with the exception of a few detailed facts, they are vague and mysterious as Delphic oracles,[95] but that I hold them sacred to the very *mysticism* they profess. In style they are almost / too fanciful, light, and delicate, even for a woman's dictation, though at the same time in substance obscure as diplomatic cyphering. In short, I am lost in wild conjecture.'

'Oh! I see Queen Mab hath been with you,'[96] observed the general, laughing, and amused by the visionary credulity of the noble idealist, which seemed to have lost nothing of its eccentricity since they had parted. – 'Are you, then, become a devotee to a more philosophical sect than the school of *faëry,* one of the illuminati, the invisible brothers, the *fratres roris cocti,* whose communion is confined to sprites, sylphs, and gnomes, and whose secret of all human good lies in the *essences of concocted dew?*'[97]

'Nay, you, may laugh as you will; but I hold the principles of the Rosicrucian philosophy in high respect. Whatever elevates the imagination, whatever raises / us above the groveling lot of earthly existence, unites us to a spiritual world, shakes off the dross of mere humanity, and purifies and refines our nature, are at least glorious illusions.[l] I have always loved the poetical and religious grandeur of the Rosicrucian doctrines, their 'divine energy,' or SOUL, diffused throughout the frame of the universe; their '*Archæus,*' or universal spirit;[98] the influence of their bright starry Providence; the government of light and harmony; their brilliant dæmons and delicious sylphs. I do not,' he continued, as his imagination heated with its own workings,[m] 'I do not, I confess, blush to own myself the dupe of those high-wrought dreams of physical possibility which inspired NUMA in his grotto, or SOCRATES in his cell;[99] and I wish not, at this moment, to dissipate the impression that there may, that there *does* exist for me, some crea- /ture of æther and light, some legitimate child of the spheres, which, always invisibly nigh, watches over my sunless life-path, throwing a ray over the heart's dark desolation, and shining upon the ruins of memory, like the gleam that now falls upon that tottering pile before us.'

'It talks well; but one *real* lovely woman is worth it all,' said the general, reddening as he spoke, from the energy of his feeling – 'But your invisible sylph, if sylph you will have her, seems to me a malicious little imp, and more like the '*shrewd and knavish sprite called Robin Goodfellow,*'[100] than a delicate aeriel; for she has led you a dance

"Over hill, over dale,

Through bush, through briar,

Over park, over pale,

Through flood, through fire,"[101]

without any apparent object in her / agency, if it be not to amuse her own splenetic gaiety, or to work upon your imagination.'

'Of you, at least,' said Lord Fitzadelm, 'whether *gnome* or *sylph,* or woman, she merits well, for *you* are the object of her *special* protection.'

'I!' said the general, starting – 'indeed!'

'Judge for yourself. Of three billets received from my lovely invisible (for lovely she must be, whether mortal or sprite), one led me from Portugal to Ireland, by informing me of my mother's intrigue to smuggle me into the borough of Glannacrime, *bon gré, malgré!*[102] another fixed my residence in the neighbourhood of Kilcolman, by announcing it the native region of my guardian spirit, (where, by the bye, I vainly waited her brilliant apparition), and the third urged my instant departure for Dunore, by intimating that my / travelling companion, General Don Fitzwalter, the illustrious South-American chief, was about to become the victim of the loyal suspicions of the petty despots of the place. I was not surprised to find that you belonged to history, and immediately hastened to your assistance; too late, indeed, to warn you of your danger; but, I trust, in time to avert its consequences.'

'This looks like magic indeed,' said the general, after a moment's pause. 'I had no reason to suppose I was known to any human being in this country: for wishing to avoid the inconveniences which follow the éclat[103] of a public character, I have concealed my name, profession, and title, which might have reached even this remote spot, through the medium of the newspapers, now that the eyes of all Europe are directed on the glorious struggles of South-America.[n] But I can only be an / object of interest to this powerful spirit, in as much as she supposes me your friend. It is you whom she has led from Portugal to Ireland through the solitudes of the Galties, amidst the shades of Court Fitzadelm: it is for you that she has called spirits from the vasty deep[104] in the questionable shapes of Mrs. Magillicuddy and Mr. Owny. She had provided you a lodging too in the neighbourhood of Dunore, in case she found it necessary to preserve your incognito; and by this arrangement I have profitted; for my host O'Leary, till he saw us together, insisted on my being Lord Adelm Fitzadelm, and as such received me for his tenant, which he would not otherwise have done.'

The general, as he spoke, was occupied in searching among some papers for the mysterious letter which had preceded his arrival at the priory: 'Here,' he said, 'is a letter from your sylph, / not, however, breathing and blushing roses, but written in human characters, on a material substance, and respiring turf smoke. O'Leary, who is a Rosicrucian in his way, insists that it came from *the good people,* the designation of Irish faéry.'[105]

Lord Adelm took the letter in surprise, and read it with emotion. 'It is,' he said, 'the writing and the seal. May I keep this letter?' he asked after a pause.

'Oh, certainly,' replied the general, carelessly: 'it does not concern me; you of course will find out who this invisible agent is; and then –'

'That is not so certain,' interrupted Lord Fitzadelm: 'she wraps herself in impenetrable seclusion, throws a veil of mystery over her motions, as over her person, and in her fanciful epistles, though there is much to excite wonder, there is nothing to feed hope / further than the interest she takes in me.'

'Interest indeed! but you cannot for a moment consider this adventure in any other light than as a mere *bonne fortune*,[106] however singularly it has been conducted.'

'O! there is satiety in that thought, in that term at least; and to confess the truth, I do not wish to *dull* the delight of this mystic union by exploring its causes, or assigning it a motive or object. I love to think that in the pauses snatched from the *tedium* of society, I may inhale the sigh, and listen to the song of this nymph of the air, as I caught the one on the ruins of Holycross, and hung upon the other, amidst the desolation of Court Fitzadelm, for I am convinced of her presence on both occasions, and to believe that our communion is divine, and that our alliance will become immortal.' /

'And I,' said the general, with warmth, 'I would not give up the idea of this *invisible correspondent* being a woman, a true devoted woman, were I in your place, to be an object of adoration to a *"world of spirits."*[107] Were I the object of such zeal, vigilance, and devotion, had *I* called forth such talent, spirit, and inge- nuity, I would not long remain ignorant of my invisible guardian. I would force my way through the mystery which conceals her, I would follow her from pole to pole, over alps and oceans, or remain fixed and rooted to the spot she inhabited; woo her, win her, cling to her, cherish her ....'

'And – *marry her* –' interrupted Lord Adelm, yawning.

'Marry her!' repeated the general in a tone as if some sudden association of ideas were abruptly awakened by this proposition; then, after a pause, he asked abruptly – 'What do you think / of that pretty, but extraordinary, looking, Lady Clancare? Her appearance was altogether sudden and singular.'

'Oh! she struck me to be a mere *minaudiere!*[108] some stale *engouement*[109] of my mother's, who came in this extraordinary way upon the scene, merely to make a sensation, and startle back Lady Dunore into a faded prepossession. You may *trust* me on the score of my mother's fancies. This wild Irish peeress has been one of the *lions*, I suppose, of a London season,[110] has been exhibited for her brogue or her howl, or shewn off *"as the lady,* whose father was hanged in the rebellion;" for my mother, who is one of the reigning autocrats of fashion, brings people into vogue upon her *own* emotions, as the old Dutchess of G. did upon a fiddle-string;[111] and *weeps* or *wonders* them into notoriety, as her grace *danced* them into ton. This Lady Clancare has "fretted *her* hour upon / the stage" and was heard no more;[112] and she now issues from her own castle, a prisoner *with her own consent* into ours, merely to get up a scene, and occasion a *réchauffee,*[113] in my capricious mother's "promptly cold affections."'[114]

'She seems, however, to have succeeded, for she carried off Lady Dunore, even from you, who were so little expected, so freshly arrived, and so rapturously received.'

'Oh! that is quite my mother. She is an excellent person in her way; but in her *engouemens* [115] her feelings are –

"Momentary as a sound,
Swift as a shadow – short as any dream."[116]

Be not you, therefore, misled by her favour. You are made to win it; but even you will find it "sweet, but not permanent."[117]

'I shall not remain here to put her ladyship's stability to the test. I expect / my little vessel round by the first fair wind, and then I am off.'

'No, no,' interrupted Lord Fitzadelm, 'you do not mean that. You will not leave me here with dawdling dandies, and cast coquettes; for, save my excellent uncle DALY and Eversham, who, though a coxcomb, is a perfect gentleman, the whole *set-out* at Dunore castle is, I saw at a glance, perfectly detestable: but that I am spell-bound here, I would fly off with you to South America to-morrow.'

'And your election?'

'I have not even thought of that yet. If I am returned, however, I shall pursue my own course: if I am worsted I shall be left to follow it; but all depends upon how my mother stands implicated: what is done cannot be undone: for the present, however, other objects touch me more nearly:'

The castle bell (for they were still / pacing backwards and forwards beneath the rampart)° now intimated the hour for dressing; and Lord Adelm, urging the general's quick return, subjoined an ardent request that he would take up his residence at the castle, while his business detained him in the neighbourhood.

This Fitzwalter, with his wonted tone of decision, promptly refused. He insisted upon their original stipulation, which had guaranteed mutual and perfect freedom of action.

'How necessary it is to me,' he continued, 'yourself shall judge.' He paused for a moment, placed himself between Lord Adelm and the postern gate, at which he was about to enter, and with a low voice and rapid but emphatic enunciation, he continued – 'I am here in this neighbourhood for the purpose of recovering my birth-right, of which, in my boyhood, I was fraudulently bereaved. I am here for the / purpose of dispossessing a powerful family of princely property, title, honours, and influence of vast extent, which, but for my unexpected re-appearance on the scene, would in right be theirs. To effect this, the testimony of the lowly, and proofs in possession of the illiterate and the prejudiced, are necessary. My agents lie amongst those, purchaseable by their poverty or assailable by their simplicity. My opponents are among the great, the powerful, the noble, and the wily. Vigour, promptitude, perseverance, and secrecy, are the arms given me to contend with. Judge then how necessary to my views are perfect freedom, obscurity of position, and disengagement of mind. I am here collecting witnesses, whom I dare not trust with the secret of their own evidence. Brought forward in society in this country, I should come into contact with those whom I am bound, *not to injure* / (for I come but to claim my rights), but *to dispossess*: it may be to receive their hospitality in the common intercourse of the world, or to awaken suspicion by rejecting it. I might, perhaps, too, so ally myself to some one interesting member of that family, who, united to me by blood, and endeared to me by splendid qualities, would eventually weaken my efforts in the cause of justice, general as well as personal: in a word –' he stopped abruptly: his eye darkened, his under lip trembled, and his silence was that of strong emotion; a seeming struggle between the impulse of a generous frankness, and the caution of necessary prudence.

'Pray go on,' said Lord Adelm, impatiently: 'your story interests me;' and he seated himself upon an abutment of the rampart, forgetful of the time, the place, of every thing, but the extraordinary person who stood before him; / and who, now, like a creature restored to its native element, was energized by strong passion, and animated by emotions best adapted to his nature and existence.

'In a word then,' continued the general, firmly, and after a pause, 'such a person as I have described exists; and I have suddenly but *decidedly* resolved to make him, who must chiefly suffer by my claims, the sole confidant of my strenuous efforts to establish them; to relate to him a story which will cover those nearest to him with ignominy, and tend to deprive him of the greatest objects of the world's ambition. Imagine how highly I think of the honour and the spirit of this person, of the truth of his character, of the elevation of his mind, of the disinterested generosity of his nature.'

'By heavens! I would rather be that selected person,' said Lord Adelm, im-/petuously – 'I would rather merit and obtain such proofs of esteem, confidence, and admiration, than possess the highest sounding titles, which eventually await me, or lord it over these rich domains, which must one day be mine.'

'Would you?' exclaimed the general, catching his extended hand in a grasp of iron; 'would you –' he stopped short: a slight convulsion passed across his countenance, and, suddenly letting fall the hand he so firmly held, he added – 'But you shall hear my story: I will confide to you events, and names blasted by those events, consigned to shame and ignominy, which have long lain deep buried in my heart with feelings of indignation, stifled, indeed, but not extinct. In *my* person justice has been set aside, right overthrown, nature's holiest ties violated; my nearest kindred have been my deadliest foes, and the legal guardians of my youth / have torn me from my natural position in society, exposed me to misery, to slavery; through them I have been bought and sold like beasts of burden; through them –' He paused abruptly: he clenched his hands with a violence that proceeded from acute and powerful feeling, seeking vent in physical sensation, acute even to pain; then with a flashing eye, and an illuminated countenance, he added – 'But it is passed, and I have asserted all the rights of man, recovered and protected them for myself and others: I have broken the chain of oppression wherever I have found it galling the oppressed: I have fought my way to glory and success; and now, I trust, I come to illustrate the name I claim, to add to the splendour, not to darken the brightness, of hereditary nobility. This, however, is no moment –'

'Yes, yes,' said Lord Adelm, catch-/ing his enthusiasm, and borne away by the energy and rapidity of his manner, 'go on; this is the time.'

'Will you,' said General Fitzwalter, after a long pause, 'will you trust yourself to-night in my lodging among the ruins of Monaster-ny-Oriel?'

'To night! at what hour?'

'The tide will be out at midnight: by taking the strand you will reach the Friary in less than twenty minutes.'

'At midnight, then,' said Lord Adelm, shaking the hands of his companion; and, for the first time in his life, interested in the details of a story of which he was not himself the hero; for till this moment he had never been associated with one, whose high qualities and superior endowments assimilated with his own. The singularity and mystery of the stranger's position had also fastened with tenacious influence on his imagination; and a secret mid- /night interview, for the purpose of receiving a momentous confidence, in the ruined towers of a desolated abbey, on the wild shores of the vast Atlantic, had each their due effect; and, for the moment, the invisible sylph was superseded, if not forgotten, in the interest excited by the stranger chief.ᴾ

The dressing bell had now ceased to ring; and the new, but firm friends, parted for the moment. /

CHAPTER III.

'Rongé de fiel et bouffi d'orguil.'¹¹⁸

As the judges were to proceed on their journey early in the evening, dinner had been advanced by nearly an hour earlier than the ordinary time, and the last bell had rung before any one had descended to the saloon. The judges alone were impatiently observing the gradual refrigeration of soups, fish, and patés, as the party dropped into the dining-room, one by one. Lord Adelm and General Fitzwalter were among the last. They came in together, and all were standing in expectation of the entrance of the marchioness, / when a servant presented a note to Lady Georgina.

'Oh!' said Lady Georgina, as she finished a few lines, written with a pencil on a bit of twisted paper, 'here is a note from Lady Dunore: she desires me to offer apologies to all for her absence, to take the chair, and to say that she will join us at the dessert. – She dates from Castle Macarthy,¹¹⁹ the seat of Lady Clancare.'

Some smiled at this last intelligence, and some looked sad: among the former were Lord Frederick and Mr. Daly: the latter were exclusively composed of the Crawleys – all took their places at the table. The presence of the servants prevented the turn the conversation would otherwise have taken from the circumstances of the morning; and the dinner passed off with a heaviness, which not even some occasional flashes from Baron Boulter could en-/liven. Lord Adelm, with his look of habitual haughtiness and abstraction, sat silent and reserved. Judge Aubrey talked only in a low voice with General Fitzwalter, who sat next him. The Crawleys, formal and constrained, equally by the presence of Lord Adelm, who did not notice them,[120] and of a person whom they had calumniated, and would have injured, scarcely concealed the chagrin and vexation under which they laboured. Lord Frederick murmured soft nonsense and satirical remarks into Lady Georgina's *'pleased ear,'*[121] Mr. Heneage was too fine, Lord Rosbrin and Mr. Pottinger too busy to speak, while the absence of Lady Dunore's restless vivacity was evinced by the general quietude of the table, which was solemn and dull as any fashionable dinner of extreme London bon-ton could have been.

The announce of the judges' carriages / before Lady Dunore's return, and while the fruit was still upon the table, induced the whole party to rise, and adjourn to coffee and the drawing-room, *à la francaise*;[122] and Mr. Daly, shocked at the want of all bienseance[123] in his niece towards her high judicial guests, endeavoured to apologize for her absence, by jokingly remarking that she had fallen into the thraldom of some enchantment; and that he did not doubt that the pretty Lady Clancare was some 'Irish night-tripping fairy,'[124] who had carried her off, for special reasons, known only to the high court of faéry.

'By the bye,' said Lord Frederick, 'I should like to be better acquainted with that same Lady Clancare, who chose to be made a prisoner, just *pour s'egayer!*[125] Does no one know any thing about her?'

'Not a great deal, I believe,' said Miss Crawley, eagerly and pointedly, / 'at least in this neighbourhood, my lord.'

'More than is good,' muttered old Crawley; while Lady Georgina, not perhaps quite satisfied with Lord Frederick's inquiries, replied,

'Oh, you must have seen her last season in London. Lady Dunore shewed her off for a night or two, and took her from old Lady Newbank, who picked her up, as she picks up all odd people and old china, nobody knows where.'

'What does she do?' said Lord Frederick, sipping his coffee. 'Is she one of the *'Guitararie,' the 'Tu mi Chamas'* ladies, who thrum'd us to death, when Spain was in vogue?[126] *"Et Dieu sait la raclerie que c'étoit."*[127] Or does she play the *'devil?'* or is she a waltzer, or a quadriller? or does she invent Chinese puzzles?[128] or make mottos and draw trophies,[129] or what?' /

'I think she was brought about for writing books,' said Lady Georgina, languidly, 'as well as I remember.'

'Writing books!' re-echoed Lord Frederick in a tone of alarm: 'you don't really mean that?'

'Not absolutely books, I believe, but *tales, stories*, something about Ireland, and Spain, and South America.[130] I almost forget what; but I fancy people thought they were very amusing and odd.'

'*De tout mon cœur*,'[131] said Lord Frederick, 'I have no objection. But with respect to ladies that write books, '*en tout et par tout, je quitte la partie*.'[132] It's a pity too, for she's a pretty, odd, shy, sly looking concern enough. But really Lady Dunore's bringing a live author down upon us, *à porte fermée*,[133] as we are living at present, is too bad; and the worst of all authors, a *noble* author. 'Tis misprision of treason, against / all ease, comfort, and enjoyment. Has she a husband belonging to her, do you know?'

'Oh dear, no,' said Miss Crawley, eagerly. 'She is *a peeress in her own right*[134] – he! he! he! She has nothing belonging to her; she is a very independent sort of person:' and she laughed affectedly.

'In fact,' said young Crawley, 'we know nothing of the lady whatever, except that such a person came down to this neighbourhood two years ago; took an old ruined mansion, called *Castle Macarthy*, in the village of Ballydab, *passed* herself as the grand-daughter and heir of old Denis Macarthy, commonly called the titular Earl of Clancare, who died in Dublin in jail about that period; and with no other inheritance than an old greyhound, and no other proof of the truth of her story than her own assertion, entered / at once upon a scheming course of litigiousness, broke some leases, and –'

'Took my iligant mountain of Clotnotty-joy from me,' interrupted old Crawley, despondingly.

The pathetic tone in which this was pronounced excited some mirth; and Mr. Daly observed, 'if then she breaks leases, and made good her claim to Clotnotty-joy, there can be no doubt, I suppose, that she is the personage she asserts herself to be.'

'There is *none* whatever,' said Judge Aubrey, who had sat silently listening, while Baron Boulter went to the stables, to look after a favourite mare, ridden by his crier,[135] 'there is none whatever. I have had opportunities of knowing something of this young lady; but I did not know before that she labours under *the odium* of writing books, for there is certainly no personification of authorship about her – no pretension whatever.' /

'And that's the *pity of it*,' said Lord Frederick: 'there is, on the contrary, an odd melange of the shy and the comic in her countenance, that one would think pretty if she was not an author.'

'Comic!' interrupted old Crawley, gradually resuming his wonted tone of spirits, by mere force of temperament, while his eye occasionally turned on the stranger with a look of doubtful anxiety, as if some vague, unsatisfied suspicion still lurked in his mind – 'Och! she's comical enough; – a little *too* comical, like Paddy Mooney's goose,[136] full of fun and nothing to play with.'

The coarse vulgarisms of Mr. Crawley always excited unrestrained mirth in the finer part of the society at Dunore Castle; and Lord Frederick, laughingly replied,

'I should like then to know Mr. Mooney's goose most particularly: for I vote *fun* the best thing alive; and if / your Lady Clancare has this talent in common with Mr. Mooney's goose, I believe I should almost be inclined to pardon the possession of others, even though they went as far as writing books. Pray, is this literary peeress in her own right rich?'

'Rich!' said young Crawley, 'nobody knows how she exists; and people laugh at her pretension to rank. The person last bearing the title of Clancare died abroad without issue: and in Ireland titles are so frequently claimed by pauper pretenders, that little attention is paid to such events. We had, not long since, a basket boy[137] a viscount, and a turf-cutter a baron; and have still, occasionally, all sorts of adventurers returning to claim pennyless rank in this country, in the hopes of obtaining a pension from government along with it.'q

'The statement which appeared respecting the extinction of this title was / incorrect,' said Judge Aubrey; 'for although the former Earl of Clancare died in Italy without issue, yet a representative of the title was found to exist in the person of the late Mr. Macarthy, whose lineal ancestors were included in the general attainder of the Catholic peers who supported James the Second in the war of the Revolution.[138] These attainders, however, have, with a few exceptions, been reversed. I sat upon the Clancare cause, which terminated in the success and the ruin of the old chieftain. He obtained his title, which descends in the female line, but died, as Mr. Conway Crawley states, a few days after in prison, where he had been detained for costs for two years, having ruined himself for the honour of his family. Since that event, I have had the pleasure of once meeting Lady Clancare upon an occasion that did equal honour to her heart and her head. She inte-/rested herself in the fate of a person condemned to perpetual incarceration, under the shameful Irish BYE-LAW called a RULE of BAIL.[139] She came to me last spring assizes twelvemonth, and made so clear and undeniable a statement of the man's innocence, and adduced so many proofs, that there was little difficulty and great justice in reversing the order under which he suffered.r He is now gaining an honest livelihood, and runs a chaise and pair of his own, I understand, on some of the bye-roads between Cork and Kerry. Every one knows Owny, the Rabragh,* and is glad to employ him; for he occasionally realizes all that has been said of the shrewdness and humour of an Irish postillion.' /

General Fitzwalter and Lord Adelm exchanged glances of significance.

---

* An Irish scholar translated this term for me – a 'hearty fellow:' it in fact means a rustic 'gay Lothario.'

'A little hanging would do him no harm for all that, with great deference to your lordship,' said old Crawley; 'for there was neither *pace* nor *quiet* while he was in the barony, setting up the fairs and patterns[140] after they were put down by *milithary law*, and burning *me* in *elegy*,[141] and thinking a *beau-maison*[142] of himself, as the French says; with his white shirt sleeves and green ribbons, at all the hurling matches[143] that never would have been but for him, and the likes of him, in the place; and *too* many of them there are, without having him turned on our hands again.'

'I am glad of it,' said Mr. Daly; 'and I wish with all my soul we had more rabraghs. The Irish peasantry are not only more indigent than they were forty years ago, but they have lost much of the gaiety and cheerfulness / of spirit which set sorrow at defiance. Their wakes and fairs, patterns, and Sunday evening cake,[144] are almost wholly laid aside: these, and the hurling matches, that noble, athletic, and national sport, are quite gone by: and of the troops of pipers and harpers that used to perform daily in their villages, or resort to the houses of the gentry, where welcome entertainment and ample remuneration awaited them, there scarce remain any of the order.[5] I remember as if it were but yesterday, fifty years back, heading the Leitrim boys against the Kerries, who were led on by old Florence Macarthy, the very grandfather of this Lady Clancare, in an hurling match between the counties.[145] Macarthy won the match, and more than the match, for he won the heart of the pretty Honor O'Connor, the toast of the two provinces, whom he afterwards married, and who, with / all the reigning beauties of the day, followed the fortunes of the contest.

'It warms one's old blood,' continued Mr. Daly, starting up, with animation, 'even at seventy-three, to think of the native energy, force, and spirit of the genuine Irish character; and it chills it,' he added, with a sigh, and retaking his seat, 'when one thinks upon the means which must have been employed within the last thirty years to weaken and turn it from its natural bias. To see that it is only great, vigorous, and fortunate, when transplanted from its native clime; but withering, drooping, and fading at home. – I doubt, Sir,' he added, turning to General Fitzwalter, 'that had you remained at home (for I take it for granted you are one of those gallant Irishmen, who are forced by religious proscription to seek glory in a foreign land), I doubt that *you* would have de- /veloped those great qualities in this devoted country, which have obtained for you, elsewhere, the epithet of *the liberator*, and have enabled you in a land of strangers to fight your way to high command, and higher consideration.'

General Fitzwalter had given to the details of this desultory conversation that animated and earnest attention which betokens deep interest. Thus personally addressed, he replied, with the abrupt frankness of one who rather courts than shuns observation,

'I *am* an Irishman, Sir, and have been long *an exile*, but not from religious proscription, (for my family were of the *master cast*), but by circumstances connected with the political state of the country, through that demoralization which the misrule of centuries has impressed upon all the branches of its population. Turned adrift upon the / world without compass or rudder, without a home to love, friends to cherish, or a country to defend or serve, I became by necessity a commoner of nature; and unfettered by the distinctions of clime, country, or kindred, I have early claimed alliance with all who suffer, whatever might be the region they inhabited.

'The chances which threw me on the shores of America brought me early in life in contact with Don Narino.*[146] Engaging in *his* glorious enterprise, when the possible emancipation of Spanish America was yet little more than a philosophical speculation,' it was my good fortune to share his dungeon in Santa Fe, his escape to Europe, and his mission to England. I accom-/panied him also in his venturous return to New Granada, where, backed by English protection, he again risked his life in his country's cause. Proscribed, marked out for destruction, pursued, discovered, taken, he expiated the crime of patriotism by a long series of misery and incarceration. Narino has since appeared before the world in all his original splendour; and I, in common with many of my gallant countrymen,(†)[147] have continued to follow the standard of liberty, from the moment it was openly unfurled among the mighty regions of the Cordelliras.'

'*Borne* it, not followed it,' said Lord Adelm.

'The stranger,' said Fitzwalter, 'who risks his fortune in a foreign land on general principles of right and liberty, usually becomes the favourite of the more interested partizans. I have, therefore, occasionally *led*, as well as / *served*, in almost every part of Spanish America, where the glorious impulsion of freedom has been given. In a late action, more than half the corps I commanded were massacred in a pass of the Cordelliras;[148] for the war of Spain against America is named, even by the Spaniards, a 'war of death.' As their chief, I was reserved for torture, and for an ignominious death. It was a romantic event, that one of the guards, placed over me, had in early life done me an injury that weighed heavily on his conscience. He took this moment for reconciling himself with heaven, released, and fled with me. I escaped from the Caraccas to Demerara, where, through the channel of the public papers, an event of great personal interest accidentally reached my knowledge, which the remoteness and occupation of my scene of action, together with my more immediate incarceration, prevented me from sooner learning. – This event has / brought me to my native country: and though, as an Irishman, I should, on general grounds, lament the circumstances

---

* Narino visited England in consequence of certain plans entertained by the British ministry for separating Terra Firma from Spain.

† See Note (1) at the end of the volume.

which introduced me to the castle of Dunore, yet upon principles of personal gratification I am not sufficiently disinterested to regret them.'

This brief sketch of auto-biography was thrown off with a frankness and energy of manner that gave it singular effect, and bestowed upon it all the evidence of truth, and all the graces of modesty, while it obtained for the brilliant and singular narrator an admiration variously felt and expressed.

'Go on, General Fitzwalter, go on,' cried a voice from the door: 'you have no idea how you remind me of Kosiusko, when I went to see him in London,[149] lying wounded upon a sofa. You *raconter*[150] so like him; doesn't he, Georgy love? I must say, after all, that patriotism and freedom and things always sound delightfully.' /

This speech drew every eye to the spot from whence it proceeded; and Lady Dunore appeared, leaning her back against the half-open door, concealing the figure of Lady Clancare, whose dark eyes were just seen peeping over her shoulder.

The ladies had entered thus far unobserved, for the company sat with their backs to the door, at the moment when Mr. Daly had addressed General Fitzwalter; and Lady Dunore, who loved to hear every thing about every one, and loved it the more in proportion as events were extraordinary, stood spell-bound while the general spoke, as forgetful of her 'dear delightful judges,' as if they had never existed. They were now, however, recalled to her recollection by the entrance of Baron Boulter, bearing the intelligence that all was ready for their departure; and Lady Dunore, translating the reproachful look and shake of her uncle's head, came for-/ward with a multitude of apologies for her absence, many anxious intreaties that they would prolong their stay, and as deep-formed wishes that they would return, with *all their wives and all their children*, to pass some time at Dunore, where she was going to have private plays and a chapel of ease, and Lady Clancare, and perhaps *more trials*.

The judges, however, seemed perfectly satisfied with the trials they had already witnessed; and Baron Boulter, as spokesman, received and returned her ladyship's compliments with all the ardour and earnestness with which they were made. The judges were then conducted to their carriages by Lord Adelm and Mr. Daly, and departed.

Lady Dunore now led, or rather forced forward, the really, or affectedly timid Lady Clancare, who, with the / manner that resembled the graceful awkwardness of a pretty but froward child, still held back. Lady Dunore, heated and dishevelled, was still in her morning dress, with her *sautoir de cashmir*[151] rolled round her head, and a grey cloak of Lady Clancare's on her shoulders, exhibiting a most sybil-like[152] appearance. Lady Clancare, on the contrary, had exchanged her coarse unbecoming costume of the morning, for a black Spanish dress and

mantillo,[153] which were then still in fashion, for whatever was *peninsular* in sentiment or habiliment had not yet fallen 'into the sear'[154] of popularity.[u]

Lady Dunore, whose eyes were fixed upon her new protegée with delight
and admiration, now turned them on the company, to observe the effect she had
produced, and at last fixed their eager glances upon General Fitzwalter, with an
expression, which, if not attributable / to her wonted extravagance, was wholly
untranslatable. There was in this intense stare a hope, a fear, something expected,
something dreaded. General Fitzwalter, whose eyes, like those of the rest of the
company, were turned on Lady Clancare, in mere curiosity, at last met those of
Lady Dunore. For a moment they returned her fixed look, till reddening under
the intensity of her gaze, he turned away, and picking up a screen, which lay at
Lady Georgina's feet, he seized on this little act as an opportunity for addressing her. Lady Dunore whispered something to Lady Clancare, who smiled, and
threw down her eyes; and Mr. Daly, entering with Lord Adelm, was commencing his attack on his inconsequent niece, with 'how could you, my dear Emily,
leave your own house and the judges?' when Lady Dunore, impatiently putting
her / hand on his mouth, interrupted him with – 'there, there, I know all you
would say, all any one *can* say, on the subject; but you don't really want me to
bring the etiquette and tiresome forms of the world into the wilds of Ireland.
Besides, if I have done wrong, I bring my excuse in my hand;' and she drew forward Lady Clancare.

'You could not bring a fairer,' said Mr. Daly, with an air of gallantry; 'and had
I been so tempted, I too should have so sinned I fear, though the whole bench
of bishops, and all the judges of the land, had been making claims on my attention. I had the honour,' he added, addressing Lady Clancare, 'of knowing your
ladyship's venerable grandfather, some short half century back. He was not very
venerable then: – he was, indeed, as he is now present in my recollection, of a
race of men, in stature, look, and cha/racter, now almost passed away in this
country – we shall not look upon their like again.'

Lady Clancare bowed to this recollection of her grandfather; and though she
spoke not, there was something passed across her countenance, which induced
Mr. Daly to take her hand, under pretence of leading her to her chair; and he felt
(or he fancied he felt) a gentle pressure of his, which he returned with an ardour
that did not *quite* belong to seventy-three.

'Oh! par exemple, for fine men,' said Lady Dunore, throwing herself into an
arm chair, 'I think they are really quite extinct with us altogether. You know,
Georgy love, we were observing at the opera, the last night we were there, that
we thought all the presumptive heirs of the great names were pigmies. There is
nothing coming forward now at all like the Dukes of A. and H –, / the Marquis
of A –, and the old Earl of E –, in his coronation robes, and that sort of thing.
The fact is, though no one can be *more devoted* to the present ministry than I

am, I must say they are by no means distinguished looking men. None of that school at all "*shew blood*," as the old Duchess of B. used to say. However, men may govern the state very well without being beauties, or poets either; for, as Lady C. says, if the opposition have all the *wit* on their side, the *joke's all on our's*.[v] But with respect to those magnificent creatures that one used to meet in London, I think all that sort of thing now is confined to the patriots, that is the Poles, and South American chiefs. Don't you think so, Georgy, love?' and she turned her eyes on General Fitzwalter.

To get rid of the awkwardness of this pointed compliment, which evidently distressed its object, Mr. Daly addressed / General Fitzwalter, with some observations on a country where he had played so distinguished a part. 'South America,' he observed, 'is well known to us in the Spanish histories of its early discoverers, when Spain invaded it under the simoniacal pretext of *religion*; letting loose, at the same time, *blood-hounds* and *apostles*, while they opened its mineral veins, and exterminated its population. But[w] it is only *now* that it has become an object of interest through the exertions of those states, which are seeking to shake off the yoke, that has almost deprived these great regions of a place in the history of nations; the impulse, however, must have been given long since.'

General Fitzwalter replied. 'The oppression and cruelty of the colonial legislatures, which have so long bathed the richest country of the world with the tears and the blood of her children, / had excited, even as far back as the middle of last century, events, which seemed remotely to prepare a new destiny for a population of fourteen millions of its inhabitants. To a torpid acquiescence of three centuries succeeded a gathering tempest, a kindling resistance. The spirit of freedom, once vivified, rapidly brightened into flame, shining from north to south; and the period soon arrived, when every American heart beat in union under its influence. The oppressor and the oppressed stood before the world's eye, opposed and armed. The Americans would have made it a war of justice and of mercy; for they had suffered much, and have learned to pity; but the ferocity of Spain has made it a war of extermination.[*155x] Internal divisions may / render this conflict long and uncertain; but the cause belongs to humanity: it springs from the laws of nature, and is inevitable; it is borne along by the spirit of the age and the progress of illumination, and it must finally succeed.'

'To be sure it must,' said Lady Dunore. 'Don't you think so, Georgy, love?'

'For my part, I don't know,' said Conway Crawley, with his brogue and his effrontery, 'what *parsons* mean about *giving liberty and independence* to an unformed race like the South Americans; a race defined by one of the Spanish FISCALS as creatures destined by nature to work like moles in the mines.[156] We have all read the solemn declaration of the CONSULADO, or board of trade, in

---

*   The Spaniards term their contest with America, *la Guerra a muerta* - the war of death.

Mexico, that the Indians are a race of monkies, filled with vice and ignorance;[157] and they have extended / their remarks, I believe pretty justly, to the creoles,[158] or degenerate descendants of the first Spanish settlers.'

'*That*, indeed, changes the thing altogether,' said Lady Dunore, 'not but a race of monkies must be very amusing and very mischievous. Don't you think so Georgy, dear?'

'It was,' said Mr. Daly, 'these *same sagacious fiscals*, who ordered the olive and the vine to be rooted out of Chili, to compel a commerce with the peninsula.[159] And it was in the bosoms of these American automata,' he continued, 'of these MONKIES, that the British government, in 1797, resolved to cherish the spark of independence,[160] already awakened there. We all know Mr. Pitt's plans of giving freedom, and a political existence, to Terra Firma; and that the promises of assistance against Spain, *then* made, were nearly realized, when the British cabinet paid / the expedition of the gallant Miranda to Venezuela.'[161]

'Poor, dear Pitt!' said Lady Dunore, 'he was a clever creature. Mr. Heneage, move the lamp a little from under his engraving. He happened to be my most particular friend.'

'Temporary measures of expediency have nothing to do with general views,' replied young Crawley, to Mr. Daly's observation. 'What is wisdom *to-day*, in the conduct of a government, may be madness *to-morrow*.'[y]

'What is, generally speaking, the condition of the lower orders?' asked Mr. Daly, turning cooly away from young Crawley, and evidently anxious to draw out the general.

'Borne down,' he answered, 'by long slavery and injustice, the native Indian submits to his vexatious existence, with an affected patience, a seeming apathy, which veils the cunning / and ferocity of the enslaved and degraded in all countries; for as, whatever be the colour of man struggling against oppression, the language of energetic minds is still the same; so every where[z] the slave exhibits the same vice, jargon, and policy: and it *does* happen, that when a native Indian rises by low arts to petty power, and becomes the alcade, the magistrate, or loyal man of the colonial government,[162] supported by that government, and backed by the SUDELGADO[163] or priesthood (for in South America, as elsewhere, the priesthood are usually on the side of oppression),[a] he makes common cause with his superiors, and adds by misrepresentations to the sufferings of his country.'

'Och! the thief of the world!' said old Crawley, while his son changed colour, for he felt the full force of the remark. 'If we had him in Ireland, / we'd soon take away his commission of the *pace* from him.'

A burst of good-humoured laughter in Lady Clancare excited a pretty universal sympathy; and young Crawley, trembling with acrimonious emotion, continued.

'The South Americans are naturally, by temperament, a bloody and inhuman people. Their very religion is a religion of blood.'

'Oh, horrible!' said Lady Dunore: 'if that's the case, I wonder how Pitt could propose their liberation.'

'The Spaniards,' said Crawley, 'found them sacrificing human beings in their temples.'[b]

'Yes,' interrupted Miss Crawley, 'so we read in the abridgment of the life of Columbus.'[164]

'And there exists a sect,' said young Crawley, ransacking his school-boy erudition, 'who preach purification by / blood. Such are the people who are to overturn a Christian dynasty, a legitimate sovereignty, and talk of rights, humanity, and that sort of *trash*, that one is sick of.'

'They are all naturally Atheists, and Deists, and Idolaters,' said Miss Crawley, triumphantly.

'Georgy, love, did you ever hear any thing so shocking?' said Lady Dunore. 'How can any one wish well to such a people. Mr. Heneage, bring me my *eau de luce*[165] *bottle*.'

'Such facts,' said Gen. Fitzwalter, 'are a proof of the feebleness of the human mind. In South America, as in all parts of the world, atonement by human sacrifice is the dogma of nations in their infancy; because the first religion of man is the religion of fear. He suffers more than he enjoys, and he propitiates accordingly. The early Britains stained their sacred groves / with human blood;[166] the benevolent Hindoos shed it on the altar of their dark goddess *Cali*; the enlightened Egyptians rejected not such sanguinary rites; and the polished Romans performed them. Jeptha, like Agamemnon, vowed away the life of his only daughter;[167] and Spain still has her *auto da fé*,[168] and heaps her hecatombs on burning piles for the love of God, and the recreation of the court.'

'Yes,' said Lady Dunore, 'and a charming opera it is. That is not the *auto da fé*, but *Ipiginie in Aulide*.'[169][c]

'But I believe,' continued the general, 'we must not look too deeply into the history of man; whatever region he inhabits, it is a fearful and an humiliating history; and when backed by fanaticism, it is more than ordinarily blood-stained and terrific. But let us take him when we can, in his best aspect, free and enlightened; so blessed / by singularity of temperament, so formed of happy elements, that, like the mild Peruvian, he performs the rites of the heart, whose incense smells to heaven, and heaping on his sunny altars the fruits and odours of his luxuriant soil.'

'How beautiful!' said Lady Dunore: 'there is nothing like those Peruvians, par exemple, and their odours.'

'Peruvians or Mexicans, they are all a detestable race,' said young Crawley, 'unworthy of a better government; and any one who knows their history, and has read their absurd mythology, their deluge of Coxcox,[170] and their – –'

'Is he any thing to the Coxes of county Kilkenny?' interrupted old Crawley, taking snuff, and always anxious to say something to shew that he was not ignorant of any thing. This question, asked in great simplicity, for he had / only caught the word 'Cox,' produced a very general laugh, in which Miss Crawley and her nephew alone did not share.[d]

Lady Dunore, now a very violent South American patriot, exclaimed – 'Good heavens! General Fitzwalter, I hope you are come to recruit here for your *grand cause*.[171] I dare say there are a quantity of young men among our tenantry would go for nothing at all; don't you think they would, Mr. Crawley?'

'Upon my credit, my lady, I can't take upon me to say,' returned Mr. Crawley, quite unconscious of the laugh he had excited; and now fearful that as he had already bailed his own prisoner, he would next be compelled to recruit in the cause of rebellion; 'but I don't think they have any *turn* to fighting among the negers;[172] and then, I suppose, it is a *good step* off, Madam.' /

'Nothing to signify, my dear Mr. Crawley,' interrupted Lord Frederick; 'and provided you will take the command of the Ballydab and Dunore heroes, I don't care if I accompany you as a volunteer whenever you please to sally forth; for I look upon it, Mr. Crawley, that you are one of those ancient *preux, pour fendre géant, derompre harnois, et porter en croupe belles démoiselles sans leur parler de rien*.'[173]

'Many thanks for your compliment, my lord,' said old Crawley, believing Lord Frederick must be civil, as he spoke in French. 'I never was much given to travel; only oncet was going to LISBURN for my health, after my sufferings on duty with the yeomanry in the rebellion of ninety-eight.'

'To Lisburn, my dear Mr. Crawley,' said Lord Frederick, 'is Lisburn the MONTPELLIER of Ireland?'

'Not at all, my lord; I mane Lis-/burn, the capital of Spain,'[174] replied Mr. Crawley.

'If I were twenty years younger, Mr. Crawley,' said Mr. Daly, covering out the general titter by addressing its object, 'I should myself be tempted to go forth in this glorious cause. South America is the great stage upon which the world's eye is now fixed.'

'A stage,' said Lord Rosbrin, shaking his head, 'where every man *must* play his part, and *mine* a sad one.'[175]

'See that now,' said Mr. Crawley, 'and never heard tell of it before, only the Yankey-doodles and New-York, and the likes.'

'Man,' said Lord Adelm, starting up from a reverie, in which he had indulged while leaning over the back of Lady Georgina's chair, 'man, in whatever region he is found, may best be typified by a squirrel in a cage.'

'A squirrel in a cage! the Lord save / us!' exclaimed Mr. Crawley, in astonishment.

'His little sphere is so planned,' continued Lord Adelm, 'that he can be nothing but what he is, do nothing but what he does. He goes round his circle, and repeats his rotations, with no difference in the performance, but a little acceleration or a little retardment. These South Americans, therefore, but repeat an old story: they are savage and unprotected, they are conquered; – they are slaves, and degraded, they endure; – they are pressed to the quick, they turn and resist; – they struggle and succeed, become great, prosperous, illumined; conquer and oppress in their turn, moulder away, and leave to posterity the unheeded moral that in every clime, state, or being, man is neither to be praised nor blamed, admired nor abhorred. He is what he is; otherwise he cannot be; for, after / all, he is but an engine, a mere engine.'

'A steam-engine,' said old Crawley, shaking his head, and anxious to agree with Lord Fitzadelm, of whom he stood in awe; 'sorrow a thing else.'

'Faith, pretty much,' said Lord Adelm, with a gravity none preserved but himself, 'except that a steam-engine has this superiority over him, that it is neither susceptible of caprice nor distraction. It turns also upon a beneficial principle, while the mainspring of the machinery of man inevitably turns on evil.'

'Evil to him as evil thinks,' reechoed old Crawley; '*honey swa key molly panse*, as the French says.'[176]

'That's not ill put, Mr. Crawley,' said Mr. Daly, while every body else laughed; 'but, my dear Fitzadelm, you, at least, admit the principle of good to exist conjointly with that of evil. You will not establish a doctrine / less consoling than that of the dark demoniac, Indian mythology.'

'Oh, I deny good as a principle altogether,' said Lord Adelm: 'good is merely relative, evil is positive. Evil is necessary to man as the air he breathes; an inherent part of his existence: deprive him of his principle of evil, and he becomes a *vegetable*.'

'A vegetable!' repeated old Crawley; 'see that now.'

'Evil is the source, food, end, and object of the passions; or, to give them their proper names, the *appetites*. It is the grand agitator of life, its food and occupation: without evil there would be neither genius, virtue, nor valour; for what is virtue but an effort against vice? What genius? – the nisus[177] to overcome suffering. What valour? – the necessity of massacre and bloodshed.'

'Christ save us!' exclaimed Mr. Crawley.

'What is ambition? – the selfish wish / of rule. What friendship? – helplessness. What love? – a want. Whence arise the liberal professions but from the innate tendency of man to evil? Law, for instance,' continued Lord Adelm, while old Crawley drew back, 'from the villainy of the species. Physic from its infirmities; the arts from vanity; the sciences from physical pressure.ᵉ The whole business of life, then, is but one sustained effort against evil: and without evil, in a supereminent degree, those talents and properties on which we most pride our-selves, – skill, wisdom, virtue, and courage, could not be developed, because they would not be called for. Taking then a just view of things, there is little to move either our wrath or admiration. He who feels little and digests well; he who has a *bad heart* and a *good stomach*, is, after all, the true sage and the happy man.' /

Here Lord Adelm was interrupted by a servant, who gave him a note. It filled the room with perfume, and covered Lord Adelm's face with blushes, warm as the hues of the paper he perused. Every one smiled as he hurried out of the room; and though the established laws of bon-ton prevented the slightest notice being taken of this incident, Mr. Daly could not help saying, with an arch smile – 'So much for the philosophy of indifference.'

'Philosophy!' repeated Lord Rosbrin, laying down his play-book:
'There never yet was found philosophy
Could bear the tooth-ach patiently.'¹⁷⁸

The quick eye of Lady Dunore had rested on the face, and observed the emo-tions of her son. Her feelings of maternity had been so little influenced by his return, that the first pleasure over, which surprise always occasioned / in her, she had not been induced to retire with him for a single half hour since his arrival, but had been quite satisfied with the few words he had said to her in the hall, stating the motive of his journey to have been his wish to preside at his own election. Since then, other objects had arisen to ingross her attention, and oblit-erate the sensation his return had roused into transient existence.ᶠ His sudden emotion and exit now seized on her imagination. She was not yet exhausted by the events of the day; and after struggling for a moment in contest with her own feelings, she arose and followed him.

The servant who had delivered the note met her in the hall; but to her inquir-ies whence it had come, the answer was, it had been left in the porter's lodge, and had come from the post-house.

Meantime, Mr. Daly had ordered / the brag table; and while the party stood waiting for Lady Dunore to join them, Lord Rosbrin proposed reciting 'Col-lin's Ode on the Passions,'¹⁷⁹ which was by common consent over-ruled in favour of his imitations of the favourite actors of the day. With Miss Crawley's scarf bound round his head, a cashmir of Lady Georgina's wound round his body, a row of candles placed at his feet, and the company circled round him, he gave a very close imitation of some of the best modern tragedians, in the parts of Othello, Richard III. Macbeth, and Hamlet, successively. This imitation was, indeed, so faithful, that it not only rendered look for look, and tone for tone, but every inflection, gesture, and grimace, was preserved precisely the same as in the original he copied. It was curious, however, to observe, that the representation, which in public had ex-/cited admiration, in private elicited only ridicule: that, which on the stage was called *fine acting*, was in the drawing-room rank buffoonery; and tones, gurgling in the throat, as in a cauldron, heaved from the lungs as from a sepulchre, or growled forth from lips distortingly compressed, with a chin elevated to the nose, an eye sunk under a projected brow, or starting from its socket, and teeth ground, till they are almost broken, with starts, pauses, groans, strides, drags, drawls, and contortions, so often termed '*true to nature,*' and '*original conceptions,*' when viewed on a great theatre, and with a mind ruled by conventional judgment, now, when exhibited in the midst of real life, appeared ludicrous, broad, and coarse, as scene-painting compared to the cabinet pictures of a master.

The audience could, however, have 'better spared a better man;'[180] for if / the tragic throes of Lord Rosbrin did not make them weep, it did better, it made them laugh. No delicate feeling on their part inhibited the indulgence of this enjoyment; and no sensibility of his own ridiculous position on the part of Lord Rosbrin rendered him alive to the ridicule he excited. To have pitied such folly, would have been to have surpassed it.[g]

This exhibition, so well adapted to the idle and the gay, as combining (what the great love) amusement and ridicule, had so entirely occupied the minds of the audience, that nearly two hours had been passed in recitations, accompanied by bravoes and encores, (for the noble Roscius was always encored, in proportion as he was ludicrous) without Lady Dunore's protracted absence becoming a subject of notice to her pre-occupied guests. When at last she returned to the drawing-room, her / countenance was disturbed; there was a cloud on her brow, and her cheek was stained with tears.

The lights on the floor, however, the turbaned head, and draped figure of Lord Rosbrin, operated as talismans on her oppressed spirits. He was commanded to go over the course again, and was again rewarded with vociferated bravoes and hysterical laughs. Plans and schemes for building a new theatre became an animating subject of discussion, which occupied the general attention,[h] until Lady Georgina observed that both Lady Clancare and General Fitzwalter had disappeared during the representation.

'Gone! and together?' asked Lady Dunore, starting up in emotion: 'when, where, how?'

'Together!' repeated Lord Frederick. '*On crie à la scandale!*'[181] Lady Dunore repeated her question, but no / one could give any answer. While Lord Rosbrin had strutted his hour,[182] none had eyes or ears but for him; and the marchioness, in an agitation no one could understand, left the room.

'There she goes, like a sky-rocket,' said Lord Frederick. 'I should like to know her impulsion.'

'If her ladyship means to watch the extraordinary disappearances of Lady Clancare,' said Miss Crawley, 'she will have something to do. Her stealing away with General Fitzwalter was, however, a strong measure, if this was their first acquaintance.'

'You don't mean that, my dear Miss Crawley,' said Lord Frederick with a significant look. 'If this little shy thing has had an *illustre foiblesse*,[183] we must forgive her her authorship.'

'I don't wish to say any thing inju-/rious of the pseudo Lady Clancare,' said Miss Crawley, 'but it will certainly surprise *the people of consequence* in this neighbourhood, when they hear of her being received at Dunore. She has now just returned *from a mysterious disappearance* of some months.'

'Oh! you are raising her cent. per cent.[184] my dear Miss Crawley,' exclaimed Lord Frederick; 'if you prove this Irish Sappho is a Sappho,[185] head, heart, and all. You redeem her to all intents and purposes.'

Lady Dunore now re-entered, her countenance brightening into smiles. 'It is very extraordinary,' she said, 'that none of you could tell me Lady Clancare went away twenty minutes before General Fitzwalter, which I find is the case.'

'Are we your lady's keeper?'[186] asked Lord Frederick. 'But, marchioness of my soul, what is your extraordinary / anxiety about these new *god-sends*,[187] who seem to have arrived here for the sole purpose of keeping up the ebb and flow of your solicitude? Your secret, lady. Pray "let me not burst in ignorance."'[188]

'Secret!' said Lady Dunore, laughing: 'why should you think I have any?'

'Well then, Lady Clancare's secret; for we know, as Rosbrin would say, only he is now too tired to say anything, you "*could a tale unfold*;"[189] and Miss Crawley has just been giving us some hints of *l'aimable sceleratesse*[190] of your Irish peeress. In short, it seems that the inhabitants of our good city of Dunore do not visit her. It seems she has come no one knows whence, goes no one knows where, and, *pour trancher le mot*,[191] is just a *little equivocal*.'ⁱ

'And does Miss Crawley presume,' said Lady Dunore, turning full upon the shrinking Miss Crawley, (the only / one, save Lord Frederick, at that moment not engaged at the card table,)ʲ 'does Miss Crawley *presume* to throw a breath of slander upon a friend of mine, to talk over in village *commerage*[192] a person of Lady Clancare's rank and celebrity?'

'I assure your ladyship,' said Miss Crawley, pale with mortification and fear, 'I did not say – did not mean..'

'No, no,' said Lord Frederick, half amused with the consternation he came to relieve, 'they are rather *my* surmises than Miss Crawley's assertions, who merely hinted that

"Lips though lovely must still be fed,"[193]

and that if this lady were not fed by the gods with nectar and ambrosia, her mode of existence was a mystery, if not a miracle, unknown to any one.'

'Yes,' said Lady Dunore triumphantly, 'there is a miracle and a / mystery in Lady Clancare's retreat from the world; but its secret is known to one person; and I am that person: for the rest you may trust me. I would not present in my own exclusive circle one who was not in all points *comme il faut*.[194] One thing, however, I must generally observe to you all, good people, – Lady Clancare must not be obtruded on: she receives no visits from either sex; admits no strangers; and I alone have obtained permission occasionally to join her in her solitude. Meantime I stand pledged that no constraint shall be put upon her movements. She is to have free ingress and egress, *à plaisir*,[195] at Dunore Castle, and is to creep in and creep out like a pet kitten, as she expresses it, '*without let or molestation*.'

'But dear love,' said Lady Georgina, as she dealt round the cards with sparkling fingers, 'your *kitten* will at least *pur* a little, I hope, for us. Do / you know she was not the least in the world entertaining to-night.'

'By the bye,' said Lord Frederick, 'now I think of it, she sat staring her pretty round eyes out, like one of the little *sourds et muets* of the Abbè Sicard,[196] looking unutterable things, but speaking not a word. I thought the female author species always talked as it wrote, for the amusement of the public, and got up things cut and dry for the occasion; quotations, sentiments, *impromptus à loisir*,[197] and all that.'k

'Well!' said Lady Dunore, 'don't judge her hastily; leave her to time and to me.' – She looked oracularly mysterious as she spoke, cut in as Mr. Heneage cut out; and having convinced the company she had some profound secret in her keeping, and won fifty pounds from old Crawley, she retired to bed at three in the morning, in great elevation of spirits, repeating to Lady / Georgina, as they parted on the corridor, –

'Well, after all, sweetest, there is nothing like these wild, barbarous, rebellious countries, *par exemple*: and gay as we are now, and amused as we are with all these judges and *Padreen Gar's* boys, and Peruvian chiefs, and things, there is no saying but we may be all *murdered* before morning.'

With this consolatory reflection, she kissed the forehead of her sleepy, smiling friend, and retired. /

CHAPTER IV.

– For I will tell you now
What never yet was heard in tale or song,
From old or modern bard, in hall or bower.

Milton.[198]

GENERAL FITZWALTER had alone observed the retreat of Lady Clancare. Amused as she had appeared to be in common with the rest of the company, by the buffoonery of the noble amateur, the perpetual folly might at length have wearied her; for she had taken the advantage of an open door to escape, half an hour before the general had himself retired.[1] There was something in the popularity which she enjoyed under the rude title of the BHAN TIERNA, some- /thing in her story, as the representative of an illustrious but ruined family, something in her sudden and unexpected appearance in the hall of Dunore, which, taken together, and contrasted with her youth, her very feminine person, unprotected state, and extreme reserve, powerfully interested him. He had once or twice also, as he stood opposite to her, met her eyes, and they were not eyes to be met with impunity; nor were their glances less impressive, from being suddenly and bashfully withdrawn. Still he fancied that he could trace something sinister in her looks; and the singular mobility and intelligence of her peculiar countenance (a countenance whose character was not unknown to him)[m] were strangely opposed to her timid and unbroken taciturnity, leaving it doubtful which was her natural habit, the reserve of a recluse, for the acuteness of a practised observer. /

That she had '*written books*,' as Lady Georgina termed it, was a proof she possessed either talents or pretension; yet there was nothing in her address or manners that bespoke the consciousness of the former, or the importance of the latter.[n] While, therefore, General Fitzwalter pursued his way along the strand, he continued to puzzle himself in the research after the cause of her attraction (her attraction for him at least, for after the first surprise of her appearance, she seemed to have excited little interest in others), he at last summed it all up in her eyes. He had somewhere met such eyes before; and which ever way he now turned his own, whether upon the stars, which seemed to start from the heavens like wandering fires, or downward upon their fairy reflection in the smooth ebb tide, still the full, dark, and fixed eyes of Lady Clancare were before him. /

He had not proceeded many paces from the rampart wall of the castle when Lord Adelm overtook him.

'You are an hour before your appointment,' said Fitzwalter, 'for the castle clock now tells eleven.'

'How could you remain so long among those tiresome people?' returned Lord Adelm, petulantly.

'I came away as soon as decency would permit. I waited for the return of Lady Dunore.'

'She had not then returned when you came away?'

'Not to the drawing-room; but I heard her voice in the gallery as I passed through the hall.'

'You can have no idea how she has crossed my way to-night,' said Lord Adelm, in a tone of vexation: 'you saw me receive a note?'

'Yes, most appropriately. It produced in your countenance a refutation / of your doctrine; and eloquently proved that mind is not wholly dependant on a *good stomach and a bad heart* for its happiness.'

'Yes, I felt I was shewing up most confoundedly. But the *circulation* is still stronger than that moral mover we call reason, which, after all, means nothing, but more or less of temperament. You guess who the note was from.'

'Certainly, by its *hue* and *odour*.'

'Well, she who has led me here, has followed me here, or rather has preceded me.'

'And where is she?'

'Perhaps bedded in that rock, or perched on the wing of the sea breeze that whistles by us, for aught I know. Now imagine, if you can, a contre tems[199] like this. The prettiest little French billet,[200] inclosed in an envelope, which bore the post-mark of Dunore, summoned me to a rock under the castle / terrace, called the *Hag's Tooth*. I was to come alone; not before ten, nor after eleven: this was the only stipulation: I was to be astonished – this was the only promise. The rest was supposed; but hope was not idle.° I found the spot with some difficulty. All was solitary and silent; not even the rippling of the wave, nor the sigh of the gale. I had been at my appointed post but a few minutes when I perceived a female form, gliding like a sea nymph over the glittering sand, light as air, and rapid as light. The dupe of my heart, or my hopes, or what you will, I stood spell-bound. Had I beheld a vision descending from the clouds, it could not have held more influence over my imagination. I had scarcely power to breath, to stretch forth a hand, to clasp that which was presented to me. – I did however clasp it.' /

'Then it was a mortal hand, true flesh and blood, after all?' interrupted the general, eagerly.

'It was,' said Lord Adelm, stamping his feet, and grinding out his words: 'it was my mother's hand.'

'Then the promise of *astonishment* was at least fulfilled.'

'Lady Dunore, it seems, had herself received a note,' continued Lord Adelm, 'advising her to watch my steps this evening. I half suspect it was some trick of those delectable Crawleys. She followed me out: I was annoyed, bored beyond all expression, and not over guarded in concealing my feelings. A scene, often repeated, ensued between us. I condemned and contemned her interference upon all occasions: she reproached, retorted, and wept; then grew hysterical as usual; and in this way I conducted her home. Trembling with apprehension and solicitude, I / again issued forth, when that *petite évaporée*,[201] my mother's new Irish caprice, appeared in the portico, getting into her mule cart. I had now to make a second retreat, and saw her take the strand road with such feelings of patience and pleasure as you may suppose; at last, literally speaking, the *coast* was *clear*, and I bent my steps towards the rock of my disappointed hopes; for there I found only this black handkerchief or scarf, a token of my ill luck, and an indication, of course, that my sylph had been true to her appointment, and had kept it, while I was conducting my mother home. Now what think you of all this?'

'Think! why, that your sylph is some devoted woman; so ingenious, so zealous in her devotion, that did there exist for me such a being –'

'I have examined the handkerchief,' interrupted Lord Adelm, 'and I should / think there was "magic in the web of it;"[202] but that it bears a sign to conjure away all magic: a red cross is embroidered on its centre; it is too of Spanish manufacture, of true Barcelona workmanship.'

"'Tis altogether most strange, most romantic, and most flattering,' returned the general, thoughtfully, as they proceeded arm in arm, and in silence, each apparently wrapped in profound musings, till they arrived beneath a sweep of irregular and massive cliffs, above which, dark and indistinct, rose the ruins and cemetery of MONASTER-NY-ORIEL.

The pathway to the coast, cut centuries back by the monks, and the round topped perforated cross, which they had raised at its entrance, to the honour of St. Peter, the fisherman, and as a land-mark to distressed mariners, still remained. The friends ascended this rude rocky avenue by a flight of / steep unevenly hewn steps, piled on either side with a stratum of human bones – a gloomy order of architecture not unusual in the ancient burying grounds of Ireland, and terminating in a circular and spacious mandrae (2).[203] The night was still and dark; a few stars only glimmered in the cloudy firmament.

The peculiar genius of Lord Adelm was well adapted to scenes and seasons characterized by images gloomy and fantastic as his own morbid fancy. He paused frequently in his wearisome ascent, while his more active companion strode on rapidly before him: and when he had reached the summit of the rocks which formed the site of the monastic ruins, he halted, and looked around him. The scene was wild, desolate, and silent – rocks, ruins, remote mountains, bounding the land view; while the steep Atlantic spread wide and dark, and lost itself in the distant clouds. He / measured the tower, under which they now stood, with his eye: a light was streaming from its loophole casement, and it beetled over the cliff like some lone watch-tower of the deep.[p]

'These are scenes,' said Lord Adelm, 'that transport us beyond the present, that bear us into regions of thought and feeling, beyond all mean ambition and human cares.'

'They are the better adapted to prelude the tale I would unfold to you,' said Fitzwalter, impressively.

'This tower,' continued Lord Adelm, 'resembles the cell of the "*Subtil Archimago*" of Spenser, whose scenes in the Fairy Queen are, indeed, all Irish.'[204]

'Far from resort of people that did pass,
In travel to and fro. A little wyde
There was an holy chapel edifyed,
Wherein the hermit daily wont to say
His holy things each morn and even-tide.
* * * * * * * * * * * /

He told of saints and popes, and evermore
He strowed an Ave-Mary after and before.'[205]

'The tale to which you are about to listen,' said the general, as he raised the latch of a low arched door, 'is nothing less than of saints and popes: 'tis of men and sinners.'[q]

'Your story!' said Lord Adelm, in a tone of recollection, for over the mirror of his imagination reflections passed rapidly; and it was only now he recollected the purpose for which he accompanied his new friend to the Friary of St. John's at an hour so unseasonable. Oh! aye, I had half forgotten your story.'

They now ascended the spiral stairs of the tower. O'Leary, from above, held forward a lamp, whose light produced uncertain shadows upon the dark damp wall; but when he perceived by its flickering ray that his guest was accompanied by Lord Adelm Fitzadelm, / he started back, then came again forward, and drew up against the doorcase to let them pass, changing the lamp to his left hand, that he might make the sign of the cross on his breast with his right, as a sort of exorcism of an event, which, to his confused and wandering mind, appeared little less than miraculous. He then followed them into the room, where a fire had already been kindled in the open hearth; the candles, also, stood ready lighted; yet, under various pretences, he lingered in the apartment, occasionally coming forward with the snuffers, and snatching hasty and anxious looks at the two gentlemen, who were already seated at a little deal table, both leaning on their elbows, both earnestly conversing in Spanish. O'Leary, as he gazed on them with an half-murmured exclamation, crossed himself devoutly, and made new causes for delay; till the general, / telling him that he had no further occasion for his services that night, peremptorily desired him to retire to rest: he then slowly retreated; and was twice called back to shut the door before he obeyed.
* * * * * * * *

The morning after this midnight interview had taken place, O'Leary, at an hour later than usual, entered the apartment of the general to attend at his toilette and breakfast. He found him, however, asleep in Friar O'Sulivan's great chair, where he had left him seated the night before, and his bed had not been occupied. His repose was so profound, that O'Leary had rekindled his turf fire, and got ready his dressing things, without awakening him. But the heavy pacing about the room, and murmured ejaculations of the pedagogue, at last aroused him from his slumber.

'I'm afeared I put the sleep astray / upon your honor,' said O'Leary, with an anxious look.

'It is time, I believe, to rise, O'Leary, is it not?' said the general, starting up, and shaking off his *'obedient slumbers,'*[206] as one accustomed to snatch repose, when, where, and as he could, and to dismiss it at will.

'*To rise!*' said O'Leary, shaking his head, 'and your honor not in bed, gineral, the whole live long night, Sir!'

'How do you know that, O'Leary?'

'How do I know it? Why, the day was breaking on th' Atlantic, plaze your honor, when I saw the young lord going down the rock there, and you looking after him from the top of the friar's leap, as it is called; and wonders but he'd be afeared to be wandering his lone that away in the country. It's little his father, Baron Gerald, would dare it, great a *Calebalaro*[207] as he was; for he / was a *sould* man, Sir, from the time he planned the ruination of young De Montenay; and its only for him your honor would be alive and hearty this day: not all as one – that's his own nephew I mane; and when I saw you both sated cheek by jowl last night, and my Pacata Hibernia[208] between yez, it minded me the last time I seen the two brothers at Court Fitzadelm together: it was a little time after the Honorable Gerald had married the great English lady, th' ould marchioness that is now, and came over his lone to Ireland. They were seated together in th' oak parlour, that's the two *Tiernas*, with a tankard of claret, and a bottle of brandy to qualify it, between them. I was only called in about a date, being then at the court, and comed to see the child; for the rumour was, he was going to be carried to Dublin by his uncle, and his mother only buried the / week before: and the *Tierna Dhu* handed me a glass of wine, saying, pleasantly, *he believed I'd rather the whiskey.*'

'I'm afraid,' said the general smiling, and who was preparing for a sea bath before he went to breakfast, 'I'm afraid, O'Leary, *that* preference still clings to you; and I was sorry when I looked in on you this morning to find you sleeping in your clothes, with a bottle of spirits half consumed by your side. This is not the way to recover your health, and compose your mind, O'Leary.'

'And did your honor look in on me?' said O'Leary, in a softened tone. 'And never felt*you, gineral, dear; for when I went to my truckle,[209] I fell asleep like a rock, Sir. But as to the whiskey, Sir, you need not fear it, and / only laves it by way of two-milk-whey at my bed-side; for whiskey, plaze your honor, is so qualified in the making, that it dryeth more, and inflameth less, than other hot confections. It sloweth age (saith the philosopher), and helpeth youth; it reviveth the heart, lighteneth the mind, quickeneth the spirits, keepeth the veins from crumpling, the bones from aching, and the marrow from soaking.[210] Musha! it's the elixir of life, and only for it, I'd be dead long ago. For when the world deserted me, *that* staid by me, and when I lost joy elsewhere, sure its there I found it, Sir.'

O'Leary had pronounced this eulogium on his favourite beverage, as he followed the general down the rocks to a little creek, or basin, which was always sufficiently full to afford a bath; and then having left him his dressing gown, at his desire he went back to / prepare his coffee. When the general returned, and had seated himself at the breakfast-table, with a book in his hand, as he was wont, O'Leary, who attended him, took his place in a window-seat, at a respectful distance. He drew forth an old tattered volume, which for a few minutes fixed his attention; but, habitually wandering and unsettled, his rapid eyes glanced frequently from his studies to the general, who, like himself, seemed incapable of giving a continued attention to the book which he held open in his hand. O'Leary, perceiving that his guest had laid down the volume, and leaned thoughtfully on his elbow, closed also his own; and advancing to pour out some coffee, observed –

'I think, your honor, the Memoir I am perusing of the Fitzmaurices of Lixnow, a great branch of the Geraldines, and Lords of Muskerry, would plaze you intirely. Och! its a great legend! / It's done into rhyme, Sir, Irish rhyme, by a priest, who was confessor to the family. The argument runneth thus. The young Lord Thomas Fitzmaurice, of Lixnow, was in foreign parts fighting against the Pagans, when the Barony of Muskerry fell to him by right.[211] And it being reported that he was captured by the Turks, an usurper, a bastard of the family, did forthwith start up and seize his title and domains. And the Lord Thomas, when the wars were over, would have returned a beggar, but for his faithful fosterer, one Joan Harman, Sir, an ould Irish servitor of the family, married to an English bowman. She was aged and infirm; but when the rumour was spread of the devised usurpation, she took ship at Dingle, then a great port, and was landed in France, when the young lord was at court, as became his nobility, having changed the service of the Emperor of Austria / for that of the French king. And there Joan sought him out, and made him acquainted with the ill tidings, and brought him back without delay; and saw him cross the threshold of his own

---

*   A common Irish idiom.

castle, and restored to his fair possessions. And one calendar month, from the date of her mission, as she foretold, she died, being the day of the young lord's investiture in his ancient rights. For I've heard tell the heart will break with joy as well as sorrow; and shews the room to this hour where Joan Harman died. Och! it would not grieve me a taste to be old Joan Harman this day, if it was the will of God; for it's remarkable, that affections of fosterage never weaken, but

'Ner longas invaluere moras.'[212 r]

And there was little use in making gossipping and fosterage treason, by the famous statute of Kilkenny;[213] for they / both only just flourished the more, though the queen, that's Elizabetha regina, sent down the great Earl of Thomond, to abolish that same in his palatinate; and he entered recognizances, and bound himself to her majesty in a thousand pounds, that he should not marry, foster, nor gossip, contrary to the statute in that behalf provided, without the special license of the lord-deputy for the time being.[s]

Now gossippred, or confraternity, [214] plaze your honor, was said to produce confederacies of actions in all things, whether lawful or unlawful; but foster-age proved an iron link to bind the affections for laudible purposes, not only of the *fosterers* and *fostered*, but of the friends and relations on each side; and it bound the Irishry to the English by descent; as the O'Callighans to the Butlers formerly, and the O'Learys to the Fitzadelms to this blessed hour, / do you see, your honor; for says ould Stanihurst, and your honor knows him well, Lib. p. 49,[215] says he, you cannot find one instance of perfidy, or deceit, or treachery, among them. Nay, they are ready to expose themselves to all manner of dangers, for the safety of those who sucked their wives' or mothers' milk. You may beat them to a mummy, you may put them upon the rack, you may burn them on a gridiron, you may expose them to the most exquisite tortures, that the cruelest tyrants could invent, yet you will never remove them from that innate fidelity which is grafted in them; you will never induce them to betray their duty. And Cambrensis addeth (who was loath to afford a good word for the poor Irishry), 'if any love or faith be found among the Irish, you must look for it among the fosterers and the foster childre.'[216 t] /

'But,' said the general, throwing down his book, which he had for a moment resumed, rising in agitation, and placing himself opposite to O'Leary, who had resumed his seat, but who now rose also – – 'but, O'Leary, love and faith are not alone sufficient, where there is a perilous confidence to place, where the point at issue may be property, freedom, *life itself*; there must also be discretion, pru-dence, firmness, vigilance, command of thoughts, of looks, of feelings, and of language.'

As he spoke, O'Leary advanced step by step, but trembling, and gradually folding and compressing his hands, his mouth half open, his colour livid, as if he expected something he almost feared to learn. 'O'Leary,' continued the general in a calmer voice, and throwing himself back in his chair, 'O'Leary, sit down, compose yourself, and hear me.' /

O'Leary in part obeyed. He sat down, but his composure was irrecoverable. He remained for a few minutes silent. Suspense, hope, fear, almost to agony, were pictured in his countenance; while with a mechanical motion, he stooped to pick up a black silk handkerchief which had fallen from his breast, to wipe the cold drops that now bedewed his furrowed forehead, and rolled down his colourless cheek, when a crimson cross worked in its centre caught General Fitzwalter's eye. He started up, and snatched the handkerchief from O'Leary's hand.

'How came you by this handkerchief?' he asked eagerly.

O'Leary, with a wild and wandering look, his mind bent upon other objects, made an effort at recollection, then replied,

'The kerchief, Sir? is it the kerchief with the cross on it? Oh! plaze your / honor, I did not mane to purloin it, only return it, Sir, to the right owner, plaze God.'

'And who is that?' demanded the general with impatience.

'Is it who owns it, gineral?' replied O'Leary, endeavouring to recover himself. 'If it is not the Spanish American nun, Sir, owns it, one Madam Florence Macarthy, I don't guess who can own it, that's in respect of the blessed and holy crucifix.'

'Did you say Florence Macarthy?' asked the general with great emotion, and in a voice scarcely articulate, – 'a nun *from Spanish America?*'

'I did, your honor,' replied O'Leary in a low voice, as he contemplated with apprehension the change which had taken place in the general's countenance, – 'Florence Macarthy, Sir. Did you know her, gineral, in foreign parts? Her father was son to the ould Earl / of Clancare's brother. He went to be made a merchant of in some of the West India islands; and was the first of the family that turned his hands to business, which made a great bruite[217] in the country; and then he went into South America, and joined the wars there when they first broke out, as I heard tell, and was killed or died there I disremember me which. And his daughter, Florence Macarthy, his only child, went into a convent, her aunt being an abbess somewhere in Spain, so Father O'Sulivan tould me; and when it was broke up by the French army, who let loose the craturs, she fled back to Ireland, to her people in her own barony, which she had quit when a child; and none was in it left, only the *Bhan Tierna*, and one Mrs. Honor Macarthy, called *Honor ni Sancta*, or Holy Honor, who is the superior of "our Lady of the annun-/ciation," near the Abbey of the Holy-cross: and when there was a place vaquent in the convent, which was soon, Madam Florence Macarthy went to the convent, and was brought there by the countess, who has no vocation that way, the little sowl, with her *caen-cothar*, as her ould grandadda used to call her curley black head;

and the mouth and teeth of her, just like a young hound's, in regard of her red gums, gineral.'

A silence of many minutes succeeded to this information, and accompanying digression of O'Leary's, who usually '*drew the thread of his verbosity finer than his argument*.'[218]

At last the general, who was walking up and down the apartment in great agitation, stopped opposite to O'Leary, and asked, 'Where did you find that handkerchief? How came you by it?'

'How came I by it, Sir, is it? I / came by it, Sir, when I was just creeping out for a mouthful of fresh air, before dawn, this morning, and was looking up at the light in your casement, gineral, and thinking there must be great shanaos* between you and the young lord, would keep you up talking all night, and my foot caught in this kerchief, Sir, and I thought it was my own; only when daylight came I saw it was not, for by the cross marked on it in the centre I thought it must be Madam Florence Macarthy's, in regard of the cypher done in donny red letters, Sir.' O'Leary pointed to the small F. M. in the corner as he spoke. 'But the wonder of the world,' he added, 'is, what would be bringing her here among the rocks, and she settled down in her own convent, in Tipperary county, Sir, and is to take the vow in the begin-/ning of the month,, and a great sight it will be.'

'Did you ever see this Florence Macarthy?' asked the general after a pause, and standing opposite to O'Leary, with his eyes fixed on him.

'I did, gineral, often, when she was for a month at Castle Macarthy, and afore she went into her convent, and used to come down here to the great Macarthy-More's tomb in the monastery, and remained half the length of the day on her knees before it. Och! Sir, that's the voteen†, and the saint, if there's one upon earth: and it's extraordinary, but her cousin oncet removed, Lady Clancare would be taking a turn that way too, – and she brought up in a convent too, and never had a calling, only laughing, and shewing them white teeth of her's, and circum-/venting the Crawleys, and has great learning and fine Irish for all that, to say nothing of her being mighty comical.'

'Does Miss Macarthy resemble her cousin, Lady Clancare?'

'Why then, gineral, I could not well tell you that, in regard of never seeing her face, only with a thick black veil over it, and never shewed it to sun or moon, they say, barring Fra O'Sulivan, who confesses both ladies?'

The general now resumed his seat and book, requesting O'Leary to return to his school.

'You may lay out my writing desk, O'Leary,' he added, 'and – no; don't take away that handkerchief; and pray shut the door after you: I wish to be left alone.'

---

*   Family tradition, genealogical details.

†   Devotee.

O'Leary sighed deeply, and laid down one writing article after another; at last, taking up a pen to mend it, he observed: – /

'I thought, gineral, when I was brushing your coat yesterday, Sir, and you dressing for the castle dinner, that I heard you mintion a word of going away in a day or two, if the wind was fair, Sir; and a bit of a ship coming into port at Cork; and that – and then – and I thought your honor said something, Sir, about the *say* sickness being good for my complaint; and that you was going to – and the kerchief then came in the way; that's this morning, gineral, a bit ago.'

'And would you, O'Leary,' said the general, in a voice of great kindness, 'would you leave your home, your country, to follow me, uncertain as you must be whom –'

'Would I?' interrupted O'Leary, with a burst of emotion, in which consciousness and insanity seemed to struggle for supremacy – 'would I?' and he fell at the general's feet, and seized his hands, while his tears fell fast. / 'Would I follow you, is it? Did not I lose my senses for you? Did not I leave home, and kin, and friends, to wander the world over for you, when you were'nt in it? And now that you are before me with your mother's smile, see here, gineral,' and he attempted a tone of firm composure; 'if you are'nt yourself, and would tell me *that* at once, there would be an end of all; and I would be what I was before I met you in the mountains, and still would go on quietly, and would just, some fine morning, lie down in the sun, like old Cumhal, and die.'

The general, in irrepressible emotion, with difficulty released his hand from the maniac grasp of O'Leary: then drawing from his breast an ancient missal, he opened its clasps, and shewed, opposite to one of its illuminated pages, two certificates of a marriage and a birth. O'Leary seized the sacred vo-/lume, and kissed it eagerly and devoutly, with a look of anxious recognition. The general hurried it back to his breast.

'You stand pledged to God and to me, O'Leary,' said the general, in a deep and affecting voice.

O'Leary remained silent, but his lips moved rapidly; his eyes wandered wildly over the face that fascinated his gaze, till at last his clasp relaxed its firmness, his eyes closed, and he would have fallen to the earth, if the general had not received him in his arms.

'O'Leary, my old boy!' he said, bearing him to the fresh air admitted at the open window; and at this well remembered epithet, O'Leary, shaking off his faintness, cried, with a burst of hysteric laughter –

'That's it! that's the voice I have heard in the lone mountains by day and by night. They tould me it was my / fitch.[219] My fitch! oh, Jasus!' and he wept freely. Then suddenly drying his eyes, and throwing their rapid glances over the face of Fitzwalter, whose hand he still held, new lineaments seemed to start forth to his recollection, and he continued to repeat: – 'And there was a mole under the curls of the left temple; and axes your honor's pardon – yes, there it is; and the curls too, only far blacker. Shoosheen used to call it the fairy's lock, because the world would not take the curl out of it: and weren't drownded after all; sure I said so. And them transport ships off the coast, from Cork. And how was it, gineral, dear? And the boat there, turned upside down, when we went out to look for you; and your fostermother had sat up all night, and had a warning. And not many nights she sat up after – barring at her own wake, God help her: and that was too much for any man; and twenty-two years / ago! and all that time never to claim your own, nor just write one's own foster-father a line from foreign parts; and so ready at the pen formerly, in respect of them *themes* and *exercises!*'

'O'Leary,' said the general, in a firm and imposing voice, 'let it suffice that I live, and am here; that I have returned to my native country with a name as distinguished, through my own exertions, as that which I received from my fore-fathers; a name too not assumed, but inherited: for, after the ancient manner of my family, I have but given the Norman prefix to my father's baptismal appella-tion.'

O'Leary started, 'Fitzwalter! Walter, the Black Baron, and never thought of that. Och! I've a poor head now, and a beating in it that wears the life out of me by times. – To be sure, Walter de Montenay Fitzwalter; the ould Geraldine fashion evermore.'

'For the rest, O'Leary, secrecy the / most profound of my present existence in this neighbourhood is necessary. It is for the interest of many that I should never re-appear. My presence here, if even suspected, might endanger my life or lib-erty: besides, I wish to avoid all publicity – to compromise rather than contend, and to save the honour of my family, by touching lightly on the crimes of one of its members; or, if possible, by burying them in eternal oblivion.'

'That's the Honorable Gerald,' interrupted O'Leary, 'the Marquis, and Lord Adelm's father.'

'It matters not whom, O'Leary,' said the general eagerly; 'and now leave me for the present; resume your ordinary habits; be secret – – be circumspect – my life is in your hands; but hold yourself in readiness to depart at a moment's warn-ing. Had it not been for a circumstance that has become accidentally known to me this morning, / I should have left this country to-night, and even as it is perhaps.'

'To-night!' repeated O'Leary, who had moved a few paces, but who still loi-tered at the door.

'To-night. I must first, however, see the Countess of Clancare; and I think I will try my fortune at her door in an hour hence.'

'You will, Sir!' said O'Leary, in astonishment. 'See that – and in *amity*, plaze your honour?'

'Certainly not in *enmity*,' returned the general, smiling. 'But you seem surprised by my intention, O Leary.'

'No, plaze your lord –, your honour, I mane; not a taste; for sure 'twas just the same anno 1321, when the ENGLISH BY BLOOD leagued with the IRISH MERE in the common cause,[220] that's ould Ireland, Sir; and enemies before, became fast friends sithence, as *Ayphraim* against Menasses, and Me- /nasses against *Ayphraim*; and both united against the tribe of Judah,[221] that's the Crawleys, Sir, the land pirates! – and will step down and order your fine new charger from Cork, Sir, to be brought from the Dunore Arms, and will put on my Sunday apparel, and mount the little Kerry asturiones, and ride after your honor in the capacity of an ecury,[222] as is right and fitting, till you're Lord –, till you have a better – and will just induct Teague Rourke, my head Homer, into the office of my coadjutor and assistant in the seminary: that is, gineral, he'll tache the classes, while I'll attind your honor.'

'No, O'Leary,' said the general, shaking his head, 'that will never do. You must return to your learned runagates,[223] of whom I found you so justly proud when I arrived here: and if you do not wish me to repent of the confidence I have placed in you, you / will in no respect change your wonted habits.'

'Then I'll engage I won't, Sir; replied O'Leary, emphatically, 'and never will call you my lord, till the day of judgment; that is, till all's proved; and your lordship, the great Marquis of Dunore (which you are at this blessed moment), taking possession of your castle: for fortune, though she be pourtrayed to stand upon a rolling stone, as being flighty by nature, yet for the most part she helpeth such as be of courageous mind, and valiant stomach. – Did not Thomyris the Scythian queen, and collateral ancestor of the Macarthies, by her great spirit, with a few hundred followers, bate Cyrus intirely,[224] with many thousands? and did not –, but I will not bother your lordship with needless tediousness, only just will defy the world, from this day out, to prove that I care a testoon / for you; and thought, Sir, that I'd ride the asturiones[225] after you, to shew you the way, Sir, to Castle Macarthy.'

'I should, for many reasons, prefer going alone,' said the general.

'Och! very well, gineral: sure I have no control over you now, Sir, why would I, only in respect of finding out the Bhan-Tierna, who does not care to be in the way of the quality; foreby being always in the fields, or on her own mountains, from sun-rise to sun-set, just like a little grasshopper, the sowl! chirping and hopping, and living on dews and air, as one would say; that's as Anacreon says,[226] Sir: – and remembers your construing that same into mighty pretty Latin; and you only twelve years old and three months.'

'You may order my horse in an hour hence,' said the general.

O'Leary now drew towards the door, throwing back one eager, anxious, and / affectionate look, which the general returned with an expressive smile. O'Leary raised his eyes in thanksgiving, murmured an Irish prayer, dashed the gathering tears from his eyes, and crossing his hands behind him, retired muttering to himself as he slowly descended the steep stairs, 'And Cumhal the cratur, not alive to see this day!'

An hour had scarcely elapsed when O'Leary, mounted on the fine horse he had alluded to, appeared under the window of the general's apartment. He had thrown off his pedagogue costume, was habited in his gala dress of many coats, had put on a new wig and hat, was shaved unusually close, and exhibited a countenance far indeed from placid, but from which every trace of anxiety and solicitude was banished. The flutter of new-born, unexpected happiness still distinguished his manner. He had given his boys an holiday, and / was incapable of fixing his attention to his daily habits; but there was an air of contentment about him which indicated an evident revolution in feelings and ideas. His short cough, and expressions of kindness to the animal on which he was mounted, drew General Fitzwalter to the window; and he stood for a moment contemplating this warm-hearted, zealous, and devoted being, with an emotion of pride and benevolence, as one, who true to human sympathy, beholds with triumph the happiness he has created.

In a few minutes he was mounted on his steed; and O'Leary continued to walk beside him, with one hand behind his back, and the other leaning on the horse's flank.

'I'll just step on a taste with your honor,' he observed, to excuse his intrusion, 'to shew the good road, Sir, and open the little gates, and remove / the brambles that stop up the gaps in the mearings betwixt the *pratie* grounds[227] of the Dunore tenants.'

To this the general made no objection; and O'Leary continued,

'And so, you are going, gineral, jewel, to make your courtesies, and to pay your obeysance to the Countess of Clancare, which makes the friar's words come true, anno 1505.'

'What friar; and what words, O'Leary?'

'Och! an holy man your honor,' said O'Leary, lowering his voice, and raising his head towards the general's ear, 'who was superior of the order here, in the time of the first Lord Dunore, who got the castle after the Macarthies, and who chased away the brotherhood. He left a curse on Dunore castle, which remains unredeemed to this day. His prophecy, which is in Irish, may be thus construed:
/

Macarthy More shall have his won,
When, after battles lost and won,
The Norman shall cross the threshold floor,
To woo the heir of Macarthy More:
When the dexter hand from the clouds shall bend,

And the moose deer* to its home shall wend;
When he shall return, who was dead and gone,
Macarthy More shall have his own –
Such are the words of Friar Con.'

'The prediction of your friar, O'Leary,' said the general, smiling, 'like most prophecies, is sufficiently vague and indefinite. It may mean anything or nothing.'

'Anything or nothing!' returned O'Leary, quickly. 'Does *battles lost and won* mane nothing? And the retrate of Masha-na-glass, and the Foray of Dooghna-go-hoone, between the Fitzadelms and the Macarthies, about a prey of cattle, and divers other com-/bats, as will be seen in my Genealogical History, written in the Phœnician vulgo vocata Irish; do *they* mane nothing? And does the *Norman crossing the threshold floor, to woo the heir of Macarthy More*, mane nothing, gineral? and your honor' (here he lowered his voice to a whisper), 'and your honor going to make your obeisance to the *Bhan Tierna* of the world? And does

> "*The dexter hand from the cloud shall bend,*
> *And the moose deer to its home shall wend*,"

mane nothing? when the dexter hand's the device of the Fitzadelms; and is going, in lowly suit, to tender itself to the Macarthy's heir: and the moose deer, the crest of the Macarthies, which was found cut beautifully in stone among the rubbish at Castle Macarthy, and set up over the portal, by Lady Clancare, when she came home, a wandering *deer* herself, the / cratur! the wide world over? And then –' he added, in emotion, "*for him who shall return, being......*"'

'Yes, yes,' interrupted Fitzwalter, 'that is plain: but it is by no means so certain, because a Norman stranger visits the heiress, or representative of the Macarthy family, that he is to *woo* her. And if the restoration of the greatness and property of the Macarthies rests upon that part of your Friar's prophecy, I'm afraid, O'Leary, the whole falls to the ground.'

'If she chooses it, plaze your honor, she'll make you woo her, and win her too,' said O'Leary, with an air of mysterious doggedness.

'Indeed!'

'Troth! and deed, Sir. Sure she rules the world intirely, Sir: and has greatly quelled the Crawleys since she came into it. – And is like her great ancestor, the famed Illen Macarthy,²²⁸ the / first Countess of Clancare, only child to the great Florence: she, who rescued the title from Daniel the base-born, and bestowed it upon her own husband (the queen consenting thereunto), Sir Donach Macarthy Reagh of Carberry; and like her the Bhan Tierna isᵘ sharp witted, a great lover of learning, capable of any study, and has, at this present speaking, my Irish and Latin dictionary, which she walked down herself to borrow, the very evening

---

*   The dexter arm, the crest of the Fitzadelms: – the moose deer, that of the Macarthies.

of the day your honor set off to Cork; which was the day, Sir, she arrived from England, where she had been sojourning, to the intire loss of the country; and the Crawleys waxing cockish the moment her back was turned; and brings me home this piece of antiquity; *and thinks it will plaze you, O'Leary,* says she, here it is, plaze your honor.' He pulled from his breast a tattered volume, adding, 'It is entitled '*Tom / Loodles' rhymes*, Sir, '*nipping by name divers honorable and worshipful of the realm, and certain officers of the deputy's household, for grieving the land with impositions – bearing* date Jan. 28, Anno Dom. 1576.'[229] Making, with the deputy's answer, and a speech of one James Stanihurst, an Esquire of worship, Warder of Dublin, but eight sheets closely indited – which,[v] with your lave, gineral, I'll peruse aloud to beguile the way, which is bare and bleak.'

'I would rather you would explain to me, O'Leary,' said the general, alighting, and throwing the bridle of the horse over his arm, 'why, talking as you did, so much and so frequently of the ancient state and fortunes of this Macarthy family, you should have said nothing of their present existence; of this Lady Clancare, for instance, whom you merely mentioned as an *ancient* / lady, absent from the country, and whom I naturally supposed to be the widow of the late earl.'

'And isn't she an ancient countess, though a young faimale, your honor? Anno, 1565; estates regranted by letters patent, to hold them of the crown after the English fashion; and sat in parliament afore 1584: and as for not *coshering*[*][230] about her with a stranger in the mountains (no stranger to the heart if strange to the eye), would you ax one of the Pobble O'Leary's to betray their Tanista, their Bhan Tierna? and her last words, laving the country in Owny, the Rabragh's ould chay, being –'

'Owny, the Rabragh!' repeated the general, with a little start.

'Yes, my lord, Sir, I mane; the last words laving the country, and the first when she came back was, not to / be talking her over with strangers; nor, 'bove all, with any of the Fitzadelms, who were expected over every day them two years: and when I tould her that I was sure I had the Lord Adelm houselled under my roof, and described your honor to her *verbatim et literatim*,[231] she swore me over again that I would not sell her to yez.'

'Sell her! but what was her object in this concealment?'

'Pride, Sir; what else would it be. The pride of the Macarthies, Sir, the proudest race in Christendom, dead or alive, this day: and didn't choose, the sowl, to be overshadowed by them Dunores and their greatness, in her poor ould castle, (3)[232] without her tiernas or clans, her bonagh, sorohen, cuddy, shragh, or mart; without her warder, or constable, or gallowglasses, or calivers; or hand weapons; but only just Ulic Macshane, the cow-boy, and Sibby, her / little bit of a handmaid, with only thirty pounds per annum, chief-rents of great estates on

---

[*]   Coshering, literally, gossiping.

the Kerry side of Clotnotty-joy, that are worth thousands to their owners; and
that's all coming to her now, who by right is king of the Corianddi; and all that's
left of her barony, town-lands, plough-lands, castle, and manor, with all royalties,
mines, quarries; suit and service, knight's fees, wardships and marriages, escheats,
waifs, strays, goods proclaimed, persons of bondmen, estovers, villains and their
followers, fairs, markets, tolls, and all franchises and privileges whatsoever, with a
court baron at Ballydab for the Cork estates, and another at Claneare for Kerry;
to say nothing of chieftainries all through the province, sowled scrubal by scrubal to such land pirates as the Crawleys; and broke some of their sword-blade
company bargains since she came home.ʷ Now to see her / rinting her own castle, and going a foot to mass, barring when the mules isn't at work, and has them
put to her cabriole, made by ould Cormack the wheel-wright. Mules! Bachal
Essu! she that had her Spanish jennets, and her Hobellers, and Asturiones, and
Arabians, sent over by Don Jacobus Macarthy as a gift to the great Florence;
foreby her steeds ready caparisoned afore the rack in case of a sudden foray, and
the O'Driscols coming down the mountains to make a prey of kine; and that is
the raison, plaze your honor, why she'd wish to keep aloof of them English quality, who might stand upon the pantoufles[233] of their English rank, and treat her,
as she pithily observed to me, as the Saxon King John and his Norman gallants
did the great Milesian O'Connors, and O'Briens, and O'Byrnes, and Macarthies, who set the Irish chiefs at nought, laughed at their man-/tles and truises,
mocked their glibbs and beards, and with flaps on their lips, and thumps on their
backs, discourteously received the courtesies of the native nobility of the land.[234]
ˣ Besides, she might not like, being a lone lady, to come in the way of the young
Lord Adelm, who is, according to rumour, a rake and raparee,[235] one in whom
there is no stay, no sobriety, likening his father the Honorable Gerald.'

'And yet,' said the general, 'Lady Clancare chose to let herself be taken prisoner to Dunore, when a word would have saved her the mortification of standing
in so humiliating a position before those persons she was so anxious to avoid.'

'And if she did,' said O'Leary, with a significant look, 'I'll ingage she had her
reasons for that same: and did not you mind, that secret and drifty[236] as them
Crawleys was, to ruin / the world round, and your honor to boot, they were all
outwitted and circumvented every step; and mark my words, the Bhan Tierna
was at the bottom of all, overthrowing their complots and their policies; and
when I saw your honour there in the midst of them, your natural kin, it minded
me of the secret enemies of the great ould Earl of Kildare, and their accusations
against him, deposed before Henry the Seventh, anno 1501, charging him with
burning the cathedral church of Cashell;[237] and he, baited at the stake, did confess the fact: and when it was looked for that he should justify the same, 'By
Jasus,' quoth he, 'I would never done it, plaze your majesty, had they not tould
me the archbishop was within; and merrily laughed the king at the plainness of

the man, the archbishop being present; and when it was deposed that all Ireland could not govern this earl, /

"No!" quoth the king, "then in good faith shall this earl govern all Ireland;" and forthwith he made him lord-deputy and knight of the garter, to the discomfiture of his enemies, and is ancestor to the young Duke of Leinster to this day.'

O'Leary chuckled over this anecdote; and though General Fitzwalter could perceive no parallel between the Earl of Kildare's case and his own, yet there was such animation and cheerfulness in O'Leary's manner, out of the abundance of whose heart the mouth now spoke, that he was unwilling to chill it by a dissentient opinion upon a subject which it seemed to give him such pleasure to maintain.[y]

They had now passed the last fence of the potatoe grounds, had got upon the highway, the general had mounted his horse, and was declining O'Leary's offer of accompanying him to Castle Macar-/thy, when Lord Adelm, followed by a groom, appeared galloping towards them. He stretched out his hand to General Fitzwalter, who rode up to him, and took it cordially. O'Leary stood with his head uncovered, and with something between amazement and consternation painted in his looks.

'I have met with a great loss,' said Fitzadelm, as they rode on together.

'You bear losses with such philosophy,' said Fitzwalter, 'that it would be throwing away sympathy to offer it to you. But what further trials has your disinterested generosity been put to?'

'I have lost,' said Lord Adelm, with a melancholy look, 'my sybil's kerchief.'

General Fitzwalter rode close up to him, and throwing his arm over Lord Adelm's shoulder, said – 'And what, if I / have discovered the sybil who owns that handkerchief?'

'Discovered!' said Lord Adelm, almost springing from his horse, and taking the bridle of the general's, so as to draw them still closer together – 'discovered, say you! how? when? where? what is she, sybil, sylph, woman, maid, widow, or wife? Speak, I conjure you.'

'A woman and a wife; *almost*, at least, a wife,' replied Fitzwalter, with a half-repressed sigh.

'Whose wife?' demanded Lord Fitzadelm, with the blood mantling to his cheek.

'Mine,' was the abrupt reply.

A short silence succeeded to this singular and most unexpected answer; till Lord Adelm, recovering from the shock a reply so mysterious was calculated to give, at last, with a look, in which some faint indication of plea-/surable triumph was discernible, observed: –

'Every thing about you is extraordinary. You are out of the pale of every-day creation. All things connected with you are calculated for amazement or admiration: but that any one you have deigned to – to – should turn her eyes on me! – in short, you trifle with my folly; you play with my credulity – you –'

'At the present moment,' said the general, 'I cannot satisfy your doubts, or clear up your perplexities. I am myself doubtful and uncertain; perplexed in the extreme. If the owner of the mystic kerchief is the person I suspect she is, or might be still – but I demand your indulgence, and the suspension of your curiosity. To-night it may be in my power to become more explicit. Till then, or till that moment arrives when I can fully explain my-/self, confide in my truth, rely on my friendship, and believe that my feelings are not more at ease than your own. Where can I see you this evening?'

'Where! where, but at the castle? My mother's dinner card of general invitation is now on its way to you. It was with difficulty I could confine her to *that*; not but that I consider your delicacy as morbid and sickly upon this point.'

'It must not, and it ought not to be,' said the general.

'It must, and ought. It's folly to act otherwise. To me it is privation, and in you suspicious. I will call on you in my way home, and we will return to dinner together; or, rather, I wish you would accompany me now.'

'Where are you bound to?'

'To Glannacrime. This morning, at breakfast, I thought I perceived a little intelligence between my mother / and her election agent, to keep me for some time out of the scene of action; so I ordered my horse, and came off to canvass the '*most sweet voices*'[238] of those purchaseable worthies, in person. But this most extraordinary intelligence, mysterious and unsatisfactory as it is, which you have now communicated to me, leaves me without thought or view for any other object, save that which has so long occupied my existence; that which .... Your wife! Oh! you jest. Impossible! you never mentioned, never hinted, that you were married before; and now ....'

'To tell the truth,' said Fitzwalter, shrugging his shoulders, 'I had almost forgotten it myself. It was an event in my life brief and fantastic as a dream, made up of circumstances as wild and as discordant; occurring amidst scenes, perilous and foreign to such an engagement, amidst the crash of war, / the groans of the dying; when the vow, half breathed, remained unratified; the benediction, half pronounced, was unfinished; and the ceremony, all but concluded, was broken off in time to render the forms which had passed binding only to faith, to honour, and to gratitude. These ties all remain; and if they are to be irrevocably broken, 'tis not by me. This you are going to say is all enigma; and so it is. Yet now I will be pressed no further. To-night perhaps ... till then, farewell.'

He now spurred his horse, and in a moment was out of sight. There was in the tone, the air, and the manner, more than in his words, an imposing firmness, and indisputable decision upon all occasions, when he chose to be peremptory, which left persuasion hopeless.

'He is his own destiny and mine,' said Lord Adelm' with a sigh, as he / looked after him. 'To contend with him, or to oppose him, were to struggle with fatality.' In this conviction there was something extremely accordant to the habits of mind and morbid imagination of him who embraced it. Mystery was his element; and whatever was wild or terrible, dark or extraordinary, whatever roused profound emotion, or gave feeling to extraordinary conjecture, was calculated to ingross and interest him. The commander of *Il Librador* did both. /

CHAPTER V.

Even so, this happy creature, of herself is all sufficient.
WORDSWORTH.[239]

There stand – for you are spell-stopp'd.
SHAKESPEARE.[240]

IT was a bright, warm September morning (one of those days so rare in a climate impregnated with the vapours of the greatest ocean of the earth),[z] that, for the first time since his arrival in the country, General Fitzwalter entered the village of Ballydab. But neither the noon-day sun which shone on its views, nor the mountain breeze that blew over them, rich in the perfumes of plants peculiar to the southern mountains of / Ireland, could lend a charm to this ruinous retreat of indigence and misery. Ballydab, the EL DORADO[241] of O'Leary; the once fair dependency of its own feudal castle, an ancient borough, which had formerly sent two members to parliament by prescriptive right (for its charter was not upon record), Ballydab, once noted in military and ecclesiastical history, was now a desolate and ruinous village, scarcely less imposing or less miserable in its appearance than the deserted city of Kilmallock in the same province (4).[242] The remains of a wall which once surrounded the town were still visible. The site of a Dominican abbey of Black Friars, erected in the fifteenth century, by 'the sovereign, brethren, and commonalty,' was yet ascertainable; and the ruins of other castles and monasteries afforded shelter to many wretched families, who had built their perishable / huts against the walls of edifices, whose strength had stood the shock of ages. Ballydab, which had been founded by the Macarthies, had long since been transferred to the Dunore family, and had been included in the great sale of boroughs, which, while it sanctified the principle of corruption, by acknowledging the landlord's pecuniary interest in the votes of his tenantry, and his *possession* of the borough, had purchased the transfer of all right in the annihilation of the national legislature.[a] Desolate, impoverished, and neglected, the surrounding land given up to jobbers, it bore all the signs, not only of distress, but of squalid and hopeless pauperism. Its inhabitants were deemed lawless, they were, indeed, occasionally desperate; no natural demand being made upon their native activity, their restlessness had sometimes degenerated to mischief: and it was, perhaps, as much / their misery that they had few wants, as that they had still fewer means of supplying them. Their cabins were, for the most part, ruined hovels; and in the centre of the town, a swampy marsh, where an annual fair was held by ancient usage, sent up ordinarily a pestilential vapour, though now unusually dry.

Yet, amidst these symptoms of general wretchedness, evidences of recent and progressive improvement were to be seen. The mountain which sheltered the town was cultivated and green to its summit. Several of the hovels were newly whitewashed: and, in a few instances, freshly plaistered chimneys emitted the smoke, which more commonly found egress at the door. In the front of one cabin, a poor man was employed in filling up a stagnate pool, and an heap of manure was removing from before another. At the / door of a barn a number of children were employed in making green rush matting, and at a little shebeen house, a piper sat upon a stone bench playing a gay Irish lilt.

The general as he passed along had to return the low bows of all he met, for there were strangely mingled with the general aspect of misery and wildness an air of courtesy, and a civilization of manner, which formed a curious contrast.[b] From every point of the village the castle was conspicuous, for it stood on the brow of a hill that overhung it, and upon a precipice which immediately arose from a river, formed of many tributary streams, and flowing into one of the many bays, which, a mile further on, indented the coast. All that now remained of the original edifice of Castle Macarthy was a coarse square building, rude, inelegant, and wholly destitute of the architectural ornament which / distinguished the beautiful and perfect Castle of Dunore, a building more modern by about a century. The ballium, the barbican, the parapets, the embrazures and crenelles,[243] described by O'Leary, and existing only in the memory of what he read, or the imagination of what he wished, were vainly sought for in the chapter of realities. His castle was literally 'a castle in the air.'

As General Fitzwalter approached more closely, and ascended the steep and rutted lane, or approach, he perceived a fosse partly filled up, and a flagged causeway crossing it. The stone pillars of the gates still remained; and the castle bawn, the demesne of feudal recreation, lay to the left, and was still fenced round with a low wall of mud and brambles. It was now, however, planted with potatoes, rich in their bright silver and orange flowers. The / mountain rose almost perpendicularly above the castle; and to the left a romantic glen, wild, irregular, and rocky, afforded a passage to the many mountain brooks which swelled the greater streams and fell into the sea. Two or three irregular sashed windows appeared scattered over the front of the castle, but it was principally lighted by loophole casements. The hall door of black bog oak lay open, and the crest of the Macarthies, alluded to by O'Leary, the moose deer, cut in stone, was raised above it, with the date of 1500. A knocker would have been vainly sought for; nor was any person visible, except two women, who appeared at a distance, weeding a patch of ground at the extremity of the potatoe ridges; while a venerable greyhound, which lay basking in the sun before the door, the sole guardian of these ruined towers, only growled at the / stranger's approach, half raised himself, and then lay down again to sleep. General Fitzwalter entered the stone-roofed hall; and in the hope that some one might accidentally appear, occupied himself in examining the singular ornaments with which it was decorated. A wolf's head, the last caught in Ireland, as was inscribed on a brass plate, bearing date 1710,[244] hung from the centre of the ceiling. Beneath it, on an old stone table, the enormous fossil horns of a moose deer were extended: a few old pictures were dropping from their frames; and on either side of the hall, two narrow arched ways led to dark, damp, stone passages. He was at last tempted to proceed through that on the left, guided by the sound of a voice, which had suddenly raised a lilt, and as suddenly stopped it, when some one ran forcibly against him, hastily drawing back and exclaim-/ing, 'The blessed Virgin save us, Amen!' The general followed the person whose surprise or fears had extorted this ejaculation, and found himself at the door of an old spacious smoaky kitchen. In removing the alarm he had just awakened, he increased the surprise of the intimidated person. It was a young woman, who courtesied and blushed, with something like recognition in her looks; and putting back her locks beneath her round-eared cap, she remained silent and confused. On the inquiry whether Lady Clancare was at home, she courtesied, still lower, and said, 'Is it my lady, Sir? Oh yes, to be sure she is, your honor – I ax your pardon. This a way, if you plaze, Sir. Have a care, there is a little stooleen in your way. I'll but step afore your honor a taste,' – and still engaged in arranging her dress, she led the way to the stone passage, on the / other side the hall, and passing under a gothic arched way, she threw open a door at the further extremity of the passage, and ushered the visitor into a low-roofed but spacious room. His conductress having wiped a large arm chair, and pulled it near the dying embers of a turf fire, which she replenished from an huge turf-box that stood near the hearth (for the room was chill, notwithstanding the warmth of the day), she was retiring, when he called her back, and giving her his card, desired her to carry it, with his respectful compliments, to the Countess of Clancare. The girl looked at the card, and then at him, and a smile just visible stole over her features as she retired.

The room into which he had been shewn occupied his attention during the moment of waiting. It was of dimensions disproportionate to its height, and from its dark and irregular figure, / and the immense width of the wall (marked by the deep recess of its only window), it appeared to occupy one of the towers which flanked the castle towards the precipitous glen, and was not, therefore, perceptible from the front.

The walls, neither wainscotted nor papered, were partially covered with faded tapestry, the figures of which were antique and grotesque. It was the work of Irish nuns, whose looms a century and a half ago had contributed to the decoration of many Irish castles.(5)[245c] Above the ample and ungrated hearth, a lofty, cumbrous, but handsome chimney-piece of grey marble, the produce of the adjoining quarries, arose nearly half way to the ceiling. For two feet above the floor, it was incrusted with brick, and seemed to have been but lately discovered. On its entablature was carved the following / inscription: DONAGH MACARTHY COMES DE CLANCARE ME FECIT, 1565:[246] The floor was of beaten earth, mixed with free-stone sand, and was covered near the fire-place with some new rush matting: an oak table, a tattered Indian skreen, a high ponderous japan chest,[247] and a few long-backed curiously carved oak chairs, composed the whole furniture of this antique and gloomy apartment: a spinning wheel stood near the hearth, and a Spanish guitar, and a parasol, oddly contrasted to it, lay on the table. The recess window was evidently devoted to the purposes of a study. The view it commanded was enchanting, for it hung immediately over a glen; and a river seen sparkling through the rich underwood brawled beneath; and rushed through a cleft in the rocks towards the distant bay.

The floor of this recess was covered with a piece of old but once rich Turkey / carpet: the table, which nearly occupied it (leaving space only for a chair), was heaped with books and manuscripts; the latter, however, not bearing the stamp of antiquity, but fresh written; for the humid pen was evidently but just laid down. Two books stood open, marked with a pencil and a flower. The one was *Hanmer's Chronicle*, the other *Campion's History of Ireland;*[248] an Irish and Latin Dictionary, and an odd volume of Lopez de Vega, Burn's poems,[249] and a small edition of Shakespeare, with an antique missal, bound in crimson velvet, with the arms and coronet of the Clancares, formed the whole of this little collection. Some flowers, seemingly just gathered, in a handsome china vase, stood upon the table, and an embroidered work-bag, such as are worked in foreign convents, with a silver cross and rosary, hung over the / back of the chair, and compleated the paraphernalia of this little recess, which might have served equally for the retreat of the sage or the saint, or as a reposoir for the fantastic taste of a petite maitresse. The flowers and the work-bag were at once assignable to the *gout musqué*[250] of the timid,[d] but evidently affected Lady Clancare – for Lord Adelm's epithet of the *petite evaporeé* seemed not ill-placed. The rosary and the cross, and the missal, were as markedly appropriate to the Spanish nun, Florence Macarthy, who had been so lately an inmate at the castle. General Fitzwalter had learned, by experience, to distrust the extravagant exaggerations of O'Leary, when the family of his hereditary Tiernas was concerned. He had no doubt that the character of Lady Clancare had been confounded in his wandering imagination with that of the celebrated / *Illen Macarthy*, of Queen Elizabeth's days; and that the

learning and potency, attached to this female *Tanaist* in his descriptions, had
no more certain existence than the balliums, crenelles, and barbican, which he
had given to her dilapidated castle. Even the exertions she had made to liberate
an oppressed man, through her application to Judge Aubrey, while it evinced
great goodness of heart, was deemed sufficient to explain the popularity she so
evidently enjoyed among a people equally alive to kindness and neglect. But
whatever might be the character of this fair recluse, her tastes, like her appearance, were manifestly delicate and feminine: and there was something peculiarly
touching, and even pitiable, in the indigence betrayed in this ruinous asylum, of
one so young, so nobly born, so destitute, and so unprotected. Her assumption
of a title / she had no means of supporting, her retirement from the world to a
solitude so dreary, shewed at least the pride of birth; and pride, from whatever
source it springs, when at variance with poverty, forms one of the most painful
contests of feeling to which humanity is subject.

As these thoughts passed rapidly through the mind of Fitzwalter, he almost
unconsciously took down an antique sword, which hung against the wall; and
mused, as he examined its curious structure, on the untowardness of a fate, in
which he found some parallel to his own.

'Man,' he involuntarily exclaimed, brandishing the weapon, and clasping it
with a warrior's grasp; – 'man, with such an instrument as this, can always cut his
way to fortune or to death; and rushing forward to meet the evils of his destiny,
by *opposing, end* them: but woman! hapless woman! what is / *her* resource when
fortune *deserts*, when adversity *assails* her? Desolate and unguarded, with scarce
one path open to her exertions, scarce one stay left to her weakness, endangered
even by her perfections, risked and enfeebled by all that makes the delicious
excellence of her nature, – woman! –'

The door opened, and she, whose destiny had probably given birth to this
apostrophe, interrupted its conclusion. There was a sort of half start, a sudden pause in the approach of Lady Clancare, as if the visit and the visitor were
equally unexpected, which communicated something of its brief confusion to
her guest. He bowed, then stood for a moment, slightly embarrassed; and still
armed with the antique sword of Macarthy-More, he not inaptly realized to the
eyes of his fair descendant the picture left on historic record, of that magnificent
chieftain. (6)[251] Lady Clancare, with that promptitude and pre-/sence of mind,
which peculiarly belong to woman's quick perception, was the first to recover
herself, and, slightly courtesying, addressed her guest by name, motioned him
to a chair, and advanced with a light quick step to the centre of the room. With
a disengaged air, she gradually disencumbered herself of a deep straw bonnet, a
grey cloak, gloves incrusted with earth, and a black apron full of mountain ash
berries, all of which articles were deliberately laid upon the table. Thus engaged,
she stood with her profile towards General Fitzwalter, who had not taken the

chair she had pointed out to his notice. He remained looking at a person and countenance, that seemed to have changed much of their character since he had last seen them; but where the change had occurred, he could not detect.ᶜ

Lady Clancare, as she now stood, was the very personification of health, in all / its force and freshness, vigour and elasticity. The crimson of haste and exercise glowed in her cheek; and there was a life palpitating through the whole frame, throbbing in every pulse, and vibrating in every fibre, that was visible to the observer's eye. But whether she was *animated* or *agitated*, breathless from hurry, or from emotion, it would have been difficult to ascertain. Her countenance had lost nothing of its peculiar modesty; but from her half-closed eyes one glance met his, that, to him at least, seemed charged with triumph; a sort of smiling malicious triumph; the triumph of conscious success, of conscious superiority, and infelt power; such a look as he had seen her wear, when, in carrying off Lady Dunore, she had bowed her laughing and almost insolent salutation to the dis-comfitted Crawleys. This look, whether real or fancied, was, however, / transient as lightning; and now, disencumbered of her coarse out-of-door garments, she turned round a face dimpled with a thousand smiles; and, with the ease of a woman of the world, but the naïveté of one beyond its forms and formalities, she apologized for having so long detained him. 'This is,' she added, pointing again to a chair, and throwing herself into an immense old fashioned fauteuil,²⁵² 'this is my farming season, and farming hour. We are digging our potatoes to-day; for you must know, General Fitzwalter, the *potatoe vintage* is to us poor Irish of as great moment and interest, though not quite so susceptible of picturesque description, as the gathering of the rich grapes in the luxuriant vineyards of the Loire and the Garonne. I always preside on these occasions myself,' she added, carelessly untying a silk handkerchief which encircled her neck, / 'for I dare say you will agree with me, that no work goes on so lightly as that which is shared by the master.'

To this proposition General Fitzwalter returned no answer. He had mechan-ically taken the chair assigned him, and sat with his right arm thrown over its back, and his left leaning on the old sword. His eyes were rivetted on Lady Clancare, with that eager, animated penetrating gaze natural to them, when he sought to discover or dive at once into the secret of a character that appeared to elude observation. Her's, however, as it now equivocally appeared through her easy, animated, disengaged manners, opposed to her 'outward seeming'²⁵³ at the castle of Dunore, was all enigma. Her childish shyness, her timid and affected carriage, which had induced Lord Adelm to give her the epithet of a *minaudiere*, had disappeared. There was now something / of the sybil in her looks; and her incomprehensible change of manner assimilated with the present character of her person and character. Meantime his silence, though marked and singular, scarcely confused, and seemed not to displease her; and she sat demurely patting and caressing the old greyhound which had followed her into the room, as if she awaited an explanation of the visit, which appeared wholly unexpected, and which, it was natural to suppose, was not without cause or excuse. At last, as if to relieve the awkwardness of the pause, she stretched forth a very pretty little hand, and asked smilingly –

'Shall I take that sword from you? 'tis a cumbrous article.' He laid the sword upon the table, and she drew it towards her. 'Have you examined this antique weapon, General Fitzwalter? I am told it was found in a bog in 1748. / It was sent to me the other day by a neighbouring farmer, into whose hands it fell accidentally, for he was pleased, poor man, to consider me as the lady of the manor. What makes these brazen swords a valuable relic to the Irish antiquarian is, that they serve to corroborate the opinion that the Phœnicians colonised this country; for they insist that the sword-blades found upon the field of Cannæ[254] were of the same metal and construction, and being used by the Carthaginians, who were originally Tyrians, they establish the certainty that these Irish weapons were Phœnician also. Consequently, you know, General Fitzwalter, something more than a mere presumption arises that Ireland had her arts and letters from the country of Cadmus, as all her traditions affirm, in spite of all Dr. Ledwich has said to the contrary.'[255]

All this was uttered with a sort of / mock emphasis, that left it very doubtful whether she believed a word she spoke, or whether it was mere ironical badinage, or antiquarian credulity – it served only to involve General Fitzwalter in deeper perplexity.

'Now, what is your opinion?' she added with emphatic gravity. 'Do you really think we are *Tyrians by descent?*' Then laughing, and resuming her gay tone, she added, 'O! I see you are no antiquarian, though you are the guest of my friend O'Leary. Well then, neither am I; and to confess the truth, the present state of this poor country interests me more than its ancient real or fabled greatness; and I should rather see my neighbours of Ballydab succeed in reclaiming and cultivating that mountain, to the right of the casement (my dear Clotnotty-joy), or improve in the rush and straw work, I am endeavouring to teach their / idle, helpless, naked children, than establish, beyond all controversy, that the *Macarthies* are descended from the Tyrian Hercules, or that Ireland was the seat of arts and letters, when the rest of the world was, according to my family genealogist, the sage O'Leary, buried in utter darkness. Do you know – apropos to ancient greatness,' she added with a quick transition of voice, 'that as I entered this room, there was something in your appearance, as you stood brandishing that antique weapon, that reminded me of a picture I have seen, of our family hero, (7)[256] Florence Macarthy; though to Miss Crawley's deep-read mind, and ready literary associations, I dare say you would have recalled the image of Achilles, in the court of Lycomedes.

"In questa mano,
Lampeggi il ferro ah recomineio adesso, /
A ravissar me stesso, ah! forse a fronte,
A mille squadre, e mille!"²⁵⁷

'And if I were,' said General Fitzwalter, interrupting her impulsively, and borne away by her animation, for she had repeated these lines with an almost dramatic effect; 'and if I were *"a fronte a mille squadre e mille!"* my position, perhaps, would be less hazardous than that I at present occupy.'

'It would at least be more in your WAY,' she replied significantly.

'How do *you* know that?' he asked eagerly.

'Oh! I *know* nothing. I merely guess it. I have a true woman's mind: no judgment, no reflection, no *knowledge*, but some intelligence, and a rapidity of perception, that goes before all experience, and lights upon facts by accident, which it would take an age for philosophy to puzzle at.' /

'Then perhaps,' he returned, 'you are already intuitively aware of the cause of this intrusion upon proscribed ground, where the soles of unblessed feet are not, I understand, permitted to press.'

'Oh! to be sure I am. The cause *is*, – that of most of the untoward things men do; – heroes, as well as others, – a woman –'

'*That*, my visit to your ladyship sufficiently indicates. But the purport of this visit *to a woman,* whose dwelling is forbidden to a stranger's steps – to all male intrusion I understand –'

'*That* I confess,' returned Lady Clancare, laughing, 'surpasses my oracular divinations. I trust, however, it is sufficient to sanction the infringement of one of the most strictly observed laws in the statute book of – Ballydab. -- But whatever be the pur-/port of your visit, I honestly confess you owe your admission to the simplicity of my maid -- a little Tipperary nymph, and a stranger, whom I have just brought to this country, and whom I have not yet had time to initiate into all the mysteries of her vocation. My seclusion,' she added earnestly, 'is no *affectation,* no lure to quicken curiosity, or attract attention. It is indispensable that I should live much alone; my peculiar situation demands it, my circumstances enforce it, my avocations require it. You, however, have taken me by surprise; may I, therefore, beg to know the purport of the visit so unexpected?'

'The purport, Madam,' said General Fitzwalter, 'of this visit, which certainly demands an apology for such unwarranted intrusion, is to return *this handkerchief to its right owner.'* /

He arose as he spoke, and drawing from his breast the handkerchief, dropped by Lord Fitzadelm, presented it to Lady Clancare. Her complexion, which had varied to hues of every shade of red as she spoke, now faded to an unearthly paleness. The ardent eyes of General Fitzwalter pursued its flight, and contributed, perhaps, by the intensity of their gaze, to recall it to the surface it had deserted.

'And to whom, then,' she asked, in a low and unsteady voice, 'do *you* suppose this handkerchief belongs?'

'I did,' he replied, emphatically, 'suppose this morning, from particular circumstances, that it might belong to a lady of the name of Florence Macarthy, a kinswoman of your ladyship, a refugée nun from Spanish America, and now, as I have just accidentally learned, a resident in a convent in / the neighbourhood of Holy-cross. Her father served for a short time in the Guerilla war of South America: his death, which was the purchase of my life, imposed on me an obligation I *would* have requited to his daughter; but –' he paused in some confusion, then rapidly added – 'Of the early part of this gallant man's story I know little; for he had assumed a Caraquian name, having in horror and disgust abandoned the royal and persecuting army. It was from his death-words only that I gathered his connexion with the illustrious house of Macarthy in this country. That he was high-spirited and brave, I collected from my own observation; that he was unfortunate, and in exile, it was natural to suppose, for he was an Irishman, and a catholic.'

Lady Clancare had listened to this detail with an averted head; she now turned round, with the deep inspiration / of one who suddenly recovers from a shock in which the mind and body had alike participated. She opened the handkerchief, ran her eyes rapidly over it, and observed, carelessly – 'There is no doubt this little scarf must be Florence Macarthy's: here is the cross, the holy device of these fanciful saints, who you see, general, must have their *prettinesses in piety,* and are women even to the last; and here are the initials of her name, F. M. Now Florence is spelled with an F, and Macarthy with an M. Here, then, you see are proofs incontrovertible, internal evidences. I know the *caligraphy* of her needle: this is *her work;* there is her favourite stitch; take two threads, drop three, and cross over.ᶠ I remember it well. I have seen it thrown over her shoulders an hundred times in our stolen twilight walks; for these cloistered creatures are coy even to the very / air; "the chartered libertine,"[258] which blows on all alike, the sinner or the saint: and yet, to my knowledge, my cousin has not been in this part of the country since she took up her residence with our lady of the Annunciation; and though she has not yet renewed her vows, I believe she holds herself religiously bound

"For aye, to be in shady cloister mewed,
Chaunting faint hymns to the cold fruitless moon."[259] g

Besides, she is so sober, stedfast, and demure, that she would scarcely step out of her way to woo a soul to heaven, much less to *fling the handkerchief.* Come, confess; have you then been besieging her convent, opposing your military tactics to the whole army of martyrs, and has she sent you this appropriate device as a flag of defiance or of truce, / till further parley, and am I to be the *herald,* the negotiator?'

The sudden transition of Lady Clancare's look, the playful ease which suc-ceeded to her evident but transient consternation, the rapidity of her utterance, and the directness of her question, confounded General Fitzwalter. A new-born surmise, which for a moment had arisen out of her confusion, was stifled in its birth; and his suspicions, as to the mysterious and invisible mistress of Lord Adelm, were lost, or rather no longer remembered, as he listened to a rallying pleasantry which he was wholly unprepared to answer, and unconsciously took up the handkerchief which Lady Clancare had thrown on the table.

'I have only this morning learned,' he replied, 'that Miss Macarthy was in this country: nor do I hold myself at liberty to reveal more of the strange / circum-stances connected with this handkerchief, which your ladyship insists to have been her's, than that it came by romantic and singular means into the hands of a person who prized it much, who knows not that it is now in mine; and that we are both, though from different motives, interested in discovering the real owner.'

'I think the initials sufficiently indicate,' said Lady Clancare, gravely, 'that it is, or has been, the property of Florence Macarthy: but, after all, the fact may be that she has bestowed it upon some young novice, or convent boarder; some fondled little friend *de par l'eglise*.[260] These feminine interchanges of good-will are perpetually passing between the ladies and their laical companions. It makes a part of the occupation of their pious idleness: and the young worldlings frequently exhibit in a ball-room what has been / worked in a cell.[h] If the hand-kerchief, therefore, *has been thrown at you,* General Fitzwalter, as you loitered in some country town, or reproachfully sent to you with the pretty device of

"When this you see,

Remember me,

Though far asunder we may be,"[261]

or if you yourself took it, the owner nothing loath to wipe away tears worth an Hebe's smiles,[262] and now wish to return it, with an heart wrapped up in it, no longer of any use to the present owner; or if you –'

'To spare your ladyship any further conjectures,' said General Fitzwalter, with a countenance rather expressive of annoyance, 'I must repeat to you, the hand-kerchief is not mine, was neither sent to, nor intended for me; and the object of this intrusion goes no further than to learn from your ladyship if – / that is, where, or how –' he paused and coloured. The eyes of Lady Clancare now archly fixed his, and again confounded him. He threw himself back into his chair, and petulantly, but with the naïveté of one whose feelings goaded him beyond all power of disguise, added, 'The fact is, Madam, I scarcely remember what was the object of my visit.'

'Pray, do not hurry yourself,' said Lady Clancare, resuming her serious and demure look. 'I will await your leisure, General Fitzwalter. It is now sufficient for me to know that you were the friend of the gallant Colonel Macarthy, that you are interested for his daughter. You may, therefore, of course, command me. Her interests, her happiness, are mine. I might almost say her story is mine; and add with Celia, of her cousin Rosalind, who was, like myself, *one out of sorts with fortune*, /

"We still have slept together,
Rose at an instant, learned, played, eat together,
Still coupled and inseparable."[263 i]

I would do much to effect the happiness of Florence Macarthy: I have done much; – too much, perhaps; but hitherto I have failed, wholly failed.'

She spoke with a voice of great emphasis, a countenance of great emotion, indicating a capability of powerful and passionate feelings: then *hemmed* away a sigh, drew forward her spinning wheel, and gave up her attention very strenuously to arranging the cobweb thread upon its real: then placing her little foot upon the pedal, and turning the wheel rapidly round, she gave one sly demure look at General Fitzwalter, and awaited in patient expectation the narration which she anticipated, but which he was less than ever enabled to make. He had hung earnestly upon her emphatic declaration of friendship for / Florence Macarthy; he had watched the arrangements of the primitive and picturesque task on which she was now engaged.[j] The quick motion of the prettiest foot he had ever seen, carelessly, but inevitably displayed, the delicate fingers which twisted and drew out the fine-spun thread, with fairy nimbleness, the occasional throwing back of her dark divided hair, and the changing hues of a complexion which bore testimony to the consciousness of being gazed at, rendered even her silence eloquent, and combined to form a picture new, and, therefore, fascinating to her sole observer. His modes of existence had indeed led him but rarely into those walks of society in which woman appears with all the superadded attraction of mind, talent, and the graces.

He now leaned on his arm, with his eyes fixed on her figure, silent, intent, and yielding to the fascination of an in-/fluence, of which, at the moment, he was scarcely conscious. All that he heard and saw was new to him; his own position was a novelty; and his fresh unworn feelings, his vehement and impetuous passions, took warmly and deeply the impressions, which, an object to him so extraordinary and so attractive, was so unsuspectingly making. The conventional tastes of certain circles were no indisputable guides to his preferences; his feelings, not his vanity, decided his prepossessions: he was a man whom the world had not yet spoiled; passionate, ardent, energetic.[k] He saw before him a woman betraying her vocation, to feel and to please in every fibre, lineament, feature and motion: he beheld her distinguished by spirit, feeling, softness, and gaiety; and by that talent, so pardonable even in a woman, the talent of amusing, by that charm so delightful in all, in every thing / that possesses it, the charm of endless variety; the whole guarded by a modesty which even licentiousness dared not violate, and set off with an occasional shyness, the lingering habit of seclusion sometimes dispelled, but never totally overpowered. He saw all this, and saw – nought beside. Lord Adelm, the handkerchief, Miss Macarthy, the purport and object of his visit, were all alike forgotten; even O'Leary's prophecy and assurance of the potency of his liege lady were no longer remembered. There was now but one object in creation for him, and that was the Bhan Tierna. Meantime the wheel went merrily round; many a circling thread was spun off, many an impulse given to the twirling reel, and its monotonous hum was alone interrupted by Lady Clancare's carelessly adverting to the primitiveness of her occupation, probably for the purpose of breaking an awkward silence. /

'This is a rude rustic work,' she observed, 'for *ladies*' fingers, but our grand-mothers of the highest rank in Ireland were all spinners. This wheel belonged to the last Lady Clancare, who had the blood royal of Ireland in her veins. My grandfather preserved it for me, and he had little else to bequeath me. It has already obtained me some celebrity. I am reckoned an excellent spinner; and in fact I like it beyond all other work. I like its humming noise, which disturbs the dreary tranquillity of the long winter evenings, which I pass here alone in my "*Val chiusa.*"[264] It relieves my worn-out eyes from the dazzle of the paper, on which necessity has urged me to trace so much nonsense, that I may live, and others may laugh; for possibly you *have* heard, General Fitzwalter, that I am, by *divine indignation,* a – a *sort* of an author *un maniére d'esprit*, and it is quite true. With / Ireland in my heart, and epitomizing something of her humour and her sufferings in my own character and story, I *do* trade upon the materials she furnishes me; and turning my patriotism into pounds, shillings, and pence, endeavour, at the same moment, to serve her and support myself. Meantime my wheel, like my brain, runs round. I spin my story and my flax together; draw out a chapter and an hank in the same moment; and frequently break off the *thread* of my reel and of my *narration* under the influence of the same association; for facts will obtrude upon fictions, and the sorrows I idly feign are too frequently lost in the sufferings I actually endure.'

'The sufferings you endure!' interrupted Fitzwalter. 'You! gracious heaven! You, who look the very personification of health, spirit, and enjoyment!'

'Enjoyment!' she repeated, shaking / her head, and throwing her eyes significantly from the bare walls of the gloomy apartment to its cold earth floor.

'Yes,' he said, replying to her look, 'if external objects were any thing to *you,* that may be true: but with a spirit apparently so buoyant – a spirit that sparkles in your eye, varies your complexion, gives life, soul, and animation to every feature, and every word you utter; with an imagination to create around you a perpetual Paradise, an imagination –'

'An imagination,' she interrupted eagerly, 'to exalt every anguish, to exaggerate every suffering, to embellish the distant good, and embitter the present evil, to oppose the dreariness and privation of a rude and ungenial solitude, to all the refined and elegant tastes of polished social life, whose details passing through the prismatic medium of fancy, like the broken and / worthless particles flung into the kaleidoscope,[265] arrange themselves in symmetric beauty and harmonic colouring, to charm and to deceive, and to assume forms, hues, and lustre, beyond their own intrinsic qualities.'

'But, good God!' he exclaimed, seduced by a frankness so flattering, struck by a detail, which in delivery opposed the energy of strong feelings to the playfulness of constitutional gaiety, 'your solitude after all must be an act of choice, an election made for the noblest purposes – for serving your compatriots; for cherishing in retreat the enthusiasm, the true source of genius, and which is so soon lost in the passionless trifling circles of society. You have only to appear in the world and to –'

'And to be shewn off like a wild beast; as *the woman that writes the books*; to be added to the ménagerie of such lion leaders as that half ma- /niac Lady Dunore; to "con wit by rote,"[266] and "*desennuyer la sottise;*"[267] and then, having worn out curiosity with novelty, to be sent back to my den, with an assurance from my keeper that I am perfectly harmless, and not half so dangerous as might be supposed. Oh! no, better, far better, that I should be shut up with my Irish inheritance of pride, poverty, and talent; better leave the mind in the spacious circuit of its own musing, to feed upon its own resources, to associate only with the deep loneliness of its own feelings: better remain amidst the scenes of my wild, uncultivated childhood, and unknown, unseen, steal silently through an insignificant life, watch through each successive

– "Drizzling day
Again too trace the wintry brake of snow;
Or sooth'd by western airs, again survey
The *self-same* hawthorn bud and cowslips blow.'"[268] /

She smiled, paused, and then continued: – 'Here, at least, I stand aloof from debasing protection, from the taunt of envy, and the sneer of malignity, the overbearing of upstart pride, the contumely of self-satisfied ignorance. Here, too, I still do some good. I thwart the evil genii of the place, the OGRISH Crawleys; immortalize the supercilious folly of my neighbours, which, even here, *would* look down upon me with that hatred, "*all blockheads bear to wit*;"[269] colonize my dear little Clotnotty-joy; encourage the arts, by allowing two and eightpence halfpenny per week to a piper; and give "*my little senate laws*"[270] – the Cato and Lycurgus[271] of the flourishing city of Ballydab. Besides, I do much in giving an example of constant ceaseless industry and activity to my people. When I am not writing, for I write for bread, I am planting potatoes, or presiding over turf /

bogs; or I am seated with my wheel in a barn, in the midst of the would-be loitering, lounging, lazy matrons of Clotnotty-joy; and when the Bhan Tierna's wheel goes round, every wheel in the parish turns with it. For in these remote districts, as all through Ireland, a long train of unhappy circumstances, political and local, greatly increased since the Union by the absence of our nobility and gentry, have reduced the peasantry to an indigence only to be estimated by being seen; and from the very inadequate remuneration of labour, have introduced inveterate habits of sloth. Labour is pain, and idleness must naturally prevail, wherever the incitements to industry are wanting to overpower the constant tendency of human nature to inertness. A few insulated examples of well-meaning individuals are not sufficient to effect a very general reformation, which will not take place till / artificial wants become as pressing as the natural ones. Yet poor and unassisted as I am, I think even I could do much, could I only persuade the people about me to want bacon for their dinner, and shoes for their feet. But as long as they are content to subsist on potatoes, and are satisfied to go barefooted, there is nothing to be done. What must have been the state and government of that land, in which a vigorous and spirited population, a people naturally so acute, so active, and ingenious, are reduced to submit, without repining, to privations the most degrading, and to wretchedness below the unaccommodated ambition of beasts of the field.[m] With the prejudices which run so strongly in favour of the representatives of their ancient chiefs on my side, born and reared among them, speaking their language, and assimilating to them in a thousand ways, I / have excited rebellion against my sovereign authority, by the innovations of erecting chimneys and filling up pools; and all my arguments are answered with – "*Och! long life to you, my lady; sure you'll lave us our taste of smoke, Madam, any how, that keeps the heat in us through the long winter, and not a skreed to cover us. And musha! sure the pool, why, is the life of us, Madam, in regard of the little ducks and pigs; for what would we do with them, only for the pool, my lady? and only them to pay the rint, and keep a rag on the childre.*" The worst of it is that it is all true,' she added, shaking her head. 'But pray, what do you think of me, General Fitzwalter, in the character of Mrs. Larry Hooleghan, pleading the cause of her *pigs and poultry?*'

As she asked this question, she laid her laughing face on her arms, which / were now folded on her silent wheel, and fixed her dark, round arched eyes on those of her auditor.

'*What do I think of you,*' he exclaimed abruptly, and drawing his chair closer to her's, yet with an air of eager impressiveness, which shewed him unconscious of the act. 'To tell you all I think of you, would perhaps be as impossible as to follow the changes of your character and your countenance, which have all the brightness and evanescence of a rainbow. What I think of you now is lost in what I think of you a moment after. Nor can I, in the Lady Clancare of to-day, trace one feature of the Lady Clancare, whom I beheld, for the first time, a prisoner in the hall of Dunore castle.'

'Well,' she replied laughing, 'I sometimes almost lose my own identity; for I am absolutely beyond my own control, and the mere creature of cir-/cumstances, giving out properties like certain plants, according to the region in which I am placed; and resembling the blossom of the Chinese shrub, which is red in the sunshine and white in the shade,[272] and fades and revives under the influence of the peculiar atmosphere in which it is accidentally placed. The strong extremes, and wild vicissitudes of my life, have perhaps given a variegated tone to my character, and a versatility to my mind, not its natural endowments. Abandoned in my infancy by my parents, who went to Spain, my mother's native land; left to the care of my genuinely Irish, improvident, and enthusiastic grandfather; brought up with all his Irish pride and prepossessions, among his greyhounds and finders,[273] on the mountains; left a charge upon the rent-roll of Providence; forced by poverty, and the prejudice of my mother, into a Spanish convent; / breaking the thraldom which held me in bigotted slavery; and joyfully following a widowed father amidst the privations of a military life, in a distant land, reduced to close his eyes among the dying and the dead; helpless, hopeless, returning to my native land, to seek the protection of my aged grandfather – to find it in a jail; to labour for his support and my own; and, by the light which shone through his prison bars, to trace scenes of fancied joy and ideal happiness; thrown upon life, friendless, unprotected, and dependent upon my own exertions for subsistence, I have continued always before the world, yet always in seclusion; known to all in my public capacity, to none in my private character; carrying into society the awkwardness of a recluse, the susceptibility of sensitive feeling, equally alive to notice or to slight; but in the freedom of intimacy, to the touch / of sympathy, in communion with kindred minds, borne away by the ardour of my nature, and indulging the easy, extravagant playfulness of my constitutional gaiety; still loving the world, yet unable to live in it; *enduring* solitude, not *enjoying* it; living without hope, as without fear; blessed with health, and animated by a spirit, that never yet struck sail, to vileness, dependence, or oppression; noble by chance, an author by necessity, and a woman –' she paused for an instant, and then hastily added, 'I have given you this little auto-biography, General Fitzwalter, to save you the trouble of *guessing at me*, for I see you have been conning me over, as children do conundrums, beginning with my first, and getting on to my second, but quite in the dark as to the strange combination which makes my *tout*.[274] It now lies before you; and I have thus intruded upon the right of / intimacy, and kidnapped you into an unsought confidence, because you have been long known to me; because your position, with respect to Florence Macarthy, is known to me: this is my sanction, my excuse. I know you are going to employ me, and I thus put you in possession of my *bearings*, before you instal me in my agency.'

They had now both arisen; General Fitzwalter in amazement, in emotion, and admiration, he had no power or inclination to conceal; Lady Clancare, with the colour heightening in her cheek, and her manner less collected, less easy, less disengaged, than when she had first began to speak. There was a breathless anxiety in her countenance when she paused; an apprehensiveness that seemed relieved by the door opening, and entrance of the maid, who stepped up and whispered something in her ear. Whatever this communi-/cation might be, it excited considerable confusion; and when the girl had received her answer, and had hurried out of the room, Lady Clancare, turning round in great embarrassment, said, 'General Fitzwalter, you must leave me instantly. Whatever you may have to say relative to Colonel Macarthy's daughter, it must be reserved for another moment; not now – pray go. This may seem strange, but it is inevitable; and let me entreat –' she clasped her hands, and spoke with great earnestness – 'let me entreat you will not take the road you came – the Dunore road. – Turning to your left, you will come out upon the beach. My maid will conduct you. The tide must be *out, or in:* if *out,* you can ride along the strand; if in, my boat is moored among the rocks. You can paddle it easily: I do myself – and your horse shall be sent after you to O'Leary's. I / had it put up as I entered. Now then go – farewell.' He took the hand she extended to him, and holding it firmly, though it gently struggled in his grasp, he said, 'I will go in any way you wish me to go; but tell me as frankly as I ask the question, is Lord Adelm Fitzadelm the person you expect? for I perceive I am in somebody's way.'

Lady Clancare interrupted him with the quickness of lightning, and haughtily liberating her hand, she repeated, 'Lord Adelm! – General Fitzwalter, you are the first person of your sex and rank who ever obtruded upon this solitude, where pride and poverty have sought an asylum which delicacy and prudence should have rendered inviolable.'

She turned away her head; but not before he had perceived her eyes glistening with tears, prompt as her smiles, but infinitely more dangerous. They were the first tears he had ever brought / to a woman's eye; and from whatever source they sprang, however inadequate their cause, and he felt they *were* inadequate, their effect was electric: they left him shocked and confounded, covered with shame and self-reproach. Lady Clancare was moving towards the door: he followed, and prevented her exit.

'Lady Clancare,' he said, 'you must take me as I am, as one under the influence of tyrannical feelings, habitually but vainly combatted. You have thrown me off my guard. I have offended you unwarily: hear me a moment; I will explain to you ....'

'No, no, not now. You must leave me; you must not be seen here,' she answered in a hurried voice.

'I will *not* leave you be the consequence what it may, till you promise me another, an immediate opportunity of seeing you. I *must* see you, for my / own sake, for Florence Macarthy's sake, for your sake, perhaps.'

Lady Clancare turned aside her head as he spoke. Something between a smile and a frown struggled on her countenance, and she replied,

'I ought not, I cannot receive you here by appointment under my own roof. You can write to Florence Macarthy: I will convey your letter: I will do every thing to forward *her* happiness, short of endangering my own character; but leave me now, I entreat, *I insist.*'

'I have written,' he said, producing a letter, 'but –' he hesitated, and still held it back, as if unwilling to part with it, – 'but I know not how far this letter may now –'

Lady Clancare snatched it eagerly, and placed it in her bosom. 'There,' she said, 'she shall have it immediately: you may depend on me where she / is concerned, and I will forward you her answer. I told you you would employ me: but remember, this visit, so *unexpected on my part*, so unwarranted on your's, is not to be repeated, and never to be revealed – remember that.'

'*Never to be revealed!* I swear solemnly,' he replied with energy: 'but by all that is sacred, I will not leave this country without seeing you again; without seeing you *here*. Observe me, Lady Clancare, I am a man who has fought against a wayward fortune: by the force of perseverance, firmness, decision, and enterprize, success has followed the bias of these natural impulsions. I have no other guides, and I shall still obey them. If you are the owner of that handkerchief; if you are the person who –' He paused, and then added in a hurried tone, 'that ascertained, I shall then come once more, and bid you an eternal farewell. If Florence / Macarthy, on the contrary, is the invisible demon or angel who follows, or rather leads the steps of Lord Adelm, then –'

'The marchioness is walking up the court, my lady, and has left her coach at the gates below,' said the maid, putting in her wild head with a fluttered look. Lady Clancare stamped her little foot with impatience. 'Go now, for God's sake,' she cried.

'Do *you* then,' he said, seizing her hand, and with a countenance which had undergone a rapid change since the maid had announced Lady Dunore as the expected visitor, 'do you return to the castle with her – with Lady Dunore to-day?'

'Yes, yes, I dine there; but if you notice me there, or any where, without my special permission, you lose me for ever – that is, you lose the benefit of my agency with Florence Macarthy. / Now then, pray follow the servant, she will conduct you to the beach.'

He had half raised her hand to his lips while she was speaking, but he suddenly dropped it and followed the maid, who led him through the stone passage to a little door that opened on the strand. There he found his horse fastened by the bridle to an iron anchorage ring in the rocks. The tide was coming in, but he out-galloped its stealing progress, and arrived with incredible celerity at Monaster-ny-Oriel.

He found O'Leary before the door of the chauntry, exposing to the air a large open deal box, lined with pictures of saints and devils, sacrifices and canonizations, his countenance full of bustling importance, and his voice raised to the highest pitch, singing Carolan's famous '*Receipt for Drinking.*'[275]

'I was just, plaze your honor,' said O'Leary, coming forward to take the ge-/neral's horse as he alighted, 'I was just airing my chest, Sir, in respect of getting ready for our journey, and was conning in my own mind, when your honor galloped up, whether it would contain my Genealogical History of the Macarthies, or whether I'd divide them into two turf kishes, just to make a shew travelling through the country; for when *Carte* got lave to take the Ormonde papers out of the evidence chamber at Kilkenny castle, to compose the life of the great *Duke of Ormonde*, he filled three *Irish cars* with them;[276] and I'd be sorry, troth, but the documents of the real Irish Macarthies-More, Kings of Munster, would be of less bulk than the papers of them Saxon churls, the Butlers.'

'I am afraid, however,' said the general, smiling, 'we must dispense with their honourable burthen in our immediate journey, O'Leary.' /

'*We must, gineral?*' replied O'Leary, in a tone of mortification, 'and there being mixed through the Macarthy papers many notes and codices,' he added, in a whispering voice, 'that might be sarvicable on the trial; for they'll fight a great fight afore they give up, Sir, and right vanquisheth might.'

'I am not so certain of that,' said General Fitzwalter; 'but at all events, O'Leary, I shall not leave this country so soon as I expected.'

'You won't, gineral?' he replied, with a countenance expressive of curiosity and surprise; then, after a pause, he added, 'och, then I'll have my documents home from the lord-deputy before we start. And thinks Moriagh will plaze you the day in regard of a dinner, Sir, and ordered a bottle of Portugal wine from the Dunore Arms for myself, your honor, just in honor / of the day,' and he looked at the general significantly.

'I'm glad of it,' said the general; 'but I shall not dine here; I dine at Dunore castle.'

O'Leary started, put his hand under his wig, with a look of perplexity, but only repeated 'at Dunore Castle!' then giving the horse to one of his scholars, who was waiting about the ruins, he followed the general to his tower, observing, 'Well, gineral, so you didn't see the Bhan Tierna after all, I'll ingage.'

'Why should you think that?'

'Because, plaze your honor, I heard she was in the mountains the morning, seeing the praties got in, and sorrow a foot she'd lave that for the King of England if he was to come to see her. Och! she's a great farmer, and has done more for Clotnotty-joy in a year and a half than the Crawleys ever could, in / respect of the hearts and hands of the whole country being with her, and her giving every man his own little lase.'

To this observation the general made no reply; and they ascended the stairs together; the guest to dress, and the host, under pretence of assisting him, to loiter about his person. /

NOTES.

(1) Page 121. – It is natural that the natives of an oppressed country should sympathize with the oppressed wherever they may exist. Many Irish names are to be found among the gallant advocates of liberty in South America.

Colonel O'Higgens was appointed commander-in-chief of the patriot army in 1813, and afterwards was made supreme director of Chili. Colonel *M'Kenna* was appointed second in command; and Mr. Brown, with the title of admiral, took command of a flotilla, and blockaded Montevidio.[n]

(2) Page 170. – 'Though the number of monks and nuns now recited is by no means to be depended on, yet it suggested to their presidents the necessity of stone inclosures or classes; these in the east were called mandrae. The word originally imported a sheep-fold, and was applied to those monastic buildings, wherein the archimandrite presided over his disciples, as the shepherd superintended his flock in the fold. /

There are many of these mandrae dispersed over this kingdom, hitherto unnoticed. One remarkable is Dun Aengus. This is in the greater Isle of Arran, on the coast of Galway, situated on a high cliff over the sea, and is a circle of monstrous stones, without cement, and capable of containing two hundred cows. The tradition relative to it is, that Aengus, King of Cashel, about 490, granted this isle, called Arrannaomh, or Arran of the Saints, to Saint Enna or Endeus, to build ten churches on.'

Ledwich.[o]

(3) Page 211. – 'These tiernas were what Davis calls confinues, canfimies, con finnie – *the heads of clans*. We had our Clanbreasil, Clancarty, Clanaboy, Clancolman, Clanfergal, and many more. In most cases the tierna's sirname was that of his clan. Macarthy was Riagh, or King of Desmond; his tiernas were the clans O'Keefe, O'Donaughu, O'Callaghan, O'Sullivan, and the last by his tenure was obliged – First – To aid Macarthy with all his strength, and to be marshal of his army. Second – He was to pay for every arable plough-land five galloglasses or kerns, or six shillings and eightpence, or a beef for each, at the option of Macarthy. Third – Macarthy was to receive half-a-crown for every ship that came to fish or trade in O'Sul-/livan's harbour. Fourth – O'Sullivan was to give Macar-

thy merchandize at the rate he purchased it. Fifth – O'Sullivan was to entertain Macarthy and all his train two nights at Dunbay, and whenever he travelled that way. Sixth – O'Sullivan was to send horse-meat to Paillice for Macarthy's saddle horses, and pay the groom three shillings and fourpence out of every arable plough-land. Seventh – O'Sullivan was to find hounds, greyhounds, and spaniels for Macarthy, whenever he came, and one shilling and eightpence annually to his huntsman out of every plough-land.'

 Ledwich's Antiquities of Ireland.

The first head of O'Sullivan's tenure proves that a military association and subordination universally prevailed, and these were the essentials of the feudal system. His being marshal of Macarthy clearly evinces that grand serjeantry was in use. As this is a tenure in capite, and could only be held from a sovereign prince, if this was a feudal tenure, as it must be allowed it was, then there can be no doubt but the other services were likewise feudal. Through all the subinfeudation, there was the same obligation of military duty. If any from neglect or perfidy disobeyed the call of their lord, he compelled them by force of arms, or expelled them from their possessions, for they owed military service / by their tenures. An ancient poet thus expresses the feudal call and penalty.[p]

'The original exactions of the Irish kings were:

Bonaht – a tax for the maintenance of the galloglasses, kerns, and other military.

Scrohen – a tax on freeholders for the entertainment of soldiers.

Coshery – a custom of exacting entertainment for the king and his followers from those under his jurisdiction.

Cuddy, or suppers.

Shragh and mart – imposed at the will of the lord, and levied partly in cattle or food.[q]'

(4) Page 225. – Kilmallock, in the County of Limerick, a city of conspicuous figure in the military history of Ireland, and still exhibiting one of the most curious monuments of antiquity, being a desolate and nearly uninhabited town, with castles, antique mansions, ruinous indeed, but preserving extant the peculiar features of domestic architecture in Ireland as it existed many centuries back.[r]

(5) Page 234. – Specimens still remain of this manufacture in many ancient Irish mansions. / The author believes that some of the tapestry in Kilkenney Castle was done by Irish nuns.[s]

(6) Page 240. – 'When Florence Macarthy submitted to the queen, in the midst of a troop of forty of his clan, himself, like Saul, higher by an head and shoulders than his followers, the president entertained him greatly, hoping by his submission that the wars were ended in Munster. Florence left two hostages, his base-brother and his foster-brother, both of whom he held in precious esteem.

'Among all the Irish septs in Desmond, or South Munster, the Macarthys, before the arrival of the English, were by far the most eminent, being sovereigns of the whole country; but after their best lands were subdued by the English adventurers, the chief of this potent clan retired into Kerry, as to a place of security, the southern part of the country being then almost inaccessible, because of its mountains, woods, and fastnesses. His successor, Daniel Macarthy-More-ni-Carra, so named from the river Carra in this country, concluded a peace with the English in 1196. Their posterity were very eminent people, and great disturbers of the English, particularly the Fitzgerald family, who dispossessed them of a considerable part of their / country. In these contests great numbers were slain; and at Callon, in this country, the Macarthys gained a complete victory, anno 1261, over the Fitzgeralds; but at length dissensions arising among the followers of Macarthy, the Fitzgeralds (or Geraldines) prevailed in their turn, and kept them under for many years. However, a great regard was always paid to the chiefs of this family, who retained the title of Macarthy-More, one of whom, named Donald, was ennobled by Queen Elizabeth, who, in 1565, created him earl of Glencare, a tract of land in this country between the Bay of Dingle and the River of Kinmare. This earl having resigned his estates to the queen, had it restored and re-granted by letters-patent, to hold it of the crown after the English manner. She also conferred many ample privileges on him, and paid the expense of his journey into England; but by the advice of O'Neil, who rebelled in Ulster, Macarthy pursued his example in the south, and even assumed the title of king of Munster. These chiefs joined their forces together in 1560, but before the expiration of the year Macarthy was forced to submit to the lord-deputy, and craved the queen's pardon. This earl afterwards sat in a parliament held at Dublin on the 26th of April, 1584, by Sir John Perrat, who, from the presidency of Munster, was ap- /pointed lord deputy of Ireland. He gave the government of the county of Desmond to this earl of Glencare, who died soon after, leaving behind him an only daughter, Ilin or Ellen, and an illegitimate son, called Daniel, who assumed the title of earl, but was dispossessed of it by Florence Macarthy, son to Sir Donough Macarthy, Reagh of Carberry, in the county of Cork, who marrying Ellen, took possession of the estate, and assumed the title of Macarthy-More, which was confirmed to him by O'Neil, who called himself king of Ireland. Florence and his followers joined O'Neil, who, by the queen, was created Earl of Tyrone, and also the Earl of Desmond, in their rebellion, as may be seen in the annals of this country.'

*See Smith's Cork and Kerry.*ʳ

END OF VOL. III. /

FLORENCE MACARTHY:

An Irish Tale.

by

LADY MORGAN,

AUTHOR OF 'FRANCE,' 'O' DONNEL' &c.

Know thus far forth:
By accident most strange, bountiful fortune,
Now, my dear lady, hath mine enemies
Brought to this shore: and by my prescience,
I find my zenith doth depend upon
A most auspicious star, whose influence,
If now I court not but omit, my fortunes
Will ever after droop.
SHAKESPEARE.[1]

Les femmes ne sont pas trop d'humeur à pardonner de certaines injures, et quand elles se promettent le plaisir de la vengeance elles n'y vont pas de *main-morte*.
DE GRAMMONT.[2]

IN FOUR VOLUMES.

VOL. IV.

LONDON:
PRINTED FOR HENRY COLBURN,
PUBLIC LIBRATRY, CONDUIT STREET, HANOVER SQUARE.
1818.
B. CLARKE, Printer, Well Street, London. /

FLORENCE MACARTHY.

CHAPTER I.

He seems to have the quotidian of love upon him.
                                        SHAKESPEARE.[3]

I'll venture – for my new enlivened spirits prompt me.
                                        MILTON.[4a]

GENERAL FITZWALTER was dressed for dinner a full hour before the usual time of assembling at Dunore Castle. All his motions were involuntarily accelerated: a feverish restlessness urged his most trivial actions: his whole existence had received a new impulsion by the operation of one unaccustomed and absorbing sentiment: an overpowering motive had unexpectedly sprung up to actuate his conduct, and the obedient / will followed its spring with a promptitude and energy consonant to his nature and his habits.

Woman, who had hitherto imperiously governed his senses now, for the first time, obtained a moral influence over his mind, and became, not the object of a caprice, but of a passion; and passion, whatever might be its cause, was his element.

The person of Lady Clancare was not particularly distinguished by its beauty, but it was characteristic. Fresh, healthful, and intelligent, she had neither the symmetry of statuary loveliness nor the brilliant colouring of pictured charms; but she was piquante, graceful, and vivacious: her mouth and teeth were well compared by O'Leary to those of a young hound; her head was picturesque, and her whole appearance the very personification of womanhood. Silent, and at rest, she was scarcely dis-/tinguishable from the ordinary class of women; but when her countenance was thrown into play, when she spoke with the anxiety or the consciousness of pleasing, or under the impression of being pleased, there was a mobility, a variety of expression and colouring, which corresponded with the vigour, spirit, and energy of her extraordinary mind.

This indication, which might have repelled others, was the charm that fascinated Fitzwalter. The kindling susceptibility it betrayed harmonized with his own prompt and impetuous disposition, bespeaking a congeniality of feeling, and a reciprocity of intelligence, which he had never found in man, which he had never sought for in woman, and which, whether it took the calm and steady form of friendship, or the bright intoxicating aspect of love, was still the object of his uncon-/scious research, and the indispensible ingredient of his permanent schemes of happiness. Hitherto he had lived unassociated and solitary in the midst of the universe; his deep and lonely feelings preying on a mind left to its own resources, unanswered, unreciprocated. He now found one, like himself, vigorous in intellect and rapid in action; full of that life and spirit which suited his own habits and modes of being; devoted to that country whose interests was the object of his future life; and drooping, like himself, in that feeble and futile society, whose very atmosphere is fatal to the elevation of great minds, or the vivacity of lively and energetic ones.[b]

This conviction struck at once upon his imagination with that force which accompanied all its strong and promptly received impressions. It awakened his passions in all their natural vehemence; / and, impatient of all suspense, ill-brooking even inevitable delay, he would have gone at once to the 'head and front'[5] of his views and hopes; he would, in his own language, have followed their object 'from pole to pole, over alps and oceans, or have remained fixed and rooted to the spot she inhabited, wooed her, won her, clung to her, and cherished her;' and, according to the startling conclusion of Lord Adelm, 'married her,' but that he was *already married;* married, at least, he considered himself, in honour, in gratitude, until she who shared his bondage voluntarily broke it.

There was too another barrier to the impulse of his passionate feelings. It was just possible that all he admired and all he sought was devoted to another. Those powers and endowments, so attractive in his eyes, might be applied to the subjection of one, who / would only prize them so long as their versatility and ingenuity could confirm and feed his visionary tastes and metaphysical delusions; so long as they could excite ideal prepossessions in favour of the invisible agent, which the actual woman would probably neither awaken nor perpetuate. From several corroborating circumstances, Fitzwalter was almost convinced that Lady Clancare was the Egeria, the demon[6] of Lord Adelm, who had either watched over or bewildered him, had made him the object of her care, or the victim of her caprice, since his arrival in Ireland. Her knowledge of himself, his name, and profession, which she had revealed to Lord Adelm, might have come through details received from her cousin Florence Macarthy; but where she could have seen him in Ireland, or how Miss Macarthy had learned his arrival, were still enigmas. /

That talent and love for the embroglio,[7] which Lady Clancare had herself confessed to have inherited from her Spanish mother, and which took from the simplicity of her character what it added to its spirit and ingenuity, pointed her out as the agent of mystery, who had directed the conduct and led the steps of the accomplished ideologist; and who had summoned around her 'most willing spirits to do her service'[8] in the incongruous forms of Mrs. Magillicuddy, and Owny, the Rabragh. The object of employing so clumsy an agent as the former was not very obvious; but the latter personage was manifestly devoted to her orders, and might for many reasons be deemed capable of promoting her still inexplicable views. He was her foster brother, that bond of service and devotion so sacred in Ireland. She had also relieved him from misery and incarcera-/tion by her exertion and interference. He had conveyed her from Dunore to Dublin, according to O'Leary's account, and he might, on her return to the south, have been naturally summoned to meet her at Cashel, either to carry her home, or to 'do her behests.'[9]

Alert, adroit, gay, humorous, and deviceful, as he evidently was, he might unite to these personal peculiarities qualities inherent in the lower Irish in general. Warm friends and revengeful enemies, inviolable in their secrecy, devoted in their attachments, inexorable in their resentments, entertaining such notions of honour that neither threats nor recompense could induce them to betray a confidence to which they have once pledged themselves, they are obviously adapted to the service of a mysterious agency, whether for a political or a private purpose. Owny, who was a genuine / Irishman of this class,[c] endowed with zeal, activity, and evasion, the qualities of a finely organized, but socially debased people, as one too who owed every thing to Lady Clancare,[d] might, with great probability, have engaged in any scheme to forward the interests of his benevolent patroness, as he would be true to any trust reposed in him, but more especially by that popular Bhan Tierna, whose health he had pledged at the cottage at Lis-na-sleugh with a solemnity almost religious.

This act had not escaped the observation of Fitzwalter, and these suppositions and inferences, quite possible, and more than probable, were gradually worked out, distinctly examined, and rapidly combined in his fluctuating thoughts, as he pursued his way on foot to Dunore castle. To a mind so quick in its perceptions, so energetic in all its workings, slight data were sufficient / to lead to a just result; and his natural acuteness got the start in this, as in many other instances, of progressive investigation.

To detect Lady Clancare in her concealed and mysterious character was one thing; to ascertain the motive to arrive at the object of her singular, and almost equivocal conduct, was another. His life had not been a life of reflection; and woman, though frequently an object of his devotion, had never been to him a subject of analysis. Yet he knew enough of the general principles of human nature to understand that human conduct must be motived by passion, and he could conceive but one passion incidental to female existence – and that was love. All that he had known of the sex or the sex's tendencies had been acquired under the voluptuous influence of tropical climes, among the moon-eyed beauties / of India, the languid dames of Mexico and Peru; and he^e would have decided at once that Lady Clancare was in love with Lord Adelm, but that the supposition was too painful to indulge. He knew not why, but it maddened him; and he was rescued from its poignancy by the reflection that Lord Adelm had never seen her, but on her first appearance in the hall of Dunore, when she had given him the impression of being a mere *minaudiere,* a caprice of his mother, having recourse to stratagem to procure an introduction to the insipid circle which Lady Dunore had grouped around her. As a woman of talent, one too who had obtained celebrity by that talent, Lord Adelm would have detested her; and that spirit and vigour of mind, which made her charm with Fitzwalter, would have rendered her insupportable in the eyes of one who placed the perfection of woman in her / fatuity, and who knew no medium between the *pretenders* of the *Hotel Rambouillet,*[10] and the unideaed beauties of a Turkish seraglio.^{f} Still he believed, that in spite of her equivocal and playful evasion, the handkerchief found by Lord Adelm was purposely dropped by Lady Clanclare. The motive of this mystery, as well as the train of events in which he had in some respects been involved himself since his arrival in Ireland, remained unfathomable. The agent and chief mover was still (he reflected himself into the conviction) the singular Bhan Tierna, whom O'Leary represented as one endowed with the art of vanquishing whom she pleased, and whose powers were darkly sketched, according to the genealogist of the Macarthies, in the obscure and remote prophecies of Friar Con.^{g}

The suspicions which now gradually lighted on the head of Lady Clancare / were necessarily withdrawn from Florence Macarthy, the refugee of the Convent of the Annunciation. With this person, the fate of General Fitzwalter was strangely linked. His connexion with the daughter of the brave Colonel Macarthy, to which he had alluded in his conversation with Lady Clancare, and with which, to his amazement, and a little to his confusion, that lady had confessed she was already acquainted, was a romantic episode in the strange history of his eventful life. To that event memory referred with a painful sensation, that originated in feelings not at rest with themselves. If there was one circumstance in his life which had left a shadow behind it, it was his connexion with Florence Macarthy. His efforts to become reconciled to himself were reduced to a proposal, which hastily conceived, and as hastily executed, was contained in the letter which / he now lamented having trusted to Lady Clancare. The misery or happiness of his future life might depend upon the answer that letter produced; meantime he was the slave of feelings new to his nature, uncongenial to his habits, but powerfully assimilating with his vehement and restless passions. He was the victim of a suspense intolerable, and wholly at variance with a character formed alike to suffer and to enjoy; but unequal to hang upon the slow course of probabilities, for the sentence which would consign him to bliss or to misery, which he could neither hasten nor control, and which, for the first time, took his destiny out of his own hands, and placed him in subordination to the will or caprice of others.[h] The business which had brought him to Ireland was effected. It was his interest to return immediately to England, and he could give to himself no / plausible cause of delay, but the necessity, he fancied, or believed himself to be under, of waiting an answer to the letter he had dispatched to Florence Macarthy: it would have been more consonant to his habitual modes of acting to have flown himself to her convent, and sought a personal interview, and immediate and decisive sentence: but his feelings opposed themselves to a conduct so natural; and he was more inclined to defer than to expedite personal communication with one, whose presence could only awaken ungracious association, and who was perhaps the only human being in existence before whom he would have blushed to present himself.

After a long slow-paced circuitous rout, considerably lengthened in fact, but apparently shortened in idea by the agitation of his thoughts, and the pre-occupation of his mind, he at last arrived at the portico / of Dunore; and, with the exception of old Crawley, who had left Dunore that morning for Dublin, and of Lord Adelm, who had not yet returned, he found the usual party assembled in the great hall of the castle, and disposed in a manner as ludicrous as it was unexpected.

Lady Dunore occupied the foreground. She stood, with a coarse bib and apron tied over her superb dinner dress of crimson satin, and filled with green rushes, which she was fastening in sheaths. The floor was spread with the same materials, which Mr. Heneage, Mr. Pottinger, and Miss Crawley, were engaged in peeling; while Mr. Daly and Conway Crawley were reading the papers; and Lord Rosbrin, covered with rushes, was spouting 'Mad Tom;'[11] Lord Frederick and Lady Georgina, as usual, were lounging on an ottoman, and laughing together / at the whole party. At the sight of General Fitzwalter, Lady Dunore sprung delightedly forward, and welcomed him with an ardour, for which, even vanity itself, could find no adequate cause.

'This is so good of you,' she said, 'so unexpectedly kind! Fitzadelm endeavoured to persuade me this morning that you were bored to death with us all; that we did not in the least amuse you; that you were engaged in business, and law, and things; that, in short, you would neither breakfast, dine, nor sup with us; and that, as to sleeping, you would as soon take up your lodging in Bedlam. You can't imagine how this fretted and annoyed me, because I wanted you for a particular –' She paused abruptly, and added, 'that is, I wanted you to, to – help me to peel rushes. You see we are all occupied with this rush manu-/factory. I hope, if you settle in this neighbourhood, which perhaps,' she added with a significant look, '*you may*, that you will encourage the rush manufactory; for the whole misery of this country, General Fitzwalter, arises out of the want of work, and food, and things. Isn't it so, Lady Clancare?'

General Fitzwalter followed the direction of this question, and not without emotion perceived Lady Clancare seated in the arm chair at the back of the hall, which the preceding day had been occupied by one of the judges. She looked pale and spiritless, as one exhausted, and under the reaction of over excitement. She coloured, however, slightly at Lady Dunore's appeal, and returned an affirmative, but silent nod of the head. Every one smiled, and this smile increased the colour in her cheek. /

'The fact is,' continued Lady Dunore, following the general's eyes with triumphant satisfaction in her own, 'no one knows any thing of the real state of this country but Lady Clancare. She has given me an entirely new view of things. It is too dreadful, too heart-rending. It is all a tragedy *du plus beau noir*.[12] I have cried myself sick as I drove here.'

Every one tittered; the Crawleys almost audibly; and Lady Clancare coloured deeper than before. 'The miracle is,' said Lady Dunore, in a vehement manner, and wholly ingrossed with her own sensations, 'the miracle is, that they don't all arise and murder us. They will do so soon; and I think they are quite justified. I would not bring them to trial if they were to murder my whole household. I will have no more secret committees, no more green bags, and special com- /missions; "*employ*, not *hang*," *that's my maxim now*. It is, however, curious enough to see people troubling their heads about elections and evangelical schools, and private theatricals, and chapels and Bible societies, and things, when the people to be represented are starving; the people to be edified, amused, and instructed, are literally perishing for want. Give them something to eat first, and then instruct them; teach them to labour, and then to read; give them wants that civilize humanity, and that raise them above the brute creation, and then edify them: for, after all, the first law of nature is *to exist*. People must *live*, in order to live piously; and it is a fact that bread is as necessary as books; and if people will die of the typhus from cold, want, and filth, why they cannot then read the multitude of evangelical tracts which are written for their use, / and population will thin, as tracts multiply. Is it not so, Lady Clancare?'

This question, asked with emphatic gravity, excited new smiles of ridicule or amusement in some, of gratified malignity in other; for all were quite aware, that Lady Dunore's inspiration and authority came from the same source; a source which now, for the moment, ruled the ascendant. Meantime Lady Clancare's downcast, but rapidly moving eyes, seemed to take in the suffrages of the whole circle. She coloured, and only replied to Lady Dunore's parrotted details, with another oracular nod, while the officiating priestess went on, under the influence of her delphic deity.[13]

'No one can be more devoted to the Irish government than I am, and all their measures; and I think our Irish secretary[14] the cleverest little creature in / the world, as I said to the premier,[15] after he made his maiden speech. I said he would distance all the rising young men, none of whom, by the bye, have risen at all; but disappointed us, like the young Roscius, and the boy that told the sums and things; and those tiresome musical children,[16] that did all by rote.[i] As to the vice-regal B –'s, they happen to be my particular friends, and I was quite delighted they got such a good thing, poor dears; and, in fact, they could not have gotten on at all, if they had not been sent over here, and got their thirty thousand a year. But when it comes to considering Ireland in its actual state; and when one hears *you*, Mr. Pottinger, talk of your *Lady-Lieutenant's* encouraging the Irish manufactures, because she wears a tabinet gown on St. Patrick's night,[17] or St. Patrick's day, or in St. Patrick's church; or, what is it, Lord Fre-/ derick, about the *kettle-drums* and things, and Noodle and Doodle?[18] And *you*, Mr. Conway Crawley, talking of the chief secretary's *expedients, and measures of necessary coercion*; *his eminent worth, splendid talents, unremitting zeal, consummate wisdom, and transcendent merit,*[*] and that sort of thing; when all he *can* know of Ireland must be collected from such people as *you* and your *father*; or as he whirls through the country in a chaise and four, to shoot partridge or grouse, or to hunt at Lord *Clon – this,* or Lord *Kill – t'others,* some of your new made lords, par exemple, who are excellent people, only no one cares much about them with us; it's quite too ridiculous! /

Don't you think so, Lady Clancare? and when the prettiest rush-work in the world might be done, and encouraged by them all, as it is done at that very ancient ruinous town of Ballydab, the Irish Balbec,[19] as one may call it. For my part, I shall employ ALL the poor at Dunore at rush-work. I'll have rush sofas, rush chairs, rush mats, rush fillagree, rush lights, and rush carpets; every thing, in short, that can be made of rushes.'

'Then,' said Lord Rosbrin, flourishing about the hall,

"Then shall we wantons, light of heart,

Tickle the senseless rushes with our heels."[20]

Here dinner was announced, and Lord Adelm alighted at the door at the same moment, and went to dress. The rest of the party proceeded to the dining room.

Mr. Daly officiated at the head of / the table, in the place of Lord Fitzadelm. Lady Clancare took the seat her rank assigned her, on his right hand. Lady

---

* The ready-made addresses of the most loyal corporation of Dublin, to all secretaries, past, present, and to come, abound in such epithets of universal eulogium.

Dunore took her's by the side of Lady Clancare; and she contrived to place General Fitzwalter opposite to both, by directing him to a seat, most mal-apropos,[21] between Miss Crawley and her nephew. There was something in the presence of this extraordinary stranger which had become extremely irksome to the Crawleys. They had received a sort of half-given confidence respecting him, from old Crawley, which had terrified and confounded them. He had let fall hints, and suggested possibilities, which broke upon them an event of which they had no suspicion; and though, either in timidity or distrust, he had never fully and explicitly opened his heart to them on a subject which began to oppress his conscience, in proportion as it awakened his / apprehension, they had yet gathered enough to inspire considerable alarm; and they had urged the old man to go to Dublin, previous to the election for Glannacrime, for the purpose of anticipating or frustrating a discovery, which could not long be retarded, and was pregnant with evil to the character, influence, and property, of the whole Crawley family.

Miss Crawley and her nephew now sat silent on either side of their ill-boding neighbour; while Lady Dunore, with her mouth in Lady Clancare's ear, and her eyes fixed on General Fitzwalter, continued wholly inattentive to the rest of her guests.

Lord Adelm entered the room with the second course.

'How did you get on at Glannacrime, Fitzadelm?' asked Lady Dunore, carelessly, as soon as he had finished his soup. /

'I don't know exactly what your ladyship's question points at: but I got off as soon as I could.'

'Did you speak to them?' she returned, with a look of nausea. 'I mean to those horrors, the forty shilling freeholders?'

'Speak! oh, yes, of course, "in wholesome manner,"[22] Madam.'

'Indeed; well, and what did you say, my dear Adelm?' continued Lady Dunore, with a little increasing interest.

'*I bid them wash their faces, and keep clean their teeth, and so troubled them no further.*'[23]

'That must have surprised them,' said Lady Dunore, much pleased with what she took very literally; 'but it was excellent advice.'

'I think it must have astonished them a little,' said Mr. Daly, laughing.

'Yes,' observed Lord Rosbrin, 'it must: but you might have chosen a / better speech, Fitzadelm. You should have said, as I did from the hustings of Kilrosbrin, before they got me into the upper house:

"Your voices. For your voices I have fought:
Watched for your voices: for your voices bear
Of wounds two dozen odd. Battles thrice six
I've seen and heard of. For your voices have
Done many things, some more, some less."'[24]

'And did they believe you, my patrician Coriorosbrin?' asked Lord Frederick, languidly.

'Yes,' replied Lord Rosbrin, abstractedly. 'The first citizen said –

"He has done nobly."

The second citizen –

"Therefore let him be consul.

The gods give him joy, and make him friend

To the people."

And *all* cried –

"Amen! amen! God save the noble consul." [25] /

And then exeunt O. P.[26] I speak from Covent Garden prompt-book.'

Every one laughed but Lord Rosbrin, who was beyond the reach of ridicule, engaged in muttering parts of Coriolanus.[k]

'Had I known of your lordship's intention of visiting Glannacrime this morning,' said young Crawley, 'I should have accompanied you.'

'It was quite unnecessary,' said Lord Adelm, coldly.

'How were you received, Fitzadelm?' asked Mr. Daly.

'Not at all; they did not know me. I look upon it as against the freedom of election to come forward personally. I went, however, to their sessions-house, where a committee was sitting in my favour. I told them Lord Adelm's opinion in a few words: that he was aware they would elect him if they could make any thing of it; but that / they would sell him and their votes together, if they could make more by the bargain.'

'That must have widened the little eyes of the *yellow buttons and peacock's feathers*,'[27] observed Lord Frederick, laughing.

'It is a new mode of electioneering,' said Mr. Daly, evidently pleased with his grand-nephew.

'And will doubtless succeed,' said Conway Crawley, in a whisper to Mr. Pottinger.

Conversation now took a desultory turn; and the ladies retired early. Lady Dunore and Lady Clancare walked from the dining-room into the court, though it was after night-fall. Lady Georgina went to sleep, as usual, in order to call up her looks for the evening: and Miss Crawley retired to brood over her own venom, which every hour was increasing by the events of the day. /

Mr. Pottinger had scarcely bowed out the ladies, and closed the door after them, when Lord Adelm beckoned General Fitzwalter to the window.

'Well!' he said, with a look of anxious impatience.

'Well!' said the general, something perplexed. 'I have nothing to tell you, save that the person to whom I alluded this morning *is* not, *cannot be*, your sylph, your *woman*.'

He dwelt with a species of inveteracy on the latter word; and Lord Adelm, pronouncing with a sigh of disappointment and a look of mortification, 'I thought so; – and I am now as far as ever from the ideal presence,' they both resumed their seats.

The gentlemen sat late: conversation had taken a wide range. The general politics of Europe, the actual and relative position of their own country, the spirit of the age, and determination of / popular opinion, were discussed ably and energetically by Mr. Daly, Lord Adelm, Lord Frederick, and General Fitzwalter. Mr. Pottinger edged in a few feeble common-places, gleaned at castle dinners; Lord Rosbrin quoted and spouted where he could, and as he could; Mr. Heneage said nothing, except that the imperial Arctic Dandy was reported to employ a French *Schneider*;[28] and Conway Crawley rather marred and thwarted the conversation, than joined or promoted it, pouring forth an infinite deal of nothings with great fluency, and arrogantly contradicting what he could not ably controvert.[1] When they adjourned to the drawing-room, even the most temperate were a little animated, if not flushed by Lady Dunore's excellent claret; yet scarcely more wine had been taken than served to dissipate the apathetic dulness, which, in spite of Lady Dunore's own impe-/tuous spirits, and vivacious character, habitually presided over the circle at Dunore.

When the men, however, entered the drawing-room, they found it only occupied by Lady Georgina and Miss Crawley; the former, with her elegantly draped figure, lying apparently half asleep on a canopied couch; the latter, seated near her, was so occupied in some narration she was muttering, that the gentlemen had advanced into the middle of the room before she observed them. Lady Georgina, with a pretty affected start of astonishment, opened her soft, languid eyes, and made an effort to rise. Lord Rosbrin meantime hanging over her, exclaimed, –

'Her body sleeps in Capulet's monument,
While her immortal part with angels lives.'[29]

'I think,' said Lord Frederick, taking his coffee, and throwing himself / on a divan, near Lady Georgina, 'we all appear to be buried in the tomb of the Capulets. I had no idea the divine Marchesa[30] meant to consign us all to such immortal dulness. The castle of *Le bois dormant*[31] faintly images the quietude of our provincial chateau;[32] and one of these fine days we shall all be found, by a new generation, fast asleep in the costume of the *then* last century, like the court of the Sleeping Beauty.[33] We are already almost reduced *aux muets entreprétes*,[34] and shall gradually fall into the eloquent silence of that round-eyed, tongue-tied Lady Clancare, who *par parenthese*,[35] looks as if she were extracting us all for her common-place book, and will doubtless bring us out in hot-press,[36] *sans dire gar!*[37]

'I doubt she will ever bring out any thing half so good,' said Conway Crawley: 'as yet, that is not in her line; she has had too few opportunities of / studying fashionable life to attempt any thing in that way. Her position here, at least, is so extremely obscure, that I believe the castle of Dunore is the first fine house in the country into which she was ever admitted.'

'And,' said Miss Crawley, smiling, and in spite of her former discomfiture unable to contain her acrimonious spirit, 'and perhaps it may be her last.'

'Her principles,' continued young Crawley, 'as disseminated in her "*National Tales*," as she calls them, are sufficient to keep her out of good society here.'

'I thought I had heard you say, Mr. Crawley,' observed Mr. Daly, 'that you did not know Lady Clancare was an author?'

'I did not till this morning,' said Crawley, a little confused. 'When Lady Dunore mentioned the titles of her works, and the initials representing the / author's name, I recollected having looked over those *tomes of absurdity and vagueness, of daring blasphemy, of affectation, of bad taste, bombast, and nonsense, blunders, ignorance, jacobinism and falsehood, licentiousness and impiety, which it now seems are the effusions of the pseudo Lady Clancare*.'[38]

Young Crawley, already flushed with wine, grew still more red with rage as he spoke.

'Oh, my dear Mr. Crawley,' interrupted Lord Frederick, with unusual vivacity, 'say no more, or you will make us in love with the author and her work together; for, really, a book that could combine all these terrific heterogeneous qualities, and yet be read, must be very odd and extraordinary: *pour le moins*.'[39]

'Very extraordinary, indeed,' said Mr. Daly, 'considering that with all / these vices and faults they have been so read and bought, as to realize an independence for their author, and enable her to carry on a suit which has deprived the elder Mr. Crawley of his dear Clotnotty-joy. It would at least appear, that in spite of professional criticism, the public are *always* with her.'

'O, her flippant and arrogant ignorance has its market,' returned Conway Crawley, hatred and envy of Lady Clancare, reanimated by the position she now held in a circle from which it was his object to have excluded her, getting the better of all presence of mind, and giving the direct lie to his recent declarations of ignorance;[m] 'and the *sylphed* Miss Macarthy, the *elegant* Lady Clancare, is, in fact, a *mere bookseller's drudge*. Her *impudent falsehoods*, and *lies by implication*, the impious jargon of this *mad woman, this* audacious worm –'[40] /

'Are you speaking of Lady Clancare, Sir?' said General Fitzwalter, who had been talking to Lord Adelm, but who now turned shortly round upon young Crawley, with a tone and look that stunned the hardy railler; 'are you applying such language to a *woman* – to *any* woman?'

'I – I – I was speaking, Sir,' said young Crawley, nearly sobered at once, and growing pale at this address, 'that is, I was repeating the criticism of a celebrated periodical review,[41] which may, perhaps, be deemed severe, but which is edited by men of the most –'

'*Men!* do you call them,' said General Fitzwalter, with a sharp contemptuous laugh, and turning on his heel. '*Men*, indeed!'

A momentary silence ensued. The indignant contempt with which General Fitzwalter had fixed his eyes on Crawley was observed by all. Crawley was physically timid; he shrunk back and / took up a book; Miss Crawley changed colour; and at that moment the marchioness entered, leaning on Lady Clancare's arm. They were both wrapped in their shawls; and the freshness of the evening air, and the deep colouring of exercise, gave a vivid brightness to their complexions.

'We have had a delicious walk of some miles; two or three, I believe,' said Lady Dunore, sinking into a fauteuil, and calling for coffee; while Lady Clancare modestly took her seat rather behind than beside, so as just to raise her face over the back of Lady Dunore's chair, in a position equally shy and observing. For a moment she attracted every eye, and all sought to trace in her countenance some indication of the audacious, lying, profligate, ignorant, and pretending jacobin.

'There is nothing, after all,' said Lady Dunore, gradually unmuffling her- / self, 'like the security, and moonlight, and things of that kind, of Ireland. I am so in love with my Irish solitudes, that I am not certain I shall not remain here through the winter.'

'Then, marchioness of my affections,' said Lord Frederick, 'I must beg my *bouquet d'adieu*;[42] for though I agree in the old sentimental tag of *La solitude est une belle chose*,[43] yet –'

'Oh, sweet love,' interrupted Lady Georgina, addressing the marchioness, and who, as well as Lord Frederick, had her reasons for disliking the extreme smallness of the *petit comité*,[44] in which they had lived at Dunore, and which placed every one so constantly before the eyes of the others – 'oh, sweet love, you have no idea what an excellent society you have about you, if you would but let in the *Aborigines*. Miss Crawley has been amusing me this evening with a description of your / neighbours for twenty miles round. I dare say they would amuse *you* greatly. Now do, Miss Crawley, pray shew your list to Lady D. Miss Crawley has made out a list for you, *Ma Reine*.'[45]

'Oh, you may let in who you like,' said Lady Dunore: 'I shall not in the least object, if there are cups and saucers and things for the Irish ladies, who are monstrously particular I hear; and provided they won't expect me to go to them in return, they may come and welcome. Who shall we have? Who shall we let in, Lady Clancare? Who is there really presentable and amusing? But mind, I won't have any *circulars*; I won't have those Chinese hieroglyphics, with their tails in their mouths,[46] that is, the serpents. What is it, Lord Frederick, about eternity you know? The Chinese Mandarin? You have no idea how that word "*eternity*" ennuies[47] / me. Now come, Lady Clancare, do speak: who shall we have? Is there no one at Balbec, at Ballydab I mean?'

The Crawleys laughed *(aside)*, but were yet heard and seen by all, Lady Dunore excepted, who was now arranging her dishevelled hair at a mirror over the chimney-piece.

'I should like to make you, my dear Lady Clancare, my returning officer, as old Mr. Crawley says, of the electioneering business. Now who shall we have?' and she resumed her seat.

Lady Clancare begged, in her low soft voice, to have the office assigned to Miss Crawley, who was so much better known in the neighbourhood.

'Oh, dear! no, Ma'am,' minced Miss Crawley: 'I could not think of obtruding on your *ladyship's* province.'

'Now pray do as Lady Clancare desires you, Miss Crawley,' said Lady Dunore, with her usual *inconsequence*[48] / and peremptory tone. 'Rosbrin, draw the writing-table near me: you shall be secretary to the committee; you shall name the persons, Miss Crawley; and then we'll talk them over, and elect accordingly.'

Miss Crawley now advanced in implicit obedience to the commanding fiat of her future Neophyte; for the certain conversion of the marchioness still appeared in the perspective, and beckoned her on, through every gradation of servility, to her grand object.[n] Every one gathered round the table placed before Lady Dunore, except General Fitzwalter and Lord Adelm. The one stood aloof, looking, partly in curiosity, and partly, perhaps, in contempt, on this group of grown children; the other was stretched upon a sofa, occupying a recess window, and partly shadowed by its drapery.

'Let us see,' said Lady Dunore, / taking a paper out of Miss Crawley's hand, on which she had written some names. 'Who is this? Lady Lisson! Who is she, Miss Crawley?'

'She is a young widow lady, Madam, of large fortune. They say she has more diamonds than the queen; and is niece to our bishop, with whom she is now on a visit.'

'Do you know anything of her, Lady Clancare?' said the marchioness, turning cooly to her '*Cynthea of the minute*.'[49]

'I have *seen* her,' said Lady Clancare, in her wonted tone and look of real or affected simplicity.

'Is she *presentable?* What is she like?'

'Like?' said Lady Clancare, with a look of great naïveté, as if searching for some object of comparison – 'Like a diamond beetle[50] – small, shining, and insignificant. You would find her tire-/some for anything exclusive, but she might answer for a *ball* – you might ask her to that, on the strength of her diamond necklace; it helps to dress a room.'

This was the first sentence Lady Clancare had uttered aloud since her introduction at the castle; and its oddity, contrasted to her naïve air and timid look, had its due effect.

'Oh! put her down, by all means, Rosbrin,' cried Lord Frederick, laughing. 'Down with the *diamond beetle*, with a N. B.[51] the necklace to be included in the invitation.'

'And who is this, my dear Miss Crawley? – You write such a very pretty precise cramped hand – oh! Mr. and Mrs. Wiggins of Fort Wiggins. – That sounds bad,' added Lady Dunore, shaking her head.

'However it may *sound*, Madam,' said Miss Crawley, a little piqued, / and resolved not to be worsted by Lady Clancare, to whose talents she now believed herself to be purposely opposed in the arena of contest by Lady Dunore. 'However it may *sound*, Mr. Wiggins holds a distinguished office of trust under government; and Mrs. Wiggins is supposed to have more titles at her parties than any one, except Lady Kilgobbin.'

'I wish somebody would kill Lady Kilgobbin,' said Lady Dunore, 'for I am sick of her name. I suppose if these *Wiggins people* are government folk, we *must* have them. I wish particularly to distinguish the friends and supporters of the present ministry. But I hope *your Mrs. Wiggins* is not a quiz,[52] Miss Crawley. Do you know her, Lady Clancare?'

'I saw her in Dublin, Madam, at a few assemblies.'

'And what is she like? Now do / throw her off for us, *à trait de plume*.[53] Now pray what is she like?'

'Like – like a scarlet flamingo, lean and lank, all legs and neck, in an eternal *red velvet* gown.'

'I'll have nothing to do with your flamingo, my dear Miss Crawley. The *eternal red gown* would destroy me in two nights. I cut the flamingo and the velvet gown, positively, legs, neck, and all.'

'No, no,' interrupted Lord Frederick, 'the flamingo must go in with the beetle. Only conceive; you will stand here like your mother Eve, surrounded by all the birds of the air and beasts of the field. – Rosbrin, down with the flamingo, as a *pendant*[54] for the beetle: they are charming; and here is,' he added, looking over Lady Dunore's shoulder, 'here is Mrs. Randal Royston – delicious name! and the three Miss Roystons.' /

'There were originally *seven* Miss Flambroughs, with seven China oranges,'[55] said Lady Clancare, with kindling spirits, and now evidently *piquée au jeu*,[56] but Mrs. Randal has married, or rather *lunched off* four.'

'Lunched off! Good God, how good!' said Lady Dunore, laughing; 'but how lunched off, my dear Lady Clancare?'

'Why, when maternal speculation, with balls, dinners, and suppers, wholly failed, Mrs. Royston advertised sandwiches to morning saunterers, and got rid of her Westphalia hams and her marriageable daughters together.'

Everybody laughed. Miss Crawley made an effort to speak, but was overpowered by the loud shrill voice of Lady Dunore.

'Here, read on, Lord Frederick: do you read: go on. This is too amusing.'

'Here is,' said Lord Frederick, / 'General and MRS. GENERAL Jenkins.'

'But not the *general* Mrs. Jenkins,' said Lady Clancare, whose spirits apparently grew with what they fed on, and who gradually came more forward on the scene, with increasing confidence. 'Not the *general* Mrs. Jenkins: on the contrary, she is the *exclusive* Mrs. Jenkins, one who discriminates by the indices of the Red Book,[57] estimates qualities by the nobs on coronets,[58] and ranges all worth and talent under the privilege of walking at a coronation: for the rest, she is fussy, fidgetty, and fretful, but useful in getting up balls, to extract names from a porter's book; and might herself pass the muster-roll of gentility unnoticed, but for her *idears, winders, Mariars, Mirandars*, and all the whole race of r's in the Cockney vocabulary of Bow-bell.'[59]

'Now, Lady Dunore,' interrupted / Miss Crawley, more annoyed at the amusement Lady Clancare was exciting, than by the abuse of Mrs. General Jenkins, 'now I must observe to you, that this Mrs. Jenkins, the object of Lady Clancare's ridicule, happens to be her own friend; and if her ladyship ridicules her own particular friends –'

'My own particular friends!' said Lady Clancare, gravely; 'and if I don't laugh at my *own* friends, whose friends can I take the liberty of laughing at, Miss Crawley?'

'Really, Madam,' said Miss Crawley, sneering, 'I at least do not see the necessity –'

'Necessity! Oh, pardon me, – the necessity is obvious, inevitable, *plus fort que moi*,[60] and does not leave a shadow of free-will[61] in the case.'

'My aunt, Madam,' said young Crawley, 'must decline all logical disquisition with you on *necessity* and *free / will*. She is not quite so *learned* in metaphysics, and does not advertize her study of Locke for the benefit of the public. I believe, and hope, indeed, *she never read him.*'

'Did not she?' asked Lady Clancare, with simplicity; 'then she must not *speak* of him, Mr. Crawley: for there's no getting at Locke *by deputy*. There is no quartering review of *him*! no opinions to be picked up at second-hand, no cut and dry criticisms, neat, compact, and portable, made up in small parcels, and ready for immediate use, as soon as delivered to the purchaser – you understand, Mr. Crawley. To speak of Locke, to criticise *him*, one must absolutely read him – a gone-by sort of practice unknown to the retailers of literature of the present day, the pedlars and hawkers of the cast-off observations of hireling umpires. But,' she added, with a total change of coun-/tenance and manner, and a sort of fondling voice, opposed to the sharp acute accent she had first spoke in, 'you must *not believe, my dear Lady Dunore, that I am the ingrate and cankered Bolinbroke.'*[62]

'Henry Fourth, act first, scene third,' observed Lord Rosbrin, raising his eyes from his list to Lady Clancare's face, with pleasure and surprise.

'I am not,' she continued, following up her blow on the heart of Lord Rosbrin and the temper of the Crawleys at the same moment – 'I am not guilty of this "ungrateful injury," as Coriolanus has it,[63] against Mrs. General Jenkins. She is *not* my friend: judge if she merits that name. On my coming down to this country, some two years back, Mrs. Jenkins, herself then a stranger, came to visit me, on the strength of my title, and did not get into my ruined towers, to view the / "nakedness of the land;"[64] so she sent me an invitation to her house. I went, *pour voir ce que cela deviendra*,[65] and accompanied her to an assize-ball, where she suddenly dropped me; for, having found out that I was but a *pauper* peeress, and fitter for the parish books than the red bench,[66] she charitably consigned me to my destiny; and now meets, stares at, and passes me; while I, with my *"good den, Sir Richard,"* am answered with, *"a gad have mercy, fellow"*[67] But I advise you to ask her to your fête,[68] whenever you give any, for she twines holly and ivy wreaths for garlanding the walls, cuts flowers out of turnips and carrots for ornamenting supper-tables, and has a recipe for making very tolerable lemonade, without the expensive addition of lemons.'

'No, no; no Mrs. General Jenkins,' was the *general* cry: while Lady Dunore, equally delighted with the amusing / powers of the awakened Lady Clancare, as with the discomfiture of her ex-favourites, the Crawleys, who, it was evident, were gradually losing ground in her changeable opinion, cried out louder than all, 'Go on, go on, Lord Frederick. Who have we next? Now, Lady Clancare.'

'Mrs. Wilkinson,' pronounced emphatically Lord Frederick.

'A great favourite of our late lord-lieutenant,' said Mr. Pottinger, who was on the Crawley side, 'quite a beauty in the grand style.'

'Yes,' said Lady Clancare, laughing, 'a very Mammoth of loveliness,[69] ponderously pretty, with no more joints than an elephant, and quite as heavy and as mischievous withal; for she'll tread the nap off your carpet while she talks down the character of your friends, and never moves or breathes, but to injure.'

'She's mighty pert,' said Mr. Pot-/tinger, in a half whisper to Conway Crawley, whose looks replied in the affirmative.°

'Yet for all that,' said Lord Frederick, 'we must have the *elephant* to compleat the menagerie. Put her down, Rosbrin, with the beetle and the Flamingo: so, – here are Mr. and Mrs. Twiggle, too: I like the name – it bodes well.'

'Mr. Twiggle is one of our great Irish financiers,' interrupted Miss Crawley, endeavouring to get the *pas*;[70] 'for our rich army agents here answer to the financiers of France, as described by Marmontel in his sweetly written Memoires.'[71]

'I shall say nothing of the army agents,' said Lady Clancare, 'till *there's a peace*.'[72]

'Scrub! hem!' said Lord Rosbrin, chuckling.

'*Peace or war,*' said young Crawley, / much irritated, 'the *Twiggles* must always hold a situation of trust and emolument. The government will always take care of *them:* and as to Mrs. Twiggle, she's first cousin to that distinguished parliamentary leader, and *will-be* minister, who reflects such lustre upon this country, by his extraordinary talents and wit; which family endowment indeed she shares. Mrs. Twiggle *is*[p] a woman of first-rate abilities, and, like her illustrious kinsman, one of the best critics, and one of the most eloquent persons, I ever listened to. She has indeed none of that flippant smartness, which is rather the pertness of pretension, than the ebullition of genuine ability; but she has a flow of language –'

'*Flow*, do you call it?' said Lady Clancare, in surprise: 'a *flow*, a *flood*, that carries down with it all sorts of rubbish. In fact, the eloquent Mrs. / Twiggle is not *ill* represented by a long-necked bottle, shallow and noisy. My dear Lady Dunore, you would die of it. A windmill is an hermitage to the neighbourhood of the *eloquent* Mrs. Twiggle.'

'Away with her, away with her!' cried Lord Rosbrin, theatrically. 'No Twiggle,' was the general cry; while young Crawley, without temper or taste to enter into this idle playfulness, without art or talent to counteract the growing popularity of Lady Clancare, who was now triumphantly under weigh, and sailing over the prejudices excited against her authorship, rudely snatched up the paper from Lord Rosbrin, and said in a tone of great irritation, 'I believe, Lady Dunore, my aunt will rather decline giving any further assistance on this occasion. For as *she* happens to *know* and *visit* all the persons of distinction who inhabit this / neighbourhood, it is rather mortifying her to hear calumnies launched against all the leading gentry and principal people of the province.'

'Calumny!' reiterated Lady Clancare, with mock solemnity, and solemnly spreading her little hand on her bosom, 'I deny the accusation. I deny that the *Lissons,* and *Wiggens,* and *Jenkins*, and *Roystons*, and *Twiggles,* are the gentry of the province. Though some be nieces of embarrassed English clergymen, suddenly become Irish bishops, who, having dropped the birch in their own country, snatch the crozier[73] in our's;[q] though they be placemen and pensioners, and army-agents and revenue commissioners, yet their very names were unheard of in this country a few years back; and I therefore deny that they are the *genuine* nobility and *gentry* of this country. My dear Lady Dunore, if you would / invite only the Irish aristocracy to your castle, you must deliver your cards to king's messengers, and send your invitations to every court in Europe, except our own, where alone the *Irish nobility are not to be found.* But if the true *gentry* of the country will satisfy you, the descendants of her brave chiefs and princes, the O's, and the Mac's,[74] there is no province in Ireland can furnish a more *national* or delightful circle than Munster. I promise you, you will be delighted with them. You will, perhaps, find more brogue and bows than you would meet with in your English assemblies; but you will also find something of the refined courtesy, and gay spirit of the Irish cavalier, still extant in the inheritance of temperament, when all other inheritances have been swept away:ʳ prompt, indeed, to suspect slight, but ardent to repay kindness;ˢ for, like the Irish / wolf dog,[75] the *Irish people* are devoted when caressed, and fierce only when provoked. I propose then, in this great election for the independent borough of your ladyship's favour, the O's and the Macs as worthy candidates.'

'I second the motion,' cried Lord Frederick.

'The O's and the Macs,' echoed on every side, while Lord Rosbrin, flourishing his handkerchief, cried out, 'a mug, a mug, a mug!'*[76]

Lady Dunore, delighted with the noise, because noise always delighted her, charmed by the transition in Lady Clancare's manner, because all transitions gave her sensation; gratified by the amusement it had, and still might afford her, embraced her new favourite *a la francoise*, and cried out –

'You are quite charming. I told / you how popular you would become whenever you would shake off your *mauvaise honte*.[77] You shall ask who you like to the castle, and nobody but *whom* you like; for I now constitute you mistress of the revels of Dunore.'

'Do you?' said Lady Clancare with vivacity; 'then I'll make the "*welkin dance*,"[78] or at least Clotnotty-joy; and if I could find out a co-partner in my labours, I would get up a series of festivities that should last out your banishment here. We would perform a masque for the amusement of the nobles of the castle, as in the older times: we would have the most lamentable comedy and cruel death of Pyramus and Thisbe;'[79] and her countenance now assumed the dull stupidity of Peter Quince; [80] 'or we would try –'

Lord Rosbrin, as if touched by an electric spark, here interrupted her with the rejoinder of Bully Bottom, / 'a very good piece of work, and a merry –'[81] Then taking her hand, to the amusement of all, he added, with great gravity,

> 'Come, my queen, in silence sad,
> Trip we after the night-shade.
> We the globe can compass soon,
> Swifter than the wand'ring moon;'[82]
> while she replied significantly,
> 'Come, my lord, and in our flight,
> Tell me how it came this night,
> THAT I SLEEPING HERE WAS found
> By these mortals.'

---

*   Mayor of Garret.

'Sleeping indeed!' said Lady Dunore; 'but you have awakened us all now, I trust,'

'*Macbeth* hath murdered sleep,'[83] added Lord Rosbrin. 'But what mirth, what revelry, shall we begin with?'

'A mask presented at Ludlow Cas-/tle, 1634, on Michaelmas night, before the Right Honourable John Earl of Bridgewater, Lord President of Wales, called Comus,'[84] said Lady Clancare, looking at Lord Rosbrin; who replied, fluttering about in an ecstasy,

'Music by Henry Lawes. Here, we'll cast it forthwith;' and he dropped on his knees and seized the pen. 'What are the characters? I have not looked into Comus these six months.'

'There is the elder brother,' said Lady Clancare, dictating gravely. – 'General Fitzwalter – younger brother, Lord Adelm – the lady, by Lady Georgina – Comus, your lordship; and the Crew, Mr. and Miss Crawley, Mr. Pottinger, &c.'

'And Euphrosyne, Lady Clancare,' said Lord Rosbrin.

'Now then,' said Lady Clancare, with all the spirit and sportiveness of the character assigned her, /

'Welcome song and welcome jest,
Mid-night shout and revelry,
Tipsy dance and jollity.
Braid your locks with rosy twine,
Dropping odours, dropping wine.'[85]

'Brava! brava!' re-echoed on every side.

'For the audience,' she continued, 'Lady *Bridgewater,* seated under a canopy, and dressed in the old *English habit,* shall be represented by the marchioness.'

'I have one,' interrupted Lady Dunore, 'made for the last opera masquerade.'

'The Lord-President will be admirably done by Mr. Daly; and the *O's* and the Macs will look stately and quaint in the boxes; while the Wiggins, and Twiggles, and Roystons,

'*Will fill a pit as well as better men,*'[86]

'To be sure they will,' said Lady / Dunore; 'we'll parade them all on the occasion; and that won't be the least part of the fun.'

'We must have an afterpiece,' said Lord Rosbrin, gravely, and in a thoughtful attitude.'

'Let it be something Spanish,' said Lady Dunore, 'in compliment to General Fitzwalter.'

General Fitzwalter was leaning over the back of a chair, pursuing the variations of Lady Clancare, who now was light and fantastic.

'Like some gay creature of the element,
That in the colours of the rainbow lives.'[87] t

He started at this application to his *amour propre,* and bowed slightly and in some confusion, while Lady Dunore, her eyes still fixed on him, whispered something in Lady Clancare's ear, who blushed, threw down her eyes, and shook her head incredulously. This / was not the first time he had observed a mysterious communication between these two ladies, of which he was evidently the object, but he had never been struck so forcibly as now; for the deep blush of Lady Clancare gave it no trifling effect.

In the meantime, Lord Rosbrin, puzzling his head for a *Spanish American piece,* could thing of nothing but Pizarro,[88] which it was impossible to cut down into a farce; and so, as a succedaneum,[89] he proposed the Spanish farce of the PADLOCK, in which Lady Clancare offered to play *Mungo* to his Leander,[90] except Mr. Heneage had a preference for that part. Mr. Heneage declared that he would not blacken his face for any earthly consideration; and Lord Rosbrin observed he should much like to try his talent at singing, but that he had no wooden leg among his properties for Leander.[91] Lady Clancare / suggested that the wooden leg was a worn out *common-place; that tying up* the limb in a handsome blue scarf would be a new reading; and that, with the help of a cane, he would manage it admirably.

'Exactly,' said Lord Rosbrin, charmed with the idea of a *new reading*: 'such a scarf as this,' and he took one from off Miss Crawley's shoulders. 'Here, Heneage, lend me your arm. Now, Pottinger, fasten this round my ankle, so; and then round my neck, so. Thank you, Lady Clancare, for your assistance: how well you understand these things: that's a little too tight though; not quite so many knots. Oh, the devil! your ladyship's tying my heel to my head. Stay, I'll try a few bars of the serenade:

'Oh thou whose charms have won my heart.'[92]

D — n it, *this* is torture. I – I –' and suddenly seized with the cramp, Lord / Rosbrin now fell to the ground, almost screaming with pain, and crying, 'By the Lord I have got the most intolerable cramp: loose me, for pity's sake, or I shall die of it.'

Every one now hastened to relieve him, but Lady Clancare's nimble fingers had tied a Gordian knot:[93] no one could loosen it. Lord Rosbrin roared, and Mr. Daly at last *cut boldly* what could not be untied. Every body laughed, as if the sufferings of the noble amateur were 'sport for ladies.'[94] Miss Crawley received back her mangled scarf with a look of vexation and dismay. Lady Dunore, equally amused by the sufferings of one friend, the annoyance of the other, and the *espieglerie*[95] of the third, turned round, after a fit of laughter that brought tears to her eyes, to reproach Lady Clancare for not assisting at a *denoument*[96] she had rendered so difficult to effect, but – she was gone. /

CHAPTER II.

But yet I say,
If imputation and strong circumstance,
Which lead directly to the door of truth,
Will give you satisfaction, you may have it,
                              SHAKESPEARE.[97]

GENERAL FITZWALTER retired early from the circle at the castle, and was passing rapidly through the hall to his carriage, when the figure of Lord Adelm
caught his attention, moving under the projecting corridor, and tearing some
paper in a thousand pieces, which he had trampled under his feet. His countenance was marked by strong traces of passion, and his obvious confusion and
embarrassment, when his eyes met Fitz-/walter, almost tempted the latter to
pass on without addressing him; suddenly, however, turning back upon his steps,
under the influence of a prompt and ardent sympathy, as easily excited as it was
uncontrollable, he demanded,

'What is the matter? You appear to suffer. Has any thing happened to annoy
you?'

'Annoy me, indeed!' he repeated, while the general took his arm, and walked
for a minute in silence by his side.

'What can have occurred within the last hour, when I saw you smiling in
mockery at the buffoon, Lord Rosbrin? Fancies, not facts, I trust: for I would
rather believe your nymph had discovered herself, and so dispelled your illusions
than –'

'Discovered herself with a vengeance! she has discovered herself.'

'Ha! has she so?' /

'Oh! with a frankness perfectly original. For, with an ingenuous confession
that she has made my vanity and credulity the dupes of her devices, and the
instruments of her own views, she absolves me from her spells, restores me to
my freedom of agency, releases me from leading strings, and with a mysterious
allusion to the convent of Nuestra Señora de las Augustias, the ruins of the Holy-
cross, and my visit to Court Fitzadelm, she signs herself mine *au revoir*, MARY
MAGILLICUDDY. And thus,' he added, tearing to atoms the fragments of the
letter he still held – 'thus ends a dream I would not have exchanged for any real
good life could have bestowed, which was to me as the spirit of the sun-beam to
Tasso, as the airy voice to Des Cartes, as the resplendent light, which hovered
over the shadow of Cellini.'[98 u]

'I'm glad of it,' replied the general, / emphatically; and there was a beaming
satisfaction in his animated countenance that ratified the assurance, as if he was
himself relieved from some unpleasant conjecture, which weighed heavily on his
mind. 'All that is mystery is bad,' he added; 'you will now be restored to yourself.

Passion, genuine and correspondent to your age and character, will succeed to distempered fancies; realities to visions; and the heart will act, where the imagination has so long exclusively operated.'

'You think, then,' said Lord Adelm, 'that I am to rest here, to return solemn thanks for my delivery, and to sit down quietly in the pleasant conviction of having been the dupe of some idle or wilful person, who construes the enthusiasm and elevation of my character into vanity and credulity, and insolently laughs at the simplicity with which I / have submitted to the imposition. No, by heavens! time, accident, or perseverance in the research, must yet discover this arrogant unknown. If it be a man, the result is obvious, and if a woman –' He clenched his hands, and ground his teeth. 'To be revenged, I would pursue her under every form, device, and stratagem, that could woo and win; to punish, I would even marry her, and thus make her future life the slow-working expiation of her momentary insolence.'

Either the general saw the folly of contending with the first burst of suffering of wounded self-love, or his own thoughts so deeply ingrossed him, that he permitted a long silence to succeed to this singular denunciation; then starting, as from a profound reverie, he said,

'I shall be detained here a few days longer, contrary to my intention. Your / election may be determined in the interim; and the revelation, which must then take place –'

'Yes,' interrupted Lord Adelm; 'but it is an object with me that this revelation be protracted. Nothing effectual can be done till the opening of term.'

'Nay, you shall name the time, the moment, yourself. I too have my reasons for prolonging my incognito yet a little longer.'

'What!' said Lord Adelm, with a bitter smile, 'have you too a phantom to contend with?'

'No: my object of *contention,* as you call it, is, simply, *a woman.*'

'The betrothed wife to which you alluded?' asked Lord Adelm.

'You shall know all at a future moment,' was the reply.

Here the opening of the drawing-room door, and the sound of ap- /proaching steps and voices, separated the friends. Lord Adelm retreated to his dressing room, and the general threw himself into the Dunore chaise, and returned to his tower.

Solitude, the nurse of genius and enthusiasm, is the true sphere of passion; and silence and meditation communicate a contagious energy to the feelings and fancy, which fades and becomes enfeebled in the bustling and noisy communication of the world. The wild shores and mountain headlands, the solitary ruins and shadowy glens, which diversified the scenery of Dunore, were appropriate sites and associations to him in whom a sentiment, ardent in proportion to its novelty, had arisen.ᵛ This sentiment, inspired by one as much an object of suspicion as of admiration, occupied General Fitzwalter with a despotism, which a sense of honour, and of his own peculiar situation, could / alone repress or resist. Still it possessed, it ingrossed him: it chased repose from his pillow by night; it agitated and disturbed the dream of the morning; and it drove him into scenes of solitude, wild as his passions, and lonely as his existence.

It was his wish, and might almost be called his principle, to avoid the castle of Dunore; yet he had no power to accomplish the purpose; and though in the interim which must necessarily elapse before the arrival of an answer from Florence Macarthy he escaped the invitation of the marchioness, by the pretence of a visit to the romantic, and, locally, celebrated glen and hermitage of the Gougane Barra,[99] yet in four days that he had ridden about the country, he had seldom lost sight of the turrets of Dunore, or the ruined towers of Castle Macarthy.

On the afternoon of the fifth day, / he found himself on the edge of a wild moor, or what in Ireland is called a shaking bog, which skirted the heights of Clotnotty-joy. He alighted from his horse to inquire for a bridle-way more safe than that he pursued, from a man, who appeared white-washing the walls of a wretched hut, which arose lonely and desolate amidst the bleak and dreary scene. As he advanced, he perceived a woman, in a grey cloak and straw bonnet, standing near the cabin, and seemingly giving directions. The sound of his horse's feet caught her ear. She took off her bonnet, shook back her dark hair, and discovered the glowing countenance of the Lady Clancare.

General Fitzwalter started at this unexpected vision, and then advanced and moved his hat; but with her upraised hand she beckoned him back, and exclaimed with much earnestness: /

'No, no, pray don't come here: go back, General Fitzwalter, I beseech you.'

'For what reason?' he demanded coolly, and still advancing. 'This is my road.'

'For a thousand reasons,' she replied, moving rapidly away; and speaking with her head turned over her shoulder.

'One will suffice,' he rejoined, still approaching.

'There is a fever raging in that house. Nay, it may not be safe even to come in contact with me.'

'In contact *with you!*' he answered, with a voice full of emotion, and now walking beside her, with his horse following at bridle's length. 'But if a fever rages here, why then are you here yourself?' he demanded anxiously.

'Oh, because I bear a charmed life,' she returned, laughing, but quickening / her pace, as if to get beyond the sphere of contagion; 'because if I did not come, four wretches who lie there, dying for want of proper care, would perish. The neighbours hold this typhus[100] in such dread, that though they come and leave a little drink at the door of the cabin, they dare not enter. No, no, you shall not speak what you are going to say about charity and, *a good heart; that* virtue always ascribed to those who have none – the capricious and the unregulated.

The fact is, these poor people are my tenants. I induced them to settle in this swampy tract, and feel myself in part answerable for their existence.'

'But if there is infection here?'

'I laugh at the idea of infection; that is, in my own person. The fever which sweeps away the poor people is, in my mind, the pure result of their poverty and its concomitants, filth and / starvation. Their moral and physical ills are closely linked, and arise out of the same cause. Repeal the act which banished our land-lords, and exhausts the country of its revenue and resources, and then disease will disappear, with the want that fosters it. People will die, to be sure, and of typhus fever sometimes; but it will no longer be to Ireland what the yellow fever is to the West Indies, or the plague to Constantinople.'ʷ

'But how is it you warn others of a danger you contemn yourself?'

'The imagination,' she returned, smiling, 'goes a great way in this business; and I keep mine exclusively for my books. This disease I believe to be epidemic, and not infectious. I have exposed myself constantly to it these two years, and here I am, still directing Lawrence Toole how to white-wash his hut. But as I may be singular in my / opinion, I should not be justified in exposing others uncon-sciously, where, after all, there may be something like danger.ˣ But,' she added, suddenly pausing, and slackening her rapid pace, 'is not this rencontreʸ a breach of our original stipulation? We were not, I think, to hold any communication till the arrival of –'

'I did not understand that accidental rencontres came under the head of your prohibitions, which, you perceive, I have otherwise religiously observed.'

'You take the advantage of the *letter,* and neglect the *spirit* of the enactment, I observe, and neither keep the promise to the sense, nor the ear.'

'No, in this instance, as through life, I merely give myself up to the tide of circumstances as they flow; adapt them to my wishes and my views as I can; render them serviceable to my purposes as I may; turn them to the best account / of which they are susceptible: but when they become wholly untractable and adverse, then I trust I shall stand the brunt of their resistance with fortitude, and, with Milton's dæmon-hero, acknowledge, that "*to suffer, as to do, our strength is equal.*"[101] I had no hope of meeting your ladyship this morning; but most assuredly I will not neglect the good the "gods provide me."[102] I am too selfish, perhaps, to consult your wishes; but still you will not find me unprepared to obey your commands. Do you desire me to leave you?'

'Wishes, obedience, and commands!' repeated Lady Clancare, shaking her head. 'You are resolved to leave me no female doubling to escape by. You bring me to my purgation at once, and put to rout the host of little diplomacies with which we habitually come at our object, without any visible interference on our own part. Suppose / now I did not *wish* you to go, and yet thought it right to *command* your departure. You see,' she added, with her brilliant laugh, 'to what you have reduced me, and plenary confession is all now that remains.'

'If for one moment,' he added, with warmth, 'I may suppose you *do not wish* me to go, even your commands should not banish me. Will you take my arm, and permit me to see you home?'

She declined the offer with a slight bow, and after a short pause, observed, 'You seem, General Fitzwalter, to have lived but little with women?'

'So little, Madam, that I fear I am scarcely fit to live with them; and yet am unable to live without them. Woman is to me, the spring in the desert, precious and rare, seldom found in my life's wild and dreary track; but when found –' /

Lady Clancare looked full in his eyes, and laying her forefinger on his arm, pronounced emphatically, 'Florence Macarthy!' A deep crimson rushed over his face. 'Since,' he said, 'you revert, yourself, to that strange circumstance, you will allow me to enter fully on an explanation of conduct, governed only by that inevitable course of events, which in human life governs every thing.'

'Not one syllable,' she interrupted eagerly. 'I am one of those legislators, the first to break the laws they make, but withal, rigid as to the infringement of others: a perfect Lord Angelo.[103] But raise your eyes to the right. Do you not see an abrupt conical hill?' His eyes followed the direction of her hand.

'It is called,' she continued, '*Cahir Conreagh,* the fort of the king, and is the scene of much romantic / story. It rises, as you see, in a plain, open and sunny, like the life-path of the prosperous: that is *your* way: – and here, to the left, behold, is a little gloomy glen, obscure and cloud-capp'd – it is rude and obstructed, and leads to solitudes and ruins – that is *mine*: farewell.'

She turned abruptly away, towards the spot she had so singularly described, and moved on with rapidity: but Fitzwalter as rapidly followed, and overtook her.

'Lady Clancare,' he said, imperatively, 'you *must* hear me. I will not neglect the opportunity afforded me by accident – accident is fate, is fortune; and fools or cowards only neglect its favours, or miss its tide, I am not much in the habit of governing myself, or of being governed – more practised in command than in obedience; yet I have obeyed you, / without reservation, as far as your orders were directed by prudence, discretion, or any other cold, necessary quality, which the world takes upon trust, in place of better feelings. I am prepared to obey you still in the world. There, reject and banish me, as you will, if it must be so; but here, in this place, so lonely, no eye to watch, no tongue to wound, no malice to misrepresent, why should you refuse to hear me, on a subject connected with the future destiny of one whose happiness you hold so dear to you? Hitherto I have lived the creature of my own fortunes, independent of any human being for my conduct, without one object to interest, one tie to bind me –'

'Without *one* tie?' interrupted Lady Clancare, emphatically, yet obviously intimidated by the impetuosity of his manner; for he spoke with vehemence; his eye flashing, his cheek glowing. /

'Well then,' he said, 'if you persist in calling that a tie, it is to that tie I would allude. I would account to you for an act so romantic, that even the feelings which led to it can scarcely excuse it – my strange, equivocal, uncompleated marriage with Florence Macarthy.'

'Then, General Fitzwalter,' replied Lady Clancare, with firmness, 'on this subject, neither here nor any where ought I to hear you, until impowered to do so by Florence Macarthy herself. A few days must put you in possession of her own sentiments and determination. But in the interim,' she added with a smile, 'like other diplomatic agents, I must neither act nor speak without instructions.'

'Then, Madam,' he replied with petulance, 'it were, perhaps, best to relieve you from your over cautious agency. I will fly myself to Florence / Macarthy; overtake, perhaps anticipate, a letter, which never should have been written before a personal interview had taken place; and learn, *vivá voce*,[104] what it is idleness to wait for in dilatory suspense.'

'Are you sure she will receive you?' asked Lady Clancare, coolly.

'She *must* receive me,' was the stern reply.

'True, even a convent's bars yield to a husband's intrusion.'

'Husband!' repeated General Fitzwalter. 'Husband to a woman I scarcely looked upon! whom I might not even again recognize!'

'Yet so earnestly did *she* look at you,' said Lady Clancare, in a voice full of softness and reproach; 'so well are *you* remembered, that from her description alone I should have known you among a thousand. Nay, I did instantly recognize you, from the pic-/ture she had drawn, even before you were announced in the hall of Dunore. So much for the rapidity of a woman's perceptions, the fidelity of a woman's memory, where the heart is engaged.'

'The heart! the heart engaged?' he interrupted, 'in one sudden, short, agitated interview! under such circumstances too!'

'The circumstances of that interview quickened and deepened the impression, and were calculated to affect and influence a woman's feelings and imagination. A soldier's daughter was well fitted to be interested in a soldier's virtues. She had long heard of you as a hero, in *an army of heroes:* as one combating *for,* not *against,* the rights of humanity.[z] She beheld you for the first time, flushed with conquest, soothing a father's death-bed anxieties, for the fate of his friendless child, by the offer of all you had to bestow, your hand and fortune, / and a name destined for immortality: and when Florence Macarthy described you as bearing her wounded, dying parent in your arms, from the field of battle to the neighbouring convent, from which she herself had beheld the fatal conflict, when she painted you as generously answering all his parental solicitudes, by offering to give his child the only protection a man of your age could afford a woman of her's, when she dwells upon your valour and disinterestedness, your prompt, uncalculating, romantic generosity –'

'Lady Clancare,' said General Fitzwalter, in great emotion, and colouring deeply, 'I cannot hear you out. That Miss Macarthy should have received such an impression, that you should thus recapitulate –'

'Me!' she replied, carelessly: 'you don't suppose I was imposed upon by the representations of a love-sick girl? / No, I have little respect for military heroes. Luck and temperament usually form the compound of a hero; and for one Cæsar on the list of military immortality there is many an illiterate Marlborough, without education sufficient to spell his own despatches,[105] and many a brutal Saxe, without intellect enough to compose them. O! your heroes follow a fearful and an hireling trade, at best: sometimes the butchers, sometimes the gaolers of the species; rarely its advocates or benefactors. Vainglorious abroad, worthless at home, despotic in the camp, dull in the circle.[106] It has been well, though quaintly said,

"Hercules was a fool, and straight grew famous,
For fool's the stuff of which heaven makes a hero."'[107]

'If a man,' said Fitzwalter, with a bent brow, and a compressed lip, 'ambitioned the character of a hero, your / ladyship's description would but little flatter his passion,'

'I admit exceptions, however, and would make one in favour of *the Librador*, to whom American gratitude may yet raise statues; but I do not admit them to Florence Macarthy. It has long been my system to oppose *her* fatal, fruitless prepossession in your favour, by representations calculated to weaken them; and when she would excuse your desertion, by the untoward circumstances of a party of the royal troops rushing down upon the convent, at the moment when the marriage ceremony was performing in its chapel, which obliged you to drop the hand of the weeping (and, *entre nous*),[108] maudlin bride, and to seize the sword – when she dwells upon your being forced from the altar to the field, upon your bravely opposing, repulsing, pursuing, a sanguinary foe, being surrounded, taken pri-/soner, condemned to death, rescued by your own devoted troop, then *I* take up the tale, to add – and once more free and crowned with fresh laurels, did he return to lay them at your feet, to claim his half-widowed bride, to ratify his imperfect vows!'

She paused, looked under her eyes; and there was a malignant archness in her countenance which had its effect. In a tone of irritation and impatience, he replied: 'I was the victim of circumstances. I did, however, return.'

'When?' asked Lady Clancare hastily.

'At the expiration of some months, and found the convent, where Miss Macarthy had been placed by her father, during the campaign in which he fell to save me, razed to the ground by the Spanish army.'

'And with the convent,' continued Lady Clancare, laughing, 'fell your / hopes and wishes, and all the et cetera of disappointed love. War was, in fact, your mistress, for glory was your passion; and now Florence Macarthy is left to find herself the "spouse of God in vain:"[109] for though, after your desertion, she struggled hard in her vocation, the human feeling was superior to the heavenly calling, *"not on the cross her eyes were fixed, but you:"*[110] for you were still before her, and always under circumstances favourable to her unhappy prepossession.[a] She followed you through all the public events of the day. Every gazette was a register of your actions and heroism; every newspaper *"prated of your whereabouts."*[111] [b] The Guerilla chief, II Librador, became the hero of her imagination, that first strong-hold in the pregnable garrison of a woman's feelings.'

She paused. The general sighed / deeply, walked on with a slackened pace and folded arms, and lent not a pleased but an ardent attention, interrupted by occasional starts of amazement, while she again continued: 'Unwooed, unsought for, forlorn, abandoned, poor, and friendless, the destruction of the convent which had afforded her an asylum urged her return to Ireland. Since *then* her life has been a blank, with one bright object glittering upon its surface, like the brilliant spot, self-formed, in the retina of the eye, when all around is darkness. You, however, I trust, have come to dispel that darkness, and to give to that bright speck a more definite form and a steadier lustre; for I take it for granted you are returned in search of a wife,

"*Lost or mislaid,*
Stolen or strayed,'

as the crier[112] of Ballydab has it:[c] though / I confess you negotiate the recovery with a *sang froid*[113] that renders your ardour in the research very doubtful.'

'I came to this country,' he said, thoughtfully, and with a countenance marked by painful embarrassment, – 'upon a very different business; upon a mission less generous, less *just,* than you suppose.' He pressed his hand to his forehead, and abruptly broke off: then, after a few moments silence, interrupted only by a deep inspiration, he added, 'I will see Miss Macarthy, Madam. I will leave Dunore for her convent to-morrow; and if her feelings are disposed as you describe them, if her religious, like her marriage vows, are still unratified –'

'If they were ratified,' interrupted Lady Clancare, eagerly, 'with her great uncle, a cardinal of considerable influence with the pope, and resident at Rome, Don Dermutio Macarthy, there / would be no difficulty in procuring a dispensation.' Then, after a long pause, she added, with earnestness, – 'Go then, General Fitzwalter, and hear your destiny from the lips of her whose life and happiness lies, I fear, in your decision; and take with you my prayers for your happiness, my hopes that whatever may have drawn you to this poor country, it will yet benefit by your talents and philanthropy; and the liberator of the enslaved in other lands may become the advocate of the oppressed in his own.'

She spoke with a feeling, an energy that was infectious; and when she pronounced 'farewell,' and extended her hand to Fitzwalter, he seized it with a grasp, almost painful in its pressure: his eyes were fixed upon her as he searched, or would have searched, her inmost soul; and the agitation of his countenance evinced the conflict of / deep and strongly opposed emotions by which his own was torn; yet he continued silent.

'Should Miss Macarthy's answer arrive in your absence, inclosed to me,' demanded Lady Clancare, gently, but vainly endeavouring to liberate her hand, 'where am I to forward it?'

'If,' said he, dropping her hand with a deep sigh, and recovering from his abstraction, – 'if you expect an answer so soon –' he paused.

'I must have one in a day or two at furthest,' she replied. 'I did not trust your embassy to our uncertain cross-posts: I despatched one of our Irish pedestrian couriers, who, if not quite as graceful as "a feathered mercury,*" [114] [d] are always trust-worthy. He / will return with an answer in the shortest possible time, that the surprise, I may say joy, of poor Florence will permit, in order that she may cooly sit down and reply to your unexpected proposals; for be they what they may, coming from *you*, after a silence of three years, they must surprise her, and cannot fail to be unexpected.'[e]

'Then,' he said, 'I will remain here, as I first intended, until this – answer – arrives.'

'Perhaps it were best,' replied Lady Clancare, carelessly; 'but you must now leave me. I know not how I have been thus led on to enter upon a topic forsworn: a woman is always the slave of circumstance and her own garrulity.'

'But I have still much to say,' / replied Fitzwalter, with earnestness, 'much to ask.'

'You must not say it now, not here, for we are near the high-road to Dunore. I must not be seen walking with you by the persons of this neighbourhood, who have no quadrant to take the altitude of my character,[115] and yet affect to calculate my conduct. I have set out in life with wind and tide against me; and now, that by prudence and circumspection I have been enabled to anchor in a safe but rude harbour, I would fain have no enemy to contend with but "*winter and rough weather.*"[116] Yet, even here, calumny has reached me.'

---

* These foot-messengers perform long journies with a celerity quite incredible; and for a recompence that marks the poverty of their state and the industry of their habits. They will carry a letter thirty Irish miles (near forty English) for sixpence, and perform this journey two or three times a-week.

'But if you forbid my intrusion elsewhere, you will at least release me from an observance of your orders of reserve at the castle of Dunore. Will you permit me to address you there when we meet?'

'Not for a wilderness of monkies,' / she replied, eagerly, and smiling; 'for I hold my tenure in Lady Dunore's favour by a clause, in which, somehow or other, your not appearing to know me makes an item.'

'Indeed! but good God, what object can her friendship be to you or –'

'Her friendship! the maniac!' she interrupted, with an indignant laugh that changed the whole expression of her countenance. 'She my friend! – she is my instrument, my agent, my tool, my any thing. You look amazed, General Fitzwalter: it will not lessen your amazement when I tell you that I am playing a part upon which all the prosperity and happiness of my life depends. It was necessary that I should get into the castle of Dunore and obtain an influence over its mistress. This was effected by means as wild and extravagant as her mind and habits. I was to / astonish her into prepossession, and secure her by a series of events which should gratify her love of strong excitements, and keep up the constitutional fever of her being; which should make her mine, give me the use of her house, the sanction of her authority, and keep aloof the idle frivolous circle, which, privileged by the charter of society, would, out of mere curiosity, without besieging or beseeching, have gained admission to my den, intrude upon the time they could neither compensate nor occupy, and then have left me to oblivion and neglect. As it is, I counteract the pernicious influence of the Crawleys on her mind, serve the poor of my neighbourhood, by directing the caprices of Lady Dunore to relieve their wants, keep off her train by her own prohibitions, and have obtained ample '*scope and room enough*'[117] for all my machinations: for to tell you a secret, / at this moment I move more puppets by my art than one.'

As she spoke, she looked like the magician she described herself. 'I perceive,' she continued, with a voice and glances which became every moment more acute and penetrating, 'that while I gain upon your imagination I lose in your esteem; but I shall recover it: "*Le tems et moi*," as Cardinal Mazarine used to say.[118] When you become acquainted with the object, you will admit the legality of the means, extraordinary as they are, extraordinary as they will appear to you; for when you know that I have imposed myself upon Lady Dunore as your wife –'

'My wife! he exclaimed, starting with the look of one thunder-stricken. 'Yes, your wife,' and she laughed, but coloured deeply, and turned pale in the succeeding moment. 'In a word, I have assumed the story of Florence / Macarthy; have persuaded Lady Dunore that I have found my renegade husband in her circle, without being recognized by him; for with a little dramatic license, such as being much changed in my person, having only been dimly seen through the shade of a Spanish mantillo by my unknown bridegroom, with all those combinations which might have existed in the instance of Florence Macarthy, nay, which *did*, according to her own account, I have imposed on her by facts extraordinary beyond the utmost daring of fiction; as the events of real life always exceed the power of invention.[f] Her object is that I shall win this cold insensible husband as Lady Clancare, whom, as Florence Macarthy, I could not secure. While engaged in the perpetration of this scheme she is wholly in my power. But if you really should fall in love with me; General Fitzwalter,' she / added playfully, 'it would be the ruin of all my plans, by curtailing the time necessary for its accomplishment; that is, if you betray your unhappy passion; – for a married man, the husband of my own, dear, long suffering Florence, must be unhappy, you know, for the sake of the *moral* of poetical justice.'

General Fitzwalter, stunned in the first instance, continued to listen to her with increased emotion; but when he would have spoken, she interrupted him, and continued:

'I am playing a desperate card: I have set my all upon the chance. I am actuated by the two strongest passions of which a woman's heart is capable. They have each their object. One has already almost succeeded; the other –.' She pressed her hand upon her heart, as if to check the violence of its throb, suddenly awakened by some singular association. At that moment / her quick eye discovered some person moving slowly under the stone fence which separated the heath on which they were walking from a car road; but the figure instantly disappeared, and the deep cuts in the bog in the other side the road favoured concealment, if that were an object.

'We are observed,' said Lady Clancare, anxiously: 'no retirement here is sacred from observation. There are two parties in this country in a continual state of espionage on each other, the oppressor and the oppressed. Communications are conveyed from remote extremities with inconceivable rapidity.[g] I suppose you are aware that you are an object of suspicion and of attention to Mr. Crawley?'

'What, now?' said Fitzwalter: 'why should you suppose it?'

'I know it. Many respectable, but timid persons in the neighbourhood, / observing your residence in the country, without any ostensible object or occupation, are anxious to have you removed, even although you are received at Dunore, the ordinary criterion of all worth and distinction. Your reception there is attributed to the predilection of Lord Adelm, whose half genius, half mania, whose mixture of poetry and paradox, has simply set him down with these good loyal people as a *jacobin outré*,[119] not to mention his conduct about the election, and the speeches he made to his committee.'

General Fitzwalter listened with that half-lent attention which accompanies pre-occupation of mind on other more interesting subjects.[h]

'Lord Adelm,' he observed, after a pause, 'is one whose virtues are overshadowed by his follies. He is noble, just, generous, and disinterested.'

'Vain, capricious, fanciful, and heartless,' she added. /

'And yet,' said General Fitzwalter, turning abruptly his eyes on Lady Clanclare, 'he is the star that holds the ascendant, that governs the conduct of one, who otherwise seems above all human control. Lady Clancare,' he added, rapidly, 'I have now not the slightest doubt that he is the object of what you have yourself termed *your machinations*, of the part you are playing, and of the agency so ingeniously, whimsically, and singularly conducted; so singularly conducted, that it cannot be surprising, with his heated imagination, and unregulated fancy, he should ascribe it to superhuman influence. All that you have so candidly confessed deepens and confirms this suspicion; and that he is the object of the passions by which you are actuated, the strongest of which a woman's heart is susceptible.'

Lady Clancare interrupted him: 'May I beg your assistance,' she said, offer-/ing him her hand, for they had now reached a stile, at which her cabriolet stood, attended by a boy. Then seating herself, and taking the reins and whip, she turned her laughing eyes full round on Fitzwalter, and nodding her head significantly, she said, '*Le tems et moi*,' and drove off.

Fitzwalter stood transfixed to the spot on which Lady Clancare had left him: his eye still followed the rustic carriage that conveyed her, till it descended into the glen she had pointed out to his notice, and was lost in its windings. He then turned shortly round to mount his horse, and came abruptly in contact with some person who stood close behind him. It was O'Leary. There was a shrewd, sly glance, lurking in the old man's eyes, mingled with the surprise and pleasure expressed at the general's appearance, which did not escape him at whom it / was levelled. He coloured slightly, and said, with some coldness, 'So, O'Leary.'

'Agus cead mille faltra,[120] your honor,' said O'Leary, moving his hat: 'ten thousand welcomes, and ten million welcomes home, and hopes the Gougane Barra plazed you, Sir, and Father O'Mahonny's hermitage.'

Fitzwalter was never less in a mood to withstand the annoyance of unseasonable intrusion. His thoughts were deeply occupied, and beyond the power of interest or distraction from any other subject. The presence of O'Leary, and the peculiar and significant expression of his countenance, embarrassed and provoked him. He mounted his horse in silence; but the tremulous and boggy surface he was treading obliged him to walk the spirited animal slowly and cautiously over the irregular and undulating turf. O'Leary / walked beside him for a few minutes in silence, raising his eyes at intervals to his face, with an affectionate and apprehensive look, as one who feared to have offended; at last, with a deep sigh, he said,

'I'm afraid I'm not agreeable to your honor.'

'It is certain, O'Leary,' said the general, with a petulance of temper he could not command, 'that you do not leave me many moments to myself.'

'Don't I, gineral, jewel?' said O'Leary sorrowfully. 'Then arnt it quite *natral*, that where the heart is, there will the body be also; troth it will.'

'But, my dear O'Leary,' said the general, in a voice of kindness, 'you must be aware that there are moments when the presence of the dearest friend may be felt as intrusion.'

'His dear O'Leary!' murmured the schoolmaster to himself. 'Why, then, / see here, gineral, jewel, sorrow bit but I'd throw myself from the top of Mangerton, afore I'd be a burthen to you, dead or alive; and axes nothing better in life than just to sarve you by day and by night, and to be looking in your face, when your back's turned, not to be unplazing to you; and wasn't thinking of you at all, at all, only wondering when you'd be back; and was going on an errand to the Bhan Tierna from Father Mulligan, about his dues owed to him by a poor family on Clotnotty-joy, that hadn't a scrubal nor a crass to buy a *station*;* and heard from little Ulic Macshane, her boy, who was leading round the cabriole by the bog road, that she was here convenient at Larry Toole's cabin, a fever house,' (and he crossed himself). /

'And here is the items I set down of Father Mulligan's dues, your honor, if you don't give credit to me.'

As he spoke, O'Leary presented the general a bit of dirty paper, on which was written

Shane Gartley, to the Rev. Patrick Mulligan, Dr.[121]

	s. d.
To two Confessions	2 2
To one Christening	1 8
To Sundries	1 6
	5 4[1]

'I should like to know what these devotional *sundries* were,' said the general, returning this account, furnished for salvation.

'Och! I'll ingage there was value received,' said O'Leary; 'and many a sore trot the priest had, by day and / night, over bog, and moor, and mountain, for their sowl's savetie, and to earn that trifle. But trifle as it is, Shane Gartly wasn't able for it, in respect of great sickness, and none to get in his potatoes for him, and he on the broad of his back, only just for the Bhan Tierna, the blessing of God and the Virgin Mary light on her, every day she sees the sun. When she got Clotnotty-joy into her hands, it was a desolate neglected place, with only a little handful of cattle grazing on it in the autumn time. The first ever she settled on it was this

---

*   In remote districts, where the Catholic chapel is at a considerable distance, the priest performs service in some poor man's cabin. This ceremony is termed a *station*.

Shane Gartly, whom she found big, bare, and ragged, walking the world* with a
wife and four childre, and a blanket and kettle: and says she, if you'll settle down
here, my lad, and labour, I'll give you a taste of land to / be your's for ever, and
help you to raise a shed, and lend you three pounds to stock and begin the world
with; and so she did. Under God, and her ladyship, Shane was doing bravely,
and many a one followed his example, and Christians were seen now, where only
bastes thriv before; but,

> Haud facile emergunt quorum virtutibus obstat,
> Res angusta domi,[122]

as the Roman poet sayeth, and it's true for him, for with all the labour and
pains and industry of the craturs, let them work night and day, and let them have
never such good friends to back them, its hard for them to get before the world:
and then if any accident happens, if the cow dies, or the rood of barley fails, its
the greatest of distress that comes over them, and so it was with Shane, when the
hard summer and the fever overtook him. But I'll / ingage with God and the
Bhan Tierna on his side, he'll fight it on yet.'

'From your account, O'Leary,' said the general, interested in a conversation
that took for its topic the object which exclusively ingrossed him – 'from your
account, Lady Clancare is the tutelar genius of the soil and its inhabitants.'

'Why then its just that she is, the lares and the penates[123] of the poor man's
cabin, long life to her; and if there were many of the likes of her, plaze your
honor, who would be after staying at home with us; why then the reformed and
civil sort would be cherished, and the poor and the ignorant would be instructed
and well exampled; and sorrow one of us would be beholding to them Crawley
pirates, bad luck to them, and their likes, who, by polling and pilling[124] the poor
to make good their own fortunes, and carrying on many false and cautelous[125]
practices, ruin the / land, like the escheators, and undertakers, and grantees of
Elizabeth's, and Charles's, and James's days. For its all one in Ireland, gineral,
dear, ould times or new: the men changes, but the measures never: and so, if
your honor don't believe me, being myself Irish mere, and thinks me a party
man, only look in a taste to the *Desiderata curiosa Hebernica*,[126] and then see the
Declaration, anno 1560, secundo Eliz. and see Lee's brief declaration of the Irish
government, opening many corruptions in the same, discovering the discords of
the Irishry, and the causes moving those troubles, anno Regni Reginæ 37; and
if that won't content your lordship, being English by descent, and of Norman
blood, why then dip into the English lords' remonstrances and appeals, see the
'*Humble Apology of the Lords, Knights, Gentlemen, and other inhabitants of the
English / Pale, for taking up arms in their own defence*, 1641; and Curry's Civil
Wars.[127] Och! Musha! it was all the same, English or Irish, Catholic, Protestant,

---

*   Walking the world, is wandering without a settled habitation.

or Presbyterian, when once their hearts warmed to the soil, and their spirits rose in its defence; then they were marked men, and sowld.[i] But though they send strangers to rule us,*[128] strangers I mane to our history, our natures, and our ways, that neither know, nor read, nor study us, and though, as Sir Henry Sydney said to the Queen, they pound us as in a mortar:[129] though they perish us with want, and burn us with fire, still the Irish spirit is to the fore; and until the sword of extermination passes over us, as was once proposed, it is not in the breath of the English to blow it out, or extinguish it.'

'I doubt, however, the existence of this *Irish spirit*,' returned the general, / gratified to observe that the mind of O'Leary was becoming hourly more collected, as the cause of its derangement was removed, 'The result of this misrule and oppression of ages, of this religious disqualification, of this arraying one-half the people against the other, by fanaticism and jealousy, is to extinguish what you call *Irish spirit*, by which, assuredly, you do not mean the spirit of idle unfounded discontent.'

'Unfounded!! Bachal Essu!' interrupted O'Leary, vehemently: 'when ould Elizabeth herself said of the government of Ireland, it will be objected to us, as to Tiberius by Bato, concerning the Dalmatians, "you it is that be in fault, who commit your flocks, not to shepherds, but to wolves."[130] Unfounded! when three-fourths of the people are, as it were, branded on the forehead, like the descendants of Cain,[131] and wandering in foreign lands, because / they profess the faith of their forefathers. For, as I said to Lord Adelm Fitzadelm when he scoffed at Butler's Lives of the Saints[132] this morning, when I found him seated his lone in your chamber, gineral, and the blessed and holy book in his hands –'

'Lord Adelm! was he at the Friary to-day?'

'He was, gineral, and yesterday – and did not much like his turning espial on you, like Jemmy Bryan, who watches your very shadow.'

'Indeed! But did Lord Adelm leave no message for me?'

'None in life, plaze your honor. Only hearing you might be expected this morning, sat him down, and took up Fra Dennis O'Sullivan's books, one by one, and held a disputation with me, wherein he shewed more wit than faith, until Madam Florence Macarthy's handkerchief caught his eye, lying on / the table, where you left it, gineral, and forthwith he put me on my trial.'

'What do you mean by that?' asked the general, impatiently.

'Crass examining me all about it, gineral, how it came there, and marveling that it should belong to Madam Macarthy, and she not in it.'

'And did he take it away?'

'No, plaze your honor, gineral, he did nat; and minded me of the honourable Gerald with his curling auburn hair, and toss back of the head, as if the world was made to be his slaves, – the very moral of the father of him; a great calabalero*[133] in his time.'

At this moment, a turn in the path brought them upon the high road to Dunore, by a causeway formed over a bog dike by branches of trees and sods of turf: and Lord Adelm himself ap-/peared, followed by a groom, and rode up to them. He looked somewhat confused, as if the rencontre was neither pleasant nor expected. It was, however, inevitable, and he drew up as the general approached him. To his abrupt inquiry of whither Lord Adelm was going, he replied, carelessly,

'To follow your example: change the scene for a day or two, get rid of time, myself, and of the society with which I have, for my sins, been for some days shut up; in a word, *promener mes ennuis ailleurs.*'[134]

The general threw his eyes over the valize strapped behind the groom; and Lord Adelm, as if to avoid all further interrogation, came close to him, and continued, in a low voice, –

'I congratulate you on your escape these few days back. Those who were fools before, are now mad, stark-staring mad; bitten by Rosbrin, and that artful / little adventuress, Lady Clancare, who has now brought them all round to her side, even Lady Georgina and Lord Frederick, and who is taking the short cut to Rosbrin's heart, by flattering his stage-struck vanity.'

'Lady Clancare! -- adventuress! – Lord Rosbrin's heart!' repeated Fitzwalter, breathlessly.

'Did you not observe it the other night, when she *debuted*[135] in that way, that he was the Prometheus that awakened the statue?[136] that it was for him she kindled, sparkled, and blazed forth? All her words were addressed to him, and all her dramatic airs and citations, and setting my mother afloat, on the article of private theatricals, her flippant cast of the characters of Comus, her assigning the daudling parts of the prosing brothers to us, and giving the hero to him; all go to the same tune of / Kilrosbrin, and the great house in Portman Square.'

'I perceived her *kindling*, as you call it; but that Lord Rosbrin was her inspiration, 'tis preposterous to suppose.'

'Why had she ears or eyes but for him?'

'She certainly did not do the honours by your self-love, or by mine, for she noticed neither,' said Fitzwalter, endeavouring to smile through the air of thoughtfulness which had taken possession of his features.

'Yes,' said Lord Adelm, biting his lips: 'as she tied up Rosbrin's leg I heard her call us *"the two gentlemen of Verona;"*[137] and the fool laughed as if she had said the cleverest things in the world: the sobriquet too has stuck to us ever since; for when you were missed you were inquired for by the title of *"Sweet Valentine;"*

---

*   Quere, cavalier.

and I was addressed / as "*Gentle Proteus.*" You will find them all in the paroxysm of the dramatic mania at Dunore, at least they have been so these four days; and Lady Clancare will keep up the epidemic till she is secure of exchanging her castle Ballydab for the mansion of Kilrosbrin, while to those who do not see, *dessous les cartes,*[138] she is merely *prima donna*[139] of the troop:'] so saying, he gallopped off, followed by his groom, who had been talking to O'Leary; and the general, as one who had undergone a sudden revulsion of ideas and feelings, heaved a deep sigh, and continued his route to the Friary.

By a few indirect questions he discovered that O'Leary had given Lord Adelm sufficient notices on the proprietorship of the handkerchief to induce him to learn the address, situation, and story of its supposed owner; and he entertained no doubt that his friend / was now engaged in a pursuit of errantry, in the supposition of having discovered the unknown spell which had governed his recent life. But nothing could come of nothing.[140] If Lady Clancare, the frank, though mysterious, unaccountable, incomprehensible, Lady Clancare, could be depended upon, the devotion of Florence Macarthy to himself, ideal and romantic as it appeared, would sufficiently frustrate the hopes of Lord Adelm, whether they sprang from vengeance or from love. If, however, contrary to all expectation, prepossession yielded to ambition, he would himself stand released from an engagement to which honour alone now bound him. In either case the pursuit and absence of Lord Adelm boded him no ill; it was, indeed, a subject dwelt upon but for a moment, and rapidly forgotten, for one which gradually possessed itself of his mind with an uncontrolable influence. /

Lady Clancare's views on Lord Rosbrin, as detailed to him by Lord Adelm, he could neither credit nor disbelieve, for he had not yet been a witness of the operations upon which Lord Adelm's inferences were founded. He saw at once, that like all vain persons, Fitzadelm was easily piqued by the semblance of neglect, even in women, who neither interested nor attracted him; and that his suspicions might have originated in the discolouring source of wounded self-love. He resolved, therefore, to judge for himself; and for this purpose once more join the circle at Dunore, painful as it was, to become involved in Lady Clancare's strange intrigue, and to support the character assumed by her direction.

An object of romantic fondness to one woman, to whom he was perfectly unattached, and of indifference to another to / whom he was ardently devoted, bound by ties of honour to the one, and by consequence, to avoid all intercourse with the other; his position new, singular, and uncalculable, left him no thought for any other subject of reflection. In the conflict of passions and principles, thus opposite and contradictory, and wrapped[k] in reverie, he was still seated before the untasted dinner which O'Leary had provided for him, when a note from Lady Clancare increased the pulsation of his heart, and propelled the blood with a violence that induced O'Leary to observe, as he stood watching him:

'No bad news, I hope, gineral, Sir? It was a bit of a gassoon, give old Morraigh that missive, your honor, while I was attending on you, Sir; and hope the Crawleys have no hand in it. Devil speed the whole *kish* of them, I pray Jasus!' /

'Inquire if the messenger waits,' said Fitzwalter; and when O'Leary had left the room he re-perused the note, already hastily read. It ran as follows:

'General Fitzwalter's letter has been received and acknowledged. The struggle of contending feelings prevents an immediate decision; and an interval for reflection is consequently required. Love and pride, hope and fear, are all at variance. Meantime it is expected General F. will not present himself at the Convent of the Annunciation without special invitation. Should Lady Clancare have the honour of meeting General Fitzwalter this evening at Dunore Castle, she may find some moment, *à la derobée*,[141] for being more explicit.'

Castle Macarthy,
Monday, Six o' Clock.

In the calendar of love, the moment of receiving the first line traced by the / object of adoration is a memorable epoch. It is a festival of the heart, always commemorated with transport so long as that object holds its empire.[1] The handwriting of Lady Clancare, the paper folded by her, fluttered the pulse of him to whom it was addressed, and for a moment even the nature of the communication was forgotten. When at last reverted to, the contents of the note came like a reprieve: he believed that there was now a necessity for remaining where he was, to receive the sentence by which he was resolved to abide. He had arisen from the table, and was about to replace the note in its envelope, when the seal caught his attention; its motto was

'Sou utile ainda que bricando.' /

CHAPTER III.

Su, svegliatevi da bravi,
Su, corraggio o buona gente.
Vogliam star allegramente
Vogliam ridere e scherzar.
                    IL DON GIOVANNI.[142]

I know you all – and will awhile uphold
The unyok'd humour of your idleness.
                    SHAKESPEARE.[143]

IN the brief sketch which Lord Adelm had made of the social economy of the castle of Dunore, he had scarcely exaggerated the epidemic influence of the reigning folly of the day. The dramatic mania which had seized the marchioness, indirectly or directly, favoured the views, interests, or vanity, of every member of her / circle. It broke through the spell of that all pervading demon, ennui, and provided that something to do or to discuss, so essential to those who are habitually dependent upon external circumstances for occupation and interest, and who, from their elevated position in society, are unpractised in the exercise of their own resources. It removed likewise the prying eye of concentrated observation from those who wished to elude its glances; and by opening the door to strangers, it enlarged a circle whose members had long become weary of each other. Even Conway Crawley and his aunt, the only persons of that family then at the castle, found their account in an event, which afforded to the poetical vanity of one an opportunity of writing an opening address, while it left him a more undisputed management of the Glannacrime election, in which Lord / Adelm took no interest;[m] and to the other it held out means of operating the conversion of Lady Dunore, which overcame her conscientious aversion to theatricals, private or public, and reconciled her to the sin as the instrument of contingent good. It is a dogma of the sect to which Miss Crawley belonged, that the deeper the sinner, the greater the saint; – that there is a necessary probation of iniquity to qualify for the expected grace, and to render the dispensing power of mercy the more manifest upon earth. In Miss Crawley's eyes private theatricals now stood high in the calendar of offences; and according to her system of *reculer pour mieux sauter*,[144] she was satisfied that in proportion as Lady Dunore risked the little virtue time and the world had left her, she would more perfectly fit herself for that state, in which the '*nothingness* of good works'[145] is but as a sounding brass and tinkling cym-/bal.[146n] Meantime her own little frippery tastes and paste-board talents had ample scope in planning decorations for the proscenium of the new theatre, in assisting Lord Rosbrin in the getting up of stage *properties*, and in suggesting devices and mottos to ornament the frontispiece. She disapproved, it is true, and spoke against the whole business with edifying eloquence; but she seized not the less willingly the scissars and the pencil at the command of Lady Dunore, domineering over the dress-makers of the theatrical wardrobe, as over the sempstresses of the cheap repository, dictating to machinists as she had done to Neophytes, and flattering herself that she was forming a balance to the preponderating influence of Lady Clancare, who had so nearly turned the vacillating scale of her patroness's favour against her.

From the night of the first dramatic / discussion, every circumstance and subject had yielded to the important interests of the private theatricals. Expresses were despatched by Lord Rosbrin for the histrionic amateurs in the neighbourhood of Kilrosbrin, whom he had drilled to the exercise of the art; dress-makers, mechanists, and carpenters, arrived with incredible rapidity; and the few English and Irish families of rank resident in the country were invited to the castle, and readily obeyed the summons.[o]

The difficulties, obstacles, and contrarieties, which were to be overcome or reconciled, made up the whole charm of the arrangement to Lady Dunore, who, in her capacity of manageress, had to contend with that inordinate vanity, that overweening *amour propre*, usually attributed to actors, public or private, which, though it wearied, fatigued, and fevered her, was not less a source gratification than of annoyance. /

It was in vain that plays were selected, proportionate to what Lord Rosbrin technically called 'the *strength of the company*,' and that parts were judiciously cast, according to the talents of the respective actors. The corps dramatique[147] of Dunore was a company of first-rates; all stars, all chiefs, either of the sock or buskin,[148] or of both: none were subalterns; and, with a profusion of supernumerary Romeos and Doricourts, Macbeths and Macheaths,[149] there were none to take the inferior characters.

A young lady from Cork, introduced by Miss Crawley, an Irish *gentlewoman bred and born*, but who was soon to come forward on the Dublin boards, and by the stamp of *private* opinion, was already superior to the Barries and Siddonses[150] of other times, took possession at once of the tragic heroines, with a spirit of monopoly that was not without opposition. Not content with the / natural importance of Desdemona, she refused to perform the part, unless she was allowed to double it with some of the best speeches of Othello. To this, the Othello (Lord Rosbrin) solemnly objected, declaring, that so far from giving up the *ghost of a letter* of his own part, he meant to restore to it some lines from the part of Iago, according to an old edition, of which no one had heard but himself. Iago's resistance to this *restoration* was unvanquishable; and he conceived that his own *scenes* stood so little prominent, that he proposed ekeing it out with the best speeches of Zanga, in the tragedy of the Revenge.[151]ᵖ

Contentions ran so high on the subject of Othello, that at last it was laid aside, and three tragedies were placed in the stock list, in which each of the tragedians were in turn to play the principal part, and ingross exclusively the attention of the audience. /

Lady Dunore, meanwhile, far from reconciling these dramatic disputes, endeavoured by every species of *tracasserie*[152] to nourish and perpetuate them.

Alternately chosen by the contending parties as referee and umpire in these 'fierce vanities'[153] she became the very genius of discord; and before the first rehearsal, one half the company had sent the other to Coventry,[154] and held no communication, but in their assumed characters of heroes and heroines.

In this floating capital of vanity and exhibition, the largest portion of stock seemed to have been contributed by Lady Clancare. The first line in comedy had been assigned to her by Lord Rosbrin; and the oddity, whim, and originality, with which she delivered certain passages in the Rosalinds, Beatrices and Roxalanas,[155] whether they were or were not true to the author's conception, obtained universal admiration. /

A countenance, whose extraordinary mobility was susceptible of every expression, a certain sly simple solemnity of look and air, which possessed itself of every feature, and ranged every muscle on the side of humour, and a taste for mimickry, with a keen sensibility to absurdity, naturally capacitated her for being a good comic actress.[q]

The influence, however, which she had obtained, was not exclusively through her histrionic talent. She had made herself necessary to the amusement of those so difficult to amuse, and she consequently assumed an overweening importance, which never fails to succeed with indolence or mediocrity in all ranks. She now affected to consider acting as the first of talents: she spoke, as if a great tragedian or comedian, male or female, was of more consequence to society than the philosopher who instructs, the genius who en-/lightens, or the artist who improves it: and she, who as an author, an inventor, or an originator, as one who took life and nature for her guides, rejecting conventional rules and assumed tastes,[r] had appeared in this bon-ton circle, modest, nervous, timid, and unpretending; now, in her newly assumed character of an actress, an imitator, a detailer of other persons' ideas, became imposing, self-sufficient, and inconsequent; taking, without hesitation, the place which the new prepossessions of the frivolous society in which she lived had assigned her, and giving that boundless fling to whim and caprice, in which the *spoiled* of every class indulge, at the expense of those who make them what they are. Always surprising or disappointing, she set calculation at defiance; and the certainty that the corps dramatique could not do without her, rendered them submissive to all her oddities. /

She still refused to sleep at Dunore; and a carriage, horses, and servants, were kept in continued requisition to go between that mansion and Castle Macarthy, a journey which they performed a dozen times a-day. Not unfrequently she was superintending her turf clamps, while her Solyman the magnificent fretted his hour upon the stage in expectation of his Sultana, or was busied with literary composition, or in getting in her potatoes, while Orlando stood in the forest of Arden in vain attendance on his whimsical Rosalind:[156] but while she thus illtreated her *co-partners,* for authors she had no mercy. Seemingly occupied with the idea that she alone could amuse or interest the audience, her efforts to stand supereminently forward, to secure the leading points, and 'clap traps,'[157] as Lord Rosbrin called them, were incessant and extravagant. She cut, interpolated, subjoined, trans-/posed, and changed the text of her part, until scarcely an original intention of the mangled author remained: and in this sacrifice to her monopolizing ambition, Shakespeare and O'Keefe, Ben Jonson, and Moreton,[158] the author of the day, or the poet of ages, were treated with equal severity, or rather with equal indifference. Still, however, dissatisfied with all she could effect by efforts, naturally opposed by the contending selfishness of rival candidates, she finally resolved (and her versatile talents forwarded the intention) to write a monologue for herself, in which, uniting various characters, she would alone occupy the stage and the audience. The sketch she gave of her interlude, then new and original, met with general approbation. Even the literary talent expended upon its composition was forgiven, in favour of the more highly prized ability which was / requisite to enact it: and they, who would have scarcely inquired the name of the person who produced the clever thing, were wild in praise of the actress who only realized the conceptions.

'But, good heavens! my dear Lady Clancare,' observed the Marchioness, as Lady Clancare, the centre of a circle of listeners, concluded the reading of the rough sketch of her monologue; 'why don't you write plays instead of those romantic tales about your own country, which every body reads, and nobody believes?'

'Aye, why indeed?' said Lord Rosbrin.

'Because,' replied Lady Clancare, 'if I wrote plays, I am afraid I must draw characters.'

'To be sure,' said Lady Dunore; 'and what then? Is there anything so delightful as characters?'

'Provided they *resemble nobody*,' said Lady Clancare. /

'How do you mean?' asked the Marchioness.

'Simply, that should I ever abandon my high strain of romance by the advice and supplication of my dear friends, *les belles et bonnes dames de par le monde*,[159] and hold the mirror up to life, you would all fancy you detected in it your own reflection, and each

"Would cry, that was levelled at me."'[160]

'Certainly,' said Lady Georgina, 'if one saw one's self shewn up, one would feel and resent it, and so too I hope would all one's friends, at least I should expect it.'

'But what is the *genre* of character,' said Lady Clancare, 'which, if in true keeping to life and manners, should not be found to resemble any body? There is no *beau ideal*[161] in human life: combine qualities as you may, to the very verge of extravagance, the world will furnish models, trace like- /nesses, and assign originals – let your conceptions be as general as they can – paint classes and describe genera: – classes and genera are still made up of individuals; and even vanity will find out resemblances where satire could not trace similitude. There, indeed, my patience quite fails me. Conscious vice, conscious absurdity, and apprehensive eccentricity, when combined with masculine energies and decided volitions, may be excused for indulging in such fanciful appropriations; but that the walking no-characters of every-day life, the dear, dull,

"Unfinish'd things one knows not what to call,

Their generation's so equivocal,"[162]

should imagine themselves fit subjects for indignant reprehension or sportive caricature, and live in fear of authors, lest they should *put them in their books!* – put *them* in our books! who then would read us? or who would review us? – / Which of the worthy *we's*, [163] the *weekly*, the *monthly*, the *quarterly* drudges, would "*let loose their dogs of war*"[164] on works safe from the world's notice and applause. – No, *they* war not with dulness and the dead; it is living, buoyant, and, above all, prosperous merit, animates their zeal; and their malice is worth courting: for, next to the spontaneous burst of public applause, an author's ambition should be the unqualified, unmanly, ungentlemanlike attacks of some party, hired anonymous reviewer. I speak with warmth, for I speak from experience. I have not the vanity to think you have all read me, "*pour les beaux yeux de mon mérite.*"[165] No, I have been lashed into note by these "*waspstung and impatient critics:*"[166] their attacks have been patronage, their malice kindness; and it must be allowed they have been

"Very, very, very kind indeed."[167] s

'But why write at all?' exclaimed / Lord Rosbrin, who was now considered as the professed admirer of Lady Clancare, and who took an interest in all she said or did.

'Simply,' she replied with naïveté, 'to live – you may perhaps add, *quelle necessité*:[168] and, perhaps also,' she added significantly, 'you are right.'

'No,' answered Lord Rosbrin, 'I should reply no such thing. I would have you live to be the first actress of the day; which you would, should you ever be tempted to go on the stage.'

'One never did see a peeress on the stage,' said Lady Dunore, delighted with the new idea – 'it would be quite curious, charming.'

'So it would,' said Lady Clancare, as if suddenly struck with the proposal, and inclined to adopt it.

'You would have made the first actress in the world,' continued Lord / Rosbrin, 'and, perhaps, would net ten or twenty thousand pounds in a year or two.'

'More than you could make in a long life by writing,' observed Lady Dunore, 'the best book that ever was read.'

'A great deal more,' replied Lady Clancare.

'Besides,' continued Lord Rosbrin, 'so far from derogating from your rank, it would probably promote it. – The green-room is now the shortest road to the red bench.'[169]

'Exactly so,' replied Lady Clancare.

'And many English peers,' continued Lord Rosbrin, with meaning in his looks, 'who would not think of you as a gentlewoman, or a genius, would be happy to lay their honours and their fortunes at your feet, as a celebrated and popular actress.' /

'*On peut se rapporter à vous par exemple*'[170] said Lord Frederick.

'Then,' said Lady Dunore, 'you would be so much more *fétée*[171] as an actress than as a genius.'

'Besides,' said Lord Rosbrin, 'who cares when an author dies?'

'Nobody,' said Lady Clancare, shaking her head.

'What is there in the death of twenty celebrated writers to the solemnity of one great tragedian taking leave of the stage? Handkerchiefs streaming, eyes winking, sobs heaving, laurels flying, awful pauses, broken sentences, and hysterical screams. I'd rather be a great actor taking leave of the stage than die the greatest hero of the age. Then when you do die,' continued Lord Rosbrin, heated by his subject, 'what honours await you! dukes hold the pall, earls chief mourners, dead march in Saul,[172] monument in West-/minister,[173] dust mingled with kings and conquerors.'

Here a sort of Irish howl, bursting from the lips of Lady Clancare, produced a shout of laughter from all present, save Lord Rosbrin, to whom she replied, shaking her head, and wiping her tearless eyes – 'No, never did I think I should weep so much at my own funeral; for I am now determined to adopt your lordship's advice, and, like other *dramatis personæ*, "*to that complexion must I come at last.*"'[174]

'Then,' said Lord Rosbrin, 'I promise you complete success,' and he added, in a low whisper, 'more than that.'

'In that case,' said Mr. Pottinger (who, since Lady Clancare's popularity with the *people of quality*, had taken her into special consideration), 'in that case I fear your ladyship cannot go to the castle, that is, on public days. / You could not well take your place on the red bench as an actress, although you are a peeress.'

'That, indeed,' said Lady Clancare, as if suddenly struck with the mortifying conviction, 'that makes all the difference.'

'But,' said Lord Rosbrin, 'in that case you will not come to Ireland, except as a star, in the after season, when Covent Garden is shut; and I'll answer for it, the vice-regals will be enchanted to give you *les petites entrées* at the Phœnix.[175] I remember when the arrival of an Italian opera singer in Dublin turned the heads of the court, and of all the officials, major and minor. Imagine then how another Farren, another Abingdon,[176] would be received.'

'I wish, Lady Clancare,' said Lady Georgina, with her usual supercilious high-dame-of-quality air, 'I wish you would *raconter* a little of your history: / I dare say it would be very amusing and odd.'

'*A mourir de plaisir*,[177] no doubt,' said Lord Frederick, raising his glass to her face.

'No,' said Lady Clancare, conceitedly throwing herself into an arm chair, 'I am not equal to details to-night: besides, should my story be serious, you would yawn over it; should it be romantic, you would quiz[178] it; if philosophical, you would not understand it; if common-place, you would abuse it; if extraordinary, you would doubt it. Now it happens to be all this, and I should thus unite every species of criticism against me.'

'I have not a doubt,' said Lord Rosbrin, 'that your life would be quite as amusing as George Anne Bellamy's apology, or Mrs. Baddely's memoirs.'[179]

'And as edifying too?' asked Lady Clancare. 'But I appeal to Lady Du- /nore, if it be possible for me to reveal all the circumstances of my life?'

'By no means,' said Lady Dunore, with a mysterious air, and throwing her eyes to that part of the room where General Fitzwalter stood, and she instantly gave the conversation another turn.

After a short struggle, Fitzwalter had yielded to the temptation of Lady Clancare's indirect appointment, and had joined the evening circle at Dunore, where he was received with courtesy by the marchioness, but with indifference by all the rest. Mr. Daly, the only person capable of appreciating him, had departed; driven away by the noise, confusion, and discomfort, the bustle and contentions of the private theatricals. The little society that had been enjoyed at Dunore Castle was now quite broken up; conversation was at an end; and even cards and billiards / were suspended, the whole intercourse being confined to criticisms on the drama, compliments between the actors on their respective merits, or complaints of rival monopolists: for, as Touchstone says, they '*quarrelled in print by the book; and retorts courteous, quips modest, replies churlish, reproofs valiant, and counter-checks quarrelsome,*'[180] were echoed and re-echoed in every quarter.'

The hope which had led General Fitzwalter to the castle was wholly frustrated. Lady Clancare had afforded him no opportunity of addressing her. On entering the saloon he beheld her the *primum mobile*[181] of the circle which surrounded her. During the evening she scarcely noticed him by a look; and when she retired, which she did early, Lord Rosbrin led her to the carriage, and took her willing hand, with the air of Henry the Eighth handing out Anne Bulleyn at Cardinal Wolsey's / banquet,[182] and murmuring as they passed Fitzwalter,

'The fairest hand I ever touched. Oh, beauty,
Till now I never knew thee.'[183]

While she, humouring his folly, replied:

'I do not know
What kind of my obedience I should tender,
More, than my all is nothing.
Beseech your lordship, &c. &c.'[184]

The words were lost as she disappeared; and a conviction of the truth of Lord Adelm's observation struck forcibly on Fitzwalter's mind. He turned away in indignant irritation, while Lady Dunore, with her eyes fixed expressively on his, observed:

'Is not Lady Clancare an excellent actress?'

'Excellent!' he replied, in a tone of ironical significance. /

'Lord Rosbrin is amazingly in love with her,' added Lady Dunore, emphatically.

'It is a proof of his taste,' replied the general, coldly.

'What do you think of her?' demanded Lady Dunore, with an inquisitorial look.

Aware of the object of all these remarks and questions, General Fitzwalter felt confused, and indignant at the strange situation into which Lady Clancare's embroglio had thrown him. Lady Dunore evidently enjoyed his confusion; but without reiterating the question, added, 'she is extremely clever, but by no means does the honours by her own talents; and until we hit on these delightful theatricals, had no success whatever with my set. Since then, she has come out wonderfully. She is the most delightful Beatrice I ever saw, and capable of making a benedict of / the most obdurate wife hater.'[185] With these words, uttered with a mysterious air, she fluttered away, and joined in a conversation in another part of the room.

General Fitzwaiter, governed by passions, over which neither reason nor will held any influence, found himself for two or three successive evenings in the saloon of the castle, a spectator rather than a member of its society, where there were none to communicate with him since the absence of Mr. Daly and of Lord Fitzadelm. His visits, however, were apparitions. He came and disappeared abruptly, as if in search of some object never obtained, yet still pursued. His character was more than usually energized; and though he commonly stood wrapped in silent but acute observation, in sullen and marked abstraction, yet he occasionally came forward in conversation, with a boldness / and originality, that chequered the monotonous flow of some modish opinion, and startled common-place remark from its wonted track. His first appearance at Dunore as a guerilla chief insured him that species of favourable reception, given equally to learned pigs, and French conjurers, Esquimeaux warriors, and Irish giants:[186] but first prepossessions faded away in proportion as it became known that he was engaged in a cause wholly inimical to the sentiments of the greater part of Lady Dunore's circle, who took their opinions from graver parrots than themselves. Upon the subject of public affairs they held no discussion; and the manner and matter of his conversation were equally out of their beaten track; for the law of bon-ton enforced the necessity of never being energetic upon any subject, of never deserting that half dead-alive suavity which simpers its / flat medium between pleasure and pain, the gentlemanlike and melancholy habit of *ennui* and self-sufficiency. On subjects of lighter moment there was still no reciprocity, for he was ignorant of the philosophy of dandyism, unpractised in the cold routine of fashionable gallantry, and unstudied in the dull memoirs of fashionable characters. A patriot warrior combating for the rights of humanity, for the emancipation of a long debased and enslaved people, and opposing a bigotted, ferocious, and imbecile tyranny,ᵘ he had upon the whole, after the first surprise occasioned by his abrupt and splendid appearance, become an object of some-what less consequence than Thady Windham Crawley, with his peninsular honours, bivouacks, wigwams, and the Ragent's levee.

The absence of Lord Adelm had been noticed by all, though not com-/mented upon by any. To his mother it was in fact a relief rather than a privation. To the other women he was cold and *brusque*;[187] to the men, haughty and super-cilious. He stood aloof from all; and his refined tastes, singular habits, and his powerful vanity, found no account in the private theatricals, which, as he neither could nor would take a part, he openly ridiculed with a wit and an asperity that could neither be rebutted nor retaliated. His immediate return (for the election drew near) was therefore expected with apprehension rather than hope; and his mother was not among the last to pray for its prorogation.ᵛ

The night of the first representation was now arrived. The play of 'As you like it' was to be performed; and a crowded audience, furnished from the guests of the castle and the neighbourhood of Dunore, had already assem- /bled, when a note from Lady Clancare, returned by the carriage which had been sent for her, informed the marchioness that she could not play Rosalind that night, and hint-ing that she had been seized with a typhus fever.

The confusion which this unexpected circumstance created was excessive. Persons had arrived from immense distances; expectation was at its height. The first music was over, and all was consternation. Lady Dunore stamped her feet and wrung her hands, as if the most dreadful affliction had befallen her: she abused Lady Clancare, as if her misfortune was her fault; and would have set off for Cas-tle Macarthy, but for the apprehension of the infection, so long the object of her terror. In the midst of this dilemma Lord Rosbrin, already dressed for Orlando, proposed to undertake the part of Rosalind; while the *second Amoureux*, who / was to have performed Sylvius,[188] should assume Orlando. The *second Amoureux* declared that Orlando was the part he had originally intended for himself, and that he was perfect for it. One of the foresters[189] engaged to perform Sylvius, delighted to escape from the mortification of enacting a mute.[190] Lord Ros-brin's proposed arrangement was accepted with transport by Lady Dunore. If he played the part with propriety, Lady Clancare would not be missed: if he did it ridiculously, her place would be still better supplied.

The place *was* still better supplied; and the shouts of laughter, which hailed the entrances and exits of Rosalind, were testimonies that the audience were sat-isfied and amused up to their bent. The play went off brilliantly: bravoes and archi-bravoes marked every speech; and the original Rosalind was left extended on her bed of sickness / without one thought of her situation, and given to instant oblivion. The disappointment she had occasioned Lady Dunore in the first instance had overthrown the frail structure of her prepossession at a blow; and the creature who could no longer amuse, no longer interested or lived in the memory of her *soi-disant*[191] friends and admirers. /

CHAPTER IV

Stand not amaz'd – here is no remedy.
                                                SHAKESPEARE.[192]

I speak not this in estimation
As what I think might be, *but what I know*
Is ruminated, plotted, and set down,
And only stays but to behold the face
Of that occasion which shall bring it on.
                                                SHAKESPEARE.[193] w

LADY DUNORE, wearied and exhausted, was the last to quit the scene of festivity, and the most anxious to prolong it. She had presided at a splendid supper after the play, and had reluctantly bowed out her guests, and bestowed her usual *embrassades*[194] on her / dear friend, Lady Georgina: she was now taking one lingering look at the silent and deserted theatre in her passage to her own apartment, when the sound of a footstep closely following her own, alarmed her, she knew not why. Without 'casting a look behind,'[195] she was hastily ascending the stairs, when a voice called after her, 'Aisy, aisy, my lady, if you plaze. I'd just beg a word with your ladyship *incornuto*[196] for a moment.'

At the well-known voice and accent of Darby Crawley, Lady Dunore turned round. 'Good God!' she said, 'Mr. Crawley, is it you? When did you arrive from Dublin? Were you at our play? – Conceive my not seeing you.'

'I was not, my lady; but came here a few hours back, and has been lying ' he whispered – '*per dor*[197] in Anne Clotworthy's room till the play was over, and the company gone, not / wishing to shew myself for *raisins* of state. Would your ladyship just turn in here for a moment, and grant me an hearing on very particular business?'

'Certainly,' said Lady Dunore, following him into the dark spacious dining-room. Crawley shut the door cautiously, took the chamber candlestick out of Lady Dunore's hand, and placed it on a table; then drew forward a chair for her, and another for himself, picked up her ridicule,[198] and presented it with a bow, and drawing his hand over his face, as if at a loss how to begin, he at last abruptly inquired,

'Does your ladyship know any thing of Lord Adelm Fitzadelm, for he is not here it seems?'

'Gracious heavens!' exclaimed Lady Dunore, suddenly alarmed: 'if any thing has happened let me know it at once;' and she started from her chair. /

'Where is Fitzadelm, and what do you know of him?'

'Nothing in life, I give you my honour, Lady Dunore; and wouldn't keep you in suspince half a minute if I did: only just axed out of curiosity, if he's at a distance; that's all, I give you my honour.'

'I don't know where he is,' said Lady Dunore, between the hope and the fear of having some cause for alarm and agitation: – 'he is upon one of his wild rambles.'

'*Tom-Mew*,[199] as the French says, Lady Dunore; for he has a mighty odd quick way with him, and isn't always inclined to hear raison.'

'Nor I neither,' yawned his disappointed auditress. 'At two in the morning, my dear Mr. Crawley! Surely your coming at so unseasonable an hour must have some extraordinary motive,' and she took up her candlestick. /

'No ways extraordinary at all, at all, Madam; for such things happen every day; for what brings me here to your ladyship, masquerading at this hour of the night, is about a *hitch* in the election. I suppose Conway has tould your ladyship that the sheriff's precept for the election is issued, and the polling will begin to-morrow.'

'I believe he did; but really,' and she yawned again, 'I have been so deeply engaged of late; and Fitzadelm's absence, and my dependence on you, and your son, and things, that I did not particularly think about it; but –'

'But,' continued Crawley, gently taking the light out of her hand, 'he did not tell you, and how could he, and he never near Glannacrime this fortnight, that, contrary to our expectation, there will be a violent opposition; and that isn't no ways impossible but the / Dunore interest will be trodden down by those O'Mahonny whigs.'

'Trodden down!' interrupted Lady Dunore, indignantly, and reseating herself – 'The Dunore interest trodden down!'

'Except, in addition to the *thousands* already distributed, there is a couple of thousand pounds more, to carry on the war during the polling,' added old Crawley, with some hesitation.

'And is that all?' asked Lady Dunore, languidly.

'All!' repeated Crawley, with a look of pleased surprise.

'Oh! if that does not *shoot* (suit) you, Ma'am, your ladyship may follow the bend of your generosity, and make it *double* or *quits*. But the *murthur* of it is, Lady Dunore, that after you have expended thousands upon thousands, and after Lord Adelm is elected, which he will be as sure as eggs is eggs, and no / thanks to them, it seems his opponent manes to petition against him in parliament, on the score of what they, the spalpeens, call his bribery and corruption, his *trates* and his presents, and other illegal practices to which he has had recourse; that's if you'll believe the likes of them, the rebelly thieves.'

'Bribery and corruption! illegal practices! My son, Lord Adelm Fitzadelm guilty of this, Mr. Crawley,' interrupted Lady Dunore, with a mingled expression of anger and surprise. 'What does all this mean, Mr. Crawley?'

'Why it manes, my lady, plain enough, that in Ireland, as throughout the world, a little bribery goes a great way. The people, Ma'am, are used to it. It's the way of the place, time *in-memorial*, and will be evermore. The voters and freeholders, and corporation of Glannacrime, require a taste of a / *dewshure*[200] as well as their betters, why wouldn't they; and nothing has been done here, that hasn't been done since the beginning of the *Europayan* world, at all elections; and would pass muster any where, only for them jacobin whigs, the O'Mahonneys, that are just ready like *drownded* men to catch at a straw. It's only them and the likes of them that is always open mouthed against loyal men, or would go to call a little trifle of a prisent made to the burgesses of Glannacrime a bribe.'

'I don't care what *they* call it,' said Lady Dunore, rising in violent emotion, as the high honour and lofty spirit of her son started to her recollection, coupled with these accusations – 'I don't care what your Irish creatures call it; but what will my son say? What will Lord Adelm Fitzadelm say to this imputation on his honour and principles?' /

'What can he say, Madam?' returned Crawley, endeavouring to keep pace with Lady Dunore, who was now walking in agitation up and down the room: 'What can his lordship say, but that while he was star-gazing in Lisburn, the capital of Spain,[201] among them Papists, his friends at home was working for his interests, like gallows slaves,[202] sparing neither time, money, nor labour, to keep out the ould enemies of his family, and get in himself?'

'He will *murder* you, Mr. Crawley; I *promise* you *that*,' said Lady Dunore, cooly, and stopping short in her quick pacing,

'The Lord save us!' ejaculated Crawley, looking round him fearfully.

'You know,' she continued, 'he already holds you and all your family, *en franche et belle aversion*.'[203]

'He does!' said old Crawley, guessing rather than understanding the pur- / port of this sincere assurance. Then with a low, half insolent, half mysterious tone, he added, 'Why then, in spite of all that, Lady Dunore, it's me and my family can be the saving of him and his yet.'

'Indeed!' said Lady Dunore, with a laugh of irony.

'Indeed!' repeated Crawley, unintimidated; 'and, Lady Dunore, will you just hear me for a minute, and then I'll never spake more, if I don't contint you to your heart's desire.'

There was something imposing in the manner of Crawley, which induced the Marchioness to resume her seat, and to grant him (what she so rarely granted any one) a *patient hearing*.

'Now, Lady Dunore,' he continued, 'it will tell ill for the greatness and grandeur and honour of the Fitzadelm and Dunore families, that him, who may be said to be their representative, / should be little better than a rogue and a rapparee, and give handle to the whigs in the house of commons, to be talking of the corruptionists and Irish electioneering bribery, and the likes. But as sure as Lord Adelm is returned, all this will come to pass. He'll be petitioned against in the House of Commons, to the intire satisfaction of the whigs.'

'I would not for a thousand worlds,' interrupted Lady Dunore: 'I should never stand London, and the insolence of the opposition women.'

'Then, my lady, sorrow thing there is to be done at all, at all, in the business but to withdraw Lord Adelm altogether for the present, who takes no pleasure in the election, and instead of being canvassing, is at this moment *philandering* it, like a *beau maison*,[204] after some skittish young fawn of a famale. Just, you see, consint to set him fairly / aside; and then, you see, Lady Dunore, we'll get another person *agraiable* to all parties, to set up in his stead, who will be elected forthwith, and sorrow word you'll hear of corruption or bribery, or the likes, I'll engage.'

'And so save our honour,' said Lady Dunore, 'and lose all our money.'

'No, but save both,' interrupted Crawley, 'for we'd take care to set up a person that would be a follower of the family, and just keep the *sate* open for the real member till the *desolution*, which will soon come, for all the world as your ladyship's footman keeps your box for you at the theatre till you arrive yourself.'

'This all sounds plausibly, Mr. Crawley; and you certainly are a very longheaded person, in spite of your *teinture de ridiculité*,[205] which renders you very amusing. But where could we get a person to take Fitzadelm's / place, in whom we could rely, in whom we could confide, who would act for the time being as our deputy, and vote as we bid him.'

'Why then, I'd offer myself with all the veins,* Lady Dunore, only that *crassing* the *say* just fairly kills me.'

'You!' said Lady Dunore, bursting into a fit of laughter.

'And what would ail me?' he answered, in a tone of mortification.

'Sure, many a man as isn't fit to hold a candle to me, Lady Dunore, has been sent over from this country a ready cut and dried parliament man: and what is in it after all, only just to take your cue, and know when to cry aye, and when to say no, according to order. And if you let out a blunder, or cut a joke, don't you carry the day? And *pales* of laughter from the treasury / bench, as the papers say,

---

*   i. e. veins of my heart.

and hear him! hear him! from the whigs.[x] I give you my honour, I'd do as well as the best of them if I was in it, and make them split their sides laughing, which is all the go now. But if it's eloquence and poethry you want, and one ready made to their hands, and just in their own way, quite *ministarial*, isn't there Con, Counseller Con, the darlint of the corporation, and would prefar him 'bove the world. I'll engage he'd be returned as soon as nominated, and has been merely known, as law agent for the election, and has nothing to do with what the whigs calls bribery, but stands with clane hands; and would lay down his life for the Dunores, though Lord Adelm trates him *de ho-on baw*[206] as the French says.'

Here Crawley paused, looking from under his shrewd little eyes on Lady Dunore, and puckered up his mouth, in / silent expectation of her answer to this hazardous proposition.

Lady Dunore, after a few moments silent cogitation, exhausted alike in body and spirit, and already weary of a subject which now ceased to agitate her, at last observed, 'Well, Mr. Crawley, you have hitherto conducted this business your own way. I am quite ignorant of the details; but all I know is this, the deputy member for Glannacrime must be a staunch thorough-going friend to the present ministry.'

'Lave him alone for that,' interrupted Crawley: 'sure isn't he after their own heart?'

'And the honour and intentions of my son must never even be called in question.'

'How can it, when there will be no petition against him if he is not elected.'

'As to Lord Adelm,' continued / Lady Dunore, 'the borough of. Glannacrime is evidently an object of indifference to him, *pour le moins*,[207] and I now despair of his ever setting up again for any borough while things remain as they are. I shall be the less anxious, as I shall command the voice of your son, in addition to my other voices in the house; for Conway is, after all, and notwithstanding what people call his vulgar effrontery, a very clever, and, as you observe, eloquent creature.'

'Why, then, he is that same every taste of it; and without wishing to alarm your ladyship, or give you unaisy drames to-night, I must just say that the time may not be far off –'here he paused, looked cautiously round, advanced to the door to see if it was fast, and then returning on tip-toe, continued – 'when you can't have too many voices in the house, nor too many friends in court, as the saying goes.' /

'What do you mean?' demanded Lady Dunore, startled, and amazed more by his manner than his words.

'Och! It's no matter what I mane now,' said old Crawley, coolly: '*on times uncertain date eternal hours depends*;[208] but I won't now detain your ladyship another moment.'

The clock at this instant struck three.

'I shall not leave this room now, be the hour what it may,' said Lady Dunore, throwing herself back in a chair, and putting her feet on another, to mark her determination, 'until you explain to me the mysterious words you have just uttered, Mr. Crawley.'

'Why then, see here the *dilemia* I have reduced myself to,' said Crawley, with an air of perplexity. 'I give you my honour, Lady Dunore, I would rather walk with paize (peas) in my shoes than annoy your fine feelings; and it three in the morning and you tired' /

'I am not in the very least tired, Mr. Crawley. I am equal, at least I fancy I am, to any communication you have to make to me; so pray go on.'

Old Crawley, with hesitation, and a marked reluctance, either affected or felt, began and broke off several sentences, hemmed, cleared his voice, and cried – 'Well, to be sure:' at last he began with: 'Of course my late noble friend and patron, your ladyship's late, dear, and ever to be lamented *concert*, has often mentioned to you an idle story, set about by his enemies, in regard of a claimant of the title of Fitzadelm, for there was then nothing else to claim; and who –'

'Not a word,' interrupted Lady Dunore, impatiently.

'Not a word!' repeated Crawley, with surprise. 'And never tould your ladyship that his elder brother, Walter, / Lord Fitzadelm, commonly called the Black Baron, had a son, an only son?'

'Never.'

'Who was drowned; but about whom there were some mighty ugly reports?'

'What reports?'

'Oh! just that his uncle and his father connived to put him out of the way to raise money; that, at one time, his uncle thought to bastardize him, by proving him the son of a nurse who first suckled the young Fitzadelm; that this attempt failed; and that after his brother's death he had the boy kidnapped, and sent no one knew where, among the black negers, and then trumped up a story of his drowning.'

''Tis a most curious romance!' said Lady Dunore, interested in the story in proportion to its wildness, and forgetting / the part her husband had been accused of playing, or how deeply it affected her own sons.

'Oh, mighty interesting,' said old Crawley, ironically.

'But no one ever believed a word of it, only the enemies of the Fitzadelms. But I suppose my lord tould your ladyship that the herald's office in Dublin refused him for a long time the style, title, and arms of Baron Fitzadelm?'

'Never a syllable.'

'Nor of the conversation he had with the Ulster king at arms,[209] whom he knocked down, and stood his trial for it afterwards in Dublin; my brother, the serjeant, acting as counsel, and I the attorney, and brought him off iligently?'

'Never,' said Lady Dunore, with increasing amazement and interest: 'he never would allow me to accompany him to Ireland. It was a subject of eternal / contest with many others.' (she sighed.) 'I led a most miserable life with poor, dear, Lord Fitzadelm, Mr. Crawley; yet upon the whole I have known no happiness since his death: but go on; your story is a most extraordinary one.'

'The most extraordinary part is to come, Lady Dunore: for after all had died away, and poor Lord Fitzadelm dead with the rest, and your son Marquis of Dunore, and every thing going on fair and aisy, at the end of three and twenty years, and when people were thinking of nothing at all at all, the story is revived again; and go which way you will, there is nothing but whispering and coshering, more particularly among the lower orders, that the son of Walter Lord Fitzadelm has re-appeared to several persons, with the intent of making good his claims to the Dunore estate and title, and of throwing out your ladyship's sons, the / most noble the marquis, and his brother, Lord Adelm Fitzadelm.'

To this observation a silence of many minutes succeeded. Lady Dunore sat thunderstruck, with a succession of strange and contradictory emotions flitting over her strongly working countenance. There was something in this wild and romantic tale that harmonized with her unregulated imagination, with her love for the marvellous, and her passion for excessive sensation: for there was a probability at least of the story being true, and a chance of conflict and vicissitude, of defeat or success, which flattered her feverish necessity for excitement, exertion, and occupation; but there yet remained a sufficient source of annoyance, apprehension, and anxiety, to counteract emotions of a more fanciful nature. Old Crawley sat deliberately gazing on her, his hands folded, his thumbs / twirling, his round vulgar bronzed face in strong relief from the light of the taper; while the pale and haggard countenance of Lady Dunore, half thrown in shade by the surrounding darkness of the spacious and gloomy apartment, stood opposed in picturesque contrast.

At last, after a long-drawn inspiration, Lady Dunore again exclaimed, 'This is a most extraordinary tale, Mr. Crawley.'

'It is indeed, Lady Dunore, mighty extraordinary, if it is true.'

'You do not believe that it is so?'

'Believe! the Lord forbid! If it was true, my lady, what would become of the marquis your son? What good would there be in all the mortgages, bargains, leases, and purchases, made under the Black Baron and your ladyship's dear late lord, and the present marquis? Why, if it was proved to / be true, Lady Dunore, wouldn't it be the murther of the world, the ruin of us all? Sure we must *prove it isn't true*, if we spend the last tinpenny we have in the world.'

'Prove! then you really think claims will be made – pretensions urged?'

'I think, and is certain sure of it. All kinds of *manyeuvering* and *checanery's* going on at this present moment to prove it.'

'But where – how – who is the pretender?'

Old Crawley passed his hand over his face; then looked round, as if he feared a witness of what he was going to say. He drew his chair closer to Lady Dunore, and continued in a low tone, 'Where is he! Why then, for all I know, Lady Dunore, he's under your roof at this moment. Any how he was in it this evening.'

Lady Dunore's exclamation almost / amounted to a scream; and Crawley, terrified at the vivacity of her emotions, cried,

'Hush! hush! for the love of the Lord. Keep down your fine feelings, Lady Dunore, dear, and smell your *O de Lucy*, or your *Sally Volatile*;'[210] and he searched her ridicule for a smelling bottle, which he had often seen her use under any agitation. Holding the salts to her nose (for Lady Dunore, like all hysterical persons, became violent in proportion as she was noticed), he continued, –

'Aisy now, aisy, Lady Dunore, honey; what will I do if you give way to your *asterisks*, and nobody up in the house to get you as much as a sup of water, or a thimble full of hartshorn?'[211]

The effect of the sal volatile, which he poured up her nostrils, was so powerful as to absorb for a moment every / other sensation; and when she could speak, which she did between laughter and sobs, she observed, 'Under my roof, Mr. Crawley? The kidnapped injured son of Lord Walter Fitzadelm under my roof, did you say?'

'Not at all, Lady Dunore, not the ra'al son of Baron Walter, but an *imposture*, a vagrant, a rebel, who came and bullied me in my own house, in my *sate* of Mount Crawley, and wanted to force Court Fitzadelm from me, and refused to drink the "Glorious and immortal," and snapped at Conway, and put his *commether* upon Clotty, and passed on her for a Methodist preacher, as he did afterwards upon your ladyship for a great officer from the Yankies; and is neither more nor less than the bastard, saving your ladyship's presence, of Judy Laffan, who was first nurse to the young Master Fitzadelm that was drownded. A little bit of a bye-blow of my lord's, / a JEW *d'esprit*,[212] as the French says; which was the raison why Lady FitzAdelm turned her away, when she found she was a *forepaw*[213] of my lord's, and she gave the child to that rebelly thief O'Leary's wife. And now, after every body has lost sight of him, that's MICKY Laffan, for he turned out a vagabond, was transported, and said to have died in Botany-Bay, he comes to pass himself for the ra'al young lord that was drownded, and he goes about chicaning the lower orders, and buying them over; and conniving with Lady Clancare, his great crony, though he daren't let on to know her here, gallowanting her in the bogs, and getting in with her into every cabin in the barony, and shewing himself as the raal Marquis of Dunore. Isn't he here, playing the great don with your ladyship, and calling himself General Fitzwalter, and laying down the law to yez? / all as one as if he was the king of the place already: and what's more, my lady, Lady Clancare is no more sick than I am; and as soon as the curtain was up and the play begun, the gineral was off like a shot, and Jemmy Bryan, who never loses sight of him, followed him to Castle Macarthy. Oh, troth, it's little of your ladyship's play she's thinking; no, but of her own: and was humming you²¹⁴ all the time, for the Devil is not able, for that one, the Lord pardon me!'

This information, so extraordinary, so out of all calculation, had the effect of sobering Lady Dunore, and of giving, for the moment, a tinge almost of rationality to her ideas; for wounded self-love effected more than reason or even self-interest could have produced. That she had been duped, deceived played upon, was the predominant feeling of her mind; deceived by Lady / Clancare, at the moment when she was endeavouring to serve her, and to forward her views, and who now turned out to be the agent of an adventurer, who had come under her roof for the purpose of defrauding and dispossessing her children of their rank and property.

'I see your ladyship is a little amazed,' said Crawley.

'Amazed!' she returned, collectedly, 'yes, a little, but not confounded, not overcome, as you shall find, Mr. Crawley: you shall see that I can shuffle and cut and deal my cards as well as another: you shall find that neither the villainy of an impostor, nor the arts of an adventuress, shall be too much for me. It is not the first time, my good Mr. Crawley, that I have been placed in situations where a little policy, a little management, disguise, and intrigue were necessary. I have already made up my mind to the event.ʸ / The conspiracy of this hero and heroine is, I suppose, a fair subject for legal prosecution; but that's not enough. They must be shewn up, upon their own scene of action, and it will go hard with me if I don't make examples of them.' Her eyes darkened with expected vengeance, as she spoke.

'Why then, see here, Lady Dunore, Divil a bit, but I give you credit for shewing a proper spirit: for hasn't that fellow made you the talk of the country round, for letting him into the castle, when not a house would let him crass the threshold, and was obliged to take up his lodgings with that marked man, O'Leary, because the Dunore Arms thought him a suspicious character?'

'I wish we had your son Conway here,' said the marchioness, musing.

'Och! there's no occasion in life for him. Haven't he and I been holding a council of war in Clotty's room, while / the play was going on, and every thing settled and planned between him and I and only waiting your ladyship's *veto*, as the Papists say?²¹⁵ I haven't come from Dublin without my credentials, I'll ingage.'

'What do you mean, my dear Mr. Crawley?'

'Why I mane, that I have a warrant to bring the body of this young gineral, who is an ould soger, to Dublin, afore the Lord Chief Justice.'

'Oh! but remember your last warrant, Mr. Crawley. You do not *briller par là*.[216] You must not again involve us in your ridiculous mistakes and conspiracies, and things in Queen Elizabeth's days.'

'I'll ingage there is no fear, Lady Dunore, and Judge Aubrey not in the country to back his jacobin friends; and has my charges made out in due form, and sworn to.' /

'What charges, *par exemple?*'

'Only for a trifle of murther, that's all.'

'Murder!'

'Aye, faith, ra'al and undoubted murther. Did'nt your ladyship hear Conway read out of th' Hibernian journal,[217] one morning at breakfast, of a rising in the mountains about a still-hunting party, and of a fight between the country people and the sogers, and a stranger on horseback, getting among them to settle the difference, as it was to appear, and taking part in the disturbance, and a shot fired, and a soger killed, and nobody ever able to tell by whom, until a lad turned king's evidence th' other day, and is ready to swear that this gineral was the murtherer; that he was seen going into a cabin before the fight, and drinking with the people, and saying he was the ra'al Lord Dunore; and that on going away, / under pretence of relieving the people, who were very poor, he gave them, as he thought, a golden guinea, which turned out to be a Spanish coin, the very same that the gineral gave your ladyship a prisint for card counters;[218] and here it is, and a great evidence it will be on the trial.'

So saying, he produced the coin.

'This is most extraordinary! This is a special intervention of providence. It is indeed the same,' said Lady Dunore, 'that this *murderer* gave me.'

'Now,' said old Crawley, 'a man who is convicted of murder, and I believe we have witnesses enough to prove *that*, will have but a poor chance of proving his claims to a title and property in the possession of a noble family, as is hand and glove with the ministry.'

'But you have not got him yet,' / said Lady Dunore, impatiently: 'he may still elude us all.'

'He is now, I believe, quietly asleep in O'Leary's lodgings. Jemmy Bryan saw him safe home at half past ten, from Lady Clancare's, and then came here to inform Conway of it. But what would ail your ladyship but to write him a line in the morning to beg he would step down to you, as you are unaisy about Lord Adelm, whom he flatters himself he's bit fairly.'

'And then?' said Lady Dunore, reddening with the ardour of her newly awakened feelings.

'And then, my lady, we'll just nab him *nately* as he stands all alone by himself in your ladyship's dressing-room; for he has become so *populous* with the lower orders, that if he were arrested at O'Leary's, that is the ringleader of the country, there would be a / rising of every riband man and every *functionary*[219] in the place round. But here, sorrow a taste of any mortal will know about it; and we'll have a poshay at the little *posture* gate,[220] under the tower on the strand, and a military escort.'

'No,' said Lady Dunore, whose feelings, all personal, had nothing but private vengeance in view, 'that will never do, I will have him arrested and exposed in the presence of the party assembled in the castle (whom he has imposed upon), and confronted with that artful adventuress, Lady Clancare, who I now see, while she was serving her paramour, was upon the point of taking in poor dear Lord Rosbrin, persuading me, the little wretch, that she did it to pique that Fitzwalter; but don't talk of her – it maddens me to think how I have been duped, laughed at, played upon; and that –' /

'Now keep yourself cool, Lady Dunore, honey,' interrupted Crawley, fearful of a return of her hysteric paroxysm, 'and just go to bed and –'

'I will not go to bed till I write a note of invitation to the *general*, whom, we shall *out-general* in the end, and leave it to be sent early in the morning; and as to the *Countess* of Clancare,' and she laughed hysterically, 'a countess, indeed! a gypsy countess! with her typhus fever; I will have the honour of going for her myself, and bringing her, *vi et armis*,[221] to the castle.'

Cheered by this resolution, Lady Dunore now took up her candle, and with her cheek colourless, her eyes inflamed and staring, and her head wrapped in a lace veil, she not inaptly imaged the sleep-walking and conscience-stricken Lady Macbeth.[222] Old Crawley meantime, with a tip-toe step, / groped his way by the moonlight to the bed-room of his son, who had sat up to receive him, and learn the result of his extraordinary interview with the lady of the castle. /

CHAPTER V.

How could'st thou find this dark sequestered nook? MILTON.[223]

Now does my project gather to a head;
My charm crack not; my spirits obey; and time
Goes upright with his carriage.
                    SHAKESPEARE.[224a]

THE solemn consequence given to every thing connected with the drama, by Lord Rosbrin, had rendered the disappointment occasioned by the illness or caprice of Lady Clancare an event of the most important and mortifying nature; and he insisted on announcing it to the public in all the set form and phrase usual upon such occasions in the / public theatres. He came forward, therefore, with a countenance in which he hoped 'men would read strange things;'[225] and, after a long pause, he commenced an apology for the non-appearance of Lady

Clancare, put forth his own claims to indulgence, in assuming, by particular desire, and for that night only, the part of Rosalind; and concluded by reading aloud the letter of the comic heroine, to whom he had undertaken to act as *double*. It ran as follows:

My dear Lady Dunore,

    I am obliged to decline the pretty part of the fantastic Rosalind this evening for one of a less agreeable nature; and I trust you will not think I am playing the *Malade Imaginaire*,[226] when I assign indisposition as an excuse for my absence from the castle. I would, perhaps, ask you to / come and judge for yourself of my situation, but that the nature of my feelings at this moment, and my recent visits to a house where the typhus fever rages, might render it as unsafe for you, as embarrassing to me, to receive you at Castle Macarthy.

I am, my dear Lady Dunore, &c.

F. Clancare.

The apology was received with plaudits; the audience, better pleased with the Rosalind which chance and folly had given them, than with the Rosalind of which a dangerous malady had deprived them, 'bound up each corporeal faculty'[227] to expected mirth and laughter.

    Miss Crawley declared the excuse of Lady Clancare was all affectation and assumed importance; and Lord Frederick observed to Lady Georgina that he saw *la petite personne*[228] was, from the be-/ginning to the end, playing another part than that assigned her, and that it was very clear her intention had never been to play at all.

    Contrary to his first intentions, General Fitzwalter found himself in the theatre of Dunore; but upon the reading of Lady Clancare's letter, he suddenly disappeared. The carriage in which he had arrived had returned to the Dunore Arms, and, notwithstanding the roughness of a singularly inclement night, he wrapped himself up in a long travelling cloak, lent him by one of the grooms of the chamber, and proceeded on foot to Castle Macarthy.

    As he walked forth from the illuminated hall of Dunore, and lost the glitter of the sparkling lights that gleamed from its casements, the rude savage scene through which he proceeded seemed to scowl a gloomy contrast. The night was unusually dark, but the / roar of the waves indicated their agitation; and in the pauses of the shrill gusts of wind which whistled among the rocks, under whose shadow he was moving, the rain fell heavy, cold, and penetrating. Opposed to the brilliant images and mirthful scenes he had quitted, those he now occupied became marked by a character of supernatural horror and desolation.[b] He found and ascended with difficulty the little defile in the cliffs through which Lady Clancare's maid had formerly led him to the strand; and when he stood before the gates of Castle Macarthy, he felt that there also was the silence of dreary sequestration, and of desolate privacy. A faint stream of light issued from the half open portals of the hall. He entered, without finding any human being to impede his steps or to announce his arrival.

A flickering rush-light stood upon / the old stone table, and its expiring ray flashed upon the skeleton wolf's head that hung suspended above it, and then sunk and died into utter darkness. Fitzwalter stood for a moment, his hand resting on the table, on which the rain, dropping through the roof, fell with heavy plashes. Unable to proceed, his feelings all tumult, his spirits depressed, one image, gloomy, painful, and affecting, still occupied his mind. The young, friendless mistress of this silent and dreary dwelling, she who so late had appeared beyond the reach of suffering, so brilliant, so wooed and won by adulation and attention, now neglected, abandoned, unpitied, left on a bed of sickness by those to whom her spirit and talents had recently afforded occupation, and supplied amusement – no eye to watch her, no tongue to sooth her, no hand to seek the feverish pressure of her's. All her follies, all her / faults (if the conduct which had thwarted his passion could be so construed) were forgotten, and nothing was now remembered, not even her talents, her charms, save the unpitied situation to which her too intrepid benevolence had reduced her.

Almost suffocating from excess of emotion, still struggling with himself, in the midst of darkness and of silence, he hesitated as to the manner in which he should seek to announce himself, when the heavy creaking of a door, slowly shut, footsteps approaching, and a faint flash of light, proceeding from the narrow dark stone passage, which led to the sitting-room he had once occupied, caught his attention. A man advanced, holding a dark lantern; the light, turned on himself, burnished his face and figure with it's yellow rays, and threw them into strong relief. He was humming an old melancholy Irish cronan,[229] and proceeded cau-/tiously across the hall to the door, without perceiving the general, whose dark figure and garb were confounded with the profound shadows of the place. The full and strongly lighted view of his person instantly awakened a perfect recognition in the general's mind. It was the *Rabragh*.

'Owny!' he exclaimed, advancing eagerly, and seizing his arm. Owny dropped his lantern from one hand, and a letter which he carried from the other, and clasping both, mingled a broken *ave-maria* and *mea-culpa*,[230] in utter consternation and superstitious fear, the only fear by which his hardy spirit was assailahle.

'Do you not remember?' asked the general, in an impatient tone, and letting go his arm. 'You cannot have forgotten the traveller whom you drove from Cashel, bewildered in the Galties, and imprisoned in Court Fitzadelm.'

The habitual gaiety of the Rabragh's / countenance, and the natural ruddiness of his complexion, returned together; and picking up his lantern, and turning it full on the apparition which had scared him into the belief that he stood in the unearthly presence of the famous *Macarthy-More*, he replied, with a smile: –

'Know your honor, is it, Sir? May be I don't; and never will forget yez, till the hour of my death, if I was to live a thousand years and more; and took you now for ould *Fogh-na-gael*, in regard of the surprise, Sir, and the place, and the ould shanaos, Sir. And sure wasn't I going to your honor this very minute, with a letter for you from the Bhan Tierna, long life to her ladyship! and if I didn't find you at O'Leary's was to follow you to the castle, and lurk about till you came out, Sir, and slip this into your hand, Sir; and thinks it great luck, plaze Gad, to find you in / it here, in regard of not caring to crass the church-yard of Monaster-ny-oriel, and the night dark and stormy, only in respect of the Bhan Tierna, who has a right to my life, Sir, if she chooses, and am bound to serve her till death, and more.'ᶜ

During this speech, the general had opened the letter alluded to, and read as follows.

'You stand accused of murder. Depositions to this effect have been laid against you, by one, who, in betraying the circumstance to his comrade, the noted Padreen Gar, persists in its veracity. Officers of justice are furnished with a warrant to take you. Though your conscience be at rest, confide not in your innocence, for you are powerfully beset. A chaise with a driver, on whom you may depend, will be ready to receive you at three in the morning, / and conduct you to a port from whence you may sail. Announce your arrival and future intentions to Lady Clancare, they will then securely and speedily reach your wife,

FLORENCE MACARTHY.

'This for the present is all the answer I can return to your letter, and its general proposal.'

Fitzwalter read this letter twice, with a confusion of ideas and feelings that scarcely left him power to comprehend its contents. The increasing paleness of his cheek, the rolling of his eye, the tremulous motion of his under lip, fixed the shrewd but sympathizing gaze of the Rabragh, as he held up the lantern before him; and as the general stood silent and motionless, he observed, significantly: –

'Hasn't your honor better step into the dining-parlour, Sir, and see the / Countess herself? and ingages, if she backs you, Sir, sorrow taste there is to fear. And didn't she save my life, Sir, entirely, when I fell into trouble, and none to take my part against the Crawleys, only God and her ladyship, Sir. Shall I shew your honor the way?' and he stepped lightly on before. Fitzwalter followed mechanically, and, as the door stood half open, Owny pointed to it, and retired.

The unexpected visitant paused at the threshold, and the interior of the apartment was exposed to his view. It was dimly lighted by a rude lamp which stood on the table, before which Lady Clancare sat writing. Her appearance almost justified the account she had given of herself; for her unusual paleness of complexion was accompanied by the worn, anxious, and exhausted look of one who suffered much. One hand was spread and / pressed upon the forehead it supported; the other was guiding her pen with the rapidity of lightning; while at intervals she raised her head, addressing the interrogatory of 'well,' to a person who appeared dictating to her in Irish. He presented a gaunt tall figure, and fearful aspect; but he stood with his head uncovered at a respectful distance, and traces of a reverential feeling softened the harsh lines of his wild and marked countenance. It was Padreen Gar. In another part of the room Lady Clancare's youthful attendant, assisted by an old woman, was engaged in packing up a small travelling trunk. Struck by a combination so extraordinary, by the peculiar situation of Lady Clancare, and by the presence of her singular associates, Fitzwalter stood for a moment unnoticed, and wrapt in profound observation; when the eyes of Lady Clancare sud-/denly and accidentally turning to the spot where he stood, with his dark pale countenance just visible above the cloak which wrapped his figure; she uttered a faint, exclamation, smiled, attempted to rise, and would have sunk to the earth, but that the arms of Fitzwalter received her, with a clasp that seemed almost indissoluble. Her efforts to rally back her fading spirits and declining strength were instantaneously successful. She resumed her seat, affected to laugh away her weakness, ascribed it to exhaustion and surprise; and then having abruptly observed, that General Fitzwalter could not yet have received the letter she had dispatched to him, she turned to her attendants, desired her maid to wait in the adjoining room, and dismissed Padreen Gar and the old woman till they should be called for. All this was done rapidly but collectedly, and was observed by / Fitzwalter with silent amazement; for the feverish hectic that burnt in a red spot on one of her cheeks convinced him that the excuse she had made for her non-appearance at the castle of Dunore was not without foundation. He took her hand in emotion; and as he applied his fingers to its throbbing pulse, she gaily observed, while she struggled to release it, 'Oh, you are not to believe a word it tells you. I have *no leisure* to be ill now, nor shall I *have time* to die these twenty years: then, indeed, having retired from the world, with the first wrinkle, and moped through a few years of age and ugliness, I may some day or other be found here dead of the sullens, like an old bird in its cage.'

'But you are ill,' he replied, anxiously: 'your hand burns, your complexion varies. Where is there a physician? Have you not sent for assistance?' /

'What!' she said laughing, 'my equivoque[231] of the typhus fever succeeded with you as well as the rest? But in that case, if I am indeed imagined ill, where are all my *"friends fast sworn,"*[232] my admirers, my Orlandos, my Solymans! Ha! not even *l'amie d'honneur!*[233] My dear Lady Dunore! Then have *I* touched the highest point of all my greatness,

"And from the full meridian of my glory
I haste now to my setting;"[234]

so sit down, General Fitzwalter, and tell me how it comes, that *"left and abandoned by my velvet friends,"*[235] you, who never ranged yourself among their number, have deserted the festive hall of pleasure to seek the supposed infectious air of these ruined towers?'

'You suffer and are here,' he replied eagerly, and taking a hand, which she now struggled not to withdraw – /

'You did not then, of course, receive the letter which I have just despatched to you from your guardian angel, from Florence Macarthy?'

Fitzwaltcr let fall her hand, and after a moment's pause, replied, 'Yes; but that is not the question now. Will you permit me to go to Dunore for such medical advice as I can procure: or, if you prefer sending your mysterious agent, Owny, whom I left in your hall, and who has been employed in the service of a life much less valuable than your own –'

'No, no,' she interrupted, 'I am not ill. I do not deceive you. I am harassed, anxious, a little exhausted, and burning more with indignation than fever. With your life, the life of any human being at stake; with the happiness, the existence of Florence Macarthy in my hands, – is her name, then, so abhorrent to your ears that you turn thus in disgust away?' /

'You have not chosen your moment wisely; but I am ready to fulfil my engagement to that lady,' interrupted Fitzwalter, vehemently, and starting from his chair. 'I will marry her, protect her, and while I live, live with her. What more does she require, or do you demand, Lady Clancare?

He paused, and fixed his stern eyes on a countenance marked by the profoundest agitation.

'I require! I have no right to require any thing. I speak in her behalf, not in my own. Oh! you know not,' she continued, with a supplicating earnestness, 'the devotion with which she has pursued you – silently, unobtrusively pursued you. You know not what zeal she has displayed, what ingenuity she has exerted, to keep you within her view; to behold you, to listen to you, to study you, to obtain you.' /

'Well,' said Fitzwalter, throwing himself back in his chair, 'she has succeeded – I am her's. I acknowledge her worth: in time I trust I shall feel it,' – and he sighed profoundly.

'Her worth!' replied Lady Clancare: ''tis of her love I speak, and of all the romantic energy which has accompanied it. It was her determination, when she heard of your captivity, to return to South America, to endeavour to effect your escape, or to share your dungeon; for the woman is unworthy of the sacred name of wife who is not prepared to follow the husband of her choice and her affections to slavery, to death; oh! more than all, to follow, to cling to him even in shame, in ignominy. Nay, hear me out, and look not thus on me. The report of your escape had reached her when she was on the point of embarking from England, to share, or offer to share / your destiny. Then she lost sight of you until you presented yourself to her eyes in Ireland, breathing the same air, inhabiting the same room, exchanging glances, yet still instinctively shrinking from her. Ha! you start. It will not lessen your surprise to learn that Florence Macarthy was the rejected, the formidable Mrs. Magillicuddy, something disguised, indeed, and changed. You laugh incredulously. But love would have recognized its object even under that concealment. Young, well looking, and unprotected, she has often sought safety in the assumption of age and ugliness, during her inevitable wanderings. Her flexibility of voice, and mobility of countenance and gesture, her powers of imitation, and acquaintance with the character she assumed, favoured her disguise. But your intercourse stopped not here. It was she who contrived to play upon the / vanity and credulity of Lord Adelm, whom she had once seen in Spain, whom she had afterwards seen in England, though unnoticed by one so self-occupied and self-involved – it was she who summoned him from Portugal – at once avenging a friend she had dearly loved, whom he had sacrificed, and making him an instrument in her own schemes. Her's was the irrepressible sigh, the malignant laugh in the ruins of Holy-cross. It was she who placed you in the Fitzadelm chaise, under the guidance of her agent, the Rabragh, had you carried to Lis-na-sleugh, where her knowledge of the Spanish language put her in possession of your views and intentions. Thus she anticipated you at Court Fitzadelm, imprisoned you to afford herself time for escape, and provided you a lodging at O'Leary's, by an equivoque of which he was the dupe. From that moment you became / my charge. The proximity of your residence favoured the trust I embraced. Acquainted with your departure for Cork, your intended return to Dunore, and with the arrest which waited you there, I was enabled to forward the views of Florence Macarthy, by witnessing your first appearance in the castle of Dunore; to effect which, as much as to surprise the favour of Lady Dunore, I suffered myself to be taken prisoner by Mr. Costello, and even paid him for his trouble. It was I who kept your friend Lord Adelm in play, by dropping the handkerchief, whose initials first discovered to you the residence of Florence Macarthy in Ireland, and again brought on a negotiation by means scarcely calculated on. I see you are amazed, confounded, stunned, because the omnipotence which belongs to the affections of a devoted woman is unknown to your sex: still less can you / judge of its disinterestedness, of its power to abnegate self, to confound its identity with the object beloved. It is you, you alone, Florence Macarthy prizes. It is for yourself you are estimated: and now, ignorant of all concerning you, save the part you recently played in America, beholding you in this remote place, wrapped in mystery, suspected, accused, your life in danger, whatever may be your innocence or fate, that fate she is ready to share with you.'

'I cannot, dare not hear you on,' interrupted Fitzwalter, in a burst of passion amounting to agony. 'Why should I deceive her, you, myself? 'Tis not on Florence Macarthy my thoughts are bent, admirable and wonderful as you paint her. 'Tis on you my existence at this moment depends; my soul, my senses, my life, are your's. 'Tis on your eloquence I hang, on your counte-/nance I gaze, on your eyes I look. I confound you with her, and become unworthy of both. Were *you* this devoted creature, whose cause you plead – spoke you, looked you thus *for yourself*, the struggle would be at once decided. Florence Macarthy should not be deceived, nor I –. In a word, Lady Clancare, I love you to madness, to folly, to dishonour; you, only you, against my better reason, my happiness and sense of right. Now then, knowing my state of feeling, speak on, if you will; but remember, I do not answer for myself. Every word you utter, every sigh you breath, every glance you emanate in another's cause, confirms my crime, and devotes me to yourself. Were you the creature you paint another, were you capable of this devotion, this zeal, and for me –'

'I am capable of it,' interrupted Lady Clancare, breathlessly, and clasp- / ing her hands in passionate emotion, while she half averted her face to conceal its expression. 'Could I thus describe if I had not felt? In pleading the cause of Florence Macarthy, see you not that I but delineated my own feelings, my own strong, tender, and indestructible emotions. You say you love me, and I dare not doubt it. You deny not your danger; I am ready to share it: this is no moment for details: let it suffice to know that she who thus throws herself on you, is –' she paused, turned away her head, while Fitzwalter encircled her half retreating form with his arms, and hung wildly over her, 'is – FLORENCE MACARTHY!'

His arms lost their power of supporting her, and he sunk motionless upon the chair from which she had just arisen; while Lady Clancare, after a moment's struggle, turning full round, fixed her eyes on him with that expres-/sion of triumph with which she had first received him where she now stood, and gently putting her hand on his shoulder, said, '*Now, infidel, I have you on the hip.*'[236]

The story of Florence Macarthy, Countess of Clancare, the daughter of Colonel Macarthy-More, whose life had been sacrificed in the South American cause, had already been gradually detailed, and little was left to reveal. The story of her kinswoman, Florence Macarthy Reagh, a Spanish nun, resident in the Convent of our Lady of the Annunciation, as partly related by O'Leary, had given rise to that *quid pro quo*[237] which had enabled Lady Clancare to follow up her innocent schemes on the heart of him she considered as her husband, while apparently acting as the agent of another.

Florence Macarthy Reagh was the / young novice of Nuestra Señora de las Angustias, to whom the eccentric Lord Fitzadelm had addressed his love,

'Stealing her soul with many vows of faith,
   And never a true one;'[238]

and who had since expiated her credulity by years of religious sacrifice. Misled by the embroidered handkerchief, and by O'Leary's description of its owner,
Lord Adelm had flown to her convent, and, in the person of the mistress he had
abandoned, sought the invisible torment who had so long eluded him. He arrived
at the convent the day preceding that on which his supposed sylph was to take
the veil; and the certainty of not obtaining her increased his ideal and romantic
passion to the desperate height of proposing, unknown, unseen, to marry her.
The answer to this proposition revealed the name and story of the person he ad-/
dressed, and inclosed a drawing of a cenotaph, on which was inscribed

'Sic me Phœbus amat.'[239]

For the rest, he was informed that his proposal should be forwarded to
Mrs. Mary Magillicuddy, the person whose invisible, but ardent attentions, had
induced him to make it.

Florence Macarthy Reagh, though much of the saint, was more of the
woman; and in spite of herself, secretly rejoiced in the innocent vengeance procured her by the playful agency of her cousin, who, like the rest of her sex, made
common cause, and conceived an injury done to one woman a slight to all.

The town clock of Dunore had struck eleven, as General Fitzwalter, dogged
by Jemmy Bryan, reached his tower of Monaster-ny-Oriel; and O'Leary, who
had been watching his return, expressed / his amazement at his doing so on foot
in so dreary a night, and informed him, with a mysterious air, that things were
getting wind, and that Lord Adelm was just arrived at Monaster-ny-Oriel a few
moments before, and awaited his return in his chamber. Fra Denis O'Sullivan
was also, he said, returned, to his utter amazement, to his lodgment in the tower,
and was now *solus cum solo*[240] with the young lord. /

CHAPTER VI.

Yea, even that which mischief meant most harm,
Shall, in the happy trial, prove most goodly.
Evil on itself shall back recoil.
                              MILTON.[241]

THE following morning, an hour after sun-rise, the ruined chapel of *Monaster-
ny-oriel* exhibited a singular and unusual scene: for before the high altar, at whose
feet reposed the ashes of the great chief, Macarthy-More, the young descendant and inheritor of his title and name gave her hand to the representative of
his hereditary enemies. The ceremony was performed by the Reverend Denis
O'Sullivan, / titular Dean of Dunore, assisted by the parish priest.

The protestant rector, who was to repeat the rites, according to the forms of the protestant church (the parties being of different persuasions), also attended, at Lady Clancare's particular request, to represent her grandfather, to whom he had been a fast firm friend, and to give her away. The only persons present upon the occasion were O'Leary, who, between every response, muttered some part of Friar Con's prophecy; and Lady Clancare's maid, who was her foster sister. Lord Adelm, who had passed the night in a conference with General Fitzwalter, to which Mr. O'Sullivan was latterly admitted, had left O'Leary's before day-light, informed of the event which was about to take place, but declining being present, from feelings originating in his actual state of mind, the mortification he / had recently undergone, and some well-grounded suspicions of the share Lady Clancare had contributed to it.

The celebration of the wedding of the Bhan Tierna in the chapel of Monaster-ny-oriel, some vague reports that the distinguished stranger on whom she was bestowing her hand was the real and long-lost Marquis of Dunore, had circulated with incredible celerity, and the old Fitzadelm chaise, with four horses in attendance at the gates of the cemetery, the white cockade mounted in the Rabragh's hat, who rode proudly on the coach-box, a similar distinction in the *caubeen* of Padreen Gar, who had forcibly dismounted the ragged postillion, and thrown his huge limbs over the back of the leader, and a chaise and pair in attendance for the countess's maid and O'Leary, all served to confirm the hints

'*Loud rumour spoke.*'[242] /

By the time, therefore, that the bridal party issued from amidst the grey ruins of the abbey, a multitude of persons, with the whole population of Clotnotty-joy, had assembled round the gates, and shouts of joyous emotion, mingled with the cry of the Macarthies and Fitzadelms, rent the air.

Lady Clancare, as she ascended the carriage, addressed a few words to those nearest to her: she said she was about to leave them for a short time, but she trusted it was only to return, with the power as well as the will she had always felt to be of use to them; – she recommended sobriety, industry, and peaceable conduct; and amidst fresh shouts of approbation and joy was placed in the carriage by the catholic dean and protestant rector. The cavalcade was now taking the road to Cork, still followed by the multitude, when a party of military, led on by / several officers of the civil power, commanded the drivers to stop; and General Fitzwalter was arrested in the name and on behalf of his majesty the king. The arrest was instantly observed by the peasantry, who prepared to resist it with their usual uncalculating warmth, while *Padreen Gar*, still mounted on the foremost horse, rose his gaunt figure from the stirrups, and cast round a significant look, which operated like electricity. In a moment the scattered multitude, contracted into a close phalanx, rushed with one impulsion through the military party, and environed the chaise: stones and turf sods, suddenly torn up, flails and scythes brandished in the air, and countenances fixed, stern, resolute, and ferocious, declared the event of an intended rescue. In a momentary pause, Fitzwalter, sternly, as one accustomed to command – Mr. O'Sullivan, mildly, / as one accustomed to conciliate, endeavoured to address the mob, and induce them to return quietly to their work or their homes: both were only answered by shrill wild shouts, which convinced them of the inefficiency of their interference.

The military loaded their pieces, but behaved with great moderation, till urged by the interference of the civil officers, who ordered them to disperse the mob, *vi et armis*;[243] and a general engagement was about to take place, when the voice and interference of Lady Clancare produced an effect, as unexpected as singular. She addressed them in Irish; but it was evident neither in command nor supplication. Whatever she said produced bursts of laughter and applause; every eye, flashing humour and derision, were turned on the constables and their satellites. A new impulse seemed to be given to / the susceptible feelings of the auditory she addressed. Rage was turned to contempt; anticipated triumph shone in every eye. They drew back, suffered the military to close round the carriage, dropped their missiles, and followed in regular order the track of the carriages, as they now proceeded to the castle of Dunore.

'There are two, and but *two* short roads,' (said Lady Clancare smiling) 'to Irish feelings, – pathos or humour: you may weep or laugh them out of any thing.'

Notwithstanding the earliness of the hour, every window, every loop-hole, in the castle of Dunore, was crowded, when the bridal carriage and its singular cavalcade wound up its gloomy court: and when the party (evidently expected), alighted in the hall, and were received and conducted by the grooms of the chamber to the saloon, Lord / Adelm stood at the door: he appeared pale, and much worn in his appearance; but he came anxiously forward, and observed in a low voice to Fitzwalter, 'It is unnecessary to say I am unprepared for *this*. I knew nothing of it. I have had a few minutes conference with my mother. Reports of your story have reached her through the Crawleys, distorted however and vague: act now as you please, but spare the memory of my father for my sake.'

Fitzwalter wrung his hand in expressive silence, and the whole party entered the saloon together. Lady Clancare, supported by her husband's arm, and partly veiled by the Spanish mantillo, which fell from her head over her whole person, excited evident amazement by her presence.

The titular Dean of Dunore followed, accompanied by the rector; and the wildly expressive countenance of the / agitated O'Leary, agitated almost to the return of his former malady, and the black rough head and grim visage of Padreen Gar, were seen among the many curious faces which filled up the door. The saloon was already occupied by all the guests of the castle, with the exception of Lord Rosbrin, and some of the *corps dramatique*, who were either wearied beyond the power of being roused at so unseasonable an hour, or had no inclination to appear on a scene in which they were not to act the *principal* part *themselves*. The summonses, however, of Lady Dunore had been given to all, and were for the most part punctually obeyed; for Lady Dunore had personally solicited the attendance of the ladies, and despatched Mr. Pottinger to the gentlemen to request they would be present on an occasion which involved some of the dearest interests of her being. /

Lady Georgina, in a wrapper of India muslin, and a drapery of Brussels lace shading her face, yawning and peevish at being disturbed, when the *dearest* interests of her *dearest* friend were concerned, reclined on a sofa, on which Lord Frederick, in a robe de chambre,[244] and embroidered Turkey slippers, had taken his wonted place beside her.

Mr. Heneage and Miss Crawley had descended in such a hurry that the one appeared without his stays, and the other without her frizette.[245] Mr. Pottinger was habited in a yellow silk banyan,[246] presented him by an ex-lady-lieutenant. Old Crawley, ghastly and agitated, stood in a remote window, taking snuff and pulling down his wig. His son had left the castle before day-light, under the excuse of attending the election; and Lady Dunore, pale and flushing alternately, moved about in restless / agitation, till on the entrance of her son she seized his arm, and, with a countenance charged with irony, and malicious, yet doubtful triumph, stood observing the entrance of General Fitzwalter, Lady Clancare, and their two clerical friends. A pause ensued, which Lady Dunore at last interrupted, and dropping her son's arm, she came forward, and addressing Lady Clancare with a sort of half ironical, half hysterical laugh, she said, 'If there be any truth in the report which has just reached us, that your *ladyship* has this morning bestowed your fair hand on –, the gentleman whom you now accompany, may I hope I am among the first to congratulate you on the event, and to wish you all *the joy* it is likely eventually to produce?'

Lady Clancare, who stood the image of her own first appearance in the hall of Dunore, the same shy, sly ex-/pression of countenance, and bashful embarrassment of air, replied to this ironical congratulation by a low respectful courtesy, as one who took this mock civility *tout de bon*,[247] and was grateful for it.

Provoked at this unlooked for interpretation, Lady Dunore, wholly overcome by her ungovernable temper, went on with increasing acrimony: 'Had I, Madam, known the *extent* and *cast* of your *ladyship's* theatrical abilities, I should have undoubtedly induced you to undertake the part of Estifania, and we should have had no difficulty, it now appears, in providing a *copper captain*.'[248] She laughed convulsively; and then yielding gradually to the violent impetuosity of her temper, provoked by the modest self-satisfied air of Lady Clancare (who seemed scarcely to attend to her ravings), she added in a loud shrill voice: /

'Mr. Crawley, why don't you come forward?'

Crawley, with an air of timid perplexity obeyed.

'I turn over those two adventurers, those conspirators to you, and to the laws they have violated; and I now thus publicly acknowledge my imprudence in receiving them under my roof, and beg forgiveness of the friends into whose society I obtruded them. Lady Georgina, Miss Crawley, we will if you please, now retire. Mr. Crawley, the officers of justice may do their duty. Fitzadelm, give me your arm.'

'No, Madam,' said Lord Fitzadelm, firmly, and leading her back forcibly to her seat, 'you must not go. Neither shall I, until the defamation you have indulged in is either substantiated or disproved; until my friend, General Fitzwalter, is afforded (and in / the presence of these, before whom he has been so grossly insulted) an opportunity of clearing himself of the aspersions with which you have blasted his gallant character.'

'*Your friend! your friend!*' repeated Lady Dunore, bursting into a fit of hysterical tears. 'Are *your friends* then to be always my enemies? Am I always to find an adversary in my son; or is it only to thwart, oppose, and distract me, that you now involve yourself in the guilt of an *impostor and a murderer*, by publicly acknowledging him *as your friend?*' – A general murmur of amazement and consternation arose. Lord Fitzadelm, with the air of one whose feelings seemed to find their own level in the extraordinary and unprecedented part he was now called on to play, turned to General Fitzwalter, and said: 'now then is your moment – I hold myself answerable / for the truth of all you shall assert.'

Fitzwalter gently released himself from Lady Dunore's arm; while Lord Frederick, in good-natured consideration of the anxiety and emotion painted in her countenance, led her to a chair, and took his place beside her. A silence of a moment ensued, and Fitzwalter advancing, with his wonted disengaged and elevated air, towards Lady Dunore, placed himself before her, and, leaning his hand on the back of a chair, addressed her with his usual rapid energy of utterance.

'Making a journey on horseback, Madam, a short time back on business of emergency, I was overtaken in the Kilworth mountains by a storm, which induced me to take shelter in a miserable hut. I found it occupied by men, whose countenance and appearance were of that wild resolute cast which / in such scenes induces suspicion. The poverty of the mistress of this hut, and of her naked children, led me to an act of perhaps imprudent liberality at such a moment; I meant to have given her a guinea. I gave her by mistake a golden coin. Proceeding on my journey, I fell in with a small military party: they stopt and questioned me. While thus engaged, the men I had left, accompanied by a hundred others, well mounted, and rudely armed, overtook the soldiers, who were employed in the service of the revenue, or, in the language of the country, still-hunting. The conflict was desperate. I endeavoured to interfere, failed, and rode on.

'The papers have since announced the death of one of the military party: the murderer remained for a time unknown, and after the expiration of some weeks, it appears that I stand accused of this murder; of joining the party who op-/posed the military, for the purposes of canvassing popularity, and obtaining false witnesses to prove, or credulous persons to believe, that I am the *son* of the elder baron of Fitzadelm, whose death was supposed to have occurred three-and-twenty years back. This, I believe, Mr. Crawley, is the spirit of your indictment.'

'Pon my credit, Sir, I can't take upon me to say just in a moment, but *believes* it is,' returned old Crawley.

'And now,' continued Fitzwalter, 'having been brought forward for the purpose of being exposed to shame, obloquy, and ridicule; a refinement upon the severity of the law, a propitiatory sacrifice to the distinguished persons on whose indignant nobility a murderer and a conspirator has been unwillingly obtruded, may I beg to know from you, Mr. Crawley (who seem the acting and active agent in this prosecution) where I am now to proceed?' /

Old Crawley, gradually edging himself out of his way as he approached him, sidled towards one of the officers of justice, who stood at the door, and twitching him by the sleeve, whispered him a few words in his ear: the man respectfully approached his prisoner, and bowed.

'I suppose,' said Fitzwalter, 'Lady Clancare, as whose husband I have the honour to announce myself, may be allowed to accompany me. – Is it not so, Mr. Crawley?'

'Give you my honour, Sir, I don't know: if it's in the warrant, and Mr. Lynch has no objection,' replied Crawley, gradually taking shelter behind Lady Dunore's chair, and directing many significant looks to the constable, while Miss Crawley whispered Lady Dunore,

'Sure such a pair were never seen'[249]

A pause of a moment ensued: every / countenance was marked either by curiosity, amazement, or anxiety; when Mr. O'Sullivan advanced into the room, and was presented to the marchioness by the rector, as the Catholic dean of Dunore, and superior of the friary of St. John's, as a gentleman to whom, in the course of his professional duties, a wicked and black conspiracy had discovered itself, which he was desirous of revealing before the gentleman who stood there accused of murder should be dismissed from her ladyship's presence.

Lady Dunore's countenance brightened into triumph. She cast a look of reproach and indignation at her son: old Crawley, on the contrary, turned deadly pale, and sunk on a seat beside his sister, whose whispers and sneers were all directed *at* Lady Clancare, though addressed to Lady Dunore.

'Pray sit down, Mr. Dean,' ex-/claimed Lady Dunore. 'I am happy to make your acquaintance. Georgy, love, move a little, and make room for the dean. Pray speak, I am all attention.' Mr. O' Sullivan declining the honour of the seat intended him, briefly entered on the business which had brought him to the country, at some personal inconvenience, and read from a paper, which was afterwards handed about, the dying declaration of a man of the name of Teague Connor. This person had been two days before wounded to death in a riot, and had sought to purchase remission of his crimes under the influence of a death-bed remorse, by confessing his recent conspiracy against the life of an innocent man, a stranger, of whom he knew nothing, but that he had seen him give money to a poor woman in a cabin. To the crime he had confessed, he had been instigated by the arts of the notorious / Jemmy Bryan, who purchased his acquiescence by the sum of fifty pounds, and the protection of a great gentleman in the country.

'The name of this *gentleman*,' continued Mr, O'Sullivan, 'is in my possession; and this declaration is signed by three magistrates, who were present when it was made, and who were persons of the *highest* respectability and consideration. The unfortunate man who made it still lives; and the woman who received the golden coin from General Fitzwalter had deposed that she sold it, a few days back, for forty shillings, to the said Mr. Jemmy Bryan, who has escaped the vigilance of the most active research; and except Mr. Crawley can give us some assistance in the pursuit, may finally elude the grasp of justice.'

The triumph which had flashed from Lady Dunore's eyes now gave way to / a look of deep mortification and disappointment, while the appeal of Mr. O'Sullivan turned every eye on old Crawley, who, during the singular *denouement,* had nearly crept to the door: there he was stopped by Lord Frederick, who springing after him, and catching him by the arm, led him back into the room.

'Stay, my Ching-foo,' he cried: 'it is now very evident we cannot get on without you, my mirror of magistrates. We cannot yet dispense with your presence.'

'Give you my honour, was only just stepping out for a little *thieves' vinegar*[250] in respect of the *hate*,' replied old Crawley, as he took his seat, muttering, as he passed his sister, in a tone of agony – 'and Con to desert me in this *dilemia,* and think only of himself and his election!'

'I have only to add,' continued Mr. / O'Sullivan, 'that it is my firm belief that this conspiracy against the character and life of a brave and high-spirited gentleman had been contrived for the sole purpose of preventing his making claims to title and property of which he has been long deprived by the most iniquitous proceedings; and I am also ready to declare upon oath, in a court of justice, that I believe the person who now has the title and name of General Fitzwalter is Walter de Montenay Fitzadelm, son and heir to the late Baron Walter Fitzwalter, and that he is the *true Marquis of Dunore*.'

'And *I* declare,' exclaimed old Crawley, worked up by the exigency of the moment, while universal emotion and amazement were pictured in every countenance; 'I declare, that the *gentleman,* if it's *gentleman* you call him, Mr. O'Sullivan, is Micky Laffan, a bit of a bye-blow of my Lord Fitzadelm, / by one

Judy Laffan; and if I don't prove it, and many respectable witnesses along with me, I'll just give my head for a Cronobane halfpenny.'[251]

'How can that be?' exclaimed a voice from the door, 'and I, Micky Laffan, here to the fore.'

The gaunt figure of Padreen Gar strided forward, and he continued:

'And you thought, Mr. Crawley, I'd never come back from transportation; but I tould you I would, Sir, when you laste expected me, and am here, you see, to make good my word.' As he spoke he wiped off the yellow stain that covered his face, and removing the black hairs which concealed a handsome auburn head, he asked, with his wonted air of resolute intrepidity, 'do you know me now, Mr. Crawley, Sir? Isn't that the *coolin*[252] of the family all the world over?' and he run his coarse fingers through locks / curled and burnished as Lord Adelm's own: 'and hopes I have too much of a gentleman in me, Mr. Crawley, and too much of the blood of my father in my veins, to do the unhandsome thing, or save myself from trouble by bringing ruination on the head of an innocent man and a fine gentleman; and you may *sind* me back to Botany now, if you plaze, Mr. Crawley, for another *ruction* at Ballydab, as yez did before, but defies the world to say I ever injured man or baste, barring a tythe proctor, or a bit of an exciseman, or cropping a taste off Jemmy Bryan's odd ear, just for fun, and carries my mark with him to this day: and if you don't believe what I say, there's the certificate of my birth, and there's the gentleman, God bless him, that signed it, and was minister at Fitzadelm church the day I was born.'

Padreen Gar presented a piece of / dirty paper to the rector, who acknowledged the signature, and recollected the baptism of an illegitimate son of Lord Walter Fitzadelm, at the period of the date, whom, like many others of the offspring of that lord's illicit loves, he had abandoned to the want and misery which eventually led to a life of lawlessness and desperation.

Old Crawley sunk back in his chair, and either was unable or unwilling to make any further effort. Lady Dunore was motionless and silent from fear, doubt, and consternation; her eyes, almost starting from their inflamed sockets, wandered alternately from the face of her son to Fitzwalter and Padreen Gar; and, differing as they all did in personal appearance, she beheld, or fancied she could trace, a resemblance, such as is often seen in members of the same family, however vague or indefinite. /

The rest of the company were silent from amazement and anxious expectation, while eager curiosity was apparent in the looks of those even least interested in the results of this curious scene.[d]

Fitzwalter turned his eyes on Lord Adelm, as if, before he himself occupied attention, he wished to give *him* an opportunity of playing a part, distinguished in proportion to its singularity and disinterestedness. Lord Adelm, though languid, and occasionally abstracted as one self-involved and distressingly preoccupied, understood the appeal made to all his better feelings, and came forward to reply to it.

'It may,' he said, addressing his mother, 'it may tend to put a speedy termination to a scene naturally calculated to distress and agitate you, Madam, if, without further discussions, at a moment when they are scarcely available, I, who have been so / long supposed the presumptive heir of the Dunore estates and titles, come forward to assert my solemn belief in the actual existence of my uncle's only son, De Montenay Fitzadelm: further, it is my belief, that the celebrated and distinguished man, who now stands before me, is that person; and I am proud to confess, that I have been possessed of the secret of his existence, and of the efforts he had been making to establish his just claims since he first arrived in this country – claims which it would be impolitic as vain to oppose or resist. The perilous confidence his noble and generous nature thus placed in me has been the purchase of my everlasting esteem and gratitude. I will not say I am *happy,* that is not human nature; but I am *proud* to be enabled to welcome the long injured Marquis of Dunore to the possessions of his ancestors.' He held out his hand to Fitzwalter, and the / embrace of the distinguished cousins was a signal to the prompt feelings of O'Leary and Padreen Gar. Their cry of long live Walter de Montenay Fitzadelm, Marquis of Dunore, and *Gal-Readh-Aboe,* was echoed by persons who had forced their way into the hall, and re-echoed by the multitude who occupied the court without.

Lady Dunore, now agitated '*up to her bent,*'[253] wrung her hands in convulsive emotion, exclaiming, that Lord Adelm sought only to oppose and distract her, calling on Mr. Crawley to come forward, and intreating her friends to stand by her to secure the conspirators, and to discredit a tale in which there was not, there could not be, a shadow of truth.

Every eye was turned on the hero of the scene, who waited evidently for the first burst of Lady Dunore's passion to exhaust itself before he addressed her. / He then said – 'that a story so extraordinary, so strongly opposed to your ladyship's maternal interests and ambition, should startle your belief, is natural and excusable; of its truth, however, there is one witness in this room, whose testimony you cannot doubt; I mean Mr. Crawley.'

Old Crawley, faint, ghastly, the victim of his constitutional timidity, and of facts which were bearing all before them, shrunk back, and seemed almost to diminish to the eye, as every feature, every limb, yielded to gradual contraction. General Fitzwalter, however, advanced, drew him forward, and led him for a few minutes on one side. Whatever had been the subject of their conference, when old Crawley turned round, though still agitated and trembling, the colour had returned to his livid cheek; and when he was led forward to his patroness, who was weep-/ing on his sister's shoulder, Lady Georgina being too much amused to lend her friend any assistance, he endeavoured to address her.

'Lady Emily Fitzadelm,' he began; but the wild start of the person he thus addressed, the flash of indignation which sparkled in her haughty eyes, again annihilated his returning courage; and uttering an inarticulate – '*The Lord save us!*' he hastily retreated.

'Mr. Crawley, Madam,' said the Marquis of Dunore, 'would have sought your ladyship's forgiveness for having so long concealed an event in which you are so deeply interested. He would plead in excuse, *that* zeal for you and your children, which originated his acquiescence in a crime, it is now his intention to expiate by a full and complete discovery. His testimony, however, may be dispensed with: the evidences in my favour are sufficiently / numerous and strong to leave me independent of his assistance. His liberty, perhaps *his life,* was in my power – they are so no more. I have pledged my honour for their safety, on certain conditions. His reputation, his ill acquired property, I cannot save. I have now little to add. It will depend upon the prudence and discretion of your ladyship's counsellors, whether in acting as the representative of your suffering son, Robert Fitzadelm, commonly called Marquis of Dunore, you shall bring our mutual claims before a court; when it is for the honour of our family that they should be referred to private decision.

'For what purposes, and at whose instigation, I was in my boyhood torn from my country and my birth-right, and sold to slavery, Mr. Crawley can best tell you, for the rest, my story may be briefly related. /

'The generous person into whose hands I fell rescued me from the horrors of a condition which still exists among the professors of christianity, to the shame of humanity. The precosity of intellect, which had been nourished by the lessons of my good and learned fosterer and preceptor, O'Leary, told powerfully in my favour with him whose property I became. I was soon made the companion and instructor of his only son, saved the boy's life in a surprise attempted by some native Indians, who surrounded us in a distant sporting journey; received my manumission as a recompence; grew unconsciously on the father's affections; became the child of his adoption on the premature death of his only son, and succeeded to his property on his demise.

'The cause of liberty was my natural vocation, and I hastened to the South / American continent, to join its standard, then slowly beginning to unfurl in the land of oppression. My own story lay rankling in secret at the bottom of my heart; and I had almost to abhor the name and title which had been the cause of my being reduced below the state of man. When I arrived in England, however, with Don Narino,[254] in my inquiries after my own family, I found there only existed an empty title, without property, rank, or consideration, and a representative whom my re-appearance would blast with eternal infamy. There was nothing to be gained by a discovery, but the destruction of those nearest to me by blood. I returned to South America without reclaiming a name I almost blushed to own, that I might make one I should glory in wearing.

'In justice to myself, I must observe, / that the protector of my infancy, the instructor of my youth, was never forgotten – my dear foster-father O'Leary.' He paused, and a smile of mingled emotion and beneficence threw its radiance over his splendid countenance. O'Leary hustled forward, and passing the tears from his swimming eyelids, he stood with a look of proud triumph beside him, swinging his hat, and humming away his emotion.

'Of the persons of respectability in my father's service, I could only remember the son of our land steward, Darby Crawley, an attorney in the neighbourhood of Court Fitzadelm. To this person I wrote, requesting him to forward an inclosed letter to Terrence O'Leary, (whose wife had been in the service of the Baroness Fitzadelm), containing five hundred pounds; but in case of his death to return it / to my banker in London. In my letter to O'Leary, I entrusted the secret of my existence, and my intention of coming forward to claim my right and title *on the death of my uncle.*'

'The murthuring pirate!' interrupted O'Leary, shaking his hand at old Crawley, who sat behind the chair of his trembling and now agitated sister. 'And never gave me a scrubal of it, as I tould your lordship before; but had me flogged in the *rebellion for a latin note* he found in my pocket – the *Ignoramus!*'

'The event of my captivity in the Caraccas,' continued Lord Dunore, 'is already before the public. One incident arose from this event, which it is curious to mention, as bearing forcibly on the circumstances of the moment. The keeper of my dungeon was a Spaniard, who spoke a little English. He had occasionally addressed me in that / language, and eyed me with a curiosity which indicated an interest beyond that of our present relation – it was the interest of recognition: and inquiries, mutually made and answered, discovered in the person of the keeper of my dungeon a sailor, one of the crew who had assisted in kidnapping me in my boyhood from the Irish coast.

'This man had suffered much in the interval which had elapsed: he had been taken by Barbary pirates – sold to slavery, and, in the vicissitudes of his life, had entered into the service of Spain, been wounded, disabled, and made one of the keepers of a royal prison in Spanish America. He had considered his sufferings as retributions for the crimes he had assisted in committing on the Irish shores; and in the hope that he was now about to be reconciled with heaven, he effected my escape from prison, accompanied me in / my flight, and is at present my mate, and on board my own vessel, which lies in harbour near Cork. In confirmation of these facts, he can produce a letter, dropped on the deck by one of the disguised persons who had brought me out to the vessel, which he had preserved, in the hope of one day expiating his crime by being of use to me. The signature of this letter I have shewn to Lord Fitzadelm. Its address is to Mr. Crawley, from

Court Fitzadelm, twenty-three years back, and the post-mark is a town in the neighbourhood. Witnesses, no less efficient than this letter, are – a groom of my father's who carried me in the chaise, which now awaits at the door of this castle, and who has been reduced to beggary, under the Irish epithet of the *Baccah;* Terence Oge O'Leary, my foster-father; the Reverend Denis O'Sullivan, my mother's kinsman and confessor, to whom / she bequeathed the certificate of my birth and her own marriage (urged to this cautionary proceeding by the intrigues of which she died the broken-hearted victim); – the miniatures of both my parents in their youth in his possession, to both of which I bear a strong resemblance; – and the Reverend the Rector of Dunore, who remembered me in my childhood, when he was himself a young man, just gone into orders, and made curate of the parish of Court Fitzadelm. I have nothing more to add, but that my story, strange and improbable as it may appear, belongs to the history of a long disorganized country, where, under the influence of political misrule, the moral relations of society too often sit loosely: and where the demoralization of the people is a necessary dogma in the code of those who rule by national debasement and disunion. /

'Happily, the national spirit and national virtues, founded in strong and warm affections, and in that animal courage which rarely allies itself to baseness, has always formed a barrier to systematic degradation: but it is melancholy to add that my story is not without its parallel in the private history of the land.'*[255 e]

Then, after a brief silence, preserved by the amazement of some, and the still eager curiosity of others, he added, in a voice full of conciliation and respect, and more especially addressing himself to the weeping and exhausted Lady Dunore, 'This is not a moment to press upon your ladyship's credence the facts of a story it can neither be your interest or inclination to admit. But I would at least induce your to believe that the / mother of Lord Adelm Fitzadelm must always be to me an object of respect, of interest, and consideration; and that whether you persist to refuse, or yield to the claims I have now briefly stated, you will, at least, I trust, remain mistress of this castle, so long as it may be your convenience or pleasure to continue in Ireland.

'And now, Mr. Crawley,' he added, with his radiant smile, 'if you insist on the execution of your warrant, I must obey, and accompany your officers of justice to Dublin. I confess, however, I had planned a journey of a very different description.' He coloured deeply, and threw his eyes on Lady Clancare, who, down-cast and blushing, was deserted in this moment of prosperous triumph by that gaiety and elasticity of spirit which in less fortunate hours had borne her above the adverse circumstances of her forlorn destiny. /

---

*　　See the great Ansley trial for the title and estates of Althams and Anglesey.

The bashfulness of a bride, fresh from the altar, and the powerful emotions incidental to her peculiar position, as she now stood, the mistress of the superb mansion, where she had first appeared a prisoner, where she had lately stood accused of conspiracy and imposture, left her confused, silent, and shrinking from the glances which the slight allusion of the Marquis of Dunore to their respective situations had drawn to her person. A few words having passed between the agitated Crawley and Lord Fitzadelm, the latter addressing his cousin, observed aloud, that Mr. Crawley had referred every thing to him for the present.

'Then, in that case,' observed Lord Dunore, stepping back, and drawing the arm of the new and bridal marchioness through his, 'we shall pursue our route according to our original intention.' /

Lady Clancare, now letting go his arm, advanced timidly to Lady Dunore, and took her hand with that fondling and playful manner which had once such charms for her capricious friend.

'No,' said Lady Dunore, snatching it hastily from her, and in a tone of angry indignation; 'whatever may happen, I shall always consider your conduct as false and deceptive.'

'How!' said Lady Clancare, all her wonted spirit rallying to her eyes and countenance. 'False! Was it false to confide to you the sole important secret of my life? Was it deceptive to confess to you the motives which led me to your castle to seek and to accept your hospitality? If I have deceived *you*, Madam, it was by the frank relation of facts, calculated indeed by their improbability to win on your attention, but yet confided to you at some risk, because, though I may have / availed myself of some mysterious truths, I disdained falsehood even for the purpose of effecting my dearest interests – and now,' she added, with a sudden burst of gaiety flashing over her whole countenance, and animating every gesture, 'I would fain, like one of my own heroines, wind up the denouement of my story with some touch of humour or pathos – some appeal to the feelings I address, which should enable me to retire with applause: but hitherto adversity has been my muse, and now,' placing her hand in Lord Dunore's, 'she deserts me.

'What remains, therefore, to say of myself, must be deferred to calmer moments, when as *ennuyée*, as other great personages with the "*toujours Perdrix*,"[256] I shall seek to diversify the calm of my dull prosperity by a recurrence to the vicissitudes of my early life: – then seated by my Irish turf fire, / with my own amusement for my object, and my husband for my critical reviewer, I shall take the liberty of *putting myself in my own book*, and shall record the events of this last month of my life under the title of – *Florence Macarthy*.' /

CHAPTER VII.

And thus the whirligig of time
Brings in its revenges.
MILTON.[257]

CONCLUSION.

THE eccentric and visionary, but high-minded Lord Adelm Fitzadelm, had just remained in Ireland long enough to learn that his law agent, Conway Crawley, had been elected member in his stead for Glannacrime; and the papers soon after announced his departure for the North Pole.[258]

Meantime, his mother, backed by powerful friends, and urged by interested counsellors, refused, on her return to England, to acknowledge the claims / made by the gallant guerilla chief to the title and property in possession of her insane son: a suit was commenced, which ended in her defeat, and only served to expose the infamy of her late husband to '*the glarish eye of day*.'[259] The trial, however, had occupied, amused, and agitated her; and the overthrow of her hopes furnished her new sources of real affliction and complaint, in place of the ideal sorrows she had loved to create and to deplore.

As Miss Crawley had prudently separated herself from her brother Darby, with the desertion of his success and fortunes, and had accompanied Lady Dunore to England, she availed herself of the depression of mind to which that lady, for a time, resigned her variable feelings; and, to her infinite triumph, she had the happiness of seeing rouge, Almacks, and 'Georgy love,' sacrificed to round-eared caps, / religious conversaziones, and the society of the elect and hungry in the Lord, who eat their way to their patronesses' conversion with true gastronomic, as well as polemic zeal; while Miss Crawley, the directress of her conscience and her house, gradually assumed a power over both, to which the unregulated imagination of Lady Dunore, easily worked on by terror and mysticism, made no resistance.

The leases and mortgages, inevitably rendered unavailable by the unexpected re-appearance of the real Marquis of Dunore, with the loss of his agency, nearly reduced old Crawley to a state of ruin, which an investigation of the *commissioners of enquiry* into his official emoluments finally completed. His military son had been ordered abroad. His eldest son, under an accumulation of gambling debts, occupied an apartment in a prison over which he / had once presided; and old Crawley, in his extreme distress, was reduced to applying for relief to his favourite son, Conway, who had, however, on the first turn of his father's fortunes, shaken him off, on the plea of his *immoral conduct* and *lost character*.

Conway Townsend Crawley, Esq. member for Glannacrime, had found an early opportunity of attracting the eyes of persons in power, by serving in a cause in which they were interested, and had purchased a situation of trust and emolument, at the expense of every manly and every gentleman-like feeling. Pushing his way into high society by the same intrepid *effrontery* as he had pushed his way through life to fortune, he happened one day to be seated at the head of his sumptuous table, entertaining a select party of official grandees, when Mr. Darby Crawley from Ireland was announced, and, to his horror and con- /sternation, his vulgar, blundering, but unfortunate father, entered the room, and, throwing his arms round him, exclaimed: –

'Con, honey, sure you won't turn your back on your poor ould father, like the rest of the world? – he that made a counsellor and a member of parliament of you, and that warned you against poethry, and pathritism, and ganius; and owes to him what you are at this minute, if you were twenty times as great.'

The ridicule of this scene, prolonged by the good-nature of his guests and friends, was *ineffacable*; and from that moment, Conway Crawley resolved on getting rid of a relative, who blended a disgraceful vulgarity and lost character with an effrontery which, like his own, was unconquerable.

In a few weeks, therefore, Mr. Crawley, through the interest of his son, / being still *a loyal*, though almost *a lost* man, was appointed consul to His Britannic Majesty at a *Turkish port*. Meantime, consigned by that son to the back stairs, and housekeeper's room of his house in London, he felt the indignity with parental pride: but his natural cheeriness of temperament prevailed over his misfortune; and while he sat with the priestess of conserves, enjoying a *sup of hot*, his head full of turbaned Turks, and the elephant in Blue Beard,[260] on which he expected shortly to ride, with some acrimonious reference to the political power, and unnatural conduct of his son, he occasionally was heard to sing forth –

"'Tis a very fine thing to be father BY law,

To a very magnificent three-tail'd bashaw.'[261]

His son, meantime, becoming a servant of all work in his political voca- / tion, and remunerated accordingly, in his various capacities, literary, official, and diplomatic, *used*, not *respected*, *tolerated*, not *esteemed*, continues to live

'With *pay*, and *scorn* content,

Bows and votes on in court and parliament.'[262]

On the successful termination of the great Fitzadelm cause, which had for some months occupied the public attention, the Marquis and Marchioness of Dunore took possession of their ancient castle and vast possessions in Ireland, and fixed there their chief residence. For, convinced by a close and attentive observation, that the land of their birth was hourly sinking in the scale of nations, under the oppression of petty, delegated authority, and by the neglect and absence of its natural protectors, they acted, with their accustomed energy and perseverance, upon the / dictates of experience, and illustrated, by their example, the truth of a maxim now more generally felt and admitted, that

IRELAND CAN BEST BE SERVED IN IRELAND. /

NOTE.

(1) Page 118. – The constant cry of Sir H. Sydney to the queen was, 'Your majesty must plant justice here.' His manner of giving in his resignation was singular, as coming from an Irish lord-lieutenant. 'If,' he says, 'that cowardly policy be still allowed to keep the Irish in continual dissension, for fear lest through their quiet might follow I know not what, then my advice to your majesty both is and shall be, to withdraw me and all charge here. It is flattering to Ireland, that the few men of talent who have been sent to govern that kingdom became ever after her firm friends. Of this Sir H. Sydney, the unfortunate Lord Essex, [*263] and Lord Chesterfield, are proofs.[f]

ERRATA.

VOL. I.

Page 4	line 19	for	aouthern	read	southern
	20		arbor		ardour
29	5		Marlemont		charlemont
41	14		Smart'		Smart's
145	ult.		settling		setting
157	1		trouble		trouble you
196	21		furzes		frizes
256	13		subjiciant		subjiciunt
290	penult		dele now		-
301	18		Bellianus		Belliains

307	11	One	one's
308	ib.	tombrua	tonitrua

VOL. II.

1	5	parvent	parvient
45	15	Of	off
60	18[illeg]	genius	genus
92	5	liquor	liqueur
137	10	dele now	
152	20	observed	and observed
165	17	his	her
191	12	dele soon	
246	1	Italien	Italian
256	ult.	pooh	Proh[illeg]!

VOL. III.

85	4	read	is at least a glorious [illeg]illusion
104	1	orguil	orgueil
177	5	dele and	
181	19	her	per
227	21	stagnate	stagnant
260	15	real	reel

VOL. IV.

[illeg]79	12	the	to the
117	10	Hebernica	Hibernica
133	17	recular	reculer
143	14	belleve	believes
264	7	passing	pressing

Some errors in punctuation which affect the sense will be perceived, which the reader is requested to correct en passant.

*   The Earl of Essex here alluded to is not the favourite of Elizabeth's court, but the unfortunate nobleman who was, murdered in the Tower. – *See Essex's Letters.*

THE END. /

*   See Young's Tour. Their priest's dues form the smallest portion of the religious taxes paid by these poor people.

EDITORIAL NOTES

Volume I

1. *Know thus far ... SHAKESPEARE*: Shakespeare, *The Tempest*, I.ii.207–14.
2. *Les femmes ... DE GRAMMONT*: From ch. 8 of *Mémoires de la vie du Maréchal de Gramont* (1713), an account of the life and social circle of Philibert, comte de Gramont, by his brother-in-law Anthony Hamilton (1644/5–1729). The first English translation, by Abel Boyer, appeared in 1714 as *Memoirs of the Life of Count de Grammont: containing, in particular, the amorous intrigues of the court of England in the reign of King Charles II*. A prominent member of James II's court in exile in France, Hamilton was a grandson of James Hamilton, first Earl of Abercorn – and thus also related to Owenson's patron, the ninth Earl of Abercorn. The passage from which Owenson's epigraph is taken concerns the slanders against Anne Hyde after her marriage to James, Duke of York (later James II). It is translated in a revised edition of Boyer's version as: 'Women are seldom accustomed to forgive injuries of this nature; and, if they promise themselves the pleasure of revenge, when they gain the power, they seldom forget it'. See *Memoirs of Count Grammont, by Count A. Hamilton. A New Translation, with Notes and Illustrations* (London: S. and E. Harding, 1794), p. 167.
3. ratio ultima regum: 'the last resort of kings' (Latin).
4. *the master cast*: members of the Anglo-Irish 'Ascendancy', being mainly the descendants of Norman settlers in Ireland.
5. *Glorvinas, O'Donnels and MacRorys, of former compositions*: Refers to major characters in Owenson's earlier novels: Glorvina, heroine of *The Wild Irish Girl* (1806); and Roderick O'Donnel, eponymous hero of *O'Donnel* (1814), and his foster-brother, McRory.
6. *T. C. M*: The initials of (Thomas) Charles Morgan (1783–1843), Sydney Owenson's husband. Born in London, he was educated at Eton, Charterhouse and Cambridge, and received his medical diploma in 1809. His first marriage ended after only a year, with the death of his wife following the birth of a daughter. Morgan met Owenson when both were members of the household of the Marquess of Abercorn, by whom Morgan was employed as a medical attendant. He was knighted immediately before his marriage to Owenson in 1812; and subsequently appointed physician to the Marshalsea Prison, Dublin. His published works on moral philosophy included *Sketches of the Philosophy of Life* (1818), and *Sketches of the Philosophy of Morals* (1822).
7. La Grange ... 1818: Charles Morgan's Advertisement is dated from the Château La Grange, seventy-five miles east of Paris in Seine sur Marne, France, the country seat of Lafayette, where he and Owenson were staying as they travelled southward toward Italy.

8. *Whom when ... Spencer*: From Edmund Spenser, *Colin Clouts Come Home Againe* (1595), 64–7.
9. *the Channel*: the Irish Sea.
10. Il Librador: Since the 1780s, revolutionary movements against Spanish rule had been taking place throughout the Spanish provinces of South America. Revolutionaries' main demands included legislative independence, free trade and improved education for the native and creole populations. General Fitzwalter, the owner of *Il Librador*, is a fictional example of those foreign sympathizers with the cause of South American independence who became actively involved in the rebellions against Spanish rule.
11. *Plymouth Sound*: the confluence of the mouths of the rivers Plym and Tamar, off the coasts of Devon and Cornwall.
12. homme comme il faut: '[a man] as he should be'(French). Used here and elsewhere in *Florence Macarthy* to mean correct; conforming to fashion or etiquette. The first cited instance in *OED* is that which appears in Volume III, Chapter 3, p. 7.
13. *manière d'être*: 'manner of being' (French).
14. *alembicated*: Over-refined, over-subtilized (as if distilled in an alembic). This is the second instance of usage of this sense recorded in *OED*.
15. *ideologist*: One who has ideas; an idealist, theorist or visionary. This is the earliest usage of this sense recorded in *OED*.
16. '*nothing is, but thinking makes it so*': recalls *Hamlet*, II.ii.259–60 ('There is nothing either good or bad, but thinking makes it so').
17. physiognomists ... intellect: Physiognomists were proponents of the pseudo-science of physiognomy, and claimed to be able to gauge traits of personality from the shapes and proportions of subjects' facial features.
18. *valet de chambre*: literally 'chamber-valet' (French); a gentleman's personal manservant or attendant (*OED*).
19. *Spencer's 'Fairy Queen,' and 'State of Ireland'*: The two major works in which the English poet Edmund Spenser (1552–99), employed within various capacities in Elizabeth I's Irish administration 1580–98, engaged with issues relating to Elizabeth I's government of Ireland. *The Faerie Queene* (1590) was the unfinished epic poem of which six books of twelve cantos were completed, each of them allegorizing a different princely virtue. Spenser drew most upon his experiences as a crown administrator in Ireland in Book V. *A View of the Present State of Ireland* was the prose treatise in which Spenser not only described the history and geography of Ireland, but also argued that conflicts between the new English, Protestant settlers, and the traditionally Roman Catholic, Gaelic and Old English (or Anglo-Norman) communities in Ireland, could only be resolved by the uniform imposition of English laws, social conventions and religion. The work took the form of a dialogue between two characters, Eudoxus and Irenius. Probably completed during 1598, it was not published until 1633, when it was included by Sir James Ware in his collection of *Ancient Irish Histories*; see also n. 141 below.
20. '*communing with the skies*': a variation on a line in Thomas Cowper, 'Charity' ('When one who holds communion with the skies').
21. *the morning star*: the planet Venus, as seen in the eastern sky before sunrise.
22. *The* cross of the south: the constellation Crux Australis, visible only in the southern hemisphere, the four brightest stars in which form a cross shape.
23. ennui: 'boredom' (French); in English usage, weariness with life.
24. '*his poor estate of man*': source unidentified.

25. *tacking*: steering a ship obliquely against the wind, in alternate directions, so as to proceed in a windward course (*OED*).

26. *lubberly*: clumsy (*OED*).

27. *Spencer, the deputy of a deputy*: Edmund Spenser was first employed in Ireland as private secretary to Arthur, Lord Grey of Wilton, appointed Elizabeth I's lord deputy (equivalent to a viceroy) in Ireland in 1580. In 1586 he acquired the estate connected to the Norman castle of Kilcolman, Cork, on lands confiscated from the Earl of Desmond; and in 1590 Elizabeth I conferred the manors, lands, castle and town of Kilcolman upon Spenser and his heirs. In late 1598, Spenser had to flee from the estate when it was overrun by rebels. Spenser never returned to Kilcolman, as he died in England in January 1599.

28. *the dreadless might ... one of Ireland's Herods*: Arthur Grey, fourteenth Baron Grey of Wilton (1536–93), lord deputy of Ireland 1580–2, was admired by Protestant supporters, including Spenser, for decisiveness in suppressing the rebellions of Roman Catholic earls including Gerald Fitzgerald, fourteenth Earl of Desmond. However, he became notorious among Irish Catholics, and earned disapproval at court, for his massacre of around 600 Spanish and Italian troops belonging to the rebels, after their surrender at Smerwick, on the Dingle peninsula, in November 1580. The Commodore compares Grey to Herod (73 BC–4 BC), king of the Roman protectorate of Judaea, whose anxiety on hearing that a new king (Christ) had been born in the province prompted him to order the precautionary slaughter of all male children under the age of two; see Matthew 2:1–16. The Commodore also quotes from Spenser, *The Faerie Queene*, book V, canto 4, stanza 1, concerning the need for strength and boldness in government: 'For vain it is to deem of things aright, / And makes wrong doers justice to deride, / Unless it be performed with dreadless might: / For Power is the right hand of Justice truly hight'.

29. *his Irish Kilcoleman*: Owenson's footnote names the MacCarthy More, the most powerful of the MacCarthy clans of Co. Cork, which also included the MacCarthy Reagh. Also mentioned in the footnote is Walter Raleigh (1554–1618), who served as a captain under Grey at Smerwick in November 1580, and oversaw the executions of the surrendered rebel troops. In 1586 Elizabeth I presented Raleigh with extensive properties on the confiscated Desmond lands in the province of Munster. Raleigh was a guest of Spenser's at Kilcolman in 1589, and encouraged the publication of Books I–III of the *Faerie Queene*. He was also the dedicatee of Spenser's *Colin Clout's Come Home Againe* (1595). Owenson alludes here to the common identification of the knight Sir Artigall, hero of Book V of the *Faerie Queene*, as an allegorical portrayal of Grey. In her endnote (1), accompanying this footnote, Owenson quotes at length from Charles Smith, *The Antient and Present State of the County and City of Cork*, 2nd edn, 2 vols (Dublin: n. s., 1774), vol. 2, pp. 59–61. In her allusion to Toney Lumpkin', Owenson appears to be thinking of the passage in Act V of Oliver Goldsmith's *She Stoops to Conquer* (1773), where Tony Lumpkin tells his disappointed mother, Mrs Hardcastle, 'all the parish says you have spoil'd me, and so you may take the fruits on it'.

30. *'He sat ... far about'*: Paraphrases Spenser, *Colin Clouts Come Home Againe*, ll. 56–7, and 62–3.

31. *Magna Charta ... emancipated nation*: 'Great Charter'(Latin), signifying any document establishing rights, after the charter of English political liberty obtained from King John of England by his rebellious barons in 1215 (*OED*).

32. *darkling*: 'Darkling' here is the present participle of the verb to darkle, 'to become dark with anger, scorn etc' (*OED*).

33. *Holyhead packet*: A packet boat, a vessel travelling at regular intervals between two ports, for the conveyance of mail, goods or passengers. The term originally referred to boats which carried 'packets' of state letters and dispatches, chiefly between England and Ireland (*OED*). Holyhead, on the Welsh island of Anglesey, was and is the principal port for British shipping to Dublin.

34. *land-waiter*: A customs officer.

35. *'c'est a nous' 'ce n'est pas a nous'*: '[It's] ours,' '[it's] not ours' (French).

36. *'got dam'*: i. e. 'god damn'.

37. *Figaro*: The hero of Pierre-Augustin Caron de Beaumarchais' comedy *La Folle journée, ou le Mariage de Figaro* ['The Follies of a Day, or The Marriage of Figaro] (1784), Figaro is the outspoken and resourceful valet of Count Almaviva. In a dialogue in Act III, the Count tells Figaro that he has reconsidered a plan to take Figaro to London with him on the grounds that Figaro knows no English. Figaro retorts that he can say 'God damn', further remarking that this expression seems to be useful in all circumstances in England.

38. *on ne manquede rien, nulle part*: 'one need lack nothing' (French), Figaro's words to the Count, concerning use of the expression 'God damn', in Act III of *La Folle Journée, ou le marriage de Figaro*.

39. *jingle*: A covered, two-wheeled car used in the south of Ireland (OED).

40. *brogue*: 'strongly marked dialectical pronunciation or accent', particularly used to refer to the English speech of Ireland (*OED*).

41. *lazzaroni*: singular of *lazzarone* (Italian), members of the lower classes, originally in Naples, who lounged about the streets, living by begging or odd jobs (*OED*).

42. *hackney*: Vehicle for public hire.

43. *handy by*: 'Conveniently situated for' (*OED*; first recorded usage 1825).

44. *pelisse*: A fur-lined mantle or cloak (*OED*).

45. *'the many hotels ... the banished nobility'*: alludes to the conversion of many Dublin townhouses to hotels, following the passage of the Act of Union in 1800, after which numerous politicians and grandees who had opposed the Union abandoned public life, and thus also their city residences.

46. *laquais*: literally 'place-servant' (French): A manservant temporarily hired during a visit to a foreign city (*OED*).

47. *the Pedrillos ... Spanish comedy*: Owenson may be referring to two comedies, set in Spanish locations, by Irish dramatists of the previous century: *The Castle of Andalusia* (1782) by John O'Keeffe (1747–1833), which featured a servant named Pedrillo, and *Two Strings to Your Bow* (1791) by Robert Jephson (1736–1803), characters in which include Lazarillo, also a lively, outspoken servant. The name Lazarillo meanwhile had a long association with the Spanish comic tradition in prose fiction, following the success of *La Vida de Lazarillo de Tormes* ['The Life of Lazarillo de Tormes'] (1554), a picaresque novel by Diego Hurtado de Mendoza (1503–75).

48. *all the embarrass ... the portable toilette*: *embarrass*, obstacle (French); used in English in sense of an excess of objects (*OED*); *necessaire*, necessary (French), here in English sense of small carrying case for personal grooming implements (*OED*); *toilette*, literally 'small cloth', or towel (French); here in contemporary French and English sense of a set of items used in dressing and grooming (*OED*).

49. *Zamora's Spanish plays*: It is not clear which of two Spanish dramatists named Zamora, both of whose works were available in various editions by this period, is being referred to here. Antonio de Zamora (1660?–1728) was a notable dramatist of early eighteenth-century Spain; his major dramatic works included a version of the Don Juan myth, and

Nuevas Comedias (New Comedies), first published 1726. Gaspar Zavola y Zamora (1760–1812) was one of the most prominent Spanish dramatists of the late eighteenth, and early nineteenth, centuries, who authored highly emotional, dramatic allegories of Spanish national identity including *Los patriotas de Aragón* (The Patriots of Aragon), and *La alianza española con la nación inglesa* (The Spanish Allegiance with the English Nation), both published in 1808.

50. 'sacre,' 'diantre,' or 'Peste de moname': i.e. *sacré*, 'Hell' (French); *diantre*, 'Damn it!' (Spanish); or *Peste de mon ame*, 'Plague of my soul' (French).

51. *'paix! paix!* 'peace! peace!' (French); 'Quiet!'. Phonetically similar to 'Pay! pay!' as heard by the Irishman.

52. *daddle*: English slang: the hand or fist (*OED*).

53. *lounger*: 'One who lounges, an idler' (*OED*).

54. *'May travel ... Balin-robe'*: an inaccurate allusion to the opening four lines of a song performed by the patriotic Irishman Murtock, in William Macready, *The Irishman in London; or, The Happy African. A Farce* (Dublin: G. Perrin, 1793), vol. 2, p. i:

    > If you'd travel the wide world all over,
    > And sail across quite round the globe,
    > You must set out on horseback from Dover,
    > And sail unto sweet Balinrobe.

55. *Bon, bon ... Bon, j'en suis charmé*: 'Good, good ... Good, I am charmed [with it]' (French).

56. *her beautiful eye ... her hill of Hoath*: refers to 'Ireland's Eye', a small island off the Co. Dublin coast; and, just to the south of this feature, the Hill of Howth, which rises 560 feet from the peninsula of Howth, which extends into the Irish Sea to the north east of Dublin port .

57. *Marino, the great earl of Marlemont's sate [seat]*: Situated in in the northern Dublin suburb of Clontarf, Marino House was the coastal retreat of the Whig grandee James Caulfeild (1728–99), first Earl of Charlemont, a leading Patriot in the 1782 Parliament.

58. *Bryan Borough ... the Musaum of Trinity*: Brian Bórama (Boru), high king of Ireland (d. 1014), was killed during the Battle of Clontarf, a decisive victory against the Danish occupiers of Dublin in 1014. A medieval harp reputed to have belonged to him is still displayed in the Old Library (1712–13) at Trinity College Dublin.

59. *Comment donc*: 'indeed' (French).

60. *Comment donc ... que tu es*: 'Indeed, beggar that you are' (French). 'Que tu es' is phonetically similar to 'cut away', as heard by the Irishman.

61. *mais voila ... qui est bien*: 'There now, my good friend' (French).

62. *sirs let ... and the likes*: the sailor appears to mean that 'mounseers' ('monsieurs', Frenchmen) are 'let alone' by 'sirs' (Englishmen) for their courtly manners; that the French are unusual or unique for such manners among people of all nationalities.

63. *never a dancing dog at Bartlemy fair*: One of the major fairs traditionally held in London, Barthlomew Fair was particularly associated with street entertainments, such as performing animals.

64. *portly*: Here meaning stately or imposing (*OED*), rather than corpulent.

65. *surtout*: 'above [or over] all' (French); man's greatcoat or overcoat (*OED*).

66. *true blue*: Faithful, staunch (*OED*).

67. *the Howes ... wooden walls of old England*: The sailor refers to the British naval heroes Richard, Earl Howe (1726–99); William, first Baron Hotham (1736–1813), and Horatio, Viscount Nelson (1758–1805); and alludes to Henry Green, 'The Wooden Walls of Old England: A Naval Ode' (1773).

68. *Demerara ... Cadiz merchantman*: Now part of modern Guyana, Demerara was one of the South American colonies acquired by Britain from the Dutch in 1814, and merged with Berbice and Essequibo as British Guiana in 1831. Cadiz is a major seaport on the Atlantic coast of Spain.

69. *aloft on the mail*: sense unclear.

70. *lubber ... goes our halves in hard work*: Lubber, conveys both a clumsy, stupid fellow; and a clumsy seaman or unseamanlike person (*OED*). *Goes our halves*, a variation on the expression 'to go halves', to share something equally with one or more others (*OED*).

71. *the Spanish Don*: Used in this period as a courtesy title for a Spanish man of high rank, 'don' could also refer to a Spanish lord or gentleman (*OED*).

72. *a bird of passage ... a God send*: *bird of passage*, literally a migratory bird, here in figurative sense of an itinerant person who never remains in the same place long (*OED*); *a God send*, i. e. a 'godsend', usually meaning a desirable thing received unexpectedly, but here apparently used ironically (*OED*).

73. *Edystone lighthouse*: the lighthouse, built in 1699, which stood on Eddystone Rocks, a reef off the Cornish coast, south-west of Plymouth.

74. *palarvering*: Used here in the sense of chattering foolishly or inconsequentially (*OED*).

75. *yard arm ... fore and aft*: The expression 'yard arm to yard arm' usually refers to ships, when so close together that their yard-arms touch (*OED*), and so here indicates the extent of intimacy between two friends. 'Fore and aft' refers to the entire length of a ship.

76. *like the town of Babylon*: The sailor means the Tower of Babel (the Hebrew name for Babylon), referred to in Genesis 11, and subsequently proverbial for any confusing situation in which many languages are being spoken at once. The tower was constructed by the descendants of Noah, who hoped to reach heaven by climbing it. God punished their presumption by making the builders all speak in languages incomprehensible to each other.

77. *Dungarvon*: Dungarvan, a town on the coast of Co. Waterford.

78. *sorrow bit of Ringsend*: 'Sorrow bit', 'hardly any'. Originally a small village, Ringsend was by this period a slum district close to the disembarkation point for travellers arriving in Dublin from Holyhead.

79. 'toiled after him in vain': From Samuel Johnson, 'Prologue on the Opening of Drury Lane Theatre' (1747), referring to Shakespeare: 'Existence saw him spurn her bounded reign, / And panting time toil'd after him in vain'.

80. *my morning*: 'Morning' is recorded in *OED* as a colloquial expression, in chiefly Scottish use in the period, for a (usually alcoholic) drink taken in the morning.

81. *gin or glory 'leads but to the grave'*: Adapted from Thomas Gray, 'Elegy Written in a Country Churchyard', 36 ('The paths of glory lead but to the grave').

82. *'lonely misery retired to die'*: Misquoted from Samuel Johnson, 'On the Death of Mr Robert Levett, A Practiser in Physick', 20 ('And lonely want retired to die').

83. *bravely*: Used here in the sense of well, or healthy (*OED*).

84. 'an unwearied spirit of doing curtesies': Shakespeare, *Merchant of Venice* III. iii. 294–95.

85. *the fine new streets, Sir, that is'nt built*: a reference to the short-lived period of speculation in land and town development in Ireland following the Union, much of which was halted as economic depression set in following the end of the war against France.

86. *wait a taste*: *taste*, small amount; 'a little' (not recorded in this sense in *OED* before 1894).

87. 'And sure it is a most beautiful and sweet country': De Vere reads from the passage in which Irenius describes the attractions of Ireland for English settlers, in Edmund Spens-

er's *View of the Present State of Ireland*, in J. Ware (ed.), *Ancient Irish Histories* (1633; Dublin: Hibernia Press, 1809), pp. 28–9.

88. *Irishtown*: a district of Dublin, south of the river Liffey.

89. *suburban*: Of the suburbs; suburban, often with reference to licentiousness (*OED*).

90. *Crabbe's Borough Scenery*: Refers to George Crabbe, *The Borough* (1810), twenty-four verse letters describing aspects of everyday English provincial and institutional life, at all levels of society. 'Letter XVIII' ('The Poor and Their Dwellings') contains agraphic depiction of the sordid living conditions endured by paupers and the unemployed.

91. *'The brave … of vapours'*: Adapted from Shakespeare, *Hamlet*, II.ii.319–20.

92. *Merrion Square*: Stillincomplete in 1818, Merrion Square was developed from the 1760s, from an earlier residential terrace. It was favoured by Dublin's wealthier inhabitants both before and following the Union. On this, and other Dublin locations in notes below, see entries in Christine Casey, *The Buildings of Ireland: Dublin* (New Haven, CT: Yale University Press, 2005).

93. *Sir John's fountain*: The fountain in Merrion Square was one of many installed in Dublin as part of improvements to the city's water supply led by Sir John de Blaquiere (1732–1812), a commissioner of the Dublin paving board who became notorious for profiting from the sale of offices, in 1786.

94. *by Jagers*: the origin of this interjection is not clear.

95. *Sackville Street*: Sackville Street was the site of Dublin's most exclusive, Ascendancy residences from the earliest development of its upper section in 1749. During the 1780s it was extended southward to the River Liffey, Carlisle Bridge (now O'Connell Bridge) being added to its south end in 1795. 'Edifices' located on Sackville Street in 1818 included Nelson's Pillar, a Doric column commemorating the British victory at Trafalgar (erected 1812; destroyed 1966); Charlemont House (grand neoclassical townhouse of the earl of Charlemont), and the General Post Office (completed 1818, to design of Francis Johnston). The entire thoroughfare was renamed O'Connell Street, after Daniel O'Connell, in 1924.

96. *coup d'oeil*: a 'glance'; a 'general view' (French).

97. *the area flanked by … its venerable university*: i.e. College Green, site of both the former Parliament House, and Trinity College Dublin, and a traditional space for civic ceremonies, including receptions of newly-appointed viceroys. The Parliament House, here 'silent' owing to the transference in 1801 of Irish government to Westminster, was begun in 1729, to the designs of Edward Lovett Pearce, with later additions by others including James Gandon. An outstanding example of Irish Palladian architecture, the building became the headquarters of the Bank of Ireland following the implementation of the Act of Union in 1801. Trinity College was founded by Elizabeth I in 1592, originally to provide Protestant university education in Ireland. Its iconic grouping of neoclassical buildings, including the entrance front on College Green, was developed from the 1750s.

98. *the night of the UNION*: refers to the evening of 1 August 1800, when the Act of Union was passed. The final sitting of the Irish parliament took place on 2 August 1800.

99. *the Freeman's*: *The Freeman's Journal* was founded in 1763 by the Patriot author Henry Brooke (1703–83), and became the major organ of liberal opinion in late eighteenth-century Dublin, welcoming submissions from its readers. See Robert Munter, *The History of the Irish Newspaper 1685–1760* (London: Cambridge University Press, 1967), p. 188.

100. *counsellor Grattan*: The barrister (hence 'counsellor') and politician Henry Grattan (1746–1820) became the most vocal and distinguished of the Whig politicians who

worked toward the establishment of the Irish Parliament in 1782. Having been called to the Irish bar in 1772, he first entered the Irish House of Commons as MP for Charlemont in 1775. He was especially famed for the eloquence and energy of his rhetoric, as displayed in his 1779 address to George III, requesting that Ireland be granted the right to free trade. During the 1790s Grattan advocated Catholic emancipation as an expedient to avoid the spread of French revolutionary ideas in Ireland, but he also recommended religious toleration in Ireland as an end in itself. After the passage of the Act of Union, which he had energetically resisted, Grattan retired from politics for some years; but later, asMP for Dublin City (1806–20), he brought forward successive bills for Catholic emancipation, the last being in 1816, 1817, and 1819 (*ODNB*).

101. *counsellor Gallagher's iligant* [*elegant*] *speeches*: 'Counsellor Gallagher' not identified.

102. *the bank of Ireland*: see n. 97 above.

103. *some future Volney ... this little Palmyra*: an allusion to the opening passage of *Les Ruines, ou Méditations sur les revolutions des empires* (1791; translated as *The Ruins, a Survey of the Revolutions of Empires*), by the French traveller and republican politician Constantin François de Chasseboeuf, comte de Volney (1757–1820), in which a traveller contemplates the ruins of the ancient Syrian city of Palmyra, before meditating further upon the operations of power in different times and places. The work gained wide currency among English radicals in particular from the 1790s. Also mentioned here are the Ohio and Susquehanna, two rivers of the north-eastern regions of North America.

104. *Collagian* [*Collegian*] *Barrett*: possibly refers to the eccentric John 'Jacky' Barrett (1753–1821), who, after undergraduate studies at Trinity College Dublin, resided there as a fellow from 1778 until his death, holding posts including librarian (1791–1808), and professor of Hebrew and vice-provost (1806–21).

105. *Smart's Temple of Dulness ... find no favour*: De Vere refers to 'The Temple of Dulness', a verse satire, originally composed in Latin, on the supposedly complacent and hidebound intellectual culture of Trinity College, Dublin, by Christopher Smart (1722–71), which appeared in Smart's *Poems on Several Occasions* (1753) along with a translation by Francis Fawkes. The Irish authors Jonathan Swift (1667–1745) and Oliver Goldsmith (1728?–1774) both attended Trinity College, Dublin. Swift was refused a degree 'on account of insufficiency,' according to John Boyle, earl of Orrery, in his *Remarks on the Life and Writings of Dr Jonathan Swift*, fourth edition (London: A. Millar, 1752), p. 10. Possibly in part due to his having had to perform so much menial work in the college as a sizar in order to support himself there, Goldsmith, too, was not a successful undergraduate (though he did graduate BA in 1750), as had been documented in the many accounts of his life published by 1818.

106. *the equestrian statue of King William the Third*: A statue of William III on horseback, by Grinling Gibbons, was installed at the centre of College Green in 1701. It commemorated William's defeat, as the Protestant Duke of Orange, of the Roman Catholic James II (whose supporters were known as the Jacobites), at the Battle of the Boyne on 1 July 1690. William's accession to the throne led to both the consolidation of a Protestant succession to the English throne, and the impositions of penalties and civil disabilities upon both English and Irish Catholics. As well as being frequently decorated by Unionists and Protestants, as here, the statue was regularly attacked by Irish nationalists. It was finally destroyed in 1929.

107. *Mr. —*: 'De Vere' apparently omitted either at MS or print stage.

108. *orange and green*: respectively, the colours traditionally associated with the Protestant and Catholic interests in Ireland, orange representing William III's background as Duke of Orange, in the Netherlands.

109. *shew-board*: Sign-board (*OED*).

110. *a pendant to Holyhead*: 'pendant' is here apparently used in the sense of one item (usually a picture, or other decorative object) in a matching pair (*OED*).

111. *a country which they dislike to visit, and are impatient to quit*: Owenson's footnote quotes, slightly inaccurately, from John Bush, *Hibernia curiosa. A Letter from a Gentleman in Dublin, to his Friend at Dover in Kent. Giving a general view of the manners, customs, dispositions, &c. of the inhabitants of Ireland ... Collected in a tour through the kingdom in 1764* (London: W. Flexney, 1769), p. 19 (Bush has 'strangers and travellers'). Before *c*. 1788, the single hotel in Dublin appears to have been the Marine Hotel, George's Quay.

112. *Killarney and the Giant's Causeway*: The two major tourist attractions in Ireland during the early nineteenth century: Killarney, co. Kerry, a district famed for spectacular lakes and mountains; and the Giant's Causeway, co. Antrim, a promontory formed of thousands of basalt columns, extending five kilometres from the coast. Morgan's previous 'Irish' novel, *O'Donnel* (1814) had featured a party of pleasure to the Giant's Causeway.

113. *'Mais, comment donc, mon amiqu'est ceque c'est'*: French: 'But indeed, my friend, that's what it is.'(French).

114. *out of pledge*: out of a pawnbroker's possession.

115. *the Post-Office*: The General Post Office, with its imposing, Greek Revival portico, was completed in 1818 to the design of Francis Johnson. The declaration of the Irish Republic was issued from there in 1916.

116. *a Scena*: literally, the words and music of a scene in the Italian opera; here used ironically in the sense of an encounter between two or more persons involving exhibitions of strong feelings (*OED*).

117. *a lounger*: Here apparently used in sense of an item of furniture for relaxing on, not recorded in *OED* before 1969.

118. *in a jiffy ... her pochay was ordered*: *in a jiffy*, Colloquial (origin untraced) in a very short space of time (*OED*). *Pochay*, i.e. a post-chaise, a horse-drawn, usually four-wheeled carriage used for carrying mail and passengers (*OED*).

119. *the whole province of Munster*: The south-western Irish province of Munster, comprised of the counties Clare, Cork, Kerry, Tipperary, and Waterford.

120. *a tête*: literally a 'head' (French). A woman's hairstyle, or wig, dressed high and elaborately ornamented, in the fashion of the second half of the eighteenth century (*OED*).

121. *chitterling*: A frill, ruff, or ornamental pleating, named for its resemblance to chitterlings, the smaller intestines of pigs (*OED*).

122. *camblet-joseph*: A'joseph' was a long riding-cloak with a small cape, fastened by buttons down the front, and worn chiefly by women in the mid-eighteenth century (*OED*). In this instance, the joseph is made ofcamblet (otherwise camlet), a fabric of mixed wool and silk (*OED*).

123. *pillion*: . A type of light saddle used by women (*OED*).

124. *whose parish ... as many protestant families*: This observation refers to the imposition of taxes (tithes) for the support of the Established Church in Ireland, payable by all, regardless of denomination, with Protestants forming the minority of the population.

125. *Cashel ... Doneraile and Buttevant*: The town of Cashel, Co. Tipperary, was once a royal seat of Brian Boru (see n. 58 above). Its major features and monuments include the limestone Rock of Cashel, an outcrop 200 feet tall; and the twelfth-century Cormac's

Chapel, named after Cormac mac Carthaig (MacCarthy), king of Munster (d. 1138). The Galty (or Galtee) Mountains span the Limerick-Tipperary border, and were highly regarded by nineteenth-century travellers for their imposing and picturesque scenery. Doneraile and Buttevant are towns in Co. Cork, formerly within the Kilcolman estate granted to Spenser.

126. *reposoir*: 'repository' (French).

127. géne: i. e. *gene*, past participle of *gener*, to embarrass(French); in English usage in the period, embarrassed or constrained.

128. *Oronoko*: the Orinoco, a river rising in south-east Venezuela, and flowing into the Atlantic Ocean.

129. '*still hanging in the stars*': slightly misquotes Shakespeare, *Romeo and Juliet* I. iv. 108 ('Some consequence yet hanging in the stars').

130. *the ancient* Ogham: the earliest form of writing in Ireland, Ogham was composed of lines and strokes representing letters of the Latin alphabet, and carved into wood or stone. Each letter was named after a different tree or plant.

131. *a black silk ... cardinal cloak*: a 'cardinal cloak' was a travelling garment worn by women in the early nineteenth century. An article on 'Fashions for the Month of February' in *La Belle Assemblée* no. 80, (January 1816) states that the 'cardinal cloak' is 'generally of a tea colour, or some other chaste and unobtruding hue'; see p. 37.

132. Thomas Street: Site of the arrest of the United Irishman and rebel leader Lord Edward Fizgerald in 1798, and of the assassination of Lord Kilwarden in the rebellion of 1803, and so possibly invoked here (along with the magpie, as a 'bird of ill omen') as being ominous in its associations for Patriots and Unionists alike.

133. *her enquiry as to their being 'serious' ... her calling*: serious, 'earnest about the things of religion; religious' (*OED*). The remark regarding the 'particular new light' refers to the liberal, 'New Light' Irish Presbyterianism that emerged during the eighteenth century, in opposition to the more conservative, strictly Calvinist 'Old Light' Presbyterianism.

134. *the Krudner or Johanna South-cote*: Owenson's narrative refers to two noted, female religious enthusiasts of the period. Barbara Juliana, Freifrau (Baroness) von Krüdener, née Wittinghof (1764–1824; otherwiseJulie de Krüdener or Juliane von Krüdener), renounced a hedonistic life in European court society following her conversion to the mystical teachings of Jung Stilling. By 1818 she had become a prominent preacher and millenarian prophet. She was befriended by Tsar Alexander I of Russia, whom she regarded as having been chosen by God to lead the nations of Europe into a new, Christian era. Before her conversion she authored a novel, *Valeria*; see Stewart J. Brown, 'Moments of Christian Awakening in Revolutionary Europe, 1790–1815,' in *Enlightenment, Reawakening, and Revolution, 1660–1815*, ed. Stewart J. Brown and Timothy Tackett (Cambridge: Cambridge University Press, 2006), pp. 575–95; 585. The maidservant Joanna Southcott (1750–1814) became a millenarian prophet when aged 42, after experiencing visions predicting war in Europe. Having published the first of many pamphlets detailing her prophecies, *The Strange Effects of Faith*, in 1801, she attracted disciples from all levels of society both in London and throughout England. By 1816 she had become one of the most popular published authors of the period. She died in December 1817, having claimed to have become pregnant with a new incarnation of God.

135. *bohea tea*: variety of fine black tea (*OED*).

136. *the sickle ... will yet be reaped*: could refer to Revelation 14: 14–19, where an angel prepares to harvest ripened 'grapes' (souls) with a sickle, though does not quote any Biblical

passage directly. Imagery of harvesting with a sickle to represent the last judgement recurs throughout the Old and New Testaments of the Bible.

137. *Naas*: the county town of Kildare, 15 miles south of Dublin.

138. *He that giveth to the poor* lendeth *to the Lord*: recalls Proverbs 19: 17 ('he that hath pity on the poor, lendeth unto the Lord').

139. *Oh! quel homme superieur! ... VOLTAIRE*: ('Oh! what a superior man! what a great genius, this Poco-curanto!Nothing can please him.') From *Candide, ou L'Optimisme*(1759), by Voltaire [François Marie Arouet] ((1694–1778).

140. *Ossian*: refers to the 'Poems of Ossian'(1760–63) by the Scottish poet James Macpherson (1736–96), a series of fabricated 'translations' from fictional ancient manuscript works narrated by the Gaelic warrior Ossian, and comprising atmospheric tales of heroic deeds in an imagined, primitive Celtic world. The character Ossian was based on the legendary Scottish Gaelic hero Oisín.

141. *the Campions, Spencers, and Hanmers*: Edmund Campion (1540–1581), the Jesuit scholar and priest canonised by the Roman Catholic Church following his martyrdom, composed his *History of Ireland* over ten weeks whilst staying in Dublin as the guest of James Stanihurst, Speaker of the Irish House of Commons, during 1571. The Church of England clergyman Meredith Hanmer (1543–1604) received various appointments in Ireland under the patronage of Thomas Butler, tenth earl of Ormond, from 1591, and authored *A Chronicle of Ireland* in 1594. Along with Spenser's *View of the Present State of Ireland*, both Campion's and Hanmer's works were collected, and first published, by the Dublin-born antiquary Sir James Ware (1594–1666), in *Ancient Irish Histories* (1633).

142. '*Out of the common roll of men*': recalls a line in John Tobin, *The Curfew*, fourth edition (London: R. Phillips, 1807), V. iii ('A man, struck from the common roll of men').

143. *lazaretto*: A house for the reception of the diseased poor (*OED*).

144. *a Whitewashing under the insolvency act*: a clearing of a bankrupt's or insolvent's debts under the terms of the Insolvent Act (1814).

145. *to America*: 'the land of Canaan,' mentioned in Owenson's note as a name used by the Irish to refer to America, was an ancient name for the region between the Mediterranean and Dead Seas, now occupied by modern Lebanon and Israel. It was regarded as the 'Promised Land'by the Israelites during the period of their bondage in Egypt, and was where they settled having escaped from Egypt, as described in Exodus.

146. baroque: whimsical, odd (*OED*).

147. '*They eat, and drink ... eat again*': adapted from lines in Elizabeth Thomas, 'A Midnight Thought, (On the Death of Mrs E. H. and Her Little Daughter, cast away under London-Bridge, Aug. 5. 1699.),' published in*Poems on Several Occasions* (London: T. Combes, 1726), p. 115('We*eat*, we *drink*, we *sleep*, and then / We rise—to do the same again'). The lines seem to have been misattributed here to Matthew Prior, author of 'Old Darby and Joan,' a piece included in Prior's *Poems* (Manchester: G. Nicholson, 1795).

148. *the Rotunda ... the statues*: The Rotunda Hospital was established by Dr Bartholomew Mosse (d. 1759) as a charitable maternity ('Lying-In') hospital. Building commenced at the north end of Sackville Street in 1751, to the designs of Richard Castle. The Lying-In Hospital site included a public pleasure garden which generated revenue; and in 1764 the 'Rotunda' itself, a round assembly hall, was added for use as a venue for benefit concerts. Two further assembly rooms, one of which later became Dublin's Gate Theatre, were built in 1784. The Royal College of Surgeons was founded in 1784, and its council members met in the Rotunda boardroom before the site of its present headquarters was acquired at York Street, St Stephen's Green, in 1810. The Dublin Society House, South

William Street, was built 1765–71, for the accommodation of the Society of Artists and its exhibitions. Following the failure of the Society due to lack of funds, the building was leased for public assemblies in 1791, and was subsequently used by the city Corporation (1809).

149. *the Back-lane division auxiliary yeomanry corps*: The yeomanry, a part-time force, was first raised in Ireland in 1796, to counter the perceived threats from the United Irishmen, and radical sympathisers with the French Revolution. It attracted a largely Protestant membership, especially after 1800, and became associated with sectarian violence and general lack of discipline.

150. *the Phanix [Phoenix]*: Located at the western end of Dublin city, the Phoenix Park was created as a royal deer park in 1662. Its name was originally an Anglicisation of the Gaelic *fionn uisce* ('clear water'), referring to a well near the site. A ranger's lodge built in the park from 1752 was purchased in 1782 to serve as the official viceregal residence; it is now the residence of the President of the Republic of Ireland. Other houses built in the park during the eighteenth century became residences for senior government officials including the Chief Secretary. The Lord Chesterfield mentioned in Owenson's note was Philip Dormer Stanhope, fourth earl of Chesterfield (1694–1773), appointed lord lieutenant of Ireland in 1744. He erected the 'Phoenix Column'(1747), which still stands in the park, and which features a visual pun on the park's original name in the form of a sculpture of a phoenix rising from flames.

151. *a Barry, a Shee, and a Tresham*: Three of the major Irish-born artists of the period: James Barry (1741–1806), history painter and Royal Academy professor of painting 1782–99; Sir Martin Archer Shee (1769–1850), portraitist, novelist and poet, later appointed President of the Royal Academy (1830); Henry Tresham (bap. 1750/51, d. 1814), history painter and art dealer, appointed Royal Academy professor of painting in 1809.

152. *such a grouping*: In the contemporary discourse of picturesque landscape aesthetics, 'grouping' referred to the arrangement of objects, such as trees, animals, or human figures, for the best visual effects.

153. *the Royal Barracks*: The Royal Barracks (now the Collins Barracks) was commissioned in 1701 to accommodate four foot, and four horse, regiments. The Islandbridge barracks, by the Islandbridge gate of Phoenix Park, was built in 1798, as the Royal Artillery Barracks.

154. *Musha*: Irish-English, possibly derived from Irish *múise*: interjection expressing surprise, disbelief, or angry renunciation; 'Well!'; 'indeed!' (*OED*).

155. *in Elizabeth's day ... Irish enemy*: refers to the period of the Nine Years' War, or Tyrone's Rebellion, the Irish earls' campaign of rebellion against the imposition of English laws and customs in Ireland, which lasted from 1593 to 1603.

156. *'Of trumpets loud, and clarions'*: Milton, *Paradise Lost* I. 532.

157. *Look at Turkey*: In 1818, Turkey continued to rule Greece, and was widely associated with tyranny, as well as with an aesthetic culture aspects of which had become fashionable in Britain following the success of literary works such as Byron's 'Turkish Tales'.

158. *'Full of pomp ... for deities'*: Milton, *Paradise Lost* I. 372.

159. *Familiars and inquisitors ... auto-da-fes*: De Vere refers to the practices of the Spanish Inquisition, which subjected those it found guilty of heresy against the Roman Catholic Church to the public ritual of the *auto-da-fé*, execution by burning as the culmination of a ceremony also including a street procession , and the saying of Mass.

160. *a handsome square building … almost a town*: The 'extensive barracks' at Naas is mentioned in Thomas Walford, *The Scientific Tourist Through Ireland* (London: J. Booth, 1818), no p. nos . Naas was the site of a major rebel defeat on24 May 1798.

161. *the jail … a croppy's head spiked on the top of it*: The jail and courthouse at Naas are described as 'lately erected' in *The Traveller's New Guide Through Ireland* (Dublin: J. Cumming, 1815), p. 111. 'Croppy' or 'croppy boy' was a derogatory nickname for Irish rebels who cropped their hair to indicate their democratic sympathies (*OED*).

162. *Vinegar-hill*: Vinegar Hill, near Enniscorthy, 15 miles north of Wexford town, was the site of a major encampment of rebels during the 1798 rising. On 21 June 1798 the rebels suffered heavy losses when the camp was stormed by government forces, which incident was remembered as the 'Battle of Vinegar Hill'.

163. *a ruined monastery of Dominicans*: The Dominican monastery, founded by the Eustace family in 1353, and dedicated to St Eustachius, located at the centre of Naas.

164. *'an ounce of civet … my imagination'*: Shakespeare,*King Lear* IV. v. 126.

165. *William Lithgow … 'head upon'*: Owenson refers to William Lithgow (1582–1645?), *The totall discourse, of the rare adventures, and painefull perigrinations of long nineteene yeares travailes from Scotland, to the most famous kingdomes in Europe, Asia, and Africa* (London: N. Okes, 1632). She quotes loosely from Lithgow's description of the homes of the Irish poor, in which he writes: 'There Fabricks are … erected in a singular Frame, of smoak-torne straw, greene long prick'd turffe, and Rain-dropping watles … where, when in foule weather, scarcely can they finde a drye parte, whereupon to Repose, their cloud-baptized heads'; see p. 429.

166. *the proclaimed districts*: areas which had been proclaimed by the lord lieutenant to be in a state of civil disturbance, in accordance with the Peace Preservation Act (1814). This Act also provided for the use of special constables to help police such areas.

167. *'the world … the world's law'*: Adapted from Thomas Otway, *The History and Fall of Caius Marius. A Tragedy* (London: T. Flesher, 1680), act V, in which Marius junior, contemplating suicide, tells the impoverished apothecary who has hesitated to supply him with poison: 'The World is not thy Friend, nor the World's Law'.

168. *'sheweth a greater … have in living'*: unidentified.

169. *'a country's boast and pride'*: from Catherine Jemmat, 'On the Return of the Right Honourable Lord Viscount Charlemont, from his Travels, to Ireland, in the Year 1755,' published in her *Miscellanies, in Prose and Verse* (London: printed for the author, 1766), and in which Charlemont, returning from his Grand Tour to Italy, is apostrophised as 'Illustrious youth!thy country's boast and pride'; see p. 27.

170. *the undertakers of … the Elizabeths, the James's, and the Charles's*: Owenson refers to those English settlers who were granted properties in Ireland during the reigns of Elizabeth I, James I, Charles I and Charles II, over a period spanning the years 1558–1680.

171. *'man delight'*: after *Hamlet* II. ii. 329 ('man delights not me').

172. *'Nature wanted … with fancy'*: Adapted fromShakespeare,*Antony and Cleopatra*V. ii. 116–17.

173. *the 'Firehouse' … sacreligiously extinguished*: In her endnote (2) to the volume, Owenson cites Giraldus Cambrensis' account of the perpetual fire tended by the nuns of St Bridget at Kildare in *Topographia Hibernica* (1186–87). Her source appears to be not Giraldus himself, but Sir James Ware, who in *The Antiquities and History of Ireland* (Dublin: A. Crook, 1705)quotes from the salient passage from Giraldus Cambrensis, *Topgraphia Hiberniae*, which text Owenson reproduces in the note; see Ware, p. 45. From 'From hence that Nunnery' to 'wherein he lived,' Owenson quotes verbatim from the continu-

ation of Ware's account. Along with Sts Patrick and Colum Cille, Bridget of Kildare (*c.* 450–*c.* 525) is one of the patron saints of Ireland. Some folk practices honouring St Bridget are regarded as possible survivals of the worship of the Celtic goddess Brigid, who, like St Bridget, was a patron of poets, blacksmiths, and healers.

174. *the feudal castle of the Butlers ... its abbies*: The county town of Kilkenny was also the centre for the Ormond lordship, and the Butler (Ormond) family established a cathedral and several monastic foundations there. Kilkenny Castle remained the Butler family seat from the 1300s, until 1935. Owenson came to know the area during the mid-1790s, while her father was manager of a theatre at Kilkenny.

175. *'eremites ... trumpery'*: Milton, *Paradise Lost* III.474–75.

176. *'Irish kernes and galloglasses'*: In medieval and early modern Ireland, 'Kernes' and 'galloglasses' (or 'gallowglasses') were Irish soldiers, often in foreign service. Kernes were cavalry troops, and galloglasses foot soldiers.

177. *Irish posting*: i. e travelling by 'post', by hired transport, through Ireland.

178. *Longford-pass*: identified as a small village in Co. Tipperary, on the road approaching Kilkenny, in Thomas Walford, *The Scientific Tourist Through Ireland* (London: J. Booth, 1818), no p. nos.

179. *making Thurles their sleeping stage*: Thurles is a town in Co. Tipperary, on the river Suir. A 'sleeping stage' may be either a place in which rest is taken on a journey by road, such as a roadside or coaching inn; or the distance travelled between two places of rest on a road (*OED*).

180. *a dony bit further*: 'Dony' is the name of a dwarf appearing in Book V of Spenser's *The Faerie Queene*; see Canto II, stanza 3. Neither the word 'dony', nor its variant 'donny', are recorded in *OED*.

181. *cousin-germain*: (otherwise cousin-german) first cousin (*OED*).

182. *Holy Cross ... the religious romance of its name*: Owenson's endnote (3) is taken verbatim (with variant punctuation and spelling) from the account of Holy Cross Abbey, Tipperary, in James Ware, *The Antiquities and History of Ireland* (1705), p. 105. Holy Cross is described as 'a desolate hamlet' in *The Traveller's New Guide Through Ireland* (Dublin, 1815), p. 262. The abbey is situated on the western bank of the river Suir.

183. *Carbrogh O'Brien, King of Limerick*: apparently refers to Donnchad Cairprech O'Brien (d. 1242), referred to as Donogh Carbragh O'Brien in the account of Holy Cross Abbey by Francis Grose in *The Antiquities of Ireland*, 2 vols (London: S. Hooper, 1790), vol. 1, pp. 67–8; see n. 192 below.

184. Raison de plus: 'all the more reason' (French).

185. chimœra dire: a 'dreadful monster'; probably recalled from Milton, ('Of dire chimeras and enchanted isles').

186. *the degout of an atmosphere of Irish snuff and marrow pomatum*: *Degout* disgust(French); *marrow pomatum*, hair oil made with marrowfat from animal bones (*OED*).

187. oiseau de mauvais augure: 'bird of ill omen' (French).

188. *convent of Our Lady of the Annunciation*: not identified.

189. *the TONTINE or principal hotel of the town*: a 'tontine' is a scheme in which subscribers to a common fund each receive life annuities which increase as each member of the scheme dies (*OED*).

190. *a mere Shebean house*: an inn selling exisable liquor without a licence (*OED*).

191. *the biographer of St Rumoldi*: St. Rumold (d. 775) was a bishop of Dublin, before settling in Mechlin. Owenson may refer here to the Irish Franciscan Hugh Ward (d. 1635),

author of a Life of St Rumold published in 1662; see Benignus Millett, *The Irish Francis-cans, 1651–1665*(Rome: Gregorian University Press), pp. 487, 489.

192. *Donagh Carbraigh O'Brien: ... the Cistertian order*: refers to Donnchad Cairprech O'Brien (d. 1242), referred to as Donogh Carbragh O'Brien in the account of Holy Cross Abbey by Francis Grose in *The Antiquities of Ireland*, 2 vols (London: S. Hooper, 1790), vol. 1, pp. 67–8.

193. the *relic of the cross ... to Mac Morragh*: In *An Introduction to the Study of the History and Antiquities of Ireland* (Dublin: T. Ewing, 1772), Sylvester O'Halloran states that the Irish king Murtough, a grandson of Brian Boru, 'received from pope Paschal II in 1110, a gift of a piece of the cross, covered with gold, and ornamented with precious stones' (no p. nos), but does not provide a source. In *The Antiquities of Ireland*, 2 vols (London: S. Hooper, 1791),Ledwich dismissed this story as 'a monkish fiction'; see vol. 1, p. 67.

194. *the devotion paid to the relic ... an English minister*: Sir Henry Sidney (1529–86), father of the poet Sir Philip Sidney, served two terms as lord deputy of Ireland, in 1566–69, and 1575–78. He was a keen promoter of Irish self-government under English law. In a letter to Elizabeth I of 1567, describing travels through Munster, he mentioned the '[people's] Suffrance of most detestable Idolatrie, used to an Idoll, called the *Hollie Cross*, whereunto there is no small confluence of people daielie resorting'; See *Letters and Memorials of State in the Reigns of Queen Mary, Queen Elizabeth, King James, King Charles the First, Part of the Reign of King Charles the Second, and Oliver's Usurpation*,ed. Arthur Collins, 2 vols (London: T. Osborne, 1746), vol. 1, p. 20.

195. *Darkness ... source of the true sublime*: According to Edmund Burke in *A Philosophical Enquiry into the Origin of Our Ideas of the Sublime and Beautiful*(1754), darkness, or obscurity, was one of the conditions most conducive to the 'sublime' sense of pleasurable terror or awe.

196. *'Solemn and slow ... gloom around'*: From James Thomson, *The Seasons*, 'Summer,' 519–21.

197. *the choir ... the dormitory*: In a medieval monastic complex, the choir was the area within the church from where services would be sung; therefectory was the dining room, and the dormitory was where the monks slept.

198. *Fanaticism ... destroyed them*: In her footnote, Owenson quotes verbatim (with variant spelling and punctuation) from Sylvester O' Halloran, *An Introduction to the Study of the History and Antiquities of Ireland* (London, 1772) p. 86. Donough O'Brien, fourth Earl of Thomond (d. 1624) served in the campaigns to subdue the rebellious Catholic earls Hugh O' Neill (in 1595–97) and Florence MacCarthy Reagh (in 1600); so his monument in Limerick Cathedral would have been an unlikely target for the Cromwellian destroyers of images in churches.

199. *Nuestra Senora de las Angustias*: a church in Grenada noted in the period for its chapel decorations; see *A History of the Campaigns of the British Forces in Spain and Portugal*, 5 vols (London: T. Goddard, 1812–14), vol. 1, pp. 194–95.

200. *a famous picture ... its own lute*: Apparently a reference to 'Musician Angel' (or 'Angel with Lute'; c. 1520s), the fragment of a larger oil painting by Giovanni Battista di Jacopo di Gasparre ['Rosso Fiorentino,' the Redhead of Florence'] (1494–1540). Acquired by the Medici family by 1605, the painting is now held in the Uffizi Gallery, Florence.

201. *'her spouse in vain'*: after Pope, 'Eloisa to Abelard', 177, where the speaker Eloisa describes herself as 'believed the spouse of God in vain'.

202. *Cordelliras*: The names of many chains of mountains in South America and elsewhere include the word 'Cordilleras' (meaning a chain of mountains, from Spanish *cordilla*, 'little cord'); so it is unclear which location is being referred to here.

203. Sic me Phoebus amat: 'thus Phoebus loves me' (Latin). Phoebus is one of the names of Apollo, the sun god who in Greek mythology was also a patron of creative artists.

204. *'Rocks, caves ... MILTON*: Milton, *Paradise Lost*, II.621–5.

205. *BUTTEVANT, the Bothon ... the Kilnemullagh of Spencer*: Charles Smith explains that Buttevant was called 'Bothon' in the 'ecclesiastical books', and that 'the Irish and Spenser' called it 'Kilnemullagh'; see Smith, *County and City of Cork*, vol. 1, pp. 312–13.

206. *Gaul Bally ... Agherlow*: the narrative refers to further real locations: Galbally, Co. Limerick; and the Glen of Aherlow, through which flows the river Aherlow, separating the Galtee Mountains and Slievenamuck Hills.

207. *the rock* [of Cashel]: see b. 125 above.

208. *sangfroid*: literally 'cold blood' (French); in English usage, coolness (of temperament or demeanour).

209. *Mitchels town*: i. e. Mitchelstown, a market town in Co. Cork.

210. *Mangerton*: a mountain in Co. Cork, described by Smith as 'one of the highest in Ireland'; see *County and City of Cork*, vol. 1, p. 289.

211. *these cross roads in Munster*: 'cross roads' here refers to roads crossing each other, or running between main routes, as by-roads (*OED*).

212. *alow backed car*: in this period, and especially in Ireland, 'car' could refer to any ordinary wagon or cart (*OED*).

213. *thegrate [great] stillhunting ... fining the townlands to ruination*: A reference to the strict government measures imposed against illicit distillation, in a period of increased taxation on legally-produced whiskey and other spirits. The suppression of illicit distilleries (referred to as 'stillhunting' here) was one of the functions of the new police forces sent into districts under the Peace Preservation Act (1814). See S. J. Connolly, 'Union Government, 1812–23', in *A New History of Ireland*, ed. W. E. Vaughan et al. 9 vols (Oxford: Clarendon Press, 1989), vol. 5, p. 64.

214. *frize coat*: A coat made of frieze, a kind of coarse woollen cloth manufactured in Ireland in the period; 'frieze-coat' also a designation applied to an Irish peasant (OED).

215. *from Galtimore ... to the reeks in Killarney*: Galtymore is the highest mountain in the Galtees, located on theborder of Limerick with Tipperary. MacGillycuddy's Reeks is a mountain range in Co. Kerry.

216. *Cormac Mac Coleman's travelling landau ... the pilgrimage to Holy-cross*. May refer to Cormac mac Cuillenan (846–908), a notably pious king of Cashel; the vehicle is being jokingly referred to as old enough to have been used by the figure named.

217. *King Flann*: Flann Sinna [Flann mac Máele Sechnaill] (847/8–916), high king of Ireland 879–916.

218. *'I am a rake ... near Aughnaghcloy'*: Apparently a variant of 'The Rambling Boy', a song printed in *An Excellent Garland* (Manchester: G. Swindells,?1800), with the opening lines: 'I am a rake and a rambling boy, / Lately come from the town of Cloy'; see p. 5.

219. *the tithe-proctor's business*: a tithe-proctor (otherwise tythe-proctor) was an official employed to collect a parson's tithes (*OED*).

220. set-out: a 'turn-out'; a complete equipage of carriage and horses (*OED*).

221. *a glass coach*: Originally a coach with glass, as opposed to unglazed, windows; later applied especially to a coach let out for hire (*OED*).

222. *a dexter arm ... a naked sword, all proper*: In heraldry, dexter, 'right' (Latin) refers to the right side (opposed to *sinister*, Latin for 'left'). The heraldic term 'proper' describes an object represented in natural or realistic colouring (*OED*).

223. the motto, Vigeur de dessus: *vigeur de dessus*, 'strength from above' (French) was the motto of the clan O'Brien, to which belonged the kings of Limerick.

224. Dieu est toujours pour les gros bataillions: 'God is always on the side of the heavy batallions' (French), a variation upon Voltaire's remark that *Dieu n'est pas pour les gros bataillons, mais pour ceux qui tirent le mieux* ('God is not on the side of the heavy batallions, but of the best shots').

225. from Henry the second ... chiefs of kings of Desmond: Owenson appears to have derived these names from the account of Henry II's distributions of Irish lands in James Ware, *The Antiquities and History of Ireland* (London: A. and J. Churchill, 1705), p. 121.

226. *Strongbow*: the soubriquet of Richard fitz Gilbert, otherwise Richard de Clare (d. 1176), who, after being deprived of the earldom of Pembroke by Henry II, was recruited to the cause of Diarmait Mac Murchada, the exiled king of Leinster. After landing at Waterford in 1170, Strongbow led a successful campaign for Mac Murchada, taking the cities of Waterford and Dublin. He married Mac Murchada's daughter, and succeeded him as lord of Leinster on his death in 1171.

227. *'melancholy and gentlemanlike'*: a quotation from the Preface to Miles Peter Andrews, *The Songs ... Introduced ... in the Pantomime Entertainment, of The Enchanted Castle* (London: printed for the author, 1786), p. iii('the chosen *Lover* slides across the Stage, melancholy and gentlemanlike').

228. the pathetic grotesque of chrononhotonthologus: Refers to Henry Carey (1687?–1743), *Chrononhotonthologous*. First performed 1734, and published unde the pseudonym 'Benjamin Bounce' this piece was a satire on the overwrought manners of contemporary opera and tragedy.

229. *'the groves ... so charming'*: Opening lines of 'The Groves of Blarney' (1800), Richard Alfred Milliken's mildly ribald(and radical-sympathizing) parody of the anonymous lyric 'Sweet Castle-Hyde' (1790s). Castle Hyde was situated on land confiscated from the earl of Desmond, andsubsequently granted to the Hyde family by Elizabeth I as a reward for loyalty. Although not named in *Florence Macarthy*, Castle Hyde is in the direct vicinity of the Hag's Bed, the next ancient site to be mentioned in the narrative (see n. 244 below).

230. smithereens. Small fragments, as defined in Owenson's footnote. The word is not recorded in *OED* until 1829.

231. Laissez aller. Absence of restraint (French); unconstrained ease and freedom (*OED*). The first recorded instance of English usage of this expression in *OED* is that appearing in Volume 2, chapter 3.

232. *the stage plays at court Fitzadelm*: This is the first mention in the novel of the fashionable pastime of staging private theatrical performances, which will become a major motif in Volumes III and IV. 'Private theatricals' had been staged at several Irish aristocratic and gentry seats since the 1750s, and by the 1780s they were being attended by royalty. Some enthusiasts (such as the fictional Fitzadelms, in this instance) had small, but fully-equipped, theatres constructed in their country seats; while other groups took over public theatres between seasons, as at the Fishamble Street theatre in Dublin during 1793–95. The most famous centre for private theatricals in the period was at Kilkenny, where performances began in 1802. See *The Private Theatre of Kilkenny, with Introduc-*

tory Observations on Other Private Theatres in Ireland, before it was Opened (n. pl, 1825), pp. 1–9.

233. *the Gotroes, and the Balli-Howries*: refers to the Ballyhoura Hills, which extend west of the Galtee Mountains. The reference to 'Gotroes' is unclear, possibly due to an error in the text.

234. *the castle bawn*: a bawn, derived from Irish *báblum*, is a fortified enclosure; or the fortified court or outwork of a castle (*OED*).

235. *screed*: A fragment cut, torn, or broken from a main piece; a torn strip of textile material (*OED*).

236. *cloud-cap'd*: recalls the 'cloud-capp'd towers' spoken of by Prospero in Shakespeare's *Tempest*, IV. i. 152, one of many allusions to and echoes of the play throughout the text.

237. sore bits: 'sore' in this sense corresponds most closely to the *OED* definition of the adjective 'sore' as 'involving great hardships, unusual difficulty'.

238. *the Cloghniagh-Cluain* ... noisy water: A location of this name is mentioned by Edward Ledwich, in *A Statistical account of the Parish of Aghaboe, in the Queen's County* [now Co. Laois] (Dublin: G. Bonham, 1796), p. 32.

239. cotamore: Not in *OED*; and no earlier instances identified.

240. caubeen: a hat, possibly from Irish *caipín*, diminutive of 'cap' (*OED*). The earliest cited instance of usage in *OED* is from 1831.

241. *my ould father's before me, Sir*: the 'scratch-wig' mentioned in Owenson's note denotes 'a small, short wig' (*OED*).

242. *'a fine, gay, bold-faced villain'*: Not in Shakespeare, but in Thomas Otway's tragedy *Venice Preserv'd* (1682), I. i. , spoken by the character Pierre, describing himself.

243. *a band of Shanavests ... the Caravats*: Names of opposing factions active in the south of Ireland from the early 1800s. The Shanavests were dominated by farmers and shopkeepers, and the Caravats, who formed an agrarian militant organisation, by members of the labouring class. The name 'shanavest' derived from the Irish for 'old waistcoat ['vest']', while 'caravat' was from 'cravat' (see *OED* entry for 'shanavest').

244. *the 'Hag's Bed'*: Smith identifies this location as Labacally, 'i. e. the Hag's Bed', two miles north of Castle Hyde; see Smith, *County and City of Cork*, vol. 1, p. 349.

245. *bon gré, malgré*: 'whether willing or not' (French).

246. Whiteboys or Threshers: The 'whiteboys' were originally the members of an agrarian rebel organisation formed in Tipperary in 1761, who customarily wore white shirts over the rest of their clothing. They committed acts including arson, in protest against tithes and excessive taxation. Their activities prompted legislation, during the 1760s and 1780s, which made criminal acts committed in association with such organizations punishable by death. The Threshers were members of another protest organization (though one loyal to the state), which emerged in Connaught during 1806–7. By 1818, the terms 'whiteboys' and 'threshers' were used generically to refer to members, or presumed or suspected members, of any agrarian rebel organisation. See S. Connolly, 'Aftermath and Adjustment,' in *A New History of Ireland*, vol. 5, pp. 17–20.

247. *ma vourneen*: 'my darling' (Anglo-Irish; from Irish *mo muirnín*).

248. *gassoon*: 'lad' (Irish slang).

249. *the amatory history of* 'Cooleendas' 'Croothenamœ': 'Cooleendas Croothenamoe' is the title of a pastoral ballad about a milkmaid whose suitor persuades her to break a vow not to marry before she has become rich. It is printed along with (and under the title of) 'Patrick's Day in the Morning. A new song on the Tipperary militia'(Limerick, ?1800).

250. '*The Connaught Daisy*': ('*Noinin Conactach*') is a tune included in Edward Bunting (1773–1843), *The Ancient Music of Ireland Arranged for Piano*(Dublin: Hodges and Smith, 1840), with the note that it is 'Very ancient, author and date unknown'; see p. x.

251. *the last dying speech of Captain Dreadnought*: Unidentified.

252. 'Ma chere amie', *as sung by* Mrs Billington: 'Ma chere amie,' apparently written to be sung in a male character, appears in various published collections of popular songs from the 1770s onward; no published version has been located naming 'Mrs Billington' as having performed it. Elizabeth Billington [née Weichsel] (1765–1818) was the major English soprano of her generation. She began her stage career at Smock Alley, Dublin, in 1783, subsequently achieving fame in both Britain and Italy. She is generally accepted to have been the daughter of two German musicians employed at the Vauxhall pleasure gardens during the 1760s, though Owensonhinted in her memoirs that Robert Owenson, then also a singer at Vauxhall, may have been Billington's father. See *Lady Morgan's Memoirs*, vol. 1, p. 82.

253. *that curious coiffure ... the name of a* calesh: *calesh*, from French *calèche* (a kind of light carriage with a removable folding hood on top) a woman's hood, made of silk and supported with whalebone or cane hoops, projecting beyond the face (*OED*). *Coiffure*

254. *Rabragh*: Not in *OED*; no earlier instances identified.

255. *tête-a-tête*: i.e. *tête-à-tête*, literally 'head to head' (French); in English usage, a private or intimate conversation between two persons (*OED*).

256. *wentherself to the judges ... in regard of her being his foster-sister*: In 1809, Owenson had herself successfully appealed against the sentencing to death of a convicted felon, Barnaby Fitzpatrick, personally petitioning the judge who had tried the case. See *Lady Morgan's Memoirs*, vol. 1, pp. 353–62. In this fictional case, Lady Clancare's concern for Owny is largely motivated by her having,as an infant or young child, been partly brought up ('fostered') by his mother, in the manner which remained customary among the aristocratic and ascendancy classes in Ireland into the nineteenth century. She thus considers herself to be connected to the foster-mother's own children in a quasi-sibling relationship.

257. *Dunkerron ... in Kerry*: a real town in Co. Kerry.

258. *hobby*: A *small* or middle-sized horse; a pony (*OED*).

259. *St Crohan's cell ... his own hands*: Owenson's footnote is based on the account of the 'cell' by Charles Smith in *The Antient and Present State of the County of Kerry* (Dublin: s. n. , 1774), p. 93.

260. corragh: A small boat made of wickerwork covered with hides, used from ancient times in Scotland and Ireland; a curricle (*OED*).

261. *bathers ... the salt wather*: the 'medicinal waters' of Co. Kerry, used during the eighteenth century in the treatment of disorders including scurvy and jaundice, are described in chapter 9 of Charles Smith's *County of Kerry*, pp. 336–49.

262. *his* Shanaos *of the Macarthies More*: i.e. his family history, family lore of the MacCarthies More (cf. Irish *seanchas*, lore; tradition; storytelling).

263. whipper-in: A hunstman's assistant who keeps the hounds from straying by driving them back with the whip into the main body of the pack (*OED*).

264. the hunt of Kilruddery: Refers to a ballad by Thomas Mozeen (fl. 1750, d. 1768), popularly referred to as 'The Kilruddery Hunt', and first published in Mozeen's*A Collection of Miscellaneous Essays* (London: printed for the author, 1762) under the title 'A Description of a Fox-Chase, That happened in the County of Dublin, 1744, with the Earl of Meath's Hounds. ' Set to the tune of 'Sheila na Guira', the piece became widely popular during the eighteenth and nineteenth centuries. See Andrew Carpenter (ed.), *Verse in*

English from Eighteenth-Century Ireland (Cork: Cork University Press, 1998), p. 314; and James N. Healy (ed.), *The Second Book of Irish Ballads* (Cork: Mercier Press, 1962), p. 110.

265. *en chemin faisant*: 'on the way' (French).

266. comether: A dialect pronunciation of *come hither*, used as a coaxing invitation to cows or horses. In nineteenth-century usage, 'to put one's [or the] comether on' meant to exercise persuasion or coaxing on someone, or to get someone under one's influence (*OED*, with no instances of usage in this sense cited from before 1838).

267. *night-mare*: used in the original sense of 'a female spirit or monster supposed to settle on and produce a feeling of suffocation in a sleeping person' (*OED*).

268. *hag-ridden*: afflicted by night-mares (*OED*); De Vere plays on this sense, in conveying that he is being pestered by a hag, in the sense of 'an ugly, repulsive old woman' (*OED*).

269. *your motions are retarded ... She rules the ascendant*: the Commodore speaks in terms drawn from astronomy.

270. 'In her bright radiance ... not in her sphere': Paraphrases, and misquotes, the words of Helena, on Bertram, in Shakespeare's *All's Well That Ends Well*, I.i.100–1 ('In his bright radiance and collateral light / Must I be comforted, not in his sphere').

271. *her Bardolph's nose*: A reference to Falstaff's ridicule of Bardolph's red nose in Shakespeare's *1 Henry IV*, II.ii, where Falstaff's succession of quips on the theme includes 'I never see thy face but I think upon hell-fire' (ll. 23–4).

272. *tower of horse hair*: refers to Mrs MacGillicuddy's elaborate, and apparently artificial, 'tête'.

273. '*chewing the cud of sweet and bitter fancies*': Misquotes Shakespeare's *As You Like It* IV. iii. 104 ('Chewing the food of sweet and bitter fancy').

274. *what Peter the Great called 'Irish wine' ... pure falernian*: falernian, of or pertaining to the *ager Falernus* in Campania, Italy, which produced a wine celebrated among the ancient Romans (*OED*). The anecdote concerning the Russian Tsar Peter the Great's appreciation of whiskey appears in Thomas Campbell, *A Philosophical Survey of the South of Ireland, In a Series of Letters to John Watkinson, M. D.* (Dublin: W. Whitestone, 1778), p. 142.

275. *friandise*: 'a delicacy' (French).

276. caubeen: see Volume 1, n. 240.

277. *a Spanish Posada*: *posada*, 'inn' (Spanish; *OED*).

278. kead mille faltha: i.e. *céad mille fáilte*, 'a hundred thousand welcomes' (Irish).

279. 'si tout n-y est pas bien, tout est passable': 'if all is not well there, all is acceptable' (French).

280. *This Eden ... SHAKESPEARE*: partially (and inaccurately) quoted from John of Gaunt's lament for England in Shakespeare, *Richard II* II. I, giving variations on lines 42 ('This other Eden, demi-paradise); 57, 59 ('this dear, dear land ... Is now leas'd out'), 60 ('Like to a tenement or pelting farm').

281. *What harmony ... IBID*: from Shakespeare, *The Tempest*, III.iii.18–20.

282. *Were such things here ... IBID*: Shakespeare, *Macbeth*, I.iii.83–5.

283. *cabaret*: A drinking-house or pot-house (*OED*).

284. *their picturesque grouping*: see Volume I, n. 152.

285. *his own* Mole: The Mole is the name by which Spenser refers to a mountain representing the Ballyhoura Hills (see n. 233 above) in *Colin Clouts Come Home Againe*, 56–9, 106–13.

286. 'unprofitably gay': From the description of the 'blossom'd furze' by the schoolmaster's house in Oliver Goldsmith, *The Deserted Village* (1770), 196.

287. *meerings*: boundaries, formed of earth or fencing, the term being especially used in Ireland in rhe modern period (*OED*).

288. *his own rood*: A rood was a unit of land area usually equal to forty square rods (a quarter of an acre, approx. 0. 1012 hectare); or a plot of land of this size (*OED*).

289. *the Idyls of Theocritus ... the Arcadia of Sannazaro*: De Vere alludes to Theocritus (*c.* 310 BC–*c.* 250 BC), the Sicilian-born Greek poet whose *Idylls*, a series of songs and dialogues of lovelorn rural characters, have been regarded as the founding text of pastoral poetry; and Jacopo Sannazaro (1457–1530), an aristocratic Neapolitan poet and art connoisseur whose romance *Arcadia* (1504) developed the pastoral genre through descriptions not only of nymphs, satyrs, and classical landscapes, but also of imaginary paintings.

290. *Georgics of Virgil*: Composed between 39–29 BC by the Roman poet Publius Vergilius Maro [Virgil] (70–19 BC), the *Georgics* form a series of poems instructing on various aspects of agriculture and animal husbandry. Admired in all later periods for their richly descriptive, philosophical evocations of natural landscapes and everyday human endeavour, they also stand as a statement of Roman national pride following a period of civil war, and of belief in a Providential design in nature.

291. soubriquet: 'nickname' (French); in English usage, otherwise *sobriquet*.

292. *friezesand entablatures*: parts of an architectural structure from a level above its pillars. The frieze can form part of an entablature, or may otherwise be a band of sculptured decoration (*OED*).

293. *Alleen ma chree! Alleen deelish!*: Ellen ! Ellen darling!(Irish).

294. : *Alleen ma vourneen*: *ma vourneen*, 'my darling' (Anglo-Irish; from Irish *mo muirnín*).

295. *a poor* innocent ... *she's a* natural: *OED* records usage in this period of both 'innocent', 'a simpleton ... a half-wit'; and 'natural,' 'A person having a low learning ability or intellectual capacity' (Irish English).

296. cute: acute, clever (*OED*).

297. *catering*: procuring food (*OED*), here apparently in the form of donations.

298. *wallet*: bag for provisions (*OED*).

299. *terrace gardens ... nobility of Munster*: A famous example of such garden design is still to be seen at Lismore Castle, Co. Waterford.

300. *fantastic little buildings ... of rock-work*: garden follies. The most famous example in this region of a garden shell house, an outdoor room or grotto decorated with sea-shells, isat Curraghmore, Portlaw, Co. Waterford, seat of the earls of Tyrone. The shell house in the gardens was built in 1754 by Catherine Power, Countess of Tyrone.

301. *'And with their boughs ... rankness did deface'*: Spenser, *The Faerie Queene*, book V, canto 1, stanza 1.

302. *put it up to the hammer*: offer it for sale by auction.

303. *You know but little of Calista*: An allusion to Nicholas Rowe, *The Fair Penitent* IV. i, ('Oh! thou hast known but little of Calista').

304. *the house was to be seen*: i. e. the house could be viewed by prospective purchasers.

305. *Portrieve*: Originally, the governor or chief officer of a town or borough; later a person equivalent in rank and office to a town mayor (*OED*).

306. *down in a crack*: down in a short time (*OED*).

307. *wailing, and gnashing of teeth*: Matthew 13:42 ('The Sonne of man shall send forth his Angels, and they shall gather out of his kingdome all things that offend, and them which doe iniquities: And shall cast them into a furnace of fire: *there shall be wayling and gnashing of teeth*').

308. *whom the Lord loveth, he chasteneth*: Hebrews 12:6 ('For whome the Lord loveth hee chasteneth, and scourgeth every sonne whom he receiveth').

309. *Is my strength ... flesh of brass*: Job 4:12 ('Is my strength the strength of stone? or my flesh of brass?')

310. *a watch-tower in a wilderness*: 2 Chronicles 20:24.

311. *seeking whom yez* [you] *may devour*: an allusion to Peter 5:8 ('Be sober, be vigilant: because your adversary the devil, as a roaring Lion walketh about, seeking whom he may devoure'); 'the old one' meaning the Devil.

312. *an house of clay ... before the moth*: Job 3:46 ('How much lesse them that dwell in houses of clay, whose foundation is in the dust, which are crushed before the moth').

313. *Babylon*: An ancient Mesopotamian city and kingdom which acquired negative connotations in both Hebrew and Christian culture, being the place of the Hebrews' exile following Nebuchadnezzar's capture of Jerusalem in 597 BC. Also associated by the Hebrews with luxury and moral degeneracy, the name of Babylon was subsequently attached to any place or culture regarded as decadent or corrupt, with New Testament authors referring to Rome as 'Babylon'.

314. *James the Second ... his way through Munster*: After William of Orange arrived in England to pursue his claim to the throne in November 1688, James II fled to France, from where he travelled with his supporters to Ireland, arriving on 12 March 1689. After his defeat at the Boyne in 1690, James returned to permanent exile in France.

315. *by abandoning the scarlet lady ... their lands and rights*: i.e. the Fitzadelms renounced their Catholic faith in order to retain properties and privileges that would otherwise have been removed from them under William III. The 'scarlet lady' is the 'woman arrayed in purple and scarlet' in Revelation 17:3–4, traditionally identified, in some Protestant interpretations, as a prophetic personification of the Roman Catholic Church.

316. *the royal astonishment*: The anecdote of James II looking out of a window at Lismore Castle, and '[starting] back in terror at contemplating its precipitate elevation above the river' appears in William Fordyce Mavor, *The British Tourists: or, Traveller's Pocket Companion, Through England, Wales, Scotland, and Ireland*, 6 vols (London: R. Phillips, 1809), vol. 4, p. 350.

317. *the Franchinis ... its noble mansions*: the brothers Paul and Philip Franchini, Italian stuccodores who came to Ireland around 1739, and whose skills in decorative plasterwork design remained in demand among wealthy Irish homeowners throughout the mid-eighteenth century.

318. *the delightful Memoires de Grammont*: *Memoires de la vie du comte de Grammont: contenant particulierement l'histoire amoureuse de la cour de L'Angleterre, sous la regne de Charles II* (1713; first published in English translation 1714), was an account of the life and social circle of Philibert, comte de Gramont, by his brother-in-law Anthony Hamilton (1644/5–1729). The first English translation, by Abel Boyer, appeared in 1714 as *Memoirs of the Life of Count de Grammont: containing, in particular, the amorous intrigues of the court of England in the reign of King Charles II*. A prominent member of James II's court in exile in France, Hamilton was a grandson of James Hamilton, first earl of Abercorn – and thus also related to Owenson's patron, the ninth earl of Abercorn.

319. *Lilly and Kneller ... ad infinitum*: Sir Peter Lely (1618–1680), was a major portrait painter to the courts of Charles I and Charles II; the German-born Sir Godfrey Kneller (1646–1723), was also a major portrait painter at the courts of Charles II, and of James II. The frescoes by John Souillard in the chapel at Lixnaw Castle are mentioned by Charles Smith, in *County of Kerry* (1774), p. 216, as being copies of cartoons by

Raphael, depicting Biblical subjects, at Hampton Court. The portrait artist James Gandy (1618/19–1689) came to Ireland under the patronage of the first duke of Ormond. The Ormond art collection included works by Gandy.

320. *'la plus jolie taille du monde' of the coquettish Countess of Chesterfield*: *la plus jolie taille du monde*, 'the loveliest figure in the world', translated by Boyer as 'she had a most exquisite shape' (p. 140). Elizabeth, countess of Chesterfield (1640–1665), was a daughter of James Butler, first duke of Ormond. She was married to Philip Stanhope, second Earl of Chesterfield (1633–1714) in 1660, and died of a fever in 1665.

321. *'La Muskerry faite comme la plupart des riches heritieres'*: 'Lady Muskerry made like most of the rich heiresses' (French). The salient passage from the Memoirs, with its continuation, is translated in 1794 as 'made, like the generality of rich heiresses, to whom just nature seems sparing of her gifts, in proportion as they are loaded with those of fortune'; see p. 116, where Lady Muskerry is also described as having one leg shorter than the other, and the figure of a pregnant woman, despite not being pregnant.

322. *'the fair Hamilton, "grande et gracieuse dans les moindres de ses mouvements"'*: refers to Grammont's description of Elizabeth Hamilton as 'grande et gracieuse jusque dans le moindre de ses mouvements' ('grand and graceful down to the least of her movements'), translated in 1794 as 'majestic and graceful in all her movements'; see p. 113. Elizabeth Hamilton, Countess de Gramont, known as 'la belle Hamilton' (the beautiful, or fair, Hamilton) (1641–1708) was born probably in Ireland, the sister of Anthony Hamilton. She became one of the most noted beauties of Charles II's court. Following her marriage to Philibert, comte de Gramont (1663), she was also prominent within the court of Louis XIV of France, and her home at Meudon became an important Jacobite centre in the early 1700s.

323. *'la belle Stewart'*: 'the beautiful Stewart' (French). Frances Teresa Stuart (or Stewart), duchess of Lennox and Richmond (1647–1702) grew up at Queen Henrietta Maria's court in France, and in 1662 was appointed maid of honour to Charles II's queen, Catherine of Braganza. A devout Catholic, she rebuffed the advances of both Charles II and the Duke of York (later James II), before marrying (in 1667) Charles Stuart, third duke of Richmond and sixth duke of Lennox.

324. *'la blonde Blague,' now literally 'plus jaune qu'un coing'*: 'La blonde Blague' ('Blague the Blonde') refers to Henrietta Maria Blague, or Blagge, who was appointed maid of honour to the Duchess of York in 1662, and shortly afterwards married Sir Thomas Yarborough. Her younger sister Margaret was the intimate friend of the diarist John Evelyn both before and during her marriage to Sidney Godolphin. 'Plus jaune qu'un coing', 'yellower than a quince', is translated in the 1794 version as 'more yellow than saffron', in an account of 'Miss Blague' when dressed in yellow ribbons and gloves; see p. 129.

325. *liken*: resemble, represent.

326. they that plough iniquity ... reap the same: Job 3: 8 ('Even as I have seene, they that plow iniquity, and sow wickedness, reape the same').

327. *such shameless Jezebels*: Jezebel, formerly a princess of Tyre, became queen to King Ahab of Israel. A worshipper of pagan gods, and a ruthless schemer, she was assassinated by her own attendants after they sided with her enemy Jehu. Her name subsequently became proverbial for female immorality. See 1 Kings 16: 31; 19: 1, 2, 21; and 2 Kings 9: 30–7.

328. *the beautiful Duchess of Cleveland*: Barbara Palmer, née Villiers, countess of Castlemaine and *suo jure* duchess of Cleveland (bap. 1640, d. 1709) the wife of a Royalist lawyer, became the mistress of Charles II shortly after his restoration to the English throne in 1660. Charles compensated her husband by creating him Baron Limerick and earl of

Castlemaine. As Lady Castlemaine, Barbara Palmer retained considerable influence over Charles and his court into the 1670s. Lely painted her in characters including a Magdalen and a Sultana.

329. *that happy satrap, Charles*: *satrap* originally denoted a governor of a province under the ancient Persian monarchy; a subordinate ruler; often suggesting an imputation of tyranny or ostentatious splendour (*OED*).

330. *the Embevecidos ... made up of love*: *embevecido*, 'drunk with love' (Spanish). The 'embevecidos' were not women, but Spanish cavaliers at the court of the queen of Spain who had pledged themselves to love, and who were traditionallypermitted by their mistresses to dispense with certain points of etiquette. The custom was described by Marie-Catherine, comtesse d'Aulnoy (1650/51–1705) in her accounts of (unconfirmed) travels in Spain, *Memoires de la cour de l'Espagne* (1690–91), which had been through several editions in English translation by 1818.

331. *all vanity and vexation of spirit*: Ecclesiastes1: 14 ('I have seene all the workes that are done under the Sunne, and behold, all vanitie, and vexation of spirit').

332. *I walked in utter darkness*: Ecclesiastes 2: 14–15 ('The wise man's eyes in his head, but the foole walketh in darkness ... Then said I in my heart, As it happeneth to the foole, so it happeneth even unto me').

333. *antique japanned chest*: *japanned*, lacquered with japan, or other material giving a hard black gloss (*OED*).

334. *The Prince of Orange ... the Pretender*: refers to William of Orange, crowned William III of England in 1690, and his cousin James Edward Stuart (1688–1766), son of James II, and the 'pretender', or claimant, to the throne occupied by William.

335. *a fine lob*: a 'lob' is a colloquial expression meaning a 'throw' (*OED*); the sense here seems to be of 'a good go at'.

336. *cicerone*: A guide who shows and explains the antiquities or curiosities of a place to strangers (*OED*).

337. *a Venetian domino*: A 'domino' was a kind of loose cloak, apparently of Venetian origin, chiefly worn at masquerades, with a small mask covering the upper part of the face (*OED*).

338. *affliction cometh not ... out of the ground*: Job 5: 6.

339. *uterine cousin*: a cousin related by blood through the mother (*OED*).

340. *scuded off*: i. e. scudded off, moved rapidly off (*OED*).

341. *a preclusive division*: division is used here in the sense of 'the execution of a rapid melodic passage' (*OED*), a preclusive division being such a passage sung as an opening or prelude to a piece of music.

342. *the long extirpated Irish wolf*: The wolf, indigenous to Ireland, was hunted to extinction during the seventeenth and early eighteenth centuries, with landlords offering tenants rewards for helping to exterminate them. The last known rewards for the killing of Irish wolves were claimed in Cork and Kerry in1710.

343. *'Did ever mortal mixture ... enchanting harmony?'*: Misquotes Milton, *Comus* 244–5 ('Can any mortal mixture of earth's mould / Breathe such divine inchanting ravishment?').

344. *the Gobelin manufacture*: i. e. it was made at the Gobelin, a major tapestry factory in Paris.

345. *his Gloriana ... other Calidores and Sir Tristrams*: In Spenser's *The Faerie Queene*, Gloriana is the female figure representing Elizabeth I, and Calidore is the Knight of Courtesy, whose adventures are narrated in book VI. No Sir Tristram appears in *The Faerie Queene*;

but Owenson may have in mind Tristram the lover of Isoud, and hero of several romances dating to the twelfth century, as well as of a narrative by Thomas Malory.

346. *embrogleo*: a state of great confusion and entanglement; a complicated or difficult situation (especially political or dramatic). This is the earliest instance of usage recorded in the *OED*.

347. '*Function is smothered … what is not*': Misquotes or adapts Shakespeare,*Macbeth* I. iii. 140–41, 'function is smothered in surmise, / And nothing is but what is not'.

348. *amour-propre*: 'self-love' (French); in English usage, self-respect; pride.

349. '*trifles, light as air*': Shakespeare,*Othello* III. iii. 325–27 ('Trifles light as air / Are to the jealous confirmations strong / As proofs of holy writ').

350. '*Dove … Rinaldo stassi*': Lines from the 'Argument' to Canto XVI of Torquato Tasso's *La Gerusalemme liberate*, describing Rinaldo's confinement in the garden of the enchantress Armida, which opens: 'Entrano i due guerrier nell'ampio tetto, / Ove in dolce prigion Rinaldo stassi'. Philip Doyne translated the passage as follows: 'The two knights enter the enchanted gardens of Armida … arrive where Rinaldo lies dissolved in effeminate pleasure and love'; see *The Delivery of Jerusalem. A Heroic Poem. By Torquato Tasso*. 2 vols (Dublin: G. and A. Ewing, 1761), vol. 2, p. 141.

351. *the Armida … 'Sorrizi, paroletti*': In Tasso's *Gerusalemme Liberate*, Armida is the pagan enchantress who holds the Christian hero Rinaldo captive in her garden of sensual temptations, until he is rescued by two other knights, who restore him to a sense of his duties. Owenson quotes (with some inaccuracies) from *La Gerusalemme liberate* Canto XVI, stanza 25 ('Teneri sdegni, e placide e tranquille / Repulse, e cari vezzi, e liete paci, / Sorrisi, parolette … . '). Doyne translated the same passage as follows: 'mild denial, tender scorn, and sweet / Repulses, soft contention, and glad peace / And smiles, and dear discourse'; see *The Delivery of Jerusalem*, vol. 2, p. 150.

352. '*done their spiriting gently*': Adapted fromShakespeare,*The Tempest* I. ii. 297–98, in which Ariel says to the enchanter Prospero, 'I will be correspondent to command, / And do my spiriting gently'.

353. compagnon de voyage: 'travelling companion' (French).

354. *the hypochondriacal egotism of Rousseau … enmity to the whole world*: Toward the end of his life, the Swiss philosopher and author Jean-Jacques Rousseau (1712–78) suffered increasingly from mental illness, being troubled especially with paranoid anxiety.

355. *the Avonbeg … 'a muse's lyre*': The river Awbeg is a tributary of the Blackwater, and is referred to by Spenser as the Mulla. Owenson also quotes here from Pope's *Windsor-Forest*, 275–6. These lines in fact refer to Abraham Cowley, but are quoted in Henry John Todd's note accompanying *Colin Cloutes Come Home Againe*, 59, in his edition of *The Works of Edmund Spenser*, 8 vols (London: F. C. and J. Rivington, 1805), vol. 8, p. 8.

356. *some Ariel 'correspondent to command' of a concealed Prospero*: *Tempest* I. ii. 297.

357. *the foul witch Sycorax*: *Tempest*, I.ii.258, where Prospero describes the banishment to his island of Sycorax, a sorceress, who has given birth there to a deformed son, Caliban.

358. point d'appui: 'point of support' (French), a fulcrum (*OED*). This is the second instance of English usage cited in *OED*.

359. '*Not framed … restless ecstasy*': Misquotes Shakespeare, *Macbeth*, III.ii.21–4 (' … better be with the dead, / Whom we, to gain our peace, have sent to peace, / Than on the torture of the mind to lie / In restless ecstacy').

360. '*The flighty purpose … deed go with it*': Shakespeare, *Macbeth* IV. i. 145–6.

361. '*I never may believe … MIDSUMMER NIGHT'S DREAM*': Shakespeare, *A Midsummer Night's Dream*, V.i.2–3

362. *'But I have cause ... Taming of the Shrew*: Shakespeare, *The Taming of the Shrew* III. i. 85–6.
363. *viaticum*: provision for a journey (Latin). The Eucharist, as administered to or received by one who is dying or in danger of death (OED).
364. *a Cromlech ... a cairn*: *cromlech*, a structure of prehistoric age consisting of a large flat or flattish, unhewn stone resting horizontally on three or more stones set upright (OED); *cairn*, a pyramid of rough stones, raised for a memorial or mark of some kind.
365. *St Olan's cap ... St Olan's abbey*: In his *County and City of Cork*, Charles Smith explains that 'St Olan's cap', is a stone located in the churchyard at Aghabollogue, Co. Cork, 'by which the common people ... swear on all solemn occasions; and they pretend, that if this stone was carried off, it would return of itself to its old place'; see vol. 1, p. 177).
366. *The Fairy's Rock*: Mentioned by Smith in *County and City of Cork* , vol. 1, p 182.
367. *The ruins ... bended knee*: In his account of the village of Ballyvourney in *County and City of Cork*, Smith describes the 'ruined church ... dedicated to St Gobnate, who, in the 6th century was made Abbess of a nunnery of regular Canonesses here, by St Abhan'; see vol. 1, p. 185. He also mentions local customs of visiting a nearby well, also dedicated to St Gobnate, on Whit-Sunday and the feast of St Gobnate (14 February); and of praying, on the same occasions, before an image of the saint, displayed on the church 'rood' (cross) which pilgrims 'go round on their knees'. Smith adds: 'Near this cross is a stone fixed in the ground, and worn by the knees of those who come here in pilgrimage'; se vol. 1, pp. 185–6. St Gobnate, or Gobnait, appears in lives of other early Irish saints including Abbán, founder of the convent at Ballyvourney. She is believed to have lived in the sixth century; though it has also been suggested that her cult was the survival of the worship of a local Celtic goddess.
368. *hung with ragged offerings*: A reference to the folk practice of tying shreds of clothing to the branches of trees overhanging holy wells. Smith describes a well dedicated to St Dominic at Glanworth, co. Cork, where pilgrims have hung a nearby tree with rags 'as memorials of their devotion to this water, which they affirm has performed several miraculous cures'; see Smith, *County and City of Cork*, vol. 1,. p. 344.
369. *benedicite*: 'Bless you'; 'God bless' (Latin).
370. *the Peninsula of Dunore*: a fictional location, corresponding to the Dingle Peninsula, Co. Kerry.
371. *an hundred thousand welcomes*: In his *County and City of Cork*, Smith refers to the stone, found near to Clodagh Castle, Co. Cork, with an Irish inscription 'signifying to all passengers, to repair to the house of Mr Edmund Mac Swiney, for entertainment,' adding: 'This stone still lies in a ditch'; see vol. 1, p. 195.
372. *a false concord*: In grammar, 'a breach of any of the rules for the "agreement" of words in a sentence' (*OED*).
373. *'airy voice ... men's names'*: Misquoted from Milton, *Comus*, 207, which has 'airy tongues, that syllable men's names'.
374. *like the cloak ... both wind and sun*: A reference to Aesop's fable of the contest between the wind and the sun, in which each exerts its strength in order to be first to cause a traveller to remove his cloak.
375. renage: this is the second of only two instances of usage in the sense of 'to withdraw or retract (a former statement)' in *OED*; the first is from 1679.
376. *That's a reyal ASTURIONES ... them same Irish Hoblers*: O'Leary's observations on the Kerry-bred horse serve to introduce his enthusiastic attachment to the longstanding, but by this period largely discredited, theory that the Gaelic Irish were descended from the

Phoenicians, a seafaring, northern African race who had moved west via Spain. Dating back to the medieval period, the Phoenician theory of Irish origin had remained current during the seventeenth century, and had been espoused by some eighteenth-century antiquarians. The Latin name 'asturiones', otherwise Asturian, denotes something of or pertaining to the northern Spanish province of Asturias, settled since prehistoric times (see 'Asturian,' *OED*). In discussing the 'hobillers' O'Leary cites Paulus Jovius (1483–1552),and Joseph Pitton de Tournefort (1656–1708). The main source for this passage, however, would appear to be Ware (1705), p. 20, where the belief that the 'Hobbies' were descended from Spanish horses 'brought from the Asturians of Spain into Ireland' is noted, as is Paulus Jovius' account of seeing such horses *'led in the Pope's train.'* The same passage also includes mention of the'27 Hobellarii' (horsemen riding the Asturians, or Hobbies) in Edward III's army at the siege of Calais in 1347.

377. *'Infroenant alii currus ... in equos'*: Virgil, *Aeneid* XII, 287–8 ('infrenant alii currus aut corpora saltu / subiciunt in equos [et strictis ensibus adsunt].' / 'The others rein their chariots or leap onto their horses [and with drawn swords stand ready]'). See *Aeneid VII-XII*, trans. H. Rushton Fairclough (Cambridge, MA: Harvard University Press, 2000).

378. fetch: defined in *OED* as 'The apparition, double, or wraith of a living person'.

379. *Mr Camden, a Saxon churl*: O'Leary refers to William Camden (1551–1623), English antiquary and historian, whose*Britannia* (1586), a major, early survey of the British Isles, included an account of Ireland.

380. *blood relations to the Tyrian Hercules*: Charles Vallancey asserts, citing Herodotus, that Hercules founded Tyre before establishing Phoenecian colonies in Spain and elsewhere in Europe in 'An Enquiry into the First Inhabitants of Ireland,' *Collecteana de rebus hibernicis*, 2 (1786), pp. 58–75; pp. 63, 73–4.

381. *Maleeh-Cartha ... ould Bochart*: Samuel Bochart (1599–1667) was a Frenchhistorian and orientalist who argued in his *Geographia Sacra* (1646) that the ancient Phoenicians had settled in Ireland, as well as on the Iberian peninsula, and that the Irish language was derived from the Phoenician. Bochart was the major influence on the eighteenth-century Irish antiquaries, including Charles Vallancey, in their developments upon the Phoenician theory of Irish origin.

382. *defies Geraldus Cambrensis ... ould Saxo Grammaticus to boot*: Giraldus Cambrensis, or Gerald of Wales (*c.* 1146–1220x23), a Welsh-born clergyman and historian, was appointed one of Henry II's royal clerks in Ireland in 1184. His*Topographia Hibernica* (1186–7) and *Expugnatio Hibernica* (1189) presented a view of Ireland biased in favour of the Anglo-Norman colonists. The Dublin-born antiquary Edward Ledwich (1739–1823), another apologist for the Anglo-Normans, began publishing articles on ancient Irish history during the 1780s. His influential monograph, *Antiquities of Ireland*, appeared in 1790, and was revised and expanded in 1804. From an extremely conservative, Ascendancy family, Sir Richard Musgrave (c. 1755–1818) was the author of *Memoirs of the different rebellions in Ireland from the arrival of the English* (1801). This workbecame an influential account of the 1798 rebellion in particular, locating its cause in Irish Catholic aggression against Protestants. As High Sheriff of Waterford (from 1786) Musgrave was draconian in his implementation of anti-insurrection laws. Saxo Grammaticus (1180–1208) was a Danish historian, author of the *Historia Danica*, composed during the first decade of the thirteenth century, which included an account of the Danes' settlement of Ireland.

383. *degendered*: past participle of degender, to degenerate, obsolete by this period (the last instance of usage cited in *OED*is from 1597).

384. *that's Florence Macarthy I mane*: The Gaelic chieftain Florence MacCarthy Reagh [Finia Mac Carthaigh Riabhach] (1562–*c*. 1640) was born at Kilbrittan Castle, Co. Cork, his father Sir Donough MacCarthy Reagh being lord of Carberry, west Cork. The family was loyal to the English crown, but remained Catholic. For many centuries they dominated south-west Ireland as the lords of Desmond, but they lost much of this power following the granting of the earldom of Desmond to the Norman Fitzgerald family, whose members became long-standing rivals to the clan MacCarthy. After fighting for the crown against the rebellious earl of Desmond in 1578, Finia MacCarthy spent five years at the court of Elizabeth I, anglicizing his name to 'Florence' while there. Having relatives at the Spanish court, and being a lover of Spanish culture and proficient speaker of the language, he was suspected at court of pro-Spanish political sympathies, and confined in the Tower of London for questioning in 1591. He had meanwhile married Eileen ('Ellen'), daughter of Donal MacCarthy More, first earl of Clancare, in 1588. After defeating Donal in 1600, Florence MacCarthy Reagh was inaugurated as the Mac-Carthy More. The same year, he both formed an alliance with the rebel earl of Tyrone, and declared loyalty to the English crown. After resisting the despoilment of his lands by crown commissioners, he was defeated in a battle with crown troops between Kinsale and Cork city in April 1600. While he continued to pledge loyalty both to the crown and to Tyrone, MacCarthy is thought to have spent late 1600 preparing for the Spanish landing at Kinsale, on the Munster coast. He was arrested again in 1601, and confined in the Tower of London, where he spent the rest of his life, apart from two short periods of release within England. During his confinement, MacCarthy composed 'A treatise on the antiquity and history of Ireland,' covering periods from the prehistoric to the Norman (*ODNB*).

385. *anno 1565, Elizab. reginae six*: 'the year 1565, the sixth of Queen Elizabeth' (Latin, with abbreviations), i. e. 1565, the sixth year of Queen Elizabeth's reign.

386. *on their way from Scythia*: a reference to another long-standing tradition concerning Irish origins. That the Irish were descended from peoples originating in the Black Sea region of Scythia had been first claimed in ancient pseudo-histories of Ireland, most notably the *Lebor Gabála Érenn* ('Book of Invasions'). Surviving in a twelfth-century manuscript, this charted the arrivals, of successive waves of colonists in Ireland, including the Scoti, who arrived via Egypt, and the Milesians, who arrived from Spain (both groups being originally from Scythia).

387. *the O'SULLIVAN BEARS*: refers to the Co. Kerry clan, the O'Sullivan Bear. Donall Cam O'Sullivan Beare (1560–1618) was an associate of Florence MacCarthy Reagh, and involved in the plot for a Spanish landing at Kinsale on 2 Oct 1601. Tyrone appointed O'Sullivan commander of rebel forces in Munster in 1601. Following their defeat by James I's forces, O'Sullivan settled in Spain, where he helped to found the Irish college at Santiago de Compostela. He became a pensioner of the Spanish court at Madrid, where he resided until he was killed by the English spy John Bathe in 1618, ostensibly in a quarrel over money (*ODNB*). Another member of the clan, the historian and author Philip O'Sullivan Beare (b. *c*. 1590, d. in or after 1634), settled in Spain with his family in 1602, following the ending of the 'Nine Years' War' in the defeat of the Irish rebels. He was educated at Santiago de Compostela, served in the Spanish army and navy; and was involved in the fight which ended in John Bathe's killing Donall Cam O'Sullivan in 1618. In 1621 he published *Historiae catholicae Iberniae compendium*, which included an account of the rebel defeats in Munster during the 1580s and 1590s. His other works

included the manuscript *Zoilomastix*, which was intended as a corrective to Giraldus Cambrensis' and James Stanihurst's claims regarding Ireland (*ODNB*).

388. *Florianus del Campo*: A Latinized version of the name of Florian de Ocampo (1499–1555), the Spanish historian who was appointed official chronicler to the court of Charles I of Spain in 1539. He is cited by Camden as a proponent of the theory that the Irish people were descended from ancient Spanish settlers, which he discussed in his *Crónica General de España* (1541).

389. *the surrender of Condé*: The surrender of Louis II de Bourbon, Prince de Condé (1621–86), a formidable French military commander, took place in 1652, following the defeat of his attempted insurrection against the French government. An account of Cormac Mac Carthy's involvement in the campaign as commander of an Irish regiment, and his subsequent move to a command post in Flanders appears in Thomas Carte, *The History of the Life of James Duke of Ormonde, from his borth in 1610, to his death in 1688*, 3 vols (London: J. Bettenham, 1736), vol. 2, p. 173.

390. *the popular cause of South America*: see n. 10 above.

391. *the Phenecian tongue, vulgo-vocato Irish*: *vulgo-vocato*, 'commonly called' (Latin). Like eighteenth-century historians such as Charles Vallancey, O'Leary believes the Gaelic language to be derived from that spoken by the Phoenecians who colonised Spain, and then Ireland.

392. *the seventy-two languages of Babel ... Magh-Seanair, near Athens*: O'Leary refers to the myth, derived by antiquarians from the *Lebor Gabála*, that sixty years after the building of the Tower of Babel, Feniusa Farsa, king of Scythia, travelled southward from Scythia and founded a university at Magh Seanair, near Athens. Therehe developed the Greek, Latin, and Hebrew alphabets from the seventy-two languages of the world. Magog was the son of Noah's son Japheth, and regarded as the father of the Scythian people.

393. Hannibal, Hamilcar, Asdrubal: refers to Hasdrubal (d. 207 BC) and Hannibal (*c.* 247–*c.* 183 BC), both Carthaginian generals, and the sons of Hamilcar Barca (d. 228 BC), also a Carthaginian commander.

394. *the Bethluisnion-na-Ogma*: the ancient Irish Ogham alphabet, also known as 'Beth-luis-nion' after its first three characters, named for the birch (*beithe*), rowan (*luis*) and ash (*nin*) trees.

395. *some sceptics of opinion ... identity between the Irish and the Anglo-Saxon*: The most notable historian holding this view in the period was Edward Ledwich (1739–1823).

396. *'O tribus ... insanabile!'*: 'O head incurable by all the hellebore at Anticyras!' (Latin). Paraphrases Horace, *Ars Poetica*, 300, in the passage satirizing poets who supposedly believe that neglect of personal grooming may enable them to achieve fame in their vocation, and who bring to the barber 'a head that all the hellebore of Anticyras could never reduce to sanity.' Hellebore, obtained from the island of Anticyras, was a reputed cure for madness. See 'On the Art of Poetry,' in *Classical Literary Criticism*, trans. and ed. T. S. Dorah (London: Penguin, 1965), p. 89 and n. 1.

397. *testoon*: In English usage since the sixteenth century, could refer to the shillings of Henry VII and Henry VIII, and coins from the reign of Edward VI; to the Portugese *testão* or *tostão* (silver coin from c. 1500), or to an obsolete Italian coin (*OED*).

398. *Bachal essu!*: a corruption of *Baculus Iesu*, 'the staff of Jesus' (Latin). The crozier believed to have belonged to St Patrick (see n. 399 below) was preserved and venerated, firstly in Armagh, and subsequently in Dublin, until 1538, when it was publicly burned as an object of superstition. See J. B. Bury, *The Life of St Patrick and his Place in History* (London: Macmillan, 1905), p. 320.

399. *St. Patrick*: The patron saint of Ireland, Patrick lived in the fifth century AD, and was traditionally believed to have been responsible for the conversion of the Irish to Christianity. According to the *Confessio* purportedly written by himself, he was born into a Roman British family in a region which has been variously identified as being located in England, Scotland, or Wales. He first arrived in Ireland as a slave, having been captured by Irish raiders when aged 16. He discovered his religious vocation whilst working as a shepherd, possibly in modern Co. Antrim, and after making his way back to Britain, trained for the priesthood. He returned to Ireland as a Christian missionary, but is now considered not to have been the first to establish Christianity there, though his ministry was exceptionally successful, and well documented. His saint's day has traditionally been celebrated on 17 March, believed to be the date on which he died.

400. *ould* [*old*] *Strabo ... Dr Ledwich*: The Greek-born, Roman author and traveller Strabo of Amaseia (b. *c.* 64 BC) developed the discipline of geography as a necessary aspect of the training of soldiers and statesmen. His seventeen-book *Geography* was valued by later scholars for its detailed, contemporary accounts of places within the ancient world, including those inhabited by Celtic peoples, and its quotations from earlier, lost authors.

401. *the school of Ross Alethri*: A reference to Ross Alithri ('field of pilgrimage'), formerly the name of Ross, or Ross Carbery, Co. Cork. The location is mentioned by Smith in his *County and City of Cork* as having been a centre of learning, with St Brendan named as having been a leading figure there; see vol. 1, p. 257.

402. *the learned Monk Ealfrith*: refers to Edfrith or Eadfrith (d. 721), an English monk, who studied in Ireland before being appointed bishop of Lindisfarne, Northumberland, in 698. He is believed to have both transcribed and illuminated the Lindisfarne Gospels.

403. *Agelbert ... retired to Ireland to study*: St Agilbert (d. 679x90), the Frankish-born bishop of the West Saxons, was recorded by Bede as having studied in Ireland before his arrival in England (see Ledwich p. 170). St Egbert [Ecgberht] (639–729), was a priest of noble, Anglo-Saxon birth who established a monastic base in co. Carlow, Ireland, and became an influential church reformer. The English-born St Wigbert (d. *c.* 738) is mentioned by Ledwich as having retired to Ireland in *The Antiquities of Ireland* (Dublin: A. Greuber, 1790), p. 171.

404. *an old SENACHY, or genealogist*: See n. 425 below.

405. *BALLYDAB*: The name of this fictional location is possible derived from 'Ballydehob', a real town in Co. Cork town.

406. *videlicet*: 'that is to say' (Latin).

407. *pending the visitation*: 'Visitation' here refers to an official visit by a bishop to inspect the state of a diocese (*OED*).

408. *plagosus Orbilius*: O'Leary jokingly refers to himself by the Roman poet Horace's nickname for his tutor, the grammarian Lucius Orbilius Pupillus (*c.* 112–*c.* 17 BC), *plagosus* being Latin for '[to] lavish with blows'.

409. *St Jago de Compostello*: The apostle St James the Great, patron saint of Spain, whose body was reputed to have been miraculously transported to Compostela, Spain, following his martyrdom in Jerusalem in 44 AD.

410. *the ancient bawn*: (in n.) a bawn, derived from Irish *báblum*, is a fortified enclosure; or the fortified court or outwork of a castle (*OED*). 'Swift's Hamilton's Bawn' refers to Jonathan Swift's satirical poem 'The Grand Question Debated: Whether Hamilton's Bawn should be Turned into a Barrack or a Malt-House' (1729), 'Hamilton's Bawn' itself being the home of Swift's friend Sir Arthur Acheson.

411. *protestant colony*: In her endnote (7), Owenson quotes (with slight variation) from a 1662 letter of the Earl of Orrery to the Duke of Ormond, in *A Collection of the State Letters of the Right Honourable Roger Boyle, the first Earl of Orrery, Lord President of Munster in Ireland* (London: J. Bettenham, 1742), p. 74.

412. *the pin-money of his daughter-in-law*: In 1640, Boyle acquired the college house that had belonged to the collegiate church of the Blessed Virgin Mary of Youghal, Cork, placing the property in trust as a 'jointure' for Lady Elizabeth Clifford, the wife of his son and heir, Viscount Dungarvon. Owenson's source for this detail would appear to have been Smith, *County and City of Cork*, vol. 1, pp. 83–90, p. 90n.

413. *in statu quo*: 'in the current condition', or 'in the same state as formerly' (legal Latin).

414. *quondam*: 'former' (Latin).

415. *English lords of the pale*: Descendants of the first English (Norman) colonists of Ireland, who from the twelfth century settled in areas within a boundary (the 'pale') separating them from the native, Gaelic chieftains' territories.

416. *chauntry*: A chapel, altar, or part of a church for use in the offering of masses for the souls of the dead (*OED*).

417. *Shakespear's description ... in a church*: Refers to *Twelfth Night* III. ii. 72–3, where Maria describes Malvolio in his yellow cross-garters as looking 'Most villainously; like a pedant that keeps a school i' th' church'.

418. *'GLORIA DEO IN EXCELSIS' ... some Norman de Barri, or de Grosse*: Gloria Deo in excelsis, 'Glory to God in the highest' (Latin); *Giste ici. Dieu de son ame ait merci* 'Here lies ... God have mercy on his soul' (Norman French). De Barri (de Barry) and De Grosse, and Boyle and Petty, recall Norman and English settlers' names appearing in Smith's *County and City of Cork*, including those of Roger Boyle, and the land surveyor Sir William Petty.

419. *Conal Macarthy More*: not identified.

420. *the picture of an Irish school, given by Campion ... 'lessons piecemeal'*: Edmund Campion wrote, in his *History of Ireland*: 'I have seene them where they kept Schoole, ten in some one Chamber, grovelling upon couches of straw, their Bookes at their noses, themselves lying flatte prostrate, and so to chaunte out their lessons by piecemeale, being the most part lustie fellowes of twenty five years and upwards.' SeeWare (ed.), *Ancient Irish Histories* (1809), pp. 25–6.

421. *dishabille*: 'partly undressed' (French); in English usage, either 'dressed in a negligent or careless style,' or 'a dress or costume of a negligent style' (OED).

422. *'his customary suit'*: alludes to Shakepeare, *Hamlet* I. ii. 78, where Hamlet refers to his 'customary suits of solemn black'.

423. pandies: (plural of 'pandy'; probably after Latin *pande*, as in the command *pande manum*, 'stretch out your hand') beatings to the palm of the hand, given as a punishment to children in schools (*OED*).

424. *the hedge schoolmaster*: After the 1695 Act of Parliament prohibiting Roman Catholics to run or to teach in schools, many Catholic schoolmasters worked clandestinely from such spaces as were available to them, these being sometimes in the open air. These makeshift establishments became known as 'hedge schools', and remained a feature of Irish rural life throughout the eighteenth century, and into the nineteenth century. The hedge schoolmasters varied in competence and professionalism. Some were of genuinely scholarly training and abilities, while others lacked experience or qualifications, and set up their schools simply in order to profit from fees charged to pupils or their parents.

425. *an ancient Senachy*: In her note, Owenson quotes, inaccurately, from Joseph Cooper Walker, *Historical Memoirs of the Irish Bards* (London: T. Payne, 1786). 'The Seanachidhe were antiquaries, genealogists and historians. They recorded remarkable events, and preserved the genealogies of their patrons in a kind of unpoetical stanza. Each province, prince and chief, had a Seanacha. And we will venture to conjecture, that in each province there was a repository for the collections of the different Seanachaidhe belonging to it, with the care of which an Ollamh-Re-Seanacha was charged. The ancient college of arms at Ulster is still maintained'; see pp. 12–13. Owenson's note also mentions the Flemish-born Charles Vallancey (c. 1726–1812), who took up antiquarian studies in Ireland after a period of army service there, and Duald Mac Firbis (c. 1600–1671). Probably born in Co. Sligo, Mac Firbis came from a family which had for generations served the chieftains Ó Dubhda (O' Dowd) as historians and poets. He transcribed many Irish manuscript chronicles of law and genealogy; and between 1665–66 was employed as a translator by Sir James Ware.

426. *the black letter plan*: 'black letter' signifies that the studies contemplated will be based in texts old enough to have been printed in the 'black letter' type used before the seventeenth century (*OED*).

427. *'Words that ... Raleigh spoke'*: Pope, Imitation of Horace II. 2, 168.

428. *his philological riches*: (in n.) 'A bold expressive phrase ... some hundred years', Pope, Imitation of Horace II.2.165–6.

429. *when, says Campion ... the civil institutes of the faculties*: Edmund Campion wrote of the hedge-school pupils he encountered: 'Without either precepts or observations of congruity they speake Latin like a vulgar language, learned in their common Schooles of Leach-craft and Law, whereat they begin Children, and hold on sixteen or twentie years conning by roate the Aphorisms of Hypocrates, and the Civill Institutions, and a few other parings of these two faculties. ' Ware (ed.), *Ancient Irish Histories* (1809), p. 25.

430. *'Keklute ... ed epikouroi'*: a transliteration of the words of Hektor from Homer, *Iliad* VII, 67 ('κέκλυτέ μευ, Τρῶες καί ευκνήμιδες Αχαιοί'); 'Listen to me, you Trojans and strong-greaved Achaians'. See the *Iliad*, trans. Richmond Lattimore (Chicago, IL: Chicago University Press, 1961).

431. *matcher*: A truant (*OED*).

432. *getting him up for Maynooth*: St Patrick's Seminary, for the training of Roman Catholic priests, had opened at Maynooth, Co. Kildare, in 1795.

433. cordaries: not identified.

434. *Leprehauns*: In a note to her previous novel, *O'Donnel*, Owenson had defined the leprechaun as 'a supernatural agent, who holds a distinguished place in the Irish "Faerie"'. It was, she noted, said to resemble 'a shrivelled little old man,' whose presence marked 'a spot where hidden treasures lie concealed, which were buried there in the "troubles". ' She further noted that the name of leprechaun was 'a term of contempt. ' See Sydney Owenson, Lady Morgan, *O'Donnel*, 2 vols (London: H. Colburn, 1814), vol. 2, pp. 328–9 n.

435. *extemplo*: 'immediately' (Latin).

436. *Hector and Andromach*: O'Leary wishes his pupils to learn the passage toward the close of Book VI of Homer's *Iliad*, where Hektor bids farewell to his wife Andromache before returning to the war in Troy.

437. *'looped and windowed raggedness ... that which passeth shew'*: Shakespeare, *King Lear*, III. iv.31; and *Hamlet*, I.ii.85 ('But I have that within which passeth show').

438. *ferule*: a rod for use as a pointer, or as an instrument of punishment (*OED*).

439. in casu incognito: 'in unknown state' (Latin); in disguise.

440. *tranglers*: may mean 'floggers,' from the verb 'to triangle,' or to flog someone bound to the triangle, the apparatus formerly used in the army for such purposes (though this sense of the verb to triangle is not recorded in *OED* until 1879). That O'Leary could mean the word in this sense seems possible on account of his having been flogged as a suspected rebel conspirator in 1798.

441. *the berring [burying] ground of the pobble O'Leary:* A fictional location the name of which is based on those of other Irish regions associated with particular, old families, and containing the word 'Pobble' (meaning region, or country, but from Old Irish *popul*, people or community). These areas include the Pobble O'Healy ('O'Healy's Country'), in the barony of Muskerry, Co. Cork, the O'Healys having been a family associated with the MacCarthys, the Muskerry chiefs. See Michael C. O'Laughlin, *Families of County Cork, Ireland: From the Earliest Times to the Twentieth Century* (Kansas City, MO: Irish Genealogical Foundation, 1999), p. 91.

442. *sou utile ainda que Bricando*: '*Sou útil ainda que brincando*' would be more correct Portugese for 'I am useful even when at play', *brincando* being the present participle of *brincar*, to play, frolic, or coquet; while *ainda* may also express 'yet', 'still' or 'more'.

443. *maigre days*: days of abstinence from meat, as appointed by the Roman Catholic Church (*OED*).

444. *carding*: preparing wool for spinning, by combing it to straighten the fibres and remove impurities (*OED*).

445. *That's my* Girleen: In colloquial Irish and Irish English, the suffix 'in' or '-een' represents the diminutive of a word, often used in endearments; hence 'girleen' here means 'little girl'.

446. *imp his flight*: strengthen his wings, and his flying ability (*OED*).

447. *Don Bellianus ... Plae racca na Rourke: The History of the Seven Wise Masters of Rome* and *The Honour of Chivalry. Or the Famous and delectable history of Don Bellianis of Greece* were popular chapbook romances, frequently reprinted from the sixteenth century. They were noted as being often used in Irish schools to teach reading, or simply to entertain children, from the late 1600s. See Raymond Gillespie, *Reading Ireland: Print, Reading and Social Change in Early Modern Ireland* (Manchester: Manchester University Press, 2005), pp. 85; 162. *Plae racca na Rourke* refers to 'Pléaráca na Ruarcach' ('O' Rourke's Feast'), a Gaelic poem by Hugh MacGauran which told the story of a feast hosted by the sixteenth-century rebel chieftain Brian O'Rourke. It was set to music by Turlough O'Carolan, and Jonathan Swift composed an English version, 'The Description of an Irish Feast' (1720). Owenson included a note on the piece in *O'Donnel*; see vol. 2, p. 329n.

448. *Milesian born*: descended from the originally Spanish, 'Milesian' colonists led by Míl Espáine, believed by some antiquarians to have arrived in Ireland as the last of the waves of invaders chronicled in the *Lebor Gabála*.

449. *the Luceni in Spain*: The Luceni are mentioned in many eighteenth-century histories of Ireland as having been a prehistoric people inhabiting the Munster region. Camden was among earlier historians who believed that they had originated in Spain.

450. *insensed*: *OED* does not record usages for 'incensed' in the sense given in Owenson's note.

451. *the grate [great] Skelegs*: the Skellig (*Sceilg*) Islands, a group of rocky islands off the south-west coast of Co. Kerry. They include the Great Skellig island, site of a monastery dedicated to St Michael from the ninth to the eleventh centuries.

452. *a thousand* ullalues: *ullalues*, cries of lamentation.

453. *'Auditque ruentes ... tombrua calcat'*: slightly misquotes Claudian [Claudius Claudianus] (b. *c.* 370 AD, d. after 410), *Panegyric on the Consulship of Fl. Manlius Theodorus*, 209–10 (*auditque ruentes / sub pedibus nimbus et rauca tonitrua calcat*; 'and [the summit of Olympus] hears the hurricane rushing beneath its feet while it treads upon the thunder's roar'). These lines are part of a simile describing the 'patient mind' of Manlius. See *Claudian*, trans. M. Platnauer, 2 vols (London: Heinemann, 1922), vol. 1.

454. say [*sea*] *dogs*: May refer either to the common or harbour seal (*Calocephalus vitulinus*), or to a kind of dogfish (*OED*).

455. late tyranni: 'rulers far and wide' (Latin).

456. *gabbion*: (otherwise *gabion*) wicker construction filled with earth or stones, used for fortification (*OED*).

457. *his only son ... in the Lord President's power*: This anecdote is based on an account, in *Pacata Hibernia*, on a confrontation between the rebel earls and The Lord President (George Carew)'s forces on 5 July 1600. In this account, it was the six-year-old son of the Knight of the Valley (a member of the Fitzgibbon family) who was placed on a gabion as a human shield by the Lord President. See Thomas Stafford, *Pacata Hibernia; or, A History of the Wars in Ireland, During the Reign of Queen Elizabeth*, 2 vols (Dublin: Hibernia-Press Company, 1810), vol. 1, pp. 114–16.

458. hoeretpede pes ... viro vir: either a misquotation or mistranscription from Virgil, *Aeneid* X, 361 (*'haeret pede pes densusque viro vir'*). The line translates as: 'foot against foot, and man pressed close against man.' See *Aeneid VII–XII*, trans. H. Rushton Fairclough (Cambridge, MA: Harvard University Press, 2000).

459. *'the vile squeaking ... wry-necked fife'*: Shakespeare, *Merchant of Venice* II. v. 30.

460. *the tune of 'the Protestant Boys'*: A song of this title is among pieces collected in *Constitutional Songs* (?Dublin, ?1798), exhorting loyalty to Church, King, and the memory of the Boyne victory ; see pp. 16–17.

461. 'Croppies lie down': 'Croppies Lie Down,' a song urging the defeat of the Irish rebel cause, published in *A Collection of loyal songs, as sung at all the Orange lodges in Ireland* (Dublin: s. n. , 1798), and included in many subsequent, similar published collections of songs. 'Croppy' or 'croppy boy' was a derogatory nickname for Irish rebels, originally applied during the 1790s to those who cropped their hair to indicate their democratic sympathies (*OED*).

462. *'Misused the king's press most damnably'*: from Falstaff's account of his troops in Shakespeare's *I Henry IV* IV. ii. 12–53. As he explains, those he initially 'pressed' into military service have 'bought out their services,' leaving him with only such unpromising recruits as the 'revolted tapsters' and 'hostlers trade-fallen.'

463. *'No eye had seen such scarecrows'*: *I Henry IV* IV. ii. 41, from Falstaff's description of his 'pressed' troops (see n. 462 above).

464. *their court baron*: a 'court baron' was a manorial court held periodically by local lords or their stewards, to settle land and tenancy disputes.

465. *the retrait* [*retreat*] *of Xenophon*: Refers to the 1,500 km retreat led by the Greek soldier and historian Xenophon (*c.* 435–*c.* 354 BC) following the loss in battle of his leader, Cyrus the Younger, as recorded in Xenophon's *Anabasis*.

466. *the 'excellent quality of discretion'*: source unidentified.

Volume II

1. *Know thus far ... SHAKESPEARE*: See Volume I, n. 1

2.   *Les femmes ... DE GRAMMONT*: See Volume I, n. 2
3.   *Having both ... TEMPEST*: Shakespeare, *Tempest*, I.ii.83–5.
4.   *Rampant ... BEAUMARCHAIS:* Beaumarchais, *Le Mariage de Figaro*, III.v (typically translated from the nineteenth century as 'be commonplace and creeping, and you will achieve all things').
5.   *wyat windows*: 'Wyat,' or Wyatt' denotes windows in the Gothic Revival (pointed) style, as developed in architecture and interior design by the English architect James Wyatt (1756–1813) (*OED*). Here, they have been incongruously adopted along with the neo-classical, Grecian portico, in a mixing of styles indicating the Crawleys' lack of cultivated taste.
6.   levee: A reception of visitors on rising from bed; morning assembly held by a person of distinction (*OED*).
7.   *land jobber*: A person who buys and sells (land) as a middleman (*OED*)
8.   *at the expense of the —* county: i.e. Crawley has raised his militia on his own initiative, as had been traditional within the rural landlord and middle classes in Ireland, where little official support for local policing had existed, apart from deployment of troops, prior to the Peace Preservation Act (1814).
9.   *en robe de chambre et bonnet de nuit:* 'in his dressing-gown and nightcap' (French). *Robe de chambre*, a dressing gown or nightdress (*OED*); *bonnet de nuit*, a nightcap (*OED*).
10. *drivers*: Landlords who impounded ('drove' to pounds) the cattle of tenants whose rent payments had become overdue (*OED*).
11. *spalpeans*: 'common workmen or labourers' (Irish; *OED*); otherwise, and used contemptuously, 'rascals' (*OED*).
12. *acts for preserving the public peace ...* insurrection acts: In July 1814, Parliament passed the Insurrection Act as a reintroduction of an Act of the same name of 1796. It enabled repressive measures including the suspension of trial by jury, and the imposition of curfews, in areas affected by agrarian unrest or suspected rebel activity. The same month, Parliament passed the Peace Preservation Act, which enabled the lord lieutenant to proclaim districts as being 'disturbed', and to send special constables to reinforce policing of these areas.
13. *Rule of Bail*: an order enabling the release from custody of persons accused of crimes, on condition of their being bound over to keep the peace for an appointed period of time, having found sufficient security.
14. *'the protestant boys' and 'croppies lie down'*: see Volume I, ns 473, 474.
15. *Jemmy Bryan, ci-devant driver:* This character's name is possibly intended to recall that of Jemmy (James) O'Brien, a notorious government informer, who was hanged for murder in Dublin in 1800. *Ci-devant*: 'former' (French).
16. *en evidence*: ' in evidence' (French), conspicuous (*OED*). This is the earliest instance of English usage cited in *OED*.
17. *encouraging the manufactory of the country*: From the early eighteenth century, Irish institutions such as the Dublin Society (founded 1731) and (before 1800) the Irish Parliament had forwarded various initiatives for the encouragement of home production of commodities such as cotton and linen, many of which were imitated on local levels.
18. *raised his soul above buttons*: To have 'a soul above buttons' became a commonplace expression in nineteenth-century literature, for feeling oneself to be above one's duties or station. It seems to have originated in George Colman's one-act comedy *Sylvester Daggerwood* (first performed 1795), in which the aspiring actor Daggerwood says: 'My father was an eminent button-maker ... but I had a soul above buttons ... I panted for a

liberal profession'. See George Colman, *Sylvester Daggerwood; or, New Hay at the Old Market* (London: J. Cawthorne, 1808), p. 10.

19. *fugle me those haroes through all them system of tictacs*: In military parlance, to 'fugle' is to lead soldiers through particular procedures, a 'fugleman' being an individual who demonstrates such new procedures to soldiers (*OED*). 'Tictacs' here seems to refer to set manoeuvres or procedures.

20. *my invisible fence*: An 'invisible' fence in this period consisted of thin, horizontal wires stretched taut between regularly-spaced posts. It excluded grazing animals from pleasure gardens, without interrupting the view across the gardens or land. The 'invisible fence' was invented by J. Pilton, a Chelsea wire-maker, who describes it in *Gentlemen's Magazine* 79, part 1, (1809), pp. 313–14.

21. *Is it to Jericho ye are marching*: Possibly a variation upon the English slang expression to 'go to Jericho', meaning (especially in the imperative) to 'go to the Devil' (recorded from c. 1635). See Eric Partridge, *A Dictionary of Slang and Unconventional English*, eighth edition, ed. Paul Beale (London: Routledge, 2000), p. 616.

22. 'ruction': Irish English shortening of 'insurrection', in continued usage as 'ruction'. The use of this word in Volume IV, ch. 6 is the second instance recorded in *OED*.

23. *a square hollow*: a hollow square, a military formation in which troops form a square around an empty space (*OED*).

24. *trevailly*: i.e. reveille, the signal to wake or rise, sounded on trumpets or drums (*OED*).

25. *Judith ... her country's cause*: Miss Crawley refers to the story in the apocryphal Book of Judith, concerning how the Israelite widow Judith saved the city of Bethulia by seducing, and then beheading, Holofernes, the Assyrian general besieging it.

26. *that great leviathan*: In the Old Testament, the leviathan is a mythical sea-beast, and an embodiment of evil, being associated with the Devil in Isaiah 27:1.

27. *reconnoitre*: To make an inspection or take observations (especially of an enemy) (*OED*).

28. *biding the keen encounter of the eye*: Apparently an allusion to Shakespeare's *Richard III*, I.ii.120 ('this keen encounter of our wits').

29. *slip-shod muse*: Recalls the 'slip-shod sibyl' of bad poetry who inspires the king of the dunces in Pope's *Dunciad* III, 15.

30. *Dulce Domum*: sweet home (Latin).

31. *much of the Sappho*: Born on the Greek island of Lesbos in the late seventh century BC, Sappho was the most famous woman poet of classical antiquity. She authored highly personal, passionate lyric poems, only one of which survives complete, along with other fragments. The (unsubstantiated) legend that she committed suicide when the male poet Phaon rejected her love inspired Ovid's epistle of Sappho to Phaon (*Heroides*, 15), and versions of this piece by John Donne and Alexander Pope, as well as Mary Robinson's sonnet-sequence *Sappho and Phaon* (1796). The name 'Sappho' became proverbial for any woman of poetic accomplishments or pretensions.

32. *This Olla Podrida*: Olla Podrida, otherwise an 'olio', a spiced stew containing various meats or vegetables, and originating in Spain and Portugal; and hence, a miscellaneous collection of things or elements, especially different languages (*OED*).

33. *religious calls*: works of admonitory religious literature aimed at effecting the conversions of readers.

34. *Philosophy ... the true faith at seven*: Owenson burlesques, or loosely cites (at times conflating them), the titles of several published works of fiction and religious instruction, possibly including: Francesco Algarotti, *Sir Isaac Newton's Philosophy Explain'd for the Use of the Ladies*, 2 vols (London: E. Cave, 1739); Charles Dibdin (as 'Castigator'),

The Lion and the Water-Wagtail: A Mock-Heroic Poem (London: s.n.,1809), a satire on the recent corruption scandal involving the Duke of York and his mistress Mary Anne Clarke; Abbé Gabriel François Coyer, *Bagatelles morales* (London and Paris: Duchesne, 1754); Anon. [John Macken], *Minstrel's Stolen Moments, or Shreds of Fancy* (Dublin: J. Cumming, 1814); Anne Clarke, *Small Literary Patchwork, or a Collection of Miscellaneous Pieces, in Prose and Verse, written on various occasions, chiefly on Moral and Interesting Subjects* (Shipston: T. Smith, 1805; 2nd edn (London: Bentley, 1814); Joseph Alleine, *An Alarme to Unconverted Sinners* (Edinburgh: M. Duncan, 1695; and much reprinted and abridged); Ralph Venning, *Mr Ralph Venning's Alarm to Uncoverted Sinners* (London: W. Miller, 1675); Anon., *Delicate Crimes. In a Series of Letters*, 2 vols (London: S. Hooper, 1777); James Naylor, *Milk for babes: and meat for strong men* (London: R. Wilson, 1661); *The Beauties of the Poets. Or, a collection of moral and sacred poetry*, compiled Thomas Janes (London: J. Fry, 1777). 'The History of a Child' recalls typical titles of the many accounts of the lives, conversions and deaths of pious children published during the seventeenth and eighteenth centuries, with examples including 'E. C.', *Some Part of the Life and Death of Mrs Elizabeth Egleton, who died … In the fifth year of her age* (London: s.n., 1705); Anon., *An Account of the Admirable Conversion of one Sarah Howley, a Child of Eight or Nine Years Old* (Edinburgh: J. Reid, 1704), and G[eorge]. B[urder]., *Early Piety; or, Memoirs of Children Eminently Serious* (London: s.n., 1777; frequently reprinted into the early nineteenth century).

35. *Elegant Extracts … with two hands*: Owenson burlesques typical titles of instruction manuals for amateur musicians, and mass-market language textbooks, contemporary and recent examples of which included: *The Preceptor, or A Key to the Double Flageolet* (London: s.n., c. 1815); Nicholas Salmon, *A Footstep to the French Language* (London: printed for the author, 1787); and Peter Prelleur, *An Introduction to Singing: After so Easy a Method, that Persons of the Meanest Capacities May (In a Short Time) Learn to Sing (In Tune) Any Song that is Set to Musick* (London: J. Simpson, 1747).

36. *catalogue raisonnée, or rather dé raisonée*: In English usage, a 'catalogue raisonnée', meaning literally 'explained catalogue' (French), is 'a descriptive catalogue of works of art with explanations and scholarly comments' (*OED*). A 'catalogue déraisonnée' would be literally a 'non-explained', or a 'garbled', catalogue (from French *déraisonner*, 'to talk nonsense').

37. *sanctum sanctorum*: 'Holy of Holies' (Latin).

38. *taught his young idea how to shoot*: Adapted from James Thomson, *The Seasons*; *Spring*, 2.

39. *: the trifling events … jacobinical*: The events referred to here are the signing of 'Magna Carta', a charter of rights obtained by a grouping of barons from King John of England in 1215, and the English revolution against Charles I, both which occurrences would be troubling to the Crawley family's anti-democratic sensibilities.

40. *chapeau de bergere*: 'shepherdess hat' (French).

41. *Sol*: In Roman mythology, the name of the Sun, personified as a god.

42. *bon ton*: 'good style' (French). In English usage, good style, good breeding (*OED*).

43. *Glengariff*: a picturesque, wooded valley in west Co. Cork, which had become a popular tourist destination during the eighteenth century.

44. *en passant*: 'in passing' (French).

45. *a sergeant-at-law*: Along with King's (or later Queen's) Counsels, sergeants-(or serjeants-)at-law were the highest ranking members of the English bar, from the fourteenth to the nineteenth centuries. Appointed by the Crown, they had the exclusive right to speak in the Court of Common Pleas. They also had exclusive rights to appointment as

judges in the Courts of Common Pleas and King's Bench, and occupied a social status equal to that of knighthood.

46. *a peninsula hero, covered with orders*: 'Orders' here refers to badges or insignia demonstrating membership of an order of knighthood, honour, or merit (*OED*). Miss Crawley's brother has been awarded his 'orders' for service in the 1808–12 campaign to liberate Spain and Portugal (countries forming the Iberian Peninsula) from Napoleon.

47. *cadet*: 'youngest child' (French; and in English genealogical usage).

48. *Magnus Apollo*: 'great Apollo' (Latin). In Greek mythology, Apollo was both god of the sun and of prophecy, and patron of musicians, poets and physicians.

49. *élève*: 'pupil' (French).

50. *darling without end*: Milton, *Paradise Lost* II, 870.

51. *The word 'serious'*: see vol 1, n. 133.

52. *the beauty of holiness*: from Psalm 29:2.

53. *prominent ses ennuis*: 'parading his or her ennuis' (French).

54. *some male Huntingdon, some imitative Wilberforce*: *Huntingdon* refers to Selina Hastings, née Shirley (1707–91), countess of Huntingdon, who became an energetic promoter of Methodism among the English upper classes in London and Bath, and who in 1783 founded the strictly Calvinistic sect known as the Countess of Huntingdon's Connexion. *Wilberforce* refers to the Tory MP and abolitionist William Wilberforce (1759–1833), who was a leading member of the 'Clapham Sect', a grouping of wealthy evangelical Christians.

55. *personal advantage*: In her note, Owenson quotes from Pope, *Moral Essays*, I ('To Sir Richard Temple'), 136.

56. *on the qui vive*: on the alert, on the lookout (*OED*). *Qui vive*, literally 'who lives?' (French)

57. *Sublapsarians ... Muggletonions*: *Sublapsarians*, Calvinists who believed that God foresaw the fall of Man; *Baxterians*, followers of Richard Baxter, whose teachings combined both Arminian and Calvinist doctrines; *Necessarians*, those believing that human actions are dictated by circumstance, rather than by free will; *Antinomians*, those believing that Christians were bound not by moral law, but by the 'law of grace'; *Sabalarians*, not identified; may refer to the Sabbaterians, a Baptist congregation founded in New England in 1665, whose members observed the Sabbath on Saturday rather than Sunday; *Swedenbourgians*, i.e. Swedenborgians, followers of the Christian mystic Emanuel Swedenborg (1688–1772), who asserted that the physical world corresponded to a spiritual one; *Independents*, English nonconformists who formed independent congregations, and asserted independence of conscience, and whose movement gained popularity in Ireland during the 1650s; *Universalists*, those believing that all human beings would finally be saved after death; *Destructionists*, those believing that the punishment of the damned would be temporary, but followed by the destruction of their souls; *Hutchinsonians*, (in Britain) followers of John Hutchinson (1674–1737), who taught that all languages had originated in Hebrew, and who rejected the scientific theories of Isaac Newton; *Millenarians*, those believing that an end time, or millennium, was at hand, which beliefs emerged within various Irish Christian denominations from the late eighteenth century; *Shakers*, otherwise the United Society of Believers, a puritanical, millenarian sect settled in New York by the English factory worker Ann Lee (1736–84), whose members' practice of physically shaking during worship earned them their nickname; *Jumpers*, Welsh Calvinistic Methodists, who separated from the Established Church in 1795; *Dunkers*, members of a Baptist sect founded in Germany in 1708, and later settled in America,

whose nickname derived from their practice of baptism by triple immersion in honour of the Trinity; *Fifth-Monarchy men*, millenarians who believed that the four empires of the ancient world (Assyria, Persia, Greece, Rome) would be succeeded by a 'fifth monarchy' of Christ, culminating in the Last Judgement; *Muggletonions*, i.e. Muggletonians, followers of the visionary prophet Ludowicke Muggleton (1609–98) who founded his sect in 1652.

58. *curricle*: a light, two-wheeled carriage, usually drawn by two horses abreast (*OED*).

59. *two barouches and four*: A barouche was a four-wheeled carriage with an adjustable half-hood behind, having a seat in front for the driver, and seats inside for two couples to sit facing each other (OED).

60. *Crime gave ... impudence*: paraphrased from Pope, *Satires of Dr Donne Versified* II, 45–6 ('One, one man only breeds my just offence; / Whom crimes gave wealth, and wealth gave impudence').

61. *that period ... rod of extermination*: i.e. the 1798 rebellion and its aftermath.

62. *green bag*: a bag, traditionally made of green fabric, used in the period by barristers and lawyers for carrying case briefs.

63. *silk gown*: the traditional court dress of a barrister after promotion to King's or Queen's Counsel.

64. *the Union parliament*: the parliament formed at Westminster following the implementation of the Act of Union in 1801, and incorporating Irish MPs into the British House of Commons and House of Lords.

65. *this most filthy bargain*: Shakespeare, *Othello*, V.ii.155.

66. *the BUREAUCRATIE, or office tyranny*: *Bureaucratie*, 'government by bureaux [offices]' (French). This is the first example of English usage cited in *OED* (the first example of usage of the anglicised 'bureaucracy' cited in *OED* is from 1837).

67. wise men of Gotham: In English folklore, the inhabitants of the village of Gotham, near Nottingham, were remarkable for their stupidity. Various stories about them featured in plays and narratives from the fifteenth century onward, including a seventeenth-century chapbook, *The Merie Tales of the Mad Men of Gotham*. In some of the stories, the men affected their stupidity as a stratagem.

68. *a crown-solicitor*: a lawyer involved in preparing criminal prosecutions for the crown.

69. *ad libitum*: 'at will'; 'at pleasure' (Latin).

70. *that subtilty of littleness ... 'left-handed wisdom'*: i.e. cunning, as expressed in Francis Bacon, 'Of Cunning', *Essays*.

71. *the cause of its independence*: 1782 was the year in which the Irish Parliament achieved what would be a short-lived (and always ultimately limited) legislative independence, free trade having been secured in 1779. Lords lieutenant were still appointed from England; and the English Privy Council was still technically empowered to veto Irish parliamentary acts during the period 1782–1801 (though rarely did so); but the 1780s in particular would be regarded by Irish Whigs like Owenson as a time of optimism for the further extension of independence.

72. *slip slop*: A blunder in the use of words, or the habit of making such (*OED*); also trifling, foolish talk (*OED*).

73. *the long vacation*: the three-month summer break customarily taken in this period by law courts (*OED*).

74. *my new hair-bottoms*: Crawley refers to what are evidently 'hair-bottomed' chairs, items of furniture common in the period, with wooden frames, and seats ('bottoms') stuffed with horse-hair.

75. 'Hints for a Magistrate,' *or* 'Mach Nally's Justice of Pace [Peace]': Crawley alludes to legal manuals of the period. The reference to Leonard MacNally, *The Justice of the Peace for Ireland: Containing the Authorities and Duties of that Officer*, 2 vols (Dublin, 1808) is clear; but 'Hints for a Magistrate' is not precisely identifiable.

76. *rattan*: A walking-cane made from the stem of the rattan plant, obtained in south-east Asia (*OED*); also 'a drumming or beating noise' (*OED*).

77. *my iligant [elegant] Northumberland table*: The Northumberland table, a large and often ornate piece of domestic furniture popular in Ireland during the late eighteenth century, was named after Hugh Smithson, second earl of Northumberland, and lord-lieutenant of Ireland 1763–5, who became a leader of Dublin fashions.

78. *cuddy would you taste*: cuddy (corruption of Irish *cuid oidhche*, 'evening portion') originally referred to 'a supper and night's entertainment due to the lord from his tenant'; but by this period also had the sense of a gift or bribe from a tenant to a landlord (*OED*).

79. *a dewshure*: i.e. a douceur, a bribe.

80. *bougie*: 'candle' (French). Darby means to say 'bijou', 'jewel' (French), also in English usage in the period for 'trinket'.

81. apropos *de* bot: possibly an erroneous rendering of *a propos des bottes*, 'with regard to something quite irrelevant' (French).

82. bull-veasied: Darby appears to mean '*bouleversé*', 'turned upside down' (French)

83. *Irish volunteers ... catholic bill*: The 'Volunteers' was a part-time military force initially established in Ireland during the late 1770s, to maintain a national defence, and to preserve public order, while the regular troops were mainly engaged in the American war of independence. From the early 1780s, the Volunteers became increasingly linked to the Patriot movement, with membership being especially popular among the middle classes. The 'Catholic bill' could refer to any of the parliamentary bills, and acts, which relaxed various civil restrictions upon Roman Catholics, including the Relief Acts granting Catholics education rights (1782), the right to practise as lawyers (1792), and the parliamentary franchise (1793).

84. *counsellor Curran*: The leading Irish Whig politician and barrister John Philpot Curran (1750–1817) first entered the Irish Parliament as MP for Kilbeggan, Co. Westmeath, in 1783. A noted orator, he made his first major speech in support of Henry Flood's motion for parliamentary reform. Throughout the 1780s and 1790s he continued to protest against government corruption in Ireland, and to demand full Roman Catholic emancipation. Following the 1798 rebellion, he appeared as counsel for the defence at many of the trials of suspected rebels, which activity in particular gained him a wide popular following, and the familiar name 'counsellor [lawyer] Curran'.

85. *ould Lord Charlemont ... his popularity*: James Caulfeild, first Earl Charlemont (1728–99) was actively involved with the formation of the Volunteers during the late 1770s, and in 1780 became their commander-in-chief. His Dublin home became a centre for Irish Patriot activity toward the establishment and continued promotion of the 1782 Parliament. Charlemont was a noted connoisseur and patron of arts, and his houses in Dublin and Clontarf have been regarded as outstanding examples of Irish Palladian architecture (see Volume 1, ns 57, 95).

86. *Mr. Grattan ... Irish eloquence*: Henry Grattan (1746–1820) became the most vocal and distinguished of the Whig politicians who worked toward the establishment of the Irish Parliament in 1782. He was especially famed for the eloquence and energy of his rhetoric. See also Volume 1, n. 100.

87. *Gally-my-jaw*: Crawley mispronounces 'Galimathias' an originally French word for 'nonsense', or 'gobbledegook', which can also mean a confusion or mixture of items (*OED*).

88. *a deputy remembrancer*: in this period, a deputy to the King's Remembrancer, the principal clerical officer in the Exchequer of Pleas, who dealt with business relating to crown revenue, and the collection of debts due to the exchequer.

89. *a seneschal of the Dublin liberties*: *seneschal*, a governor (of a city or province), or other administrative or judicial officer (*OED*).

90. *the whole boiling*: slang expression meaning 'the whole lot' (*OED*).

91. *bone-bush*: ie *bonne bouche*, literally 'good mouth', 'a pleasing taste in the mouth', and used in sense of 'tasty morsel' or 'titbit' (French); in English usage, also literally a 'tasty morsel' (*OED*).

92. *enfant trouvé*: literally 'a found child'; a foundling (French), with connotations of illegitimacy. Darby means to say *enfant cheri*, 'beloved child', meaning a 'favourite' (French).

93. *if you will just mind your P's and Q's*: 'if you will just mind your manners'; 'P's and Q's' being a colloquial expression referring to 'please[s]' and 'thank you[s]'.

94. *speaking French like a Nabob*: the origin of this saying is unclear, but that it was current in Ireland by the late eighteenth-century period is indicated in the United Irishman Wolfe Tone's journal entry for 25 April 1796, in which he records, regarding his progress in learning French, 'I begin to speak French like a Nabob'; see *The Life of Theobald Wolfe Tone*, ed. W. T. W. Tone, 2 vols (Washington, DC: Gales and Seaton, 1826), vol. 2, p. 100. 'Nabob', from Urdu *nawab*, referred in the period to any foreign person (whether British, Irish, or of another nationality) who had gained wealth or power in India (*OED*).

95. *wigging*: OED does not record 'earwig' in Owenson's sense as a verb; but gives 'an ear whisperer, flatterer' as a figurative sense of the noun, the latest recorded usage of which is dated 1758.

96. *an epithet*: Darby Crawley means to say 'an epitaph'. 'An epithet', in general usage meaning simply 'an adjective expressing some [characteristic] quality or attribute ... of the person or thing described', could also take the specific sense of 'an abusive or derogatory expression used of a person' (*OED*).

97. Momenti mori: 'remember death [remember that you must die]' (Latin; *OED*), a typical epitaph intended to induce reflections upon mortality.

98. *dirt we are ... we must return*: Paraphrases Genesis 3:19.

99. *the port surveyor*: perhaps intended to recall that John Wilson Croker's father had served as surveyor of the port of Dublin (1800–7); see also Volume II, n. 105.

100. *Windham Crawley ... their baptismal appellations*: The eldest Crawley son has been named after William Windham (1750–1810), who served as chief secretary for Ireland for only two months following his appointment in May 1783. He is thought to have resigned on account of a lack of confidence in his own fitness for the post.

101. *dasher*: One who 'cuts a dash'; a dashing person (*OED*).

102. *service in America ... in the peninsula*: Thady Crawley has served in the 'War of 1812' (1812–14) between Britain and America, causes of which included American opposition to the British blockade of Napoleonic Europe, and which saw the British occupying Washington during 1814; and in the British campaign to liberate the countries of the Iberian peninsula (Spain and Portugal) from Napoleon (1808–14).

103. *BIVOUACKING ... pipeclay*: 'Bivouacking' is a military term for overnight camping without tents or covering (*OED*); 'wigwam' originally referred to the traditional tents of some Native American peoples, but could ultimately also refer to other forms of tents or temporary structures, such as those used by the military (*OED*). The exact sense of

'making *the ould one* come *down with the pipeclay*' is unclear. 'The ould [old] one' is Irish slang for the Devil, while 'pipeclay' has some reference to soldiers, the term being used as an adjective describing good military presentation or order, a white paste made from pipeclay having been widely used in the period for whitening or polishing parts of the military uniform (*OED*).

104. I am the man for the leedies: source unidentified.

105. menage: 'establishment' (French).

106. *Conway Townsend Crawley*: Conway Crawley is modelled on the Galway-born barrister, politician and author John Wilson Croker (1780–1857), whose father John Croker had been an exciseman before being appointed surveyor general of Dublin port in 1800. J. W. Croker's strongly anti-jacobin sensibilities were formed while he was a student at Trinity College Dublin, during the1798 rebellion. He supported Catholic emancipation, however, as an expedient to ensure stability in Ireland. He was called to the Irish bar in 1802, and by 1818 had sat as Tory MP for Downpatrick (1807–12) and Athlone (1812–18), as well as substituting for Arthur Wellesley as Irish chief secretary from 1808, while Wellesley was serving in the Penisular campaign. From the early 1800s, Croker published several satirical pamphlets and verses, and in 1809 he helped to establish the *Quarterly Review*, the inaugural number of which featured a damning review of Owenson's *Woman; or, Ida of Athens* widely attributed to Croker. Conway Crawley's names recall those of Edward Conway (*c.* 1623–83), a Tory politician prominent in the administration of Ireland under Charles II, who was rumoured to have paid £10,000 to the Duchess of Portsmouth for his elevation to Earl of Conway in 1680; and George Townshend (1724–1807), first Marquess Townshend, and the first lord lieutenant of Ireland to reside there continuously (1767–72). Liberal in his distribution of offices and pensions, Townshend was accused of using bribery to secure support for Castle policies in the Irish House of Commons. Conway Crawley's middle name also recalls Richard Townsend (*c.* 1618–92), a Parliamentarian commander close to Cromwell, who was instrumental in effecting the submission of Cork to Parliament in 1649, and who acquired lands in Munster during a subsequent career in Irish administration, in which he actively opposed the Jacobite interest in Ireland.

107. a plus haute voleé: a higher flight (French); i.e. on a more elevated level.

108. *overflowing of the pancreatic juices:* in Laurence Sterne's *The Koran*, a woman character is described as '[having] no gall to boil over – her overflowings were of the pancreatic juices only'. See *The Works of Laurence Sterne*, 8 vols (London: C. Bathurst, 1799), vol. 8, p. 75.

109. wisely shunning *the broad way and the green*: Adapted from Milton, Sonnet IX ('To a Virtuous Young Lady'), ll. 1–2 ('Lady! That in the prime of earliest youth / Wisely hath shunned the broad way and the green').

110. *he would 'have blushed to find it fame'*: Adapted from Pope, 'Epilogue to the Satires', ll. 135–6 ('Let humble ALLEN, with an awkward Shame, / Do good by stealth, and blush to find it Fame').

111. *going the Munster circuit*: Early in his career as a barrister, John Wilson Croker also appeared at assize hearings on the Munster circuit.

112. *dulcis et utilis*: 'agreeable and useful' (Latin).

113. *étalage de sensibilerie*: 'display [as in shop-window] of sensibility' (French).

114. *Died of a rose in aromatic pain*: Adapted from Pope, *Essay on Man* I, 199–200 ('Or quick effluvia darting thro' the brain, / Dye of a rose in aromatic pain?')

115. *card-racks*: racks for holding visiting cards (*OED*)

116. dernier resort: last resort (French); originally (in reference to legal jurisdiction) the last tribunal or court to which appeal can be made; hence, a last or final resource or refuge (*OED*).

117. *Minerva*: Minerva was the Roman goddess of learning and creative artistry, known as Athene in Greek mythology.

118. *bench of the Common Pleas, and Exchequer*: in this period, the Bench of Common Pleas was a court for the hearing of civil cases. It was one of the three main courts of common law, another being the Court of Exchequer (concerned with issues relating to the national revenue), the judges sitting in which were known as Barons.

119. *moins bannales*: 'less trivial' (French).

120. *her vaulting ambition, which might o'erleap itself*: Alludes to Shakespeare, *Macbeth*, I.vii.27.

121. *the soft green of her soul*: An allusion to Edmund Burke, *A Philosophical Enquiry into the Origin of our Thoughts on the Sublime and the Beautiful* (London: R. and J. Dodsley, 1757), part III, section 10 ('How far the idea of beauty may be applied to the qualities of the mind'): 'Those persons who creep into the hearts of most people … are never persons of shining qualities, nor strong virtues. It is rather the soft green of the soul on which we rest our eyes, that are fatigued with beholding more glaring objects'; see p. 93.

122. *elected to the bench*: appointed a judge.

123. *What dust we doat on when 'tis man we love*: Pope, 'Eloisa to Abelard', l. 336.

124. *tent-stitch*: Embroidery in which the pattern is worked in a series of parallel stiches arranged diagonally across the intersections of the threads. Also called petit-point (*OED*).

125. *agacer*: 'to annoy'; 'to irritate' (French).

126. *recherché*: 'outlandish, affected' (French); in English usage (*OED*).

127. *petites maitresses*: 'young ladies [of fashion]' (French).

128. *Heaven's own proper dye*: source not identified.

129. *coquelicot*: The colour of the common red poppy; a brilliant orange-red (*OED*).

130. *breathing a browner horror*: an adapted quotation from Pope, 'Eloisa to Abelard', 165; 170, in which 'Black Melancholy … breathes a browner horror on the woods'.

131. faste: 'pomp' (French).

132. *in propriâ personâ*: 'in his own person' (Latin); in person.

133. *the Irish red bench*: Red was the traditional colour of the upholstery of the benches in the House of Lords.

134. *alpha and omega*: 'The beginning and the end', originally referring to God as the Supreme Being, alpha and omega being the first and last letters in the Greek alphabet.

135. *Not yet* come out: i.e. she has not yet been presented in society as a marriageable woman (*OED*).

136. *wousky-looking*: sense unclear.

137. *What hempen … SHAKESPEARE*: Shakespeare, *A Midsummer Night's Dream*, III.i.73.

138. *He gives … IBID.*: Shakespeare, *King John*, II.i.463–4.

139. *I abhor … IBID.*: Shakespeare, *Love's Labours Lost*, V.i.17–19.

140. *Old Bailey counsel*: An 'Old Bailey' counsel could be any barrister engaged in criminal defence or prosecution, the Old Bailey being London's principal court for the hearing of criminal trials. From the mid-eighteenth century, such lawyers began generally to attract disreputable associations, whilst also being particularly stereotyped as bullying interrogators who indulged in pompous or sarcastic rhetoric.

141. *proneur titré*: 'acknowledged flatterer' (French).

142. *the young legal Bobadil*: Captain Bobadil is a conceited soldier in Ben Jonson's comedy *Every Man In His Humour* (1598).

143. *That's nate*: i.e. 'That's neat' ('That's good').

144. *'But what's in a name' as Romeo says*: Miss Crawley alludes to Shakespeare's *Romeo and Juliet*, II.ii.43.

145. styptic: A remedy for costive bowels; or any substance with a binding, contracting effect on organic tissues (*OED*). Darby Crawley appears to have confused this word with 'sceptic'.

146. *a magdalen asylum*: 'Magdalen' asylums were originally charitable institutions for the housing and rehabilitation of 'fallen' women, so named in reference to the legend that St Mary Magdalene had been a prostitute before becoming a disciple of Christ.

147. lethargy:' liturgy', in Darby Crawley's pronunciation.

148. *King Pomarre ... Otaheitee Islands*: Could refer to either of the first two kings of the Pomare dynasty, whose members ruled the Kingdom of Tahiti 1773–1880: Pomare I (ruled 1773–1803), or his son Pomare II (ruled 1803–21).

149. *king of the Mummers ... king of the* hummers: 'Mummer' appears to be used here in the sense of a bad actor or performer (*OED*); 'hummer' here means 'one who "hums" or hoaxes; a humbugger' (*OED*).

150. *the man in the Guardian ... out of a fever*: An allusion to the essay on puns in the *Guardian*, 36 (Wednesday 22 April 1713), which includes a story about a man who recovered from an 'ague' by amusing himself in punning on the word 'abracadabra.'

151. 151. *one of the Dunore hack chaises*: A hack chaise was a carriage kept for public hire (*OED*).

152. *demi-toilette*: 'half-dress' (French); in English usage, semi-formal, rather than full, evening or dinner dress (*OED*).

153. *perplexed in the extreme*: Shakespeare, *Othello*, V.ii.345.

154. *the very moral of Paddy Duigenan*: 'The very moral of' was a colloquial expression current in the period, meaning 'the exact likeness of' (*OED*). Darby Crawley also refers to the ultra-Protestant lawyer and politician Patrick Duigenan (1735–1816), who, as MP for various Irish seats during the 1790s and early 1800s, energetically opposed Catholic emancipation both in speeches and published pamphlets.

155. cheval de bataille: 'battle-horse' (French); an obsession, or favourite topic (*OED*).

156. *the* pas: *pas*, the right of going first (French); the right of precedence (*OED*).

157. done the state no service: a common form of words in legal documents and reports of the period.

158. état: 'state', 'condition' (French).

159. *let us eat ... to-morrow we die*: A version of the English proverb 'Let us eat, drink, and be merry, for tomorrow we die,' which conflates Ecclesiastes 8:15 ('a man hath no better thing under the sun, than to eat, and to drink, and to be merry'); and Isaiah 22:13 ('Let us eat and drink; for to morrow we shall die').

160. *malversations*: corrupt activities in official posts or other positions of trust (*OED*).

161. *the 'last fool's as welcome as the former'*: adapts a line from Thomas Rowe's *The Fair Penitent*, I.i ('One lover to another still succeeds, / Another, and another after that,/ And the last fool is welcome as the former').

162. rélevés: literally 'raised up' (French). In French cookery, a dish or course brought in to replace one that has been removed (*OED*).

163. *making a Judy Fitzsimmons of myself*: The exact origin of the expression 'to make a Judy Fitzsimmons of onself', meaning to make a fool of oneself, is unclear. It is, however,

believed to be possibly Anglo-Irish, and to date from the early nineteenth century; see E. Partridge, *A Dictionary of Catch Phrases*, ed. P. Beale, 2nd edn (London: Routledge and Kegan Paul, 1985), pp. 111–12.

164. mille fois repetês: 'a thousand times repeated' (French).

165. *the Temple*: the area in London, between the Strand and the Embankment, in which are situated three of the four Inns of Court (Inner Temple, Middle Temple and Gray's Inn). Membership of one of these Inns is a condition of training and qualifying as a barrister.

166. C'est clair: 'it's clear' (French), phonetically similar to 'see Clare', as heard by Darby Crawley.

167. *See Clare*: Darby thinks that his son is referring to the lawyer and politician John Fitz-gibbon, first earl of Clare (1748–1802). As lord chancellor during the 1790s, Clare was a vigorous opponent of Catholic emancipation. His support for measures such as the Insurrection Act (1796), and his encouragement of the use of terror to enforce state authority during the rebellion, made him widely unpopular. Many of his speeches in favour of the Union, and against Catholic emancipation or relief, were published as pamphlets.

168. *Lyttleton upon Coke*: i.e. 'Coke on Littleton', the name by which *The First part of the Institutes of the Laws of England, or, A Commentary upon Littleton* (1628), by Sir Edward Coke (1552–1634) came to be most widely known. The work was only partly a gloss on Sir Thomas Littleton's 1481 treatise on tenures, known as 'Littleton' (the first law book printed in England). It ranged widely across many aspects of English law, and formed the first of the four volumes of Coke's *Institutes of the Laws of England*. Although 'Coke on Littleton' was regarded as over-long and idiosyncratic, it became one of the major commentaries on English law.

169. *the* 'idle visions of the brain': Miss Crawley alludes to Richard Graves (1715–1804), 'On Fancy', in *Euphrosyne; or Amusements on the Road of Life*, 3rd edn, 2 vols (London: J. Dodsley, 1783), vol. 2, p. 217, where Reason demands of the nymph Fancy: 'Why, maniac-like, pursue in vain / The idle visions of your brain?'

170. *Watt's Hymns*: Isaac Watts (1674–1748), *Hymns and Spiritual Songs* (1707), which had been through many subsequent editions throughout the eighteenth century.

171. *Themis and Apollo ... their* liaisons: In classical mythology, Themis was the daughter of the Titan deities Gaia and Ouranos. She became the mother of Prometheus, and was honoured as a personification of justice. Miss Crawley is thinking here of Apollo as the god of creative artistry; though he, too, was also with law and justice.

172. liaisons dangereuses: 'dangerous liaisons' (French), alluding to the title of Choderlos de Laclos' novel of aristocratic sexual intrigues, *Les liaisons dangereuses* (1782).

173. *Blackstone ... was a poet*: The legal writer and judge Sir William Blackstone (1723–80), later best known for his *Commentaries on the Laws of England* (1765–9), won a prize for Latin verse composition whilst a pupil at Charterhouse, and in his twenties authored poetical works including 'The Lawyer's Farewell to His Muse,' and *The Pantheon: A Vision* (1747).

174. *Shenstone ... the English bar*: The poet William Shenstone (1714–63), who developed a famous landscape garden at The Leasowes, the Shropshire estate where he was born, was reported to have worn the gown of a student of civil law during his last three years of study at Pembroke College, Oxford (1732–9).

175. *the wool-sack*: Miss Crawley refers to the wool-stuffed seat in the English House of Lords, traditionally used by the Lord Chancellor (now the Lord Speaker), and said to have been

installed during the reign of Edward III, to remind the monarch and lords of the importance to England of its wool trade.

176. *I have found out ... wood-pigeon breeds*: In this and the succeeding quotations ('But let me
... of his young'), Miss Crawley quotes from 'Hope' in William Shenstone, 'A Pastoral
Ballad, in Four Parts' (1743). The piece was published in *A Collection of Poems in Six
Volumes, by Several Hands*, second edition (London: R. and J. Dodsley, 1758), and was
set to music by the English composer Thomas Arne (1710–68). The full stanza quoted
from runs as follows:

> I have found out a gift for my fair;
> I have found where the wood-pigeons breed:
> But let me that plunder forbear,
> She will say, 'Twas a barbarous deed.
> For he ne'er could be true, she aver'd,
> Who could rob a poor bird of its young:
> And I lov'd her the more, when I heard
> Such tenderness fall from her tongue.

See vol. 4, p. 351.

177. fadaise: 'twaddle' (French).

178. *the Della Cruscan school*: refers to a group of English poets resident in Florence during
the mid-1780s, foremost among whom was Robert Merry (1755–98), who published
lyric poems under the pseudonym 'Della Crusca'. The works of Merry's circle were characterized by sentimentality of tone, and ornate diction. Mocked by many commentators
for their supposed artificiality, the Della Cruscans were in fact concerned with exploring
poetic possibilities beyond the strict forms of Augustan verse. Many of them, like Merry,
also held radical political views.

179. *my friend of the Baviad and Mæviad*: Crawley refers to William Gifford (1756–1826),
author of the literary satires *The Baviad* (1791) and *The Maeviad* (1795).

180. *your friend of the Baviad ... 'a wretched woman'*: In his Introduction to *The Maeviad*
(London: printed for the author, 1795), William Gifford attacked both Robert Merry,
and 'Anna Matilda' (Hannah Cowley; see n.181 below) for what he regarded as the stylistic pretensions and superficiality of their poetry, referring to 'Anna Matilda' as 'this
wretched woman'. This phrase would be exactly echoed in the review of Owenson's
France in the *Quarterly Review*, 17 (April 1817), where she, too, was referred to as 'this
wretched woman'; see p. 280.

181. *Anna Matilda was ... Mrs Cowley*: enfant gaté, i.e. 'enfant gatée', a 'spoilt child' (French).
'Anna Matilda' was the pseudonym adopted by the poet and dramatist Hannah Cowley
[née Parkhouse] (1743–1809), in her exchange of sentimental lyric poems with Robert Merry (as 'Della Crusca') in *The World*, a daily newspaper. The phrase 'enfant gatée
of a particular set' meanwhile closely echoes the description of Owenson herself as 'the
enfant gatée of a particular circle', referring to her association with the Abercorn household, in the review of her novel *Woman; or, Ida of Athens* (1809) in the *Quarterly Review*,
1 (February 1809), pp. 50–2; 52.

182. *the Belle's Stratagem*: Crawley refers to Hannah Cowley's comedy *The Belle's Stratagem*,
first staged in London in 1780. The piece remained popular during the early nineteenth
century, with revivals including one at Covent Garden in September 1817. Its heroine,
Letitia Hardy, adopts a series of deceptions and disguises in order to woo Doricourt, the
sophisticated young gentleman who has agreed to the arranged marriage proposed for
them by her wealthy father, but who does not return Letitia's feelings. Robert Owenson

played the minor role of Silvertongue the auctioneer in *The Belle's Stratagem* when it was first performed in Dublin, at the Smock Lane theatre in 1781.

183. *Belle ... the Rape of the Lock*: Samuel Johnson's *Dictionary of the English Language* defines 'belle' as 'a young lady', noting the French origin of the word, and citing as his example of usage Pope's *The Rape of the Lock*, ll. 7–10.

184. *ruse de guerre*: 'a stratagem in war' (French). In English usage, also a stratagem intended to deceive an enemy in war; or any artifice or scheme for gaining advantage (*OED*).

185. *Zoilus*: The original Zoilus was an ancient Greek literary critic born at Amphipilis, Thrace, and active in the fourth century BC. He became notorious for the malicious invective with which he attacked the works of many eminent authors, most particularly Homer, whose 'scourge' he styled himself in his (mainly lost) *Censure of Homer*. As Thomas Parnell (1679–1718) noted in the account of Zoilus which accompanied his 1717 translation of *Batrachomyomachia* ('The Battle of the Frogs and Mice'), a mock epic poem then attributed to Homer, the name of 'Zoilus' came to be applied to any critics who indulged personal malice in their writings on others' literary works.

186. *'never ending, still beginning'*: Quoted from John Dryden's *Alexander's Feast: or, The Power of Musick; An Ode, In Honour of St Cecilia's Day*, l. 101.

187. *ergo*: 'therefore' (Latin).

188. *cum grano salis, as the French say*: *cum grano salis*, 'with a grain of salt' (Latin).

189. *his political principles ... the last fifty years*: Crawley refers to the committed republicanism of John Milton (1608–74), who was active in Cromwell's administration, serving as his foreign languages secretary, as well as authoring treatises such as *Tenure of Kings and Magistrates* (1649), in which he argued the legality of deposing or even executing a monarch. Milton's greatest poetic work, *Paradise Lost* (first published 1667) was also widely admired by radicals, who saw in his characterisation of Satan a supreme expression of republican resistance to monarchy and the Established Church.

190. *As when the sun ... Perplexes monarchs*: Milton, *Paradise Lost* I.594–9.

191. *the Suspendeas Corpus Act ... the law of libel*: Darby Crawley refers firstly to *habeas corpus*, the writ requiring production of any detained person in court, a procedure established in England in 1679, and in Ireland in 1782 (under the Liberty of the Subject Act), to protect individuals against imprisonment without trial. This right of habeas corpus was suspended in Ireland, by act of parliament, for most of the period between 1796 and 1806, in response to the perceived threats from the United Irishmen and other radical movements. Darby Crawley's garbling of the term represents a grim joke of the potential for punishment, as well as imprisonment, without trial of individuals during the suspension of habeas corpus; for an example involving flogging, rather than hanging, see Volume 2, n. 210. By 'law of libel' Crawley most probably refers to the English law prohibiting 'seditious libel', the writing or speaking of words intended to diminish respect for the monarchy, which was defined as a crime in 1606.

192. *legitimate prince ... house of Stuart*: The 'legitimate prince' referred to here is Charles II, who came to the throne with the restoration of the English monarchy in 1660. The royal licenser at the time of the publication of Paradise Lost in 166 was Thomas Tomkins (1637/8–75), whose attempt to halt publication of the poem on grounds of his objection to the simile of the eclipse in I. 594–9 had been discussed by John Toland in *The Life of John Milton* (1760; London: A. Millar, 1761), p. 121, and mentioned in several subsequent biographical accounts of Milton.

193. *twice drove them from her shores*: the Commodore refers to the exile of the Stuart court in France following the execution of Charles I, and the exile of Charles's son, James II, from 1690.

194. *an ukase*: Originally a decree or edict having the force of law, issued by the Russian emperor or government; otherwise any proclamation, decree, order or regulation of a final or arbitrary nature (this is the first recorded instance in *OED* of the word in its more general sense).

195. *myrmidons*: In the *Iliad*, the Myrmidons were the followers of Achilles (see *Iliad* II 64). The name may refer to any follower, or henchman, being also sometimes (as here) intended to convey an idea of sycophancy (*OED*).

196. pierre de touche: 'touchstone' (French).

197. *the glorious and immortal memory*: Crawley refers to William III and the 'Glorious' Revolution of 1688, when he defeated the Catholic James II and ensured the Protestant succession of the English throne.

198. Beresford bob: Worn by men throughout the eighteenth century, and during the early nineteenth century, a 'bob-wig' (often referred to as a 'bob') was made of hair cut short, and curled upwards into 'bobs' (*OED*). Darby Crawley's name for his wig may be inspired by John Beresford (1738–1805), a politician noted for his opposition to the views of the United Irishmen, or his son John George de la Poer Beresford (1773–1862), a Church of Ireland bishop who in 1829 would oppose the Roman Catholic Relief Bill.

199. *that despotic bigot*: James II. As a Whig, the Commodore remembers William III less for his religious views, than for the constitutional reforms established with his accession. These reforms ended the previous assumption of the 'divine right' of the monarch to rule, and increased the powers of Parliament as a 'check' on absolute monarchical authority.

200. *'As when heav'n's fire' ... Homer and Virgil*: Crawley quotes from Milton, *Paradise Lost* I. 612–13. A 'cento' was defined in Samuel Johnson's Dictionary as 'a composition formed by joining scraps from other authors' (*OED*). William Lauder (see n. 202 below) cited the same passage from Milton as an instance of his using tree imagery in a similar manner to Homer and Virgil (to depict the 'falling of a Hero') in *An Essay Upon Milton's Imitations of the Ancients, in his Paradise Lost* (s.n., 1741), p. 24.

201. *Thrice he essay'd ... faucibus hæsit*: quotations from Milton, *Paradise Lost* I. 619–20; and Ovid [Publius Ovidius Naso] (43 BC–AD 17), *Heroides*, IV ('Phaedra Hippolyto,' [Phaedra to Hippolytus]), ll. 7–8 ('Ter tecum conata loqui ter inutilis haesit / lingua, ter in primo restitit ore sonus'). These lines have been translated as 'Thrice making trial of speech with you, thrice hath my tongue vainly stopped, thrice the sound halted at first threshold of my lips.' See *Heroides*, trans. Grant Showerman, rev. G. P. Goold (Cambridge, Mass.: Harvard University Press, 1996).

202. *Lauder ... Douglas*: In 1747, William Lauder (*c.* 1710–*c.* 1771), a teacher of Latin, published a series of articles in the *Gentleman's Magazine*, claiming that Milton had plagiarized passages of *Paradise Lost* from Latin verses by modern authors. He developed his arguments in *An Essay on Milton's Use and Imitation of the Moderns, In His Paradise Lost* (London: J. Payne and J. Bouquet, 1750) which included a preface and postscript by Samuel Johnson. Lauder's hoax was exposed by John Douglas (1721–1807), who in *Milton Vindicated from the Charge of Plagiarism, Brought Against Him by Mr Lauder* (London: A. Millar, 1751) showed that the 'plagiarized' passages had in fact been taken by Lauder from a Latin version of *Paradise Lost* by William Hog, and inserted into texts quoted as having been Milton's sources. Under compulsion by Johnson, Lauder confessed to his imposture in *A Letter to the Reverend Mr Douglas* (London: W. Owen, 1751).

203. accoucheur: a (usually male) midwife (French; *OED*). Crawley appears to have meant to say 'connoisseur.'

204. *a post one*: a letter sent through the public postal service.

205. *For now enforst* ... SPENCER: an adaptation, with misquotation, of the proem to Spenser, *The Faerie Queene*, Book I, stanza 1:
     Lo I the man, whose Muse whilome did make,
     As time her taught in lowly Shepherds weeds,
     Am now enforst a far unfitter taske,
     For trumpets sterne to change mine Oaten reeds,
     And sing of Knights and Ladies gentle deeds;
     Whose prayses having slept in silence long,
     Me, all too meane, the sacred Muse areeds
     To blazon broad amongst her learned throng....
     'To blazon far' does, however, appear at book II, canto 10, stanza 3 ('Thy name, ô sovereign Queene, to blazon farre away').

206. *maître d'hotel*: i.e. a *maître d'hôtel,* literally 'house master'; 'house manager' (French). A major-domo or steward (*OED*).

207. chefs du menage: 'household managers' (French).

208. *the fair autocrat of the north*: Catherine II (1729–96), empress of Russia 1762–96, and subsequently known as 'Catherine the Great'.

209. *a magistrate asserted* ... 'publicly disclose': On 6 April 1799, T. Judkin Fitzgerald presented a petition to the Irish House of Commons requesting that he be indemnified for 'certain acts ... not justifiable in common law' committed by him when serving as high sheriff of Co. Tipperary during the 1798 rebellion. He stated that 'he had been reduced to the necessity, in many instances ... to order corporal punishment of whipping to many persons, of whose guilt he had secret information from persons, whose names he could not publicly disclose'. See F. Plowden, *An Historical Review of the State of Ireland: From the Invasion of that Country under Henry II. to its Union with Great Britain on the 1st of January, 1801,* 2 vols (London: T. Egerton, 1803), vol. 2, part 2, pp. 950; 951. The same passage of the petition was reproduced in a review of published Parliamentary speeches on the issue of Roman Catholic claims made during 1817 by the Bishop of Ossory, Leslie Forbes and Robert Peel, in *Edinburgh Review*, 29:57 (November 1817), pp. 114–41; p. 129.

210. *What, you* ... *after sentence?*: Owenson bases this incident on a case described by Francis Plowden in his account of the petition brought by the former Tipperary high sheriff T. Judkin Fitzgerald (see n. 208 above). After the 1798 rebellion, an action for assault and battery was brought against Fitzgerald by a Clonmel 'teacher of the French language' named Wright (not a hedge-schoolmaster, but employed in local boarding schools and private homes). After receiving 'charges of a seditious nature' against Wright, Fitzgerald had sentenced him to be flogged and shot, without trial. Wright pleaded for a trial, and 'surrendered his keys to have his papers searched', to which Fitzgerald's reported response was: "'What, you Carmelite rascal, do you dare to speak after sentence?"' Wright was reported to have received a total of 150 lashes. See Plowden, *An Historical Review of the State of Ireland*, vol. 2, part 2, pp. 953–4.

211. *Delphic oracles*: an allusion to the prophecies, or 'oracles' issued by the priestess of the sanctuary of Apollo, located at Delphi, in the ancient Greek state of Phocis, from the third century BC.

212. *king Solomon's court in the* fringes: The custom of 'Riding the "fringes"', a traditional, triennial procession of the Lord Mayor of Dublin, and the members of trades and craftsmen's guilds, around the city boundaries, was discontinued in 1782. It had developed over the centuries into an elaborate pageant, in which members of particular trades traditionally represented mythological, historical, or Biblical scenes and characters, such as the 'King Solomon's court' mentioned here. See Jonah Barrington, *Personal Sketches of His Own Times*, 2nd edn, 2 vols (London: H. Colburn and R. Bentley, 1830), vol. 1, pp. 259–66. As Owenson remarks in her endnote, the custom had also continued in Shrewsbury, where it had originated in the celebration of the feast of Corpus Christi. However, in *The Stranger in Shrewsbury: or, An Historical and Descriptive View of Shrewsbury and its Environs* (Shrewsbury: Printed for the author, 1816), Thomas J. Howell had suggested that it was in decline, with apprentices the only company and guild members still taking part; see pp. 38–9.

213. *Ogygia ... Histoire d'Ireland, by Abbe' O'Gahegan*: O'Leary refers to Roderic O'Flaherty, *Ogygia: seu, Rerum Hibernicarum chronologia* (London: s.n.,1685), published in an English translation by J. Hely as *Ogygia, or, A Chronological Accout of Irish Events*, 2 vols (Dublin: W. McKenzie, 1793), which expanded upon Samuel Bochart's theories of the Phoenecian origins of the Irish people; and James MacGeoghegan, *Histoire d'Irelande, ancienne et moderne, tirée des Monumens les plus authentiques*, 3 vols (Paris: Antoine Boudet, 1758–63).

214. *Ware's Antiquities, and Lynche's Cambrensis Eversus*: O'Leary refers to Sir James Ware, *The Antiquities and History of Ireland* (London: A. and J. Churchill, 1705); and John Lynch [Gratianus Lucius], *Cambrensis eversus, seu potius Historica fides, in rebus Hibernics Giraldo Cambrensi abrogate* (?St Omer, 1662), a refutation of Giraldus's claims regarding Ireland.

215. *A curlew ... on her back:* Owenson would appear to have (loosely) recalled these lines from the account of regional fauna in *The Ancient and Present State of the County and City of Cork*, 2 vols (Dublin: s.n., 1774), in which Charles Smith records a Suffolk fowlers' proverb, concerning the commercial value of curlews' meat: 'A Curlew, be she white, be she black, / She carries twelve-pence on her back'; see Volume II, p. 344.

216. In all their glory: an allusion to Matthew 6:29, where Christ remarks upon the lilies of the field as being more beautiful than 'Solomon in all his glory'.

217. *His bosom's counsellor, and better self*: The phrase 'my better self' recurs throughout Shakespeare's *Sonnets*; though Owenson may also be thinking of John Hoole's tragedy *Cleonice, Princess of Bithynia* (London: T. Evans, 1775), in Act I of which Arsetes addresses Agenor as 'My other self, my bosom's counsellor!'.

218. exeunt manent: 'all leave, all remain' (Latin). Crawley has confused two separate stage directions.

219. *'on time's ... new clock says*: These words from the 'new clock' recall typical mottoes inscribed by clock and watch makers of the period on the dials of their timepieces. The favourite motto of the mid-eighteenth-century Liverpool clockmaker John Wyke was 'On time's uncertain date man's eternal hours depend'; see W. J. Roberts and H. C. Pidgeon, 'Biographical Sketch of Mr John Wyke', *Historic Society of Lancashire and Cheshire Transactions*, 5 (1853), p. 169.

220. *a few-de joy*: Darby Crawley means to say *feu de joie*, literally meaning 'fire of joy' (French), and referring to a rifle salute. 'Few de joy' is phonetically similar to *fille de joie*, '[a] prostitute' (French).

221. *DAME DU PALAIS*: 'lady of the palace' (French).

222. *conversaziones*: originally an Italian term, a 'conversazione' was a meeting for socializing or conversation.

223. *devotées*: i.e. devotees, people zealously devoted to religion or religious observances (*OED*).

224. *Mademoiselle Espinasse*: an accomplished French society hostess, recalled in the memoirs of Jean-François Marmontel (1723–99) as having presided over a lively and highly culti-vated salon, frequented by liberal intellectuals. As Marmontel explains in his *Memoires d'un père* (1804), Mademoiselle Espinasse first entered aristocratic and intellectual circles as the paid companion of an older woman who dismissed her when she became jeal-ous of the attention she attracted from her friends. See *Memoirs of Marmontel, Written By Himself*, 4 vols (London: Longman, Hurst, Rees and Orme, 1805), vol. 2, pp. 320, 325–30.

225. *debutée*: 'first appeared'; 'debuted' (French).

226. *like a pilgrim clad in sober grey*: recalls both the opening line of Joseph Warton's 'Ode to Evening' ('Hail, meek-eyed Maiden, clad in sober grey'); and the lines concerning John Bunyan in William Cowper's *Tirocinium: or A Review of Schools* (1784), 143–4 ('E'en in transitory life's late day, / That mingles all my brown [hair] with sober grey, / Revere the man whose PILGRIM marks the road').

227. *flame coloured taffetas*: alludes to Shakespeare, *1 Henry IV*, I.ii.11 ('the blessed sun him-self a fair hot wench in flame-color'd taffeta').

228. *shelelaghs*: i.e. shillelaghs, Irish cudgels made from blackthorn or oak wood (*OED*).

229. *in a circle at Almacks*: i.e. in a group of friends at Almack's, the exclusive private members' club. Located on King Street, off St James's Street, Almack's was the centre of fashion-able life in London in the period. It had been built in 1764–5, and named after its first proprietor, William Almack. It was at the height of its popularity in the 1810s, provid-ing entertainments including dancing and card games. See Jane Rendall, *The Pursuit of Pleasure: Gender, Space, and Architecture in Regency London* (London: Athlone Press, 2002), pp. 86–8.

230. que voulez-vous: 'what more can you want' (French).

231. *the* Balthassar ... *complete courtier*: Lord Frederick refers to the Italian diplomat and cour-tier Count Baldassare Castiglione (1478–1529), and his treatise instructing on courtly manners and accomplishments, *Il Libro del Cortegiano* (The Book of the Courtier) (1528).

232. *a young English lord of the pale*: Lord Eversham identifies himself with the Anglo-Norman settlers who first occupied lands in Ireland within an agreed boundary, under English jurisdiction, which became known as the 'pale', on the other side of which lay the territories ruled by the native, Gaelic chieftains.

233. c'est un affaire arrangé: 'it's a settled affair' (French).

234. *not purely Milesian*: i.e. not of the oldest Irish blood, the Milesians being the ancient Spanish settlers supposed to have arrived in Ireland during the prehistoric period, from whom the Gaelic Irish were traditionally descended.

235. poteen: whiskey produced in an illegal still (*OED*).

236. *ERIN GO BRACH*: i.e. *Éirinn go brách*, 'Ireland for ever' (Irish).

237. *By Confucius ... mandarin of the province*: This is the first instance of Lord Frederick's satirical analogy between the Irish viceregal administration at its local levels, and the highly complex and ceremonial Chinese system of government by provincial mandarins (senior civil servants and government officials) on behalf of the emperor. The earliest instance of the now commonplace English usage of 'mandarin' to denote any impor-

tant (or reactionary or secretive) official recorded in the *OED* is from 1907. Confucius (551–479 BC) founded the political philosophy on which the Chinese government had been developed, and which promoted both familial loyalty to the state, and ideals of personal advancement by service to government. The 'celestial empire' was the term used by the Chinese court to describe itself, in keeping with the belief that the imperial family line was divine in origin. The term was frequently adopted (often ironically or satirically) by non-Chinese commentators.

238. c'est à mourir de rire: 'one could die laughing' (French).

239. *his glass*: an eye-glass, an instrument originally designed to assist weak eyesight (*OED*), but also (as a 'quizzing-glass', 'spy-glass', or monocle), a fashionable accessory, constructed usually of a single lens, with or without a handle (*OED*).

240. *your district is proclaimed*: see Volume I 1, n. 166.

241. *the feast of lanterns*: Published accounts of the Chinese 'feast of lanterns', which honoured the new year, had been appearing in Britain from the mid-eighteenth century. A detailed description of the spectacular decoration of all outdoor spaces with colourful lanterns for the celebration of this festival appears in Jean-Baptiste Grosier, *A General Description of China*, 2 vols (London: G.G. J. and J. Robinson, 1788), vol. 2, pp. 322–5.

242. *the Jubilee*: may refer to the fifty-year anniversary of George III's accession to the throne, which would have been celebrated in 1810.

243. *transparencies*: pictures, lettering or other decorative images painted onto transparent surfaces, such as glass or fabric, and lit from behind (*OED*).

244. *Grecian* vesbitule *or portico*: Darby Crawley means to say 'vestibule,' meaning the partially-enclosed entrance-court, or portico, in front of a classical or (as here) neoclassical building (*OED*).

245. cantharides: Darby has confused *Cantharides*, the pharmacopoeical name of the dried beetle *Cantharis vesicatoria* ('Spanish Fly'), taken internally as a diuretic or aphrodisiac (*OED*), with *Caryatids*, sculpted female figures used as columns to support the entablatures of buildings (*OED*).

246. *a perfect* bougie: Darby again confuses *bougie*, 'candle' (French), with *bijou*, 'jewel' or 'gem' (French).

247. aregorical: i.e. 'allegorical'.

248. *the great Wellington ... Nelson's pillar*: The images on the transparencies commemorate the Allied victory over Napoleon at the battle of Waterloo, led by Arthur Wellesley, Duke of Wellington in 1815; and represent the monumental pillar erected in Dublin in 1808, to commemorate Horatio Nelson's naval victory over the French at Trafalgar in 1805.

249. *the Ragent's [Regent's] plume*: i.e. the three feathers of the heraldic badge of the Prince of Wales, who in 1818 was ruling as Prince Regent in place of his father George III, who had become mentally incapacitated.

250. 250. *Crawley ... I am thine*: Lord Frederick adapts lines from M. G. Lewis's, *The Monk: A Romance*, 3 vols (London: J. Bell, 1796): 'Agnes, Agnes, thou art mine! / Agnes, Agnes, I am thine!' See Volume II, p. 53.

251. *Mount St. Gothard, or Sierra Leone*: The St Gothard (or Gotthard) Pass is a mountain pass in the Alps near the border between Switzerland and Italy, located at an altitude of 2,108m (6, 196ft). It was a popular subject for Romantic-period poets and artists. 'Sierra Leone' here refers not to the West African country, but to the mountainous peninsula which forms the site of its capital city, and after which the country is itself named. *Sierra*

Leone is an Italian rendering of *Serra de Leão* ('Lion Mountain'), the name by which it was known by the Portugese traders who arrived there in the fifteenth century.

252. *lapsus linguæ*: a slip of the tongue (Latin; *OED*).

253. *slip-slop*: A blunder in the use of words, or the habit of making such (*OED*); also trifling, foolish talk (*OED*).

254. sur son terrein: 'on his terrain'; 'on his own ground' (French).

255. *Ching-Foo Crawley of the yellow button*: 'Ching foo' appears to be Morgan's particular transliteration of a Chinese honorific, variously transliterated by other English commentators in the period. In *A Dictionary of the Chinese Language, In Three Parts*, 6 vols (Macao: Honorable East India Company's Press, 1819), Robert Morrison explained that 'A man of eminent virtue and talent, on whom others may depend for support, is called … Chang-foo'; see part 2, vol. 1, p. 164; but also noted the term 'Ching-foo' as referring to 'the principal and the second'; ibid., p. 171. Morrison further mentions the term 'Seun-foo' as being 'a title now given to the Deputy, or vice-governors of provinces'; ibid., p. 720. The 'yellow button' refers to the imperial system of identifying mandarins' rank by the colour of the 'button', a badge customarily worn on their hats, described in several Westerners' published accounts of travel in China from the1790s onward. In his account of the British diplomatic visit to China in 1816–17, *A Journal of the Proceedings of the Late Embassy to China* (London: John Murray, 1817), Henry Ellis described an encounter with an arrogantly strutting 'Mandarin with a yellow button'; see p. 221.

256. par tous les dieux: 'by all the gods' (French).

257. *The raven … battlements*: Shakespeare, *Macbeth*, I.v.38–40.

258. *chop mandarins*: In imperial China, 'chop' referred to any of various kinds of official seal, stamp or document (*OED*). Such items included inscriptions of the emperor's name, to be venerated in his absence as substitutes for his person; and licenses or passes conferring various permissions, issued by designated mandarins (hence 'chop mandarins').

259. God's providence is my inheritance: originally the motto of the Boyle family (earls of Cork).

260. *petit couvert*: 'little cover' (French); *couvert*, the utensils, such as cutlery, laid for each person's use at table (*OED*).

261. *batterie de cuisine*: apparatus for preparing or serving meals (French; *OED*).

262. *delf*: glazed earthenware made at Delf or Delft in Holland; originally called Delf ware (*OED*).

263. *loungers*: articles of furniture designed for relaxing on (*OED*; first recorded usage from 1969); see also Volume I, n. 117.

264. *every thing Gothic*: By the early nineteenth century, the Gothic style of decoration, based on medieval ecclesiastical art and architecture, and featuring pointed arches and intricate, carved embellishments, had become fashionable in the designs of domestic interiors.

265. *couvre-pied*: literally 'cover-feet' (French); a rug to cover the feet (*OED*); the instance at FM III ch 3 is earliest cited in *OED*.

266. *terra incognita*: unknown land (Latin); an unknown or unexplored region; often used figuratively (*OED*).

267. Le fruit ne fait pas tomber la fleure: 'the fruit does not make the blossom drop' (French).

268. besoin de sentir: '[the] need to feel' (French).

269. par accés: 'by fits and starts' (French).

270. *like harlequin in the comedy*: A reference to the traditional, stock figure of the harlequin (or Arlecchino) of the Italian *commedia dell'arte*, and the English pantomime, who frequently took the forms of witty, cunning servant characters.

271. Unheedful ... woes: Adapted from Pope, *Satires of Dr Donne*, I, 4.

272. *muse of Camoens, in the shades of Coimbra*: A reference to the Portugese poet and travel-ler Luis Vaz de Camões (or Camoëns) (*c.* 1524–80), and the university city of Coimbra, Portugal, where he studied and lived.

273. Sou utile ainda que briccando: see Volume I, n., 442.

274. *quondam*: 'former' (Latin).

275. *selon les régles*: 'according to the rules' (French).

276. *silent and ... to heaven*: Pope, 'Epilogue to the Satires: Dialogue I', 93 (which has 'remove to heaven').

277. *Tien Sing, or the Heavenly Spot*: In his account of the 1795 embassy of Lord Mac-artney to China, George Staunton had explained that the name of the major, northern Chinese port of *Tien Sing* meant 'heavenly spot.' See George Staunton, *An Authentic Account of an Embassy from the King of Great Britain to the Emperor of China*, 2 vols (London: W. Bulmer and Son, 1797), vol. 2, p. 23.

278. faite a ravir: 'made to delight [one]' (French); delightful.

279. *the Baldassar ... of the Irish court*: see Volume II, n. 231.

280. the park: Refers to Phoenix Park, Dublin, the location of the residences of many senior government officials in Ireland; see Volume I, n. 150.

281. arbiter elegantarium: 'judge of elegance' (Latin). 'A judge on matters of taste' (*OED*). This is the first instance of English usage cited in *OED*.

282. *savoir vivre*: literally 'to know how to live' (French). 'Ability in the conduct of life; knowl-edge of the usages customary in good society' (*OED*).

283. delices: 'delight' (French).

284. merveilleux: a 'marvellous one' (French), the contemporary Parisian expression for a dandy or 'fashionable' (see *OED*, which cites an instance from Owenson's *France*).

285. *St. James's Street, or the Chaussée D'antin*: the most fashionable and exclusive thor-oughfares in London and Paris respectively.

286. *Petrarch ... 'wretched'*: A reference to the Italian poet Petrarch [Francesco Petrarca] (1304–74), whose sonnet sequence, the *Canzoniere* (*c.* 1351–3), traces the often ago-nized development of his love for a woman named as 'Laura'. It is, however, unclear which particular work of Petrarch's is alluded to here.

287. *whom folly ... please*: Pope, 'The Second Epistle of the Second Book of Horace Imitated,' 327.

288. aimer en courant: 'to love on the run' (French).

289. laissez aller: See Volume I, n. 231.

290. aux petit soins: 'in little attentions' (French).

291. *the* yellow skreen*, and castle Ko-tou*: In his *Journal of the Proceedings of the Late Embassy to China* (London: John Murray 1817), Henry Ellis, who accompanied the diplomat Lord Amherst to China in 1816, describes an 'audience' with the emperor, who was not present, but substituted by 'a table hung with yellow silk', placed in front of a 'skreen'; see p. 91. The envoys were instructed to perform the submissive ceremony of '*ko-tou*' ('to knock the head'), by kneeling and striking the floor with their heads nine times, in front of this yellow silk hanging. Amherst's refusal to comply with this requirement, which he deemed insulting to a sovereign's representative, was among causes of the failure of the embassy. Ellis does not refer to the silk hanging specifically as a 'screen'; but it is referred to as 'the yellow skreen' in the review of the work in the *Quarterly Review*, 17 (July 1817); see p. 479.

292. *Where got'st thou that goose look?*: Shakespeare, *Macbeth*, V.iii.12.

293. *Kilkenny theatricals*: The private theatre at Kilkenny became Ireland's most famous centre for amateur dramatic performances by aristocrats and other eminent persons, opening on 2 February 1802.The last performance there took place on 28 October 1819, by which time its 'seasons' had been running for as long as three weeks at a time, attracting fashionable audiences, and raising large sums for charity. See *The Private Theatre of Kilkenny, with Introductory Observations on Other Private Theatres in Ireland, before it was opened* (n. pl, 1825), pp. 8–9. Rosbrin's theatrical obsession meanwhile recalls that of Richard Barry, seventh Earl of Barrymore (1769–93), who owned extensive lands in Co. Cork, but who constructed one of the foremost private theatres of the eighteenth century at his Thameside property, Wargrave, in 1788. He made many appearances as an actor both there and at other locations, including the second theatre that he set up in London in 1790, in an old auction room. His Wargrave theatre was seized by his creditors in 1792, and subsequently demolished.

294. *Macheath's gang*: the thieves led by the highwayman Captain Macheath, in John Gay's *Beggar's Opera*.

295. *innate ideas ... the subject*: In his *Essay Concerning Human Understanding* (1690), John Locke (1632–1704) had argued that the human mind possessed no innate ideas or principles, and that all ideas were acquired through associations formed from experience.

296. *a noble infant Roscius*: Rosbrin is ironically described as having been an aristocratic version of William Henry West Betty (1791–1874), a celebrity child actor from Co. Down, who became known as the 'Young Roscius'. 'Roscius' had been a traditional nickname for famous actors in England from the sixteenth century, and recalled the Roman comic actor Quintus Roscius Gallus (d. 62 BC). Betty was hailed as a prodigy for his appearances in adult tragic roles including Hamlet and Macbeth, mainly in London, between 1804 and 1808.

297. *Ariel*: the ethereal spirit in Shakespeare's *The Tempest*, who serves the enchanter Prospero in return for being released from the power of the witch Sycorax.

298. *all the world ... merely players*: Shakespeare, *As You Like It*, II. vii.139–40.

299. *clap-traps*: Special theatrical devices designed to elicit applause (*OED*).

300. *Peers, heralds ... and lawn*: Pope, 'The First Epistle of the Second Book of Horace Imitated', l. 317.

301. *St Stephen's*: i.e. St Stephen's Hall, Westminster, the former St Stephen's Chapel, which was originally built for Edward III in 1364, and used as the chamber for meetings of the British House of Commons from 1547 until it was destroyed by fire in 1834.

302. *: went out ... the Union*: As Henry Grattan did (although, in his case, not permanently), Daly has retired from political life following the passage of the Act of Union.

303. the finest gentlemen in Europe: Owenson apparently refers to an anecdote concerning Edward IV and John, Earl of Ormonde, in Thomas Carte, *An History of the Life of James Duke of Ormonde, from his birth in 1610, to his death in 1688*, 3 vols (London: J. J. and P. Knapton, 1735–6), vol. 1, p. xlii ('That King used to say of him [Ormonde], that he was the goodliest Knight he ever beheld, and the finest Gentleman in Christendom').

304. *Time ... 'thinned his flowing hair'*: An allusion to the title of 'Time has not thinned my flowing hair,' a popular vocal duet by the English composer William Jackson (1730–1803), from one of his twelve canzonets for two voices.

305. *Charlemonts ... Floods*: As well as to James Caulfield, earl of Charlemont (see Volume I, n. 57), Henry Grattan (see Volume I, n. 100) and John Philpot Curran (see Volume II, n. 84), Owenson alludes here to two other leading Irish Patriot politicians of the 1780s, Walter Hussey Burgh (1742–83), and Henry Flood (1732–91).

306. *Gunning, Munroe, or Birmingham*: Owenson refers to three of the most noted society beauties of eighteenth-century Dublin: Elizabeth Gunning (1733–90), who, with her sister Maria (1732–60), led fashionable society in Dublin and London in the 1740s and 1750s, and who married James Hamilton, sixth duke of Hamilton; Dorothea ('Dolly') Monro, or Munro (d. 1793), who became a 'toast' of Dublin society prior to her marriage in 1775; and Lady Anne Bermingham, who in 1802 married the second earl of Charlemont, and who, as Lady Charlemont, became a friend and correspondent of Owenson.

307. *La noblesse ... George Dandin*: 'Gentility in itself is good; 'tis, to be sure, a considerable Thing; but it's attended by so many ugly Circumstances, that the best way is not to meddle with it'. From Molière's comedy *George Dandin: ou le mari confondu* (1688) ('George Dandin: or The Defeated Husband), I. i. See *George Dandin, ou le mari confondu, comédie* (London: J. Watts, 1732), p. 2 (original); p. 3 (translation).

308. far niente: 'doing-nothing'; 'idleness' (Italian).

309. little equipage of wit: An allusion to John Dryden's epilogue to his tragedy *All For Love*, 4 ('this is all their equipage of wit').

310. couleur-de-rose: 'rose-coloured' (French); coloured pink (*OED*).

311. *hands which ... 'kings have lipped'*: An allusion to Shakespeare, *Antony and Cleopatra*, II.v.29–30.

312. *jaunting car*: a light, two-wheeled vehicle, popular in Ireland, able to accommodate four (or sometimes more) passengers, and used for group excursions (*OED*).

313. *Debret's Peerage*: By 1818, *Debrett's Peerage of England, Scotland, and Ireland*, a two-volume reference work listing the genealogies of all noble families in Britain, and published by John Debrett (d. 1822), was into its tenth revised edition (1816).

314. *en masse*: In a mass or body; all at once (French; *OED*).

315. *entrée*: 'entrance' (French).

316. *Honiton lace*: lace from the Devonshire town of Honiton, a noted centre for the production of fine lace.

317. incursion of the Kalmucks: The Kalmucks were a Mongolian people inhabiting a region on the north-west shores of the Caspian sea (*OED*).

318. *his glass*: another reference to Lord Frederick's eye-glass, or 'spy-glass'; see Volume II, n. 169.

319. *chip hat*: a simple hat made from wood or woody fibres split into thin strips or 'chips' (*OED*).

320. Bergere derangée: 'dishevelled shepherdess' (French).

321. Cela a cent ans sonnés!: 'she must be a hundred [years old]!' (French).

322. tawny tight ones: adapted from George Colman's musical comedy *Inkle and Yarico: An Opera* (London: G. G. J. and J. Robinson, 1787), I. i, where Trudge, a white, male character, addresses Wowski, his black sweetheart, as 'my little tawny tight one'; see p. 25.

323. c'est impayable: 'it's priceless' (French).

324. *I must ... Ko-tou*: Lord Frederick refers ironically to the imperial Chinese ceremony of *ko-tou* (often referred to in English as 'kow-towing'), a submissive gesture of kneeling before the emperor or an object representing him, and striking the floor nine times with the head; see also Volume 2, n. 291; and (for 'Ching-foo Crawley of the yellow button'), Volume 2, n. 255.

325. embrasseur impitoyable: 'a merciless embracer' (French).

326. *taking close order*: 'close order' is a position in military drill, in which men stand at stipulated distances apart from each other (see *OED*) .

327. Marquise de mon ame: 'marchioness of my soul' (French).

328. je vous en repond, bel idol mio: 'take my word for it, my lovely idol' (French, Italian).

329. *the hieroglyphical circle ... tail in his mouth*: Images of serpents, or dragons, biting their own tails, and thus forming circular shapes symbolizing temporal eternity, occur in the texts and artworks of many ancient civilizations, including the Chinese. The use of such emblems in different cultures had recently been discussed in detail by George Stanley Faber in *The Origin of Pagan Idolatry Ascertained from Historical Testimony* (London: A. J. Valpy, 1816).

330. *'supping' ... a shoulder of mutton at Catherine's head*: Mr Daly alludes both to Shakespeare, *Macbeth*, V.v.13; and to the scene in Shakespeare's *The Taming of the Shrew*, where Petruchio seeks to subdue Katharine's temper by himself feigning rage. On being served some mutton, he complains to the servants that it is burnt, and, as a stage direction indicates, 'Throws the meat, &c. at them'; see IV.i.160–70.

331. *téte-à-téte-ing*: *tête-à- tête*, literally 'head to head' (French); as verb, 'to engage in private conversation' (*OED*).

332. Sans-six-sous: Crawley confuses *sans six sous*, 'without a sixpence'; 'broke' (French) with *sans souci*, 'without a care' (French).

333. *upon a* regiment: *regimen*, a diet, or course of treatment, for the restoration or preservation of health (*OED*).

334. *your proscription*: Crawley means not 'proscription', but 'prescription'.

335. solus cum solo: 'alone with (oneself) alone', 'all on one's own' (Latin); in English usage, alone (as a man) with an unchaperoned woman (*OED*; this instance is among examples cited).

336. *catsup*: actually a Chinese vegetable sauce (*OED*), also known in the period as 'catchup' (from Chinese *kê-tsiap*, from which modern 'ketchup' is also derived). Mr Daly refers to it to indicate the poor quality of the wine.

337. bon mot: literally 'good word' (French); a clever or witty saying; a witticism (*OED*); though Crawley appears to have confused this expression with *bon ton*, 'the correct fashion' (French).

338. *out of the wood*: out of the (wooden) cask or barrel (*OED*).

339. *Bechamelle*: A white sauce made with cream, named after its inventor, the Marquis de Béchamel, steward to Louis XIV (*OED*).

340. *chaise-marine*: a chaise (carriage) the body of which is suspended on straps, named after *chaise-marine* in the sense of a suspended seat for use on a ship, designed to prevent the effects of motion (French) (*OED*).

341. *Love in a Village*: refers to *Love in a Village* (first performed 1762), a comic opera by the Irish dramatist Isaac Bickerstaff (b. 1733), which featured a carter among the servant characters advertising themselves for hire at the end of Act I. Robert Owenson was cast as Eustace, one of the male juvenile lead characters, in a performance of *Love in a Village* at Drury Lane on 2 June 1774; see advertisement in the *Morning Chronicle*, 28 May 1774.

342. *maitresse du tripot ...* 'sermon ou Vèpres': from Paul Scarron (1610–60), *Roman comique* (1665), 4 vols. (London: s.n.,1781), vol. 1, p. 25 ('la maîtresse du tripot, qui aimoit la Comédie plus que Sermon ni Vèpres'; 'the mistress of the gambling den, who loved the comedy better than sermons or vespers').

343. *chasseur*: 'huntsman' (French).

344. *Great Glamis! Worthy Cawdor!*: Shakespeare, *Macbeth*, I.v.54.

345. *Now good digestion ... health on both*: Shakespeare, *Macbeth*, III.iv.36.

346. *I care not ... were not weary*: Spoken by Celia after she and her cousin Rosalind have fled her father's home in Shakespeare's *As You Like It*, II.iv.2–3.

347. *Mrs Siddons*: Sarah Siddons [née Kemble] (1755–1831), the leading tragic actress of her generation, whose signature roles included Lady Macbeth. As well as dominating the London stage, she appeared at the Smock Alley Theatre, Dublin, in 1783 and 1784, and returned to Dublin to play Hamlet in 1802. By the early nineteenth century her celebrity had seen her admitted to the most exclusive social circles, including that of Lady Abercorn.

348. *her old point*: a piece of point lace, a kind of lace made with a needle, rather than with bones or bobbins, or made to imitate the appearance of such lace; otherwise, any kind of fine-quality lace (*OED*).

349. one entire and perfect crysolite: Shakespeare, *Othello* V. ii. 43, which has 'chrysolite'.

350. *Apropos of the Siddons' dynasty ... Kemble the other day*: Rosbrin refers to Sarah Siddons's brother John Philip Kemble (1757–1823), also a leading performer in tragic roles, including Othello, Macbeth, and Hamlet. He first appeared in the role of Hamlet at the Smock Alley Theatre, Dublin, in 1781. During a later tour to Dublin in 1797, he appeared at Smock Alley in the title role of *Macbeth*, alongside company members including Robert Owenson, who played Hecate. The rest of the 'Siddons dynasty' included Siddons and Kemble's brother Charles Kemble, also a prominent member of the Drury Lane company.

351. *good man delver* ... wild amazement around: Rosbrin quotes from, or paraphrases, Shakespeare's *Hamlet*, V.i.14 ('good man delver'); while 'scatter wild amazement around' may be a misquotation of 'And wild amazement hurries up and down,' in Shakespeare's *King John*, V.i.35.

352. *Let Drury ...* 'state of Denmark': Rosbrin refers to the Theatre Royal, Drury Lane, London; and slightly paraphrases Shakespeare, *Hamlet*, I.iv.90.

353. That will be ... out of one weaver: Rosbrin quotes from various tragedies and comedies of Shakespeare: *Macbeth*, I.i.5; *Hamlet*, I.ii.180–1 (paraphrased); *A Midsummer Night's Dream*, I.i.11; *Twelfth Night*, II.iii.58; 59–60.

354. Take this ... by circumstance: Rosbrin quotes, with slight variations, from Shakespeare's *Hamlet* II. ii. 154; and *The Winter's Tale* V. ii. 32–3.

355. God save the King, *and* Patrick's Day, *and* Patrick's hall: 'God Save the King [or Queen]' is the British national anthem, the origins of the words and tune of which are unknown (though they may date to the late seventeenth century). It was first performed in the now well-known arrangement by Thomas Arne in 1745. St Patrick's Day is the feast-day of Ireland's patron saint, traditionally celebrated on 17 March, the reputed date of St Patrick's death (see also Volume 1, n. 399). St Patrick's Hall is a ballroom at Dublin Castle, added to the Upper Castle Yard there in 1746–7, and given its name in 1783, to commemorate the founding of the Order of St Patrick. See Christine Casey, *The Buildings of Ireland: Dublin* (New Haven, CT: Yale University Press, 2005), pp. 356–7.

356. *business of the stage for the performance of Henry the Fourth*: the characters named indicate that Rosbrin means Shakespeare's *Henry IV* part 1, rather than part 2.

357. tant soit peu: 'slightest bit' (French); 'a little bit'.

358. *bel respiro*: 'lovely retreat' (Spanish).

359. facons à la ordinaire: 'usual ways' (French).

360. tout comme une autre: 'just like another' (French).

361. en evidence: 'in evidence'; conspicuous (French).

362. par exemple: 'by example' (French); For example; for instance (*OED*; first instance cited from FM).

363. *a squeeze*: This expression possibly used here in the sense of 'a crowded assembly or social gathering' (*OED*).

364. hors de combat: Out of the battle; disabled from fighting (*OED*); figuratively, meaning to be unable to participate in an activity.

365. en grande ceremonie: 'in ceremonial style' (French).

366. *drawing-rooms and birth-days*: 'Drawing rooms' in the sense meant here were formal receptions held by monarchs or other persons of rank (*OED*). 'Birth-days' refers to royal birthdays, which in this period were often celebrated as major social occasions.

367. à toute entrance: 'at every entrance' (French).

368. Son nez en l'air: 'with his nose in the air' (French).

369. *the ribs of his South-Downs*: reference unclear; though 'South-Downs' could refer to a breed of sheep in the period.

370. *Grizzle, Noodle, Doodle*: Refers to Lord Grizzle, and the courtiers Noodle and Doodle, characters in Henry Fielding, *The Tragedy of Tragedies, or The Life and Death of Tom Thumb the Great* (1731).

371. 'chickens, come cluck,' – *to slow music*: 'Chickens, come cluck' was a children's playground game in which players followed a leader, popular throughout the nineteenth century. In *Ireland: Its Scenery, Character, &c* (1841), Mrs S. C. [Anna Maria] Hall describes a barn dance culminating in a 'finale' in which the dancers process around the room, holding onto each other's clothing, and which she compares to 'the play of Chickens, come cluck'; see vol. 1, p. 167.

372. Voyez-vous: French:

373. siesta: 'afternoon nap or rest' (Spanish); and in English usage (*OED*).

374. Ma Belle: 'my beauty' (French).

375. mignonne: 'sweetheart' (French).

376. *By, bye*: in this period, a colloquial and nursery variant of 'goodbye' (*OED*).

377. *Day, day*: a childish expression for 'good day' or 'goodbye' current in the eighteenth century (*OED*).

378. coup de grace: 'stroke of mercy' (French); the stroke by which a mortally wounded person is finally dispatched or 'put out of his misery'; figuratively, the stroke which settles or ends something (*OED*).

379. That antique song ... music hath charms: Rosbrin quotes from Shakespeare, *Twelfth Night* (paraphrased); and either from Pope, 'Sappho to Phaon' l. 14 ('Music hath charms alone for peaceful minds'), or from Congreve, *The Mourning Bride*, I.i.2 ('Music has charms to sooth a savage breast').

380. 'let us the cannikin clink,' *or* 'Troll us a catch': Rosbrin paraphrases *Othello*, II.iii.65–6; and misquotes *Tempest* III.ii.117.

381. non chalance: possibly a rendering of 'nonchalance' in the manner usual in the eighteenth century (see *OED*).

382. Did you ever ... picture of nobody: Shakespeare, *Tempest*, III.ii.126–7 (misquoted).

383. *Music ... after his studies*: Rosbrin quotes from Shakespeare's *The Taming of the Shrew* III.i.10–12.

384. ingenuous: Darby appears to mean 'ingenious'.

385. Here then ... upon our ears: a misquotation of Shakespeare, *Merchant of Venice* V.i.556–6.

386. Away with melancholy: A popular song, with the opening line 'Away with melancholy, nor doleful changes ring,' printed in many collections of songs from the late eighteenth

and early nineteenth centuries; see, for example, *Fisher's Ladies' and Gentlemen's Musical Review for 1801* (London: S. Fisher, 1800), pp. 30–1.

387. alto: 'high' (Italian); playing the higher part in the piece of music being performed.

388. *cheiroplast*: i.e. a chiroplast, 'an apparatus designed by J. B. Logier in 1814 for keeping the hands in a correct position in pianoforte playing' (*OED*; earliest usage cited from 1842); hence the previous reference to the young Miss Crawley's being out of her 'musical stocks', in which the cheiroplast is imagined as confining the wrists like the 'stocks' or pillory.

389. bravado: 'ostentatious display of boldness' (*OED*).

390. *Petruchio*: the suitor of the temperamental 'shrew' Katherine in Shakespeare's *The Taming of the Shrew*. Rosbrin goes on to quote from II.i.188–91.

391. *My Henry is gone*: A popular song, with words by 'C. E.' to a tune by Sir J. Stevenson, and with a refrain containing the lines, 'But my Henry is gone, and left me forlorn, / To deplore the most faithless of men'. See *The Vocal Magazine*, No. 7 (1 July 1815), p. 29.

392. quitte pour la peur: 'got away with a fright' (French).

393. your's au revoir: 'yours till we meet again' (French).

394. *brag table*: A table to be used for playing brag, a card game similar to modern poker, in which one player issues a 'brag', or challenge, to others to turn up cards equal in value to his own (*OED*).

395. *Citizens! your voices*: Shakespeare, *Coriolanus*, II.iii.125 (misquoted).

396. *Cruel are ... SHAKESPEARE*: Shakespeare, *Macbeth*, IV.ii.18–22.

397. *the woods of Germany*: The ancient tribes of northern Europe, as encountered by the Romans, and described by Gaius Cornelius Tacitus in his *Germania* (*c*. 98 AD), were associated by eighteenth-century Whigs with a primitive, uncorrupted form of democracy in which many positions of authority were earned by merit. An especially attractive element of the ancient accounts of these tribes was their use of natural, wooded spaces for their religious or legislative activities.

398. most filthy bargain: Shakespeare, *Othello*, V.ii.155.

399. pot-walluping: In the period before the 1832 Reform Act, 'pot-walloping' boroughs were areas largely populated by 'pot-wallopers', male householders whose possession of separate fireplaces on which pots could be boiled qualified them to vote in parliamentary elections (*OED*). From the early nineteenth century, the term 'pot-walloper' could also carry the derogatory meaning of a fool or upstart (*OED*).

400. *tour de force*: 'a feat of strength or skill' (French).

401. *the celebrated and lovely Duchess of D. ... the famous Westminster election*: Georgina Cavendish [*née* Spencer] (1757–1806), Duchess of Devonshire was a leader of fashion, and an active supporter of the opposing, Whig interest. She joined with other female Whigs in canvassing voters prior to the Westminster election in 1784. Confronted with the Whigs' success in the election, the pro-government *Morning Post* alleged that the duchess had been exchanging kisses for votes; and further slanders and lampoons against her continued to appear in the Tory press.

402. *check-string*: 'A string by which the occupant of a carriage may signal to the driver to stop' (*OED*).

403. petrie des lis et des roses: i.e. *pétrie des lis et des roses*, 'full of lilies and roses' (French).

404. vallum: Originally a defensive wall or rampart of earth or stone (*OED*); this is the first usage of this transferred sense of the term recorded by *OED*.

405. *all the irregularity ... picturesque could desire*: Irregularity of outline or features was one of the principal qualities of the 'picturesque' aesthetic, as formulated by authors such

as William Gilpin and Uvedale Price, being instanced in objects such as ruins or rock formations.

406. Cunningly ... laid: Adapted from the description of the 'house of Pride' in Spenser, *The Faerie Queene*, book I, canto 4, stanza 4.

407. *flax pit*: A pit for the soaking and rotting of flax, a plant crop, in order to extract the fibres used to make a textile.

408. *Irish forty-shilling freeholder*: Ownership of land valued at forty shillings was the lowest possible qualification for voting in elections before the 1832 Reform Act. In 'rotten boroughs' election agents made false valuations of land in order to maximise the numbers of votes available.

409. bog leave: In the 1839 edition of the text, a footnote accompanied this expression, explaining that it meant 'leave to cut turf off the landlord's bog'.

410. *Millia murthur*: 'a thousand murders' (Irish).

411. *smiled in such a sort*: paraphrases Shakespeare, *Julius Caesar*, I.ii.204.

412. *St Gobnate's eve ... holy-well of Ballydab*: see vol. 1, n. 372.

413. qui amoit terriblement les enigmes: 'who loved enigmas terribly' (French).

414. *little star-chamber*: The original Star Chamber was an English court which heard cases connected with crown interests, developed during the reign of Edward IV. Its name derived from the starred patterns decorating the ceiling of the original chamber in which sessions were held, built at the Palace of Westminster in 1347. By the reign of Charles I, the court of the Star Chamber had become notorious for the severity of its rulings on matters of public order and sedition. It was abolished in 1640.

415. *Exparte*: *ex parte*, 'on the part of one side only' (legal Latin).

416. *rebellion of 1798 ... more dreadful 1641*: refers to two of the most traumatic episodes of Irish history before the nineteenth century: the rebellion of native Irish against English and Scottish settlers in 1641, and the rebellion led against the government by members of the United Irishmen in 1798.

417. *watch papers*: discs of paper, silk, or other material inscribed with designs or mottoes, inserted as linings to watch-cases (*OED*).

418. *the siege of Drogheda ... Sir Richard Musgrave*: Refers firstly to Nicholas Bernard, Dean of Ardagh (d. 1661), *The Whole Proceedings of the siege of Drogheda in Ireland* (London: W. Bladen, 1642), an account of Oliver Cromwell's recapture of the garrison town of Drogheda, Co. Louth, from royalist control; the passages cited by Owenson appear at p. 84 (Irish use of 'charms'), and p. 84 n. (the rebel apparently unharmed by bullets). Also referred to are Sir John Temple, *The Irish Rebellion* (1646), which included graphically detailed accounts of atrocities committed by Irish rebels against English and Scottish settlers in Ireland in 1641; and Sir Richard Musgrave's highly conservative, English-biased *Memoirs of the different rebellions in Ireland from the arrival of the English* (1801).

419. *gunpowder-tea*: Fine, green tea leaves, resembling granules of gunpowder (*OED*).

420. *caffe au lait*: i.e *café au lait*, 'Coffee with milk' (French); 'white' coffee.

421. *Mais qu'est ce qu'il ya donc, belle Chatelaine?*: 'but what is the matter, fair lady of the house?' (French).

422. professeur de bavardise: 'professor of idle gossip' (French).

423. *Duke Conway ... the peacock's feather*: Among the Chinese mandarins named in Henry Ellis's *Journal of the Proceedings of the Late Embassy to China* (London: John Murray, 1817) is Ho, a 'Koong-yay,' or 'Duke'; see p. 125. The decoration of the highest-status Chinese mandarins' hats with a peacock's tail feather is mentioned in several contempo-

rary Western travellers' accounts of travel to China. Henry Ellis describes it as 'answering to our orders [i.e. insignia] of knighthood'; see p. 103.

424. *the honest gentleman ... effigy shot at*: refers to the case of John Hamilton, the Protestant curate and magistrate of Roscrea, Co. Tipperary, who in 1815 arranged for an accomplice, Robert Dyer, to shoot at a straw effigy dressed in his clothes, so that he could then attach blame to members of a local Catholic merchant family named Egan. Several members of the Egan family were brought to trial, but released when Hamilton's plot was exposed. The case was widely reported in Irish newspapers including the *Dublin Chronicle*, 29 January 1816, which report provided the basis for the account in the *Orthodox Journal and Catholic Monthly Intelligencer*, 4 (1816), pp. 78–80. Another account appeared in the radical English periodical, *Hone's Reformist's Register*, 2:8 (13 September 1817), cols 236–8. In her footnote, Owenson interjects the Latin expression *pro pudor*, 'Oh shame' (misprinted in the original as 'pooh pudor').

425. *roasted a la mode Irelandaise... so many snipes*: *à la mode irlandaise*, 'In the Irish fashion' (French); 'Irish-style'. Lord Frederick makes flippant reference to the reports of Irish rebels' roasting of Protestant victims in front of fires during the 1798 rebellion, as instanced in anon., *A History of the Irish Rebellion in the year 1798* (Dublin: Alexander Stewart, 1799), pp. 126–7; and to the tortures and killings of Protestant children by Catholic rebel pikemen, during the 1641 rebellion, several instances of which are reported in sources such as John Temple's *The Irish Rebellion* and John Curry's *Historical Memoirs of the Irish Rebellion*.

426. *Voyons donc!*: 'let's see!' (French).

427. *Oh! horror... name thee*: Shakespeare, *Macbeth*, II.iii.62–3.

428. *Confusion ... stolen thence*: Shakespeare, *Macbeth*, II.iii.64–8.

429. *Approach this ... new gorgon*: Shakespeare, *Macbeth*, II.iii.70–1.

430. *Oh! insupportable ... eclipse o' th' sun*: Shakespeare, *Othello* V. ii. 97–9.

431. *Nor left a wreck behind*: either a quotation from Shakespeare, *The Tempest* IV. i. 155–6 ('like this insubstantial pageant faded, / Leave not a rack behind'); or from 'The Contrast, a Vision,' in *The Muse's Mirrour*, 2 vols. (London: J. Debrett, 1778), vol. 2, p. 160 ('And straight the airy vision fled, / Nor left a wreck behind').

432. *ou fait la sottise, et nous sommes les sots*: From Molière's comedy *Sganarelle ou Le Cocu Imaginaire* (Sganarelle or the Imaginary Cuckold), first performed in 1660, appearing in the following couplet, spoken by Sganarelle concerning 'inconstant' women: 'Il faut que tout le mal tombe sur notre dos; / Elles font la sottise, & nous sommes les sots,' translated in 1732 as 'all the Mischief must fall upon our Backs: they commit the Folly, and we are reckon'd the Fools.' See *Sganarelle ou le cocu imaginaire, comédie* (London: J. Watts, 1732), p. 54 (original); p. 55 (translation).

433. *the mignionette harvest ... this year*: In the period, 'mignionette' could mean either the fragrant, North African flowering plant (*Reseda odorata*); or 'a type of fine French bobbin lace made in narrow strips' (*OED*).

434. *hand-screen*: a small hand-held screen for shielding the complexion from open fires.

435. *An inquest ... sport for ladies*: Mr Daly echoes the words of Touchstone on the wrestling match in Shakespeare's *As You Like It*, I.ii.147–8 ('it is the first time that ever I heard breaking of ribs was sport for ladies'). For 'shanavests and caravats', see Volume 1, n. 243.

436. *the condemning cap*: a reference to the flat black cap customarily donned by English judges before issuing sentence of death.

437. *the* Merchant of Venice *trial*: The scene referred to appears in Shakespeare's *Merchant of Venice* IV. I, where Shylock sues his debtor Antonio for a pound of his flesh, and the

heroine Portia, in disguise as a doctor of laws, rescues Antonio by ruling that only flesh, and not blood, to which Shylock is not entitled by his original bond, may be removed from him.

438. *the christening in Henry the Eighth*: refers to the christening of the infant Princess Elizabeth in the Shakespeare's *Henry VIII*, V.v, the closing scene of the play.

439. what's in a name?: Shakespeare, *Romeo and Juliet*, II.ii.43.

440. *celebrated English ecclesiastic ... crozier of iron*: Hugh Boulter (1672–1742), appointed Primate of the Church of Ireland in 1724, vigorously promoted the English interest in Ireland, advocating the appointment of only English-born judges, bishops and other senior officials in Ireland, and serving as vice-president and treasurer of a Dublin society for promoting Protestant, English-language education for Irish Catholic children.

441. we of the English ... poor Irish: Owenson refers to *Letters Written by His Excellency Hugh Boulter, D. D. Lord Primate of All Ireland*, 2 vols (Oxford: Clarendon Press, 1769), but does not appear to be quoting directly from it.

442. Ireland is only ... being divided: In her endnote, Owenson quotes a passage from James Ware, *The Antiquities and History of Ireland* (Dublin: A. Crook, 1705), p. 58.

443. a rattle and bells: a jingling toy for babies; also associated with court fools or jesters.

444. *gaité du cour*: i.e. *gaieté du coeur*, 'gaiety of heart' (French); in English usage, 'playfulness' (*OED*).

445. *fervour of an ancient Roman*: The culture of the Roman Republic appears to be denoted here by 'ancient Roman'. Reverence for the state, as expressed in the attitude of *pietas*, is a prevailing theme of much of the literature of the Roman Republic. Texts such as Cicero's *De officii* and Virgil's *Aeneid* and *Georgics* contributed to later periods' association of a particular spirit of selfless patriotism with these ancient Romans.

446. *chef de cuisine*: head cook; chef (French; *OED*).

447. *Places of emolument ... April 22 1818*: No single, specific source for these details has been identified.

Volume III

1. *Know thus far ... SHAKESPEARE*: see Volume I, n. 1.
2. *Les femmes ... DE GRAMMONT*: see Volume I, n. 2.
3. *'The council ... it is a riot'*: Shakespeare, *The Merry Wives of Windsor*, I.i.35.
4. *'Sir Hugh ... matter of it'*: Shakespeare, *The Merry Wives of Windsor*, I.i.1–2.
5. *'To vouch this ... SHAKESPEARE*: Shakespeare, *Othello*, I.iii.107–10.
6. *like sister Anne in Bluebeard... castle turrets*: In 'The Blue Beard', one of the tales in Charles Perrault's *Contes des fees* (translated as *Histories, or Tales of Past Times*, 1729) the bride of Bluebeard, threatened with beheading by her husband after having disobeyed him, sends her sister Anne to the top of his castle tower to watch for the hoped-for arrival of her brothers.
7. *bouillon*: broth or soup (*OED*).
8. *a celebrated orator ... 'by act of parliament'*: Mr Daly most probably refers to Edmund Burke (1729/30–1797), the Irish-born Whig politician who became noted for his gifts of parliamentary rhetoric. The exact source of the reference to opposition to rule by act of parliament is unclear, but throughout his writings and speeches of the 1770s and 1780s Burke expressed concerns that legislation for security could be used in manners that in fact threatened the security of those it was designed to protect, and destroyed

trust between the members of communities, as in his 'Letter to the Sheriffs of Bristol [on the 'affairs of America]' (1777).

9. *The charge is prepared ... a terrible sight*: From the air sung by Macheath before his trial in John Gay, *The Beggar's Opera* (1728), III.i.

10. *wand*: here meaning a rod or staff of office, as carried by 'an official whose duty it is to walk before a judge or other high dignitary on occasions of ceremony' (*OED*).

11. *very Daniels*: alludes to Shylock's hailing of Portia, disguised as a doctor of laws, as 'A Daniel come to judgement,' in Shakespeare's *The Merchant of Venice*, IV.1.223. That speech itself alludes to the Jewish hero Daniel, remembered as a model of piety and judicial integrity in the Biblical Book of Daniel, and the apocryphal Book of Susanna. The quotation of Shylock's words as 'a very Daniel come to judgement' appears to have been commonplace in nineteenth-century literature.

12. *the Queen Catherine of the trial*: Rosbrin refers to the trial of Katherine of Aragon in Shakespeare's *Henry VIII*, II.iii, in which Katherine , whom Henry VIII wishes to divorce in order to marry Anne Boleyn, delivers an emotional speech testifying to her devotion to her husband.

13. *rug cloak*: a cloak made from rug, 'a kind of coarse woollen cloth, frequently of Irish manufacture' (*OED*).

14. *a volume of Hogarth*: apparently a book of engravings after the paintings of William Hogarth (1697–1764), whose works frequently satirized figures from contemporary social and political life, including lawyers.

15. *mail of brass, and heart of adamant*: quotation unidentified; though 'heart of adamant' was a commonplace expression signifying hardness of heart in the period, and 'mail of brass' may recall the references in Homer's *Iliad* to the brass mail armour worn by the warriors.

16. *Now then proceed ... the indictments*: a partial quotation, with paraphrasings, from Shakespeare, *The Winter's Tale*, III.ii.6–10.

17. without loss of time or hindrance of business: a standard formulation in legal and commercial discourse and texts in the period.

18. *ten times 'told tales'*: Aubrey adapts Shakespeare, *King John*, III.iv.108 ('Life is as tedious as a twice-told tale').

19. *Lord Mansfield*: Crawley refers to William Murray (1705–93), the Scottish-born judge created first Earl of Mansfield in 1776.

20. aula regis: 'royal court' (Latin).

21. *repertorium*: a repository, treasury (*OED*).

22. *Burn's Justice ... Paley's Evidences*: Boulter alludes to Richard Burn (1709–1785), *The Justice of the Peace, and Parish Officer* (1755); William Blackstone (1723–1780), *Commentaries on the Laws of England* (1765–9); *Registrum omnium brevium tam originalem quam judicalum* ('Digest of Original Briefs'), ed. W. Rastell (1687; first published 1531 as *Registrum omniu[m] brevium*), and William Paley (1743–1805), *A View of the Evidences of Christianity* (1794), a staunch defence of the Established Church.

23. *Saxon law ... game law*: 'Saxon law' refers to English law previous to the Norman Conquest in 1066. 'Brehon law' (from Irish *breitheamh*, judge) was the English name for the early Irish legal system, the earliest documents of which date from the seventh and eighth centuries AD, covering areas including injury, theft, and contracts. These laws remained in use in parts of Gaelic Ireland until the early seventeenth century. 'Game laws' were legislative acts for the preservation of qualified individuals' rights to raise and shoot game. In force from the late seventeenth century, they were renewed, with increasing sever-

ity, throughout the eighteenth and early nineteenth centuries. By 1817 armed poachers caught at night could be punishable by seven years' transportation.

24. *de facto*: 'as a matter of fact' (Latin), denoting something existing in fact (such as possession of a title or property), whether or not by right, as opposed to something existing *de jure*, by legal right.

25. *a pitcher ... broken at last*: A version of a French proverb dating from the early fourteenth century, and cautioning against pushing one's luck too far: 'tant va pot a eve qu'il brise' ('the pot goes so often to the water that it breaks').

26. *last sizes*: i.e. during the last assizes.

27. Tully's offices: *De officiis*, comprising three books on moral duties by the Roman lawyer and rhetorician Marcus Tullius Cicero (b. 106 BC), who was frequently referred to in English as 'Tully'.

28. *Tullus Aufidius*: In Shakespeare's *Coriolanus*, Tullus Aufidius is the Volscian general with whom Coriolanus forms an alliance, but who subsequently becomes his adversary.

29. carawat: i.e. *caravat*, a cravat, and the name for a member of one of the agrarian rebel organisations formed in the south of Ireland from the early 1800s; see also Volume 1, n. 243.

30. *if your father ... a* lucky one: In Laurence Sterne's novel *The Life and Opinions of Tristram Shandy Gentleman* (1759–67), the eponymous character's father believes that the 'characters and conduct' of individuals may be influenced by their parents' choice of names for them. It is by an accident that his own son is christened Tristram, the name for which Mr Shandy has 'the most unconquerable aversion'.

31. *the art of saving your bacon*: Recorded from the mid-seventeenth century, the English idiom 'to save [someone's] bacon' means to rescue them from danger or difficulty, 'bacon' (from Frankish *bako*) having been used to refer to meat from the sides of a pig in English since the twelfth century.

32. *I did* save *it*: *OED* dates the last recorded usage of the verb 'save' in the sense of preserving (a substance) to 1728.

33. *skelps*: skelp, 'to walk, or run rapidly; to hurry' (*OED*).

34. an abridgement of Bacon: The judge plays upon two contemporary sense of 'abridgement': a reduction in the magnitude or extent of something, and a digest or shortened version of a longer text (*OED*); and upon 'bacon' as the name for a form of pork meat, and of the philosopher and essayist Francis Bacon (1561–1626).

35. attic salt: 'Attic salt' here means 'refined wit'. Current in English from the mid-eighteenth century, the term was a translation of the Latin *sal Atticum* ('attic salt'). The word 'Attic' refers to the ancient Athenian dialect which became the principal literary form in classical Greece.

36. *'had you but* smoked ... *your bacon'*: The judge puns on the sense of 'smoke' as meaning to cure or preserve meat by exposure to smoke, with the other, then-current sense of the verb as meaning 'to suspect (a plot, design, etc) (*OED*).

37. *mittimus*: a warrant committing a person to prison, from Latin *mittimus*, 'we send' (*OED*).

38. *The ravings ... at Paris*: references to Oliver Cromwell's early political career as a councillor, and subsequently Member of Parliament, for Huntingdon; to the Neapolitan rebellion against Spanish rule, led by the former fisherman known as Masaniello, in July 1647; and to the *poissardes*, or 'fishwives' (French), the working-class Parisian women who led demonstrations during the early period of the French Revolution (*OED*).

39. *the Red Book or Debrett's Peerage*: The *Extraordinary Red Book: A List of All Places, Pensions, Sinecures, &c. With the Various Salaries and Emoluments Arising Therefrom* (London: J. Blacklock, 1816) entered several successive editions from its first publication. As well as being a directory of government-funded appointments, it was intended to expose the wastefulness of government expenditure in these areas. It author was identified only as 'A Commoner.' Debrett's Peerage was the regularly updated listing of all members of aristocratic families published by John Debrett from 1769; see Volume 2, n. 313.

40. *Knights of Kerry and Glin*: families descended from separate cadet branches of the Fitzgeralds of Desmond. The titles of Knights of Kerry, and Knights of Glin, are first recorded in the fifteenth century, but their origins are obscure.

41. *Yo Mateo ... de Dublin*: Conway Crawley has quoted from the letter of the Spanish Archbishop of Dublin, of 16 January 1601, to Florence MacCarthy Reagh in Thomas Stafford, *Pacata Hibernia; or, A History of the Wars in Ireland, During the Reign of Queen Elizabeth* (1633; Dublin: Hibernia-Press Company, 1810), pp. 300–1.

42. *Bonaparte or King Joseph*: After his invasion of Spain in 1808, Napoleon I placed his elder brother Joseph Bonaparte (1768–1844) on the Spanish throne. His reign lasted until the British liberation of Spain in 1813.

43. *viva voce*: 'out loud' (Latin); orally.

44. *extracts from the Pacata Hibernia of Robin Carew*: *Pacata Hibernia: Ireland Appeased and Reduced* (1633) was an account of the defeat of Hugh O'Neill, the second Earl of Tyrone's rebellion against Elizabeth I. It was compiled from the papers of George Carew (1555–1629), who served as provincial president of Munster 1600–3, by Thomas Stafford (d. 1655), who was believed to have been Carew's illegitimate son. Conway Crawley has quoted from the account of Florence Mac Carthy's investiture as the MacCarthy More in *Pacata Hibernia; or, A History of the Wars in Ireland, During the Reign of Queen Elizabeth* (1633; Dublin: Hibernia-Press Company, 1810), p. 289.

45. *a faithful account of the insurrection ... Queen Elizabeth*: On the role of Florence MacCarthy Reagh in the Gaelic earls' rebellion against Elizabeth I, see Volume 1, n. 384.

46. *the* painals*, (*penals*)*: O'Leary refers to the 'penal laws', discriminatory acts of legislation designed to discourage the growth of Roman Catholicism in Ireland, the first of which were passed in 1695. Under the penal laws, as these were successively passed throughout the late seventeenth and early eighteenth centuries, Roman Catholics were forbidden to bear arms; to travel abroad for education or to provide Catholic education in Ireland; to practise law; to vote (from 1728); to serve in the British army or navy; to inherit land from Protestants, or to take leases on land for longer than 31 years; while the landed properties of deceased Roman Catholic landowners were required to be divided equally between their heirs. The first Catholic Relief Acts for the repeal of such laws were passed in 1778, with further repeals following in 1782, and 1792–3, prior to full Catholic emancipation in 1829.

47. *Baron of the Exchequer*: a judge of the Court of Exchequer.

48. propter dignitatem: 'for the sake of the dignity' (Latin).

49. par exemple: 'for example' (French).

50. ennuyée: 'bored' (French).

51. *Terra Firma*: Literally 'solid ground' (Latin). A name for the northern coastland of South America (*OED*).

52. Crawley pere: i.e. Crawley *père*, 'the father' (French).

53. *this* bates Banacher: Apparently a variation of the common Irish saying, 'That beats Banagher' (sometimes responded to with 'and Banagher beats the world [or the Devil]'). The most likely source for this saying has been named as the town of Banagher, Co. Offaly, though its origins otherwise remain obscure. See E. Partridge, *A Dictionary of Catch Phrases From the Sixteenth Century to the Present Day*, 2nd edn, ed. P. Beale (London: Routledge and Kegan Paul, 1985), p. 40; and the *OED* entry for 'Banagher', in which the earliest cited instance of usage of the saying is from 1830.

54. *impannel*: i.e. empanel or impanel, enrol or constitute a body of jurors (*OED*).

55. *this* Pucelle de Bally-dab: this 'Virgin of Ballydab' (French). An allusion to the character Joan la Pucelle ('Joan the Virgin'), whose trial is a major episode in Shakespeare's *1 Henry IV*. La Pucelle is based on the historical (St) Joan of Arc (1412–31) as she is represented by Holinshed, who alleged that she offered herself to supernatural 'fiends' as part of her commitment to the French cause.

56. *Rare Egyptian, the serpent of old Nile*: alludes to Antony's nickname for Cleopatra, in Shakespeare's *Antony and Cleopatra*, I.v.24–6.

57. *fancy outworks nature*: adapted from *Antony and Cleopatra*, II.ii.208–9.

58. grand succés: 'great success' (French).

59. *the frais*: *faire les frais* is French for 'to bear the brunt', from *frais*, 'cost', 'expense/s', or 'effort'. Lady Dunore is saying that the pleasure of her assemblies was obtained at Lady Clancare's 'expense', she being the main contributor to it. Owenson had previously used the expression in this sense, and partly Anglicized, in two instances in *O'Donnel*, 4 vols (London: H. Colburn, 1814). The first is where the character Mr Vandaleur says, '"I rather patronize any one who makes the *frais* of conversation after dinner, and saves one the trouble of talking"' (see *O'Donnel*, Volume 1, p. 53); and the second where ' "the two Mr and three Miss Carlisles"' are said to have ' "made the whole *frais* of the night" ' with ' "comical tricks"' and other performances (see *O'Donnel*, vol. 2, p. 170).

60. tongue-tied simplicity: Shakespeare, *A Midsummer Night's Dream*, V.i.108.

61. *Having lost ... power breathed forth*: Shakespeare, *Antony and Cleopatra*, II.ii.237–40.

62. LIONS: famous persons, celebrities (*OED*); though the term was also applied in the period to any famous objects or curiosities (*OED*).

63. *Milesian ... the Tyrian Hercules*: Among proponents of the theory that Ireland had originally been populated by Spanish descendants of the Phoenicians, led by the mythical Míl Espáine, 'Milesian' denoted people of the purest native Irish blood. The ancient, southern Phoenician town of Tyre was the origin of many Phoenician settlers who founded colonies in regions further west, including Carthage. In *A Vindication of the Ancient History of Ireland* (Dublin: L. White, 1786), Charles Vallancey claimed that the 'Tyrian' Hercules (so called to distinguish him from the mythical Hercules of the twelve labours) founded one such Phoenician colony in Ireland; see p. iii.

64. *Anno Mundi, 1525, Noah Rex*: i.e. 'the year of the world 1525 [BC], in the reign of King Noah' (Latin).

65. *Anno Domini 1166, Hen. secundus Rex*: i.e.'the year of Our Lord 1166, [reign of] Henry II' (Latin).

66. *Johannes Major Scotus ... Sir Richard Musgrave*: As well as to the English, and Anglo-Irish-biased historians William Camden (1551–1623), Edward Ledwich (1738–1823), and Sir Richard Musgrave (*c.*1757–1818), O'Leary refers to the Scottish-born historian John Mair [or Major] (*c.* 1467–1550), who is cited by Meredith Hanmer as having doubted the theories that the Irish were descended from Greek or Egyptian colonies. See

M. Hanmer, *A Chronicle of Ireland* (1594), in *Ancient Irish Histories*, ed. J. Ware (1633; Dublin: Hibernia Press, 1809), vol. 2, p. 7.

67. *Saxo Grammaticus*: Saxo Grammaticus (1180–1208) was a Danish historian, author of the *Historia Danica*, composed during the first decade of the thirteenth century, which included an account of the Danes' settlement of Ireland. He advocated a theory that the Irish had been descended from ancient Saxon settlers who arrived there centuries before the Danish invasion of Ireland in the ninth century; see James Ware, *The Antiquities and History of Ireland* (Dublin: A. Crook., 1705), p. 57.

68. Ludi Magister: 'schoolmaster' (Latin).

69. dramatis personœ: i.e. *dramatis personae*, 'persons of the drama' (Latin).

70. *cabriolet*: a light, two-wheeled chaise drawn by one horse, with a large wooden or leather hood (*OED*).

71. *cashmir*: i.e. a cashmere shawl, made of the fine wool of the Cashmere goat and the wild goat of China (*OED*).

72. *Little changeling boy... thy fairy kingdom*: Shakespeare, *A Midsummer Night's Dream*, II.i.120–1; 144.

73. My gentle Puck, come hither: Shakespeare, *A Midsummer Night's Dream*, II.i.148.

74. nom de caresse: 'pet name' (French).

75. my fat lad of the castle: either a misquotation from, or a deliberate paraphrase of, Prince Henry's words to Falstaff in *1 Henry IV*, I.ii.34 (which has 'my old lad of the castle').

76. *the old woman ... the School for Scandal*: Roxalana is the spirited English inmate of a Sultan's harem in Isaac Bickerstaffe's comedy *The Sultan; or, A Peep into the Seraglio* (1775); Urganda is an enchantress in David Garrick and Michael Arne's 'dramatic romance' *Cymon* (1767); 'the screen scene' refers to a famous incident in R. B. Sheridan's comedy *The School for Scandal* (1777), IV.iii, where the discontented young bride Lady Teazle learns of her husband's fondness for her whilst hiding from him behind a screen in Joseph Surface's library.

77. rememberest thou ... at her song: Shakespeare, *A Midsummer Night's Dream*, II.i.147–52, with line-breaks omitted.

78. That very time ... the earth –: Shakespeare, *A Midsummer Night's Dream*, II.i.155–6.

79. A fool ... a motley fool: Shakespeare, *As You Like It*, II.vii.12–13.

80. *Lovers and madmen ... SHAKESPEARE*: Shakespeare, *A Midsummer Night's Dream* V. i. 4–6, slightly misquoted.

81. *What! shall ... IDEM.*: Shakespeare, *Much Ado About Nothing*, II.iii.260–2, misquoted.

82. Nolens Volens: *nolens*, unwilling; *volens*, willing (Latin); whether willing or not; 'willy-nilly' (*OED*).

83. *the lycanthropia ... ancient Irish*: In his account of Co. Tipperary in *Britannia*, William Camden noted a prevalent belief that its local inhabitants could change into wolves every year, and stated his own opinion that they were probably suffering from lycanthropy, a condition which caused those affected to experience delusions of being wolves.

84. *the Ogygia ... Abbé O'Gahegan*: See Volume II, n. 213.

85. *Lord-Deputy ... Lord-Lieutenant*: The name for the chief governor of Ireland was 'lord deputy' from the reign of Henry VII, until 1696, after which the title of 'lord lieutenant' was adopted.

86. *Turne quod ... attulit ultro*: Virgil, *Aeneid*, IX, 6–7 (' "Turne, quod optanti divum promittere nemo / auderet, volvenda dies en attulit ultro"') which lines translate as '"Turnus, what no god dared to promise to your prayers, see – the circling hour has brought

unasked!'" See *Aeneid VII-XII*, trans. H. Rushton Fairclough (Cambridge, MA: Harvard University Press, 2000).

87. *scraws*: growths of turf (*OED*).

88. *Martingaria ... the mighty Cordilleras*: 'Martingaria' appears to be intended to recall Isla Martin Garcia, an island off what is now the Uruguayan coast, near which William Brown (1777–1857), the Irish-born commander of a small, Argentine rebel fleet, achieved a decisive victory against Spanish royalist forces in March 1814. 'Cordilleras' probably refers to a chain of mountains in the Andes, one of several different groups of mountains given this name. See also Volume 1, n. 202.

89. *Comes not within the prospect of belief*: paraphrases, or misquotes, Shakespeare, *Macbeth*, I.iii.74.

90. *my Egeria or my dæmon*: According to Roman legend, Egeria was the water-nymph consulted for advice on statecraft and religion by Numa Pompilius, the second king of Rome. 'Daemon' appears here in the Greek mythological sense of a familiar, ministering spirit or 'genius' (*OED*).

91. *sphinx*: In Greek mythology, the sphinx was a creature with a lion's body and human head. In the Oedipus myth, a female sphinx at Thebes posed a riddle, killing those who failed to solve it. The word 'sphinx' was subsequently applied to any mysterious, inscrutable woman.

92. *petite maitresse-sphinx*: 'young-lady-sphinx' (French).

93. *thoughts that breathe, and words that burn*: from Thomas Gray, 'The Progress of Poesy. A Pindaric Ode,'110.

94. *Sou utile ainda que Briccando*: See Volume I, n. 442.

95. *Delphic oracles*: The cryptic prophecies issued by the priestess of the ancient Greek temple of Apollo at Delphi (see also Volume II, n. 211).

96. *I see Queen Mab has been with you*: Shakespeare, *Romeo and Juliet*, I.iv.53, where Mercutio imagines Romeo as having encountered the queen of the fairies.

97. *the illuminati ... concocted dew*: In the Dedication (to Arabella Fermor) which precedes *The Rape of the Lock* (1712), Alexander Pope cites the 'Rosicrucian doctrine of spirits', as expounded by the Abbé de Villars in *Le comte de Gabalis* (1670). According to Villars, the Rosicrucians (or brothers of the Rosy Cross; also known as the 'Illuminati'), a possibly mythical, European occultist society, posited that the four elements air, earth, water, and fire were inhabited respectively by sylphs, gnomes, nymphs, and salamanders.

98. *their 'Archæus,' or universal spirit*: the Archaeus, or Archeus, was the immaterial principle posited by the Swiss alchemist and physician Paracelsus [Philippus Aureolus Theophrastus Bombastus von Hohenheim] (1493–1541) as regulating the animal digestive, and other, organs. Much of Rosicrucian doctrine was derived from Paracelsus' mystical and alchemical theories.

99. *NUMA in his grotto, or SOCRATES in his cell*: According to Roman legend, Numa Pompilius, the second king of Rome (715–673 BC) held trysts in a grotto at the Porta Capena with Egeria, a water-nymph who inspired him with insights into statesmanship and religion. The Athenian philosopher Socrates (469–369 BC) was reported by both Plato and Xenophon to have believed that a *daimonion*, or 'divine sign' influenced his actions and decisions. He was imprisoned for refusing to worship the official Athenian gods. He was ultimately condemned to execution by self-administered poison, his last hours in his prison cell being famously described by Plato in his *Phaedo*.

100. shrewd ... Robin Goodfellow: Shakespeare, *A Midsummer Night's Dream*, II.i.33–4

101. *Over hill ... through fire*: Shakespeare, *A Midsummer Night's Dream*, II.i.2–5

102. bon gré, malgré!: *bon gré*, willingly; *mal gré*, unwillingly (French); willingly or not; 'willy-nilly'.

103. *éclat*: from *éclater*, to burst out (French); conspicuous success (*OED*).

104. *she has ... vasty deep*: Adapts Shakespeare's *1 Henry IV*, III.1.55, where Glendower says, 'I can call spirits from the vasty deep'.

105. the good people ... *Irish faéry*: Possibly among the earliest written instances of use of 'the good people' to denote fairies; *OED* examples of usage begin at 1810 (earlier instances refer to 'neighbours' or 'good neighbours').

106. bonne fortune: literally 'good fortune' (French); a thing to boast of (*OED*).

107. a world of spirits: Probably another reference to Pope's *The Rape of the Lock*, following from the previous allusions to the Rosicrucian ideas discussed by Pope in the dedicatory letter. In a note accompanying l. 108 of canto I ('In the clear mirror of thy ruling star'), Pope comments: 'The language of the Platonists, the writers of the intelligible world of spirits, etc.'

108. minaudiere: i.e. *minaudière*, an affected or coquettish woman (French; *OED*).

109. engouement: literally, 'obstruction in the throat' (French); in English usage, 'unreasoning fondness' (*OED*).

110. *this wild Irish peeress ... a London season*: Morgan here deliberately recalls her own experiences in Dublin and London society, following the success of *The Wild Irish Girl* in 1806, and previous to her marriage in 1812.

111. *the old Dutchess of G. ... a fiddle-string*: The source of this reference is unclear.

112. *fretted her hour ... heard no more*: Adapted from Shakespeare, *Macbeth*, V.iii.24–6.

113. réchauffee: i.e. *rechauffée*, 'reheated' (French); a 'reheating'.

114. *promptly cold affections*: source not identified.

115. engouemens: see Volume III, n. 109.

116. *Momentary as a sound ... short as any dream*: Shakespeare, *A Midsummer Night's Dream*, I.i.

117. *sweet, but not permanent*: A misquotation from Laertes' words to his sister Ophelia, on Hamlet's attentions to her, in Shakespeare's *Hamlet*, I.iii.7–8, where he advises her to regard Hamlet's 'trifling' as being like 'A violet in the youth of primy nature, / Forward, not permanent, sweet, not lasting'.

118. *Ronge de fiel et bouffi d'orguil*: Quoted from the description of the mean-spirited character Arimae in Voltaire's novel *Zadig: or, la destinée* (1747): 'Il était rongé de fiel et bouffi d'orgeuil' ('He was eaten up with venom and puffed up with pride').

119. *She dates from Castle Macarthy*: i.e. she dates her letter from Castle Macarthy.

120. *did not notice them*: i.e did not acknowledge, or speak to, them.

121. pleased ear: Possibly an allusion to Dryden, *Aureng-Zebe* (1675) IV.i, where Aureng-Zebe speaks of the pleasure to a woman of hearing her intended lover named by his rival ('Then, then, it ravishes, when your pleased ear / The sound does from a wretched rival hear').

122. à la francaise: 'in the French manner' (French); 'French-style'.

123. *bienseance*: decorum, propriety (French), from *bien*, well; and *séant*, befitting (French) (*OED*).

124. *night-tripping fairy*: Shakespeare, *1 Henry IV*, I.i.87.

125. pour s'egayer: 'to amuse herself' (French).

126. *the 'Guitarerie' ... Spain was in vogue*: The 'Guitarerie' is the term coined by Anthony Hamilton in Chapter 8 of *Mémoires de la vie du Maréchal de Gramont* (see Volume III, n. 1) to denote all the guitar-players at the court of Charles II, who all wanted to learn

to play a new sarabande introduced by an Italian visitor. The term was translated by Abel Boyer as 'Guitarery'; see *Memoirs of Count Grammont, by Count A. Hamilton. A new Translation, with Notes and Illustrations* (London: S. and E. Harding, 1794), p. 177. 'Tu mi chamas', meaning 'you call me' (Portugese), was the title (and opening words) of a song by the Portugese poet Luis Vaz de Camões (or Camoëns) (*c.* 1524–80). The piece was popularized among English-speaking readers by Percy Clinton S. Smythe, the sixth Earl of Strangford's *Poems from the Portugese of Camoens* (1803), with other English versions including two composed by George Gordon, Lord Byron under the title 'From the Portugese. Tu mi chamas'(1812). Spain would have been most 'in vogue' in English fashionable society during, and immediately after, the successful British campaign to liberate Spain from Napoleon (1808–14).

127. Et Dieu sait la raclerie que c'étoit: 'and God knows the strumming that it was' (French). This is a loose quotation from Anthony Hamilton's account of the guitar-playing craze at the court of Charles II, in his *Mémoires de la vie du Maréchal de Gramont* ('Dieu sait la raclerie universelle que c'était'), translated by Abel Boyer as 'God knows what an universal strumming there was'; see *Memoirs of Count Grammont, by Count A. Hamilton. A New Translation, with Notes and Illustrations* (London: S. and E. Harding, 1794), p. 177.

128. *Chinese puzzles*: originally, physical puzzles composed of sets of interlocking pieces for fitting together or disentangling; though the expression could be used figuratively to describe other types of puzzle or problem (*OED*).

129. *trophies*: originally, structures composed of objects such as enemy weapons, arranged and displayed to celebrate victories; here, drawings of collections of objects emblematizing, commemorating, or celebrating persons or events (*OED*).

130. tales, stories … *South America*: The themes of Lady Clancare's fictions mirror those of Owenson's own, in their concerns with nationhood both in Ireland and in other countries. By 1818, Owenson had produced not only the 'Irish' novels *St Clair* (1803), *The Wild Irish Girl* (1806), and *O'Donnel* (1814), but also *Woman; or Ida of Athens* (1809), which featured a Greek patriot heroine, and *The Missionary* (1811), set in India. *Florence Macarthy* could itself be regarded as Owenson's 'South American' counterpart to the fictional Lady Clancare's work on South America.

131. De tout mon cœur: 'with all my heart' (French); 'I quite agree'.

132. en tout et par tout, je quitte la partie: *en tout et partout, je quitte la partie,* 'in everything and everywhere, I leave the field' (French).

133. à porte fermée: literally 'with door closed' (French), apparently meaning 'behind closed doors'; in private'.

134. a peeress in her own right: the female inheritor of a peerage, when this passes down the female line of a family. Such a title would be retained in marriage.

135. *crier*: 'an officer in a court of justice who makes announcements' (*OED*).

136. *Paddy Mooney's goose*: The origin of this saying is not clear, and no earlier instance of it has been identified; though a nineteenth-century variation on it appears in the *Sporting Review* (1849), in which 'your Irish member of Tattersalls or St Stephen's [clubs]' is described as being 'like Paddy Mooney's goose – never quiet but when he's making a noise!'; see p. 162.

137. *basket boy*: either a boy who carries goods for sale in a basket (as *basket woman, OED*); or a boy who carries purchasers' goods from market for them in an empty basket kept for the purpose, as in Samuel Jackson Pratt's *Gleanings in England, Descriptive of the Countenance, Mind, and Character of the Country* (London: T. N. Longman and G. Rees, 1803), vol. 3, p. 459.

138. *the general attainder ... the Revolution*: The 'general attainder' is a term more usually applied to James II's 1689 attainting (confiscation of property and titles) of supporters of William III; though from 1690–1 William similarly instigated a policy of outlawing and attainting Irish Jacobites.

139. *RULE of BAIL*: the policy of requiring securities from detainees, for their keeping the peace, as a condition of their release; see Volume II, n. 13. The case described by Judge Aubrey is based on Owenson's own experience of intervening on behalf of a condemned prisoner; see Volume I, n. 256.

140. *patterns*: In Ireland at this period, 'pattern' (from 'patron') was 'a patron saint's day, or the festivities with which it is celebrated' (*OED*).

141. *burning* me *in* elegy: i.e. 'burning me in effigy'.

142. *thinking a* beau-maison *of himself*: *beau maison*, 'beautiful house' (French). Crawley appears to have meant to say *beau monsieur*, 'fine gentleman'.

143. *hurling matches*: Hurling is a traditional sport played in Ireland, similar to English hockey, with teams of players competing with curved sticks for possession of a ball.

144. *Their wakes ... Sunday evening cake*: Wakes were often raucous or licentious gatherings held following the deaths of family or community members. 'Sunday evening cake' refers to a rural Irish custom in which dancers competed on Sunday evenings to win a large cake, subscribed to by the local community and displayed on top of a pole. Owenson provided an account of this practice in *Patriotic Sketches of Ireland, Written in Connaught*, 2 vols (1807), vol. 2, pp. 99–100.

145. *the very grandfather ... between the counties*: Owenson would repeat a version of this story in her account of her paternal grandparents' courtship in her memoirs, reporting that they fell in love after her grandmother had watched her grandfather Walter MacOwen playing on the winning team in a local hurling match in Co. Connaught. See *Lady Morgan's Memoirs*, vol. 1, pp. 41–2.

146. *Don Narino*: The Colombian revolutionary Antonio Nariño (1769–1822) arrived in England during 1796, having escaped from the convict transport in which he had been sent to Spain for his involvement in publishing Thomas Paine's radical treatise *The Rights of Man* in Colombia. He then travelled, in disguise, to New Grenada, in order to further British plans to aid the independence movement. Having been apprehended by the Spanish royalist authorities, he was imprisoned for several years. Following his eventual release, he was re-arrested when the war of independence broke out in 1808, and sent to prison in Spain, where he remained in 1817. See M. P. Fajardo, *Outline of the Revolution in Spanish America* (London: Longman, Hurst, Rees, Orme, and Brown, 1817), pp. 118–19; J. Lynch, *The Spanish-American Revolutions 1808–1826* (London: Weidenfeld and Nicholson, 1973), p. xvii; and R. C. Heinowitz, *Spanish America and British Romanticism, 1777–1826: Rewriting Conquest* (Edinburgh: Edinburgh University Press, 2010), p. 89 n. 13.

147. *my gallant countrymen*: In her endnote (1), Owenson refers to three of the most prominent of the Irish-born, or Irish-descended participants in the South American liberation movements. Bernardo O'Higgins (1778–1842) was the illegitimate son of Ambrosio O' Higgins (1720–1801), the Irish-born, and Spanish-educated viceroy of Peru. He was educated firstly in Chile, and then (from 1795) at a private, Roman Catholic school in England. He was inspired to join the South American independence movement after meeting its foremost advocate, Francisco de Miranda (1750–1816) in London during the 1790s. From 1811, he served as a senior officer in the Chilean patriot army, being appointed its commander-in-chief in 1813. In 1817, he was elected supreme dictator

of Chile, and between 1817 and 1818 he instigated a succession of radical measures including the abolition of aristocratic titles, the confiscation of royalist property, and the jailing of royalist priests. He issued a formal proclamation of Chilean independence in the spring of 1818; see *The Times*, 6 June 1818. John [otherwise Juan] MacKenna (1771–1814) was born in Co. Tyrone, and was placed in military training in Spain by an uncle who was a general in the Spanish army. Promoted to the rank of lieutenant-colonel by 1796, he transferred in that year to Peru, where the viceroy Ambrosio O' Higgins appointed him military and civil governor of Osorno, Chile. In 1810 he became associated with the republicans led by José Miguel Carrera. After being appointed military governor of Santiago in 1813, he joined with Bernardo O'Higgins in ousting Carerra from the leadership of the republican army, and was subsequently appointed O'Higgins's second-in-command in the army. He died of a wound received in a duel with Carrera's brother Luís in 1814. William Brown (1777–1857), the first colonel-in-chief of the Argentine navy, was born in Foxford, Co. Mayo, and settled in Buenos Aires in 1811, having developed a career commanding British merchant vessels in the Atlantic. Having first been commissioned by the patriots to command a privateer against the Spanish, he took charge of a small rebel fleet of nineteen ships in 1814. In March of that year he split up the Spanish naval blockade when he defeated a much larger Spanish fleet near the island of Martin Garcia; and a further defeat of the Spanish in May that year resulted in the patriots' assumption of control over the Atlantic coast of Argentina.

148. *a pass of the Cordelliras*: No source for this fictional incident has been identified.
149. *Kosiusko ... in London:* The Polish patriot Tadeusz (or Thaddeus) Kosciuszko (1746–1817) served as a revolutionary general during the American War of Independence, before returning to Poland to promote the cause of Polish independence from Russia in 1784. He was exiled by the Russians for his involvement in the Polish nationalist uprising (1794–6), and subsequently settled in France. In 1796 he visited London, where he was welcomed enthusiastically by leading Whigs.
150. *raconter*: 'to tell [a story]'; 'to recount' (French).
151. *sautoir de cashmir*: 'cashmere stole' (French).
152. *sibyl-like*: recalling the mysterious figure of the Sibyl at Cumae, who in ancient Greek mythology could not die, and who issued prophecies.
153. *mantillo*: i.e. a mantilla, a light veil, usually of black lace, worn over the head and shoulders by Spanish women (*OED*), and made fashionable in Britain following the British liberation of Spain and Portugal from Napoleon in 1814.
154. *into the sear*: Alludes to Shakespeare, *Macbeth*, V.iii.22–3, where the jaded Macbeth says: 'my way of life / Is fall'n into the sear, the yellow leaf'.
155. *a war of extermination*: *Guerra a muerta*, 'war of death' (Spanish). The expression was used by Simon Bolívar in his proclamation of liberty in the province of Caraccas, on 6 July 1816, when he announced that 'The war of death, carried on against us by our enemies, on our side shall cease.' However, after the Spanish subsequently executed a group of South American patriots at Barinas, Bolívar adopted a retaliatory policy against Spain, following which the war in Spanish America continued to be known as the 'war of death'. Owenson's source of information on this and other aspects of the wars of independence in South America appears to have been *An Outline of the Revolution in Spanish America*, by 'A South American' (Manuel Palacio Fajardo) (London: Longman, Hurst, Rees, Orme, and Brown, 1817). Bolívar's 'war of death' is mentioned at p. 88, and his 1816 proclamation on p. 105.

156. *a race defined by one of the Spanish* FISCALS ... *like moles in the mines*: refers to the Spanish fiscals' refusal of a petition presented by the city of Merida de Maracaybo, Venezuela, requesting the establishment of a university. The fiscals explained that the petition was denied 'because *it was unsuitable to promote learning in Spanish America, where the inhabitants appeared destined by nature to work in the mines*'; see Fajardo, *Outline of the Revolution*, p. 20 (italics retained from original).

157. *the solemn declaration ... vice and ignorance*: In *An Outline of the Revolution in South America*, Manuel Palacio Fajardo explains: 'After a pretended solemn deliberation of the consulado or board of trade in Mexico, the members informed the cortes, that "*the Indians were a race of monkeys, filled with vice and ignorance, automatons, unworthy of representing or being represented*"'; see pp. 20–1 (italics retained from original).

158. *they have extended their remarks ... to the creoles*: see Fajardo, *Outline of the Revolution*, p. 21, where it is explained how the Spanish American creoles (people born in Spanish America, but of non-native descent) were largely excluded from holding public offices.

159. *the olive and the vine ... a commerce with the peninsula*: refers to the Spanish prohibition of the extraction of oils, the making of wines, or the planting of vines or almond trees in any Spanish American provinces except for Peru and Chile; see Fajardo, *Outline of the Revolution*, p. 22.

160. *the British government, in 1797 ... the spark of independence*: The British government had contemplated assisting the South American independence movements, as a means to gaining trading advantages, from the time of their emergence during the 1780s. In 1790, Francisco de Miranda had met with the Prime Minister William Pitt, to discuss his plan to establish for South America a British-style constitution, and government by upper and lower houses of parliament under the monarchy. In his *Outline of the Revolution in Spanish America* (1817), Manuel Palacio Fajardo refers to 1796–7 as 'the very epocha when Mr Pitt's plan for separating Terra Firma from the Spanish government was in contemplation'; see p. 118; and also p. 17.

161. *the expedition of the gallant Miranda to Venezuela*: The Venezuelan Creole revolutionary Francisco de Miranda (1750–1816) resided in London between 1790 and 1810, seeking assistance for the independence movement from the British government, which funded his ultimately unsuccessful expedition to Venezuela in 1806; see Manuel Palacio Fajardo, *Outline of the Revolution in Spanish America*, p. 19. In 1810 Miranda returned to South America, where he formed an association with Bolívar. He briefly held dictatorial powers in Venezuela from April 1812, but was defeated by royalist forces in July of that year, and died in prison in Cadiz in 1816.

162. *alcade*: 'a magistrate of a town, a sheriff or justice, in Spain or Portugal' (*OED*).

163. *the* SUDELGADO: i.e. the *sudelegado*, local government deputy (Spanish).

164. *the abridgement of the life of Columbus*: No specific example of such an abridgement has been identified, though one simplified account of Christopher Columbus's life available in the period was Elizabeth Helme (d. 1816), *Columbus; or The Discovery of America: As Related by a Father to his Children, and Designed for the Instruction of Youth* (London: J. Johnson, 1799). An English version of a German work by Joachim Heinrich Campe (1746–1818), it referred to the native South Americans as having practised cannibalism; see pp. 114–15. It was reprinted by C. Cradock and W. Joy in 1811 and 1818.

165. eau de luce: a preparation of alcohol, ammonia and oil of amber, used as smelling-salts (*OED*).

166. *early Britains ... human blood*: The practices of ritual sacrifices in all the cultures mentioned here are discussed by George Stanley Faber in book 2, ch. 8 in vol. 1 of *The Origin*

of Pagan Idolatry: Ascertained from Historical Testimony and Circumstantial Evidence , 3 vols. (London: F. and C. Rivington, 1816), pp. 465–96. This chapter directly follows that in which the 'origin and import of the worship of the serpent' is discussed, including the use of serpents in circular imagery of eternity previously mentioned by Lord Frederick (see Volume 2, n. 329).

167. *Jeptha ... his only daughter*: A reference to the Old Testament story of Jephthah, a judge of Israel who, in gratitude for a military victory, vowed to sacrifice the first living thing he encountered on his return home. He found himself compelled to sacrifice his daughter, after she came out to meet him 'with timbrels and with dances'. See Judges 11:30–40.

168. *Spain ... auto da fé*: The Spanish practice of the *auto da fé* was public execution by burning, as punishment for heresy; see also Volume 1, n. 159.

169. Ipigenie en Aulide: Lady Dunore refers to *Iphigénie en Aulide* ('Iphigenia in Aulis'), an opera by the German composer Christoph Willibald Gluck (1714–87). First performed in Paris in 1774, it was an adaptation of Jean Racine's dramatic version of Euripides's drama about the Greek king Agamemnon's sacrifice of his daughter Iphigenia at Aulis, in order to obtain a favourable wind to convey his fleet to Troy.

170. *their deluge of Coxcox*: In Aztec mythology, Coxcox and his wife were the only human beings to survive a great flood which destroyed the earth at the end of the 'age of water'. Owenson's source for this reference was probably the account of the deluge of Coxcox which appears in Alexander de Humboldt, *Researches Concerning the Institutions and Monuments of the Ancient Inhabitants of America*, trans. Helen Maria Williams, 2 vols (London: Longman, Hurst, Rees, Orme and Brown, 1814), vol. 2, pp. 23–4; 61–8. Substantial extracts from the same work (including the passages concerning Coxcox) also appeared in the *Monthly Magazine*, 38, pt 2, (1814), pp. 608–21.

171. grand cause: 'great cause' (French).

172. *negers*: negroes.

173. preux, pour fendre géant... sans leur parler de rien: Quoted from the passage in ch. 4 of Anthony Hamilton's *Mémoires de la vie du Maréchal de Gramont* (1713) describing the friendship of Grammont and Matta, his fellow army officer. Hamilton compares the two with the knights of chivalric romances, such as Amadis de Gaule, humorously noting that though they may not have jousted or killed giants, they possessed abilities in cards and dice that their predecessors did not. The passage quoted here is translated by Abel Boyer as follows: '[who only] knew how to cleave in twain giants, to break lances and to carry off fair damsels behind them on horseback without saying a single word to them'. See *Memoirs of Count Grammont, by Count A. Hamilton. A New Translation, with Notes and Illustrations* (London: S. and E. Harding, 1794), p. 30.

174. is Lisburn the MONTPELLIER ... *capital of Spain*: Crawley means Lisbon, capital of Portugal, not Spain; Lord Frederick is thinking of Lisburn, a town in northern Ireland.

175. *A stage ... mine a sad one*: Loosely quoted from Shakespeare, *The Merchant of Venice*, I.i.78–9 (which has 'where every man must play a part').

176. honey swa key molly panse, *as the French says*: Crawley means to say *honi soit qui mal y pense* 'shame on him who thinks ill of it', the motto of the Order of the Garter.

177. *nisus*: impulse, tendency (*OED*).

178. *There never yet ... tooth-ach patiently*: Misquotes Shakespeare, *Much Ado About Nothing*, V.i.35–6.

179. *Collin's Ode on the Passions*: Rosbrin has suggested a reading of *The Passions. An Ode for Music*, by the lyric poet William Collins (1721–59), published in his *Odes on Several*

Descriptive and Allegorical Subjects (1747). The poem evokes various personified 'passions,' or states of feeling, including fear, anger, melancholy and joy.

180. *better spared a better man*: Shakespeare, *1 Henry IV*, V.iv.104.

181. On crie à la scandale: i.e. *on crie au scandale!*, 'it's a scandal!' (French).

182. *had strutted his hour*: Alludes to the simile of life as 'a poor player, / That struts and frets his hour upon the stage, / And then is heard no more' in Shakespeare's *Macbeth*, V.iii.24–6.

183. illustre foiblesse: 'illustrious weakness' (French).

184. *cent. per cent.*: 'a hundred for every hundred; interest equal in amount to the principal' (*OED*).

185. *Sappho*: An allusion to the famous, ancient Greek woman poet Sappho; see Volume 2, n. 31.

186. *Are we your lady's keeper?*: An allusion to Genesis 3: 9, where, after Cain has murdered his brother Abel, God asks Cain where Abel is, and Cain replies, 'I know not. Am I my brother's keeper?'

187. god-sends: An ironical use of the term 'god-send', or 'godsend,' meaning a desirable thing received unexpectedly; see also Volume I, n. 72.

188. *let me not burst in ignorance*: Shakespeare, *Hamlet*, I.iv.46.

189. could a tale unfold: Shakespeare, *Hamlet*, I.v.15.

190. l'aimable sceleratesse: i.e. *l'aimable scélératesse*, 'the loveable villainy' (French).

191. pour trancher le mot: 'to cut it short' (French).

192. commerage: i.e. *commérage*, 'gossip' (French).

193. *Lips though lovely must still be fed*: Quotation untraced.

194. comme il faut: 'as they should be' (French).

195. à plaisir: 'at pleasure' (French).

196. *the little* sourds et muets *of the Abbè Sicard*: sourds et muets, 'deaf and dumb [ones]' (French). Lord Frederick refers to Roch-Ambroise Cucurron, abbé de Sicard (1742–1822), an eminent French educator of deaf children who succeeded Charles-Michel, abbé de l'Epée as principal of a school for deaf children in Paris. This school was made famous in *L'abbé de l'Epée*, a play by Jean Nicolas Bouilly (1763–1842), a highly successful English version of which by Thomas Holcroft (1745–1809) was first staged in 1801, with the title *Deaf and Dumb; or The Orphan Protected*.

197. impromptus à loisir: 'compositions made at leisure' (French).

198. *For I will tell ... MILTON*: Milton, *Comus*, ll. 43–5.

199. *a contre tems*: i.e. a *contretemps*, a 'slight disagreement' (French).

200. *billet*: 'A short informal letter', a 'note' (French; *OED*).

201. petite évaporée: 'little giddy one'; 'little birdbrain' (French).

202. *magic in the web of it*: Shakespeare, *Othello*, III.iv.70.

203. *a circular and spacious mandrae*: In her endnote (2), Owenson quotes from Edward Ledwich, *Antiquities of Ireland* (Dublin: A. Grueber, 1790), pp. 139–40.

204. *the cell of the* 'Subtil Archimago' ... *all Irish*: An allusion to the character of Archimago, an old hermit representing hypocrisy, in Spenser's *The Faerie Queene*, Book I, Canto II. Eighteenth-centiry critics who commented upon the extent to which Spenser's residence in Ireland informed his composition of *The Faeries Queene* included Thomas Warton, in *Observations on the Fairy Queen of Spenser*, 2nd edn, 2 vols (London: R. and J. Dodsley, 1762); see, for example, vol. 1, pp. 210–11.

205. *Far from resort ... after and before*: Quotations from Spenser, *The Faerie Queene*, Book I, Canto I, stanzas 34 and 35.

206. obedient slumbers: Pope, 'Eloisa to Abelard', p. 212.

207. Calabalero: 'cavalier' (Irish English; from Spanish *caballero*).

208. *Pacata Hibernia*: See Volume 3, n. 44.

209. *truckle*: i.e. truckle-bed, 'a low bed running on truckles or castors' (*OED*).

210. *whiskey ... the marrow from soaking*: O'Leary quotes loosely from Raphael Holinshed's account of Irish consumption of spirits in *Chronicles of England, Scotland and Ireland* (first published 1577), 6 vols (London: J. Johnson, 1808), vol. 6, p. 8. Holinshed comments that 'Aqaue vitae' 'drieth more, and also inflameth less than other hot confections doo'. The 'philosopher' is Theoricus, who, Holinshed writes, 'wrote a proper treatise of Aquae vitae, wherein he praiseth it to the ninth degree ... it sloweth age, it strengthenth youth ... it relisheth the heart, it lighteneth the mind, it quickeneth the spirits ... it keepeth ... the veines from crumpling, the bones from aking, & the marrow from soaking'.

211. *The young Lord Thomas Fitzmaurice ... to him by right:* The basic details of the story O'Leary goes on to relate about the restoration of Thomas Fitzmaurice (b. 1502) to his birthright are given by Charles Smith in *The Antient and Present State of the County of Kerry* (Dublin: printed for the author, 1756), p. 254.

212. *Ner longas invaluere moras*: Ovid, *Remedia Amoris*, 91– 2 ('Sero Medicina paratur; / Cum mala per longas invaluere moras'), 'too late is the medicine prepared, when the disease has gained strength by long delay'. See Ovid, *The Art of Love and Other Poems*, trans. J. H. Mozley, rev. G. P. Goold (Cambridge, MA: Harvard University Press, 2004).

213. *gossiping and fosterage ... statute of Kilkenny*: The statute of Kilkenny (1366) contained thirty-six clauses intended to counter Gaelic influence upon English colonial life in Ireland. Among customs it prohibited among the English colony was that of fostering, the placement of children in family homes other than their parents', for their upbringing, and education or training. In an agreement signed on 27 September 1572, Conor O'Brien (1535–81), third Earl of Thomond, promised Elizabeth I that he would not 'marry, gossoppe, or foster, contrary to the statute in that behoof provided, without the especial licence of the Lord Deputy or Governor for the time being'. For the text of this agreement, see J. Lodge, *The Peerage of Ireland*, rev. M. Archdall, 7 vols (Dublin: J. Moore, 1789), vol. 2, pp. 30–1 n.

214. *gossippred, or confraternity*: i.e. 'gossipred or compaternity', a usual formulation expressing the practice of fosterage in eighteenth-century texts; see James Ware, *The Antiquities and History of Ireland* (Dublin: A Crook, 1705), p. 378.

215. *ould Stanihurst ... Lib. p. 49*: This reference, and the quoted text, appears to be derived from James Ware, *The Antiquities of Ireland*, in *The Works of James Ware concerning Ireland Revised and Improved*, 3 vols (Dublin: 1739–46), vol. 2, p. 73 and n. *n*.

216. *Cambrensis ... the foster childre*: This reference and the quoted text appear to be derived from James Ware, *The Antiquities of Ireland*, in *The Works of James Ware concerning Ireland Revised and Improved*, 3 vols (Dublin: 1739–46), vol. 2, p. 73 and n. *o*.

217. *a great bruite*: bruite, 'report noised abroad, rumour' (*OED*).

218. drew the thread ... his argument: alludes to Shakespeare, *Love's Labour's Lost*, V.i.18–19.

219. my fitch: i.e. my fetch, a 'fetch' being 'the apparition, double, or wraith of a living person' (*OED*).

220. *anno 1321 ... the common cause*: This is apparently a reference to an alliance, formed by 1321, between Maurice fitz Thomas Fitzgerald (1293–1356), the first Earl of Desmond, and the Gaelic lord of Thomond, Brien Bán O'Brien (d. 1350), following Fitzgerald's

being given power over former Clare estates in Cork, and the resulting conflicts between Fitzgerald and both the king (Edward II) and the Dublin administration.

221. Ayphraim [*Ephraim*] *against Menasses ... the tribe of Judah*: The rival Israelite tribes of Ephraim and Manasseh were descended from the two sons of Joseph who originally bore those names; see Genesis 48. The Old Testament also tells of a King Manasseh of Judah, who incurred the wrath of God for his idol-worship and sacrifice of his son; see 2 Kings 21. O'Leary seems to have most in mind, however, Isaiah 9:21 ('Manasseh, Ephraim: and Ephraim, Manasseh: they together against Judah: for all this his [the Lord's] anger is not turned away, but his hand stretched out still').

222. *ecury*: i.e. equerry.

223. *runagates*: vagabonds (*OED*).

224. *Did not Thomyris ... bate[beat] Cyrus intirely [entirely]*: The story of the victory of Thomyris, Queen of the Massegetai (a Scythian people), over King Cyrus of Persia, was told in Herodotus's *History*, and referred to by Spenser in *A View of the Present State of Ireland*; see *Ancient Irish Histories*, ed. Ware (1809), vol. 1, p. 91.

225. *a testoon ... the asturiones*: A testoon was an old Spanish coin; see Volume 1, n. 397. 'Asturiones' (referring to the ancient Spanish region of Asturia) is the name of a horse believed to descend from a Spanish breed; see Volume 1, n. 376.

226. *living on dews and air ... as Anacreon says*: Ethereal, sensual imagery of 'dews' and 'air' features in many of the erotic Odes of Anacreon, a Greek lyric poet of the sixth century BC. His works were brought to prominence during this period in the popular translations by the Irish poet Thomas Moore (1779–1852).

227. pratie *grounds*: *pratie*, potato, from Irish *prate*, *préata*, *preáta*.

228. *the famed Illen [Ellen] Macarthy*: Ellen MacCarthy, daughter of the MacCarthy More, with whom Florence MacCarthy Reagh eloped; see Volume 1, n. 384.

229. Tom Loodles' rhymes ... *1576*: According to Edmund Campion's History of Ireland, a satirical work entitled 'Tom Loodles Ryme' was mentioned by Henry Sidney's 1570 speech to Parliament, in which he named it as having 'seditiously promoted' a 'pretended common-wealth'.

230. coshering: cosher, 'To chat in a friendly and familiar fashion' (*OED*; first recorded instance 1833).

231. verbatim et literatim: 'word for word and letter for letter' (Latin).

232. *in her poor ould castle*: In her endnote (3), Owenson quotes from Edward Ledwich, *Antiquities of Ireland* (Dublin: A Grueber, 1790), p. 267. The list of Irish kings' 'exactions' is derived from James Ware, *The Antiquities and History of Ireland* (Dublin: A Crook, 1705), pp. 32–3. It has not been possible to identify the 'ancient poet' mentioned as the source for this list.

233. *pantoufles*: slippers or loose shoes (*OED*).

234. *as the Saxon King John ... the native nobility of the land*: An account of Prince John's attendants' mockery of the Irish chieftains' dress and manners, based on the report of Giraldus Cambrensis, appears in Thomas Leland, *The History of Ireland from the Invasion of Henry II*, 3 vols (London: J. Nourse, 1773), vol. 1, p. 144. Mantles (long fringed cloaks), truises (or trowses, a form of breeches), glibbs (long locks of hair) and beards (grown only on the upper lip by the pre-Elizabethan Gaelic Irish) are all noted as features of traditional Irish dress by James Ware in *The Antiquities and History of Ireland* (Dublin: A Crook, 1705); see pp. 6 (glibbs), 19 (beards) and 31 ('Trowses' and mantles).

235. *raparee*: Originally an Irish pikeman or irregular soldier, the term having been applied especially to those fighting for the Jacobites, against William of Orange in 1689–91; and subsequently used in the general sense of 'an Irish bandit, robber, or freebooter' (*OED*).

236. *drifty*: wily. The only instance of usage in this sense cited in *OED* is from Edmund Campion's *History of Ireland*.

237. *the great ould earl of Kildare ... the cathedral church of Cashell*: Gerald Fitzgerald (1456/7–1513), eighth Earl of Kildare, was reported to have burned down the cathedral at Cashell, Co. Tipperary in 1495, and then to have joked, when charged with this offence in 1501, that he would not have done so had he not believed that his adversary, the archbishop David Creagh (*c.* 1450–1503) was inside. Owenson has O'Leary quote from the account of this incident in Edmund Campion's *History of Ireland*; see Ware (ed.), *Ancient Irish Histories* (1809), vol. 1, p. 158.

238. most sweet voices: Shakespeare, *Coriolanus*, II.vii.

239. *Even so ... WORDSWORTH*: lines from William Wordsworth, 'Characteristics of a Child Three Years Old'.

240. *There stand ... SHAKESPEARE*: Shakespeare, *The Tempest*, V.i.65–6.

241. *EL DORADO*: 'the golden one' (Spanish); the name of the mythical city of gold believed by Spanish colonists in South America to lie in the continent's interior, on the basis of their partial understanding of stories told by the native peoples. Sir Walter Raleigh (1554–1618) was among explorers who mounted expeditions to locate it.

242. *Kilmallock in the same province*: Kilmallock is a small town in Co. Limerick. In her endnote (4), Owenson apparently draws upon T. Campbell, *A Philosophical Survey in the South of Ireland, In a Series of Letters to John Watkinson, M. D.* (London: W. Strahan and T. Cadell, 1777), pp. 211–14, which mentions the extreme poverty of Kilmallock; its returning two Members of Parliament, and its thirteenth-century Dominican abbey, and refers to it as 'the Irish Balbeck' on account of its spectacular ruins; and John Ferrar, *The History of Limerick: Ecclesiastical, Civil, and Military, From the Earliest Records to the Year 1787* (Limerick: A. Watson, 1787), p. 441, where it is remarked that 'Kilmallock makes a conspicuous figure in the military history of Ireland'.

243. *ballium ... and crenelles*: ballium, 'defensive wall of a castle' (*OED*); barbican, 'outer fortification to a city or castle' (*OED*); parapet, 'defence of earth or stone to conceal troops from the enemy's observation or fire' (*OED*); embrasure, 'a opening [in a wall] widening from within [...] for the purpose of allowing a gun to be fired through it' (*OED*); crenelle, 'one of the open spaces or indentations [...] of an embattled parapet, used for shooting or launching projectiles upon the enemy' (*OED*).

244. *A wolf's head ... bearing date 1710*: the last rewards for the killing of wolves in Ireland were claimed in Cork and Kerry in 1710; see vol. 1, n. 342.

245. *work of Irish nuns ... many Irish castles*: In her endnote (5), Owenson appears to draw upon Edward Ledwich, 'The History and Antiquities of Irishtown and Kilkenny,' *Collecteana de Rebus Hibernicus* V, no. ix (1786), p. 450, where 'Lady Anne's Bed Chamber' is described as being 'hung with tapestry, made by nuns'. It is stated in an article in the *Gentleman's Magazine*, 71, pt 1 (1801), however, that at least one of the tapestries at Kilkenny Castle, 'representing the history of the Spanish monarchy,' was 'executed by the fair hands of Spanish nuns'; see p. 21.

246. *DONAGH MACARTHY ... ME FECIT*: 'Donough Macarthy, Earl of Clancare made me' (Latin). In *The Ancient and Present State of the County and City of Cork*, 2nd edn, 2 vols (Dublin: s.n., 1774), Charles Smith describes a similarly inscribed, twelfth-century

chimneypiece discovered at Castle Lyons, with the name 'Lehan O-Cullane'; see vol. 1, p. 157.

247. *japan chest*: Either an item of furniture treated with 'japan,' a hard, black varnish (*OED*); or one decorated with 'japan work,' varnished figures in a Japanese style (*OED*).

248. Hanmer's Chronicle ... Campion's History of Ireland: See Volume 1, n. 141.

249. *Lopez de Vega, Burn's poems*: Lope Félix de Vega Carpio (1562–1635) was a Spanish poet and dramatist, who was involved in the battle of the Spanish Armada with the English in 1588. As well as being a prolific dramatist, he was noted as an author of amatory verses. The Scottish poet Robert Burns (1759–96) also owed much of his popularity to his love lyrics; while both he and Lope de Vega also expressed strongly patriotic sentiments in their writings.

250. gout musqué: literally 'musky taste' (French), usually applied to wines, but here apparently meaning a 'fragrant', or rarefied taste.

251. *that magnificent chieftain* (6): In her endnote (6) – there is no (7) – Owenson quotes at length from Charles Smith, *The Ancient and Present State of the County of Kerry*, pp. 27–30.

252. *fauteuil*: armchair (French).

253. '*outward seeming*': Source unidentified.

254. *the field of Cannæ*: Cannae was the village in Apulia, southern Italy, where the Romans were heavily defeated by Hannibal and the Carthaginians in 216 BC. Carthage was originally one of the colonies settled by former inhabitants of the Phoenician town of Tyre; see Volume III, n. 1.

255. *the country of Cadmus ... all Dr. Ledwich has said to the contrary*: In Greek mythology, Cadmus was the son of King Agenor of Tyre, and founded the city of Thebes in Boetia. He was also said to have taught the Boetians to write using the Phoenician alphabet. In a discussion generally rejecting the 'Phoenician' theory of the origin of Irish language in *Antiquities of Ireland* (Dublin: A. Grueber, 1790), Ledwich dismissed a suggestion in Roderic O'Flaherty's *Ogygia* (see Volume 2, n. 213) that this Cadmus was the same figure as the Phoenician ('Phenisius') who had brought written language to Ireland; see p. 80.

256. *our family hero* (7): In her endnote (6), Owenson quotes at length from Charles Smith, *The Ancient and Present State of the County of Kerry*, pp. 27–30.

257. In questa mano ... e mille: These lines are quoted, with some errors either in transcription or printing, from the 1736 libretto *Achille in Sciro* ('Achilles in Skyros') by Pietro Mestastasio (1698–1782), set as an opera by Antonio Caldara (1670–1736). The opera is based on an episode from Greek myth in which Achilles, sent by his mother to live in the palace of King Lycomedes of Skyros, in female disguise, in order to avoid the perils of the war in Troy, is persuaded by Ulysses to reject this scheme and fulfil his destiny as a warrior. The original passage, in II.viii, runs as follows: 'in questa mano / Lampeggi il ferro. Ah rincomincio adesso / A ravvisar me stesso. Ah fossi a fronte / A mille squadre e mille!' It was translated, with embellishments, by John Hoole, as: 'This hand debas'd / Shall wield ... the gleaming sword. / Ah! now I feel, / I know myself Achilles – Lead me, Gods! / To meet the glorious labour of the field, / And dare with single force a thousand foes.' See *Dramas and Other Poems of the Abbé Pietro Metastasio*, 3 vols (London: Otridge and Son, 1800), vol. 2, p. 51 (where it also appears as part of II. ix, not II. viii). Wendy Heller translates the lines more accurately as: 'In this hand / The sword flashes. I begin now / To recognise myself. Ah, if there were only before me / A squadron of thousands

upon thousands.' See Wendy Heller, 'Reforming Achilles: Gender, "opera seria" and the Rhetoric of the Enlightened Hero,' *Early Music*, 26:4 (1998), pp. 562–81.

258. *that chartered libertine*: Shakespeare, *Henry V*, I.i.48, referring to the element of air.

259. *For aye ... fruitless moon*: Shakespeare, *A Midsummer Night's Dream*, I.i.71–3.

260. de par l'eglise: i.e. *de par l'église*, 'of the Church' (French).

261. *When this you see ... we may be*: 'When this you see, remember me' apparently a common motto featuring on personal items presented as gifts in the period.

262. *an Hebe's smiles*: In Greek mythology, Hebe was the youthful daughter and waiting-maid of Zeus and Hera, the king and queen of the Olympian gods.

263. one out of sorts ... *inseparable*: Lady Clancare alludes to Celia's account of her intimacy with her cousin Rosalind in Shakespeare's *As You Like It*, I.ii.263; and I.iii.76–9.

264. .Val chiusa: 'enclosed valley' (Italian).

265. *kaleidoscope*: The kaleidoscope had been invented in 1817 by David Brewster (1781–1868), an expert in optics, who also coined its name from the Greek words *kalos*, 'beautiful', and *skopein*, 'to look at'. It consisted of a metal tube with panels of glass inserted along its length, and fragments of glass placed at one end, which created intricate, symmetrical patterns when reflected in the glass panels, as the tube was turned by a user looking into its other end. By the spring of 1818, the kaleidoscope had become a fashionable craze. Brewster described his invention in *A Treatise on the Kaleidoscope* (Edinburgh: A. Constable, 1819).

266. to 'con wit by rote': Apparently an inaccurate quotation from Dryden, *Troilus and Cressida: or, Truth Found Too Late* (1679), II.iii, where Ulysses imagines the companions of Thersites at a feast ('Why they con Sense from him, grow Wits by rote').

267. *desennuyer la sottise*: 'to divert foolishness'.

268. *Drizzling day ... cowslips blow*: lines from William Shenstone, Elegy XI ('He complains how soon the pleasing novelty of life is over').

269. *that hatred, 'all blockheads bear to wit'*: Source of quotation unidentified.

270. little senate laws: From Pope's Prologue to Joseph Addison's tragedy *Cato* (1713), l. 23.

271. *the Cato and Lycurgus*: Lady Clancare alludes to Marcus Porcius Cato [Cato the Younger] (95–46 BC), the Roman republican statesman who committed suicide rather than submit to the dictatorship of Julius Caesar, and on whose life Addison's tragedy *Cato* (1713) was based (see Volume 3, n. 271); and, probably, Lycurgus (fl. 625 BC), a Spartan statesman traditionally credited with establishing the laws of his state, as mentioned in accounts by Herodotus and Plutarch. 'Lycurgus' may also, however, refer to the Athenian statesman Lycurgus (*c*. 390–*c*. 325/4 BC), who was especially concerned with the management of the city's finances, and with the prosecution of corrupt government practices.

272. *the Chinese shrub ... white in the shade*: Possibly a reference to the hortensia, or round-headed hydrangea (*hydrangea hortensis*), which was introduced to England from China during the eighteenth century; see J. Kilpatrick, *Gifts from the Gardens of China* (London; Frances Lincoln, 2007), pp. 101–2. This may be the same plant as one described as having blossoms that may change colour from white to red, and referred to as a 'Chinese rose', or 'hortensia', by John Baptiste Joseph Breton in *China: Its Costume, Arts, Manufactures, &c.*, 4 vols (London: W. Lewis, 1812), vol. 3, pp. 45–8. Another Chinese plant possibly referred to here is the camellia (*camellia japonica*), previously white-blossomed specimens of which may produce red blossoms, due to a mutation; see Kilpatrick, p. 57.

273. *finders*: dogs trained to locate and retrieve game that has been shot; or to track game animals (*OED*).

274. *conundrums ... my* tout: riddles in the forms of questions the answer to which involves a pun or play on words (*OED*); hence the name of the parlour game in which players compose and solve such riddles, by identifying syllables ('my first, my second,' etc), and progressing to the whole word (*tout*, from French 'all').

275. *Carolan's famous 'Receipt for Drinking':* a popular instrumental piece by the Irish composer and harpist Turlough O'Carolan (1670–1738).

276. *when* Carte *got lave* [*leave*] *... three* Irish cars *with them*: In the Preface to his *History of the Life of James Duke of Ormonde*, Thomas Carte reported: 'I found in the Evidence-Room at Kilkenny about fourteen wicker binns ... covered with unwieldy [*sic*] books of Stewards accompts; but which upon examination appeared to be full of papers ... There being no bookbinder at Kilkenny, I was forced to transport these on three Irish carrs to Dublin'. See Thomas Carte, *An History of the Life of James Duke of Ormonde, from his Birth in 1610, to his death in 1688*, 3 vols (London: J. Bettenham, 1735–36), vol. 1, p. ii.

Volume IV

1. *Know thus far ... SHAKESPEARE*: see Volume I, n. 1.

2. *Les femmes ... DE GRAMMONT*: see Volume I, n. 2.

3. *He seems ... SHAKESPEARE:* Shakespeare, *As You Like It*, III.ii.388–9.

4. *I'll venture ... MILTON*: Milton, *Comus*, 289–90.

5. *head and front*: Shakespeare, *Othello*, I.iii.80.

6. *the Egeria, the demon*: i.e. the inspirational nymph (after the mythical Egeria), or familiar spirit; see Volume 3, n. 90.

7. *embroglio*: see Volume 1, n. 346. This is the first recorded instance of English usage in *OED*.

8. *most willing spirits to do her service*: an allusion to Shakespeare's *Cymbeline*, IV.ii. 338–9 ('most willing spirits, / That promise noble service').

9. *do her bequests*: Source of quotation untraced.

10. *the* pretenders *of the* Hotel Rambouillet: The Hôtel de Rambouillet was the Paris home of Catherine de Vivonne, Marquise de Rambouillet (1588–1665), who established a famous literary *salon* there. The Marquise's enthusiasm for philosophical conversation, and the cultivation of refined tastes, was satirized by Molière in his comedy *Les Précieuses Ridicules* (1659).

11. *Mad Tom*: Rosbrin is probably performing the speeches of Edgar in Shakespeare's *King Lear*, when in the disguise of a madman; see II.ii and III.iv. In these scenes, Edgar refers to himself as 'poor Tom,' though he is described as 'poor mad Tom' by the Old Man at IV.i.27.

12. du plus beau noir: 'of the blackest hue' (French).

13. *her delphic deity*: Lady Dunore is compared with the priestess of Apollo at Delphi, who uttered prophecies from the god in an entranced state of divine inspiration; see also Volume II, n. 211.

14. *our Irish secretary*: The post of chief secretary for Ireland had originated in the seventeenth century, when the role involved simply acting as an assistant to the lord deputy (or lord lieutenant). By the nineteenth century, however, it was one of the highest-ranking posts in the Irish vice-regal administration, with the main function of a chief secretary being to expound government policy regarding Ireland in parliament. Robert Peel (1788–1850) left office as chief secretary for Ireland in August 1818, having held the post from May 1812. His tenure had been characterised by consistent opposition to

Catholic relief, and the rigorous enforcement of law and order in Ireland through such measures as the Peace Preservation Act (1814). Peel was succeeded as chief secretary by Charles Grant (1778–1866), the first Tory supporter of Catholic emancipation to hold the post.

15. *the premier*: The Premier, or prime minister, of Great Britain at the time of the publication of *Florence Macarthy* in 1818 was Robert Banks Jefferson, second Earl of Liverpool (1770–1828), who held the office from 1812 until 1827.

16. *young Roscius ... musical children*: The 'Young Roscius' was the boy actor William Henry West Betty (see Volume 2, n. 296). 'Boy that told the sums' probably refers to Zerah Colburn (1804–40), an American boy able to calculate large arithmetical sums mentally, who performed to audiences throughout Britain during 1812–16. He later authored *A Memoir of Zerah Colburn: Written by Himself* (Springfield, IL: G. and C. Merriam, 1833). He was also remarkable for having one extra digit on each of his hands and feet, a characteristic shared by other members of his family; see Anthony Carlisle, 'Account of a Family having Hands and Feet with Supernumerary Fingers and Toes', *Monthly Magazine*, 38 (1814), pp. 154–6. No 'musical children' exposed for learning pieces 'by rote' have been identified, though many children were presented as 'prodigies' in various musical instruments in Britain during the early 1800s, including 'Masters G. and J. Ribbon', violinists aged seven and eight; and 'the two Misses Cawse', aged eight and eleven (see *Royal Cornwall Gazette*, 22 June 1816 [Ribbons]; *Morning Chronicle*, 3 April 1820 [Cawses]).

17. Lady-Lieutenant's ... *a tabinet gown on St Patrick's night*: Tabinet was 'a watered fabric of silk and wool resembling poplin; chiefly associated with Ireland' (*OED*). The lady-lieutenant's imagined choice of dress is here linked with the long-standing, eighteenth and nineteenth-century movements for the encouragements of native manufactures and other industry in Ireland. 'St Patrick's night' refers to the feast of St Patrick, Ireland's patron saint, which has traditionally always been observed on 17 March; see also Volume 1, n. 399.

18. kettle-drums ... *Noodle and Doodle*: Lady Dunore alludes to Henry Fielding's parodic drama *The Tragedy of Tragedies, or The Life and Death of Tom Thumb the Great* (1730), in which King Arthur tells his daughter, the Princess Huncamunca, that Tom Thumb, whom he intends she should marry, is 'A husband ... Whose valour, wisdom, virtue make a noise / Great as the kettle-drums of twenty armies' (II.iv). In the scene following, Lord Grizzle compares Huncamunca's 'pouting breasts' to 'kettle-drums of brass' (II.v.). Noodle and Doodle are characters in the same play, being attendants at Arthur's court.

19. *the Irish Balbec*: The ancient city of Balbec, or Baalbek (formerly Heliopolis), Lebanon, was famed for its imposing temple ruins, which ranked among the seven 'Wonders' of the ancient world. During the eighteenth century it became a popular destination for Western antiquarian tourists. The Irish town of Kilmallock, Co. Limerick, became known in the late eighteenth century as the 'Irish Balbec' on account of its own high concentration of picturesque ruins; see Volume 3, n. 242.

20. *Then shall we ... with our heels*: an allusion to Shakespeare, *Romeo and Juliet*, I. iv. 35–6 ('let wantons, light of heart, / Tickle the senseless rushes with their heels').

21. *mal-apropos*: 'inopportune'; 'inappropriate' (French).

22. *in wholesome manner*: An allusion to Shakespeare, *Coriolanus*, II.iii.64–5, where Menenius says to Coriolanus, 'Pray you, speak to 'em [the Citizens], I pray you, / In wholesome manner', from which lines Lord Adelm continues in his next quotation from the same play (see Volume 4, n. 23).

23. I bid them ... no further: Adapted from Shakespeare, *Coriolanus*, II.iii.67–8.

24. *Your voices ... some less*: Shakespeare, *Coriolanus*, II.iii.125–9.

25. *He has done nobly... God save the noble consul*: Rosbrin quotes (partially) from the speeches of the Fifth and Sixth Citizens, and 'All [Citizens]' in Shakespeare, *Coriolanus* II. iii. 139–45.

26. *exeunt O. P.*: i. e. *exeunt omnes personae*, 'exit all persons' (Latin). In Shakespeare's *Coriolanus* II. iii, all the 'Citizens' are directed to leave the stage after line 145 ('God save thee, noble counsel!'). With his reference to the 'Covent Garden promptbook' for the play, Rosbrin indicates that he has in mind an edition of the play prepared for use in particular performances at the Covent Garden Theatre, London. Such texts were often published to accompany stagings of the performances based on them. Between September 1803 and June 1817, performance texts of Shakespeare's plays were prepared for use at Covent Garden by John Philip Kemble (1757–1823), who managed the theatre during that period, as well as appearing there in leading roles. See C. H. Shattuck, 'General Introduction,' *The John Philip Kemble Promptbooks*, ed. C. H. Shattuck, 11 vols (Charlottesville, VA: University Press of Virginia, 1974), vol. 1, pp. ix–xxi; esp. pp. xiii–xviii.

27. yellow buttons and peacock's feathers: Lord Frederick recurs to his reimagining of the viceregal administration as Chinese mandarins. On the system of identification of mandarins' ranks by the colours of the buttons on their hats, and by decoration with peacocks' tail-feathers, see Volume 2, nn. 255, 423.

28. *the imperial Arctic Dandy ... a French* Schneider: 'the imperial Arctic Dandy' refers to Tsar Alexander I of Russia (1777–1825; reigned 1801–25). *Schneider*, 'tailor' (German).

29. *Her body sleeps... with angels lives*: Shakespeare, *Romeo and Juliet*, V.i.18–19, where Balthahasar tells Romeo of the drugged Juliet's apparent death, and her burial in the Capulet family vault.

30. *Marchesa*: 'marchioness' (Italian).

31. *the castle of* Le bois dormant: a reference to the castle inhabited by the princess heroine, around which a wood forms during her hundred years' sleep, in Charles Perrault's fairy tale 'La belle au bois dormant' ('The Sleeping Beauty in the Wood'), in *Contes du temps passé de ma mère l'Oye* (title translated in English as 'Histories; or Tales of Past Times', 1729).

32. *chateau*: 'castle' (French).

33. *fast asleep ... the Sleeping Beauty*: In Perrault's version of the 'Sleeping Beauty' story ('La belle au bois dormant'), the narrator observes that the style of the princess's dress has passed out of fashion during her sleep ('she was intirely dress'd, and very magnificently, but they took care not to tell her, that she was drest like my great grandmother'). See *Histories, or Tales of past Times* (London: J. Pote, 1729), p. 47. No reference is made to the clothes of the courtiers, though they also have slept for a hundred years.

34. aux muets entreprétes: 'to mute actors'; to actors in non-speaking roles (French).

35. par parenthese: 'incidentally'; 'by the way' (French).

36. *bring us out in hot-press*: Lord Frederick refers to the 'hot press' paper-finishing process developed by the printer John Baskerville (1706–75), who from the 1750s developed a method of creating a smooth finish on printed sheets by pressing them between copper sheets (some accounts mention use of copper rollers). The first instance of usage of 'hot-press' to denote printed works produced in this form recorded in the *OED* is from 1807.

37. sans dire gar: 'without telling anyone' (French).

38. tomes of absurdity ... pseudo Lady Clancare: Crawley's speech contains words and phrases from the review of Owenson's previous published work, *France* (1817), in the

Quarterly Review, 17 (April 1817), pp. 260–86. In this review, she had been accused of 'vagueness, bombast, and affectation'; of 'daring blasphemy' and of 'Bad Taste – Bombast and Nonsense – Blunders ... General Ignorance – Jacobinism – Falsehood –Licentiousness, and Impiety'. Three of her earlier novels (*Woman*, *The Missionary*, and *O'Donnel*) were referred to as 'tomes of absurdity'. See pp. 260, 285, 264, 261.

39. pour le moins: 'at the least' (French).

40. mere bookseller's drudge ... *audacious worm*: In the review of *France* in the *Quarterly Review* 17 (April 1817), pp. 260–86, it was asserted that 'the sylphid Miss Owenson, the elegant Lady Morgan, is in fact a mere bookseller's drudge', who had written *France* under contract. She was also accused of a '*lie* by implication' in claiming to have almost been arrested in France; and of committing 'the falsehood of falsehoods, the old and impudent one ... that England has been guilty of treachery and bad faith in her treatment of Buonaparte'. It was in the reviewer's discussion of her alleged blasphemies that Morgan was attacked for 'impious jargon,' and referred to as 'this audacious worm' and 'this mad woman'. See pp. 263, 280, 284.

41. *a celebrated periodical review*: intended to recall the *Quarterly Review*, the Tory-sympathising literary and political review established by John Wilson Croker and others in 1809.

42. bouquet d'adieu: 'parting gift' (French).

43. La solitude est une belle chose: 'solitude is a beautiful thing' (French). Quoted, with slight variation, from Jean-Louis Guez de Balzac (1597–1654), *Les Entretiens de Feu Monsieur de Balzac* ['Conversations of the Late Monsieur de Balzac'] (Amsterdam: Louys et D. Elsevier, 1663), p. 62 (which has 'certainement une belle chose', 'certainly a beautiful thing').

44. petit comité: 'little group' (French).

45. Ma Reine: 'my queen' (French).

46. *Chinese hieroglyphics ... their mouths*: Images of serpents, or dragons, biting their own tails, and symbolizing temporal eternity, occur in the texts and artworks of many ancient civilizations, including those of China. The use of such emblems in different cultures had recently been discussed in detail by G. S. Faber in *The Origin of Pagan Idolatry Ascertained from Historical Testimony*, 3 vols (London: F. and C. Rivington, 1816), vol. 1; see especially pp. 194, 440, 461.

47. *ennuies*: 'bores', from *ennuyer*, 'to bore' (French).

48. inconsequence: 'inconsistency'; 'fecklessness' (French).

49. Cynthea of the minute: alludes to Pope, *Moral Essays*, Epistle II ('On the Characters of Women'), ll. 19–20. These lines were also cited by Owenson in *O'Donnel* (1814), vol. 3, p. 95.

50. *diamond beetle*: i.e. *Curculio imperialis*, an insect with striking, iridescent wing-cases, originating in South America, and described in numerous natural-historical texts of the period.

51. *N.B.*: for *Nota Bene*, 'note well' (Latin).

52. *a quiz*: 'a person whose appearance is peculiar or ridiculous' (*OED*).

53. à trait de plume: 'with a pen-stroke' (French); in a sketch.

54. pendant: (French) one of two matching or corresponding items such as pictures.

55. *China oranges*: The China, or sweet, orange (*Citrus aurentium*) was originally obtained from China, and came to be referred to in the period as 'a typical object of trifling value' (*OED*).

56. piquée au jeu: 'caught up in the game' (French).

57. *the Red Book*: A regularly-updated publication listing government-funded appointments and pensions; see Volume 3, n. 39.

58. *the nobs on coronets*: i.e. the 'knobs' on coronets, the small, rounded tips of the points of the coronets traditionally worn in the ceremonial dress of British peers.

59. *the Cockney vocabulary of Bow-bell*: Traditionally, 'Cockneys', and thus speakers of the Cockney accent being mimicked here by Lady Clancare, were those Londoners born within range of the sound of the church bell at St Mary-le-Bow (or 'Bow Church'), Cheapside (see 'Bow-bell,' *OED*).

60. plus fort que moi: 'stronger than I' (French).

61. *free-will*: Refers to the discussion of will and necessity by John Locke (1632–1704) in *An Essay Concerning Human Understanding* (1690), Book II, chapters 20 and 21, both which chapters form part of the section headed 'Of Power'.

62. the ingrate and cankered Bolinbroke: alludes to Shakespeare, *1 Henry IV*, I.iii.136.

63. *this 'ungrateful injury,' as Coriolanus has it*: Shakespeare, *Coriolanus*, II.ii.35.

64. *nakedness of the land*: Quoted from *Genesis* 42:9–12.

65. pour voir ce que cela deviendra: 'to see what that will become'; 'to see how that will turn out' (French).

66. *fitter for the parish books than the red bench*: i.e. a more likely candidate for poor relief from the parish, than for elevation to the peerage.

67. good den Sir Richard ... a gad a mercy, fellow: Shakespeare, *King John*, I.iii.4.

68. *fête*: 'festival' (French), here in the sense of any celebration or party.

69. *a very Mammoth of loveliness*: Lady Clancare compares Mrs Wilkinson to the mammoth (*Mammuthus (Elephas) primigenius*), the gigantic elephant which became extinct *c.* 10,000 BC, and which was once native to countries throughout the northern hemisphere. Important, preserved specimens of mammoth had been discovered in the early 1800s, and widely discussed in scientific publications of the period. See, for example, G. Cuvier, *Essay on the Theory of the Earth*, trans. Robert Jameson, 3rd edition (Edinburgh: W. Blackwood, 1817), pp. 272–6.

70. *to get the* pas: to take precedence (*OED*), from *pas*, 'precedence'; 'right of going first' (French).

71. *Marmontel in his ... Memoires*: In his *Memoires d'un père* (1804), Jean-François Marmontel (1723–1799) described the opulent establishment of a cultured (and dissolute) financier named as 'La Poplinière,' whose home at Passy was equipped with an orchestra and a private theatre, and whose guests included leading actresses and musicians. See *Memoirs of Marmontel, Written By Himself,* 4 vols (London: Longman, Hurst, Rees, and Orme, 1805), vol. 1, pp. 331–3.

72. *I shall say nothing ... till* there's a peace: Lady Clancare's words recall those of the servant Scrub in Act IV of George Farquhar's *The Beaux' Stratagem* (1707): 'I'm resolv'd never to speak one word, pro nor con, until we have a peace.'

73. *having dropped the birch ... snatch the crozier*: i.e they exchange the birch rod (as used by schoolmasters for disciplining pupils) for the bishop's crozier, or staff of office. Lady Clancare imagines the financially 'embarrassed' English clergymen as supplementing their income by taking pupils.

74. *the O's, and the Mac's*: i.e. members of families with patronymic surnames taking either of the two main, traditional Gaelic prefixes, 'O' (from Irish *ó*, 'grandson' or 'descendant'), or 'Mac' (from Irish *mac*, 'son'); see 'O'' and 'Mac', *OED*.

75. *like the Irish wolf dog*: The Irish wolf dog, or wolfhound, had been long remarked by this period not only for its impressive size, but also for its combination of a generally docile

temperament with fierceness in hunting or defence. Irish wolfhounds had almost died out in Ireland by the end of the eighteenth century, largely owing to the extinction of the wolves they had been used to hunt; see Volume 1, n. 342.

76. *a mug, a mug, a mug*: the cry of the supporters of Matthew Mug in the hustings scene in Samuel Foote's two-act farce *The Mayor of Garratt* (first performed 1763), II.ii.

77. *mauvaise honte*: 'false shame' (French); false modesty.

78. *make the* 'welkin dance': alludes to Shakespeare, *Twelfth Night* II.iii.61.

79. *the most … cruel death of Pyramus and Thisbe*: refers to the fictional tragedy performed by the Athenian 'mechanicals' (artisans) following the wedding of Theseus and Hippolita in Shakespeare's *A Midsummer Night's Dream*, V.i., and rehearsed by them in I.ii., and III.i.

80. *Peter Quince*: In Shakespeare's *A Midsummer Night's Dream*, Peter Quince is a carpenter, in charge of producing *Pyramus and Thisbe* as the entertainment to follow Theseus and Hippolyta's wedding.

81. *the rejoinder of Bully Bottom …'and a merry'*: Rosbrin quotes from Bottom's opinion of the tragedy of Pyramus and Thisbe in Shakespeare's *A Midsummer Night's Dream*, I.ii.14–15 ('A very good piece of work, I assure you, and a merry').

82. *Come my queen … the wand'ring moon*: Rosbrin quotes (with some variations) from the Fairy King Oberon's speech to his wife Titania, following their reconciliation, in Shakespeare's *A Midsummer Night's Dream*, IV.i.101–04; and Lady Clancare responds with a partial quotation from Titania's answer, at IV.i.105–8.

83. Macbeth *hath murdered sleep*: A slight misquotation from Shakespeare, *Macbeth* II. ii. 43 (which has 'Glamis [i.e. the character Macbeth] hath murder'd sleep'); though the same scene also includes the line 'Macbeth does murder sleep' (l. 37).

84. *A mask … called Comus*: Originally published in 1637 as *A Masque Presented at Ludlow Castle*, and subsequently known as *Comus*, John Milton's masque was first performed on 29 September 1634 at the Shropshire seat of the Earl of Bridgewater, to celebrate his appointment as Lord President of Wales. Members of the Earl's family took the principal roles, and the music was provided by the Bridgewater children's music tutor, the English composer Henry Lawes (bap. 1596, d. 1662), who also appeared in the role of the Attendant Spirit. In the masque, a virginal Lady, lost in a forest, is tempted by the enchanter Comus, but is rescued by her two brothers, guided by the Attendant Spirit. However, Lady Clancare has in mind not Milton's original masque, but a one-act stage adaptation of it, also named *Comus*, by John Dalton (bap. 1709, d. 1763). This version was first performed at the Drury Lane Theatre, London, in 1738, with James Quin (see also Volume 4, n. 174) in the title role, and music composed by Thomas Arne. It remained popular throughout the eighteenth century, and was frequently performed as an afterpiece in the main London and Dublin theatres. It incorporated substantial alterations and additions to the original, including interpolated musical and danced interludes, and sections of other texts by Milton. Among the new elements introduced to Milton's text is the character of the nymph Euphrosyne, representing 'mirth', which role Lord Rosbrin will suggest Lady Clancare should take. Euphrosyne is introduced in Act III, her appearance being heralded by Comus's partial quotation from the first thirty-four lines of Milton's *L'Allegro*. She performs a series of songs and dances as part of Comus's temptation of the Lady. See *Comus, a Mask: (now adapted to the stage) as alter'd from Milton's mask at Ludlow-Castle* (London: R. Dodsley, 1738).

85. *Welcome song … dropping wine*: Quoted from a song in John Dalton's 1738 version of *Comus*, I. i (see Volume 4, n. 84), with the opening lines 'Now Phoebus sinketh in the

west, / Welcome song and welcome jest'. The song is based on a speech of Comus in Milton's *Comus*, at 102–6.

86. Will fill a pit as well as better men: Paraphrases Shakespeare, *1 Henry IV*, IV.ii.73–4, where Falstaff dismisses his unprepossessing troops as 'food for powder'; adding, 'they'll fill a pit as well as better'.

87. *Like some ... rainbow lives*: paraphrases Milton, *Comus*, ll. 299–300 ('some gay creatures of the element, / That in the colours of the rainbow live'), lines retained in John Dalton's 1738 stage version (see Volume 4, n. 84).

88. *Pizarro*: i.e. Richard Brinsley Sheridan's highly successful tragedy *Pizarro* (1799), a version of Friedrich von Kotzebue's *Die Spanier in Peru* ('The Spaniards in Peru'). It ostensibly centred upon Spanish colonial abuses in South America, but also allegorized Sheridan's opposition to British actions in India and Ireland.

89. *a succedaneum*: a substitute (*OED*).

90. *the Spanish farce ... his Leander*: Rosbrin suggests staging Isaac Bickerstaff's comic opera *The Padlock* (1768), an adaptation of Miguel de Cervantes's novel *The Jealous Husband*, with music by Charles Dibdin (bap. 1745, d. 1814). The plot concerns the efforts of a Salamanca student, Leander, to gain access to his beloved Leonora, whose jealous husband, Don Diego, has confined her to his house. The other major character in the drama is Mungo, Diego's black servant, who becomes Leander's ally. Robert Owenson played the role of Leander on numerous occasions, the first being at Covent Garden on 21 May 1773; see the *Public Advertiser*, 21 May 1773, p. 1.

91. *no wooden leg ... for Leander*: In Bickerstaff's *The Padlock*, one of the stratagems adopted by Leander in his courtship of Leonora is to disguise himself as a crippled minstrel, which he explains he will effect by 'clapping a black patch on my eye, and a swathe [bandage] upon one of my legs'. See Isaac Bickerstaff, *The Padlock: A Comic Opera* (London: W. Griffith, ?1768), p. 7.

92. *Oh thou ... my heart*: Misquotes the opening line of Leander's song to Leonora in act I of *The Padlock* ('O thou whose charms enslave my heart'). See See Isaac Bickerstaff, *The Padlock: A Comic Opera* (London: W. Griffith, ?1768), p. 15.

93. *a Gordian knot*: Alludes to the legend of the knot in the strip of cornel-bark securing a yoke to the ox-cart in which the peasant Gordias arrived in the Phrygian town later renamed Gordium after him, when he became its king. An oracle stated that whoever could untie the knot would reign over Asia. The knot proved impossible to untie; but Alexander the Great claimed to have fulfilled the oracle when he cut through it with his sword. To cut a 'Gordian knot' thus means to take drastic, direct action to overcome a difficulty.

94. *sport for ladies*: echoes the words of Touchstone on the wrestling match in Shakespeare's *As You Like It*, I.ii.147–8 ('it is the first time that ever I heard breaking of ribs was sport for ladies'); see also Volume II, n. 436.

95. espieglerie: i.e. *espièglerie*, 'mischievousness' (French).

96. denoument: i.e. a *denouement*, an 'unknotting' (French), in English usage usually referring to the resolution of a dramatic or literary plot.

97. *But yet I say ...SHAKESPEARE*: Shakespeare, *Othello*, III.iii.406–9.

98. *the spirit of the sun-beam ... the shadow of Cellini*: 'The spirit of the sun-beam' refers to a delusion experienced by the Italian poet Torquato Tasso (1544–95), during a period of mental illness. Tasso believed that he was visited by a spirit who conversed with him, but a friend who was present when Tasso looked towards a window, saying that the spirit had appeared, 'saw nothing except the sun-beams darting through the window.' See

John Hoole, 'The Life of Tasso,' in *Jerusalem Delivered: An Heroic Poem*, 2 vols (London: R. and J. Dodsley, 1763), vol. 1, pp. xvii–xlviii; xxxix. The source of the reference to the 'airy voice' and 'Des Cartes' has not been traced, though in his *Meditations on First Philosophy* (1641), the French philosopher René Descartes (1596–1650) posited the idea of a malicious demon who tricks people into a false sense of reality, in order to illustrate his argument concerning the unreliability of human perceptions. According to his biographer, Adrien Baillet (1649–1706), Descartes also believed that his commitment to philosophy had been partly supernaturally inspired, following three dreams he experienced on the night of 10 November 1619. Baillet presented an account of this episode in *La Vie de Monsieur Des Cartes* (1693), which was translated by 'S. R.' as *The Life of Monsieur Des Cartes* (London: R. Simpson, 1693); see especially pp. 35–6. The 'resplendent light, which hovered over the shadow of Cellini' refers to a form of halo which the Florentine goldsmith and artist Benvenuto Cellini (1500–71) claimed to have acquired during his imprisonment in the Castel Sant'Angelo, Rome. In his autobiography, Cellini described being visited in a dream by a figure who placed a mark on his forehead, after which 'there appeared ... a resplendent light over my head, which has displayed itself conspicuously to all that I have thought proper to show it to.' He added: 'This shining light is to be seen over my shadow till two o'clock in the afternoon.' See *The Life of Benvenuto Cellini: A Florentine Artist*, trans. T. Nugent, 2 vols (London: T. Davies, 1771), vol. 2, pp. 4–5.

99. *the Gougane Barra*: *Guagán Barra*, 'mountain recess of Barra' (Irish Gaelic); a mountainous region in Co. Cork.

100. *this typhus*: An epidemic of typhus, an infectious, feverish disease spread by parasites, and associated with insanitary and overcrowded conditions, broke out in Ireland during the spring and summer of 1817. It had spread to all parts of the country by 1819, causing an estimated 65,000 deaths. Government measures intended to contain the outbreak and relieve those affected were introduced from the spring of 1817, but it was not until April 1818 that a select committee was appointed specifically to examine the spread of contagious fever in Ireland, with an Act of Parliament in May 1818 enabling the establishment of local health boards, and the building of fever hospitals. See discussion in S. J. Connolly, 'Union Government, 1812–23,' in *A New History of Ireland*, ed. F. X. Martin et al., 9 vols (Oxford: Clarendon Press, 1989), vol. 5, pp. 61–2.

101. *to suffer ... is equal*: Milton, *Paradise Lost* II.199–200.

102. *the good the 'gods provide me'*: Paraphrased from Dryden, *Alexander's Feast; or The Power of Musique. An Ode, In Honour of St Cecilia's Day*, 106 (which has 'Take the good the gods provide thee').

103. *a perfect Lord Angelo*: In Shakespeare's *Measure for Measure*, Angelo is the puritanical deputy to the Duke of Vienna, who during the Duke's absence decides to enforce a long-disregarded law against fornication. However, when the novice nun Isabella, sister of a young man sentenced to death under this law, appeals to Angelo for mercy, he offers to spare her brother in return for her sexual favours.

104. *vivá voce*: 'out loud' (Latin); orally.

105. *for one Cæsar ... his own despatches*: The Roman general and emperor Gaius Julius Caesar (100 BC–44 BC) authored detailed prose accounts of his successful military campaigns, *Commentarii de bello civili* ('Commentaries on the civil wars [with Pompey]') and *Commentarii de bello Gallico* ('Commentaries on the war in Gaul'). John Churchill, first Duke of Marlborough (1650–1722) famously announced his victory over the Bavarians at the battle of Blenheim (1704) with a terse message to his wife Sarah, a royal attendant,

scrawled on the back of a tavern bill. Marlborough had previously been responsible for subduing Munster following the defeat of James II in 1690. Owenson's description of him as 'illiterate' may allude to the fact of his having received only a few years of formal education, in Dublin, and at St Paul's School, London.

106. *the circle*: i.e. the social or domestic circle.

107. *Hercules was ... a hero*: a quotation, with omissions, from John Dryden, *Oedipus*, III.i.

108. entre nous: 'between ourselves' (French).

109. *the 'spouse of God in vain'*: quotes from Pope, 'Eloisa to Abelard', l. 177.

110. not on the cross ... but you: Adapts Pope, 'Eloisa to Abelard', l. 116.

111. prated of your whereabouts: adapts Shakespeare, *Macbeth*, II.i.59 ('The very stones prate of my whereabouts').

112. *crier*: town crier.

113. sang froid: literally 'cold blood' (French); in English usage, coolness (of temperament or demeanour).

114. *a feathered mercury*: Quoted from Vernon's description of Prince Henry, armed for battle, mounting his horse in Shakespeare's *1 Henry IV*, IV.i.109–11 ('I saw young Harry with his beaver on, / His cuisses on his thighs, gallantly armed, / Rise from the ground like feathered Mercury'). In Greek mythology, Mercury was the god who served as a messenger to the other Olympians, communicating their commands to mortals. He was often portrayed wearing winged sandals.

115. *no quadrant to take the altitude of my character*: A quadrant is instrument used to measure the altitude of distant celestial or terrestrial objects (*OED*).

116. winter and rough weather: Shakespeare, *As You Like It*, II.v.8.

117. scope and room enough: a common construction in literature of the period.

118. 'Le tems et moi,' *as Cardinal Mazarine used to say*: Lady Clancare refers to the Italian-born French statesman Jules Mazarin (1602–61), who came to Paris as an Italian papal legate in 1634 and was appointed a cardinal in 1641. Having entered the service of Louis XIII in 1639, he succeeded his mentor, Armand Jean du Plessis, Cardinal Richelieu, as chief minister of France in 1642, and governed the country as regent during the minority of Louis XIV. Mazarin is reported to have met obstacles to his schemes with patience, saying 'Le temps et moi ... nous sommes deux grands maîtres' ('Time and I ... we are two great masters'); see Jean-François Dreux du Radier, *Mémoires historique, critiques et anecdotes des reines et regentes de France*, 6 vols (1764; Paris: M. Rey, 1808), vol. 6, p. 161.

119. jacobin outré: 'an open jacobin' (French).

120. *Agus cead mille faltra*: i.e. *agus céad mille fáilte*, 'And a hundred thousand welcomes' (Irish).

121. *to the Rev. Patrick Mulligan, Dr.*: *OED* confirms usage of 'station' in this sense, though the first instance cited is from 1843. Arthur Young provides a tabulation of an Irish cottar's expenses (based on information received in Co. Derry) which, he observes, does not include dues to the priest; see Arthur Young, *A Tour in Ireland: With General Observations on the Present State of That Kingdom. Made in the Years 1776, 1777, and 1778, and brought down to the end of 1779*, 2 vols (Dublin: Whitestone, Sleater et al, 1780), vol. 2, pp. 247–9.

122. *Haud facile ... angusta domi*: Juvenal, Satire III, 164–5 ('It's not easy anyway to climb the ladder when cramped personal resources block your talents'); see *Juvenal and Persius*, ed. and trans. S. M. Braund (Cambridge, MA: Harvard University Press, 2004).

123. *the lares and the penates*: In ancient Roman religion, *lares*, 'spirits of place' (Latin) and *penates*, 'household gods' (Latin) were honoured in all domestic homes, being repre-

sented by small figures housed in shrines. 'Lares and penates' thus referred to 'tutelary deities of a house' (*OED*), with English usages being often figurative, as here.

124. *polling and pilling*: *poll*, to rob, cheat, or 'plunder ... as by excessive taxation' (*OED*); *pill*, 'to strip (a person or place) of money or goods'; 'to oppress (a group of people) with excessive rents, taxation, fines, etc' (*OED*).

125. *cautelous*: deceitful, crafty (*OED*).

126. *the* Desiderata curiosa Hebernica: O'Leary refers to *Desiderata curiosa Hibernica: or A Select Collection of State papers; Consisting of Royal Instructions, Directions, Dispatches, and Letters*, 2 vols. (Dublin: D. Hay, 1772). This work includes Thomas Lee's 'A Brief Declaration of the Government of Ireland. Opening many Corruptions in the same. Discovering the Discontents of the Irishery; and the Causes moving those expected Troubles' (1594); see vol. 1, pp. 88–150, which O'Leary goes on to cite.

127. Humble apology of the Lords... *Curry's Civil Wars*: O'Leary alludes to 'The humble apology of the lords, knights, gentlemen, and other inhabitants of the English pale of Ireland, for taking arms,' in *Desiderata curiosa Hibernica*, vol. 2, pp. 102–13; and to John Curry (d. 1780), *An Historical and Critical Review of the Civil Wars in Ireland, from the Reign of Queen Elizabeth, to the Settlement under King William. Extracted from Parliamentary records, state acts, and other authentic materials* (Dublin: J. Hoey and T. T. Faulkner, 1775).

128. *strangers to rule us*: In her endnote, Owenson refers to Henry Sidney's letter of 20 April 1567 to Elizabeth I, concerning the need to establish 'justice' in Ireland as a means to avoiding the spread of violence. The salient passage appears in *Letters and Memorials of State in the Reigns of Queen Mary, Queen Elizabeth, King James, King Charles the First, Part of the Reign of King Charles the Second, and Oliver's Usurpation*, ed. A. Collins, 2 vols (London: T. Osborne, 1746), vol. 1, p. 28, where Sidney writes: 'As this Towne [Anrye], for Lacke of Justice, is, in a Manner totally destroyed, so will the rest of your Highenes Townes be, if with Speede you plant not Justice among them.' Owenson appears to have derived her particular wording of this citation from Francis Hardy, *Memoirs of the Political and Private Life of James Caulfeild, Earl of Charlemont*, 2nd edn, 2 vols (London: T. Cadell and W. Davies, 1812). In his discussion of the same letter of Sidney to Elizabeth I, Hardy remarks: '[Sidney's] plan for gradually improving the kingdom [Ireland] was short, simple, and, had it been followed, permanently efficacious. "Your Majesty must plant justice here." This he again and again repeats'; see vol. 1, p. 9. Sidney's use of the imagery of 'planting' justice in his letter of 20 April 1567 does indeed echo remarks in a previous letter. Writing about his government of Ireland to Robert Cecil on 17 April 1566, he had already stated: 'I intend to plante with Reason, and water with Justice; but God must give the increase'; see *Letters and Memorials of State*, vol. 1, p. 11. The further quotation of words addressed by Henry Sidney to Elizabeth I in Owenson's endnote likewise appears in F. Hardy, *Memoirs of the Political and Private Life of James Caulfeild, Earl of Charlemont*, 2nd edn, vol. p. 8. These remarks also originally appear in Sidney's letter to Elizabeth I of 20 April 1567; see *Letters and Memorials of State*, vol. 1, p. 29.

129. *as Sir Henry Sydney said ... pound us as in a mortar*: These remarks are apparently drawn from John Curry, *An Historical and Critical Review of the Civil Wars in Ireland* (1775), vol. 1, in which Sir John Davis is reported to have said of the Irish, following the end of their rebellion against the English crown: 'The multitude being brayed, as it were, in a mortar ... with sword, famine, and pestilence together, received the laws and magistrates, and most gladly received the king's pardon and peace in all parts of the realm'; see p. 56.

To 'bray' means '[to] pound, crush to powder; usually in a mortar' (*OED*), a 'bray' being 'a baker's pestle' (*OED*).

130. *you it is ... to wolves*: O'Leary alludes to Elizabeth I's remarks concerning her governors' destructiveness in Ireland, as reported by William Camden in *Annales. The True and Royall History of the famous empresse Elizabeth Queene of England France and Ireland &c.* (London: B. Fisher, 1625), p. 369. The passage was cited, with variations, by numerous eighteenth-century historians of Ireland including John Curry and Thomas Leland. Bato was a tribesman from Dalmatia, part of the Balkan province of Illyrica, which was conquered by the Romans in 168 BC. He led the Illyrican rebellion subdued by the Romans in 6–9 AD, under the military leadership of Tiberius Julius Caesar Augustus (later the emperor Tiberius). See Robin Seager, *Tiberius* (1972; Oxford: Blackwell, 2005), pp. 33, 35. Bato's remark that the rulers of Illyrica had behaved more like 'wolves' than like 'shepherds' toward their subject 'flocks,' was originally recorded by Cassius Dio (*c.* 164–235 AD) in his *Roman History*.

131. *branded ... like the descendants of Cain*: In Genesis 4:11–15, God punishes Cain for murdering his brother Abel by condemning him to become 'a fugitive and a vagabond', but places a mark upon him to protect him from attacks by others. By the nineteenth century the 'mark of Cain' was often invoked to convey the idea that someone was outcast from society, or tainted with guilt. The Biblical character of Cain also had a place in the ancient pseudo-histories of Ireland, being mentioned in the *Lebor Gabála* (see Volume 1, n. 386) as having arrived in Ireland with its first settlers from the east, and as having been the first of them to see Ireland from the sea.

132. *Butler's Lives of the Saints*: O'Leary alludes to Alban Butler (1711–73), *The Lives of the Fathers, Martyrs, and Other Principal Saints* (1756).

133. *calabalero*: 'cavalier' (Irish; from Spanish *caballero*). In Owenson's footnote, *Quere* is 'seek' (from Latin *quaere*), in this usage implying a query.

134. promener mes ennuis ailleurs: 'take my ennuis elsewhere' (French).

135. debuted: first appeared; made her 'debut'; from *débuter*, 'to begin' (French).

136. *the Prometheus that awakened the statue*: In Greek mythology, Prometheus was a Titan god who, as well as harnessing the power of fire, created the first human beings from clay. Lord Adelm's comments also recall the story of Pygmalion, who fell in love with a statue of a maiden, which the goddess Aphrodite then brought to life, as related by Ovid in the *Metamorphoses*.

137. the two gentlemen of Verona: In Shakespeare's comedy *The Two Gentlemen of Verona*, the Veronese friends Valentine and Proteus become rivals for the affections of Silvia, while both are in Milan; with Proteus deserting Julia, to whom he has made vows of fidelity, in favour of Silvia. Proteus eventually repents of his treatment of Julia, when it is revealed that the new page who has entered his service in Milan is in fact Julia, whose loyalty has led her to follow him in disguise.

138. dessous les cartes: 'under the [playing] cards' (French); meaning 'underneath', 'under the surface'.

139. prima donna: literally 'first lady' (Italian), meaning 'leading lady'.

140. *nothing could come of nothing*: An allusion to Shakespeare's *King Lear*, I.i.92, where Lear responds to his daughter Cordelia's confession that she can think of nothing that would equal her love for him, with the remark that 'Nothing will come of nothing.'

141. à la derobée: 'furtively' (French).

142. *Su, svegliatevi … Il Don Giovanni*: 'Come! rouse yourselves like good folk! Come! be of good heart, o good people! we will be happy, we will laugh and joke'. (Italian). From the libretto, by Lorenzo da Ponte (1749–1838), to W. A. Mozart's opera *Don Giovanni* (first performed 1787), trans. Ellen H. Bleiler (New York: Dover, 1985); see p. 46. The lines appear at I.iv; they are first sung by the aristocratic, Spanish libertine Don Giovanni, hosting a party for a group of peasants at which he hopes to seduce the young bride Zerlina, and are then repeated by the chorus of peasants; see p. 47.

143. *I know you all … Shakespeare*: Shakespeare, 1 *Henry IV*, I.ii.217–18.

144. reculer pour mieux sauter: 'to draw back in order to leap the better' (French).

145. the 'nothingness *of good works*': In Thomas Shadwell's comedy *The Squire of Alsatia* (1688), 'The Nothingness of good Works' is among the titles of the moralising and religious books which Isabella imagines as having been pressed upon Tiresia by her father in III.i; however, no work of this title has been traced. Tobias Smollett also alludes to a work (possibly fictional) of this title in his epistolary novel *Humphrey Clinker* (1771), in the letter of William Jenkins to Mrs Mary Jones to accompany his gift of items including 'a sarment [sermon] upon the nothingness of good works, which was preached in the tabernacle'; see *The Expedition of Humphrey Clinker*, 3 vols (London: W. Johnson, 1771), vol. 2, p. 82.

146. *a sounding brass and tinkling cymbal*: alludes to 1 Corinthians 13:1, where St Paul writes: 'Though I speake with the tongues of men & of Angels, and have not charity, I am become as sounding brasse or a tinkling cymbal.'

147. *corps dramatique*: 'dramatic company' (French).

148. *all stars … sock or buskin*: This usage of 'star' (in the sense of a celebrity, or person of outstanding talents) is not recorded in *OED* until 1824. The 'sock' and 'buskin' have since antiquity been invoked as the traditional, metonymic accoutrements of comedy and tragedy respectively. Both terms derive from the ancient Greek theatre; the 'buskin' is believed to have been a form of high-soled footwear possibly used to ensure stately height and dignified slowness of movement for actors in tragic roles, and the 'sock' a lower-soled shoe or boot associated with the lower genre of comedy.

149. *Romeos … Macheaths*: as well as to the eponymous heroes of Shakespeare's tragedies *Romeo and Juliet* and *Macbeth*, Owenson refers to Doricourt, the hero of Hannah Cowley's comedy *The Belle's Stratagem*, and Macheath, the principal male character in John Gay, *The Beggar's Opera*.

150. *Barries and Siddonses*: alludes to the distinguished actresses Sarah Siddons (see Volume 2, n. 347) and Ann Barry, née Street, later known by her second married name of Crawford (bap. 1733, d. 1801) an actress who specialised in tragic roles including Cordelia (in *King Lear*) and Lady Macbeth. She performed at the Crow Street theatre, Dublin, in the late 1750s, early 1760s and late 1770s, as well as enjoying a successful London career.

151. *the best speeches of Zanga … the Revenge*: Zanga, a Moor, is the protagonist in Edward Young's verse tragedy *The Revenge* (1721), the plot of which draws heavily upon that of Shakespeare's *Othello* (with the character of Zanga combining elements of Shakespeare's characterisations of both Iago and Othello). The role featured many impassioned speeches and soliloquies, and so was favoured by tragic actors such as John Philip Kemble.

152. tracasserie: 'fuss'; bother' (French; *OED*).

153. *fierce vanities*: Shakespeare, *Henry VIII*, I.i.54.

154. *one half … to Coventry*: The expression 'to send [someone] to Coventry', meaning to refuse to speak to or associate with them, dates from mid-eighteenth-century England,

and is thought to have originated either in the unpopularity of soldiers stationed at the English Midlands town of Coventry; or in memories of the Parliamentarians' incarceration of Royalist prisoners at Coventry during the English Civil War.

155. *Rosalinds, Beatrices, Roxalanas*: the heroines of well-known comedies. Rosalind, heroine of Shakespeare's comedy *As You Like It*, who woos Orlando in male disguise; Beatrice, the sharp-tongued heroine of Shakespeare's comedy *Much Ado About Nothing*, who in the course of the play wins the affection of the surly Benedick; Roxalana, the outspoken, English harem inmate with whom the haughty Turkish sultan Soleyman falls in love in Isaac Bickerstaff's comedy *The Sultan*.

156. *Soleyman ... Rosalind*: alludes to Soleyman and the Sultana, in Bickerstaff's *The Sultan*; and Rosalind and Orlando, the principal couple in Shakespeare's *As You Like It*.

157. *clap traps*: Special theatrical devices designed to elicit applause (*OED*).

158. *Shakespeare ... Moreton*: Lady Clancare adapts works by major dramatists from the Renaissance to her contemporary periods: William Shakespeare (1564–1616); the Dublin-born actor and dramatist John O'Keeffe (1747–1833); Ben Jonson (1572–1637), and Thomas Morton (bap. 1764, d. 1838), the prolific English author of comedies including *The Way to Get Married* (1796) and *The School of Reform* (1805).

159. les belles et bonnes dames de par le monde: 'the most beautiful and most virtuous ladies of the world' (French).

160. *Would cry, that was levelled at me*: From 'Air 30' in John Gay, *The Beggar's Opera*, X, where the prison-keeper Lockit advises would-be satirists against offending politicians likely to feel implicated by their writings.

161. beau ideal: i.e. beau-ideal, from *beau idéal*, 'beautiful ideal' (French), 'perfect type or model' (*OED*).

162. *Unfinish'd things ... so equivocal*: Pope, *Essay on Criticism*, l. 42.

163. *the worthy* we's: Lady Clancare refers to the periodical critics by allusion to their convention of writing reviews in the first person plural.

164. let loose their dogs of war: misquotes Shakespeare, *Julius Caesar*, III.i.273.

165. pour les beaux yeux de mon mérite: 'for [out of] the favourable regard of my merit' (French).

166. waspstung and impatient critics: adapts Shakespeare, *1 Henry IV*, I.iii.236, where the Earl of Worcester refers to Henry Percy ('Hotspur') as 'a wasp-stung and impatient fool'.

167. *Very, very, very kind indeed*: an allusion to lines in John Wolcot's verse satire *The Lousiad. Canto II*, 2nd edn (London: G. Kearsley, 1787), p. 20, where the King tells Madam Schwellenberg the mantua-maker, 'That thus you come to ease my angry mind, / Indeed is very, very, very, very kind [*sic*]'.

168. quelle necessité: 'what necessity' (French).

169. *The green-room ... the red bench*: i.e. the acting profession (signified by the 'green room', offstage area in which actors rest, or prepare for performance) is the best way into the peerage (signified by the traditionally red benches of the House of Lords).

170. On peut se rapporter à vous par exemple: 'one might refer to you for example' (French).

171. fétée: 'celebrated' (French); famous.

172. *dead march in Saul*: Refers to 'No. 77' in G. F. Handel's oratorio *Saul* (1738), based on the Old Testament account of the king of Judah whose envy of the young David leads to his downfall and suicide, and who is succeeded by David. The 'Dead March' accompanies the bearing away of the bodies of Saul and his son Absalom, who has been executed after refusing to murder David.

173. *monument in Westminster*: i.e. a commemorative monument in Westminster Abbey, by this period the major burial-place for persons prominent in British national life.

174. to that complexion must I come at last: A paraphrase of the closing line of the epitaph composed for the actor James Quin (1693–1766) by his friend, the actor and dramatist David Garrick (1717–1779). The last four lines of the epitaph originally read: 'Here lies James Quin! Deign, reader, to be taught, - / Whate'er thy strength of body, force of thought, / In nature's happiest mould however cast, To this complexion thou must come at last.' See D. Garrick, *Poetical Works*, 2 vols (London: G. Kearsley, 1785), vol. 2, p. 483.

175. *to give you* les petites entrées *at the Phœnix*: i.e. to provide you with introductions within vice-regal society (as represented by the Phoenix Park, where many of the official residences of senior members of the Irish administration were located). *Les petites entrées*, literally 'little entrances' (French).

176. *another Farren, another Abingdon*: Rosbrin names two popular comedy actresses of the previous century: Elizabeth Farren (1759x62–1829), of Irish descent, who retired from the stage in 1797, on her marriage to her lover, Edward Smith Stanley, twelfth Earl of Derby; and Frances Abington, *née* Barton (1737–1815), who enjoyed success in both London and Dublin from the mid-1750s, and who created the role of Lady Teazle in Sheridan's *The School for Scandal* (1777). During the 1770s, Abington was also mistress to William Petty, first Marquess of Lansdowne.

177. *A mourir de plaisir*: '[would make one] die of pleasure' (French).

178. *quiz*: satirize, mock (*OED*).

179. *George Anne Bellamy's apology, or Mrs Baddely's memoirs*: Rosbrin refers to published accounts of the lives of two theatrical celebrities of the eighteenth century. Georgiane ('George Anne') Bellamy (1731?–88), was an Irish-born, tragic actress who appeared on both the London and Dublin stages, and authored her own memoir, *An Apology for the Life of George Anne Bellamy* (1785). Sophia Baddeley, *née* Snow (1745?-1786) pursued a career in acting and singing in both London and Dublin, and lived under the protection of a series of lovers. Her biography, *The Memoirs of Mrs Sophia Baddeley* (1787) was authored by her friend Elizabeth Steele.

180. 'uarrelled in print ... counterchecks quarrelsome: alludes to the satirical speech of Touchstone the fool on the techniques of quarrelling in print and in person in Shakespeare's *As You Like It*, V.iv.94–109.

181. *primum mobile*: 'First mover' (Latin); 'first cause'.

182. *Henry the Eighth ... Cardinal Wolsey's banquet*: refers to the passage at the end of Shakespeare's *Henry VIII* I. iv, where Henry dances with Anne Boleyn, and continues to escort her as his partner when the characters all leave the stage.

183. *The fairest ... knew thee*: Shakespeare, *Henry VIII*, I.iv.74–5, spoken by Henry to Anne Boleyn.

184. *I do not know ... Beseech your lordship, &c &c*: Shakespeare, *Henry VIII*, II.iii.66–70, spoken by Anne Boleyn, not to Henry, but to the Lord Chamberlain, who has brought her Henry's offer of the title of Marchioness of Pembroke.

185. *most delightful Beatrice ... obdurate wife hater*: Fitzwalter refers to Beatrice, the witty and forthright heroine of Shakespeare's comedy *Much Ado About Nothing*, who wins the affection of the misogynist and confirmed bachelor Benedick.

186. *learned pigs ... Irish giants*: Allusions to some of the of the animal and human curiosities which had attracted public (and 'fashionable') interest in Ireland and England from the late eighteenth century. The most famous 'learned pig' was exhibited in Dublin and Belfast by Samuel Bisset (1721–1783?), who had trained it to perform tricks such as telling

the time, and spelling audience members' names, by signals. See 'Some Account of S. Bisset, the Extraordinary Teacher of Animals,' *Anthologia Hibernica*, 1 (1793), pp. 23–5 (Owenson was among subscribers to this periodical; see *Anthologia Hibernica*, 1 (1793), p. vii). The late 1700s and early 1800s saw the emergence of various successors to Bisset's learned pig, including one whose performances were advertised in *The Times*, 20 February 1817, p. 1. 'Esquimeaux warriors' appears to be a reference to John Sacheuse, a young Greenland Inuit man who arrived in Britain, having stowed away on a whaling ship, in 1816. After an apparently unhappy period spent exhibiting his skills in hunting and kayaking to the public in Leith and London, he returned home with the Arctic expedition led by Sir John Ross in the summer of 1818; see R. G. David, *The Arctic in the British Imagination, 1818–1914* (Manchester: Manchester University Press, 2000), pp. 132–3. The most famous 'Irish giant' of the early nineteenth-century period was Patrick Cotter, otherwise O'Brien (1760/1–1806), from Co. Cork, who claimed to be almost nine feet (2.74m) tall. He was exhibited in London, and elsewhere in Britain, before his death in Bristol in 1806. Patrick O'Brien was a successor 'giant' to Charles Byrne (1761–83), from Co. Londonderry (now Derry), who measured eight feet and two inches (2.54m) tall by 1780, and who was exhibited around Britain in 1782–3.

187. brusque: 'abrupt' (French); in English usage, rude or offhand in manner.

188. *the* second Amoureux ... *Sylvius*: *second amoureux*, 'second lover' (French). In Shakespeare's *As You Like It*, Sylvius the shepherd, and his sweetheart Phebe the shepherdess, form a secondary pairing to that of the hero and heroine Orlando and Rosalind.

189. *the foresters*: one of the groups of non-speaking, supernumerary characters listed in the dramatis personae of Shakespeare's *As You Like It*, others being 'Lords', 'Pages' and 'Attendants'.

190. *enacting a mute*: i.e. taking a 'mute,' or non-speaking, stage role.

191. soi-disant: literally calling-self (French); 'so-called'.

192. *Stand not amaz'd* ... *SHAKESPEARE*: Shakespeare, *The Merry Wives of Windsor*, V.v.258.

193. *I speak not* ... *SHAKESPEARE*: Shakespeare, 1 *Henry IV*, I.iii.272–6.

194. embrassades: 'huggings and kissings' (French).

195. *casting a look behind*: The exact source of this quotation is unclear, this being a common construction in English poetry of the eighteenth century.

196. incornuto: another of Crawley's bungled foreign expressions, *cornuto*, from Latin *cornutus*, horned, meaning 'cuckold'. The correct expression in this instance would possibly be either *incommunicado*, in the particular sense of not wanting communication with others (*OED*); or *in camera*, in this period a more specifically legal term meaning 'in private' (*OED*).

197. *lying* ... per dor: Crawley means 'lying perdu', hiding whilst waiting on the watch, or in ambush (*OED*).

198. *ridicule*: (otherwise *reticule*) a small drawstring handbag, decorated with embroidery or beading (*OED*).

199. Tom-Mew: i.e. *tant mieux*, 'so much the better' (French).

200. *a taste of a* dewshure: 'a bit of a douceur [bribe]'.

201. *Lisburn, the capital of Spain*: Crawley means Lisbon, capital of Portugal, not the northern Irish town of Lisburn; see also Volume 2, n. 174.

202. *gallows slaves*: Crawley means 'galley slaves'.

203. en franche et belle aversion: 'in frank and absolute loathing' (French).

204. beau maison: 'beautiful house' (French). Crawley appears to mean *beau monsieur*, with the sense of a 'fine gentleman.'

205. teinture de ridiculité: 'tincture of the ridiculous' (French).

206. de ho-on baw: i. e. *de haut en bas*, 'from high to low', from 'on high' (French); haughtily.

207. pour le moins: 'at the least' (French).

208. on time's ... hours depends: a popular motto for the dials of clocks and watches in the period; see Volume 2, n. 219.

209. *the Ulster king at arms*: the official in charge of all aspects of the practices of heraldry and official genealogy in Ireland, including granting coats of arms, and authenticating gene-alogies and claims to peerages. The post was established in 1552, and still existed in 1943, when it was incorporated into the College of Arms, London following the establishment of the Irish Genealogical Office.

210. *your* O de Lucy, *or your* Sally Volatile: i.e her *eau de luce* (see Volume 3, n. 165) or *sal vol-atile* (ammonium carbonate), preparations for treatment of hysterical, or fainting, fits.

211. *hartshorn*: generic name for preparations of carbonate of ammonia used for treating faint-ing or hysteria, and originally derived from the distilled horns of deer (harts) (*OED*).

212. *a JEW* d'esprit: i.e. a *jeu d'esprit*, a 'playful action' (French).

213. *a* forepaw: i. e. a *faux pas*, an 'indiscretion' (French).

214. *humming you*: hum, to impose upon or take in (*OED*).

215. *your ladyship's* veto, *as the Papists say*: In early nineteenth-century Ireland, 'the veto' referred to proposals to enable the British monarch to approve or reject candidates for Catholic bishoprics in Great Britain and Ireland. First suggested in 1782, the question of the veto was raised again in 1808 and 1810, and in the Catholic Relief Bill presented in 1813 by Henry Grattan (see Volume 1, n. 100). Most Roman Catholics in Ireland viewed the proposals for the veto as entailing an unacceptable degree of state interven-tion in Catholic Church affairs.

216. briller par là: 'shine in that' (French).

217. *th' Hibernian journal*: Crawley refers to the *Hibernian Journal, or Chronicle of Liberty*, a Dublin newspaper published three times weekly, 1771–1821.

218. *card counters*: tokens used in games of cards.

219. *every riband man and every* functionary: 'riband man' refers to the Ribbonmen, members of a Roman Catholic, Irish nationalist secret society active from around 1812, who iden-tified each other by the wearing of white ribbons in their hats. Like the names of other groupings, such as 'whiteboys' or 'threshers', the term came to be generically to refer to any person associated, or suspected to be associated, with a rebel organisation. A 'func-tionary' may mean any official person charged with particular duties; Crawley may have Roman Catholic priests, or other Irish Catholic community leaders in mind.

220. posture *gate*: i.e. postern gate.

221. vi et armis: 'by force' (Latin).

222. *the sleep-walking ... Lady Macbeth*: alludes to Shakespeare's *Macbeth*, V.i.21–75, where Lady Macbeth walks in her sleep, and dreams that she still has the blood of King Duncan on her hands, having connived at his murder.

223. *How couldst thou ... MILTON*: Milton, *Comus*, l. 500.

224. *Now does my project ... SHAKESPEARE*: Shakespeare, *The Tempest*, V.i.1–3.

225. *men would read strange things*: alludes to Shakespeare, *Macbeth*, I.v.60–1.

226. Malade Imaginaire: 'hypochondriac' (French); and also the title of Molière's 1673 comedy, about a hypochondriac who fears doctors, which satirized various forms of char-latanry, financial greed, and professional ambition.

227. bound up each corporeal faculty: Apparently a misquotation from Shakespeare's *Macbeth*, I.vii.79–80, where Macbeth says: 'I am settled, and bend up / Each corporal agent to this terrible feat.'

228. la petite personne: 'the little character' (French).

229. *Irish cronan*: *crónán*, drone, hum (Irish).

230. ave-maria *and* mea-culpa: 'Hail Mary' and 'my fault' (Latin), referring respectively to the traditional Roman Catholic prayer to the Virgin Mary; and words from the Confiteor ('I confess'), a prayer of contrition forming part of the Roman Catholic Mass.

231. *equivoque*: 'an expression capable of having more than one meaning' (*OED*).

232. my friends fast sworn: slightly misquotes Shakespeare, *Coriolanus*, IV.iv.12.

233. l'amie d'honneur: 'the special friend' (French).

234. *And from ... my setting*: Paraphrases Shakespeare, *Henry VIII*, III.ii.225–6.

235. left and ... velvet friends: Paraphrases Shakespeare, *As You Like It*, II.i.50.

236. Now, infidel ... the hip: Shakespeare, *The Merchant of Venice*, IV.i.330.

237. quid pro quo: Literally 'what for what' (Latin). In legal terms, the exchange of one thing or favour for another.

238. *Stealing her ... true one*: Shakespeare, *The Merchant of Venice*, V.i.19–20.

239. *Sic me Phœbus amat*: 'Thus Phoebus loves me' (Latin).

240. solus cum solo: 'all alone' (Latin).

241. *Yea, even ... MILTON*: Milton, *Comus*, ll. 596–98.

242. *Loud rumour spoke*: paraphrased from the 'Induction' to Shakespeare's 2 *Henry IV*, 2.

243. vi et armis: 'by force [of arms]' (Latin).

244. *robe de chambre*: 'dressing-gown' (French).

245. *frizette*: 'A band or cluster of small curls [of hair], usually artificial, worn on the forehead' (*OED*).

246. *yellow silk banyan*: Loose gown of a type originally worn in India (*OED*). The 'yellow silk' recalls Lord Frederick's comparison of vice-regal society to the imperial Chinese court, where yellow was the colour signifying highest distinction.

247. tout de bon: 'seriously' (French).

248. *the part of Estifania ... a* copper captain: A reference to characters in John Fletcher's comedy *Rule a Wife and Have a Wife* (first performed 1624; first published 1640). Estifania is 'a Woman of Intrigue'; and the 'Copper Captain' is Michael Perez – a 'copper captain' being 'a sham captain who assumes the title without any right' (*OED*).

249. *Sure such a pair were never seen*: the opening line of a song in R. B. Sheridan's comic opera *The Duenna, or The Double Elopement* (1775), II.ii.

250. thieves' vinegar: a mixture of rosemary, sage, and other herbs in vinegar, reputed to have been invented by thieves as a means of protecting themselves against infection when looting the homes of dead plague victims (*OED*).

251. *a Cronobane halfpenny*: i.e. a Cronebane halfpenny, a copper token struck by the Irish Mining Company in 1789, which became widespread in Ireland during the 1790s. See G. A. T. O'Brien, *The Economic History of Ireland in the Eighteenth Century* (Dublin: Maunsel and Company, 1918), p. 352.

252. *the* coolin: 'the curly hair', 'coolin' being an Anglicization of *cúilín*, 'hair or curl [of hair] on the back of the neck' (Irish).

253. up to her bent: possibly a misquotation of Shakespeare, *Hamlet*, III.ii.408 ('They fool me to the top of my bent').

254. *When I arrived ... with Don Narino*: Antonio Nariño travelled to England in order to canvass support for the Spanish American independence movement in 1796, having

escaped imprisonment in Spain, where he had been taken from Bogotá along with others arrested for spreading revolutionary ideas; see also Volume 3, n. 146.

255. *not without its parallel in the private history of the land*: The case referred to in Owenson's footnote is that of Richard Annesley (bap. 1693, d. 1761), who had his young nephew James Annesley kidnapped and sold into slavery in America, in order that he might succeed to the titles and estates of his deceased elder brother (and James's father), the fourth Baron Altham. In 1737, he also succeeded his cousin Arthur Annesley as sixth Earl of Anglesey. James Annesley later escaped from America and returned to Ireland, and confronted Anglesey at a race meeting in 1743. Despite the legal actions brought against him by James, Richard Annesley died still in possession of the Anglesey estates and titles; though further disputes surrounded the succession, with contending claims made by the sons of his bigamous marriages. The Anglesey family history had come back into public prominence in 1817, when George Annesley, second Earl of Mountnorris (1770–1844), succeeded in gaining the Lords' recognition of the validity of the marriage of his grandfather Richard Annesley to his third wife, and Mountnorris's grandmother, Juliana Donovan, in 1741 (*ODNB*).

256. toujours Perdrix: literally, 'partridge every day' (French), meaning 'having too much of a good thing'.

257. *And thus ... MILTON*: A misattribution; the source of this epigraph is Shakespeare, *Twelfth Night* V. i. 389.

258. *the papers ... the North Pole*: A topical reference. In April 1818, a fleet of four ships had embarked from Deptford on a British Admiralty-funded expedition of discovery to the North Pole. Regular reports on the expedition's progress appeared in the British newspapers throughout the summer of 1818, while Morgan was completing *Florence Macarthy*. Earlier the same year, a Parliamentary Act was passed to offer £20,000 to the owner of any ship that either reached the North Pole, or could locate a sea passage between the Atlantic and Pacific Oceans; see *The Times*, 31 December 1818, p. 3. Adventurers embarking on attempts to win the reward included a Lord Cochrane, whose order for the construction of a steamboat in which to undertake the expedition is reported in *The Times*, 24 March 1818, p.3.

259. the glarish eye of day: An inaccurate allusion to Milton, *Il Penseroso*, 141 ('Hide me from day's garish eye').

260. *the elephant in Blue Beard*: A reference to the stage elephant (constructed from wickerwork) which appeared in the procession in the opening scene of *Blue Beard, or Female Curiosity!*, a popular, and frequently revived, stage adaptation of Charles Perrault's tale of *Bluebeard* (see Volume 3, n. 6) by George Colman junior (1762–1836). The play was first performed at the Drury Lane Theatre, London, in 1798. In his version of the story, Colman transferred the action to a Turkish setting; and the elephant became one of the most frequently remarked, and longest remembered, of the effects created for the production. See Casie Hermansson, *Bluebeard: A Reader's Guide to the English Tradition* (Mississippi: University Press of Mississippi, 2009), pp. 60–6.

261. *'Tis a very fine thing... three-tail'd bashaw*: Lines from a song in George Colman's *Blue Beard; or, Female Curiosity!*, II.iii. First staged in 1798, this was a version of Charles Perrault's fairy tale set in Turkey (see Volume 3, n. 6; Volume 4, n. 260). Opening with the lines 'Major domo am I / Of this grand family', the song is performed by the character Ibrahim, father to the heroine who is about to marry Abomelique (the 'Bluebeard' character). For the text of the song, see George Colman, junior, *Blue Beard; or, Female Curiosity! A Dramatick Romance*, 6th edn (London: T. Woodfall, 1800), pp. 37–8. In

the Turkish Ottoman empire, a 'bashaw' (or pasha) was a high-ranking official, whose status was indicated by the number of horse-tails worn as part of his court regalia – a 'pasha of three tails' being one who occupied the highest rank (*OED*).

262. *With* pay... *and parliament*: Pope, 'The Second Epistle of the Second Book of Horace Imitated,' 274–5.

263. *the unfortunate Lord Essex*: Owenson refers to Arthur Capel, first Earl of Essex (bap. 1632, d. 1683), who as lord lieutenant of Ireland (1672–7) favoured toleration of Catholics and dissenters, and was critical of the culture of bribery and corruption in high politics, as well as of government policies such as high taxation in Ireland. On the accession of James II, Essex became involved with the Monmouth rebellion, with a view to replacing what he regarded as the illegitimate monarchy of James II with a republic. He was arrested and placed in the Tower of London on 9 July 1683, and died there from a razor wound to the throat on 13 July. A coroner ruled that Essex had committed suicide; but many believed that various factors, including the nature of the wound, indicated that he had been assassinated. 'Essex's Letters' refers to *Letters Written by his Excellency Arthur Capel, Earl of Essex, Lord Lieutenant of Ireland, in the Year 1675. To which is prefixed an historical account of his life* (Dublin: B. Grierson, 1770).

SILENT CORRECTIONS

Volume I

49   secretly] secretedly
77   52] Its
77   52,] hay
53   world's] worlds
55   see here] see hear
55   Oge O'Leary] oge O'Leary
56   'I mean] I mean
56   cousin] cousins
57   parlour] parlor
57   land,'] land,
64   friezes] furzes
65   lords'] lord's
67   it's] its
69   says she— "] says she—"
74   line from behind] line behind
79   pedant.] pedant."
81   ruin were] ruin vere
81   habitual expression] habitual expression
87   approached] approached
93   clamping] clamping
94   ensued] nsued
95   Dunore] Dùnore
95   Sir, if] Sir," if
95   'that even] that even
99   He paused,] "He paused
99   Macarthies] Macartnies
100n Macarthies] Macartnies

Volume II

112   substantial] sustantial
112   Mount Crawley legion] mount Crawley legion
115   every where] every were
116   faith at seven.'] faith at seven,'
118   involuntarily] involuntary
121   Mr. Commissioner] Mr. Commisioner
124   get off it] get of it
124   in the world] in the the world
126n. *i. e.*] i. *e.*
127   entailed] intailed
129   piqued] peaked
130   sweetmeats] sweatmeats
132   arrogant] ar ogant
136   it's] its
138   won't] wont
139   it's] its
140   poetical] poetica
141   a good poet.'] a good poet.

144 however,' and] however, "and
151 *by blood*] *by blood*
152 It's] Its
153 brothers'] brother's
155 interest.] interest
163 parole] patrole
164 all the] "all the
166 tant de] taut de
168 He dropped] He, dropped
170 Rosbrin's] Rosbin's
170 with me,'] with me,
173 *plus que*] *plusque*
178 She then] "She then
183 Sir, has.'] Sir, vas.'
183 counsellor's] counsellors
184 It's] Its
184 *Italian*] *Italien*
186 called] callen
189 caravats] caravasts
189 pray read it] "pray read it

Volume III

202 forthwith.'] forthwith
202 told tales."'] told tales."
204 *game laws!*] *game laws!*
214 will stand] wil stand
214 lordships] lordship's
214 attracting] attract
215 side.] side."
215 dear Lady Clancare] dear Lady Cancare
215 it's] its
218 aught] ought
221 companion's] companions
221 insignificance.'] insignificance.
222 'To me] To me
222 of belief."] of belief."
223 there *does*] their *does*
224 further than] "further than
225 affections."'] affections"
226 permanent."'] permanent."
226 title,] titl,
226 theirs] their's
235 par exemple] par example
238 life of Columbus] ife of Columbus
238 par exemple] par example
239 whenever you] whenever, you
241 villainy] villainy

243 ignorance."'] ignorance."
244 *par exemple*] *par example*
249 It's] Its
250 it's] its
252 plaze God.'] plaze God.
254 that's this morning] that' this morning
257 threshold] threshold
257 woo] woe
258 being ......"'] being ......"
266 paraphernalia] parapher alia
275 cowslips blow."'] cowslips blow."
275 *to wit;"*] *to wit;*

Volume IV

290 sex's] sexes
292 evangelical tracts] evangelica tracts
293 heels."'] heels."
294 some less."'] some less.'
313 makes a hero."'] makes a hero."
321 lying on] ying on
325 *reculer pour mieux sauter*] *recular pour mieux sauter*
325 vacillating] vaccilating
327 other persons'] other person's
328 nobody believes] nobody believe
328 levelled at me."'] levelled at me."
329 very kind indeed."'] very kind indeed."
330 *come at last."*] *come at last."*
333 perfect for it] perfect it it
338 their sides] there sides
338 ministry.'] ministry.
339 interrupted Lady Dunore,] interrupted Dunore,
339 the Ulster king at arms,] the Ulster, king at arms,
341 kidnapped] kindnapped
341 my lord's,] my lords,
344 'a countess, indeed!] a countess, indeed!
351 *quid pro quo*] *qui pro quo*
357 Pray speak,] "Pray speak,
357 all attention.'] all attention.
357 Mr. O'Sullivan] Mr. O Sullivan
358 gentleman in the country.] gentleman in the country."
358 it's] its
360 came forward] came orward

TEXTUAL VARIANTS

The first edition of *Florence Macarthy* is used as the copy text. After entering three further, identical editions in 1819, the novel was reissued in one volume by Henry Colburn in 1839, as volume 16 in the 'Colburn's Modern Novelists' series. This volume included illustrations on a frontispiece and on the title page, showing the episodes of Fitzwalter's visit to Lady Clancare in Volume III, and Fitzwalter's encounter with a priest whilst travelling in Volume 1, respectively.

Chapters were renumbered consecutively 1–22; and an apparatus of fifteen endnotes was supplied, based on the original volume endnotes. The text and notes had been comprehensively revised, with spelling regularised, some foreign expression replaced with English equivalents, and most errors in foreign spellings corrected. Syntax was simplified in many instances, and most italicisations for emphasis were dropped. Both the original 'Advertisement', and the content of many of the original endnotes, were also omitted. Given below are the most significant omissions from, and alterations and additions to, the text in 1839.

Volume I

2a	ADVERTISEMENT] *1839 omit.*
7b	ideologist] idealist *1839.*
10c	Thedelicious strains ... unequivocal despotism.'] *1839 omit.*
18d	suburbian] suburban *1839.*
19e	Counsellor Gallagher's iligant speeches] Counsellor Gallagher's iligant speeches.* [and footnote:] The number of newspapers has, however, much increased. *1839.*
21f	The capital of Ireland ... impatient to quit.* [and accompanying footnote]]*1839 omit.*
28g	The one had studied ... he had obtained.] *1839 omit.*
00h	But though he saw ... evil or to good.]*1839 omit.*
35i	dégout] disgust *1839.*
36j	that is, as they are patronized ... the capacity he despises.] *1839 omit.*
40k	The younger stranger ... founded in fact.] *1839 omit.*
41l	, the Bothon ... its neighbourhood,] *1839 omit.*
45m	but it is peculiar ... ancestors had been influences.] *1839 omit.*
45n	Her history ... far behind.] *1839 omit.*
51o	'Freedom of agency,' ... replied the Commodore.] *1839 omit.*

60p   for it appears ... she is a woman.'] and yet, she is a woman.' *1839.*

60q   compared to the creatures ... *this* a woman!] *1839 omit.*

60r   leaning against ... broad bright moon,] *1839 omit.*

62s   :for it is only ... governed for centuries.] which is refused only to the local, official oppressor. *1839.*

64t   'What I should complain ... was the reply.] *1839 omit.*

73u   This was said ... her broken nose.] *1839 omit.*

76v   ideologist] idealist *1839.*

00w   'The scenes he now ... their spiriting gently.'] *1839 omit.*

79x   *[and footnote]]*1839 omit.*

88y   Many of the better ... Anno 1563.']*1839 omit.*

89z   ;and the lords ... castles of their ancestors] *1839 omit.*

89a   He had also ... effect conversion.] *1839 omit.*

89b   The first Viscount ... God's *providence.*] *1839 omit.*

90c   who was abroad,] *1839 omit.*

91d   DualdMacFirbis ... were possessed.] *1839 omit.*

92e   'Words that wise ... philological riches.* [and footnote]] *1839 omit.*

93f   turf, Sir.] turf, Sir.* [and footnote] Getting in that useful inflammable.*1839.*

95g   break the sale.] break the sale." [and footnote] Seal.*1839.*

99h   ;for he was never ... Seven Wise Maisters] . *1839.*

100i   , the English ... breast to breast] *1839 omit.*

101j   All the circumstances ... bereft him of reason] *1839 omit.*

101k   : the idea that the stranger ... possession of his mind] . The idea that the stranger was the brother of the Marquis of Dunore had taken possession of O'Leary's mind *1839.*

105l   , where he was little better ... so you *have* me.'] . *1839.*

105m   But this fire ... Furness, in England.] *1839 omit.*

106n   S. Barr ... hair, &c. &c.]*1839 omit.*

106o   Formerly*potatoes* ... return to describe.] *1839 omit.*

Volume II

112a   : most facetiously ... *insurrection acts*] *1839 omit.*

115b   , and spoke ... purposes of display] *1839 omit.*

116c   ; for though ... of the saint] *1839 omit.*

117d   Such events ... en passant.] *1839 omit.*

118e   a mere idle ... the wilds of Munster,] a mere idle elegant English tourist of fashion, *1839.*

118f   :some male ... scenery of Dunore] *1839 omit.*

119g   The half conscious ... on the table, she] She *1839.*

119h   As saint ... *at the head.*] *1839 omit.*

120i   ; placing torture ... and emolument] . *1839.*

121j   The basis ... now exhibited.] *1839 omit.*

122k   They drew ... such bribes.] *1839 omit.*

122l   fixed aversion.] fixed aversion—in those, at least, who were not the perpetual victims of his cruel malversations. *1839.*

123k   whatever, in short ... proscription,] *1839 omit.*

123l   was then put in requisition,] were then put in requisition, *1839.*

124m   giving loose ... might still be,] *1839 omit.*

126n   God help me ... buried, and] *1839 omit.*

129o   Crawley genius,] Crawley genus, *1839.*

129p   gleaned from a class ... aromatic pain,'] gleaned from sentimental novels, *1839.*

131q   But, though dead ... in propriâpersonâ.]*1839 omit.*

133r   I abhor ... IBID.] *1839 omit.*

133s   (the one of ancient ... Protestant family):] *1839 omit.*

134t   fourpence halfpenny,] fourpence halfpenny.* [and footnote] A half-guinea of the old Irish currency, now no more. *1839.*

136u   from the manner ... impatient schoolboy,] *1839 omit.*

136v   'Does he? ... clean impossible.'] *1839 omit.*

137w   Apparently abiding ... ruined in his turn.] *1839 omit.*

137x   : for the quietude ... can procure] *1839 omit.*

144y   ; coupled, therefore ... and now] . Miss Crawley *1839.*

147z   Mothers ... endless discussion.]*1839 omit.*

147a   Protection, interference ... of others.]*1839 omit.*

148b   These mystic ... Crawley regime: meantime O'Leary] O'Leary, meantime, *1839.*

149c   primmer jargon] primer jargon *1839.*

150d   ;out-rivalling ... as follower] *1839 omit.*

000e   The beautiful person ... husband of his daughter.] *1839 omit.*

158f   The Earl of L. had married ... a remote connexion.] *1839 omit.*

158g   with such sums ... the gaming-table,] *1839 omit.*

158h   sometimes endured ... in a palace] *1839 omit.*

160i   Power and influence ... in the other.]*1839 omit.*

160j   who gave them ... within its walls,] *1839 omit.*

163k   During nine months ... the south of Ireland.] *1839 omit.*

163l   In Dublin ... subordinate capacities.] *1839 omit.*

164m   : he had fought ... in his, absence: for the rest,] . For the rest, *1839.*

164n   : in Dublin ... the castle of Dunore] *1839 omit.*

165o   This luxuriant coïffure ... for their object.] *1839 omit.*

166p   — With such recollections ... indignant patriotism.] *1839 omit.*

168q   all scarlet and *orders.*] all scarlet and medals *1839.*

169r   , who had for the day ... found herself,] *omit 1839.*

170s   Dinner was ... alone effect it.] *1839 omit.*

172t   I remember ... virtue of necessity.] *1839 omit.*

173u   Austrian chasseur] Austrian General *1839.*

175v   .It's very odd ... *grandeceremonie*;] :*1839.*

178w   , and propensity ... real or fancied] *1839 omit.*

179x   Cruel are ... SHAKESPEARE.] *1839 omit.*

179y   Civilization and social happiness ... agitated the sister island.] *1839 omit.*

180z   and all exposed ... sent to associate.] were added to the mass of corruption already festering in the unreformed British Parliament. *1839.*

180a   the *pot-walluping* boroughs of Ireland,] the rotten boroughs of Ireland, *1839.*

180b   , and that each ... with the other] *1839 omit.*

182c   forty-shilling freeholder; a class which is ... intriguing landlords.]forty-shilling freeholder.* [and footnote] The forty-shilling freeholder has since been abolished; but the class it created will long subsist, to plague the country, and to stigmatize the legislation, which called it into existence. *1839.*

183d   *bog leave*] bog leave* [and footnote] leave to cut turf off the landlord's bog. *1839.*

184e   , who had 'smiled ... her ladyship] *1839 omit.*
185f   A sort of ... testify against them.] *1839 omit.*
186g   and while ... read almost entirely—] *1839 omit.*
187h   pooh pudor,] moreover *1839.*
191i   But he had ... a severity that horrified.] *1839 omit.*
192j   gaîté du cour] pleasantry *1839.*
193k   He is ever the ready ... a just retaliation.] *1839 omit.*
195l   Places of emolument ... remaining unplaced.] *1839 omit.*
196m   When a temporary ... may still exist.] *1839 omit.*
196n   The system of government ... contained in this passage.] *1839 omit.*

Volume III

199a   To vouch this ... SHAKESPEARE.] *1839 omit.*
199b   Lady Dunore, who like sister Anne ... son, in another.] *1839 omit.*
199c   She was summoned ... to the breakfast-parlour.] On the arrival of Baron Boulter and
        Judge Aubrey, Lady Dunore was summoned to the breakfast parlour. *1839.*
199d   bouillon] soup *1839.*
202e   There was, also, in the scene ... the place assigned him.] *1839 omit.*
215f   , produced ... breathed forth.'] . *1839.*
219g   'What!shall ... IDEM.] *1839 omit.*
220h   the ancient Irish,] the ancient Irish.*1839.*
220i   and affirmeth ... the poor bird.] *1839 omit.*
221j   General Fitzwalter had ... his hallucination.] *1839 omit.*
222k   There is a sort ... an Irish district.] *1839 omit.*
223l   are at least glorious illusions.] is at least a glorious illusion. *1839.*
223m   I have always loved ... its own workings, '] *1839 omit.*
224n   , which might have ... struggles of South-America] *1839 omit.*
226o   (for they were ... the rampart)] *1839 omit.*
228p   The singularity ... the stranger chief.] *1839 omit.*
231q   ; and have still ... along with it] *1839 omit.*
231r   She came to me ... under which he suffered.] *1839 omit.*
232s   : and of the troops ... of the order] *1839 omit.*
233t   Engaging in ... philosophical speculation,] *1839 omit.*
235u   , for whatever ... of popularity] *1839 omit.*
236v   The fact is ... *joke's all on our's.*] *1839 omit.*
236w   when Spain ... But] but *1839.*
236x   The oppressor ... war of extermination.* [and footnote]] *1839 omit.*
237y   We all know ... madness *tomorrow*] *1839 omit.*
237z   ; for as ... so every where] . Every where*1839.*
237a   (for in ... side of oppression),] ;*1839.*
238b   blood.' 'Oh horrible!' ... 'found them sacrificing human beings in their temples.']
        blood. The Spaniards found them sacrificing human beings in their temples.' *1839.*
238c   The early Britons ... *Ipigenie en Aulide.*] *1839 omit.*
239d   'Is he any thing ... did not share.] *1839 omit.*
241e   Law, for instance ... physical pressure.]*1839 omit.*
241f   Since then ... transient existence.] *1839 omit.*
242g   It was curious, however ... to have surpassed it.] *1839 omit.*

242h   . Plans and schemes ... general attention] *1839 omit.*

243i   It seems ... a *little equivocal.*] *1839 omit.*

243j   (the only one ... card table,)] *1839 omit.*

244k   'By the bye ... and all that.']*1839 omit.*

245l   Amused as she ... had himself retired.] *1839 omit.*

245m   (a countenance... to him)] *1839 omit.*

245n   That she had ... importance of the latter.] *1839 omit.*

246o   The rest ... not idle.] *1839 omit.*

247p   He measured ... of the deep.] *1839 omit.*

247q   'This tower ... men and sinners.']*1839 omit.*

251 r   Nerlongasinvalueremoras.]Per longasinvalueremoras.*1839.*

251s   , though the queen ... the time being] *1839 omit.*

251t   ; for says ouldStanihurst ... the foster childre] *1839 omit.*

258u   the first Countess ... the BhanTierna is] *1839 omit.*

259v   ' He pulled from his breast ... indited – which,] *1839 omit.*

260w   ; and all that's ... since she came home] *1839 omit.*

260x   , who might stand ... native nobility of the land] *1839 omit.*

261y   ; and when I saw ... such pleasure to maintain] *1839 omit.*

263z   (one of those ... ocean of the earth)] *1839 omit.*

263a   Ballydab, which ... national legislature.]*1839 omit.*

264b   The general as he passed ... curious contrast.] *1839 omit.*

266c   It was the work ... many Irish castles.] *1839 omit.*

266d   assignable to the *goutmusqué* of the timid,] assignable to the timid, *1839.*

268e   Thus engaged ... he could not detect.] *1839 omit.*

271f   ; and here are the initials ... and cross over] *1839 omit.*

271g   ; and though ... fruitless moon."] . *1839.*

272h   These feminine interchanges ... worked in a cell.] *1839 omit.*

273i   I might almost say ... coupled and inseperable."] And *1839.*

273j   He had hung ... was now engaged.] *1839 omit.*

273k   All that he heard ... ardent, energetic.] *1839 omit.*

275l   , to feed upon ... cowslips blow."] . *1839.*

276m   For in these remote districts ... beasts of the field.] *1839 omit.*

281n   Colonel O'Higgens ... blockaded Montevideo.] *1839 omit.*

281o   One remarkable ... *Ledwich.*]*1839 omit.*

282p   Macarthy was Riagh ... feudal call and penalty.] *1839 omit.*

282q   cattle or food.]cattle or wood. *1839.*

282r   , being a desolate ... many centuries back.] *1839 omit.*

282s   Specimens still ... by Irish nuns.] *1839 omit.*

283t   'When Florence Macarthy ... *See Smith's Cork and Kerry.*] *1839 omit.*

Volume IV

287a   I'll venture ... MILTON.] *1839 omit.*

288b   Hitherto he had lived ... lively and energetic ones.] *1839 omit.*

289c   Alert, adroit ... Irishman of this class,] Irishmen of this class, *1839.*

289d   the qualities ... to Lady Clancare,] *1839 omit.*

290e   All that he had known ... and he] He *1839.*

290f   , and who knew no medium ... Turkish seraglio] *1839 omit.*

290g   The agent and chief mover ... prophecies of Friar Con.] *1839 omit.*
291h   The misery or happiness ... caprice of others.] *1839 omit.*
293i   I said he would distance ... all by rote.] *1839 omit.*
293j   splendid talents ... transcendent merit,* [and footnote]] *1839 omit.*
295k   Every one laughed ... parts of Coriolanus.] *1839 omit.*
296l   The general politics ... could not ably controvert.] *1839 omit.*
297m   hatred and envy ... declarations of ignorance;] *1839 omit.*
299n   ; for the certain ... her grand object] *1839 omit.*
302o   'She's mighty pert ... the affirmative.] *1839 omit.*
303p   she's first cousin ... Mrs.Twiggle*is*] she is *1839.*
303q   who, having ... crozier in ours;] *1839 omit.*
304r   , still extant ... swept away:] . They are *1839.*
304s   but ardent to repay kindness] but they are ardent to repay kindness *1839.*
305t   , who now was light ... rainbow lives.'] . *1839.*
307u   , which was to me as the spirit ...shadow of Cellini] *1839 omit.*
308v   Solitude, the nurse ... had arisen.] *1839 omit.*
310w   Repeal the act ... plague to Constantinople.] *1839 omit.*
310x   But as I may be ... something like danger.]*1839 omit.*
310y   rencontre] rencounter*1839.*
312z   She had long ... rights of humanity.] *1839 omit.*
314a   For you were still ... unhappy prepossession.] *1839 omit.*
314b   ; every newspaper ... your whereabouts."] . *1839*
314c   , "Lost or mislaid ... Ballydab has it:] ; *1839.*
315d   * [and footnote]] *1839 omit.*
315e   ; for be they ... fail to be unexpected] *1839 omit.*
317f   ; as the events ... the power of invention] *1839 omit.*
317g   There are two parties ... inconceivable rapidity.] *1839 omit.*
317h   , whose half genius ... interesting subjects] *1839 omit.*
321i   , like the escheators ... marked men, and sowld] *1839 omit.*
323j   , while to those ... of the troop:] . *1839.*
323k   An object of romantic fondness ... contradictory, and wrapped] Wrapped *1839.*
324l   In the calendar ... holds its empire.] *1839 omit.*
325m   , in which Lord Adelm took no interest] *1839 omit.*
325n   It is a dogma of the sect ... tinkling cymbal.] *1839 omit.*
325o   From the night ... obeyed the summons.] *1839 omit.*
326p   Not content with ... the tragedy of the Revenge.] *1839 omit.*
327q   A countenance ... a good comic actress.] *1839 omit.*
327r   as one who took ... assumed tastes,] *1839 omit.*
329s   ! – put them in our books ... very kind indeed] .*1839.*
331t   : for, as Touchstone says ... every quarter] *1839 omit.*
333u   , who took their opinions ... imbecile tyranny,] ; and *1839.*
333v   The absence of Lord Adelm ... pray for its prorogation.] *1839 omit.*
334w   I speak not ... SHAKESPEARE.] *1839 omit.*
338x   : and what is in it ... from the whigs] *1839 omit.*
342y   It is not the first time ... mind to the event.] *1839 omit.*
344z   But here, sorrow ... a military escort.] *1839 omit.*
344a   Now does my ... SHAKESPEARE.] *1839 omit.*
345b   As he walked forth ... horror and desolation.] *1839 omit.*

347c   , in regard of ... till death, and more] *1839 omit.*
359d   The rest of the company ... this curious scene.] *1839 omit.*
363e   'Happily ... private history of the land.* [and footnote]] *1839 omit.*
367f   The constant cry ... Lord Chesterfield, are proofs.] *1839 omit.*

For Product Safety Concerns and Information please contact our EU
representative GPSR@taylorandfrancis.com
Taylor & Francis Verlag GmbH, Kaufingerstraße 24, 80331 München, Germany